A Court of Ivory Feathers

MACKENZIE HILL

Contents

Dedication

For my father, who never got to see this story come to life—but whose love, strength, and memory are stitched into every word.

Note to the Reader

Dear Reader,

This story contains themes and content that may be upsetting or triggering to some individuals. While the portrayals are handled with care and are not excessively graphic, the following sensitive topics are present throughout the narrative:

- Physical abuse from a parental figure

- Panic attack episodes

- Underlying tones of sexual assault

- Mentions of parental death and the loss of a parental figure

- Domestic abuse of a spouse

- Mental health disorders including anxiety and depression

- Vulgar language

- Explicit adult scenes

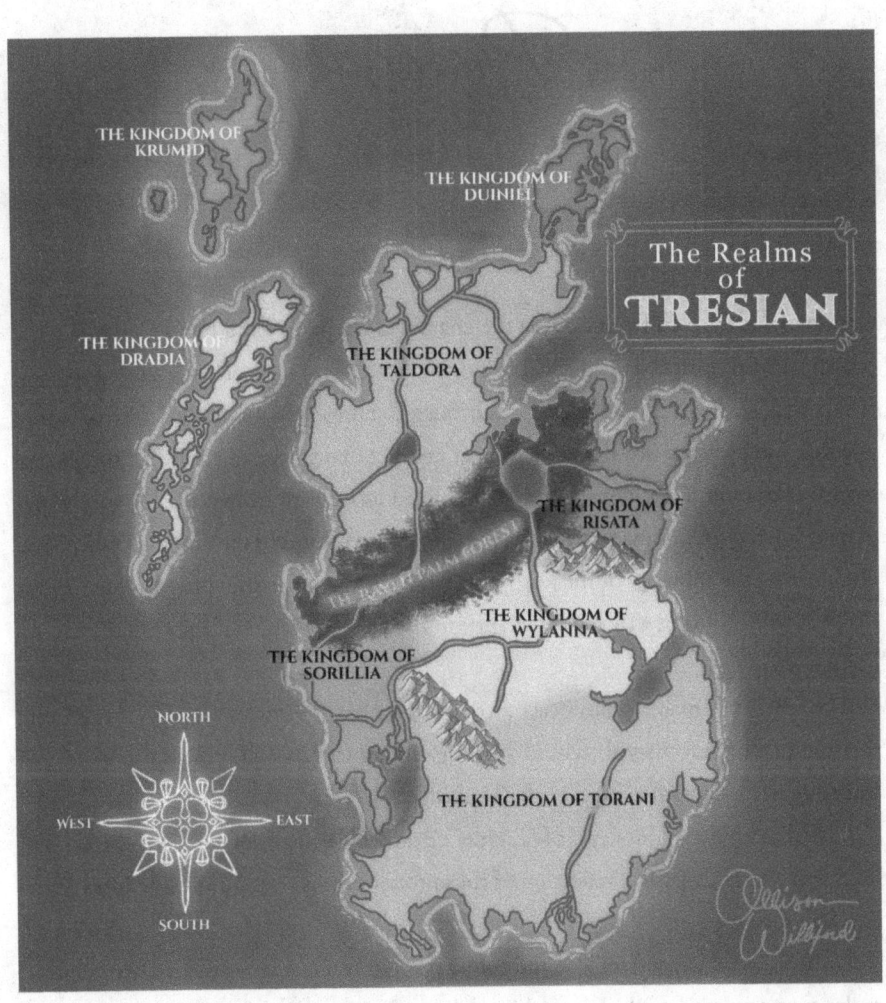

THE KINGDOM OF
KRUMID

THE KINGDOM OF
DUINIEL

The Realms
of
TRESIAN

THE KINGDOM OF
DRADIA

THE KINGDOM OF
TALDORA

THE KINGDOM OF
RISATA

THE KINGDOM OF
WYLANNA

THE KINGDOM OF
SORILLIA

NORTH

WEST   EAST

THE KINGDOM OF TORANI

SOUTH

Prologue

Cries of valor erupted from outside the chambers of the Aestival temple — where the echoing of wing beats blended with the ringing of steel in a song of war against good and evil. A trickle of a golden liquid seeped through the fingers of a delicate yet lethal hand - one that was growing deathly pale. Years of conflict, struggle, and effort had toughened the fist clutching her abdomen that constructed an empire from scratch. Ivory wings draped down the feminine warrior's back as flecks of gold caught the sunlight from above, illuminating the shimmer of the feathers. The warrior wore feather-plated golden armor that was believed to be a divine crafting from the finest metals, as if the gods themselves had made .

The armor was made to allow easy movement for her enormous wings. Not only were they useful for flying, they also could shield against attacks, as well as be a weapon, as each feather was tipped with a sharp-bladed iron edge..

Golden hair draped over eyes of ice blue, a nearly silver shade of color with an echo of lilacs and greens. A perfect reflection of the aurora borealis rested inside the irises of the Aestival queen.

Embellished with swirls of lilac and gold, a portrait of a woman with gold wings and an antler crown painted on the large, white archway door captured the queen's attention. A mural made in stainless above the archway door, one of the legendary heroine that would save all of Wylana.

The entry led to the sacred Mother Grove tree temple, magically guarded inside the castle wall of Andromeda, safely hiding the key to the Aestival's magic.

Built into the mountains, Castle Andromeda seemed impenetrable, as did its temple that lay on the opposite side of the mountains. Where the only two access points included a sky light accessible only to the Aestivals, and a hallway that led out to the battle outside its door. The walls that once was adorned with colors of lilacs, orchid, ivory, and amber.

Now, the war that rattled its walls has painted the once breathtaking castle halls in splashes of golden and thick tar-like blood , that oozed down the walls like spilled ink Despite the halls of Andromeda normally filled with music and laughter.

Barged urgently through the archway door, a tall, muscular male adorned with similar armor as the queen. Shouts from their men and the song of war rang out louder as he entered from the hallway that connects the castle to the temple. With what remained of his sword. In an attempt to hold back the enemy, he jammed the broken blade and hilt between the door handles. Pressing his weight into his palms , as his breath was ragged. An inaudible shouting came from the opposite side of the door , one couldn't have been made out but was familiar.

The deep chocolate feathers of his wings ruffled in uncertainty about the outcome of the war that shook the castle outside the temple walls. Twinges of cinnamon and tawny feathers caught on the sun rays coming in from the roof.

Turning his face towards Asteria, the sun kissed the honey beige of Gavriel's skin that was sprayed with black, oily blood from the enemies he had slain. His eyes, a golden amber, took in the sight of his wife, now barely able to stand on her two feet.

Despite the immense size of his wings, they flowed behind him effortlessly as he rushed to her side, assessing the damage swiftly to find the source of his wife's agony. His hand gently replaced hers on her abdomen, just below where her chest plate met her faulds, applying pressure to the wound to slow the bleeding down. It was a lucky hit that had turned deadly. The blade that had lacerated her, laced with the sap of a Raven Palm tree, made its mark across her abdomen, bringing her to her knees unlike any normal wound from a mundane blade.

While this toxin was potent enough to send any mortal to an agonizing death in mere minutes, it was only strong enough to weaken a seemingly immortal Aestival warrior. Bringing down their strength and slowing their ability to heal quickly, making it easy to kill them. A poison that would kill a healthy full grown Aestival in under thirty minutes.

Only in this weakened state could they be slain.

Gavriel, trying not to harm her further, kept the pressure on her abdomen even as his attention was drawn to the bellowing of his warriors and the triumphant rise of the enemy's spirit growing louder just beyond the doors. The king looked back at his beloved wife. Seeing her in this state, he needed to get his queen and himself out of there, where they could find someone to tend to her wound.

Gavriel opened his mouth to say something to her, but Asteria rose unsteadily to her feet to step away, shaking her head. "She will come, Gavriel, The prophecy said. If she doesn't, then we will fall."

Pulling away from her husband, the queen winced from the searing pain in her side before she stumbled into a pillar. Gavriel stepped forward to stabilize her as she leaned against it. The large pillar , made of white marble with swirls of lilac and gold, was now stained by the blood of his wife, who was desperately trying to keep her battered body upright.

Standing tall, despite the shaking in her legs threatening to bring her to her knees, Asteria gripped her sword. The handle was slippery under her palm from the blood coating her fingers as she adjusted her grip a few times. Gavriel, for a moment, was relieved she still carried his wedding gift to her. It was a fine sword, where the hilt was a lilac leather decorated with the ivory and gold swirled detailing. It was inscribed with the Aestival saying, *Truth is powerful and it prevails.*

It was something the royal family believed in and held close to their heart. For living a life by knowing the truth behind it, tends to make knowing your current reality is no longer the same. In turn , it tends to add complications for life's greatest warriors.

The Aestival warrior race spread throughout the great kingdom of Wylana. While the castle of Andromeda was the sole home to the Aestival people, it was not a kingdom of its own, but a large plot of land. Their various temples spread far and wide in Tresian, servicing the land by aiding and protecting its people against the Netherian inhabitants.

The Aestival were known to be proud warriors, along with the occasional healer or priest. This prideful race thrived on the saying *For there are three things that shall not be hidden for long; The sun, the moon, and the truth.*

Turning her body to face her husband, Asteria tilted her head back against the pillar and held her abdomen. "They may have the element of surprise, my love, but we have the Ivory Fawn. She will come, and when she does it, it will save us all."

It pained Gavriel to see her like this, though he was impressed by her sheer strength of will to fight the poison coursing in her veins , making her magic useless. Asteria was praised by her people for her strength in will and heart, not for being the greatest warrior, as her people praised her husband to be.

The warrior queen been suffering from her wound for nearly an hour, which was unheard of among the Aestival race. It should have claimed her life thirty minutes ago, yet here the queen was, upright, on her feet, and with a sword in hand. Gavriel admired her resilience. Somehow, death did not scare Asteria, for she was the queen of the legendary Aestival people. Warriors who were said to be no match for the Netherian people, who plagued the realm of Tresian, taking women as their blood brides. A sacrificial lamb, to appease the dark cravings of it users. They don't need these women to reverse the toll on the body. Yet they take sick enjoyment out of draining the life essence of innocent women.. These were people who took enjoyment from watching others suffer as their hands and arms turned black from their abuse of dark magic.

Everything in this world had a balance. The Aestival's magic was the purifying light praised by the Tresian to cure their sick and wounded, while the Netherian magic was nothing pure dark, malicious use of the world's darkness. Drawing natural poison and corrosive elements from the earth to be used to their own gain. Although, it had a consequence. The more it was used, the more it took from the user. It was soon learned that the Netherian people needed to consume fresh blood to reverse the effects, a life for a life, since blood was the life source of every living thing.

That was until today, when the Netherian people used Raven Palm sap to eradicate the one being in Tresian strong enough to stop them from taking over. Asteria thought the trees were a myth, since they hadn't been seen in centuries. Her great-great-grandmother had decimated their sacred grove and remaining seeds to protect her people.

"Asteria...The Ivory Fawn will not aid us...We are on our own. We need to flee if we are to save our people." Gavriel pleaded with his wife, seeing how close she was to death's door. He stepped up to her and pressed one hand against her wound again, while the other brushed her hair back to see how quickly the poison was consuming her. His heart crumbled to see its spider effect webbing creeping toward her jaw. It seemed the only thing that kept her fighting that damn toxin in her veins now was the idea of the prophecy coming true before her eyes. Just the way her eyes kept lingering back to the mural said it all.

Their people were going to fall today by the hands of their enemies, but rise again when the Ivory Fawn had risen, whenever that time would be.

He put Asteria's arm around his shoulder and ignored her cry of pain, helping his wife to their sacred Mother Grove Tree. It was where they exchanged their marriage vows. He leaned his warrior queen against it so she, too, could remember the last time they sat beneath this tree together. Looking at the mural of the Ivory Fawn on the temple door, he inhaled deeply, despite the pain from his own wounds, and recalled the prophecy that was foretold.

A prophecy that spoke about how his people would fall no matter how hard they fought to prevent it. How this Ivory Fawn, not knowing who they would be, would rise from the ashes of his home and somehow bring them back.

Part of him wished it was right at this very moment that the Ivory Fawn would appear and save them all. Although Gavriel wasn't really a believer of superstitions and prophecies, like his wife was. Yet, in this moment, it would be a relief to watch that their prophesied heroine step through the doors and wipe away the Netherian assailants.

Gavriel removed her armor carefully to relieve her of the weight. His own body screamed in protest from his wounds that he couldn't care less about at this moment. Although Gavriel knew in his heart they both would die here beneath the tree, at least they'd die together, as it should be. He removed his own armor, discarding it to the side with Asteria's, before as mindful of her wounds as he could be, brought his wife to rest upon his chest as he leaned upon the tree

Asteria looked up to the swaying leaves of lavender and orchid. Gavriel brushed sweat soaked strands of hair from her face as memories of their wedding day flashed in his mind, as well as joyous reminiscence of he and Asteria presenting their daughter Sariah to their people beneath the same tree. More blissful moments washed over him as he tried to ignore the agonizing pain coursing through him. His sole focus was to soothe his wife in her last moments. "As the ivory feathers are covered in red, the Ivory Fawn will rise from the ashes of her home guided by her," Asteria breathed out, trying to ignore the burning sensation slowly making its way to her heart.

Stifling the sob threatening to leave him, Gavriel wrapped an arm around her as he pulled her into a tight and welcoming embrace, making a more secure hold of Asteria to his chest. Without protest, Asteria leaned her head back, holding his arms across her as his heart beat thunderously on the back of her head.

Asteria gave one last glance to her husband, whose beige skin glistened from the light reflecting off the crystal-clear pool that resided under the Mother Grove Tree. Reaching up, Asteria stroked the Netherian blood splattered across his face, wiping it away. It felt as if oil was brushed from his soft, warm cheek as a silver lining formed in both their eyes.

Unable to hide behind her warrior queen persona she always used in desperate times, streams of tears erupted from Asteria's eyes, washing away the blood from her own cheeks as the poison in her veins near her heart and lungs turned black. Asteria continued fighting to keep her eyes open as she stared up at Gavriel. He held his wife close, leaned down, kissed her lips softly, and stroked a golden strand of hair from her face. Unable to stop his own tears from falling as they dropped onto her cheek.

"May the Ivory Fawn reign," Asteria strained out.

Gavriel smiled softly, stroking another strand from her face. Nodding his head, he took a deep breath. "May the Ivory Fawn reign." His voice cracked as he stared into his wife's eyes. Watching them close for the very last time, her body went limp in his arms. His queen was dead. Guttural sobs tore through the temple as the barricaded door was broken down and darkness filled the room.

Chapter One

Hazel

Shades of pinks, oranges, and yellows painted the morning sky of the village of Alexandria. Blissful calm blanketed the quiet village, and the townsfolk hadn't even stirred, still nestled cozily in their beds as the crisp autumn air danced with leaves of reds, oranges, and browns.

Rays of light peered into the cottage where Hazel lay snuggled up in her warm, sage green sheets. The fireplace crackled softly, and the room filled with the scents of vanilla and sandalwood as she continued to slumber. Her golden hair sprawled out behind her as the sun's rays warmed her golden bronze skin earned from working diligently in her gardens.

The maiden slowly woke from her slumber with such grace that she could have been mistaken for a princess about to join the autumn morning birds with a song. Hazel exhaled with a smile and turned to her small cat. Marie snuggled up near the fire, purring away in her sleep and didn't even budge as Hazel threw back her covers.

Stretching her arms up high, she let out a faint groan, and her beige cotton nightgown scrunched up showing her long, muscular legs. The front door of the cottage opened and filled the room with the smell of freshly baked bread and crisp autumn air.

"Ah, the dainty fawn princess has awoken," Hazel's uncle remarked as he carried in a bucket of freshly fetched eggs. Archibald was a stocky man whose beard was blonde as the wheat he grew, with tinges of gray, thanks to his niece, whose beauty earned her the attention of unwanted suitors. The fall sunlight caught on the scar that lined the left side of his neck from a battle years before Hazel was born.

Hazel chuckled, walked over to her uncle, and kissed his cheek before embracing him. He smelt of vanilla with hints of oranges and cinnamon as she nestled her face in his neck as she done since Hazel was a child.

Hazel took the bucket of eggs from him to put them away after pulling a few nice round ones to make them breakfast. "I am far from any princess, Uncle ... Besides, I wouldn't trade my life here with you for anything."

Archibald sat at the table watching his niece, finding himself lost in a warm memory as the morning light hit her face. It was as if his sister was alive and well, making her brother breakfast like she always did for her family. He glanced at the ring Hazel's mother passed down to her when she was younger. Hazel briefly looking over to her uncle, registering his look ,"tell me again about her... About my mother."

Thinking of all his fond memories with his darling Ashira, he let out a soft chuckle looking at his family's crescent ring. "She was kind, somehow always brought calm to anyone's mind caught in a violent storm. Hell, she calmed me from so many things when it came to our bastard father. Can't count how many times I begged her to come with me away from that life. Ash was one of the strongest-willed females I ever met. Despite how brutal our father was to her, she never let him see how much it broke her, but still shone as bright as the stars themselves."

Hazel scrambled the eggs as her uncle spoke. Glancing at her mother's wedding ring, she stroked it with her thumb before she glanced at her uncle, seeing the pain and regret in his eyes as he continued his story. "When your father came, that was one of the happiest days of her life. Although it didn't match the day she found out she was pregnant with you. I was so thrilled for her when she told me you were in her belly and that she was finally leaving our childhood home. Then there was the joy when you came into this world. Your mother radiated it. But the month after you were born, we received word your father had died. No thanks to those bastards, the Netherians. They thought and still think they can corrupt this land with their corrosive and destructive ways."

Putting their eggs on plates, Hazel carried them to the table. Marie, upon smelling the food cooking, made her way to Hazel, brushing her leg with her nimble body. Faintly smiling, she grabbed a bowl of milk and gave it to her cat before looking to her uncle once more.

"Your mother was completely devastated by his death and fell into this horrible pit of despair. That's when she came here to live with me. Your father's death ate away at her. She stopped eating and drinking, and slowly stopped tending to you as well. Ashira got so sick she passed away in my arms in the garden under the wisteria tree. That was the hardest day of my life. The only silver lining to losing my only sister was gaining a daughter." Taking Hazel's hand, he kissed it softly, rubbing it with a tearful smile as he saw the memory of his sister in Hazel's face. "I swore to your mother I was going to treat you as my daughter, and since that day I have done everything I can to make sure you have the father you deserve."

Wiping Archibald's tears away, Hazel smiled, kissing his hand before resting her palm on his cheek and looking into his eyes. "And I know from the bottom of my heart, my mother is forever grateful for what you have done for me. I am lucky to have you as a father, Uncle Archibald. Now how about we eat and then go to the market? I have been saving up some money for a new dress for my date with Darius."

Letting out a deep laugh and shaking his head, he pulled her hand off his face, kissing it before releasing it. "You will make that poor Darius boy fall over his own feet."

Chuckling, she ate her food and tucked her golden hair behind her ear with a mischievous grin. "I plan to marry that butcher boy, remember? I think after surviving this bloody village with him for four years it's time I try to settle down with him."

Archibald chuckled and began finishing his breakfast. Once they were done, he kissed her head before putting the dishes in the sink.

Chapter Two

Hazel

The market was flooded with sounds of merchants calling out to possible buyers about their foods and goods. Scents of cinnamon and nutmeg filled Hazel's nose, beckoning her toward a freshly baked pumpkin bread being sold by her Archibald and Hazel's favorite bakery. As Hazel walked the street further with her Uncle, the aroma of freshly harvested lavender filled the air mingling faintly with the nutmeg and cinnamon. Hazel adored her small village. It wasn't much to an outsider, but it was home. Sadly, the royal family treated her village as if it was the ugly stepchild of the kingdom, being so close to the Netherian borders. King Kai let the Netherian scum, along with the thieves and mercenaries, upheave the once peaceful village.

Archibald was speaking with the blacksmith about some new horseshoes, while Hazel browsed around, admiring the market quietly.

Children were playing in the street chasing a small kitten, darting past Hazel, giggling. It brought a smile to her face watching them, although the smile faded from seeing a Netherian mercenary picking up the small kitten by the scruff off his neck as it hissed and clawed at the mere. No one said anything or did anything to try help the kitten or children. A sane person who valued their life wouldn't, but Hazel wasn't like most of the scared people in her village

Stopping dead in their tracks, the little boy shielded his sister behind him, looking up at the man as the small kitten hissed at him, trying to scratch his way to escape. A deep scar ran across the Netherian mercenary's face and a patch covered his missing eye. Hazel's blood turned roiling hot as she watched.

"Release the kitten. It has no value to you, nor would it even satisfy your Netherian bloodlust. It's far too small for you to enjoy, Ratherian." One of the few Netherian mercenaries seen through out Alexandria. Just last month he didn't even drag his blood bride to the wood, He instead killed her right in the town square. Hazel hid her trembling hand as she held the young children behind her, who now clung to her beige floral skirt as if it made them vanish from the man's view.

A dark laugh escaped the mercenary's red lips It looked like they were coated in the blood of a fresh kill, the look made her skin crawl knowing some poor person or creature has suffered at his hand. All in the name of reversing the toll of his magic.

Stalking towards her, he stroked Hazel's soft cheek, and it took everything in her not to bite his plagued finger off. No thanks to the use of Netherian magic.

Leaning her head away from his touch, she held her breath as his sent shivers down her spine, making every alarm in her head scream *run* as he looked her up and down, licking his bottom lip "You look like you would make a good substitution. I wonder how sweet you will taste while screaming for mercy."

Hazel made eye contact with him and showed no fear in her eyes. Ready to punch this disgusting man right in the face for how he spoke to her, she felt a strong, callused hand touch the lower part of her back, comforting her. Salt and iron filled her nostrils as Darius's deep and calming voice spoke, "You had your fun, Ratherian... Leave the poor children and my fiancee alone."

Hazel's heart leapt out of her chest and her breath left her body when Darius called her his fiancee. However, she didn't want to look like a trembling fawn in need of protection. He has always been there for her and supported her. Has always been at her side when she needs him.

"Fine, but Darius, keep a handle on your little pet, or she may end up being the next blood sacrifice we call for." Ratherian sneered before looking Hazel up and down with pure derision.

Watching Ratherian storm away, she let out an exhale of relief and turned her face to gaze into Darius's sapphire eyes, an ocean surrounded by the sandy tone of his tan skin "Fiancee, huh?"

Holding up her hand, she smiled faintly, looking at her bare fingers, then at him. "Last time I checked, my ring finger was bare, and I had yet to have said yes."

A soft chuckle escaped his rough lips as he gripped her waist pulling her tightly, almost possessively, to his muscular chest crashing his lips to her soft, supple lips "Last time I checked, my graceful fawn, I told you to not test the Netherian scum. Such a naughty little fawn."

Hazel's cheeks flushed with the warming sensation now emanating through her, despite the chill autumn air.Resting her hands on his chest, looking up at him with a mischievous grin "Ooh, is the big bad wolf, angry? It's so cute when you get protective."

His taunting smile went away as he took her chin in his hand. "Hazel, I am serious. You cannot be so reckless as to stand up against Ratherian, of all Netherian men. He is the worst of them. If your uncle hadn't told me what was going on just now, who knows what that scum would have done to you?"

Hazel huffed, pulling her chin away, but not stepping from Darius' grip. "The Netherian run this part of the land now because our king couldn't give two shits about Alexandria's well-being. He didn't even care that we were starving because of the brutal winter last year. Most townsfolk don't think Alexandria will survive this winter since this fall's harvest wasn't plentiful. If we lose our best healer in our village, we will suffer far worse."

Hazel frowned deeply, lowering her head, feeling a twinge of regret at acting before thinking. Darius was right. She couldn't wield magic like the Netherian people or the druids who abandoned these lands after the Aestivals vanished post war with the Netherians.

Hazel didn't know why or how but for some reason, she was able to do things most healers ,like Tanja, couldn't do without help.

Darius' calloused finger tilted her chin to look up at him as he gave her a kind smile, stroking her soft skin, examining her face for any signs of blood.

Sucking his teeth, he held her tighter, kissing her temple. "I love how courageous you are, Hazy, but please don't put yourself in danger like that again. Your uncle needs you in his life, as do I."

Hazel faintly smiled before leaning in to kiss him deeply, wrapping her arms around his neck and tangling her hands in his curly brown locks. "I know, my wolf. I promise I will be more careful next time." A mischievous smirk tugged at the corner of her lips as she tilted her head, holding up her left hand. "About that ring?"

"There is no being spontaneous with you, is there?" Darius smirked, tangled his hand in her golden locks, and cupped the back of her head.

"What if I wanted to take you to your mother's tree and get down on one knee before asking you to be not only my wife but my partner in crime?"

As Darius leaned in to kiss her, Hazel tilted her head back to meet his lips and caught a glimpse of Archibald hastily approaching from the corner of her eye. Darius looked in the direction of Archibald approach and back from Hazel to look at the kids, stroking the little boy's hair before returning his eyes to Hazel.

"I am going to make sure these two little ones make it back to their mom," Darius spoke softly before leading the children away.

Hazel nodded to Darius in appreciation before looking to her uncle, preparing herself for the lecture. Archibald looked over his niece, letting out a sigh of relief. "Hazel Grace, what were you thinking? You could have been killed or worse. What if they come back to make you their next Blood Bride? I can't lose you."

Blood Bride. It was the worst thing that could happen to a maiden. With the lack of order in Alexandria, there are no guards from Castle Wylana to maintain any sort of order in their small village.

The Netherian chose a maiden at random every month for the last 4 months, to take her to the heart of their territory where they drained her slowly and painfully until there was nothing left but an empty husk of flesh.

Two weeks ago, they selected a young maiden, the tanner's daughter Esmarie. Soon another Netherian male would come to choose his bride. Although, what she had just done by standing up to that mercenary may have put her at the top of their list for stepping out of line.

Hazel could tell by her uncle's labored breathing that his heart was racing, and she was surprised she couldn't hear it.

"I'm sorry, Uncle... I just couldn't stand aside. Something in me forced my legs to move. I hate to say it, but we can only pray to whatever gods will still listen to an Alexandrian prayer to spare me this month and have them choose another."

Thinking so selfishly made her skin recoil. Hazel hated how her village was being treated as if it was just some stain on the map of Wylana.

Taking a deep, shaky breath, she looked around the market almost as if she would be taking it in one last time.

The aroma of spices, loaves of bread, freshly harvested grains, and herbs for winter. Smoke coming from the smokehouse preparing jerky from rabbit and venison. Silver lined her icy blue irises. Her throat bobbed, but she looked at her uncle as he wiped the tears from her cheeks, kissing her head.

Chapter Three

Atticus

An icy rain trickled down the foggy glass of an arched window, towering high, nearly touching the roof of the mahogany wood interior castle walls making up the Wylana castle. Ivy dangled down on either side from vases, with tinges of lilac wisteria flowers adding a pop of color.

Like the weather, there wasn't anything pleasant upon Prince Atticus's honey-tanned face. Strands of hair blacker than the obsidian filled his eyes as the night sky was slowly approaching. A hint of a black-scaled dragon's tail tattooed into his skin coiled around his wrist, peering out from the cuff of his black puffy shirt.

He typically dressed in more formal attire with his cape, lapels, and amulets, but he was exhausted after his encounter with his father, King Kai. The merciless king couldn't care less about his people, but more about what he could do to strengthen his legacy, whether it be better or worse. Lately it was for the worst.

Kai wanted Atticus to follow in his steps, as has been the tradition, going back several generations . Atticus's grandfather had been Malekith the strange, known for being a fearful ruler who came up with creative ways to torment and punish his servants, foes, and even children. Malekith's relentless pursuit of a glorious legacy and strong bloodline resulted in him acquiring a plethora of dangerous enemies and ultimately led to him being beheaded by his own council.

He feared becoming his father, and for this reason he refused to take a wife. He took a mistress to his bed, Jesinda, but that was the closest thing he wanted get to any kind of serious relationship.

Although Atticus was not anything like the kings who came before him, genuinely wanting to protect his home and help it thrive,, he made himself seem threatening, cruel, and harsh. If his enemies believed he was, then they wouldn't dare threaten to harm his home. Atticus made sure he displayed that strength to his court and to its allies.

He, alongside his brothers Heath and Kingsly. fought on the front lines of so many battles in their father's name. That is when he earned the title Immortal Dragon.

Atticus felt unease because that title did not reflect who he truly was. He was just a prince who never wished for this life, but was willing to do what he must do to inherit the throne. It was the only way to bring his people back from the brink of extermination because of the Netherian race.

His youngest brother, Reed, was only ten, and, and the last thing Atticus wanted was his innocent soul to be corrupted by the horrors seen and done on the battlefield in the name of survival. The Netherian people were becoming a more significant hassle for the Wylana fleet as their numbers increased faster than Wylana's.

Atticus pleaded with his father to recall some of the men, who were sent to take back lands gifted to the noble houses by Atticus's grandfather. They needed to come home and rid the lands of the plague of Netherian magic that was defiling and destroying not only innocent villages, but temples honoring the Aestival warriors.

The stories of these legendary winged warriors were some of his favorite historical lessons. Because of Atticus being the heir to Wylana's throne, once his father died, he was taught from a young age what it took to rule . He was now twenty-five and glad he wasn't king to the crumbling kingdom he called home. Although a part of him wished he could find the Ivory Fawn and bring them to Wylana in an attempt to save his beloved kingdom. That would be a legacy he would be willing to risk everything for.

Watching two raindrops race each other down the window glass, his mind raced on possible ways he could show his father how devastated of a state their kingdom was. Why conquer more land when he could barely handle what they had now?

Atticus brought a black wineglass to his lips, rough in appearance but smooth upon the touch. Sipping on the delicately spiced wine brought to the castle from a small village called Anniston, it known for the rich spice wines they brew with pride.

It was a very luxurious and elegant village, one of the few the Netherian wouldn't go near, because of the guards patrolling it thanks to them earning King Kai's favor for their wines and food. Every year around Kai's birthday , Anniston threw a wine festival in his honor

The sound of footsteps on marbled floors behind him reached his ears, their familiar delicate cadence on the marbled floors indicating it was his mother approaching.

Placing her hand upon his back in between his shoulder blades, Queen Sage peered up at her eldest, who stood a good foot taller than her.

Glimpsing down, he smiled at his mother. She was considered, far and wide, a beautiful woman with her white as snow complexion, lips red as the roses she tended to in her garden, and platinum blonde hair. Her natural beauty was accentuated by the crystal dangling earrings, matching necklace, and, of course, her royal crown.

Sadly in Atticus's opinion, it was common for the queen to be dressed as if she was a prized opal for all men to gawk at but never touch, for she belonged to the king. She was a captivating broodmare for him to breed the finest royal stallions that would carry on the Bromiston bloodline.

"How bad?" Was all the gentle queen asked. It was common knowledge how cruel Kai was to his own children, but Sage knew how bad it was from firsthand experience, being on the receiving end of the cruel ways of her husband she was forced to marry. Sage slowly scanned her son, who was from how his lips thinned , was fuming in the ivory covered hallway that was dimly lit by candle bras. Her handmaidens warned the queen to be cautious about approaching him in fear Atticus would harm their queen in his angry state.

Unknown to everyone, Atticus held a vow in his heart that he would never hit his mother or any woman like his father was.

He looked at his mother, and upon seeing the concern on her face she always held when she would fuss about him being careful, he gave her a faint smile to reassure her he was not harmed in any way. "Well, he didn't give me a lashing like last time. So, I will take that as a victory."

A soft sigh escaped her lip, followed by a faint nod as she took his hand where the dragon tail wound around his wrist, holding it tight.

"Atticus, you shouldn't push him. You know how he can get, and I am in no way prepared to mourn a son."

Atticus turned fully to his mother, giving her soft hand a delicate squeeze before bringing it to his lips and kissing her knuckle. He examined his mother to make sure the earlier meeting didn't cause king Kai to lash out as he had in the past/ However, thankfully Atticus saw no sign of a new bruise forming or the aroma of oils the castle healers used in their salve to tend to freshly cut wounds.

"He is letting the Netherian scum poison our home. Allowing the people who turn to him for help to suffer at the hands of those inhumane monsters. If I was king-" A warning look came from his mother's soft ice-blue eyes, making him refrain from continuing his rant. Atticus exhaled as if to rid his approaching words off his tongue, not wanting to further any trouble for himself or his mother.

"I wish that damn Ivory Fawn would show up like they were supposed to during the Blood War and get rid of those bastards so we can be done with them."

Sage let out a faint laugh, shaking her head and kissing her son's scarred hand. "You still believe the Aestivals will come back? They have been dead for almost a hundred and fifty years now. We will be lucky if they ever rise again. Your grandchildren may not even see them or *their* grandchildren. Sadly, with prophecies, there isn't an exact timeline for when they will happen."

Atticus looked out the window, watching the rain for a moment, wondering if there was any hope left for his kingdom before he faintly smiled. "I have a feeling it may be sooner than we think, Mother, and I hope I will get a front-row seat when the Ivory Fawn rises to rid the lands of the Netherian plague. To see those warriors rise once more."

The queen chuckled, releasing her son's hand before she rested her hand on his arm. "And I cannot wait for that day when we are freed of their tyranny. But for now, my son, you are the best hope for Wylana, not the Aestival's proclaimed Ivory Fawn.For now you need your rest, as do I."

Noting she was standing on her toes, Atticus lowered his head so his mother could kiss his head just as did when she wished him goodnight as a child.

Watching his mother return to her handmaiden's side, who was watching Atticus as if worried the prince would do something behind the queen's back. Atticus' brow furrowed as his eyes became sharp as his blade towards the maiden. Quickly, the maid looked down and away from the prince, hurrying after her queen. He turned his head to look out the window again, sipping another drop from his glass. The clove and cinnamon burning his throat as the wine trails down his throat. A sensation that has always helped him ground when his temper was getting the best of him.

Resting the arm that held the wine glass at his side, a delicate hand slid between his shoulder and down to the small of his back. A small framed woman with raven black hair joined his side, taking his wine glass from his grasp, trailing her finger along his jaw.

Atticus looked down at his mistress, who now stood half his size beside him. Following her head gesture towards his bedroom, he sighed softly before leaning down, kissing her cheek, taking her chin into his hand, and hovering his lips over her.

"While very tempting to have my way with you tonight, I'd rather enjoy a night of ecstasy alone."

Without waiting for her words, he straightened, turned away from her, and made his way back to his bedroom.

Chapter Four

Atticus

Morning sunlight peaked through the faintly open curtains of stained-glass archway doors that lead out to a large balcony overlooking the castle's main courtyard. The windows were so immense, they stretched up to the ceiling of mahogany that matched the walls and floor of the vast room. The sun's rays peaked in through the maroon drapes that blocked out some of its morning warmth and light, although there was a slit just enough for it to beam into his sleep-filled eyes. A small groan escaped his lips as Atticus sat up slowly in his bed, wiping the sleep from his eyes. The maroon silk sheets slipped off his sculpted chest, revealing the full aspect of a black dragon inked into his skin while he was in the battle of Strull.

One of his men had tattooed the dragon upon his arm while drinking in celebration of winning a near death battle. Its head forever inked into a snarl upon his left pectoral, its wingless body coiled down his left arm where the tip of the tail wrapped around his wrist. The title of Immortal Dragon forever grained into his skin the day he earned the name.

. It felt as if his body creaked, trying to waken from its long night. As he shifted his body in his morning ritual of stretching, causing his sore joints to pop, a satisfied groan escaped from the crown prince's lips. The dragon appeared as if it, too, was trying to wake from its slumber.

He didn't even bother to take off his deep hickory-colored trousers last night before he got into bed.

Swinging his feet over the right side of his mattress, he looked to the round, mahogany nightstand that had a turned over mead bottle, whose honey-like contents had spilled. Sighing softly, he ran his hand through his hair, raised from his bed, and made his way towards the large open archway that led into his bath chambers. Unlike his bedroom, an array of deep reds, the bathroom held an array of black, with tinges of white to highlight the marble patterns. Walking over to the oval black marble sink, where two vials of oils sat beside the spout, he picked up the vial of bergamot and cedar oils. They were something Arabella recommended to him to help with his achy muscles. Despite his youth, the countless battles and injuries he has sustained in his years fighting for his father had taken a toll on his body. Leaning now onto the sink in order to splash his face with cold water to further wake from his slumber, his mind was occupied elsewhere instead of the present. The idea of what his father was planning on doing Alexandria weighing a bit heavy on him.

Looking in the mirror, he saw the stubble of his onyx facial hair growing out along his firm jawline and slightly around his neck. Turning his head a bit to examine it, he ran his calloused hand over his skin to feel it had barely come in yet.

Exhaling slowly, he dried off his hands on a nearby black towel before reaching over and picking up the vials of oil. Pulling out the droppers, he added the suggested amount from each vial as Arabella prescribed. After rubbing his palms together to warm the cold oil, he massaged his arms, finding comfort with the earthy aroma. Setting the vials down, he washed his hands clean before turning and walking towards the main chamber of his room, where his gaze went to the fireplace and the fire that had died out during the night. Sighing, he wandered towards the left corner of his room, opposite of the fireplace, where a stack of wood was sitting. Grabbing some logs, he carefully set them on the embers them in an attempt to bring the fire back alive when there was a knock on the door.

Turning his head, he let out a faint growl in irritation as to who would dare bother him this early in the morning, before he had even had a drop of his morning coffee, let alone breakfast.

"What?" was all he ground out.

Slowly, the door opened and a small young boy peered his head in. The morning sunlight lit up the young prince's eyes as if the sun was hitting the calm ocean, although there was worry upon his face, seeing the look of alarm and panic on the young Prince Reed's face.

Atticus straightened up after throwing in a log of fire, not caring how it landed in the fire. The crown prince hurried over to his brother, kneeling before him. Before any words came out, Atticus quickly examined his younger brother for signs of physical harm. Taking his brother's face into his hand to bring Reed's eyes to look at him as he rested his other hand on the young prince's shoulder.

"What is it?" Atticus gritted out.

Reed's throat bobbed up and down as he looked at his older brother, almost scared for some reason. He was the one brother Atticus didn't treat like he was just some naïve boy with a title to a throne he may never inherit.

They always sparred together, and rode together. Atticus would tell him the stories of the Aestival people and play childish games with him when his other brothers wouldn't. Atticus other two younger brothers, Heath and Kingsly, were always caught up with their own activities to make even a sliver of time for the youngest prince.

King Kai kept Kingsly, his second-born son, busy being the general of his armies while Heath was kept busy being the king's political advisor. Although, after becoming an embarrassment in his father's eyes, Heath was sent away to search for the missing Druid clans.

Atticus thought it was a fruitless endeavor to send Heath on a wild hunt for these clans for in one had heard or or seen any hint of their existence in the hundred and fifty years since the Blood War where they were last seen battling beside the Aestivals, fighting against the Netherian to protect Wylana from their monarchs tyranny. When the Aestivals fell, it was assumed the clans were wiped out with them.

Atticus was the only brother who treated him with kindness, despite the rumors claiming he was cruel, how his heart was nothing but pure stone who didn't care who he harmed in his path of power, just as his father did. How he showed no mercy on the battlefield as the so-called dragon who took a sword to the chest and somehow still managed to win the battle of Strull.

"Father is summoning your presence to the war room." Shy, the young prince, spoke.

Atticus sucked his teeth in irritation, shaking his head. When his father *summoned* him, it was never a pleasant meeting. Either his brother had done something where he were going to be punished, and his father wished for Atticus to watch, or (other option.)

The king did this to prove to his sons his wrath would not stop at them just because they were his sons.

Atticus was hoping for a peaceful morning, but since he was a crown prince and son of a cruel father such as King Kai, there were never any peaceful mornings in Castle Wylana.

"How angry is he?" Atticus groaned out.

Reed's throat bobbing once more was all the answer Atticus needed. Standing up, he ruffled Reed's hair, took a deep breath, and headed to his large black wardrobe to grab his formal attire as Reed followed him like some puppy.

"Where is Mother?" Atticus asked with a concerned tone, hoping his father didn't harm her in one of his wrath-filled tantrums. The man often used his wife as an outlet for his anger before summoning Atticus to undoubtedly unleash any unsatisfied wrath upon him.

"She is in the sitting room knitting with her ladies." Reed replied softly as Atticus threw on a clean maroon shirt, black vest, and jacket. He turned his attention to Reed, grateful his mother wasn't alone.

"Good. I want you to wait with her, okay? Both of you stay out of father's way till I come back."

The ocean-eyed prince nodded his head before he hurried out of Atticus's chambers to find his mother. Leaning his head back, Atticus took a deep breath, mentally preparing himself for his father's tyranny. He exhaled softly as he put up his walls to prevent his father from ever reading the fear, worry, concern, and disgust that always showed on his face when in his father's presence.

Chapter Five

Atticus

Strolling into the war room, he wasn't surprised that Kingsly was already at his father's side, engaging in a battle strategy. He was overlooking the map his father had spread out along the table, examining every fine detail and figurine of his beloved home.

Kingsly's icy blue eyes scanned every detail as he took in every word his father spoke, not registering his eldest brother had come in.

It was important to the general prince to make sure he was always ready for a fight. With the king reigning with a strong hand. Many did not share Kai's ideals of ruling, leading to many enemies within the kingdom.

His long blonde hair was braided back, and laid across his shoulder, the tip of the braid ending right above his chest that was covered in silver-plated armor with a symbol of a lion with wings spread wide across it. A blue cape draped across one shoulder, and a sword hung from his belt.

The hilt looked to be normal, but the steel blade was engraved with runes to provide protection and swiftness on the battlefields.

Atticus and Kingsly were semi-matched in battle skills, but Atticus was more nimble, straight to the killing blow, while Kingsly relied solely on his brute strength and size in battle.

He over-towered Atticus by a few inches, but Kingsly wouldn't dare to be on the opposite end of his eldest brother's blade. He was once before and received a scar across his chest for it. Kingsly's sculptured jaw hardened as he looked from the map to his father.

"That village is plagued by the Netherian scum. Last I heard from a traveling merchant, Netherian men are now taking Blood Brides every month. If we allow that to spread into the other villages, what's to stop it from showing up at our gates? The number of their women are dwindling quickly."

King Kai let out a lowered snarl as his gaze slowly rose to look up at his second-born son. The pools of gray and faint green shot to Kingsly's eyes as the cruel king's muscular jaw was hidden by a thick full black well-kept beard. The only detail hinting the kin's age was the gray that grew near his sideburns, only visible when his black hair was swept back.

"That is why we are going to wipe it out. Blame it on the Netherian scum that already plagues it. Although, I want you and Atticus to be the ones to lead that charge. It will end their suffering, and we won't have to hear the Alexandrian people's constant plea for assistance."

Atticus heard how his father ordering the slaughter of innocent men, women, and children for the sake of not having to deal with their suffering. Willing to slaughter an entire village. It blew Attiucs's mind that his father dismissed them like they were cockroaches beneath his foot.

It made Atticus's blood boil as he clenched his fist in his jacket pockets, but he had to remain calm. If he lashed out, then his father could very much strip Atticus title away as heir and give it to Kingsly, who did everything his father said like a good little general he was.

Taking a deep breath, Atticus stepped forward with an unamused expression on his face, shielding his true feelings behind a steel wall. He needed to convince his father that he shouldn't go through with this, not when there were innocent children involved.

"I have a better solution. That village borders the Netherian territory they claimed for themselves for centuries after the Blood War...Why not take that village back from the Netherian people, forcing them back to their territory and let their blood paint the streets instead?" Atticus suggested, trying to stroke that possessive side of his father who obsessed over his legacy. "Perhaps take their territory completely from them. Father, you claim you want to leave this world with a great legacy. Why not be known as the king who drove the Netherian people from his kingdom?" Continuing on, Atticus saw the contemplation in his father's eyes. "Unless you don't want to leave a great legacy anymore and rather be known as a cowardly king."

Kingsly gave his eldest brother a warning look not to pick a fight with their father. He was already angry enough with the pleas for help. Atticus knew he was treading on thin ice because if his father wanted, he could whip Atticus for stepping out of line.

However, his father was never the one to deal with the lashings with his sons, it was always the general prince who would was the one to hold that whip. Kingsly did his best to make it less painful for his brothers, and always holding back and striking only certain areas to keep the pain and scarring to a minimum. Although their father was never known for holding back when it came to punishing his sons.

It was how his father taught him, so Kai treated his sons no differently , and used it to 'Make them stronger' as he always told them.

Thankfully, the only one who was spared from his punishment was Reed, because Atticus and his brothers were standing on the same stand point when it comes to taking Reeds punishments.

Although their father didn't let Reed off easily, he forced the poor boy to watch as his older brothers took his punishment and tried to hold back their. Reed would cry every time and try to look away, but his father always forced him to watch.

King Kai inclined his head back as he stared down at his heir. It was a lethal quiet, but Atticus didn't break his eye contact with his father, as if he was almost challenging his father.

The sickening grin appearing on his father's face made him want to recoil as Kingsly did, but Atticus kept up his wall to show he would not back down. "Alright then, I will spare Alexandria, but you and Kingsly will go together and access the damage the Netherian people have done to it. You will, of course, be accompanied by a few men, then you will report back to me. If it's worth the cause, Kingsly, I want your best men to patrol that village...... Dispose of them and make measures to keep the Netherian scum out... Dismissed."

Kingsly looked at his father in disbelief, putting his hand down on the map and turning to face him, shock in his eyes. "I can't spare men, Ardnaxela and I are already—" Sound of a slap echoed through the war room as Kingsly's face whipped to the side.

The king fully turned to his second born as his hand print now laid across Kingsly's cheek, who kept his face looking to the ground, at hearing the growl emanating from his father's throat.

"I gave you an order, General! You may be my son, but you are also my general, who will *not* question me. Am I clear?"

Atticus held himself back from thrusting his father into the wall with his fist and forcing him to apologize to Kingsly, but the crown prince had to keep his mouth shut. It would only make things worse, not only Kingsly but also for himself.

Kingsly stood straightened up, keeping his eyes lowered as their father once again dismissed them, this time with a wave of the hand. Atticus waited till Kingsly left before him to make sure his mouth didn't get him in trouble further. When Kai was in a mood like this, it was better to tread lightly on the ice to avoid being whipped.

Catching up to his brother was an easy task for Atticus, despite his smaller stature. Matching his pace to his brother's, he took a glance at Kingsly's face, but eyes went forward as Kingsly noticed the glance.

"I don't need your pity, Atticus!" Kingsly said sharply.

"It's not pity, but concern," Atticus replied. There was an unspoken silence between them as they shared a glance before they inhaled deeply. A few beats passed between them as they walked down the hall. Atticus's eyes caught on to a raven-haired woman, who gave him a flirtatious wink, before Atticus looked back to his brother. "So, General, what is the plan?"

There was another beat of silence before Kingsly sighed softly, pulling his braid to drape over his shoulder. "I will talk with Ardnaxela to assure our men are prepared for our message to send the regiment to our location."

A look of surprise was painted upon his face as he looked at Kingsly, raising his eyebrow. "Wait, you're not bringing the White Dragon or the regiment with us?"

"No. Like I tried to say before, I don't have the men to spare. Ardnaxela will make sure everything runs smoothly while find out how much damage there is with Alexandria. If they are past saving, you and I will find a way to get the remaining civilians out of there. If we can somehow take that village back, we will."

Atticus faintly chuckled, resting his hand on Kingsly's shoulder, admiring his brother's cleverness to go behind their father's back.

"Then we leave tomorrow morning. The sooner we get there, the sooner we can stop them from taking another Blood Bride. Rest up, brother, it will be a two-day trip."

Chapter Six

Hazel

The aroma of freshly baked cottage bread filled the small cottage, accompanied by the blend of rosemary, thyme, and garlic seasoned steaks roasting in the fireplace. Thanks to Darius's father owning the butcher, he made sure Hazel and her Uncle Archibald were never without various types of meat.Such as beef , poultry, and game meat.

She stared out the window, watching her garden as Marie, once more, curled up by the fireplace. Hazel, for a moment, was lost in her thoughts before the door opened. Turning her head, she greeted her uncle with a gentle smile. Archibald stood in the entryway that had a full view of the living room as he took off his dirty boots at the entry before removing his long trench coat and hanging it on the clothes rack on the wall beside the door. From the look on his face, he had a long day helping to tend to the autumn harvesting of wheat.

"Dinner is just about done. I made steaks with mashed potatoes and asparagus from the garden." She spoke softly to her uncle as he approached to give her their routine hug when he returned after work.

Walking over to the fireplace, Hazel went to grab the iron skillet, but without thinking or hearing her uncle's warning in her haze of her thoughts, she reached out with her bare hand.

A cry of pain escaped her lips seconds as her skin touched the hot metal, and her uncle quickly appeared at her side, taking her hand and examining it carefully. The smell of her flesh blistering made her stomach curdle.

Archibald took the mitten for the cast iron they kept beside the fireplace and removed the skillet from the fire before he led his niece away from the fire to a stool, sitting Hazel down on it before trying to pry open her hand.

"I'm fine, it's nothing," she whimpered out as she tried to act as if it was nothing.

Hazel kept her hand closed, scared to see the damage done to her hand, but her uncle looked her in the eyes. "No, you're not. Let me see," Archibald demanded

Hesitantly, she winced as she opened her hand to see for herself the damage. Seeing a good portion of her skin was burnt away, already white splotches around the burn mark and blistering on the second layer of skin. She was seconds away from burning off if she didn't release it as quickly. "Nophy." Archibald cursed the goddess of healing before looking at his niece, resting his hand on her shoulder. "Tell me what I can do to help." Panic filled his voice.

Tears formed in her eyes as the pain intensified, making hard to think. Hazel looked into the kitchen. "Grab some of the beeswax I collected, take some calendula and marshmallow root and mix it, add it to the beeswax, then you will grab some gauze I have left so I can wrap it."

Hearing her instruction, he rushed to grab what Hazel said was needed. With the items in his hands, Archibald hastily moved back to his niece. Very gently, he applied the salve, trying to ignore her yelp of pain. Once he bandaged her hand, Archibald kissed her head, resting his palm on the back of her neck, glad she would be okay now that they treated her burn.

"What was going on in your head, fawn?" All Hazel could hear was the concern in his voice as he pulled away, resting one of his hands now on her shoulders.

Hazel remained sitting, holding her burnt hand to her chest, trying to calm her shaky hands and body from the adrenaline that was slowly trickling away.

"What is going through your head my little fawn?" Archibald asked , his voice filled with concern.

Hazel swallowed before she looked at her uncle. "They return here in a few days for a Blood Bride...What if they choose me? After what I did in the village square, I am sure I am next." Hazel tried to hold back the fear in her voice, but it wobbled as she spoke.

Archibald pulled her head onto his shoulder as he kneeled before her, kissing the top of her head and inhaling a deep breath, almost as if he wanted to remember what his niece smelt of that vanilla and sandalwood oil she uses every morning, as if this would be the last time. "I won't let them take you. Leave town the night before they come, I beg of you. Please take Darius with you. He will make sure you are safe."

Pulling away, she looked at him, shaking her head with in disbelief at his suggestion. She would be leaving her uncle to the mercy of the Netherian. When they learned she left town the night before they came to collect her. Hazel knew that what she did in that courtyard with Ratherian, She most likely signed her death warrant. The idea of what they would do to him for protecting her. They would probably give him a slow and painful death.

"What?! No! You are coming with me! I won't leave you, not when they can kill you for helping me escape if they come for me," Hazel exclaimed, getting to her feet, her face draining of all color.

Archibald took her shoulder in his firm grip with a somber look as silver threatened to come forth from his eyes. Feeling him cupping her cheeks, Archibald ran his thumb under her eyes to wipe away the tear that clung to Hazel's bottom lashes.

"And I swore to your mother I would protect you, even if that meant with my last breath. I have lived a long life with so many fond memories. You are so young, my fawn princess. You must continue to live."

Hazel pushed his hand off her cheek, quickly wrapping her arms around her uncle's neck, pulling him close to her, ignoring the screaming pain in her hand as she held him. Her cheeks were now soaked with tears as she refused to let him go.

"No! No, I won't abandon you! You're the only father I have known. Please come with me! Please! I can't lose you," she cried.

Archibald held his niece tight, unable to stop his own tears from falling, holding her close to him, his grip like a bear protecting its cub.

Hazel couldn't muffle her sob as she hid her face in the crook of her uncle's neck, inhaling the scent of cinnamon, cloves, and sandalwood. She would never abandon the man who put clothes on her back, taught her how to read and write, or taught her how to ride a horse. He taught her everything she knew. How could she abandon him? Archibald took her in as if she were his daughter when she lost her mother and father. Being an only child to her parents, Archibald was the only family she had left in her life. She didn't want to let him go.

Hazel would do anything in her power to protect him as he had protected her. Pay back everything he had done for her. Leaving him here in this cottage to be at the mercy of the Netherian was an idea so sickening it made her sun kissed skin turn pale as snow. It was an insane concept to her. She would never be able to live with herself if she left him here, and he died.

They would kill him without a second thought out of not just anger he sent her away, but sheer excitement in killing him slowly to feast on his screams of pain and agony.

"I know, my fawn, I know. I would give anything to go with you, but I will just slow you both down, and I can't risk your safety," Archibald breathed out.

Unfortunately, she knew her uncle was right. If he came with her and Darius, they would have to stop more frequently to let him rest for a moment. With his leg, he wasn't able to move like the rest of the men in the village. Not with a limp in his leg due to the shattering of his knee. A wound he got in battle defending Wylana from an attack on Alexandria. He was lucky enough that could still work in the fields.

Her blood turned cold at the thought of her uncle being killed by the Netherian men who painted blood through the village square without anyone to stop them. Hazel could feel her heart starting to crumble as her uncle told her he couldn't risk her safety if he went with her.

Archibald stroked his niece's arm, trying to comfort her as their tears fall like the rain that threatened to come later in the day.

He must have known he would never see her again when she left, but at least she would be safe with Darius and away from this destructive village. Leaning back to look at his niece, he cupped her chin gently. "You have so much ahead of you, Hazel. Your mother would be proud of the woman you grew up to be."

Hearing his words was like a dagger plunging deeper into her already breaking heart. Her world was spinning so fast around her to where she couldn't breathing. Hazel wanted everything to stop, everything to go away.

"I swear to you, Uncle, I will find a way for both of us to leave...Together...We leave together," she swore to the universe.

Not wanting to argue with her, Archibald nodded before he kissed her head with a faint chuckle.

"My stubborn little fawn.... May Aena bless us with such a gift."

Chapter Seven

Hazel

The fire was slowly dying. No one stirred inside the Hilliston cottage, not even Marie, who was curled up on the foot of the bed with Hazel.

The crisp autumn night was peaceful. Not even the howls of the dogs could be heard. Moonlight filled the cottage and was the only light in the home. Hazel startled awake, clenching the sheets to her burnt yellow colored nightgown as her hair hung loosely around her after she heard a loud banging on her front door.

"Please! Please open up! It's an emergency! Fawn!"

Hazel was hesitant on answering until she recognized Darius's voice. She flung her sheets back, scrambling to pull a knitted cream blanket around her before searching for a match and a candle to light.

When she opened her door to her bedroom, Archibald was already standing there with a lit candelabra. He motioned for her to follow as they rushed downstairs.

Hazel's nightgown trailed behind her ,just at the base of her heel. Archibald and Hazel hurried down the stairs towards the front door.

Archibald opened the door as he did. Hazel's eyes widened at what she saw.

Darius had an arm of a boy , whose body hung loosely around Darius's neck, though the candle light wasn't bright enough to see him clearly. As she approached with her candle, Hazel saw a severe case of Raven Palm sap poisoning. As Archibald stepped closer with his candelabra, she could see it was the young farmer's son. "Holy Aena, bring him inside. Set him on the dining table," he instructed.

Darius nodded his head once, stepping around Hazel As he came in, the boy's father came in right behind him, helping Darius put his son on the table, who cried out in pain from the movement.

Hazel hurried over to the sick boy, setting her candle down to examine him. She then saw the source of the pain and blood seeping through his white shirt beneath a tear. As Hazel pulled back his shirt, she spied a deep puncture wound on his lower abdomen from what could have been a dagger. It was riddled with black veins leading away from the wound. Painful blood blisters were already forming around the white, blotchy skin. He had a foul stench of emesis so strong, Hazel had to keep herself from vomiting herself.

"Please, please save my boy. He is all I have." The farmer pleaded to Hazel, getting to his knees and grabbing the skirt of her nightgown.

Archibald put his hand on the farmer's shoulder, squeezing it to assure him. "Regulus, he is in good hands." The farmer looked up at Archibald and before he released her skirt and stood up, now staring down at his son, taking his hand that dangled off the table.

Hazel knew it was signing a death warrant to touch the poison, yet here was Darius, carrying the infected boy. Just touching the sap could cause painful blistering as the acidic properties interacted with the skin. Hazel noticed his hands were slightly darker at the tips of his fingers. Almost like they had been turning black. He must have been working in the butcher shop late tonight. She would have to lecture her fiance to be more wise in his decision making, but her mission now was to see if she could reverse the effect of the Raven Palm sap.

Her throat bobbed as she looked over at the boy, knowing she had a very small window to save him. Letting out a sigh, she looked at the men in the room. "Uncle, get me the milk thistle, calendula, turmeric, and dandelion I keep in the shed. Pick the freshest ones–they are the most potent. Regulus, I need you to focus so I can help your son. Can you please do that?"

Wiping his eyes dry, he nodded his head, straightening up.

"Good, grab me clean rags from the linen closet next to the fireplace, all of them." Hazel began to bark out he order in a rush of time against the poisoning.

Turning her head to Darius ,who just stood there, she motioned with her chin to the fireplace, "also, the fireplace poker. I will need to cauterize the wound when I clean it."

Turning her head to Darius ,watching him do as she directed them, Hazel took a deep breath. She had very little time to save them. The sap from the blade wasn't just eating the poor farmer boy's skin, but also where Darius's skin had met the wound. While calming herself, Archibald and Regulus did exactly as she said.

The stench of the corrosive burning flesh made her skin crawl in disgust.

Hazel watched as her uncle ground the herbs up in a white marble mortar and pestle as she hurried over to Darius to examine him, holding the candelabra in her hand wising she had more light.

"Take off your shirt." Hazel urged.

Darius nods his head without hesitation removed his tunic shirt.

Gently, she examined his bare, muscular torso. From slinging heavy carcasses, Darius was toned in his abdomen, arms, chest, and back as if he was sculpted from clay by the gods. Hazel forgot about her burnt hand for a moment as she winced from the slightest bit of pressure against her injured hand as she examined his torso to see how tender Darius's own wounds were. She needed to calculate how much time he had after his bare skin was exposed to the sap.

Darius must have seen her bandaged hand, for he took it gently with the tips of his fingers.

The swirling hues of her blue eyes intertwined with the warm depths of his walnut-brown gaze. Her throat bobbed slightly, as if trying to swallow down the lie. "I am fine."

Before she allowed him to speak, Hazel quickly made her way around the couch towards the fireplace. There she grabbed a small kettle, walking over to the sink to put water in it before hanging it over the cheerful fire. Archibald approached her with the ground herbs, putting them inside of the teakettle so the mixture could steep in the water.

The boy began to thrash, holding his abdomen as the sap further spread, causing agonizing pain. The sound that left the poor boy's body was guttural. Regulus moved to hold his son down, trying to calm him.

Tears formed in Hazel's eyes as she ran over to grab some poppy leaves from her small apothecary and ground them up with her mortar and pestle before retrieving a glass of water for the boy, dropping the poppy leaves into the water before running over to the table and handing the cup to Regulus.

"Have your son drink this. Just be careful. If you don't touch his wound, you won't get sick."

Regulus nodded his head softly before he puts the elixir in his son's mouth, encouraging him to drink every last drop of it.

It took about five minutes before the poppie's sedative properties took effect.To help the boy who once was thrashing, was now laying on the table sleeping. Hazel gave Darius a smaller dose as well to help with the pain, but not enough to make him incoherent like she needed the boy who had been thrashing moments ago. That way , if she needed his help , he was coherent. It was a blessing that his wound seemed minor compared to the boy,

The kettle started whistling from its place in the fireplace, leading Hazel to run over and remove it from the heat. Grabbing a bowl, Hazel poured the liquid into a bowl and put the pile of rags next to it, wincing as the steam irritated her burnt and bandaged hand. Gasping in the sudden sting, she set the kettle down, cradling her hand to her chest before remembering to put up a wall to block out the pain.

Darius came up from behind her, holding his side with one hand while resting the other on the small of her back.

"Fawn, tell me what to do. You hurt. If that poison-"

Hazel's eyes shot to his as she took a pained breath in from her hand throbbing. "My wolf, I shall be fine." She breathed through the pain. Drenching the rags into the content of the bowl, Hazel then handed one of the cups to Darius before she rung out the rag best she could with her hand "Drink this, no sugar or honey, then sit there with the rag on the infected area," Hazel continued before handing him the wet rag.

Darius knew it was the wiser option not to argue with her when she was focused like this. Bringing the tea to Regulus, she put her wounded hand on his shoulder. "Have him drink this. The milk thistle will remove the poison naturally from his body. The turmeric will help with the inflammation and any viruses that are in his body from the effects of the poison. The dandelion will flush his system of anything harmful."

Without hesitation, he blew on the tea to cool it before helping his son drink it. Hazel then rung out the rag meant for the boy, laying it gently over the wound, and motioned for Archibald to come to her side in.

"Apply even pressure to the wound," she instructed

Archibald's hand remained firm, the treated rag serving as the only barrier between his skin and the infectious wound.

Hazel walked over to the fire, kneeling down, trying to figure out what else she could do for the boy, if anything at all. With how deep the wound was mixed with the deadly, acidic sap, he would surely die at her dining table. How was she going to break that news to Regulus? Feeling her uncle kneeling beside her, she slowly looked up at him.

"I know I told you never to use it..." He trailed off before letting out a deep sigh. "Although in this case, I would turn a blind eye," he whispered, keeping his voice low as he pushed a strand of hair from her eyes.

A faint gasp of shock escaped her lips as her attention snapped to her uncle before glancing to the three guests at her dinner table where Darius was standing next to the farmer and his son.

Hazel had always had a radiant gift that helped heal darker wounds, such as one from the sap. However, when she first showed her skills to her mother, she was forbidden to use it..

Looking at her uncle, her voice cracked a bit as she whispered, "I swore to her-" her words got caught in her throat as she swallowed hard.

Archibald put his hand on her shoulder, squeezing it before he nodded her head. Hazel knew this boy would not survive this, not with how extensive the damage was. No healer was able to cure the Raven Palm poison once it spread to this extent. To do so would draw attention to her, and not all good. Although she couldn't let the poor boy die.

He was barely thirteen, so young and playful. Her only response to her uncle was with a nod of her head, indicating she would do it. Hazel knew her mother would understand and probably be telling her the same thing Archibald was telling her.

Walking over to the unfortunate boy, Archibald walked over to Regulus, putting his hand on his shoulder. "Come, my friend, let her work. She needs to focus if she is to save him." Archibald glanced at Darius, who joined Hazel's side as she stared down at that boy on the table barely holding on by a thread. Wrapping a protective arm around her waist as if he knew that look of dread on her face.

"You, too, Darius. Hazel is capable on her own."

Kissing Hazel's temple softly before gripping her shoulder reassuringly, Darius took his leave with Regulus and Archibald. He momentarily stopped at the door to the sitting room to glance back at her before he walked in, closing the door behind him.

Hearing the door close, waited a moment before she walked over to the couch that sat in front of the fireplace, kneeling down before it. Moving aside the coffee table, she removed a small rug before lifting up a loose floor panel.

As she takes it out, she pulled out an engraved wooden rectangle box. The initial A.A was engraved on it with leaves and branches decorating the top.

Inside was a raw amethyst crystal point that had a brown clay tree wrapping around the top. The three on the ornate both held lilac and orchid clay painted leaves. At its trunk, it had lilac mushrooms growing up from the moss that speckled around the roots that held it in place.

Rough crystal met her smooth finger as her hand reached towards the brown leather cord, one that looped through a gold ring on the top of the tree.. Pulling the amulet out of the box, she put it around her neck as a tear fell from her eye.

"Mother, please, if you still are with me, forgive me." Standing up, she hurried over to the boy. The necklace warmed the skin between her breasts. Assuming the warmth was due to its placement by the fireplace.

Hazel looked to the door for a moment before she returning her gaze back to the boy who was ridden with sweat, his skin now deathly pale, as if he was about to meet death himself.

Grasping her necklace, she took a deep, calming breath, focusing her mind on the amethyst in her hand. Closing her eyes, she began the journey into the back of her mind, searching for the smallest sliver of light to help her obtain the magic she needed to save this boy.

Images of an oak tree standing tall in the middle of a pond, its lilac leaves rustling in the wind, wisteria flowers hung from the pillars trembling in the breeze. The aroma of verbena and lavender filled Hazel's nostrils as she dove deeper into the back of her mind.

A woman approached, long golden hair draped down over her dress made of silk dyed in shades of periwinkle, orchid, and lavender colors. A floral crown made of aster flowers, lupine, and morning glories sat upon her head, and her neck was decorated with charoite, grape agate, and amethyst crystal necklace.

She looked as if she was a angelic goddess, as ivory feathers wings draped loosely behind her. The woman tilted her head before she raised a hand to Hazel, the woman's skin decorated in swirls of periwinkle and lilac.

A sensation of calm and tranquility washed over her as she approached the woman, gently taking her hand. Being guided along the marble stone path to the tree, the goddess kneeled with Hazel next to the pool of water, where she swore she saw gold shimmering light coming from the water.

Hazel's eyes locked onto the reflection in the water, expecting to see her own - but instead, a woman stared back at her. Cascading curls of molten gold framed her face, and atop her head rested a crown of gilded antlers. Four strands of Ivy wrapped skywards

, adorned with smooth amethyst and chariot crystals that glimmered like captured star dust. Strands of the same delicate flowers the goddess kneeling beside her wore woven the base of her crown, their petals swaying gently in the unseen breeze.

Ivory and gold silk fabric clung to the woman's body, cupping every curve perfectly and the deep plunge neckline where an ivory doe's head was painted between the woman's breast sculpted beautifully.

An ivory feather fell into the water from behind Hazel's head, and Hazel noticed tinges of gold in it. Slowly, the goddess took Hazel's gaze from the pool to look into her own golden eyes. Leaning forward and kissing Hazel's head, the goddess helped Hazel rise to her feet.

The goddess took her delicately painted hand placing it over her chest, where a large ball of radiant light now appeared. It danced in the woman's hand before she moved it to Hazel's chest.

Warm light filled every vein of Hazel's body. Gasping in shock, Hazel's chest involuntarily arched up towards the tree as it illuminated brightly. Then the world faded away, and Hazel, once again, stood in her cottage.

Her hand that was resting on the boy's chest was now glowing radiantly with a comforting warmth, as if the morning sun was kissing his skin. Hazel wavered, stepping back and holding her head in her good hand while the bandaged one clutched the necklace as she caught her breath.

It felt as if she was so heavily intoxicated, she couldn't see straight.

Archibald came into the room to check on Hazel. Seeing Hazel waiver clutching her head, he hurried over to her, helping her to sit in front of the fireplace.

Taking the necklace off her, he hid it back in that box where Hazel had retrieved it. Once the box was back in its hiding place, he returned the furniture to its original placement.

Panting heavily, Hazel was beginning to sweat, but Archibald wiped his niece's head clean with the sleeve of his brown tunic he wore to bed. She turned her head slightly to the boy, only to sway and lean into her uncle, and Archibald steadied her with a grasp on her arms.

"I will make a small incision with a kitchen knife and stitch it up to make it seem like your herbal remedy cured his poisoning. It will never be like you used your gift." Nodding, she lowered down into her uncle's lap, panting heavily. His only response was to stroke her hair with a proud smile.

"Rest, my fawn... You did well."

Losing the battle to stay conscious, collapsed into her uncle's arms in exhaustion from using her mother's forbidden magic.

Chapter Eight

Atticus

The smell of the morning rain filled Kingsly and Atticus's nostrils as they saddled up their horses. Both princes making sure both were tacked correctly. A palomino mare speckled with a fainter shade of beige, whose withers met with Atticus's collar bone.

Softly nickering, she nuzzled the crown prince's face in greeting. He stroked the leathery bristle muzzle of the mare, and a faint smile appeared on his lips before it was followed by a kiss to the her muzzle.

Atticus pet the star on her forehead as her blue eyes met his. Nickering once more to him, she played with his jacket pocket as if she could smell the sugar cubes he brought. Chuckling softly, he reached into his pocket and pulled out two. "Is this what you're after, Kissem?" The mare bobbed her head in answer, pawing the ground with her hoof in excitement as

strands of her white mane flapped up and down on her forelocks. Holding his palm out flat to his loyal mare, her bristling leather lips tickled his skin as she gently took the cube.

Patting her neck softly, he looked at Kingsly, who was tending to his steed. A gentle, and calm white Orlov trotter gelding, whose muzzle, socks, and beginning of its tail were blended with the gray.

The gelding stood a good five to ten inches taller than Kissem, which made sense, since Kingsly was larger in build and size than Atticus.

Kingsly didn't much care to interact with his horse other than saddle it, and the gelding returned the same treatment. His head lowered to the ground, tearing up the courtyard grass for a pre-ride snack.

Atticus stroked the mare beside him, who was now saddled with a buckskin saddle, with swirling designs burned into it. The seat was a beige color, while the skirt and back housing edges were decorated with white dyed leather. Her bridle matched her saddle, despite the cheek piece being white. The same buckskin leather cheek piece decorated with a swirl of burnt designs. Adjusting the throat latch, he couldn't help but watch Kissem play with her a bit as he did. Stroking her cheek, the mare looked at him as if she was narrowing her eyes at him.

"Don't ruin another bit, or the blacksmith will have our heads," Atticus scolded, with a faint smile on his lips.

Nickering softly in response, she ceased the toying of her bit. His attention went to Reed, who ran over to his older brothers with two satchels, likely at request by the queen, who followed behind her youngest.

"Mom had some provisions made for your trip," Reed exclaimed with pure excitement on his face as he looked up to Atticus.

Kingsly joined Atticus's side as he looked down at his younger brother, taking the satchel as he strolled to his mother. Leaning down, he kisses her outstretched cheek to her son. Hands elegantly placed in front of her.

"Thank you, Mother. We should return home within the week. It's only a two-day ride in either direction ," Kingsly promised to his mother.

The snow queen lifted her hand to her second-born son's face, cupping his cheek with a faint smile.

"You boys look after each other. That is a dangerous village. The first sign of danger, you leave, spare your mother the heartbreak of burying her two eldest sons."

Kingsly took his mom's hand, kissing it. "I swear it, Mother," he replied before stepping towards her, kissing her head once more before returning to his horse, but not before ruffling Reed's hair as a farewell. The action only made the young prince swat his brother's hand away, grimacing at the general prince in annoyance for flattening his hair.

Atticus walked over to his mother with a somber look, putting his hands on her shoulders. He didn't want to leave her without his protection against their father, but she rested her hand on his, as if knowing what was going on in her son's mind.

"I will be alright. I still have Ardnaxela if I need immediate assistance." Queen Sage laid her hand gently on Atticus's chest.

The White Dragoness was the only one other than Atticus who was brave enough to stand up against the king when he was in the wrong.

A soft sigh escaped Atticus as he pulled his mother into a warm embrace, holding her to his chest, dreading this trip and that he had to leave her behind. "I love you, Mother. Please don't hesitate to go to Ardnaxela."

Queen Sage chuckled softly, pulling away from her son and stroking his cheek before she lightly kissing it. As she looked back, there was worry and concern in her eyes for her son.

"That is my line, my son. Look after Kingsly. You know how he can get sometimes."

Nodding was his only answer as he kissed his mother's head, which was, for once, not adorned with a crown but a small metal circlet with an iced teardrop opal hanging from the middle.

Looking at Reed, who stood beside his mother, he kneeled, helping him fix his hair before resting a hand on his brother's shoulder. "Take care of our mother for me. Keep her busy with your games and stories. She loves talking about the Aestivals. If something goes wrong, you get the White Dragon and send word to Alexandria. I will ride on the fastest winds to get back here."

Reed's only response was to wrap his arms around Atticus's neck. He held onto him tightly, not wanting to let him go, scared he would never see him again.

"Please, Atti, can I come with you?" Reed begged.

Pulling away, Atticus puts his hands on his brother's shoulders with a faint frown before he playfully knocked his chin with his knuckle, causing Reed to giggle.

"Next time, Reed. For now, I need you to watch over Mom. She will need you. When I get back, I will tell you all about my trip." Atticus promised his brother. Leaning in, he whispered into Reed's ear. "Who knows, maybe I will discover the legendary Ivory Fawn," he jokingly played with his brother.

Reed's ocean blue eyes lit up in. "You think the Ivory Fawn is real? Ooo, do you think they will like flaky pastries?" the youngest prince screeched with excitement.

Atticus barked out a laugh, tilting his head back before patting his youngest brother's cheek.

"Atticus, come on, we are wasting daylight. We need to leave now, so we can hit Alexandria before the last sliver of light." Kingsly ground out.

Atticus looked at Kingsly with a confirming nod before putting his satchel in his buckskin saddle bag. The leather of the saddle groaned as he mounted Kissem, gripping her reins loosely before turning to look at his mother, who was next to Reed.

The two princes rode most of the day at a gallop, until the horses were drenched in sweat. Letting the horses rest , Atticus dismounts Kismet , stroking her neck. The sun placement putting them roughly last afternoon.

Atticus feel a twinge of guilt for pushing her so much, but he rather get this done then return back to his mother.

They still had a good ten miles left to go before they reached the city of Alexandria. Kingsly, still mounted upon his horse, looked down the mountain to the small village in the distance. It was dotted with tiny lights that could have been simple lanterns.

From what Atticus could tell, his brother was contemplating whether they would camp here under the stars, or push the horses a bit more to make their trek at night through the woods to get to the village.

Atticus rode up beside Kingsly, leaning into his saddle, rubbing Kissem's neck as she panted heavily.

Her hot breath made her seem he was riding a small wingless dragon huffing smoke from her nostrils, a sigh was huffed out of her in protest to keep going.

"We need to let the horses rest. Let's camp here, brother. We'll continue in the morning where there is more light and less danger," Atticus proclaimed.

Kingsly glanced at his brother, then back to the horse Atticus sat upon, seeing the exhaustion on her long face. He then looked to his own horse, who pulled on his reins in protest to continue.

Sighing, Kingsly nodded his head, reluctantly turning his gray steed away from Atticus, heading in the direction of a cave he saw earlier during their ride.

"Fine. There was a cave I saw earlier. Should be warm enough once we build a fire to camp."

The dragon titled named prince snapped his head to the side with a look of steel. Was his brother stupid? They were in unprotected lands now. Who knew what foul creatures roamed these woods? "No fire. It will draw attention."

Kingsly scoffed, stopped his horse, and turned his head to look at his eldest brother, who was glaring at him. "And how do you suggest we cook our dinner tonight? I hope you're not suggesting cold and raw," the general prince growled through his teeth.

Nudging his horse down the hill, Atticus joined his brother's side with a scoff. He had to remind himself that Kingsly hadn't experienced having to go without a hot meal, not when hot meals were provided in the war camps they had been.

"Yes, exactly that. Mother had the cook pack us some lunch." Groaning, the spoiled general prince rubbed his face in irritation, regretting even being ordered to join his brother in this quest. Taking a deep breath and nudging his horse into a canter was his only answer to the dragon prince.

The cave was dark , cold and damp as the sun began setting, but as they rode in further, it was surprisingly warmer. Dismounting his horse, Atticus removed Kissem's tackle, setting it down beside his bedroll. The mare nickers softly before she nuzzled Atticus's face, huffing hot air at him.

He looked in his mare's direction as he stroked the sweat-ridden mane, glancing into her blue eyes, rubbing her leathery nose and whispering to his loyal companion.

"We are both drained from the journey. It's best if we just eat and go to sleep."

Not liking his response, she nipped his hair, stomping her hoof a few inches away from his boot, nickering, almost as if she was scolding her rider.

Dodging her stomp, Atticus glared playfully at her, stroking her mane and shaking his head to her. Kissem always seemed easily irritated. Glancing to his brother, who looked exhausted. The deep circles beneath his eyes , as he removed the saddle and blanket from his horse. Atticus sighed softly peering at his mare, patting her withers.

Bobbing her head nickering before Atticus handed her the bag of oats for her dinner.

Making his way to Kingsly, Atticus brought over a bag of oats for Kingsly's horse, seeing he forgot to pack some for his companion.

"Here, I brought extra for your horse. I'll take the first watch so you can get some sleep." Atticus offered the bag to his brother.

Kingsly looked to his brother, then to the bag of oats, taking them before he stroked the gelding's neck. Hesitantly, the general prince looked to Atticus, taking a deep breath. "Thank you." Exhaling softly, the prince was relieved his eldest brother was taking first watch.

Turning to leave, Kingsly cleared his throat. "Do you know what type of sandwiches Mother sent with us?"

Stopping for a moment, Atticus paused, trying to recall if their mother ever told them. "If I know Mother well, she would have made you a chicken salad sandwich on wheat bread, knowing it was your favorite. I would think she would also have also included some pepper jack cheese and grapes for a snack."

Kingsly smiled softly, reaching into his saddlebag to retrieve the sack. As he opened it, he must have seen exactly that. Their mother was so keen about her sons and did everything she could to make sure they were well cared for, without her husband's knowledge.

Atticus, who now was sitting on a rock by the cave entrance leaning back on the cave wall, sword in his lap, held no expression on his face. After giving his horse the oats, Kingsly walked over to his bedroll and sat down to eat his food.

The sandwich was exactly how he liked it. He wondered if his mother made it herself, like she used to when they were children. The look on Atticus's face made him lower his next bite of food from his lip, frowning.

"How bad of shape do you think Alexandria is in?" Kingsly questioned.

Not removing his eyes from the cave entrance, Atticus thought for a moment, recollecting all the reports he heard from traveling merchants about the condition of the small village. None of what he heard was good. It made his stomach curdle at what the town had become. Sighing, he tilted his head a little towards Kingsly, still keeping his eyes on the entrance.

"From what I heard, people are so scared of the Netherian mercenaries and thieves that run rampant in town that no one says anything. Every month, a girl is taken from her home to be used as what they call a Blood Bride, which I believe was said to be some sort of sacrificial lamb for their magic. The maiden is essentially drained of all life. When they are done with the women, they are sent back in black bridal attire as a mockery of their families. Reminding the villagers that no one save them. "

Hearing what his brother told him, Kingsly's face looked repulsed. Kinglsy shook his head in disgust at the information.

"But just before we left, I heard rumors of a young maiden who stood up against one of them to protect some children, along with a kitten. If she is still alive, wasn't skinned right there for taking a stand, or taken as a Blood Bride..." Atticus trailed off before finally looking at his brother with a grin on the corner of his lip, chuckling softly. "she just became their sliver of hope. If she survived. Who knows? Maybe she could be the chosen one this kingdom needs."

Kingsly shook his head, laughing softly. It sounded utterly ridiculous they would find their salvation in a piss-poor town riddled with blood-lust filled thieves, mercenaries, and gods know what else plagued that village. "Oh, please, Atticus. You still believe in that fairy tale? It has been a hundred and fifty years. I am pretty sure if the Ivory Fawn existed, whoever he or she is would have risen by now. Besides, whoever that girl is, she sounds foolish and reckless. Not a glorious, legendary hero who will save us all."

Laying out on his bedroll, Kingsly rested his head on his saddle as a pillow. The general prince closed his eyes, exhaling softly, relaxing his aching body. "Enough of fairy tale legends. Wake me for the next watch." Kingsly yawned out.

Watching his brother go to sleep, Atticus looked to the cave entrance, thinking. What if she *was* the legendary Ivory Fawn? Although if the Ivory Fawn even existed, why would the gods have her in the worst town possible, as well as being so reckless with her own life? She was knocking at death's door standing up to someone who wielded Netherian magic. Their kind wiped out both the Aestival, which was the closest thing to gods to his kingdom, and possibly the druids as well, if Heath hadn't found them.

Watching the night sky and surrounding landscape, he took a deep breath, glanced at his sleeping brother, then back at the stars.

If there are any gods that still listen.

Please let me find the Ivory Fawn somehow so I can save my people.

Our people are suffering, and I want to be the best king I can, but I can't do it alone. I need the Ivory Fawn's help.

With his help, there will finally be peace for all of Wylana.

If I have to give up my crown or life to ensure my people's happiness and safety, then so be it. I just want them to stop suffering.

Atticus

The first three hours of watch were calm and quiet, to the point Atticus felt himself dozing off. Getting up from his post, he walked over to his sleeping brother and kicked his foot, waking him up. "Time to switch. I am dozing off from how calm it is."

Kingsly wanted to sleep more, but knew they both needed their rest for tomorrow. Getting up, he took his post at the same location Atticus had.

Atticus sauntered over to his bedroll, slowly collapsing on to his soft maroon bed roll. He rested his head on the saddle. Kissem was standing asleep by his bedroll.

Slowly, Atticus slipped into slumber. To his astonishment, it wasn't a nightmares that normally plague his dream escape.

Ivory feathers danced across his vision. A castle hidden in the mountains that looked run down and old came into view. It was almost like the Castle Andromeda that Sybilla, a lady and scribe to his court who held all the history, culture, and beliefs of the Aestival warriors, spent most of her time. Purple leaves fell into pools of water, causing ripples of gold.

As Atticus looked ahead, he saw a large wisteria displaying vibrant lilac, orchid, and violet leaves. A woman who came into view at the base of the tree. She stood there in a long lilac dress, two large ivory wings, and a crystal crown. Slowly, she approached Atticus, her frame much smaller than his. Her sheer presence made him want to drop to his knees, bowing his head, but his mouth was agape as Atticus stared down at this woman.

When she placed her hand on his chest, it began to glow. He felt his entire body warm with a tingling sensation at the touch.

"Prince Atticus, Son of King Kai Bromiston and Queen Sage Calirenton, you are the Crimson Dragon, the one that shall guide the Ivory Fawn to her destiny, and help her rise in order to bring peace back to the land of Wylana. You must find the Ivory Fawn deep in the Raven Palm forest within the Netherian territory before it is too late. The Ivory Fawn is in grave danger and does not know the sword of Saaos is hanging by a thread of fate against her favor."

Pulling her hand away from Atticus's chest, she stepped back from him as his dragon tattoo glowed brightly before fading back to the normal black ink.

Atticus was in awe at the woman's word that he was somehow a part of the Ivory Fawn's destiny. Was the Ivory Fawn real? What was his name?

"You cannot trust anyone in Alexandria. There will be a man who smells of vanilla with hints of oranges and cinnamon. Find him and he will tell you all you need to know about the Ivory Fawn. You must not let her stay in Alexandria, for she is surrounded by death. When you return to Wylana, have the scribe teach her our ways, for her own protection. She was sheltered from true heritage.

The day is coming where she must rise, or all will be lost. The Ivory Fawn will need to make a grave sacrifice in order to fully inherit her magic. She will need you by her side, for the journey will try to break her spirit, especially when she loses the greatest treasure in her life."

He had so many questions running rampant through his mind, hearing all this information. Raising her hand to her breast where a necklace dangled, Atticus stared at the raw amethyst crystal point that had a brown clay tree wrapping around the top of it. The tree held lilac and violet leaves, and its trunk had lilac mushrooms growing up from the moss that speckled around the roots clinging onto the crystal to hold it in place

"This necklace will warn her of any Netherian wielder near her. She must wear it at all times to protect her. If the Ivory Fawn dies, all of Wylana will. too."

Atticus felt as if two hands grabbed him from behind and yanked him into reality.

Kinglsy shook him awake before kicking Atticus's saddle where his head rested.

"Come on, wake up. It's time to saddle up and go."

Rubbing his eyes, as Atticus was blinded by the first morning light, he contemplated if that was a dream or if that was actually Queen Astoria coming to him with a warning and a mission.

Chapter Ten

Hazel

Autumn air nipped at the sweeping, draping branches of a grand lavender wisteria tree. The leaves almost seemed to danced with the fallen colored leaves of lilac and orchid. Hazel's hair brushed her rosy cheek as she pulled aside the branches from her mother's tree to look at the lovely tombstone with the etching

Ashira Hilliston

Beloved Wife and Mother.

Letting the branches close behind her, Hazel walked over to her mother's cross. Carrying a wicker basket, she removed the slowly withering flowers from her mother's clay vase.

Reaching into the basket, she pulled out a water skin, pouring fresh water into the vase before putting in the freshly cut lavender, arranging them nicely.

The young girl tried to come every month to visit with her mother and tell her everything, as if her mother would converse with her.

"I brought you some fresh flowers from my garden. I wish you could see it. Uncle told me you loved gardening, especially harvesting the lavender." Chuckling softly, she put some freshly baked lavender muffins on the plate, setting it close to her mother's cross. "He also told me how Dad used to put some in your hair when you were harvesting them together." Hazel breathed out, trying to keep herself together. Hazel wished more than anything her mother was here instead of talking to a stone grave.

Pulling out two cups, Hazel set one down by the plate for her mother before she poured some strawberry honey wine into them.

Her olive-green skirt sprawled out around her as she sat down beside her mother's grave, placing some grapes onto the plate as well. Sitting there quietly for a moment before Hazel took a deep, shaky breath.

"I wish you were here, Mom. Things are really bad. I could use your guidance. I don't know what to do. I am lost."

She leaned her head back, as if it would stop the tears from threatening to fall from her eyes, not wanting her mom to see her cry.

"I really messed up, Mom. I may be the next Blood Bride because I stood up against Ratherian in the market," Hazel confessed to her mother's grave.

Wiping the tear from her cheek, she looked down at her food, no longer having the stomach to eat it. More tears fell as she continued. "And now Uncle is sending me away. He says he will join me in a week, but I don't think he will." Her voice was so wobbly. Hazel took a deep breath, resting her hand on her sternum, trying to keep her breathing and crying in control, not wanting her uncle to hear her from inside the house..

"I want him to come with me and Darius so badly, but part of me knows that if we were to bring him on this trip, we wouldn't get far before the Netherian found us and killed both Darius and Archibald."

Putting her hand over her mouth, she took a deep breath as lavender filled her senses. Hazel needed to reach her hand up to her shoulder, feeling there was a possibility her mother was there, comforting her.

It was as if she could hear her mother's words being whispered in the wind as she turned her head. Hazel envisioned her mother kneeling beside her , putting her hand to Hazel's wet cheek and wiping away her tears with a gentle, calming smile,

A soft glow illuminated the space before Hazel , coalescing into the familiar figure of her mother. The vision shimmering , her form ethereal yet warm, as if woven from the very essence of Hazel's memories.

"Am so proud of the women you have become, my little fawn," her mother spoke softly, her voice a soothing melody. "Your father and I knew the day you were born that you would bring such light and joy to this world. You were made for great things and will change this world for better."

Hazel closed her eyes as fresh tears pilled down her cheeks. The scent of lavender wrapped around her like a comforting embrace, and for a fleeting moment, she could almost feel the gentle press of her mother's lips against her forehead.

"Things are bad now," the apparition continued, her tone filled with quiet reassurance, "but I promise you, my little fawn, they are about to change for the better. Just keep your head up. Remember my love."

The vision leaned in, her presence weightless yet profoundly real. A ghost of warmth brushed Hazel's temple as her mother's voice dropped to a tender whisper.

"Your are a Hilliston by blood, which means you are strong, compassionate, gentle-but also a gather who keeps getting up."

The apparition hummed softly, the sound like a distant lullaby, before fading into the dim glow of the room. Yet the warmth of her mother's love remained, lingering in Hazel's heart like an ember against the cold.

Hazel wished more than anything her mother was alive at this moment so she could wrap her arms around her and hold her tightly. She wished her mother could hold her frightened daughter back and make the world melt away around them, even for a moment. The rustle of the leaves pulled her back to reality as her uncle appeared, holding the branches back. Seeing the look on his niece's face, and the food she prepared for her mother's grave, Archibald walked over and knelt before her, pulling her close into his arms, holding her tightly.

Unable to hold in her sob anymore, Hazel crumbled into pieces in her uncle's embrace. He said nothing, did not even move. Just held tightly to him as he wrapped his warm cloak around her, knowing they would be in this embrace for a long time.

This morning was the morning Hazel was leaving with Darius, the morning she would leave her life here in Alexandria and start new.

Not with what they were facing. Hazel continued to remind herself he would return to her in a week, that this wasn't going to be forever. Taking his niece's face into his hands, he stroked her cheek.

"I am so very proud of the woman you have grown to be. I thank the gods every day they blessed me with the opportunity to have called you my niece. More importantly, my daughter," Archibald spoke with such joy in his heart.

Softly smiling, Hazel leaned her face into her uncle's touch, holding his hand to her cheek before she looked at him and wiped his tears away. "And I am so very proud and blessed to have not only called you my uncle, but my father as well," Hazel proclaimed to her uncle.

The Alexandria streets were very quiet and the morning sun was barely peeking over the mountain as Hazel double checked her satchel to make sure she had everything she needed for the two-day journey to the new home Darius had for them.

Archibald and Hazel both agreed it was best not to know the destination for her protection until he was sent word of where she was supposed . Checking one last time to make sure she had her blanket and pillow for her bedroll, Hazel turned to the door as her uncle cleared his throat, standing there, holding the wooden engraved box that had been hidden under the floor. After staring at the box, Hazel then appears up to her uncle's toffee caramel eyes, surprised she was being given her mother's necklace. "Are you sure?"

At his nod, Hazel gently lifted it from the box, examine over the rough crystal detailing before Archibald stroked his niece's cheek.

She threw her arms around him and held him closely, as he wrapped her in a hug, tightly holding her to his chest. "Your mother would want you to have it," he whispered, not wanting to let go.

"Little fawn, make sure to take care of yourself and stay safe. I will meet up with you in two weeks," Archibald spoke with determination in his voice.

Tightening her hold, she took a deep breath and nodded her head. "I swear. In a week, we will finally have a new and better life."

Archibald chuckled softly as he gently released himself from his niece's grasp, running his fingers through her beautiful golden hair, a faint smile playing on his lips.

Taking in every feature as if it was the very last time he was ever going to see his niece, he smiled, kissing her head. and then took the necklace, securing it around his niece's neck. "Tuck it in your shirt. You don't want to lose it or break it."

Nodding, Hazel pulled back the white, puffy shirt, tucking in her mother's necklace. It was warm against her skin before Archibald brushed past her to double check what she had packed. "You should take your mother's cloak with you. It will keep you warm, and you'll have another piece of her with you."

Hazel stared at the lilac velvet cloak hanging up. It had a light coating of dust since neither Hazel nor Archibald dared move it from where it hung, in the hope Ashira would magically come walking in to reclaim it.

Walking over, she ran her hand down the cloak, admiring the golden designs embroidered into it and how well it was made. Taking it, she wrapped it around her, tying it around her neck. The hood laid loosely on her back as Hazel pulled her two messy tied pigtails out from under the soft fabric and turning towards her uncle, who was now staring at her with silver in his eyes. "What?"

Hazel breathed, but he walked over to her, resting his hand on Hazel's shoulder. "You look just like your mother," he breathed

Faintly chuckling, she took Archibald's hand and kissed it gently then studied his worn hand then to her uncle

"Don't forget to keep using that salve on your hands. When you come back to me and they are back to being rough, I will make your other hand match," she threatened, playfully.

Which only brought out a deep laugh before he pulled her into an embrace. "I won't, I promise."

There was a knock on the door before Darius walked in. Taking in Hazel, he tilted his head to the side with a faint smile. "You ready?" It was such a soft voice from someone who was built for slinging carcasses around.

Hazel peered at her uncle, then to Darius, who was making his was to the rustic, brown fence bordering her properly . Hazel took a deep breath and nodded her head. "Yes."

Going to grab her bags that sat beside the door. At the fence there was a wagon drawn by a single dark chestnut horse. Darius took them from her and put them into the back of their wagon. Making her way to the wagon, Archibald followed her towards the entrance of the cottage, but stayed in the door frame watching his niece. Hazel stared at him long and hard for a moment before, turning on her heels and rushing over to her uncle, leaping toward him, wrapping her arms around his neck and nesting her head into his neck. Archibald held his niece tight in one last embrace, laughing full heartedly, before he kissed her temple.

"I love you, my little fawn," his voice wobbled out, not wanting to say goodbye.

It wasn't until he heard the tremble in her tone that made his heart ache in sorrow and joy "I love you, Dad." Letting go, she kissed her uncle's cheek as tears fell from her eyes. She held her hand to his cheek, taking in every detail one last time before she turned to head back to the wagon.

"You will see him again soon, my love," Darius said with gentle assurance.

With that, he cracked the reins of the horse, who then begins trotting on. Watching her uncle slowly vanish, a vision of her mother stepped from behind him and waved her goodbye.

A tear fell from her eyes when she could no longer could see either one of them.

Chapter Eleven

Hazel

During the journey, Hazel daydreamed about her life with Darius. Their wedding would be in the spring with her wearing a white floral lace wedding gown, carrying a bouquet made of lavender with hints of baby breath. Darius would be waiting for her at the altar with a wide smile on his face as Archibald escorted Hazel down the aisle. It was going to be so beautiful, a perfect way to start her new life.

The wagon shook violently, breaking Hazel's blissful sleep as one of the wheels hit a large rock. When Hazel came to blinking the sunlight peering through the leaves, she didn't realize her day dreaming was actually a dream. She didn't remember falling asleep during the wagon ride. Blinking the sleep from her eyes and taking in her surroundings, she realized where they were. As she glanced around the dimly lit forest with fog hugging the ground, panic consumed her. Her stomach twisted , a desperate thing trying to flee-to escape itself, to run home where she would be safe. Where her uncle's warmth awaited. Beneath Hazel's fingers, the familiar clasp of her mother's cloak was warm, grounded her in the storm.

They were in the middle of the Raven Palm forest, a breeding ground for the Netherian magic wielders. According to the rumors, this was the alleged location where the gruesome consumption of Blood Brides happened. This forest had allegedly been decimated eons ago, even before the Blood War between the Netherian people and Aestival people.

It was the bordering forest between Wylana and the Taldora kingdom, a kingdom that was once ruled by a benevolent king Thadeus, but after the siege by the self-proclaimed king Kennon, the benevolent king vanished. Speculation surrounded his fate, with rumors suggesting he either haunted the old Taldora castle or suffered under a curse that tormented him in his sleep.

Clenching her mother's cloak around herself to ward off the fall chill, she reached over to grip Darius's leg. Her eyes widened as Hazel caught the emotionless expression on his face, as if Darius did not concerned about their safety in these woods. The fog intensified the further they ventured into the forest, sending a uneasy sense of danger building throughout her stomach. Hazel heart pounding throughout her body as her blood raced through her body from the fear and panic.

"Darius, why are we here? We need to go back." Hazel's voice cracked as she tightened her grip on his leg, trying to get his attention., She wondered if he was under some trance. It was the only way she could think to explain why he was ignoring her. Her gaze scanned the large pine-like trees, whose needles were as black as the souls of those who inhabited this forest.

Looking back at Darius, waiting for some type of response, her heart hammered in her ears as he continued to say nothing. Instead, he pulled back on the reins of the horse to signal it to stop, and panic overwhelmed her.

"Get out." His voice was ice cold as he released the reins from his grip, tossing them aside, with no care to where they landed.

Hazel's eyes widened at his tone. Her hands trembled as she shook her head, clinging to her mother's cloak as if it were her shield.

Grinding his teeth, Darius raised his foot up and shoved Hazel out of the wagon with a kick so hard, not only did it leave a footprint the cloak, but also forced the air out of her lungs as made contact with the hard forest floor.

A never ending roaring in her ear drowned out most of her surroundings as she stared up at Darius. He stood up from the driver's seat of the wagon, getting out before making his way to the front, stroking the horse's face as it nickered softly. Hazel scrambled back before she rose to her feet, never taking her eyes off Darius as she created some distance between them. Moving around the carriage now approaching her, Darius gripped her arm, pulling her off the ground to stand. As he dragged her along, Hazel clawed at his grip, hoping he would release her. The terrified woman looked forward, past Darius, to see a partially burned, run-down cottage. It was overrun with foliage that almost made it disappear with its surroundings. The door opened, and it was who came out that scared her the most.

Ratherian stepped out onto the porch, leaning against the charred remains of the pillar that once held up the awning. He stood there shirtless, revealing more than Hazel cared to see. This man just a week ago was threatening to take a taste of her, and that was not in a way that would have been flattering. His body was like sculpted marble, with the various scars on his pale skin imitating the stone's veining. What made her breathing hitch was the sight of a crimson liquid trickling down the corner of his lip. "Darius, what a surprise," he cooed as Hazel continued to fight against Darius's grip. She lost her footing against a rock in her path, Hazel trips landing on her hands and knees slipping out of Darius's grasp. An irritated groan came from Darius as he ripped her up by her arm once more to stand on her feet, causing her to yelp out in pain.

"Darius? Darius! What is going on? Let's go!" She cried out, fighting his grip on her arm. He dragged her to the run-down cottage, closer to Ratherian, who grinned like a monster ready to consume her. Hazel's attempts of fleeing were futile against Darius as she desperately tried again and again to fight for her freedom. "Enough!" Darius growled.

He yanked her forward, nearly causing her to nearly lose her again, but she recovering her footing. Hazel could only assume the number of bruises what would surface because of his grip.

"Aww. Is little brother having some trouble with his fiancee?" Ratherian teased.

Hazel's eyes shot open wide as she whipped her head toward Ratherian when she heard him call Darius a brother. Breathing heavily, she looked between the two men before she felt the need to fight even harder to escape. Hazel was willing to take her changes surviving in the woods.

"I said *enough*!" Darius roared at her.

The sound of heels clicking on wood made Hazel stop her thrashing and turn her head to see a beautiful woman walking out of the house. Her skin was so pale, it looked like freshly fallen snow, just as her hair did, but her eyes were black as the pits of hell.

She emerged from the cottage and was now beside Ratherian, brushing her hand down the male's arm. There was a smear of blood on the right corner of her lip. This mysterious woman wiped the blood trickling from the left corner of Ratherian's lip with her finger, only to suck the blood off, with a soft moan rolling off her lips. "Easy, Ratherian. You know Darius is easily irritable when he goes this long without his fill. Wouldn't want to add anymore scars now, would you, love?"

Hazel was forced to her knees in front of the pair by Darius. Her entire body trembled, and her breakfast curdling in of her stomach. Swearing this was a horrific nightmare. She clutched her mother's necklace as it warmed even more against her chest.

"No one touches the Ivory Fawn, not yet, and *especially* not you, Lilura," Darius scorned, predatorily.

Sucking her teeth, Lilura stepped closer to Hazel before kneeling down, gripping Hazel's chin in her cold icy hand so she take a better look at Hazel. Her heart was so loud in her ears.

"Aww, but brother, she looks so delicious with all that fear and panic."

Growling viciously, Darius moved before Lilura could react. He was upon the Netherian woman, pinning her to the pillar, his hand gripping her throat as the other had pinned down the hand that dared to touch Hazel. Darius bared his fangs at Lilura.

Fangs, there were fangs now protruding from the mouth of the man Hazel kissed countless nights in her bed, a mouth that peppered her skin with love on so many occasions.

"You touch my Blood Bride, and I will make you scream, not only in your bed as I made you before, but screaming for me to spare you as I fill your mouth with your own blood." Pure venom came from Darius's throat as he glared down at the woman.

A challenging chuckle escaped Lilura's throat as she felt Darius's hot breath against her skin, pulling her leg up to wrap around Darius's hip, almost as if she was enjoying him threatening to rip her apart.

"So possessive over your brides. How did your last Blood Bride taste? I bet she won't taste as delicious as the shaking little fiancee."

Watching the interaction between Lilura and Darius, Ratherian brushed past Hazel. She turned her head towards Ratherian, and watched him undo the hose from the wagon they just arrived in.

Hazel couldn't believe what she was hearing.

This can't actually happen. Darius was one of them? But how? His hands never showed the black mark every Netherian was cursed with. That's why they needed Blood Brides.

Then it hit her. Lilura called Hazel his Blood Bride. He wasn't hunting for his father all those times. No, Darius must have been here, in these woods, feasting on a Blood Bride. How could Hazel not see the signs?

He had blamed the darkening of his fingers from the dye they used on the leather pelts sold in their shop.

The necklace reached an intense warmth against her breast that brought her to reality. Shooting to her feet, she took off running as fast as she could. Hazel needed to run for her life.

She held her skirt and ran as fast as could, her mother's cloak flaring in the wind as she ran. There was such a pounding in her legs, all Hazel could think of was running as fast and far as she could till there was an opening in the Raven Palm woods.

Before she could even think, she felt strong hands upon her waist, turning her and shoving her face into a Raven Palm tree. As she was pinned in place, the bark bit her cheek, and Hazel cried out, the wetness of her blood now dripped from the fresh wound.

There was a strong hand gripping her brown waist corset so hard that the leather groaned under its grasp. It made Hazel still as she straightened up, the pressure worsened on her waist increase.

The aroma of salt and iron filled her senses as Darius pulled hair away from her neck, exposing it. His hot breath on her skin sent shivers down her spine. As his lips brushed along her neck, sending her body ablaze, she felt the points of his canines graze her sensitive skin.

It took every bit of her not to tremble at the sensation. How many times has he had her pinned like this, pinned beneath him at his mercy, and be this close to her neck? He could easily have ripped her throat out anytime he had her like this without her even seeing it coming.

"You are a naughty little fawn, although, maybe your big bad wolf should finally properly punish you," he growled into her ear.

Before her protest could escape her quivering lips, his canines slammed into her neck. Crying out, her nails dug into the tree as her head arched back. She tried to pull away, but his arm was wrapped tight around her waist, holding her to his body. Warm blood slid down her neck now, staining her lilac cloak and white blouse.

A moan filled her ears as he pressed her harder into the tree. Pushing every part of him onto her back, her body reacted in a way she didn't want it to. In a detached part of her mind, she wanted to submit to him like she always has before, even though she wanted to get away from him so badly.

"Fuck, you taste better than I imagine," Darius, skimming his now blood-soaked lip up her ear.

To her horror, she felt something hardening against her ass. It was him. Darius was enjoying her pain and screaming in more than one way. It made her stomach want to revolt.

He released the hold of her body, and Hazel felt the world spinning around her. Holding her neck, Darius turned her, removing Hazel's hand from her neck to look at his handiwork. Lilura appeared by Darius's side, also examining Hazel's neck. She then looked at Darius's lips, pulling his chin down to engulf them with her own, licking all the blood off before leaning her head back, savoring the taste.

"Oh my. She *is* delicious! So much pain, fear, and sorrow. Like a sweet cherry pie fresh from the oven," Lilura purred.

Darius looked at Hazel, grabbing her cheek roughly, and forcing her to look him in the eyes. "I am going to enjoy every bit of life I drain from your pathetic little body, and once I do, there will be no Ivory Fawn to save anyone, not even your fucking uncle."

Hearing Darius threaten her uncle, something erupted in her, and she shoved Darius back, growling. It was as if a lioness roared in her ears as Darius now was glaring at Hazel. Lilura stepped behind him, wanting to stay clear of his path of rage. "You little bitch."

Darius slammed his teeth into Hazel's neck once more, ramming her back into that damn tree. This time, the bite was not as sensual as before, but like he wanted to rip her throat out.

Screaming out in pain, Hazel dug her nails into the bark of the tree, trying to pry off a piece of the Raven Palm bark. Once she had enough to slice into him, she took a deep breath, and shoved Darius off her. Hazel didn't waste the moment as she quickly sliced through his cheek.

Hoping it would buy her some time, she ran for the now unhitched horse as Ratherian rushed for his brother, who was screaming in agony, holding his cheek. Quickly she mounted it bare back, kicking the horse hard as she could.

It took off at a gallop not only from her kick, but also as if scared of the terrifying sound that erupted from Darius.

Ratherian roared out demands at Lilura to stop Hazel as she made her escape. Hazel didn't dare to look back as she held on to the horse's mane for dear life.

Pain rippled through her as a black tipped arrow made from Raven Palm wood now protruded from her shoulder. Hazel nearly fell off her horse as she leaned forward, holding her shoulder.

Darius bellowed at Lilura, "No! She is mine to kill!"

Chapter Twelve

Atticus

Kissem shook her mane as the aroma of freshly baked breads and pies, combined with the shouts from merchants about their freshly plucked apples from their very own orchards filled the streets of Alexandria. Atticus didn't expect this village to be so lively, considering the circumstances of current events. Unless this town found normality in their lives surrounding the Blood Bride selections every month. Atticus leaned down, stroking Kissem's neck, and chuckled softly as she nuzzled his boot with her leathery muzzle.

"Easy, girl. I will get you an apple, don't worry." Leaning back in his saddle, the two princes looked far from royalty and more like traveling merchants in their Simple brown tunics paired with brown cloaks to hide their swords. This was the best option for them in this situation, since they didn't want to draw attention to themselves.

Looking around, Kingsly scanned for anyone who might know any information about this girl they heard about. Atticus looked at his brother, nudging him with his elbow to get his attention.

"Should we get breakfast or head for Raven Palm forest first?"

Kingsly shook his head as he raised his eyebrow, pulling his horse to a halt. Looking at his brother, he let out a sigh of disbelief before dismounting his gelding, stroking the white trotter's neck. "Are you still going on about that stupid dream?" huffed the general prince.

Atticus dismounted his own horse, petting Kissem's neck. Taking her reins into his hand, he walked over to a nearby stand to buy four apples from a young sales lady, giving her a generous amount of coin with a wink before he turned to his brother.

"Make fun of me all you want. I know what I saw and I know it was a message from Queen Astoria herself," Atticus replied quietly, wanting to avoid anyone from overhearing him. After handing two of the apples to his brother, he then handed the other one to his mare while keeping one for himself, who greedily took her apple with a grateful nicker.

"You and those damn Aestivals, I swear. Mother filled your head with too many fairy tales. Let me guess, you think the Ivory Fawn is real as well?" Stepping closer to his brother, Kingsly lowered his tone as he whispered, "You will be king one day, Atticus. You can't chase fairy tales, not when Wylana needs a strong ruler. Now drop it."

Atticus scoffed in response, shaking his head.

He wanted to be king. He truly did. Although with the damage his father has done to his once beautiful kingdom, Atticus didn't know if there was ever fixing the damage his grandfather Malekith and father have done. In all of Wylana's history, it never has been this bad until Malekith began his reign.

They been walking around for about thirty minutes and the female population seems to be almost nonexistent.

Approaching a elder woman , Atticus examined her booth of herbs as well as bundles of lavender closely.

"The streets seem empty. Where are all the women?" Atticus inquired.

"You must be new here. The streets aren't safe as they used to be - especially for the women."

"Why?" He asked with a smooth measured tone.

Looking around hesitantly, swallowing audibly before speaking up

"Because of the blood brides. They been taking more this past months. More than usual."

Her eyes darted around nervously before meeting his " I shouldn't have said anything , if anything hears me talking"

"No one will," Atticus cuts in , his voice steady with a tone of authority to it. Without another, word he gave her a thankful nod, passing her a gold coin.

Walking away from the booth , Atticus spotting his bother on the other end talking with another merchant.

Atticus scans the market carefully. Seeing a stocky man who looked to be in his mid-forties dropping his basket of wheat. Atticus didn't hesitate to hand Kingsly his mare's rein before he hastily approached the gentleman, kneeling down before the man.

"Here, let me help," Atticus proclaimed.

The older man looked up in surprise. Atticus noticed while he was helping this man, "Thank you, kind man. Sorry, my hands aren't the best." His voice was deep, but the man smelt of vanilla with tinges of oranges and cinnamon. Atticus froze. A slow, creeping realization crawled up his spine, prickling at the edges of his mind like an ember catching dry parchment.

Wait... His breath hitched. Orange and cinnamon?

The scent lingered in the air , deceptively warm, wrapping around him like a ghost of something half-forgotten. His pulse hammered in his ears as the pieces clicked into place, sharp and unforgiving.

This was the man Asteria told him he could trust, he may know where the Ivory Fawn was.

Atticus shook his head, helping gather the wheat, putting it back inside of the basket for him before extending a hand to the man to help him stand. After a moment of hesitation, he accepted it. Struggling for a moment, he eventually was upright again and dusted himself off before looking at Kinglsy, who had now joined his brother's side.

"No worries. Have you seen a healer for your hand and your leg?" questioned Atticus. He noticed the man was putting all his weight on the left leg. From previous encounters on the battlefield and in camps, Atticus recognized that there was damage done to the other leg.

"I have my niece, actually. She was amazing, but she just left town this morning with her fiance. Hazel was called away by a lord to help aid his wife during her labor."

Atticus looked at this man with a raised eyebrow. If Asteria told him to trust this man , was this so called Fiance the Ivory Fawn. Looking around, seeing there were barely any women in the market, and those who were in the market stuck very close to the men with their heads lowered, almost skittish.

"Pardon me for my boldness, but there aren't really any women here in the market. Is that because of the Netherian people?" Kingsly questioned with a raised eyebrow.

Kingsly let out a grunt as his brother shoved his elbow into his ribs, earning Atticus a warning glare to the heir.

Before Kingsly could speak more, Atticus intercepted whatever insulting jabs would come from the general's mouth. "Sorry about my brother's behavior, although we heard that your women were being taken as what was called Blood Brides. We were sent by the castle to see what we can do to help stop it," He said as he looked at the elderly man.

At the mention of the word Blood Bride, the man turned somber as he looked at the two princes, then his surroundings before he leaned in, lowering his tone. "Are you *truly* from there? From the castle?"

Atticus faintly chuckled with a feline smile before pulling back his cloak to show the sword with his family crest adorned on the handle, quickly hiding it again to prevent people passing by to see it. He lowered his voice as he asked, "Yes. Is there somewhere private we can talk?" The older man nodded his head and was about to say something before Atticus continued, "I am searching for a girl."

Kingsly stepped in front of Atticus, giving him a warning glare, his back turned to this stranger. He took his brother's elbow into his hand. Atticus glanced at his brother's grip as his eyes darken before maniacally rises up to Kingsly, who, upon seeing the look, let go of his elbow, and stepped back to his eldest brother's side.

"We heard about a girl who recently stood up against one of these Netherian men, causing a bit of a stir. Well, from what I gathered from another traveling merchant. I am wanting to meet with her. I like to commemorate her for her bravery and ask for her aid," Atticus continued, resting his hand on the hilt of his sword underneath his cloak.

The man's face went from a somber expression turning into surprise before peering around, almost as if he was nervous to even mention anything about the ordeal before returning his attention to the princes.

"You're speaking of my niece, Hazel. Come on, I'll take you to our home. It's safer to speak about this in private. I live up on the hill with the large weeping birch tree." He spoke low.

Giving a smug smirk to his younger brother, Atticus followed this man out of the village with his mare in tow. Was this Hazel woman the Ivory Fawn? Should he even tell this man of who he saw in his dream and what she told him? Maybe he could help Atticus find this Ivory Fawn?

Kingsly grabbed his brother's arm tightly again, stopping him as he grumbled under his breath, "This isn't why we came here, Atticus. We were to access the damage and then leave. That was father's orders. Not to chase some girl you heard about in a dream."

Atticus narrowed his eyes at his brother's hand before a faint growl of warning escaped his lip, which lead to Kingsly pulling his hand away. Atticus then spoke in a warning tone towards his brother, "And *you* were supposed to bring your men with you on this trip. Yet, here we are just the two of us. Although. I think Father wouldn't be so disappointed in me if I brought home the Ivory Fawn to help our kingdom."

Not even waiting to see the expression on his brother's face, he turned on his heel and followed the man to his cottage. handing his uneaten apple to his mare who nickered it in thanks. Kingsly reluctantly followed Atticus.

Walking into the home, the old man set his basket down on a table next to portraits of him with a young lady. He admired it for a moment before looking at the two princes. "This is my home. It's not much, but it's home. Feel free to make yourself comfortable while I will make some tea for us."

Atticus sat down at the table, admiring the mahogany wood, taking notes of the dried blood and spots of burnt wood, almost as if someone had dropped something corrosive onto it. Kingsly remained standing as he took in every detail of the cottage, as if he was planning almost every possible escape route, It was something he always did, just in case something was to go awry during their visit, or if the older was hiding something.

Atticus was doing the same, but in a more discrete way. His eyes wandered back to a portrait of a young woman with long golden hair standing beside the stranger they just met. "Is that your niece?"

The man came back with a tray, looking at the painting before nodding and setting the tray down of tea and an array of cheeses and fruit.

"Yes, it is. She is very much like her mother. Although, after that stunt she pulled into the courtyard, Hazel fled with her fiance. Tomorrow, Ratherian will most likely come and take her away to be his Blood Bride for standing up to him. He can't stand being talked back to. Last woman who did became his bride. That stubborn girl , Hazel was

Protecting some village children and a kitten, of all things. The girl almost got herself killed."

Atticus listened how this Hazel girl stood up to not only a Netherian man, because he was being a bully to innocent children and animals.

"Oh, my apologies for my rude manners. I am Archibald Hilliston."

Kingsly turned his head to Archibald, scanning him as if there was some recognition of the older man's surname, but said nothing about it before he leaned against the wood frame near the exit, raising an eyebrow.

"When do they normally come to take their Blood Brides? Is it just one of them or multiple women?" Kingsly asked, his eyes attentively on Archibald.

Atticus glanced at Kingsly, then to Archibald, accepting a cup of tea, inhaling in the aroma of vanilla and lavender before sipping his tea, waiting for his response.

"Normally just one. We sometimes hear their screams as they are tortured and killed. Almost as a punishment to the bride's family and friends," Archibald replied.

Atticus set his teacup gently down, careful not to spill the delectable tea before peering up at Archibald raising an eyebrow

"Why doesn't anyone go searching for them or try to fight back? Surely, they don't willingly go to their slaughter,"

Archibald frowned, taking a cup of tea himself and drinking a sip to settle his nerves before he set it down. "Because no one ever comes back once they step into the Raven Palm forest. Some have tried, but all has failed." Atticus sat up straight in surprise at hearing the name, so did Kingsly, almost as if he knew what was going through his brother's mind.

Was this man's niece the Ivory Fawn he was told about? Leaning forward, Atticus rested his hand on the burn mark on the table, returning his attention back to Archibald with a wide expression.

"What do you know about the Ivory Fawn?" Atticus spoke with a bit of eagerness to his tone.

Kingsly walked over to his eldest brother and put his hand on his brother's shoulder, growling. "Atticus."

Archibald eyes widened at the tone coming from the general before he rose to his own feet, putting his hands on the table staring at Atticus with a serious look

"Why do you want to know about the Ivory Fawn?" Archibald ground out

Atticus pulled his shoulder from his brother's hold as he stood up, Kingsly narrowed his eyes at Atticus silently telling him to not proceed. But it was no use.

"Because I received a message from Queen Astoria herself last night in my dream about how the Ivory Fawn is in danger. How she is in the Raven Palm forest right now and is going to die."

The Atticus saw Archibald's heart shoot down into his stomach as his face turned pale white at what Atticus said.

"Tell me everything she told you. Do not miss a single detail." Archibald's voice wobbled as he spoke.

Atticus relayed everything he saw in his dream. How he saw the Mother Grove Tree, how the queen told him he was the Crimson Dragon in the prophecy, how he had to save her in the Raven Palm forest and bring her back here. Archibald's face drained of all color, almost as if he was going to be sick at the thought. Sitting back in his chair, Archibald rubbed his face in pure shock before his eyes met Atticus. "And you sure it was Queen Astoria?"

Atticus nodded his head. It had to be. Who else would it be? It can't be the Ivory Fawn because the Ivory Fawn is alive and in trouble.

"Yes, I swear it. It was her clear day." Atticus to Archibald.

The other man nodded his head before he walked over to his niece's apothecary, fiddled with some herbs and salves before coming back to the table with a small satchel of herbs.

"I saw my niece make these millions of times, thanks to those damn Netherian poisons. Give this to her. She will know what to do. It should buy her some time for you both to get her back here."

Handing the satchel to Atticus, Archibald looked between the brothers, then to Kingsly, who was in shock. They really found the Ivory Fawn and in a shit place like this. H how this Hazel girl treated anyone and everyone who fell ill to the poison she helped. She was their sliver of hope in this place.

"She left with her fiancee this morning, although, I have a hunch feeling that something may have gone horrifically wrong with him," Archibald continued on with a worried expression.

It was like he knew exactly what Archibald was implying, Atticus nodded his head, putting his hand on Archibald's shoulder, gripping it to reassure him that things would get better from here.

"Send word to my father. I will leave my saddle bag here for you. In it is my family crest. Use the seal to send word that my father's forces are needed here immediately. We will make sure there will not be a Blood Bride taken again." Kinglsy spoke with a calm controlled tone.

Archibald let out a breath of relief that the castle was finally sending aid to his home and the friends he and Hazel had made here in this small town. Atticus and Kingsly swiftly made their way to their horses outside.

After undoing his saddle bag, Kingsly made his way back to the cottage to hand it over to Archibald, who nodded gratefully.

Hearing a blood-curdling scream coming from the Raven Palm forest, Atticus quickly mounts Kissem , cracking the reins on Kissem, causing the mare to rear up and take off as fast as she could.

Kingsly turned to Archibald, who was making a half attempted run to his stable, though his leg objected to the action. He put his hand on Archibald's chest. "We will bring her back, I swear it," Kingsly promised the worried uncle.

Archibald looked at Kingsly before he nodded, heading inside to prepare for their return. Kingsly raced over to his horse, mounting with ease, before bolting after his brother.

Nothing but pure determination on Atticus's face. His cape flapped behind him as his mind began to race. Was he too late? Has he already failed the prophecy? Maybe it was another woman? If it was the Ivory Fawn's scream, they just heard, he would make sure whoever caused it would suffer greatly.

The Ivory Fawn was alive and in danger. It was now up to the Crimson Dragon to save the her from death.

Chapter Thirteen

Hazel

Panting heavily as blood was now dying her once white shirt and ruining her mother's cloak, Hazel leaned forward on the stolen horse as her hair and the horse's mane whipped her in the wind while it galloped.

Hazel's vision blurred as the Raven Palm poison took effect. She felt fire in her veins , and every inhale felt like she was fanning the flames in her veins. Soon, her vision blurred from the effects of the sap taking hold, only clearing when she blinked. Hazel noticed it was getting harder to stay bareback on the horse. After she had to continuously re-adjust herself on its back,

The horse eventually slowed down, feeling its labored breathing between her sweat-soaked tights. Hazel gripped its mane before she sat straight up and looked around, trying to find a way to escape this damned forest. Hazel was so turned around in these woods, she had no idea where she was.

A nearby twig snapped, causing the horse beneath her to tense. Despite her fear, she remained still, unsure of the source of the sound.

Ratherian emerged from the bushes, clapping his hands. smiling ferally as he looked at Hazel, who now appeared pale and sickly. Still shirtless, he scanned her with a predatory smirk. "What a show of bravery back there, although I am disappointed . Darius shared how your life essence tasted with Lilura, and now I wonder how you will taste."

Hazel took a deep, shaky breath, glaring at him and holding the horse tightly as its ears moved back. Ratherian must have noticed it, too, for he lunged at them, causing the horse to rear up and bolt. Hazel couldn't hold on tight enough and tumbled off the horse's back, slamming into the ground and crying out as that arrow in her shoulder snapped in half from contact with the ground. Whimpering from the pain shoulder, she rolled to her side, readying herself to fight back. However, Ratherian was too close to her before she could even get on her knees.

He slammed his foot into her stomach with enough force it sent her rolling into a nearby tree. The motion pushed the broken arrow deeper into her shoulder to where it vanished but didn't come out the other side. Grunting upon impact, she looks at Ratherian, panting heavily. This wasn't how she was going to die. Getting to her hands and feet, using the tree as support, Hazel glared at the Netherian male as he stalked her, licking his lips. "Darius will kill you if you kill me, remember?" Hazel breathed out.

Ratherian's laughter escaped his lips as he grabbed her hair, yanking her head back to expose her freshly torn neck. Darius had messed up her neck, draining her energy.

Pushing her blood-painted hair from her neck, Ratherian examined the nasty work Darius had done to her neck. He looked at her, surprised to see she was still alive despite how much blood coated her top.

Hazel held his wrist tightly, trying to pry his hand away from her

"Darius was far too rough with his meals... Making them scream too quickly... but me, well... I enjoy making my bride beg before I take her," Ratherian growled in her ear as he licked the blood from her neck.

Hazel wanted to punch him so hard that he choked on his teeth at that moment. However, she knew she would only sign a quick death warrant for herself. "So, what? Will you be a good pet and bring me back to him?"

Growling, Ratherian slammed her back into a tree, pinning her to it with his own body, causing Hazel's spine to arch in pain. She didn't want him to hear her suffering. It would give him what he was looking for. Ratherian expected her to beg for her life, and wanted her to beg for him to spare her.

His hot breath made her skin tingle. The way it smelled was so vile it made her stomach curdle. An aroma of brimstone and iron. As Ratherian licked blood from her neck, a faint growl escaped her lips. Like hell, she would let this barbarian finish her off. Not without fighting back.

He opened his lips to bite down, but she turned her head, biting Ratherian's ear so hard that he pulled back, screaming in pain as she yanked it clean off. Releasing her, he stepped back, holding the open wound as blood spewed from it.

Spitting his ear out at his feet, Hazel also wanted to puke from the horror she had just committed to break free from his grip.

Not giving him a chance to react, she ran as fast as she could, doing her best to dodge trees The cold air nipped her face, and hot tears ran down her cheeks as she held her neck. She had to survive. Hazel prayed to Aena for protection, hoping the goddess would save her.

Hazel had to return to her uncle and get him out of Alexandria. It was no longer safe for either one of them. Stumbling into a tree, she gasped in pain upon impact. Turning to look over her shoulder, she didn't see Ratherian. Coughing loudly, she held her hand over her mouth to cover her cough, but blood stained her hand.

She barely had time to react, feeling Ratherian's presence now directly behind her just before he grabbed hold of her body slamming it into the ground with his own. Her face was dragged across the dirt, and she small rocks sliced her cheek and eyebrow open.

Ratherian pushed his thumb into her shoulder wound, causing her to arch her back as she screamed in pain. Blinding white pain shot through her as she lay on her stomach, at a massive disadvantage to his size and strength. She felt like she couldn't even lift her head from the poison, sucking strength from her body.

She tried to get away from Ratherian, but the more she fought, the more pressure he applied to her shoulder. Only laughter filled her as his finger pushed deeper into the wound. She could feel the Raven Palm poisoning killing her, making it nearly impossible to open her eyes.

This was how she would die.

Hazel attempted to throw a punch by flipping her to her back, but he caught her hand and laughed at her pathetic attempt before driving his fist across her face. Her mouth filled with blood as her head slammed to the side. Ratherian latched his teeth onto her shoulder of the arm she just tried to punch with.

Hazel let out a blood-curdling scream, but was too weak to push him off with her other hand.

Ratherian was so enraged, he couldn't care less if Darius was furious with him for killing his Blood Bride. Hazel would pay for ripping his ear off. Slamming his teeth into her torn neck, he ripped into it more. She rested her hands on his chest, trying to push him off. However, her strength failed her, and Ratherian declared open season on her neck.

Hazel eyes were droopy and heavy. She wanted to keep them open, but it was hard.

Feeling blood spray across her face and hair, a horrific gurgling sound came from above her. She felt the pressure of Ratherian feasting on her neck. Unable to keep her eyes open anymore, Hazel closed them for a moment, until thunderous hooves approached, followed by male voices she didn't recognize. Panting heavily, her eyes slowly opened, but her vision was blurred. All she could make out were two tall males approaching her on horseback. Ratherian lay beside her as an arrow shot through his throat, flashing a black dragon.

A calloused hand picked up her head from her neck, pushing herbs into her mouth. She knew these herbs. They were the same herbs she used to reverse Raven Wood sap poisoning. The blood in her mouth helped her swallow it, and she hoped it be enough to keep her alive.

A male voice spoke, but she couldn't understand it. There was just a gentle stroke of across her face before whoever was at her side had an arm under her legs and neck and carried her away.

Soon, her eyes were too heavy to open, and darkness took her into a deep slumber. All she felt was a thundering heartbeat as it soothed her into sleep.

Chapter Fourteen

Hazel

Nightfall blanketed the sky with dark blues and purples as the sun sank behind the mountain. The fireplace in her bedroom emitted a steady crackling sound Looking around her bedroom, Hazel's vision was blurred, and her body felt as heavy as iron. The cream blankets were weighed down around her body, lulling her into a calm state. Taking a deep breath and enjoying the aroma of cedar wood and bergamot, Hazel tried to recollect her memory of the events. Despite her blurred vision, Hazel could see a stocky male figure relaxing in the vintage armchair in the corner of her room beside her bed. Cinnamon, vanilla, and oranges washed over her as her uncle rose from the chair, stepped closer to her bedside, stroked her sweat-soaked hair from her eyes, and gave her a warm smile. "Oh, thank the gods," Archibald exclaimed in relief. Blinking a few more times her vision sharpened. "I'm glad you are awake." The stranger said from his position at the fireplace, not even taking his attention off the flames in the fireplace. Watching the man closely, Hazel took in his black tunic tucked into tight brown trousers.

Groaning in pain as she shifted her weight, Hazel attempted to sit up, but her strength failed her, causing her body to crash back into her soft sheets she realized was the ones in her bedroom back at the cottage.. Her blankets wrapped around her, welcoming her into a smooth embrace. The pain in her neck, shoulder, and arm was unbearable, and Hazel's eyes stung with tears. Raising the heavy cream duvet to find the source of the pain reverberating through her body, she found her waist, breast, and shoulder completely wrapped in bandages, some with hints of blood on the fabric. Realization consumed her as she recalled the events that happened weren't a horrific nightmare, but reality. A shaky breath escaped her rosy lips as she turned to look at her uncle, trying to speak. Her throat was so raw from screaming, Hazel forcing herself to swallow. As her hand reached for it, she felt even the neck bandage wrap. Her eyes misted over with tears.

"Shh, it's okay. You're safe now. He can't hurt you anymore," Archibald's voice wobbled.

Hazel felt the weight and reality of everything crashing down on her, tearing a hysteric sob from body. How could she even be in this situation? Darius had always seemed to act in her best interest, but now that she knew, how long has he been deceiving her? Was it ever love? Or was she just some pawn?

Archibald pulled her into a gentle, comforting hug, cautious of his grip, not wanting to hurt her any more. Her uncle stroked her hair before kissing her forehead in an attempt to soothe her. Her eyes went to the stranger standing by the fireplace, who seemed unbothered by their presence. It made her want to hold her uncle more, worried about the intent of this man. Considering she just nearly died.

Hazel had never seen this man before , and it was unnerving that he was just standing there without a word. "Hazel, meet the Crown Prince Atticus. He saved your life," Archibald spoke gently, with a hint of gratitude. Hazel's eyes widened at the introduction. This man was the Immortal Dragon? She'd heard of how inhumane he was in his court, not to mention how heartless he was on the battlefield. Yet he saved her? Why was he even in the Raven Palm forest? Was he one of them?

Atticus turned his attention to Hazel as if sensing her fear. He straightened up, put his hands in his pockets, and flashed her the most feline smile Hazel has ever seen. "It's an honor to meet you, Hazel. I am sorry about your fiancee. We couldn't find him anywhere, and I didn't really give your assailant a chance to tell me where he was." Finally pulling away from her uncle, Hazel struggled to swallow, gripping her throat as she forced herself to speak, but it came out strained. "Dar-Darius is..."

Archibald rubbed Hazel's arm in soothing strokes, trying to comfort her. "I am so sorry, Hazel... Darius was a good man."

Hazel shakes her head as the hot tears in her eyes fell from her bottom lashes. Pushing Archibald's hand away from her, she wiped the tears away with one good arm before she looked at her uncle again. "He... He is... One... One of them." Her voice was hoarse. She needed to warn Archibald and Atticus that Darius had deceived them. That whole time, he was a Netherian wielder and not just some simple butcher boy. Grumbling, she gripped her throat from the aching feeling it gave her as Hazel forced her words out.

Archibald and Atticus both seemed taken aback by the turn of events she had just revealed. Their eyes widened , especially Archibald.

Atticus let out a faint scoff shaking his head, "So, I am guessing instead of making you a radiant bride-to-be, he made you a Blood Bride," Atticus replied, boredly.

Hazel's focus snapped to Atticus, narrowing her eyes at him for his comment as Archibald ground out, "That bastard! I should have known there was something off. I just thought for once he actually truly cared, and he wasn't one of *them*." Approaching the small round table beside the fireplace where Hazel normally read, Archibald picked up the small cast-iron kettle and poured some water into a cup with a bag of herbs. Returning to Hazel's bedside, he handed her a cup of tea while tucking hair behind her ear that had snuck out from behind the bandage on her forehead. "Here, just like you showed me. It will help your throat," Archibald said softly, stroking her head gently.

Hazel nodded in gratitude, reaching for the cup, unable to stop her cringing from the pain. There was no need to communicate as Archibald sat beside her bedside, helping Hazel drink the cup of tea. The taste of peppermint, honey, and lavender danced across her taste buds, coating her sore throat. Almost instantly, she felt such relief from the tea. Clearing her throat, she looked at Atticus, narrowing her eyes. "Why were you in the Raven Palm forest? People who go there and return are either Netherian or in alliance with them. Crown Prince or not, I want answers," Hazel demanded with a raspy, hoarse tone.

"Hazel!" Archibald warned her by touching her leg, giving it a faint squeeze.

Hazel peered at her uncle and then at Atticus, who only faintly chuckled, biting the lower corner of his lip and rubbing his jaw. "It's alright, Archibald. I don't blame her for being cautious. It's a good trait to have." Hazel's Ice-blue eyes never left Atticus's body movement weary of the stranger. To Hazel, there was no way it could be coincidental that that this prince magically showed up when she needed it most. Bowing from the waist to Hazel, Atticus lowers his head before looking up. Giving her a feline smile and slowly straightening up, he crossed his arms behind his back. "As your uncle said, I am Prince Atticus, the Crown Prince of Wylana, and the Immortal Dragon. My brother and I came to Alexandra with orders to see the condition of the village, having hearing rumors about how the Netherian wreaked havoc on it. We were supposed to report back to my father about the conditions of your village. Although, those circumstances have changed now," Atticus explained as he took a step around the bedpost, leaning against the left bedpost with sort of a swagger to his lean. "I shall leave you two alone so you can get some rest. I believe there is much you and your uncle need to speak about. I will see to it that the men outside keep up with their patrols and posts," Atticus continued raking his hand through that onyx-black hair.

Atticus's words struck a realization in her. It was at least a two-day trip on horseback. If these men came on foot, how long was she unconscious for? Atticus bowed once more before strolling to the door and opening it. Archibald helped her take another drink of her tea when he registered the look of shock on her face.

"Wait." Hazel voice cracked as she spoke up

Stopping, Atticus looks over his shoulder at Hazel with a raised eyebrow without saying a word during the moment of silence allowing her to continue. "How many days have I been laying here?" she questioned.

Hazel could have sworn there was a laugh under his breath. "You've been in bed for almost two weeks, princess. Glad to see sleeping beauty is awake at last."

Two weeks? She had been in this bed for two weeks? How could that be? Hearing she was out of consciousness for that long, there was a silence in her head, *How could she possibly be unconscious for that long?* By the time she opened her mouth to express her gratitude to Atticus, he had already taken his leave.

"Hazel, there is something we have to talk about." Archibald's voice wobbled as he spoke softly. His eyes were full of so much sorrow and anger, and was that also remorse and grief? Never had she seen her uncle like this. He was always eloquent, yet silent. Unease filled the room , leaving her uncomfortable and worried to see Archibald at such a loss for words.

"There is something I need to tell you that is long overdue," he said. Archibald walked over to a box she had never seen before and brought it over to her. There was a wisteria tree, just like her mother's, that had been painted on it with golden antlers decorating with ivory vines decorating corners. "Hazel, you are the Ivory Fawn." Sitting up in her bed, Hazel's eyes snapped towards her uncle came to stand beside her bedside table. Not once in all her years had she seen this box, yet it felt so familiar and so comforting just looking at it. "I wanted to tell you when the time was right, but part of me did not know if there would ever be a right time."

Hazel could have sworn there was a flash of guilt on his face when he spoke. It made her more weary of what else he was about to tell her. Waiting patiently seeing his hesitancy, she waited to hear what he needed to share. Watching him open it, she was shocked there were painting portraits of her mother with Hazel when she was a baby.

Picking up one portrait, she saw what she assumed was her mother wearing the lilac purple cloak Hazel treasured , holding a baby swaddled in a lilac blanket in her arms.

"You are the direct descendant of Queen Astoria and King Gavriel of the Aestival people... Your great-great-grandmother was Queen Astoria. Your mother knew it because *her* mother told her stories passed down by her mother's mother."

This news, that she was the direct descendant of the king and queen of the legendary people, rattled her world as her heart lurched in her chest. Hazel was speechless at the alteration of her reality—that she was just a simple village girl—only to learn she had royal blood coursing through her blood.

"When you were born, your mother knew the moment she held you that you were the Ivory Fawn everyone has been waiting for. When you were born, Ashira was supposed to die on the table, per the doctor's examination, but your tears somehow healed her. I offered that you, your mother, and your father were welcome to come live with me instead of by yourselves with no one they could trust if something was to happen. They agreed because it would be easier to protect you." Archibald's voice was so wavered, it was like he was choking on his words.

Archibald wiped the tears from his eyes as he scanned his niece's face, who was speechless at this information. He stroked Hazel's arm, trying to comfort her, while continuing his story. "Your mother didn't die of heartbreak. She died from Raven Palm poisoning. Some men came for you while your father was hunting. Somehow word got out of your abilities, and it didn't take much for them to assume you were the prophesied Ivory Fawn. Especially considering your abilities mirrored those of Queen Astoria while you were only a toddler. I was with your mother that day, and we fought them off the best we could, but your mother was run through by a blade covered in the Raven Palm sap."

Hazel's eyes began to pour tears from Hazel's face at the thought she had been hunted down since she was a babe, and that her mother had died protecting her.

No one had ever told her who she truly was. they knew who she was since birth. Hazel had nearly died by the same people who killed her mother, Netherian was a black stain on the Tresian history. What if she was better prepared? Maybe she had a better chance of fighting back Darius and Ratherian.

"When Ashira was dying in my arms, she asked that I hold her beneath the wisteria tree, and I did to give her a sliver of peace while she suffered from the cursed poison. We tried your tears again, but for some reason it didn't work. That was by far the hardest day of my life because when I told your father after he returned, you father blamed you for her death. Said you couldn't listen to our warning to not using your gift. He... He tried to punish you. You were only six. I couldn't let him harm you."

Hazel knew her uncle would do anything to protect her. However, knowing all this now felt like slowly a dagger was being twisted into her heart. Taking her uncle's hand, she squeezed it to reassure him even though both of their faces were stained with tears. Archibald took a deep breath to steady himself as he wiped the tears away from his eyes.

"I am so sorry I never told you sooner. I should have protected you better, shown you how to defend yourself better, and taught you how to use your abilities. You almost died because I never told you. I nearly failed you and your mother." His voice broke into millions of pieces as he begged for his niece's forgiveness.

While reaching her hand to his cheek, Hazel's shoulder screamed in protest. However, she didn't care as she stroked a tear from Archibald's cheek. "You haven't failed me or my mother. I am still here, am I not? We had no idea Darius was one of them. I still don't know how he managed to hide it so well."

Archibald watched his niece before leaning forward, kissing and stroking her head. Forcing his eyes shut, Archibald pulled himself together "You must not tell anyone but Prince Atticus. If it's true that your great-great-grandmother came to him to warn him you were in danger, that means your destinies are entwined. Trust only him," Archibald pleaded.

When she heard this, her eyes widened, and her mouth parted in surprise. The man who had just was in her room a moment ago was somehow intertwined with her destiny? Hazel didn't know what to think.

"Get some sleep, my beloved fawn. We are to join them back in Wylana, once you are in better shape to travel." Archibald wiped his tears as he spoke.

Her uncle gathered the box and portrait from Hazel before tucking it away under her pillow. Walking back over to his niece, he covered her up with the creme blanket. Hazel lay back down, slowly pulling the blanket Archibald laid over her up more so she was comfortable.

Before she could even thank her uncle or ask him more questions, sleep took her.

Chapter Fifteen

Hazel

Taking a deep breath, Hazel grumbled, shielding her eyes from the sun's rays. Turning her head, she saw a dark-haired male sitting beside her bed, reading and sipping a cup of freshly brewed coffee from the aroma filling the room. Surprised but the unexpected visitor, Hazel gasped in pain as the movement of quickly sitting up caused her body to scream in protest.

"Well, you shouldn't have done that." His voice was so husky as he spoke that it was almost alluring. His honey eyes met hers as she felt pinned to the spot.

Hazel stood, watching the stranger get up and approach her cautiously. Her body tensed as he grew closer. Atticus towered over her. She looked up at him and winced, reaching for her neck. His hand stopped her as he gripped her wrist.

"Don't. You will only make it worse." Releasing her wrist, he looked at her neck before their eyes met again. "May I?"

At first, she hesitated, not knowing if she could trust him, but Hazel trusted her uncle. If he told her to trust Atticus, she would.

Nodding her head, she slowly sat down on the bed again, and Atticus came and stood between her legs. He gently moved her hair back, and his hands were as warm as the fire he stood beside the night before.

His caramel eyes scanned over her bandages to assess if Hazel has reopened any of her wounds, holding her neck and shoulder together. His gaze lowered down to below her neck, across her chest to her shoulder. It felt degrading.

Hazel might as well have been bare-chested to this man, for his gaze heated her cheeks. His golden eyes gazed up at her. "You are one lucky princess. You didn't open up anything, and I am also glad you can stand," Atticus said softly.

Glaring at him, she wanted to slap him for calling her such a childish nickname, she looked down at her body as if nothing covered her lower half . Hazel realized she would be half-naked without the bandages covering her upper torso.

Out of instinct, she grabbed a duvet and wrapped herself up . Hazel had heard rumors for merchants and travelers he was not only cruel to, but also rough with the women he took to his bed. She didn't trust this man who was looking examining her like Hazel would be his next bed partner. Realizing she only had on her riding pants beside her bandages, Hazel's cheeks blushed at the thought of Atticus seeing her naked chest to get her wounds treated and out of the ripped up shirt she previously wore. She asked shyly, "Did you?" Silently praying he wasn't the one that dressed her wounds.

Shaking his head with a faint chuckle, the feral smile that reappeared on his face made her heart leap. "Despite what you have heard of me, Princess, I don't strip unconscious women from their clothes. Now, if they are conscious and aware, that's another story."

Hazel clinched the blanket more, looking at Atticus as he stepped back from her and returned to his previous sitting arrangement. Watching his movement carefully. From the rumors she heard of this man, he didn't earn the name Immortal Dragon because he was kind and gentle. A man didn't earn dragon status without being destructive.

"It's improper to stare at someone above your stature, Princess," Atticus purred.

Narrowing her eyes, she scoffed and shook her head before rising from the bed to grab a soft, burnt yellow cotton robe to make herself more decent in front of this crown prince. "Stop referring to me as princess," Hazel ground out

Covering herself, she gently closed her robe, pulling her hair out with a wince. The cotton felt pleasant against the small amount of skin not covered with bandages.

"What else am I to call you, then? Because I can't call you the Ivory Fawn," he replied without glancing at her.

Glancing over to him, he paid her no attention. Whatever he was reading seemed far more entertaining. It was a book she had never seen before, the cover decorated in lilac, orchid, and gold .

This couldn't be the Immortal Dragon. Not with him sitting there so relaxed and graceful, and especially not reading a fantasy book from the cover appearance. Nothing about his posture indicated that he was a cruel, brutal, heartless heir. If he, why save her and watch over her as she sleeps? Why was he being so gentle with her, ensuring her wounds don't reopen?

"Hazel is fine," she replied softly, carefully crossing her arms over her chest.

Atticus glanced up from his book and scanned her over before sucking his teeth and turning back to his book. "You will need something warmer than just a robe and riding pants," he said as he turned the page of his book.

The sound of Atticus rising from his chair drew her from her thoughts, and she watched him set his book down. "I shall let your uncle know we should prepare for our journey to Wylana," Atticus said, meeting her gaze blankly.

Hearing they were leaving Alexandria to go to Wylana, shock painted Hazel's face. What about their home? Her mother's tree? Her uncle told her they would travel when she was in better shape. Was this man insane to have her travel like this?

"Leave? You can't expect me to pack up my whole life and leave with you? The Immortal Dragon, of all people? You must be mad."

Atticus's eyes darken as he looked at Hazel, causing every muscle in her body to tense. An exhale escaped his parted lips as he stalked towards her, towering over her. Stepping backward, her back now met her closet door. Gasping at the contact and the fact she couldn't get away, Hazel looked up at him. His hands were on both sides of her head as they rested on the closed doors.

"You are the Ivory Fawn, invaluable to Wylana's future. Like it or not, Princess, you and I are stuck together because of destiny. So, either you come willingly and start your journey to fulfill your destiny, or I carry you over my shoulder, kicking and screaming, back to Wylana like an insufferable child. Your choice, Princess," the dragon prince ground out through his teeth.

A loud slap filled the air as Hazel's chest heaved angrily. He held his face, whipped to the side from the impact, and took a step back. There was a perfect imprint of her hand across his cheek. "You will not speak to me like that again, prince or not. I didn't ask to be this Ivory Fawn, and I refuse to let you speak to me as if I were a child or piece of property."

The most feral growl she had ever heard escaped his lips as he glare at Hazel. Seeing the Immortal Dragon glare from across the battlefield made grown men run for their lives. Men had been put to death at his hand for lesser offenses. Even though she refused to tolerate disrespectful behavior from anyone, not even a prince, her body trembled, preparing for the repercussions of slapping the most feared prince in Wylana.

His movement was so fast she couldn't even react before he pinned her wrist to the closet door above her head. She cried out in pain as his body pressed into her as he held her there. Panicking, she reached for his wrist as her shoulder screamed in protest.

Hazel stood stunned by the overwhelming aroma of bergamot and cedar washing over her as she realized how incredibly close he was. Her icy blue eyes met with his pools of honey. "You are incapable of defending yourself in your state," Atticus challenged.

After trying for another strike, Atticus's other hand easily caught her closed fist. He then pinned her other wrist to the closet door, restraining both wrists. Lowering his face down to Hazel's, so close they shared breaths, her heart raced as those honey-brown eyes turned deep amber. Hazel's throat bobbed as she felt defenseless.

"Princess, if you truly think you could fight in your state, you are sadly mistaken."

Pain surged through her shoulder and neck. Hot tears filled her eyes as she tried to fight out of his grasp despite her shoulder reopening. Atticus didn't even budge from her attempts.

Kingsly barged into the room and yanked his eldest brother away from Hazel, gripping Atticus's shirt collar and glaring at him. "Are you insane?!" Kingsly fumed.

Archibald appeared in the room, and ran over to where Hazel was slumped to the floor holding her shoulder, tears shining in her eyes. He dropped to his knees before her investigated her wounds.

Kingsly looked over his shoulder at Archibald, apologizing profusely as the man cradled his niece firmly to his chest.

Hazel supported her arm close to her chest to relieve some of the pain tearing through her shoulder. Breathing heavily, she closed her eyes and tried to clear her mind. Normally, she thought of how Darius would touch her to soothe her pain, but now those thoughts were tainted with betrayal and heartbreak.

Kingsly turned his attention back to Atticus, who stared blankly at the blood now soaking through Hazel's once clean bandage around her shoulder. "Clean her up. We leave tomorrow," Atticus said coldly before brushing off Kingsly's grip on his collar and quietly leaving the room.

Hazel trembled in her uncle's arm, wishing the pain would stop. It hurt so much, to the point her stomach threatened to spew out its contents.

Hazel flinched as Kingsly kneeled beside the pair, putting his hand on Archibald's shoulder with a soft expression. "Would you allow me to tend to you shoulder? You can stay in the room if that eases your mind." Looking over at this male, Hazel clung to her uncle, hesitant but soon nodding her head. There was something about him that was calming.

Archibald looked at Kingsly, unsure of him after what his brother did, but Hazel squeezed her uncle's hand and nodded. Kingsly extended his hand to her and smiled gently. "I promise you no harm."

Taking a shaky breath, she nodded again, took his hand, and allowed him to help her to stand up so they could fix the damage Atticus caused.

Chapter Sixteen

Hazel

She stared at her mother's tree and felt the chill of the first winter approaching. The way the lavender leaves swayed in the breeze was comforting to her. Kingsly restored her mother's cloak to its former glory minus the tearing, and there was no sign of blood on it. Her eyes are filled with silver tears as she stared at her mother's grave, not knowing what to say. Never once had she thought she would leave Alexandra. Hazel thought she would grow roots here with a family and a husband who loved her.

She was the proposed Ivory Fawn, who was supposed to save her home and Wylana, who was only told of her destiny after nearly dying. In the midst of all of this, Hazel discovered she was not only this legendary hero of a prophecy she had never heard of, but was supposed to trust this cruel prince to lead her down the right path. Hazel felt like her entire life was a lie. She thought she was an orphan raised by her uncle, meant to live a dull life, but now had to fulfill a prophecy and save all of Wylana, despite knowing nothing about it or the Aestival race.

Exhaling softly, she couldn't find the words to say goodbye to her mother's grave. All she could do was walk over to it, carrying the last bundle of lavender from her garden, and set it down before the gravestone. She crumbled down onto the ground, drowning in fear of the unknown of what was to become of this savior woman. Gripping her mother's cloak, she let the waves of grief and uncertainty consume her. Tears flooded her eyes, watering the soil with salt tears.

Leaning forward, she braced her hands on the earth beneath her, sobbing as the ache in her heart ripped through her chest.

Why her, of all people? Why was she chosen to take on this burden? Why couldn't it be some fierce warrior trained for battle or some princess who knew everything it meant to be a ruler?

Hazel could not stop crying. She rested her head on the earth, not caring who heard her sobbing.

A gentle hand rubbed a comforting circle on her back, causing her to weep more uncontrollably. She didn't even notice it wasn't her uncle who comforted her or that the golden-haired general prince kneeled beside her.

"Tell me about your mother," he said softly as he looked between the grave and Hazel.

She steadied her breathing, only flinching slightly when Kingsly offered her a handkerchief to dry her eyes.

Taking his offer, she wiped her eyes and gulped down deep breaths of cold air to soothe her burning throat and lungs. Looking at her mother's grave, Hazel tucked a strand behind her ear. "I don't have any memories of my own. She was killed when I was a six years old. However, from the stories my uncle told me, she was kindhearted, dedicated to her family, and didn't have a selfish thought in her mind," Hazel admitted. Sniffling, she laughs faintly, looking down at the bundle of. "I was told she loved lavender immensely, and smelled like it whenever she walked into a room. She would spend hours in the garden, tending to the lavender she grew. Used it in almost everything she made. So, I cut lavender from the garden every time it's ready to be harvested and bring it to her grave." Her voice wobbled

"And you talk to her grave every time you come?" Kingsly inquired gently.

Nodding in acknowledgment of his question, Hazel wiped her eyes as she stared at the lavender. Hazel then played with her mother's necklace hidden under her cloak, swallowing her grief. "Yes, it helps me feel close to her, knowing I am making sure her garden stays beautiful and vibrant while also telling her of my day," Hazel replied.

Kingsly extended his hand to Hazel as he spoke. "I am so sorry for everything you endured. No one shouldn't have to grow up without any parents, let alone a mother who was kind."

Looking at his hand, she stared at it for a moment before she took it, giving it a grateful squeeze.

"No, they shouldn't, but sometimes the world is cruel and dark. It tends to snuff out the light in the most deserving people while the blackest hearts never suffer for their doings." Sniffling, Hazel looked at Kingly, trying to hide a pained smile, and he offered her a kind and warm smile before giving her hand a squeeze.

"I know this is all very scary for you. I won't tell you it gets easier from here, because, unfortunately, it doesn't. Although, and I hope you will allow me to do so, I would like to get to know you as Hazel. Not as the Ivory Fawn, but as the person behind the title." Returning his handkerchief, Hazel smiled at him. "I would appreciate that very much. Also, thank you for yesterday. Stepping in between your brother and me. Is he always like that?" she replied.

Kingsly shook his head and rested his hand on hers as she offered him the handkerchief, letting her know it was hers to keep.

"Regrettably, he is like our father, direct and concise, except when addressing my mother and younger brother Reed," he replied to Hazel. "He is more gentle and caring towards them."

Taking a deep breath, she shook her head and pulled her cloak tighter around herself as the chilling wind picked up.

"Well then, if and when he takes the throne, gods help Wylana," Hazel breathed out.

"I didn't take you for the type of comparing yourself as a god, Hazel," Kingsly jokingly replied.

Hazel faintly chuckled at his comment, offering him a slight smile. "Well, I am this supposed Ivory Fawn, am I not?" Kingsly's lips curl up in amusement before he released her hand to stand up, only to offer it again to help her.

"Yes, you are, but that isn't what makes you special, Hazel," Kingsly admitted as his hand lingered in the air for her to grasp.

Smiling more, she took his hand, stood up, and brushed herself off. She looked at her mother's grave and then at Kingsly. "Well then, I think I've kept everyone waiting long enough. Shall we go?" Hazel was almost embarrassed for taking so long to her mother's grave.

Kingsly leaned over, took a lavender bud from the bundle Hazel displayed at her mother's grave, and twirled it between his fingers. "You are the one who grieves because your life was just turned upside down after nearly dying. No one should rush you through that process, not even my brother or the gods. You process grief how you want to process it, not how others tell you," Kingly mentioned to Hazel.

Smiling faintly, she took the lavender from him, spinning it between her fingers before looking at Kingsly. For a moment, Hazel was silent before planting a light kiss on the general prince's cheek. "Thank you, Kingsly. It will be a pleasure to know someone who understands what I am living through in my new arrangement other than my uncle," she replied, and a small warmth blooming on her cheeks.

Kingsly chuckled faintly, offering his arm to Hazel to escort her to their carriage. "I have learned that even healing souls need people to help them heal," he admitted with a faint smile.

Pulling herself together. Hazel went to the carriage, where Archibald and Atticus waited for them since they allowed her a moment alone with her mother's grave. Approaching arm in arm with one another, Archibald offered Kingsly and Hazel both a smile, glad his niece joined them.

Atticus's amber eyes scanned the pair before he pushed off the carriage.Narrowing them on Kingsly as Atticus walked over to Kissem, who was once again playing with her bit. Atticus climbed up easily, patting the mare's neck.

"Are you still playing knight in shining armor, brother? Or may we go now?" The dragon prince growled out in irritation.

Kingsly's jaw clenched tightly, parting his lips to reply, but Hazel responded before he could. "At least your brother has a heart dragon." Her icy tone was colder than the forthcoming snow as she narrowed her glare to the heir, whose gaze was locked with her.

Scoffing, Atticus tightened his grip on the reins and rested his hand on the horn of the saddle.

"Is that the best you have, Princess?" Atticus grumbled.

Growling faintly, Hazel went to approach Atticus to give this dragon prince a piece of her mind, but Kingsly's hand rested on the small of her back, causing her to stop in her tracks to look at him.

"Are you done with your childish pride? Or can we leave while we still have daylight?" Kingsly sighed, clearly bored by Atticus's mocking.

Huffing, Atticus nudged his horse to a walk, taking the lead, as few of his men followed. Kingsly shook his head before he looked at Hazel.

"You will be in the carriage where you will be comfortable. I would offer you a horse, but unfortunately we don't know your skill level on horseback, plus I don't want you accidentally reopening your wounds if something spooked the horse."

Resting her hand on Kingsly's arm, Hazel offered a warm smile to him, appreciative of his generosity. "Thank you. The carriage is fine. Never been in one, so it will be a nice change. Plus, I can get some more rest on the way," Hazel replied softly.

Kingsly nodded his head and handed Hazel off to Archibald, who held the door open to a brown mahogany round carriage with red curtains to provide privacy. As she stepped into it, there were three long benches covered in red velvet. It, too, was made of mahogany, as two benches faced each other while the third was on the opposite side, facing the door.

"I will be riding alongside the carriage. I don't do well in small spaces. However, you should get some rest. You still need it after these last two weeks."

Hazel smiled, nodding and kissing her uncle's cheek before Archibald closed the carriage door behind him and headed towards his solid black horse.

Mounting their horses. Archibald stayed beside the carriage, as did a few Wylannian guards on foot. Kingsly took his place beside his brother upfront, leading the small army of men back home.

Chapter Seventeen

Hazel

Barely touching the peaks of the mountain, the sun was slowly retreating behind them as the night sky crept in, battling for the right of the sky.

Dozing away in the carriage with her mother's cloak across her shoulder as a blanket from the cold, Hazel didn't once stir during the ride to Wylana.

She slept so peacefully during the first few hours of their ride. The rumbling of the carriage helped soothe her into a blissful sleep. Slowly, she began to wake as something in the air shifted. It was unnerving to not only her, but from the sound of the horse whinnying, the horses most likely sensed it too. Sitting up, Hazel's hand reached up to her mother's necklace, and noticing it was radiating a warmth to the skin in between her breasts. Sitting there momentarily, she wondered why it was so warm, she remembered the warning Archibald had forewarned her about. Shooting to her feet, she lunged for the carriage window, pulling back the curtains. "Stop the carriage!"

Almost instantaneously, everyone stopped, and Hazel urgently scrambled out. Her eyes scanned her surroundings, her heart racing as she held her mother's necklace tight in her hands.

With sheer panic on his face, Archibald dismounted his horse and went to her, brushing his hand on her arm. "Hazel, what is it?"

Rapidly, she examining the area around them. her breathing picked up when she looked up to the princes as they approached on horseback. Hazel tried to get words out, but her fear clenched her throat to where her vocal cords ceased to make a sound. All she could do was look to see if there was any movement.

"What's wrong? We can't stop for bathroom breaks," Atticus scolded.

"Atticus!" Kingsly snapped as he dismounted his horse, walking over to the trembling young lady as she clutched her necklace.

Before another word could be uttered, an arrow whistled through the air, seeing the arrow flying directly at Hazel cries out moving to dodge it, but Kingsly sliced the arrow in half before it could hit Hazel.

"Protect the girl!" Kingsly demanded with a thunderous voice.

Archibald mounted his horse again, drawing his sword and readied to fight. Frozen in fear, Hazel couldn't stop staring at the arrow split in half in front of her. Kingsly gently grabbed her non-bandaged arm, pulling her back to reality. "Listen to me. I need you to get back into the carriage." Suddenly hearing a shout in the distance, Kingsly yanked her arm to the side caging her body in-between his arms, just as the sound of another arrow whistled through the air. All Hazel heard was the impact of the arrows piercing the carriage, followed by the grunt that escaped Kingsly's lips.

Once her attention came off the arrow now piercing the carriage where her chest would have been. Realization hit once she came out of her trance, that Kingsly was holding his arm, Hazel made out a tear in his sleeve, showing a gash dripping fresh blood. Turning her head, Hazel's eyes spied the arrow that caused Kingsly fresh wounds that was pierced into the carriage door. If Kingsly hadn't moved her in time, she would have been shot between her eyes. Studying the arrow more closely, Hazel instantaneously recognized the caramel sap from a Raven Palm tree dripping from the arrowhead. Her heart lurched in her chest as she looked at Kingsly's arm, realizing in horror the grave situation they were in.

"Hazel, go!" Kingsly order through clenched teeth.

Before she could move, there was yelling from the bushes as Netherian men ambushed the small army of Wylannian guards.

An overwhelming sound of steel clashing with steel and men crying out in pain from being hit by blasts of the Netherian corrosive magic filled her eardrums. A Netherian male ran straight for Kingsly and Hazel. The general prince turned to engage with the assailant, but Atticus cut the man clean in half with his long sword. Kissem's hooves kicking up dirt as she skid to a halt.. "Get her in the damn carriage now!"

Forcibly grabbing her, Kingsly opened the door and shoved Hazel back into the carriage with an apologetic look on his face as he held his arm close. "Stay low and hidden!"

Hazel quickly got to her knees, and as the door was slammed in her face, Atticus's voice thundered from outside her carriage. "Get her out of here!"

A sudden jolt of movement made Hazel sway backward into the bench behind her, facing the door.

Her necklace was now burning her chest, to the point Hazel had to remove it. When she did, there was an imprint of the tree now on her chest. A chill creeps up her spine, panic began to claw at her throat trying to restrict her vocal cords

The carriage's sudden jolted and sent her tumbling forward. Crying out, she held her shoulder breathing through the throbbing sensation. As the sound of fighting began to fade, panic filled her bones. No, no, no! She would not lose anyone else, especially not when Archibald was fighting back there, and Kingsly took a raven sap dipped arrow for her. Getting to her feet, Hazel wobbled from the carriage motion before slamming her body through the carriage door, tumbling out of it. Gasping feeling a sharp feeling shoot up her side, she felt some of her stitching tear. Hazel forced herself up, hastily approaching the road , she had rolled away a few feet from, that leads towards the fight. She desperately needed to get back to Kingsly.

Making out the shape of a rider in the setting sun's shadows quickly approaching her, Hazel's eyes widened as she picked up her skirt to run. Before she could get away, an arm hooked under her shoulder, hoisting her up on a horse. "You are the most reckless woman—"

Hazel let out a growl as she glared at Atticus, cutting him off mid-sentence. It was like something shifted in her eye to cause him to lean his head back in shock. "Get me to Kingsly! Now!" she demanded.

Without question, He yanked Kissem's reins around, kicking her so hard she reared up , reaching an arm around towards Hazel back to keep her seated, before bolting into a full sprint to get to Kingsly.

Hazel waited until they were close before leaping off Atticus's horse, not waiting for him to slow Kissem down so she could dismount safely. A sharp pain shot up her leg when she landed, but she ignored it, limping over to Kingsly as quickly as she could.

"Shield the Ivory Fawn!!" Atticus roared at his men. There was no turning back now. Atticus revealed to the world that Hazel's true identity.

Hazel looking at Kingsly's arm, trying to see it before turning her head towards the chaos surrounding them. Turning her head to Kinglsy, she realized in horror she had no herbs or satchels prepared for this. She recklessly didn't even think of it when packing to leave until now. Thinking momentarily, she reached up ripping the sleeve ignoring the throbbing in her shoulder.

Kingsly was sweating profusely as all color leached from his face. Already there were blood blisters forming along his arm and his veins were blackening. The sap poison worked faster through Kingsly than she expected. Hazel would have to act fast.

Reaching for her necklace, she let out a groan in frustration when it wasn't there. Hazel forgot she had removed it while in the carriage. This was not good. She needed that necklace to save his life. Hazel looked to her uncle for help, but he was engaged with some Netherian men, and she couldn't distract him. There was no other choice; she had to do this alone. Necklace or not, she needed to save Kingsly.

Closing her eyes, Hazel rested her hands on Kingsly's chest as she plunged into the recesses of her mind. She searched for the tree in various shades of purple and the woman who appeared to her before, but nothing. Nothing came to her in that darkness.

Growling softly, the sounds of steel and the orders shouted by Atticus filled her eardrums. Hazel furrowed her brow in concentration and plunged deeper into that darkness to find the tree and that woman. She couldn't give up.

"Queen Asteria! I need you!" Hazel roared into the darkness, but no one responded or showed themselves. Hazel's heart beat as though nothing had happened. Hazel didn't feel the power of the necklace.

"Damn it! I am your blood, Queen Asteria! Help me save this man!"

It was a deafening silence as Hazel plunged even deeper into darkness of her mind. She delved so far into herself, she couldn't hear the fighting anymore. Roaring in frustration, Hazel wondered how she could be this Ivory Fawn if she couldn't even summon the one thing she was supposed to be good at.

"Hazel! Hazel, came back!"

There was a ribbon of crimson light appeared in the overwhelming darkness. It waved like a blood-soaked ribbon, flapping in the wind. Without hesitation, she lunged toward it, hoping it would help her with her mission. Hazel was pushed back into her body in the blink of an eye.

The blinding gold light flooded her vision before she collapse into unfamiliar arms, arms that felt like fire and steel wrapped around her. Feeling a warm wetness trickling down from her nose , she knew she pushed to hard.

Hazel had gone too far into that darkness, too far into her own magic she didn't even comprehend. Calloused hands took her face into its rough, yet gentle grip. Hazel didn't have the strength to move her head to make out as to who was holding her face.

"Breath, damn it!" a deep, thunderous voice commanded.

Hazel's chest immediately rose and fell in response. Her eyes barely opened, just enough to register that Kingsly was lying on the ground within arms reach of her , utterly still. She couldn't see his arm. "That's it, princess." It wasn't until she heard that stupid pet name that she realized it was Atticus who was holding her face. If she could move , she would shove him away, However, Hazel couldn't even speak let alone move. Soon, the blackness reclaimed her, and the world faded.

Chapter Eighteen

Hazel

Shivering, Hazel's eyes slowly fluttered open, taking in her surroundings. It was pitch black, except for the glow that filtered through the carriage curtains. She nodded approvingly. If there were camp fires, dark creatures wouldn't approach them. Not with this small force of knights and two lethal princes around. Then it hit her: Kingsly! Where was Kingsly?

Looking around the carriage, Hazel saw him , his chest rising and falling as he slept. Grateful for his torn sleeves, she had a clear view of his arm and saw no wound, just a smooth skin clear of any signs of blood..

As Hazel relaxed, her aching muscles became more apparent. Relieved that she had saved him, she closed her eyes momentarily and shifted her weight to get comfortable, letting out a pained groan.

"I swear if you damage even one thread of your newly made stitching, I will rip into your throat myself." Atticus's voice was venomous.

Hearing his words, Hazel froze as she realized he was standing outside the carriage. The Crown Prince must have been guarding her and Kingsly while they camped.

Atticus opened her carriage door. His eyes look at her, and the cold, dark expression on his face made her shrink into her seat.

It was almost as if he would rip her throat out right then and there if she moved.

Atticus glances at Kingsly, still peacefully asleep, with a fur blanket lying over him. He glares over his shoulder at his men, who howled in laughter and returned his attention to Hazel, sneering through his teeth. "You stay put while I get you food and water."

Hazel didn't dare object to his words in fear of the consequences after seeing such a deadly stare.

After Atticus closed the carriage door, she carefully shifted her weight to sit up. However, a soft, almost wheezing sound of pain escaped her lips as she held her abdomen.

The door swung open, causing Hazel to freeze once more. Atticus's lips curled upwards, showing his pearly snarl as he glared at her. "Did I not tell you that if you moved, I would rip into your throat myself, princess?" the dragon prince remarked.

Hazel's throat bobbed as he stepped into the carriage with a steaming bowl. "You told me if I ripped a single stitch, you would. You didn't say anything about moving," she barked back.

Her breath was uneven, but as Atticus took a seat , Hazel had to force herself to calm her breathing.

The rage on his face made her want to run for the hills. When Atticus looked at Kingsly, who was still sleeping, his expression softened to irritation. before Atticus' eyes met her.

The way the fire's light danced across his face from the carriage window made Atticus seem more threatening, but he sighed softly.

"You are the most reckless girl I ever met. Here, eat."

Atticus handed her the bowl , and when she reached for it, her muscles cried in protest

Atticus shook his head, dipping the spoon into the bowl before looking up at her. "And now I have to feed you because you carelessly threw yourself from a fast-moving carriage and then a horse. Here, it's probably not as enjoyable as one of your home-cooked meals, but it will help build your strength and energy the rest of the way to Wylana. he said, gritting his teeth. As he fed her what is on the spoon, she slowly pulled her head back, scanning him over.

He threatened to kill her, and now he was showing this caregiver side. It was a complete one-eighty on his character. What was happening?

Huffing, Atticus set the spoon back in the bowl, looking at Hazel. "For Larus' love, eat the blasted food, princess. It's not poison. See," Atticus grumbled once again through his teeth. He took a big gulp of the stew to prove his point, but winced at how hot it was.

Hazel smiled in amusement. "Can't handle the heat, Dragon?"

Atticus's eyes darkened as he glared at her. "Really, princess? I re-stitched your shoulder and side, and that was before you jumped out of the carriage. Now I am bring you food to help you feel better, and this is how I am thanked?" His voice slowly turned back into venom.

Hazel's throat bobbed before she lifted her head up to look at her freshly wrapped abdomen. Sighing, her head fell back on a pillow decorating the carriage seat.

"Kingsly, is he going to be okay?" Hazel wanted the topic to change away from her to avoid furthering the quickly approaching argument.

Atticus turned his attention to his brother before looking at her again, sighing softly before speaking, "He just needs to rest. By the way, what *was* that back there? You saved our asses back there."

After hearing how Hazel saved everyone during the attack, she was confused. How did she protect everyone when all she did was heal Kingsly and almost sacrificed herself while trying to save him.

"What do you mean? All I was trying to do was heal Kingsly." Hazel breathed out, confused.

Atticus faintly huffed in disbelief before leaning back in his seat and looking at Hazel. "Oh no, princess, you did more than that. Your eyes glowed. When you healed my brother, you were glowing. You grew brighter and brighter, and suddenly, there was a shield around us. The Netherian tried to get through it, but it appeared touching it made them recoil from it. It wasn't long before they fled back into the woods," Atticus explained

As she listened, all color drained from her face. Hazel saved Atticus but also created a shield to stop the fighting? How was that even possible? She only knew her power could heal.

"I heard your uncle yelling, and when I turned around and saw it was you who caused the shield, I noticed your nose was bleeding. He yelled at you to come back, as if you had departed somewhere. When you opened your eyes and finally looked at him, all I saw was ivory and gold. I stepped in and roared at you to return, and you did. Then you stopped glowing and collapsed. I thought you had died because it didn't look like you were breathing," he continued.

That voice. That voice she heard in the darkness had been Atticus's. It was his voice that broke through to bring her back. As she wandered in the darkness, he was the ribbon that helped her to return.

"When I told you to breathe, you did," Atticus admitted

Hazel reached for her necklace, relieved to feel it around her neck.

Atticus pointed at her necklace "You uncle found it in the carriage once we got it back, demanded we put it back on. Didn't really say why it was so important."

Hazel looked at Atticus, who once again handing the food to her. "I never thought I would witness Aestival magic in person," he breathed.

Hazel's eyes shot over to Atticus, hearing him say the word Aestival. her jaw dropped as she shook her head. "I am not even supposed to use it. My uncle forbade me to use it," she admitted.

Scoffing, his hand ran through his onyx hair, cocking his head to the side with a raised eyebrow. "The same uncle who lied to you your whole life? You should have been taught to use it, not fear it." He sneered.

Growling, Hazel threw her bowl to the floor, spilling the contents . "Don't you dare! My uncle protected me!"

Atticus laughed,. "And look how that turned out? You don't know how to use the one magic that will save all of Wylana. And for what? Because he didn't want to tell you?"

Hazel snapped, swinging her legs to get up, but Atticus was quick.

Quickly, he held her wrist to the seat beside her caging her in with his body.

"You are an Ivory Fawn, Hazel. He should have never kept that from you. All it did was stop you from learning how to use your gift. This has put you at such significant risk that nearly cost you your life. Twice! What would have happened if I couldn't reach you in that darkness when he couldn't? Whether you like it or not, princess, our fates are intertwined. It's now my responsibility as the Crimson Dragon to make sure you stay safe and learn your magic before it kills you," he barked.

Hazel didn't pull away or push him back. If she had learned how to use it sooner, Hazel could have thrown a shield up against Darius and Ratherian, avoiding the state she was in now.

"Now eat and rest. You must recover from what happened. When we get to the castle, I will ensure Arabella gives you a well-deserved pampering." Atticus, for once, spoke softly. Crawling off her, he left her in the carriage with Kingsly sleeping quietly and her own thoughts.

Taking the bowl that was spilled on the seat beside her. Hazel notice there was maybe a bite or two in it. Leaning her head back she drinks the strew. groaning as the hot contents slid down her throat. Rubbing her throat, a groan filled the carriage, but it wasn't Hazel this time, but Kingsly. Setting her food down, she looked at Kingsly, wondering if she misheard. Seeing him stir from his slumber. She moved to kneel beside the bench. Stroking a strand of hair from his face, she inhaled deeply. "Take it easy." Hazel's voice cracked as she looked at Kingsly, relieved he was awake.

His icy blue eyes slowly fluttered open, taking in his surroundings before they went to Hazel.

"Are you hurt?" Kingsly asked hoarsely.

Hazel shook her head with a faint smile. "I'm okay. Don't worry about me. Just a few little bumps and bruises." His eyes scanned her over before he attempted to sit up.

"Are you sure you? Because you look like hell." Hazel chuckled as she sat beside him on the bench. "I will manage, Kingsly. Can I ask you something?" Hazel didn't know why she wanted to talk to him about the prophecy. It felt silly to ask, considering she was this supposed Ivory Fawn, and yet she had no idea about the prophecy, let alone about the Aestivals.

"What do you know about the prophecy and the Aestivals?"

Kingsly paused for a moment, thinking long before side-glancing at Hazel. "How much do you know?"

She shrugged. "Little to none, other than I'm this Ivory Fawn of a race I've heard nothing about," she admitted to Kingsly, feeling even more foolish as it came out.

"From what we are taught about them, the Aestivals are winged fae-like beings who are partially immortal. Well, that was until the Blood War. There was a prophecy that said once they all perished, there would be a single being named the Ivory Fawn who would bring them back."

Taking in everything, Hazel stopped before she looked at Kingsly, her brows furrowing. "Wait? Blood War? What is that?"

"It was a war between the Netherian and the Aestivals. The Netherian somehow won, and now they run most of Thersian," Kingsly started, leaning back against the carriage wall, inhaling deeply. "Did your uncle not teach you this? Its common knowledge."

Hazel shook her head. "No, he didn't tell me until recently. What is this Ivory Fawn, though? How am I supposed to become it if I don't know it is or how to use the magic? And how is this magic supposed to save a race that's supposed to be wiped out?"

Kingsly turned his head to look at Hazel, taking her hand gently and squeezing it. "Everything will be okay. Once we get you to Wylana, you will be safe there, and we can help you learn everything you need," he reassured her as if trying to comfort her.

Hazel only inhales deeply, releasing a sigh. "That doesn't really answer my questions. What exactly is this Ivory Fawn, other than some hero who is supposed to save all of Therisan? I don't even know how that could be possible with one single person."

Chuckling softly, Kingsly rested his hand on her leg. "From my understanding, the prophecy says the Ivory Fawn will be guided by her Crimson Dragon. That doesn't sound like a single person to me."

Hazel faintly chuckled, resting her head on his shoulder. "Well, the Crimson Dragon is a pretentious, arrogant asshole. So, I'm not sure how he is going to help."

Kingsly cracked a smile, laughing softly. "Yeah, he has his moments. Trust me, I thought about putting him in the dirt a few times," he admitted before pulling his head back to look at Hazel. "Why don't you get some rest? We both had a rough day, and Wylana is still a good quarter of the day away, depending on when we leave in the morning. I can watch over you for a while." Kissing her head softly, he smiled.

It caught Hazel off guard, but she nodded. "Thank you." Getting up, she kissed his cheek and moved back to her side of the carriage, laid down on the bench, and pulled her mother's cloak over her. "Good night, Kingsly. Thank you for being so kind." Unable to stop the yawn, she closed her eyes, drifting off to sleep.

Chapter Nineteen

Hazel

Hazel slept clutching her mother's necklace. It wasn't until a calloused hand touched her shoulder that she woke from her sleep.

"Hazel, wake up. We are here." Archibald soothed her out of her slumber.

Slowly, she opened her eyes, shielding them from the morning rays now warming her face.

Sitting up, she looked around to see an ensemble of people outside her carriage. Castle staff had gathered to welcome the mysterious female guest to their home.

Archibald brushed a strand from her face as he took in her appearance, "It's okay, you're safe. Let's get you into a proper room with some hot food and a bath," he said softly.

Taking a deep breath, Hazel nodded as her uncle extended his hand into the carriage door for her to take. She gladly accepted it, pulling her mother's hood over her face to hide the dirt and exhaustion.

Kingsly was already outside the carriage, speaking with a few guards before they turned on their heels and headed inside the castle. Hazel was relieved to see him upright back to himself, as if what had happened the night before never occurred.

Atticus approached from behind the carriage over to Hazel, scanning her before turning his head to address a young woman with long, curly brown hair hanging loosely around her shoulders. She had beige skin that looked soft, like a peach.

"Hazel, this is Arabella. She will be your handmaiden. I trust Arabella more than any servant here in the castle. She will help you get cleaned up and settled here in court." Arabella bowed her head.

She just shook her head, holding up her hand.

"You don't need to do that Arabella," Hazel protested. Arabella looked at her in surprise before looking to Atticus for confirmation.

As soon as he nodded, he said, "Tomorrow we will have a celebratory dinner in the magnificent hall in your honor. Until then, let's get you settled in and cleaned up."

Arabella offering Hazel a warm, kind smile, stretching out her hand to Hazel in a gesture to take her cloak. Hazel hesitantly stepped back, shaking her head softly.

Archibald came behind Hazel, squeezing her shoulder before looking at Atticus. "Would it be any trouble to help me get an audience with the king and queen?"

A faint smirk filled Atticus's face as he waved his hand at the castle doors. "I won't be any trouble at all. I was just about to meet with them to give them a status report. You are welcome to come."

Standing there frozen, Hazel enjoyed the beauty of Wylana Castle. It looked like it had jumped out of a fairytale book she read as a child. Ivy and Wisteria wrapped themselves up around the tall stone pillars attached to a balcony

Three weeks ago, she ran away from her village to start a better life with Darius. However, now she knew Darius never loved her, her mother has been murdered, and now was this prophesied Ivory Fawn. It happened all so quickly she didn't really know how or what to feel.

"Are you alright, Lady Hazel?" The young handmaiden spoke like honey.

Lady? Did Atticus not tell anyone who she was? Taking a deep breath, she nodded her head slightly.

"Yes, I am just... overwhelmed by my travels," Hazel replied shyly. Faint chuckles escaped the handmaid's lips as she motioned to the castle

"How about we get you inside so you can take a long hot bath and get some actual digestible food in your gut? Men have no taste for herbs and spices when cooking," Arabella jokingly said.

Hazel actually laughed softly at Arabella's comment before walking to the castle doors. The staff all gawked at Hazel, whispering among themselves as they saw this mysterious lady the princes had brought home. Hazel paid them no mind. She was ready to lay down in a proper bed and get some sleep.

Making her way into the castle hall, she was flooded with the aroma of ivy and dragon's blood incense. The walls were decorated with more of the draping ivy plants with wisteria flowers she'd seen outside.

Leading Hazel to her newly acquired suite inside the castle, Arabella moved quietly and quickly through the halls, avoiding people as she does so.

Colors of ivory and gold decorated the receiving room of Hazel's new room. It was the largest room Hazel had ever seen. If she wanted to, she could fit her entire cottage in one room. Arabella swung a tall archway door inward. A tall arch window and doorway led out to a balcony overlooking the courtyard below her. As she looked out, Hazel could see a vast body of water and the forest. Ivy plants hung so far down the wall that she could hide under them. A large mahogany bookshelf was to the side of the wall where a chair and a small table sat beside it.

Arabella closed the door as she made her way to the washroom. "Would you prefer roses or lilac oil for your bath?" she asked from the bathroom's open archway.

Hazel turned slowly toward Arabella. Her throat bobbed as she looked at her hand-maiden. "Do you, by chance, have lavender and eucalyptus?" Hazel spoke with a gentle yet warm tone.

Arabella, still hearing the request, turned her head slightly in surprise before nodding. "I do. May I ask why, Lady Hazel? Those can be overpowering scents."

Hazel bit her lower lip, looking down at her mother's cloak and reaching under it to grasp her mother's necklace.

"It will soothe my nerves while the eucalyptus will help with my aches," Hazel responded.

Arabella nodded and walked to the bathroom cabinet, grabbing the bath oils for Hazel. "When Prince Atticus explained in his letter he was bringing home a special lady from Alexandria, I didn't realize he meant he was bringing home a lady who is well-versed in the art of aromatherapy," Arabella pointed out with that smooth, honeyed voice.

"I am far from a lady of nobility," Hazel admitted softly.

As Arabella busied herself preparing the bath, Hazel let her mind wander. The weight of recent events pressed on her, each memory replaying like echoes in a grand hall. The steam from the bath curled into the bedchamber, carrying the soothing scent of lavender and cedar wood, yet it did little to quiet the storm in her thoughts.

At last, Arabella walked over to Hazel, offering a warm smile with her hands crossed in front of her. "Your bath is ready."

Turning her head, Hazel nodded before removing her mother's lilac cloak and draping it over the foot of her bed, revealing her white shirt, stained with dirt and blood. Arabella stepped back in shock.. "Oh, my dear, should I call for a royal healer?" Hazel shook her head, stripping off her blouse, revealing more bandages protecting her wounds. However, they didn't cover up the nasty bruising around her ribs. They also didn't cover up the bruising on her arm from Darius.

Hazel swore she could hear Arabella's heartbreak from across the room as the hand-maiden assessed the damage beneath her clothing.

Hugging her body feeling self-conscious about what Arabella would think of the condition she arrived. Hazel looked at Arabella, frowning, "Could you help me with my bandages?"

Without hesitation, the handmaiden came over, gently unwinding every bandaged wound, starting at her waist, when moving to her shoulder, finishing with her neck. Seeing how extensive her wounds were, Arabella's eyes were lined with silver.

Hazel shook her head, covering her now half-naked body, feeling bare to this stranger. Hazel knew she needed fresh bandages to clean her wounds properly,

"Please don't...Don't look at me like that." Hazel's pleaded family

Arabella nodded, averting her eyes as she turned to a wardrobe, hastily retrieving a cotton bathing gown.

"When you are ready, put this on. It's improper for anyone but your husband and hand maidens to see you naked," Arabella turned to leave "however until you feel comfortable with me, we can have you wear the dress." calling over her shoulder before leaving the bathroom.

Hazel then walked over to the bathing dress that was provided for her assessing the fabric.It was very light cotton, soft to the touch. Removing her pants and shoes, Hazel slid the dress on over her head the only way she could, despite her body's protests.Pulling her hair up into a messy high rise bun.

Once dressed, she entered the bathing room. Hazel admired the white marble floors, the white fur rug sitting in front of a large golden oval bathtub that looked big enough to accommodate two adults. Hazel would never expect there to be a window seat on the far left of the bathroom, and a gorgeous skylight above the bathtub. Candles sat all around that, ready to be lit once the skylight no longer brightened the room. Two large oval mirrors decorated the two walls facing the bath, as if someone wanted to admire themselves taking a bath.

After Hazel made her way to the bathtub, Arabella had made her way into the bathroom extending a hand to help her into the bath, and Hazel took the assistance. As Hazel slid down into the warm water, she couldn't stop the groan that has escaping her lips. Not only did it feel good on her muscles. Her wounds stung in reaction to the warm. It felt soothing but also painful on her body. It was reminding her that she was still alive despite being targeted twice , one nearly killing her.

Arabella pulled Hazel's hair down as she picked out bits of grass and.

Taking a soft bristle brush, Arabella brushed out the tangles inside Hazel's hair. The handmaiden was so delicate and gentle.

As a result of the sensation of the soothing yet stinging feel of the cedar wood oil in the water soothing her wounds. Thanks to Hazel's mother Ashira's journals, they had all the benefits of various oils and herbs. Cedar was great to sooth possibly infected wounds. Accompanying by the faint hint of lavender to sooth her mind made Hazel felt like she could fall asleep.

"Would you want me to wash your back for you, or would you want to wash yourself, Lady Hazel?" Arabella asked softly.

Turning her head to Arabella, Hazel inhaled deeply. For once, it would be nice to be pampered like a princess.

"Could you?" she asked shyly.

Arabella smiled softly before helping Hazel sit up. She carefully washed Hazel's hair, then moved to her neck, shoulders, and arms, her touch especially gentle around the tender areas of her neck and shoulder.

When the handmaiden washed Hazel's hair, Hazel thought the sensation would lull her into sleep feeling Arabella's nail scratching her scalp. The aroma of rose water and ivy filled her senses as Arabella used fresh rose water with a tinge of ivy extract. After Hazel had finished her bath, Arabella walked over, resting a soft, warm towel beside her tub.

"You can leave the bathing dress in the tub. I will ring it out later. I will get you a clean dress. What is your favorite color?"

Looking at her handmaiden from the bathtub, Hazel thought momentarily before taking a deep breath. "I love autumn colors, especially browns and reds. So, maybe one of those, if it's not too much trouble."

Arabella nodded before gasping, "Oh, I almost forgot your robe. Would you prefer silk or cotton?"

Hazel had never been asked that before. Silk, to Hazel, was far too expensive. She felt it once in her life at the market. However, the idea of wearing an expensive piece of clothing was unnerving to her. "Cotton is fine. I wouldn't want to ruin an elegant silk robe when there isn't a special occasion," she replied sheepishly.

Chuckling softly, Arabella shook her head before walking to the tub with a warm smile. "You are nothing like the other ladies. It's refreshing. How about I get you a cotton robe for now, but surprise you with a dress? There is one that comes to mind that I think would look absolutely stunning on you," she suggested to Hazel.

It was almost impossible to keep her chuckle back, but Hazel couldn't help it. Soon, she nodded her head in agreement with the idea. Arabella took her leave, returned with a robe shortly after, then handmaiden disappeared again with a hint of a giggle on her lips.

Stepping out of the tub, Hazel did as Arabella told her. She slipped off her soaked bathing dress, leaving it in the tub, and wrapped herself in a surprisingly warm towel. Dropping it, she reached for the cotton robe Arabella had left, savoring its comforting warmth as she pulled it on.

Catching a glimpse of herself in the mirror over the sink, Hazel's breath caught in the back of her throat. Hazel was even taken aback by the visual representation of how much she had suffered these last three weeks.

No wonder Arabella had stared at her in horror. Hazel looked like she had been to war and back, with bruises, cuts, and stitches dancing across her face and body. Hearing Arabella coming into the bathing room, she quickly closed her robe, hiding her naked body and injuries from the handmaiden.

Arabella stopped in her tracks before clearing her throat, "The dress I picked out for you to wear today is on a mannequin, ready for you. Although, I would like to do your hair and polish you up a little before you meet the personal guard. Prince Atticus has chose Ardnaxela for you, from my understanding to train you" Arabella said softly.

Hazel was confused when she heard Atticus not only hand-picked her handmaiden, but also picked her to meet his personal guard that was supposed to be train her. *Why would he go through all this trouble to hand pick her handmaiden and also a guard.*

Hazel didn't really want to question him after the encounter with Atticus in the carriage the previous night.

Filling her lungs with a deep, calming breath, she smiled at Arabella. "I would enjoy that very much. I've never had anyone do my hair for me before, let alone pick out my dress." Hazel said with a warm smile on her lips.

"Didn't your mother do that for you? Or a sister?" Arabella asked with a tilt of her head.

A somber look appeared on her face as Hazel looked down, shaking her head and reaching out to play with her mother's necklace. "My mother and father died when I was a toddler, and I have no siblings." Hazel's voice wobbled slightly at the words.

Stepping back, Arabella raised a soft hand to her lips before bowing her head. "I am so sorry, Lady Hazel. I didn't mean to-"

Hazel approached Arabella, putting her hand on the handmaiden's shoulder, offering a faint, gentle smile to her. "It is alright. You didn't know. Also, please just call me Hazel. I am not much for titles." Hazel admitted.

Arabella flinched at first at the touch, but relaxed with a nod. "Well then, Hazel, let's get you dressed and ready for your meeting,"

Following Arabella to her bed chambers, Hazel's eyes fell upon a gorgeous coffee-cream-colored long sleeve dress. The upper torso was laced with swirls of various floral patterns flowing town into the sleeves. A short tulle layer feathered outward to reveal a deeper mocha color. Through the lace , the mocha padded fabric cover her breast in a heart neckline, pattern met just above her waist where the fabric-beaded belt was. As Hazel walked to the back of the dress, she understood why the padding was needed on the front, for her back was exposed by a deep plunge in the fabric that ended at the beaded belt at the small of her back.

Her breathing hitched at the breathtaking look on her face. It breathed the essence of a princess as its fabric fanned out on the floor. Hazel couldn't believe the intricate design of the dress as she ran her hand down it. "If you are to be called Lady Hazel here at court, you should look like one." Arabella's honey voice drew Hazel's attention to the amused smile on her lips. The handmaiden was proud of her choice as Hazel's eyes misted over.

"Arabella, this..." She was speechless. This was the prettiest dress she had ever seen. "This dress, I..." Trying to find the words, Hazel couldn't wipe the joyous smile off her face as she continued to examine the intricate details of the dress. It must have cost a fortune, making Hazel nervous about wearing it, afraid she would damage it.

"I saw your necklace with the tree on it" Arabella pointed out motioning to the necklace Hazel wore, "I thought lilacs would complement this dress's color," Arabella said shyly, not knowing if she had overstepped.

Hazel felt as if she was in a storybook. She was going to look like a princess in that dress. Arabella had such divine taste in dresses, that Hazel was beyond excited to see what she would do to her hair. A wide smile appeared on her lips as she walked over and hugged Arabella tightly.

At first, Arabella froze from the embrace, but hugged Hazel back.

"Thank you, Arabella. The dress are perfect." Pulling back, Hazel smiled at this potential friend, ecstatic that this was now her new home. She for a moment forgot everything that had turned horrible in her life. Sitting down at the vanity mirror, Hazel looked at Arabella, unable to wipe the joy and excitement off her face.

"What shall we do with my hair? Maybe some flowers?" Hazel beamed, and Arabella laughed softly before grabbing a soft bristle brush and began to brush out the damp hair. "I have just the right idea."

Hazel let out a girlish giggle, feeling so much joy and excitement to see what else Arabella had in store for her

Chapter Twenty

Hazel

There was a knock at Hazel's door, which caused Arabella to step back. Hazel stood up, smoothing out the ruffles with her hands. "Come on in," she called out.

To her surprise, Prince Atticus entered, looking far more polished than before. He wore a black tunic decorated with a broach of his family crest at his throat that led to golden shoulder lapels. A black and red cape rested on the right side of his shoulder. To Hazel, he looked like an actual prince, as you would see in storybooks. Her throat bobbed as his eyes scanned over her.

"Arabella's taste will help you pass as a court lady. Now, you will need to learn how to act as one," Atticus spoke in a taunting drawl, drawing out the words with exaggerated amusement..

Scoffing, Hazel rested her hand on her hip, raising an eyebrow at the arrogant prince. "I thought princes were supposed to be charming," she replied as she stood by her vanity mirror.

Smirking, Atticus shook his head, he strides over to Hazel, taking her hand. "Well, then," Atticus His voice carried a smug edge, thick with self-satisfaction, kissing her hand gently. "Is this charming enough for you, princess, or should I get my brother for you?" he mocked with a coy smirk on his lips

Hazel's cheeks warmed as her breath caught in the back of her throat. She stiffened at his touch before narrowing her eyes.

Going to slap him once more, Atticus was too quick, as his black leather gloved hand wrapped around her wrist, stopping her. "I have seen that trick before, princess. Now, come. There is someone I would like you to meet. The White Dragon." Atticus winked at Hazel, as if he was enjoying his little game with her. Arabella stepped backward in surprise, before she spoke sheepishly, "Prince Atticus, if I may? Are you sure she is ready to meet-"

Atticus whipped his head to face Arabella, growling while he still held Hazel's wrist. "Mind your tongue, Arabella. You may be allowed to speak loosely around Lady Hazel, but I will not be told what I deem is-"

Hazel growled at Atticus, moving to stand between her new friend and the dragon prince, not pulling her wrist from him. "You will not speak to her that way when I am present, am I clear?" Finally, she yanked her wrist free, glaring at Atticus..

"No, no, Lady Hazel, it's quite alright. I-" Arabella started.

Hazel twisted her head toward her handmaiden, putting her hand on the maiden's shoulder. "Please, you are like a friend now. I won't let anyone talk to my friend with such disrespect." Her head turned back to Atticus, her eyes darkened as she glared at him, causing him to straighten from its intensity. "Not even an arrogant prick this court calls their precious Immortal Dragon," Hazel challenged.

A snarl emanated from Atticus's throat as the leather of his gloves groaned from him balling his hands into fists. "Are we done here? I have other things to do aside from escorting a spoiled princess around," he gritted out, his eyes never leaving hers.

Hazel glared at Atticus, gesturing towards the door,. "Let's get this obligation over with, then."

Atticus scoffed, shaking his head before leading her out of her chambers. "Oh, I am going to enjoy you meeting the White Dragon."

After some time, Hazel found herself walking alongside Atticus, the tension between them thick and unspoken. The cold hallways stretched before her, their ivory walls stark against the dark ivy trailing from hanging pots. The air carried a faint chill, making her acutely aware of the unfamiliar stone beneath her feet. She had never wandered these corridors before, and though the beauty of the hanging greenery softened the space, it did little to ease the stiffness between them. Time felt slow, each step echoing in the quiet, but neither of them broke the silence. Atticus and Hazel approached what looked like barracks for guards. Walking into them, Hazel held up her dress, not wanting to ruin such a beautiful fabric. She also covered her nose from the overwhelming smell of sweat and body odor, along with shades of male arousal from the guards who now stared her down and made vulgar gestures to her. Hazel glanced up at Atticus to see if he was even paying attention to what they were doing, all she could see was a emotionless stare ahead. Like he didn't care.

Looking around, she saw wooden frame doors with laminate paper as windows. Some were closed, where she could see silhouettes of men being frivolous with women and some partially open doors where men stood naked, scanning her over. If Atticus had seen how these men had started, he wouldn't have said a word to them.

Walking up to a pair of double doors, Atticus swung them open before he gave out a joyous laugh. "If it isn't my White Dragon. How have you been these last three weeks?" His tone was so joyous and full of life, it surprised Hazel considering he has been nothing but a arrogant cocky prince to her. She wasn't expecting this new side of him.

Trailing in behind him, she glanced about the room, seeing the mahogany wood panel walls. In the center, there was a large black mat that looked to be used for possible sparing, while a large rectangular table was in the back of the room that looked as if it was a real-life scale model of Wylana with little figurines. A large map was on another side of the wall behind a desk that was covered in papers.

Then Hazel's eyes fell upon a woman standing beside a display of swords and a rack of long staffs. She wore a black leather halter top that was mesh up until where her breast started, covered by a black leather corset,, and a pair of black riding pants with a long sword dangling from the waist belt.

Surely, this woman wasn't the White Dragon, although watching how Atticus greeted her only confirmed it. The White Dragon was a woman!

Hazel starred in utter shock as Atticus embraced this woman in a hug, only for her to punched him in the chest. Her platinum blonde braid fell behind her shoulder from the movement, and rested at the small of her back.

"Are you fucking stupid, Atticus?" she growled.

It took Hazel by surprise to hear how she spoke to him, and how brave she was to punch him, and hard enough he grunted. Golden amber eyes fell upon Hazel as the woman scanned her over, then looked to Atticus. "You bring her here? And dressed as a fucking princess as well? Have you lost your mind?" she continued to scold the crown prince.

The White Dragon walked over to Hazel, assessing her..

Atticus held an amused look on his face, leaning back on the desk, almost as if he was waiting for something to happen.

"You have got to be kidding me. When you told me you found the Ivory Fawn, I thought you were going to bring in someone who was strapped for war and battle. Not some dainty little fawn in a pretty dress."

Hazel's jaw clenched as she ground out, "I didn't ask to be your Ivory Fawn, and I surely won't tolerate being disrespected, either."

Instead of anger or surprise on this woman's face, there was amusement. Tilting her head back towards Atticus, she chuckled. "I like her."

Hazel felt slammed to the wall from the shock. Was this woman serious?

"My name is Ardnaxela. some here at court call me the White Dragon, but I prefer White Dragoness." Her voice sounded as if it was made of steel. It was so clean and sharp as she spoke.

Atticus laughed faintly, pushing off the desk and looking at Hazel with a smirk, as he approached the two. "I told you she is feisty." Ardnaxela pushed hair from Hazel's neck to look at the damage Hazel sat still as Ardnaxela gently tilted her chin, examining the wound on her neck with cool, practiced fingers. The woman's expression remained unreadable, her touch light but precise, as if assessing the full extent of the damage. Hazel assumed Atticus must have already informed her of what had happened—why else would she be so focused on the wound rather than asking questions?

She resisted the urge to shrink away, the sensation of being studied unsettling. Ardnaxela's gaze flickered with something Hazel couldn't quite place—professional detachment, perhaps, or quiet concern. Either way, she didn't press Hazel for details, only continued her careful inspection, leaving Hazel to wonder just how much Atticus had told her.

Hazel tensed as Ardnaxela's fingers brushed over her skin, cool and deliberate. Then, with a movement so fluid it was almost unnatural, the White Dragoness shifted behind her. Hazel barely registered the change before she felt Ardnaxela's gaze settle on her shoulder—now fully exposed, thanks to Arabella's choice of dress. Hazel resisted the urge to pull the fabric back into place, suddenly hyper-aware of how much of her was being scrutinized.

"We must let these wounds heal fully before I can train her. Are you sure she is the one?"

Nodding his head, Atticus' gaze never strayed from Hazel. It was then she realized he was finally registering how she looked in her dress. Atticus's eyes were more focused on every curve and detail the dress brought out. It made Hazel's cheeks warm.

"I saw her use the Aestival magic with my own eyes." He replied to Ardnaxela, "She's the one."

Ardnaxela took Hazel's chin into her hand, turning it slightly before Hazel slapped it away. She stared at the White Dragons, who laughed at her strike.

"Well then, I will enjoy training you, Ivory Fawn." Ardnaxela crooned out. Turning to look at Atticus, she walked back to her desk. It was sprawled with papers that looked like information, but Hazel didn't know what they contained. "Get her out of here. I don't need my men distracted by her, especially when she's dressed like that."

"You mean *my* men?" Atticus corrected. His words warranted a warning glare from Ardnaxela.

"You made me Kingsly's second, so, respectfully, they are *my* men. You stick to your courtly duties, like entertaining ladies and princesses. Leave the dirty work to me, princeling."

Chuckling softly, Atticus shook his head before gesturing to Hazel that it was time to depart. "And that is why you are my favorite, Ardnaxela."

He approaching the second in command , he whispered something into her ear that Hazel couldn't make out.

Leaving the barracks, Hazel let go of her dress, flattening it out before turning her head around to see once again the cold ivory hallways lined with ivy plants hanging from planters. The refreshing aroma of ivy and dragon's blood fills her senses, cleaning her pallet of the unpleasant barracks smell.

Prince Atticus walked up behind Hazel, resting his hand on her back. Turning her head to his touch, Hazel stepped away, glaring at him. "Are we done here? I wish to check on Kingsly," Hazel snapped at him.

Atticus brown eyes met with hers. "I will take you to him. Can't have you mindlessly roaming around here without someone to protect you," he replied.

Unable to help herself, Hazel glanced at the staff as they whispered among themselves while walking by. Thanks to Arabella, Hazel wondered if her dress was too much considering how much they were whispering while staring. "Alright then, lead the way so we can proceed the rest of the evening separately," she gritted out

He laughed softly while crossing his arms across his chest. "Gladly," Atticus turned and headed down the hallway. The pair walked silently.

Hazel admired the castle's decor the best she can with the candle lit coming from the torches on the wall, ivy and wisteria flowers hanging from vases. Peering out the window, she could see a slight frost on the edges of the windows.

Atticus stopped at two large mahogany doorways. Looking up, Hazel was amazed at how large they are, as they nearly touch the ceiling, but then flinched as Atticus knocked on the door.

"Kingsly, you have a special guest," Atticus called out.

Narrowing her eyes to Atticus, he smirked. Hazel's face lightened up as Kingsly answered back, "I want to be left alone."

"Then should I return another day?" Hazel replied softly. There was silence before the doorknob turned. Kingsly still had sleep in his eyes as he blinked down at Hazel. They widened, though, as he took in her new appearance, immediately he straightening up and drinking every detail.

"Hazel, I-" Kingsly was lost for words. "Would you like to come in?"

Hazel nodded her head before looking at Atticus, who was staring in irritation at Kingsly. "Didn't you say you have other things to do than escort a spoiled princess?" Hazel snapped at him again.

Atticus gazed at Hazel, bowing his head before looking back at Kingsly. He narrowed his eyes at his brother, who remained outside as Hazel steps into Kingsly's room.

She was surprised to see such a drastic decor change from her bedroom to his. Kingsly's room was simple yet elegant in design, but instead of ivory and gold, it was darker due to the mahogany paneling around the room and floors. Hazel's eyes were drawn straight to the towering bookshelf, stretching to the ceiling, with a rolling ladder attached. Walking over to the bookshelves, she trailed her finger along the spines, reading the titles silently. Wars of Wylana, History of Wylana, and Blood War.

It wasn't surprising to Hazel to see him owning books on Wylana's wars and history, but seeing Orpheus and Eurydice on his bookshelf did. Hazel didn't see Kingsly as an unhappy romance reader.

Admiring how many books there were before directing her attention to Kingsly's arm as his approaching footsteps made her turn around. "How are you feeling?" She asked

Kingsly eyes lingered on her before following her eyes to his arm, which was concealed under his navy blue tunic.

"It feels like it never happened," replied the general prince. Feeling a relieved grin form on her lips as Hazel scanned him over to ensure he was recovering okay. "I'm glad to hear that. I was worried," Hazel exhaled in relief, she than started to notice her cheeks started to warm.

Standing before her, Kingsly pushing a loose hair away from her face, he rested his hand on her cheek, stroking it with his thumb. "Thanks to you. Atticus told me what you did. You took a great risk for me and my men. I owe you my life now, my friend."

Her breathing was interrupted as feeling his hand touched her cheek. Hazel's throat bobbed as she stood there, looking at him. "I couldn't let you die, not after you saved my life twice. I did what I needed to do," she replied , trying to slow her racing heart.

Slowly, Kingsly's hand trailed down her cheek to her jawline, and the sensation caused her breathing to become more unsteady than it already was. Soon, Kingsly's hand stopped on her chin, lifting it up.

Kingsly's ice-blue eyes scanned her face before looking down at her body. "Arabella outdid herself with you," Kingsly mused.

Smiling softly, Hazel's throat bobbed again with a faint smile on her lips as she stared up at his golden eyes. "I will have to tell her you approve," Hazel laughed. She stepped towards Kingsly, and in a bold move, rested her hands on his chest. It brought her some comfort to feel his heart was beating as fast as hers.

Their gazes were locked on one another as they stood silently, taking each other in. "Hazel," Kingsly breathed out as he wrapped an arm around her waist, pulling her closer.

Hazel's heart raced faster in her chest as his head lowered to hers, so close they shared breaths.

Craning her head back, her gaze went to his lips as she parted them in a welcoming invite to him. A second passed before he brushed his soft lips against hers. Hazel's body warmed to the touch, especially when his arm pulled her tighter to his chest. As she melted into his grip, she wrapped her arms around his neck and forgot the world around her.

Kingsly ran his hand down her body and slowly moved them to the bed, laying her down before he hovered above her. Against her will, she saw flashes of Darius's face instead of Kingsly's looking down at her, sending her into a panic. Her stomach lurched as she rolled out from under his arms, clenching the fabric above the pounding heart in her chest. Iron and salt filled her nostrils as phantom touches raced all over her body. Hazel's eyes burned as she slides off the bed to kneel on the ground, curling in on herself.

"Hazel? What's wrong?"

Hazel's eyes came to meet Kingsly, and they were not an icy blue but sapphire. She tried to plead with Kingsly to step back, but only incoherent sounds came from her clenched vocal cords. As he moves off the bed to kneel down before her Hazel scrambled back, her back met with a tall wardrobe stopping her retreat from Kingsly. Covering her mouth, Hazel's stomach twisted into knots as bile crept up her throat. The memory of the Raven Palm forest tore through her mind, along with the phantom pain of Darius ripping into her neck and the arrow slicing through her shoulder. The memories tore through her consciousness like a ravenous storm threatening to take her under its crushing winds.

"Hazel, please let me help you."

Shaking her head, she forced herself to her feet, shoving Kingsly away from her. Picking up her dress so she didn't trip, Hazel rushed out of his bedroom, tears flooding her eyes.

"Hazel, wait!" he called out to her.

She ran into the hallway, freezing for a moment in the hall, seeing everyone staring at her. Hazel's heart pounded thunderously in her chest and ears. She ran as fast as her legs could carry her. Images of Ratherian and Lilura laughing at her, blood staining their faces fueled her need to get away from everyone.

"Hazel, wait!" Kingsly called again.

The freezing air bit at Hazel's skin as she ran, her heartbeat a wild, frantic thing in her chest. The darkened corridors twisted around her, unfamiliar and endless, but she couldn't stop—wouldn't stop. Every time her boots struck the stone, the past crashed into her like a breaking wave, dragging her under.

She wasn't in the stronghold anymore.

She was back in the Raven Palm Forest, the scent of damp earth and pine thick in her nose. Darius's grip was a vice around her throat, slamming her against the rough bark of a tree. The pressure—gods, the pressure—crushed her windpipe as his nails dug into her flesh. His snarl was nothing human, his golden eyes gleaming with cruelty as he leaned in, fangs bared.

"You never should have been born."

Pain. Burning, searing pain as his teeth sank into her neck.

Hazel gasped, her hand flying to her throat as if she could still feel the punctures, the warm trickle of blood. But the memory didn't release her.

Her vision blurred as she took another frantic turn down an unfamiliar hallway. She was running now—not from the fortress, but from him. From the monster who had nearly torn her apart.

But then the scene twisted again.

She was no longer at the cabin. She was on the back of the horse fleeing for her life, the wind howling past her ears as she rode harder, faster—desperate to escape. Her fingers tightened around the reins, her knuckles white.

"You think you can run from me?" Lilura's voiced mocked from behind

Hazel's body lurched forward as the arrow struck, white-hot agony piercing through her shoulder. She cried out, the force knocking the breath from her lungs. The reins slipped from her fingers as she struggled to keep her grip, but the pain swallowed her whole.

She stumbled in the present, her boot catching on uneven stone. The world tilted, her hands slamming against the cold wall for balance. But her mind refused to let go.

The scent of blood filled her nose, but it wasn't from the arrow wound.

Ratherian.

Hazel's breath hitched as the memories shifted again. She was back on the ground of the Raven Palm forest after being thrown. She could hear him behind her, sound of the bushes rustling as he steps out, the growl that sent ice through her veins.

"Run, little fawn."

And she had. She had run until her lungs burned, until her vision blurred with pain and terror. But it hadn't been enough. Ratherian had caught her, claws digging into her back, flipping her onto the ground like she was nothing. He had loomed over her, his face twisted with a predator's delight.

"Hazel!" Kingsly voice broke through for a moment but the rushing of her heart drowned out his words.

Then came the worst part—the sharp, unbearable pressure of teeth pressing into her throat, ready to rip her apart.

Hazel choked on a sob, slamming herself against the stone wall of the hallway, her fingers gripping at the cold surface as if it could anchor her to the present. She couldn't breathe, couldn't move. Her chest tightened, panic crushing her rib cage.

"It's not real," she whispered to herself, but the words felt hollow.

The past still had its claws in her. And it wasn't letting go.

Chapter Twenty-One

Hazel

Hazel didn't care where her legs took her as long as it was away from Kingsly and this court. She needed somewhere to hide. Somewhere she could let herself fall apart without judgmental eyes. Slamming into two closed archway doors, Hazel gasped, shielding her eyes from the sunset rays, as the rays blinded her for a moment not allowing her to see the castle courtyard for a brief moment. Blinking her eyes a few time for a moment she was now able to fully take in the view of the castle courtyard. Her chest rose and fell quickly as her lungs burned.

"Hazel!"

Hearing someone yelling for her, she picked up her petticoat and descended the stairs, not wanting anyone to see her like this. Her hands trembled as she ran down the steps, heading straight toward an archway made of roses.

Not caring who was behind her, Hazel raced through the archway before taking being stopped in her tracks by the picturesque garden. Unlike her own garden at home of vegetables, fruits, herbs, and spices, this one was covered with roses of all shades.

Hazel stumbled as she remembered her cottage home, the nights she would meet Darius in the garden, him sneaking into the room to sleep with. The betrayal following those memories made it feel like the ground beneath her feet crumbled, and she fell to her knees, wrapping her arms around herself.

Hazel felt like she was unraveling, each breath pulling another thread loose until there would be nothing left of her but tattered remnants of who she used to be. The memories wouldn't stop. They came in relentless waves, each one sharper, crueler than the last, dragging her under until she didn't know where she was—who she was.

But then there was warmth. Steady. Familiar.

Archibald.

His arms wrapped around her, strong and unyielding, as if he could shield her from the horrors clawing at her mind. His scent—vanilla and cinnamon—was grounding, pulling her back from the suffocating grip of the past. He was here. He was real.

"I got you. I got you, my little fawn."

The sound of his voice cracked something deep inside her.

Hazel turned without thinking, clutching at him, pressing herself into his chest, desperate to disappear into the safety he offered. Her hands fisted the fabric of his coat as if he might vanish if she let go. His heartbeat thrummed beneath her cheek, slow and steady, an anchor against the storm raging inside her.

"Please make them stop." Her voice trembled, barely more than a whisper. "Make it all stop. I want to go back home. I want my old life back. Can we please go home?"

Archibald didn't answer right away. He just held her. His arms tightened, firm and protective, a silent reassurance that she wasn't alone. His hand smoothed over her hair, his touch gentle despite the strength in him.

"I know, Hazel," he murmured. "I know."

She squeezed her eyes shut, pressing her forehead against his chest as the sobs kept coming, no longer held back, no longer buried beneath the weight of survival. Archibald didn't shush her, didn't tell her to be strong or to push it down. He just let her grieve.

Minutes passed—maybe longer. Hazel didn't know. But when her breathing finally started to slow, when the memories loosened their hold just enough for her to remember where she was, Archibald pulled back just slightly, just enough to look at her. His gloved hands cupped her face, his thumbs brushing away the dampness on her cheeks.

"Listen to me, my little fawn," he said softly, his voice full of that steady patience he had always had with her. *"You are here. You are safe. They cannot touch you anymore. Not while I'm here."*

She wanted to believe him. Gods, she wanted to.

Hazel let out a shaky breath, her fingers still clutching his coat. *"I feel like I'm falling apart."*

His expression softened, a look she had seen so many times before—when he had patched up her scraped knees as a child, when he had held her after nightmares that left her shaking, when he had sworn to protect her, no matter what.

"Then let me hold you together," he said simply.

And for the first time in what felt like forever, Hazel let herself believe that maybe—just maybe—she wasn't fighting this alone.

There was a thud hitting the ground beside them as he held her with both arms, sitting on the ground now. "I wish we could fawn. I wish we could," his voice wobbled. Holding onto him more, Hazel inhaled his scent. Home, he smelled like home, and she reveled in the temporary comfort it provided.

"All I can see is Darius. He mocks and laughs at me. Kingsly kissed me, held me, and..." trailing off, she held her uncle tighter, breaking down more. "Why did he do all this? Why?" Hazel asked in exasperation.

Archibald pulled back just enough to cup Hazel's cheek in his calloused hand, his touch firm yet gentle. His deep-set eyes, filled with warmth and sorrow, searched hers as he spoke, his voice low but steady.

"I don't know why the world is so cruel to you, but he never deserved you," he said, his words laced with an unshakable certainty.

Hazel's throat tightened as she looked at him, her uncle—the only father she had ever truly known. She leaned into his touch, her own trembling fingers curling around his hand, desperate for something real, something solid in the midst of the storm raging inside her.

"I want to go home," she whispered, her voice breaking.

Archibald exhaled a slow, heavy breath, his thumb brushing away a stray tear that rolled down her cheek. Then, without hesitation, he kissed the top of her head before pulling her back into his arms, holding her as if he could shield her from everything.

"I know, little fawn," he murmured. "So do I."

For a long moment, he just held her, letting her breathe, letting her feel safe in the way only he had ever made her feel. His hand ran up and down her back in slow, steady motions, grounding her, anchoring her.

"I wish I could have protected you from all of this," he admitted, his voice quieter now, thick with emotion. *"I would take all of your pain if I could."*

Hazel squeezed her eyes shut, shaking her head against his chest. "I just—I feel like I can't escape it. It keeps happening, over and over again. I keep running, but it never stops."

Archibald sighed, his hand coming up to gently brush her tangled hair from her face. He tucked it behind her ear with a care that only he had ever shown her, then rested his palm against her temple, his fingers trailing down her cheek.

"I won't lie to you, Hazel," he said. "These feelings? They may never go away completely. The scars they left on you... they run deep." He let out a slow breath, his fingers tracing small, comforting circles on her back. "But the pain will lessen. It won't always feel like this. One day, you'll breathe and it won't feel like you're drowning."

Hazel swallowed hard, her fingers tightening in his coat. *"How do you know?"* she asked, her voice small.

Archibald tilted her chin up slightly so she had no choice but to meet his gaze.

"Because you're strong. Strong like your mother was." His lips quirked into a small, bittersweet smile. "She fought for those she loved, even when the world tried to break her. And you, my little fawn, have that same fire in you."

Hazel let out a shaky breath, her heart aching at the mention of her mother.

"But I'm tired of fighting," she admitted, her voice cracking.

Archibald nodded, pressing his forehead against hers for a brief moment, his warmth chasing away the last of the cold.

"Then rest, Hazel," he said gently. "You don't have to carry this alone. Not while I'm here."

She let out another choked sob and buried herself in his embrace again. And for the first time in what felt like forever, she allowed herself to believe him.

Archibald let her cry, his arms wrapped securely around her as if he could shield her from everything that had hurt her. His large, calloused hand continued to run up and down her back in soothing motions, grounding her. He never rushed her, never pulled away, just let her feel.

Eventually, Hazel's sobs quieted into soft, uneven breaths. She was exhausted—mentally, physically, and emotionally drained. Her body still trembled, both from the lingering panic and the cold that seeped into her bones from standing in the dimly lit hallway for so long.

Archibald sighed, shifting slightly. *"Come on, little fawn,"* he murmured, his voice as warm as the arms still holding her. *"Let's get you back to your room."*

Hazel swallowed thickly and nodded against his chest. But as soon as she tried to move, her knees buckled, the strength draining from her limbs.

"Whoa—got you," Archibald said quickly, steadying her before she could collapse completely. He adjusted his grip, keeping one arm wrapped firmly around her waist while his other hand caught hers. *"Can you walk?"*

Hazel hesitated, then gave a small, unsure nod.

Archibald didn't believe her. Not entirely. So he kept close as he slowly guided her forward, his arm never straying from her in case her legs gave out again. Each step felt heavier than the last, exhaustion pressing down on her like a weight she couldn't shake.

The hallway was quiet, save for the soft echoes of their footsteps. The chill still clung to the air, but it wasn't as sharp anymore, dulled by the warmth Archibald provided simply by being at her side.

After a few moments, Hazel's voice broke the silence. *"Do you think I'll ever feel normal again?"*

Archibald exhaled through his nose, glancing down at her as they walked. "I don't think 'normal' is what you need to chase, Hazel," he said honestly. "What you've been through... it's changed you. And that's not fair. It never was. But you will find peace again. You'll heal."

Hazel frowned slightly. *"What if I never do?"*

He gave her hand a reassuring squeeze. "Then I'll be here, however long it takes."

She didn't know what to say to that, but she held onto his words, letting them settle into the cracks of her battered soul.

By the time they reached her door, Hazel could barely keep her eyes open. The weight of everything—the memories, the emotions, the exhaustion—pressed down on her all at once, threatening to pull her under again.

Archibald let go of her only long enough to push the door open, then gently guided her inside.

"Sit," he instructed, helping her onto the edge of her bed. When she swayed slightly, he steadied her again before kneeling in front of her.

Hazel blinked at him, surprised by the way he stayed close, his concern etched into every line of his face.

"You rest now," he murmured, brushing a few stray strands of hair from her face. *"You've been carrying too much for too long."*

Hazel swallowed, her throat still thick with emotion. *"Will you stay? Just until I fall asleep?"*

Archibald smiled, though there was sorrow in his eyes. *"Of course, my little fawn."*

He shifted to sit beside the bed, leaning against the frame, his presence solid and reassuring. And as Hazel finally let her body relax, sleep creeping up on her, she held onto the quiet comfort of knowing he was still there, watching over her—just like he always had.

Chapter Twenty-Two

Atticus

Staring out of the tall archway windows towards the castle's east side, overlooking the village in the distance, Atticus was lost in thought. With a glass of spiced wine in hand, he paused as he heard two servants giggling among themselves about the new court lady running out of Kingsly's bedroom, sobbing as he called after her.

Recollecting how Kingsly stared at Hazel with admiration, Atticus clenched his wine glass before setting it down on the window seal. The dress Arabella chose clung to every curve of Hazel's body perfectly. Even Atticus stalled when he'd seen her.

Although he had a duty as the Crown Prince Atticus had never been one to back down from a challenge, but when it came to Hazel, it was more than just stubbornness—it was instinct, duty, and something far deeper than he dared to name. He was the Crimson Dragon, the shield forged by prophecy itself to protect the Ivory Fawn. Her safety was not just his responsibility; it was the very foundation of his existence. If she fell, if she suffered, it would mean he had failed in a way that could never be undone.

And Kingsly had already tread too close to that line.

The last thing he needed was a brokenhearted, ill-tempered, stubborn, prophesied heroine on his hand.

Banging on his brother's door, Atticus waited until Kinglsy opened it to barge in, shove his brother back, and slam the door so hard that the hinges rattled behind him. "What did you do to her?" Atticus roared.

Kingsly stumbled back as his brother shoved him, stunned for a moment as Atticus, growls at him. He moved his arm in front of him, trying to conceal his still lingering arousal from what had just transpired between Hazel and him.

"Nothing happened? We were kissing, which led us to the bed, and then she pushed me away and ran out of here, crying. I don't know what I did to scare her." Rage erupted, and Atticus slammed his fist into Kingsly's face. The general prince nearly fell on his ass as he caught himself on the bedpost, stabilizing himself.

"You bastards! You stay away from her, Kingsly! You're betrothed! What if Lady Duvessa finds out?" Atticus sneered in warning.

Holding his jaw Kingsly, creating distance between Atticus and himself, knowing he wasn't matched hand to hand with the Immortal Dragon, nor did he want to get a lashing from his father for hitting Wylana's heir. "She won't find out. I will break off the engagement with her."

Atticus grabbed his brother by the collar, yanking him in, trying not to punch his brother again. "You will do no such thing! It is my job to protect her, and you, brother, are not right for her. Breaking off your engagement with Lady Duvessa would hurt your reputation *and* our alliance with her family."

Kingly shoved Atticus away from him, smoothing out his tunic and glaring at his brother as he wiped blood from his lips.

"And what about *you*? She hates you, and for a good reason! Look at how you treat her!" Kingsly snapped back.

Stepping back, Atticus narrowed his eyes at Kingsly, closing his fist tightly to restrain his temper. "I don't care if she hates me. As long as she is safe, *that* is what I care about,"

Kingsly scoffed, walking through an archway into the simple yet elegant sapphire bathroom. Making his way over to the sink, he turned on the water to wash the blood from his mouth. "You are a horrible liar. All you have talked about is finding the Ivory Fawn, and now that you have, you treat her like some great warrior, when she isn't. Look at the state we found her in."

Atticus stepped into the archway, watching Kingsly rinse his mouth. "She is a warrior in her own way. I saw it that day in the cabin," Atticus replied, trying to calm his anger.

Kingsly looked at his brother, raising an eyebrow before holding a towel to his busted lip. "And a rightfully earned slap to your face told you that?" he responded.

Atticus stepped forward, closing the distance between them. "It wasn't the slap that made me think she was a warrior. Now, stay the hell away from her, or you will end up with more than a busted lip. Just pray, Brother, that Lady Duvessa doesn't find out what transpired between you and Hazel."

Atticus turned and left Kingsly to tend to his busted lip. The idea of his brother's hands on Hazel made his blood boil. He didn't even believe the Ivory Fawn existed till they met Hazel. Now, he seemed to be all about her. Kingsly had lost his mind if he thought he could whisk Hazel into his arms when engaged to Duvessa Forrester, of all women.

Their engagement was arranged by Duvessa and Kingsly. It took Atticus and his family by surprise that, out of nowhere, he had not only been courting Duvessa, but had already asked to marry her.

The engagement was odd, considering she was already engaged to his brother Heath. Atticus wasn't familiar with the Forrester family. Duvessa informed his father and Atticus how her family came from the other side of the Raven Palm forest, where Taldora was, that Netherian wielders were now overrunning their home, and that they needed Wylana's support.

Duvessa even presented several chests full of gold, jewels, and diamonds—money that Wylana could benefit from—and the argument that the engagement was something both families would benefit from.

Atticus didn't trust Duvessa, as something about her did not sit right with him. She was arrogant and shallow—not the makings of a noble lady.

Even when Atticus did some digging into Duvessa, his spy came up with nothing on her other than the Forrester family being wealthy beyond imagination and that her family guarded the Raven Palm forest that surrounded the Taldorian castle grounds. Before the Blood War, the Taldora and Wylana kingdoms had been aligned.

Their King, Thaddeus, was benevolent, putting his kingdom first about himself. That was, until a nobleman named Kennon took his throne from him in an assassination.

The condition of Taldora after the Blood War disintegrated slowly into a dire circumstance.

Not once in his life did he truly believe who would actually stumble upon the Ivory Fawn, let alone would he be the Crimson Dragon that would guide her. There was a mixture of wonder and excitement coursing through him, knowing the Ivory Fawn existed, but there was also a strong sense of protection for her. He didn't know if that was because of the prophecy or because she was the most reckless woman he had ever met.

Atticus couldn't shake the feeling of wanting to do everything and anything in his power to protect her. Licking his lips, he huffed in irritation. Guiding and training her would be a task as she knew absolutely nothing about fighting, other than slapping someone.

He would need to meet with his personal friend and scribe, Sybilla soon. Queen Asteria was right—Sybilla was the perfect candidate to teach Hazel everything she needed to know about being the Ivory Fawn. After all, she was the only court lady he could tolerate besides Ardnaxela, who had risen from a court lady to the second-in-command of the Wylana army. Atticus had to be honest with himself, the White Dragoness scared him.

Deep in his heart, Atticus knew they were more qualified to guide her. After her traumatic ordeal, and hearing what transpired between her and his brother , Hazel might have a slight fear of men she didn't know, which was understandable.

So, he would keep his distance from her, allowing her the time and space she needed to adjust to her new home. He knew that forcing his presence on her would only make things more difficult, and this prophecy wouldn't work if Hazel feared him.

As much as she already tested his patience with her reckless tendencies , it was his duty to protect and guide her. No matter how frustrating she could be, he couldn't afford to let his irritation overshadow his responsibility. She needed to trust him, and that trust wouldn't come if he loomed over her like an unyielding force. So, he would wait, give her room to breathe, and hope that, in time, she would come to see him as an ally rather than an obstacle.

Chapter Twenty-Three

Hazel

Archibald had escorted Hazel back to her suite after the events of the night, ensuring she was safely tucked into bed before reluctantly stepping away. She had been exhausted, barely able to keep her eyes open as he pulled the blankets over her. Though he would've preferred to stay, she had assured him she would be fine.

Now, after resting for a while, Hazel had moved to her receiving room, still shaking off the remnants of fatigue. She was surprised to find Arabella sitting by the fire, holding a yellowish-gold book with a black dragon emblazoned on the cover. The receiving room was elegantly furnished, with plush velvet chairs and intricately woven tapestries adorning the walls. A large, ornate chandelier hung from the ceiling, casting a warm, golden glow over the space. The fire crackled softly in the hearth, wrapping the room in comforting warmth.

Hazel offered a tired but genuine smile, feeling a flicker of relief at the familiar presence. "Arabella, I didn't expect to see you here."

At the sound of her voice, Arabella's head snapped up, her expression filled with concern. "Hazel." She quickly set her book aside and stood, hurrying over.

The moment Arabella grasped her hands, Hazel felt a wave of reassurance wash over her. The warmth of her touch anchored her, a silent but tangible comfort in the wake of everything that had happened. She marveled at how something as simple as a touch could convey so much care. For a brief moment, the weight of the night faded into the background.

"You're freezing!" Arabella exclaimed, her brown eyes scanning Hazel with worry. "I heard what happened with Kingsly—people saw you fleeing his bedroom." She hesitated, concern tightening her features. "Are you all right?"

Before Hazel could answer, Archibald stepped forward, rubbing his niece's arm. She didn't even see him in her groggy state until he said something

"I have some patrol duties. However, I wanted to make sure I saw you before I went." Turning his head to Arabella offering a grateful smile "Take care of her, Arabella," he said, his voice firm but gentle.

Hazel turned fully to look at him, and he cupped her chin lightly, ensuring she met his gaze. "The king and queen allowed me to return as a guard. Call me if you need me," he said. His concern was evident in the way his brows knitted together, his grip on her steady yet careful. "Will you be okay?"

Hazel nodded, touched by his unwavering support. "I'll be fine, Uncle."

He studied her for a moment longer before sighing and stepping back. "Good. Try to rest." With one last glance at her, he turned and made his way out of the room, leaving Hazel in the comforting presence of Arabella.

Hazel nodded her head, squeezing his hand. "Be careful out there, and come back after you're done. I want to reapply that salve to your leg," Hazel responded with an equal amount of concern for her uncle. As she watched Archibald leave, Hazel felt a mix of emotions swirling within her. Pride for his unwavering dedication to his duty, worry for his safety, and a deep sense of gratitude for his constant presence in her life. She took a deep breath, hoping that he would return safely. Given his limp leg , she was not only concerned by shocked Kai would allow him back into the guard. Although part of her wasn't surprised given the rumors around his reign. Kai didn't give any care or concern to his people. Living in Alexandria made that very clear.

With a kiss to her head, Archibald nodded his head before taking his leave for patrols. Walking into the bathroom, Arabella helped her out of her dress and into the tub, where the scent of lavender and eucalyptus wrapped her mind in a calming sensation.

"How was your visit with Ardnaxela?" Arabella said, breaking their silence.

Hazel relaxed in the tub as her bathing robe clung to her body, her bruises turning yellowish from when she was healing. "She is like a mirror to Atticus. Harsh and to the point. I see why they get along."

Laughing softly, Arabella continued to massage Hazel's scalp. "Believe it or not, she used to be a court lady."

Hazel's eyes opened as she turned to look at Arabella. "Could have fooled me." Relaxing again, she leaned her wet hair over the bathtub's rim.

"When Ardnaxela first got here, she was a lady-in-waiting for Queen Sage. After a time, she caught Atticus's eye. The details of *how* escape me, but she snuck into battle, winning them the battle. As a reward, she was second in command of Kingsly's army." Arabella continued before she grabbed a towel for Hazel, and assisted Hazel out of the tub with a faint smile, "Don't let Ardnaxela intimidate you. She is a sucker for a good glass of wine and a book." Hearing a knock at the door, Arabella and Hazel's heads turn to the door at the exact same moment. Arabella's attention turned to Hazel, resting her hand on her shoulder as she stood. "Get changed, and I will see who it is."

Nodding silently, Hazel removed her wet bathing gown as Arabella attended to her guest inside the receiving room. Stepping into her bedroom chamber wearing a silk robe, Hazel admired the fabric before putting it on. It still felt odd to wear it not used to the fineries that come with her new title. After retrieving a plain white flowing skirt with a simple burnt orange long-sleeve blouse, Hazel thought pairing them with a sage green corset would complement it nicely.

Arabella returned to Hazel's bedroom, wide-eyed as she cleared her throat. "It's the queen, my lady."

Hearing who was here, Hazel fussed over her attire, immediately questioning if it was appropriate. Last time, she was filthy from her journey, and now, while she felt under dressed to meet the queen, but she wouldn't make her wait.

Swallowing the lump in her throat, Hazel left her bedroom to greet the queen. Stopping in her tracks as she moved to the receiving room, her eyes widened, as she saw a gorgeous woman with snow like skin, loosely curled long golden hair, with a small opal circlet on her head standing right in the doorway as Hazel opened the bedroom door. A young blonde-haired boy stood at her side, holding a tray of pastries. "Queen Sage," Hazel breathed out before bowing. When she straightened, Hazel noticed the queen was carrying Hazel's food tray , it was surprising to see her carrying it instead of a servant.

"I wanted to bring you the dinner myself since Atticus informed me, weren't joining us tonight due , and my son Reed is a big fan."

Queen Sage lowered her hand as she stroked Reed's soft golden hair before speaking with a sweet and gentle tone "I also asked the kitchen staff to make you a lavender and chamomile teapot to help ease your nerves as you adjust to your new life," Smelling the tea from the cup on the the tray Sage was carrying, from where Hazel stood, Hazel held open the door for them both to come in, smiling widely at Queen Sage.

"Your majesty, you shouldn't have," Hazel replied.

Prince Reed ran over to Hazel, a bright grin on his face as he carefully balanced a tray piled high with various flaky pastries. He stopped just short of her, holding it up proudly.

"I brought you flaky pastries! They're my favorite, but I didn't know which kind you like, so I brought you all of them." His excitement was infectious, his golden eyes gleaming with anticipation.

Hazel tensed instinctively at his sudden movement, but the moment she took in his eager expression—so full of warmth and sincerity—her body relaxed. A soft chuckle escaped her lips, the tension melting away like frost beneath the morning sun.

She glanced down at the assortment of pastries, their golden, buttery layers stacked neatly on the tray. The gesture was so simple yet unexpectedly thoughtful, filling her chest with an unfamiliar warmth. Few people had ever gone out of their way for her like this, especially not with such unrestrained enthusiasm.

A genuine smile tugged at the corners of her lips as she reached for one of the treats. "Thank you so much, Reed," she said, her voice carrying the gratitude she couldn't quite put into words. "This is... really sweet of you."

Reed beamed, clearly pleased with himself. "Well, I do try," he said, puffing out his chest before plopping down beside her. "Now, tell me which one's your favorite so I can remember for next time."

Hazel couldn't help but laugh, warmth blooming in her heart at his kindness. Maybe, just maybe, she wasn't as alone in this place as she thought.

Queen Sage set the dinner tray down on the vanity before chuckling lightly seeing her sons wholesome remark "Reed, dear, give her some space. She's had a long, hard journey to join us here in Wylana," Queen Sage reminded the young prince.

The young prince lowered the tray, looking at his mother, frowning before he looked at Hazel with an apologetic frown. "I'm sorry, Lady Hazel."

Hazel's smile softened as she knelt down to his level, her gaze warm as she looked over the tray. Instead of rushing to pick one, she met his eager eyes with gentle curiosity. "It's alright, Reed," she said, her voice light with affection. "Which one is your favorite? I want to try it first."

Reed's expression lit up with excitement. "Ooh, I love the one with honey and sugar on it," he replied.

Hazel couldn't help but to smile at his response, taking it before breaking it in half and handing the other half to him. "Then I'd love to share it with you."

Queen Sage smiled, watching the interaction between the newest lady in the castle and her son, before she poured Hazel and herself a cup of tea. "Lady Hazel, you must come eat and have your a cup of tea. I would love to get to know you," the queen called out to Hazel.

Hazel walked over to the queen and took her teacup, inhaling the aroma of lavender and chamomile before taking a sip. The queen picked up the food tray and walked over to a table, sitting by a painting of three mountain peaks with three stars over its peak during the night sky. A simple, long rectangular claw tooth mahogany table with a white marble slab on top of it. The room was warm and inviting, filled with the soft glow of candlelight that danced off the marble slab and rich mahogany.

The scent of freshly baked pastries mingled with the soothing aroma of the tea, creating a comforting and homely atmosphere. Hazel felt her nerves ease as the friendly interaction and cozy surroundings enveloped her. The queen gently set the tray down before sitting at the table, gesturing for Hazel to join her.

Hazel hesitated for a moment before speaking, her voice careful yet curious. "I... I thought you would be with your family for dinner, Your Majesty."

Joining Queen Sage at the table, Hazel sat down across from her while Reed joined them, sitting in his mother's lap. He fidgeted slightly, excited to be part of the conversation, but comforted by his mother's presence. He glanced up at her wide-eyed, seeking approval for every little movement. As he nibbled on his half of the pastry, he occasionally peeked at Hazel, his curiosity and eagerness to engage shining through.

"My family only dines together on special occasions," Queen Sage said gently. "Normally, I share meals with my husband and Reed, but Kai is occupied with his duties this evening."

Pulling the cover off the food, Hazel's eyes widened as she salivated at its contents. A steak paired with mashed potatoes and sauteed asparagus with mushrooms. This was the most lavious meal she has ever seen. Hazel looked up to see the queen had no plate making her frown slightly. "Didn't you bring yourself a plate, your majesty?" Hazel asked shyly

Sage chuckled, waving a hand dismissively while keeping her other arm securely around Reed, who rested comfortably on her lap. "I'm still quite full from my late lunch," the Snow Queen said with a gentle smile.

Swallowing down the ocean, salivating in her mouth, Hazel looked at her plate before looking up. "Are you sure? I don't mind sharing my steak with you. I may not finish it all. It's rather large." She didn't want to eat before the queen if she had nothing for herself.

Faintly chuckling, Queen Sage shook her head, smiling. "I will be quite alright, plus you've been through a lot. Your body needs it."

The queen was just as Hazel heard, so gentle and welcome, unlike the king. Hazel's breathing hitched at what she said. Had Atticus or Kingsly told the queen who she was? Or what happened?

"If it's alright with you, I would like a proper healer to look at you. Make sure you are healing properly and aren't showing signs of any infections. That is, if you're okay with it," the queen suggested.

Hazel's hesitated momentarily, glancing down at her hands before nodding slowly. "Thank you, Your Majesty, that is very kind of you," she replied softly, touched by the queen's kindness.

Reeds jumped off Queen Sage's lap when there was a knock at the door, but Arabella made it there first, and silently opened it. Atticus walked into the receiving room quietly, his head lowered. The moment Hazel caught sight of him, her entire body tensed, and the atmosphere in the room shifted, thickening like a storm about to break.

It wasn't just his presence—it was the weight of every interaction they had shared. Since the day she had met him, he had never addressed her without that mocking lilt in his voice, always calling her *Princess* as if her very existence was some grand joke. He had restrained her once while she was still recovering from her wounds, treating her like a reckless burden rather than someone in need of care. And then there was the barracks—he hadn't forced her inside, but he also hadn't warned her. He had walked in silence, saying nothing as the men stared at her, letting her realize far too late that she was somewhere she didn't belong.

So, as he stood there now, uncharacteristically quiet, Hazel felt the air grow thick with unspoken words and lingering wounds. Her jaw tightened, her fingers curling slightly at her sides, bracing for whatever came next. Atticus had always been a storm in her life, but this silence—this unreadable posture—made him all the more unpredictable.

Hazel's heart raced because, despite his usual bravado, Atticus's solemn demeanor and avoidance of eye contact made her uneasy, as if something was off. The tension between them, fueled by past humiliations and unresolved feelings, made her nervous, unsure of what he might do or say next.

Sage's warm smile faded slightly, and she straightened in her seat, her eyes fixed on Atticus with a mixture of curiosity and concern. Arabella watched him for a moment before closing the door behind him. The young prince ran over to his eldest brother, who, to Hazel's surprise, dropped down on his and wrapped his arms around Reed and held him tightly.

"Atti! Atti! The stories were true! She is real! The Ivory Fawn is real!" Reed exclaimed with excitement.

Joyous laughter escaped Atticus's lips as Reed hugged him before he noticed the pastry flakes on his little brother's chin. "She is pretty, isn't she?" Atticus' voice was welcoming and soft. Wiping away Reed's crumbs, he chuckled softly. "Did you save any flaky pastries for her, or did you eat them all?" Atticus asked with a never-ending smile on his face.

Hazel's lips parted as she leaned back in her chair in awe. This wasn't the same prince she met before. He was kind and gentle with his younger brother. It was just as Kingsly told her. How Atticus portrayed himself with his mother and brother, he was the complete opposite of a cruel and harsh person.

Hazel watched as Queen Sage rose gracefully to her feet and walked over to Atticus, who stood up with a quiet fluidity, as if instinctively mirroring his mother's movements. The air around them seemed to soften in an instant as Atticus leaned down to kiss Sage's cheek, his hands resting gently on her shoulders. His voice, usually sharp with mockery or cold detachment, was now laced with something completely different—relief. "I'm glad you are unharmed," he said softly, his tone tender and full of warmth.

It was a stark contrast to the cruel persona Hazel had grown so used to—the arrogant prince who had often humiliated her, the one who saw her as little more than an obstacle or a joke. This Atticus, gentle and concerned, seemed like a stranger altogether. Hazel found herself momentarily caught off guard, her heart skipping a beat as she witnessed the shift in him. The cold walls he had built around himself seemed to crumble for a brief moment, and in that fleeting glimpse, she saw the true prince, one who cared deeply for those he loved. It left her questioning everything she thought she knew about him.

The queen only smiled, taking Atticus's hand and kissing it before gently stroking his cheek. "You took the words from my mouth, Atticus," she replied softly, her eyes then shifting to Reed. She offered her hand, and Reed took it with a warm smile. "Come on, my little one, we should let these two talk."

Hazel, still processing the shift in Atticus's demeanor, was caught off guard when the queen turned to her with a smile. "Welcome to Wylana, Ivory Fawn," she said warmly, her voice laced with kindness. "I do wish to continue our talk, but please eat. I will send a healer in the morning."

Hazel's eyes widened in shock. Her breath caught as the queen casually referred to her as the *Ivory Fawn*, a title that had been kept secret, known only to a select few. She quickly glanced at Atticus, her mind racing. Had he told her? The thought left her stunned, unable to mask the surprise and confusion on her face. The realization hit her like a cold wave—Atticus had revealed her identity to his mother, something she assumed would remain a secret for much longer. The weight of the moment settled in, and Hazel felt a wave of vulnerability sweep over her.

Atticus raised his eyebrow as his gaze went from his mother to Hazel. Hazel stood there her eyes locking with Atticus ,who stood there for a moment, before his mother kiss his cheek. "Be kind, Atticus. She needs a friend, not an overbearing protector," the queen whispered to her son, giving him a look that Hazel could only feel was a silent reminder from her words, before she took her leave.

The atmosphere in the room shifted to a quieter, more intimate setting after the queen's departure. Atticus and Hazel exchanged look, a mixture of curiosity and uncertainty lingering in the air. The room seemed to hold its breath, waiting for the next words to bridge the gap between them.

Chapter Twenty-Four

Hazel

Once alone, Hazel's throat bobbed as Atticus scanning her over. Swallowing hard as her mouth still salivated over the smell of her steak, Hazel licked her lips before looking down at it. She could still feel Atticus's eyes on her as she cut into her steak, trying to act as if her heart and mind weren't racing.

Taking a bite, she had to hold back a moan. Hazel couldn't help but wonder what Atticus was thinking and why he was staring so intently. Her heart pounded louder with each passing second, and she questioned whether he could hear it. As she savored the succulent meat, she tried to calm her nerves, worried that her feelings for him might be too obvious.

"Hazel, I..." His voice cracked slightly. Atticus remained where he was, running a hand through his hair as his jaw clenched. His brows furrowed in concentration. The usual steely resolve in his eyes softened, a flicker of vulnerability breaking through.

His lips parted as if struggling to release the words trapped within. His fingers twitched at his side, betraying the storm raging beneath his carefully composed exterior.

Hazel didn't know quite what to say to him. This moment marked a turning point in their relationship, revealing a side of Atticus that Hazel had never seen before. Hazel realized that this could be the beginning of a new understanding between them that could change everything. "Atti-" her words got caught in the back of her throat as his eyes met hers. A quiet, unfamiliar tension settled over her as she met his gaze. Concern—genuine and unguarded—reflected in his eyes, so at odds with the unwavering composure he usually carried. It was unsettling in a way she couldn't quite name, like seeing a crack in stone where there had never been one before

Could this be the moment she had been longing for, where Atticus actually is letting down his guard and showed his true self? Hazel had longed for this—for a moment where she wasn't an ass—but now that it was here, doubt coiled in her chest. Could she trust it? Could she trust him?

"I heard what happened with Kingsly. Are you okay?" Atticus finally asked, his voice low.

The genuine concern in Atticus's voice made her heart flutter, and she felt an unexpected surge of gratitude. For the first time, she felt truly seen by him—not as a mere ward, not as a responsibility to be managed, but as someone who mattered. Someone worth understanding. The weight of his gaze held something unfamiliar, something she had longed for yet never dared to hope for. It was recognition, not just of her presence, but of her.

"What?" She breathed, needing to make sure she heard him correctly, Her past experiences with him made her wary, and she couldn't help but wonder if this newfound tenderness was just a ploy to get her to trust him. Hazel hesitated, unsure if she could truly trust this possibility of a different Atticus.

"He told me you ran out of his room crying after you two shared a kiss." Hazel stiffened clenching her fist swallowing down the knot forming in her throat. "Hazel, you have to stay away from him." There was a bit of hesitancy to his words before Atticus continued, "He is betrothed," he admitted to Hazel with a subtle twinge of regret on his face.

Hazel's stomach twisted—she had kissed a man engaged to another. Shame and guilt crashed over her, heat rising to her cheeks. Atticus's words weighed heavy on her heart, and she looked down, unable to meet his gaze as regret burned through her.

Setting her fork down, Hazel took a steady gulp of her warm tea, hoping the lavender would calm her frayed nerves. She hadn't even been here a full day, yet she had already kissed a betrothed prince and then made a spectacle of herself—fleeing his room, running through the castle like some heartbroken damsel. No one would understand the truth—that she hadn't run from rejection, but from the crushing weight of a panic attack.

Hazel felt she made a fool of herself for letting her emotions get the better of her in a highly public and scrutinized environment. She acted impulsively, unaware of the prince's engagement, and her dramatic exit from his room only drew more attention to her actions. The thought of being judged and whispered about by the courtiers added to her overwhelming sense of humiliation.

Hazel looks out the window, not wanting to look at Atticus, as she filled her lungs with air, trying to slow down her heart and mind.

"I am sorry, Hazel," Atticus admitted leaning against the side of the table Hazel sat.

Hearing his apology, she whirled her head to look at him, causing her to wince. Hazel's mind raced with conflicting emotions.

"Why are you apologizing? It's not like you care," Hazel snapped.

A part of her wanted to accept his apology, to believe he truly meant it—that he truly cared. But another part, the one still raw from betrayal, warned her that trusting another man could lead to the same heartbreak Darius had left her with. And she wasn't sure she would survive it a second time.

Atticus exhaled sharply, raking a hand through his hair. "Look, I should've told you about Kingsly's engagement. You didn't deserve to find out like that."

Hazel let out a short, humorless laugh. "You? Apologizing?" She tilted her head, studying him as if he were a puzzle she hadn't realized was missing pieces. "What happened to the arrogant prince who thought he could throw me around like a sack of grain?"

A muscle in his jaw tensed. "I was an ass. I know that." His voice was quieter this time, edged with something almost unfamiliar—guilt. "But I'm not heartless, Hazel."

She scoffed, arms crossing over her chest. "Could've fooled me."

He held her gaze, the usual steel in his eyes softening. "You have every reason to hate me, but I'm not the enemy here. And I'm sorry—for all of it."

The words hung between them, unsettling in their sincerity. Hazel had wanted to hear them, but now that she had, she didn't know what to do with them. Trust had never come easily to her, and it wasn't about to start now.

The weight of his words lingered, unsettling in their sincerity. Hazel had wanted to hear them, but now that she had, she didn't know what to do with them. Forgiveness wasn't something she gave easily—not when trust had cost her so much before. Was it worth the risk to open herself up to someone who had already caused her pain?

She wrestled with the thought, her fingers tightening into fists against her lap. A calloused hand covered hers. She hadn't even heard him move.

Her breath hitched as Atticus's rough fingers brushed against her skin, his grip firm yet careful. He wasn't looking at her, but at her hand, his brows drawn together in concentration.

Hazel swallowed, her heart still pounding from the sudden contact. Yet, despite the shock, she felt an unexpected sense of safety in his presence. His touch wasn't rough this time. It wasn't meant to restrain or intimidate. It was steady. Grounding.

"You need to be more careful," he murmured, his voice quieter now. "If your stitches keep reopening, your skin won't heal properly. It'll scar."

There was no sharp edge to his tone, no commanding authority. Just quiet concern. And that, more than anything, unsettled her most of all.

Ice blue met with honey brown as their eyes met for a moment, and the world stilled around her. Hazel was suddenly transported back to the first time they met, when Atticus had found her injured in the forest, barely conscious from Ratherian's ambush. He had carried her to safety, his strong arms cradling her gently, despite the urgency of the situation. Even then, his presence had brought her a sense of calm she couldn't quite explain. Pulling her hand away, she looks at him, confused. "Why are you all of a sudden being nice to me? If it's out of pity, you can put it so far up your rear end—" Hazel snapped, the words spilling out before she could stop them. But as soon as they left her lips, regret settled deep in her chest, heavy and suffocating.

The truth was, his kindness unsettled her in a way she couldn't quite name. She had braced herself for indifference, for cruelty—anything but this unfamiliar softness. It gnawed at her defenses, stirring something raw and vulnerable inside her.

She looked down, unable to meet his gaze. If she did, she feared she might see something genuine in his expression, something that would make it even harder to keep her walls up. Because if she allowed herself to believe he *meant* it—if she let herself trust him, even for a moment—then what would happen when he proved her wrong?

No, she wasn't ready for this. Wasn't ready to face the part of her that *wanted* to believe in his sincerity. Because hope was dangerous. Hope had nearly destroyed her once before.

Chuckling, Atticus shook his head softly, straightening up before taking the open seat across from her. "Glad to see your attitude hasn't changed," he replied.

Hazel glared at him for a moment before yanking her hand away. Her fingers hovered briefly, then slowly relaxed. She stared at Atticus, then quickly glanced back down at her food, taking another bite of her steak to keep the words she wanted to say from slipping out.

The silence stretched between them, thick with unspoken words and unresolved tension. Hazel's mind raced, torn between gratitude and frustration. The weight of his gaze she can feel baring down on her , added to the confusion swirling inside her, yet she couldn't deny the magnetic pull that drew her closer to him.

"You said you were sorry." She glanced up at him as Atticus trailed his finger along the marble pattern, no longer looking at her. "Why did you apologize?"

Atticus' eyes meet hers , quietly thinking for a moment before looking down and trailing his finger along the marble. The dim lighting cast a warm glow across the room, the air felt charged, almost electric, as if the room held its breath, waiting for the unspoken words to be released finally.

"For last night, in the carriage. I was insensitive. It's just..." his voice trailed off as if he was searching for the right words. He looks around Hazel's receiving room as he found the right words. Atticus finally sighed, his shoulders slumping slightly. "It's just that I've always found it hard to express my feelings." Hazel's eyes softened further, and she placed her fork down, leaning in slightly. "I have dreamed of finding the Ivory Fawn since I was Reed's age. When Queen Asteria came to me in a dream to tell me the Ivory Fawn was indeed alive and in danger. It was like I took my first breath," he finally admitted to her.

Hazel leaned back in her chair, turning his words over in her mind. Was this a trick, or was she finally seeing the real Atticus? Conflicting emotions churned within her, doubt warring with the quiet, stubborn hope she wished she could ignore.

Deep down, she *wanted* to believe him—to trust the sincerity in his eyes—but the scars of past betrayals ran too deep. Letting her guard down around some she thought she could trust , has only ever led to pain. Hazel wasn't sure she could afford that mistake again.

"It made me so angry that when I found you.." His voice wavered, revealing the vulnerability he had kept hidden for so long. "I felt helpless and frustrated, knowing that the fate of our world rested on your shoulders, and there you were, not able to use that power to save Wylana." His eyes glistened with a mixture of regret and hope, silently pleading for Hazel to understand the turmoil that had driven his actions. "I took some of that anger out on you, which you didn't deserve. It wasn't your fault your uncle sheltered you from your gift and didn't teach you how to fight." He continued, "When you nearly died to save my brother, it made me furious you put yourself in danger like that. You didn't know how to use your gift, and were reckless with it trying to save Kingsly. Your uncle couldn't even pull you out of where you went. "

Hazel's expression hardened at the comment about her uncle. "Archibald thought he was protecting me," she said, her voice tinged with bitterness. Reaching her hand across the table, she takes Atticus's rough, sandy hand into hers, looking at him. "As for Kingsly, I'll do it all over again if I had to," she said.

Pulling his hand away, Atticus stood up, stepped away from her, and turned his back to Hazel, and ran a hand down his face. Atticus finally turned to look at Hazel, who braced herself for his anger, but was surprised when he only held a look of concern. "And *that* is why I ask that you not use it, except in dire situations, until I can have Sybilla help train you," Atticus implored. "If you die, then Wylana will fall into darkness. I can't let that happen."

Hazel tilted her head in confusion before she stood up. "I thought Aestival magic went extinct with its people," she replied.

This caused Atticus to chuckle faintly, scratching his chin. "It did, but Sybila has studied the temple and the Aestival scrolls and archives left behind for years. If anyone can help you with your gift, it's her. Aestival magic is the key to restoring balance to our world," Atticus explained, his eyes reflecting a deep-seated hope. "Its power is unparalleled, capable of nurturing life and healing the most grievous wounds. Without it, we stand no chance against the encroaching darkness."

Hearing this woman may be able to help her learn her gift, and about her family lineage on her mother's side, Hazel took a deep breath before tucking hair behind her ear. "When do I meet her?"

Atticus was surprised there was no argument from Hazel. "When you wish, I won't rush you on learning because you still have a lot of adjusting to do, but I ask that you go to her soon. f something happens, I want you prepared. I also want you to rest up as much as possible so Ardnaxela can start training you to fight."

Hearing she was not only going to learn to use her gift, but would also learn how to fight was a scary thought, but Hazel was willing to learn. "Alright, but, Atticus, please ease up a little on me. This is still all very new, and I can't just become this strong, powerful Ivory Fawn who knows the ins and outs of court life overnight."

Atticus smirks nodding in agreement. "I plan to. This is why I chose others to help you. Arabella will teach you how to be a lady, Sybila will teach you the way of the Aestivals, and Ardnaxela will teach you how to fight. However, till you are adjusted, I don't want you to do anything stupid that could hurt you. You are invaluable to Wylana's survival," He replied

Hazel huffed, clenching her jaw. Hearing him continue about her being invaluable again, she crossed her arms. "You said that before," she ground out.

"I know. Well, I've said what I came here to, Please finish your food and get some sleep. Arabella will bring breakfast to you in the morning. Tomorrow you will start learning how to be a court lady, try to take it easy and rest some more before any lessons. " he reply.

Nodding her head, she stepped back as Atticus approached her, causing her throat to bob. "Goodnight, Lady Hazel."

Her lips parted to speak, but it was like he stole all the air from her lungs when he took Hazel's hand, kissing it before leaving without another word. Hazel was now going to be embarking on her journey to become a court lady, she knew she would face numerous challenges. Navigating the intricate social hierarchies and mastering the subtle art of court etiquette would not be easy. Moreover, balancing her duties as a court lady with her training in combat and her unique gift would be a constant struggle. Hazel's hand lingered in the air where he kissed it, and she stared at it in disbelief. Was that from the Immortal Dragon of Wylana court or Prince Atticus? A young man who finally found hope for his kingdom.

Chapter Twenty-Five

Hazel

The birds singing filled the quickly approaching winter air as the sun's rays trickled into Hazel's room. Her eyes were flooded with morning light as Arabella pulled the curtains back, letting in the morning light. Raising her hand to shield her eyes, Hazel observed her surroundings. The silk sheets clung to her body in a warm, comforting embrace in the morning. The room exuded a sense of calm and elegance, with the faint scent of lavender lingering in the air. As the Ivory Fawn's eyes fluttered away the sleep, she took a deep breath before yawning.

"Good morning, my friend." Arabella's cheerful voice filled the silence.

Sitting up, Hazel felt like she had slept for days She looked at Arabella, squinting as her eyes adjusted to the morning light. "Good morning. What time is it?" she replied, sleepily.

Arabella walked to the side of her bed wearing a Pantone green tunic tucked into a brown skirt with a brown waist corset. Her messy array of curls was held up by a barely noticeable hair clip. Spirals of curls came out of it on top of it and trickled down like a waterfall of caramel and mocha , hiding it even more. "It's roughly ten. I let you sleep in because you needed it." The young handmaiden set a breakfast tray on Hazel's lap with a smile, and Hazel immediately noticed the small vase of lavender on it. Raising the cover off Hazel's plate, the delightful aroma of bacon, eggs, toast with butter, and roasted potatoes flooded her senses. "I wanted to help you feel more at home, so I went to the market to get a bundle of lavender for you. I also tool the liberty of buying some seeds if you wanted to plant some."

Hazel looked at her new friend in surprise before she smiled widely, taking Arabella's hand and giving it a gentle squeeze. "Thank you, Arabella, this means so much to me." Hazel's eyes glistened with unshed tears, overwhelmed by the thoughtful gesture. She took a moment to inhale the fragrant lavender, its scent bringing back fond memories of her childhood. As she looked back at Arabella, her voice trembled with gratitude. "You have no idea how much this reminds me of home. I will, of course, pay you back for the-"

Arabella cut her off with a chuckle, squeezing Hazel's hand. "No need, Hazel. Now eat up while I start your bath. Same as before?" the young handmaiden asked, rising from the bed and heading towards the bathing room.

"Yes, please," Hazel replied with a grateful smile. Digging into her breakfast, she moans in satisfaction at the taste of the eggs before she looks at Arabella.

As Arabella prepared the bath, Hazel couldn't help but feel a growing sense of camaraderie with her new friend. The simple, thoughtful gestures and shared moments were quickly becoming a deep and cherished bond.

"What color dress would you like to wear? Brown or Maroon?" Arabella asked with a faint smile upon returning to the bedchambers.

Hazel shoved another fork of eggs into her mouth, thinking for a moment before she looked at Arabella, smiling. "Something simple, but appropriate to walk around in, nothing too extravagant."

Arabella nodded her head softly before she vanished back into the bathing room. The aroma of lavender and eucalyptus was slowly filling her room. Devouring everything on her plate, there was a twinge of guilt in Hazel's stomach as she realized she hadn't saved any for her friend. Hazel knew what it was like to be in a low society and assumed the castle staff really wasn't fed as well as the royals. Hazel decided she would make it up to Arabella later by finding a way to share her next meal. She pondered how much the small acts of kindness meant in her life and wanted to extend the same to her friend. Determined to bridge the gap between them, she resolved to ensure Arabella felt equally valued.

Strolling back in, Arabella took Hazel's tray and walked to the entryway to set it down by the door, pulling on a service rope. A young maiden came in, taking the tray from the table, nodding her head to Arabella before leaving quickly as she came.

Slowly sliding her legs out from under the warm sheets, Hazel stretched her arms up towards to the ceiling. Her shoulder and side didn't hurt as much as they did before, which was good. It was a relief not to be in so much pain. This meant her body was healing.

Arabella walked over with a fresh bathing gown. "How did you sleep? I am hoping it was a good night for you."

Hazel nodded her head, rubbing her neck, careful of her wound. "I did. I don't think I've ever slept that hard," she admitted. Exhaustion from the long journey and the emotional toll of recent events had finally caught up with her. Her body needed rest to heal, and the sense of safety she felt here allowed her to truly relax.

Laying the cotton robe beside Hazel, Arabella smiled briefly before heading to the golden wardrobe to assemble Hazel's attire for the day. "Well, I am glad you needed it after your day yesterday. Thanks to Prince Atticus, he informed me that you are just to rest as much as possible, but that doesn't mean you have to stay in here all day before the banquet in your honor tonight." Arabella informed her. Hazel blinked, her mind struggling to catch up. "Wait... there's a banquet?" She paused, running a hand through her hair again, her thoughts a whirlwind. "In my honor?" Her voice faltered slightly, confusion mixing with growing anxiety. "But—why? When did this happen?"

Arabella, who had been quietly adjusting the room's curtains, paused and turned toward her. "Yes, my lady. The banquet's been planned for some time. Prince Atticus and Prince Kingsly sent word when they first learned of you , and told the King they were bringing you back with them, They've been preparing for it ever since."

Hazel's brow furrowed. "But... Atticus didn't say anything to me." Her chest tightened, and she felt a pang of frustration. "He never mentioned it."

Arabella's eyes widened in surprise. "He didn't? Oh, my lady, I thought for sure he would have told you himself." She moved closer, her voice lowering in sympathy. "It's... it's been on the calendar for several days now. I assumed you were aware."

Hazel swallowed, trying to push down the wave of unease rising in her chest. "No. I didn't know." She could feel her pulse quickened at the thought of facing so many people—so many expectations. The weight of it all pressed on her, and she exhaled sharply, trying to steady her breathing. "What... what exactly am I supposed to do at this banquet?"

Arabella hesitated for a moment before offering a reassuring smile. "You'll simply attend, my lady. Be yourself. There's no grand expectation—only a celebration. And perhaps a bit of... pressure to represent your people well." She paused, her expression softening. "But I know you'll handle it just fine."

Hazel forced a small nod, though the anxiety still clenching at her. "I suppose I have no choice but to face it, then."

"Lets get you washed up and ready for today," Arabella replies in excitement as she walked to the bathing room. Hazel's mind raced with conflicting emotions as she stood to follow. She couldn't help but wonder if she would ever truly feel at ease in this new role. The weight of her responsibilities loomed large, but she resolved to face the day with as much grace as she could muster.

Hazel changed before pulling her hair up in a bejeweled clip from her vanity mirror. Walking into the bathing room, Hazel strolled to the bathtub as she removed her robe, handing it to Arabella before getting in. The hot water enveloped her in a warm hug as she relaxed into her bath. Taking in a deep breath of the lavender and eucalyptus, Hazel smiled.

"So, what would you like to do today?" Arabella asked. "Where you go, I go."

Closing her eyes, Hazel relaxed more into her bath, thinking of what she could do before speaking, "What do ladies of court Wylana do?" Hazel was still trying to navigate the intricacies of court life, a world vastly different from what she came from. The opulence and formality already felt suffocating, making her long for the simplicity of her previous life. Yet, she was determined to adapt and find her place midst the grandeur and expectations.

Chuckling, Arabella took the soft sponge and washed Hazel's arms and legs down, making sure to be gentle when she cleaned Hazel's neck "Well, some of the court ladies like to sit at high noon tea and gossip, some like to stroll through the courtyard, and some like to read in the library," Arabella replied as she rang out the sponge.

Hazel contemplated the options, pondering what might bring her some comfort. "I think I'd like to visit the library," she said. "A quiet place among the books sounds like exactly what I need right now." Sitting up, a thought occurred to her that caused Hazel's eyes to widen. Turning to Arabella, "What about the Aestival temple? Is anyone allowed there?"

Hearing this, Arabella licked her dry lips before a bob of her throat followed. For once, Arabella's eyes averted hers. "No one is allowed there but a hand-picked few, such as the royal family and the scribes," she replied nervously.

Thinking momentarily, Hazel tilted her head a bit, looking to the marble floor and then to the handmaiden. "What about the Ivory Fawn?" Hazel asked.

Arabella's eyes shot to Hazel in shock upon hearing the name. She set the sponge down before shaking her head, stood up, wiped her hands on her skirt, and grabbed a towel. "If the Ivory Fawn was real, then yes, technically, , they would be granted access to the temple," Arabella replied

So, the banquet honored Lady Hazel and not the Ivory Fawn. This made sense, because if anyone found out who she was, then she would be in danger, and worse, Hazel would put those here in court at risk. The Ivory Fawn was a treasured symbol of the kingdom's unity and prosperity. Her appearance at the court as Lady Hazel of Alexandria at the banquet was meant to be a thank you for saving the princes. And not who she really was and what she represented.

"Would you like me to remove your necklace , my lady?" "No it's alright." Hazel replied.

Arabella walked away from the bathtub to a large white closet door, Arabella retrieved a towel before returning to the bathtub. Arabella set it down beside the tub, keeping her eyes averted from Hazel.

"Let's get you dried off and dressed, shall we?" Arabella asked shyly.

Why was Arabella acting so differently? Hazel looked at her with a mixture of curiosity and amusement. She could sense the younger woman's nerves, but appreciated her efforts nonetheless.

"Thank you, Arabella," Hazel replied warmly, a soft smile gracing her lips.

Why was she avoiding looking at Hazel's face as if she was being whipped? Did Atticus say something to her to act this way?

"Arabella?" Concern filled Hazel's voice as Arabella was about to make her leave the washing room. The handmaiden stopped, but she didn't turn to look at Hazel as she stood up in her bathing dress. "Did Prince Atticus say anything to you? Hurt you for how you acted yesterday? If so, please tell me," Hazel pleaded

before removing her bathing dress, drying off, and sliding on the robe. She walked over to Arabella and gently touched her shoulder, hoping to offer some reassurance. "You can trust me, Arabella," she said softly. "Whatever is troubling you, we can face it together." Seeing there were tears in Arabella's eyes mixed with what looked like hope, Hazel stepped back in shock. Seeing Arabella crying broke Hazel's heart and filled it with anger. If Atticus was the cause of these tears, she would carve his pride to ribbon.

"Hazel, I know. I know you are the Ivory Fawn."

She knew? Did Atticus tell her? Was that why he picked Arabella to be her handmaiden? Was it because he knew she kept her true identity secret?

"Arabella, I- " Hazel began to apologize, but there was a knock was at her front door.

Arabella straightened at the sound before she looked at Hazel. "Later, my lady, but you must get dressed. I will see who is at the door."

Hazel nodded before walking over to her outfit for the day. As she dressed, her mind raced with questions and emotions. How did Arabella discover her secret? She felt a mix of fear, anger, and relief, wondering what the future held for her now that her identity was no longer hidden.

Shaking her head, she forced herself to focus on getting dressed. The outfit Arabella chose was simple yet beautiful. It was a silk cream blouse with a coffee creme long skirt and a simple waist corset that would show off her curves in a flattering way. Sliding on a simple brown dress, she could hear Arabella speaking to someone in the receiving room. Hazel could make out a woman's voice. It was as airy and smooth, but cold as the winter's wind.

"How much longer will Lady Hazel be? I want to lay my eyes on this new lady everyone is gossiping about."

Just the way this mysterious woman spoke—syrupy and smug, her words laced with entitlement—made Hazel's fingers twitch with the urge to slap her. She hadn't even laid eyes on the woman yet, but that voice alone set her teeth on edge.

Walking over to the entryway of her bed chambers, Hazel stepped into her receiving and saw a woman wearing a black lace dress with sheer lace sleeves. It held a deep plunge, showing off her breast. Gold ivy leaf trim lined the plunge, and matching the bottom of her dress. Her black hair lay in loose curls down her back.

Hazel's eyes narrowed as she tried to place the woman. Could she be a noble from a neighboring kingdom, or perhaps a spy sent by her enemies? The woman's opulence and confidence suggested she held significant power, and Hazel felt a shiver of apprehension run down her spine. Already, Hazel wanted to slap that disgusted look off her face. "I thought Lady of Winter walked into my chambers, hearing how you just spoke to my handmaiden."

Schooling her face, Hazel tried to keep her distaste for this woman. She also tried to hide how threatened she felt by the woman's commanding presence and how she carried herself with an air of superiority. This stranger's boldness was demanding an audience, and her dismissive attitude toward Arabella hinted made her blood boil. Hazel also knew that any misstep could reveal vulnerabilities she couldn't afford to expose.

The viperous woman's eyes scanned over Hazel, taking in how she looked. A breathing laugh left the woman's throat, one that looked very tempting to strangle. Pushing her hair back from her view, an emerald engagement ring decorated the woman's hand.

Hazel took a deep breath, deciding that maintaining composure and appearing unruffled was her best strategy. She greeted the woman with a polite but firm tone, masking her wariness with a courteous smile stepping forward with an air of confidence, "To what do I owe the pleasure of your visit?"

"Lady Hazel of Alexandria, meet Lady Duvessa of Taldora," Arabella announced.

Looking at the ring, Hazel recollected what Atticus told her about Kingsly. "I presume you are the lady engaged to Prince Kingsly."

Arabella's eyes shot to Hazel, widening at the bluntness before she looked at Duvessa, whose lips curled up in a wicked grin.

"And you were the lady seen fleeing from his bed chambers, crying like a heartbroken girl. It's quite pathetic, honestly. Not even your first day at court and you already made a reputation for yourself."

If Duvessa had fangs, they would have been dripping venom. Hazel's cheeks flushed with a mix of embarrassment and anger, but she held her ground, her eyes narrowing slightly. "A reputation, you say? I suppose it's better to be known for something than to be forgotten entirely," she retorted, her voice steady despite the turmoil within. It took everything in Hazel not to punch this woman so hard that her pretty little teeth would fall out. "However, it's not as sad as you coming here thinking you can rile me up," Hazel ground out.

Duvessa let out a mocking laugh, resting her hand on her plump chest and walked over to Hazel, who stiffened at her approach.. "You should be careful who you make an enemy here at court, Lady Hazel. You never know who could be backing those you anger."

Feeling her skin shiver, Hazel narrowed her eyes at Duvessa crossing her arms over her chest, Inside, Hazel's mind was a whirlwind of conflicting emotions—rage at Duvessa's audacity, fear of the unknown alliances at court, and a steely determination not to be cowed by anyone. She could feel her heart pounding in her chest, a drumbeat of both defiance and caution. Hazel knew she had to tread carefully, but she also resolved that she wouldn't let anyone, least of all Duvessa, dictate her fate at court.

"I was going to say the same thing, Lady Duvessa. Now, if you're done with this little game you are trying to play, you can leave," Hazel gritted out in annoyance

The woman with black lips curled them up in a snarl before she huffed and leaned her head back. "Stay away from my fiance, Lady Hazel, or you will find your life will become painfully difficult," Duvessa scolded.

Hazel rolled her eyes at the threat before watching the woman leave. As Duvessa left, the warmth of the necklace she hadn't removed ,did as well.

The warmth of the necklace was more than just a comforting sensation. It was an enchanted heirloom passed down through generations of Hazel's family, meant to protect its wearer from harm. When it glowed warmly, it signaled that hidden forces were at work, either shielding Hazel or warning her of imminent danger. This subtle shift in temperature reminded Hazel that she was never truly alone, even in the treacherous environment of the court.

Turning her attention to Arabella, Hazel glided over to her friend, stroking her arm before frowning, when seeing Arabella looking a little pale. "How about we take a stroll? I could use some fresh air after that." Hazel offered a smile.

Arabella nodded her head, chuckling a bit. "I have never seen Lady Duvessa's feathers get so ruffled. You've well and truly raised her hackles. Finally, someone stood up to her," Arabella admitted, her eyes brightening slightly at the suggestion, and a hint of color returning to her cheeks. She linked her arm with Hazel. "A stroll sounds perfect. I could use a break from all this tension," she replied softly, her voice tinged with relief.

Chapter Twenty-Six

Atticus

Atticus raked his hand through his hair, still trying to line his thoughts up straight. He was to be king of Wylana, and she would become the Ivory Fawn, which in turn would be queen of the Aestival people. Despite the honor being the crimson dragon, Atticus felt an overwhelming sense of doubt and anxiety.

The weight of responsibility was immense, and he questioned whether he was truly prepared for the challenges ahead. Asteria only told him he would guide Hazel to becoming the Ivory Fawn, not what would happen after. He worried about the political intrigue that came with the throne, the constant threat of betrayal, and the need to balance the needs of his people with his personal desires. Navigating the complex relationships with neighboring kingdoms also loomed large in his mind. Most of all, he feared failing Hazel and undermining her path to becoming the Ivory Fawn.

He couldn't figure out why he was so drawn to her. There was a magnetic pull between them that he couldn't explain, a connection that defied logic. Despite her infuriating stubbornness and sharp tongue, an undeniable spark in her eyes captivated him. It was this paradox of attraction and frustration that left him in a constant state of inner turmoil, questioning his own emotions and intentions. Atticus had only known her for a week, yet he would burn villages down without a second thought if it meant keeping her safe.

However, their connection could complicate his rule and provoke dissent among his advisors and subjects.

If their relationship were perceived as a weakness or distraction, it could be exploited by those who sought to undermine his authority. Furthermore, the intertwining of their fates might place Hazel in even greater danger, making her a target for those who oppose her ascension.

Shaking his head, he groaned in frustration as he stood from his chair in front of the fireplace and paced his room. Atticus picked up a black marble vase, threw it against the wall, shattering it. As the shards scattered across the floor, he felt a fleeting moment of release, a temporary escape from the chaos in his mind. The destruction mirrored his inner turmoil, each fragment a piece of his fractured resolve, and he wondered if he, too, would shatter under the pressure of his impending duties. As Atticus rubbed his face, he could not figure out why he couldn't think clearly when around that reckless girl.

Despite the chaos she brought into his life, Hazel ignited a sense of purpose within him that he hadn't felt in years. Her presence was both a curse and a blessing, pushing him to confront his deepest fears and desires. He couldn't deny that she made him feel alive, even if it meant teetering on the edge of madness. Not once had any court lady affected him like this. He was torn between the desire to protect her and the fear of losing control over his own destiny.

The intensity of his feelings for Hazel made him question his priorities, and he worried that his emotions might cloud his judgment. Yet, in those rare moments of clarity, he realized that her influence might be the catalyst he needed to become the leader he was meant to be. Atticus had taken many women to bed to satisfy his needs, even a mistress, yet, he had never been held by a woman like this.

There was a knock at his door, followed by the sound of the it opening and then closing. "Is everything alright?" His mother's voice was laced with concern.

Atticus turned to face her, his eyes betraying a mix of agitation and vulnerability. "I'm fine," he said curtly, though his clenched fists and the shattered vase told a different story.

Sage's worried expression only deepened, as if sensing the storm brewing within her son. Atticus turned his head away from his mother, but her soft hand pulled his chin to look at her. "Did something happen?" Wearing a long simple ivory dress, her normal icy diamond circlet on her head as her brows furrowed with concern, scanning his features. The queen's eyes softened as she took in the disarray of the room and the turmoil etched on her son's face. "Atticus, you know you can talk to me," she said gently, her voice a soothing balm against his frayed nerves. She could see the weight of his burdens pressing down on him, and she was determined to help him find a way to soothe her son.

Sighing, Atticus took his mother's hand, kissing it before shaking his head. "No, everything is alright," he lied, looking at the broken marble vase before returning his attention to his mother.

Sage frowned, raising her eyebrow and giving her son a look that always melted his walls. Her frown deepened, and a flicker of disappointment crossed her eyes. "Atticus, I've known you since the day you were born. I can tell when you're hiding something," she said softly, her voice tinged with a mix of concern and frustration.

"Mother, what do you remember of the prophecy?" he finally asked.

Blinking a few times, she stared at him. "As the ivory feathers are covered with red, the Ivory Fawn will rise from the ashes of her home, guided by her Crimson Dragon."

When she paused for a moment, Atticus reflected about what Asteria told him. Releasing his mother's hand, he rubbed his face. "The prophecy speaks of a great upheaval and transformation," Atticus began, his voice heavy with the weight of the revelation. "The ivory feathers symbolize purity and peace, but their staining with red foretells violence and sacrifice. The fawn rising from the ashes suggests rebirth and resilience, and the Crimson Dragon symbolizes powerful guidance and protection." Atticus sighed, running his hand through his hair. "Queen Asteria told me that for Hazel to become the Ivory Fawn, she must sacrifice herself. I am worried. What if that sacrifice is giving up her own life, to become the Ivory Fawn."

The queen's throat bobbed, and his heart ached at the thought of losing her, yet he knew the significance of the Ivory Fawn for their kingdom. The conflict within him grew stronger with each passing moment as he searched for a way to save Hazel without defying the prophecy.

"But if she dies, what happens then? Will the Aestival people rise again after her death? Or will she come back and lead them?" Sage asked her son, her voice laced with concern.

Shaking his head, Atticus took a deep breath and sighed for a moment. He looked out the window and tried to wrap his mind around everything. "I don't know. I am worried I am just leading Hazel to the end of her life, where there is no return. I want to stay away from her to prolong the prophecy and let the others guide her. Although, it's a struggle to stay away from her. I feel drawn to her."

Sage rested her hand on Atticus's arm, looking at her son. A grounding touch his mother always did.

The weight of his responsibility pressed heavily on his shoulders, and the fear of making the wrong decision gnawed at his conscience. Every instinct within him screamed to protect Hazel, to shield her from the grim fate that seemed inevitable. Yet, the ominous prophecy loomed over him, a constant reminder of the greater good that demanded such a heartbreaking sacrifice.

"Why don't you go to Sybilla? Maybe she can help you sort out everything. She knows far more about the Aestival legends and lore than anyone," Sage offered it to her son.

Atticus looks at his mother, kissing her head, pulling her into an embrace, and holding her close. "Thank you, Mom. I may do that. I already have to fill her in on what I saw during the ambush."

Sybilla, with her vast knowledge of the ancient texts and prophecies, might be able to uncover a hidden detail or an alternative interpretation that could offer a way out. She might also provide insights into the true nature of the Ivory Fawn and the sacrifices involved, potentially revealing that Hazel's fate wasn't as grim as it seemed. Atticus held onto a glimmer of hope that Sybilla's wisdom could illuminate a path where Hazel could fulfill her destiny without losing her life.

Sage nodded her head before giving her son another stroke on his cheek, smiling. "Alright, my fire, I will see you at the banquet tonight. Please don't break anything else before then."

Looking at the vase, Atticus chuckled, "I won't."

During their journey to the Aestival temple, Kissem's mane shook. Dismounted from his horse, Atticus stroked her neck, smiling before tying her to a post. "Don't play with that bit once I am gone," Atticus warned. She nicked in response, causing him to chuckle before walking up the grand staircase.

The castle Andromeda, on the outskirts of Wylana, was run down in appearance as wild foliage crawled up the large marble pillars. Ivy snaked its way up the walls, weaving through the cracks and crevices, while wisteria cascaded down from the battlements, its purple blooms almost concealing the ancient stonework.

The once-grand castle now stood as a hauntingly beautiful relic of a bygone era, shrouded in nature's embrace. Atticus opened one of the enormous, arching double doors that stood almost nine feet tall. After entering, he saw a large lobby covered by more plant life. However, if a person looked hard enough at the dusty ivory pillars, they would find lilac marble pillars with gold patterns spidering up them.

The air was thick with the scent of damp earth and ancient stone, mingling with the sweet fragrance of wisteria. Sunlight filtered through the cracks in the walls and ceiling, casting dappled patterns on the floor and illuminating motes of dust that danced lazily in the air. The silence was almost tangible, broken only by the distant echo of dripping water and the occasional rustle of leaves. Atticus has often walked his way through the castle, even as a child. It was like a second home to him.

As children, Sybilla and Atticus would pretend they were Aestival warriors, battling the evils of this world. He couldn't remember how often Sybilla reminded him how an Aestival would act.

Making his way eagerly towards the castle library, his brown boots crunched some autumn leaves as he walked up the staircase that clung to the side of the wall. It never made sense to Atticus why they would have stairwells if they could fly.

As a child, Atticus was captivated by the tales of the winged fae warriors, their bravery and honor etched into every story he read. He would spend hours in the library, poring over ancient texts and illustrations that depicted their majestic wings and fierce battles. The idea of flight, of soaring above the world and seeing it from a bird's-eye view, filled him with a sense of wonder and longing that never quite left him.

Strolling his way to the archives, Atticus stopped, feeling a breeze coming from the hallways that lead down toward the temple. A chill ran down his spine as he grappled with the impossibility of it. How could there be a chilling breeze from a place sealed shut for centuries? His mind raced, torn between the logical explanations he clung to and the creeping dread that something far more sinister might be at play. Could an ancient force stir within?

Walking down the hallway, his curiosity got the best of him, and to his astonishment, the temple doors were open. That entrance had been locked since the fall of the Aestivals, only visible from the skylight, nestled high above the tree, was unreachable by any means but flight, its height ensuring no prying eyes could glimpse inside.

His heart pounded in his chest as he stood rooted to the spot, unable to tear his eyes away from the slight gap. He swallowed hard, a mix of fear and excitement coursing through him, before taking a tentative step forward. The only reason the scribes knew the tree lay inside was because of the inscription on the door. In Aestival writing, it was translated as *It is only when the fawn is returned to its mother that this door will awaken.* Pushing open the door to peer into it, all the breath was pulled from his chest as he stepped back in awe. He was seeing the legendary Mother Grove Tree. This tree was no ordinary tree. It was the heart of the Aestival people, the source of their magical energy that once sustained their world. For Atticus, it represented not just a link to the past, but also a beacon of hope for the future. It stood towering and magnificent, its bark shimmering with hues of lilac and gold, as if imbued with the very essence of moonlight and sunlight. Its leaves, vibrant shades of emerald and lavender, glowed softly, casting an ethereal light that danced across the ancient stone walls. Delicate flowers bloomed among its branches, each petal radiating a soft luminescence, filling the air with a fragrance that whispered forgotten tales of the Aestival people. It was untouched by time. Not a single bit of outside vegetation had made its way in here. It was as if a shield protected it against the outside environment and the passage of time.

It wasn't even cold but actually warm like it was in summer. How was this even possible? This room was untouched, unlike the rest of the temple. Atticus's mind raced with a whirlwind of emotions—wonder, reverence, and a profound sense of destiny. He felt a deep reverence for the sacred tree, knowing he was in the presence of something ancient and powerful. Tears welled up in his eyes as he realized the significance of this discovery, a pivotal moment that could change the course of history. The Ivory Fawn had returned.

Walking over to the tree, Atticus was amazed to see none of the leaves had fallen. Placing his hand on the enormous legendary tree, he had no words for what he saw. Light reflected off the water and into his eyes as a ripple appeared. Turning his head , Atticus not only saw his reflection, but also something else in the water - a sword, taking a closer look into the reflection of the water. This was not just any sword. No, this sword Atticus had only seen before in drawings. Reaching into the water to remove it, he held up the steel blade, seeing it was engraved with gold Aestival symbols. The hilt was made of the finest lilac-dyed leather with swirls of ivory and gold he had ever seen. It was surprisingly light for its appearance.

This was the sword of Asteria, the legendary queen. This temple proved to Atticus even more that Hazel was, in fact, the Ivory Fawn, and Atticus was her dragon.It's door has been sealed the entire time he has visit the door. However, with Hazel's arrival it was open. Everything now has changed. The experience of seeing her use her gift and now this. It proved the rising of the Aestival people, and the Ivory Fawn was now upon Wylana.

Atticus's heart pounded with overwhelming excitement and awe. He felt an intense connection to the ancient past, as he held a piece of history in his hands.

Footsteps sounded in the doorway before a faint gasp echoed, followed by books hitting the floor. As he turned his head, a woman with black raven hair, wearing a jade-green tunic, reached out her hand. Stepping forward, her beige-colored skirt flew behind her as she glided into the room, along the stone paths leading across the pond, and to the tree. Her emerald eyes took in every detail of the tree as if categorizing it. "Atticus," she breathed in shock. "Do you know what this means?"

A joyful smile spread across Atticus' face as he approached the young scribe woman. "It means the Ivory Fawn is home." The sheer excitement in his voice at this revelation.

Sybilla's shock was palpable as she saw the legendary sword. Her eyes were wide and her breath was coming in short, astonished gasps. She reached out a trembling hand, her fingers barely brushing the blade, as it she was afraid it might vanish if she touched it too firmly. "All these years of searching because of prophecy," she whispered, her voice tinged with awe and reverence. "I never thought I'd see this day."

"I only trust you to help her learn all of this," Atticus said, motioning with his hand to the Mother Grove Tree.

Stepping forward, Sybilla's eyes lined with silver as she put her hand to her rosy lips. "She is here? Did you find her? How?"

Atticus chuckled before resting the Aestival blade at his side "I have much to catch you up, my dear friend."

Atticus told Sybilla everything that had occurred these last two weeks. From him having Queen Asteria coming to Atticus in his dream, explaining the fawn was alive, to him saving Hazel from being killed by a Netherian male, how Hazel's fiance betrayed her, to her saving them at the ambush.

Sybilla's eyes were full of wonder with twinges of disbelief hearing all that this girl had done to her. Hearing that the Ivory Fawn was alive and, more importantly, now in court, her emerald eyes sparkled with hope.

"I need you to help her. While raising her, her uncle forbade her from using her gift. They didn't even tell Hazel that she was, in fact, the Ivory Fawn until recently. Your the only person I know that has read nearly every scroll known in the archives. Maybe those scrolls had some knowledge about how they wielded magic."

As if contemplating, Sybilla looks at the Mother's Grove before looking at Atticus. She inhaled deeply, as if trying to reel back her excitement to think clearly. "If she is to practice her gift and learn about the Aestival people, she must come here where she is safe. If she loses control, it can be here where no one is around, not at court where Hazel could put court members and herself in danger," Sybilla spoke firmly about her choice of action, and Atticus nodded his head in agreement.

"Agreed, and I asked Ardnaxela to train her. Although she wants to wait for Hazel to be in better shape before training her." Atticus looks at the tree, still amazed by it. "Their magic still lingers here. I can somehow feel it. What about Hazel sacrificing herself? Wouldn't that mean she must die to fulfill the prophecy?" Atticus asked with panic, quickly turning to look at Sybilla, who was entranced by the tree.

Sybilla's expression softened before a flicker of sadness crossed her face. She turned to meet Atticus's worried gaze. "Prophecies are often misunderstood," she said gently, placing a reassuring hand on his arm. "We must focus on guiding Hazel to harness her power safely. Sacrificing yourself doesn't always mean you have to die to be fulfilled. It can be selflessness. Putting yourself in harm's way to protect others could be seen as sacrificing yourself," she replied, her eyes not looking away from the tree.

Hope sparked in his chest. Maybe he wasn't leading Hazel to her own death. It was like a weight was lifted off his chest. "This is why I came to you. You know everything about the Aestival lore and legend like the back of your hand," he said with a wide smile as he gripped her shoulder in appreciation for clearing some of his worries.

"Don't be silly. With knowledge, it is never-ending. One simply doesn't know everything because it is impossible to know everything. The best part of learning is that it is never-ending." Sybilla looked at him finally, after being enthralled with the tree. "Are you planning to share it with her?" Sybilla asked, as she watched Atticus closely.

Shifting a bit, Atticus thought momentarily before pinching his eyebrow and sighing, "I don't understand. If I tell her she has to die to fulfill the prophecy, she may never want to become the Ivory Fawn. If I don't tell her and she finds out, she will never trust me again," he admitted

Raking her hand through her raven hair, she expressed irritation. "Atticus, it is her life. Hazel has a right to know. If I were her, I would want to know." "You can't hide something like that from her. This is her life, and she has a right to know. It sounds like she hasn't had much choice in her life. Why continue that? Hazel has already had people hide things from her. Don't be like them," Sybilla continued to counsel her friend, huffing out hot air.

He nodded, taking a deep breath. "I will tell her when the moment is right. She just got to court." He replied,

"And what about tonight's banquet? Isn't it in honor of her being welcomed to court, or is this about her being the Ivory Fawn?" she asked wearily

Atticus looked to his friend, shaking his head and rubbing the back of his neck, groaning "I completely forgot about tonight. It's being held in her honor as a lady joining the court. I told my father that her identity as the Ivory Fawn had to be hidden. We can't have everyone knowing who she is just yet. It is too dangerous with her inexperience in her gifts and fighting," he explained.

"Well, isn't that why you have Ardnaxela training her? She is one of the toughest guards you have. Do you think Hazel could learn quickly?"

"That is my hope. If she doesn't, Hazel will be at the mercy of the threats that wish to take her life," he said, a hint of concern threading through his voice. The memory of her fragile form surfaced unbidden—Hazel, deathly pale and motionless, confined to her bed for two agonizing weeks after he had pulled her back from the brink. He had sat by her side, watching the rise and fall of her breath, each one a battle hard-won. The image haunted him still, a stark reminder of how close he had come to losing her. He refused to let that happen again.

He couldn't shake how drawn he felt to her. It was like he couldn't breathe when they were not together, but he didn't know if that was because he was in the presence of the Ivory Fawn he dreamed of meeting, or if it had something to do with their destinies being intertwined. "Come on, you should meet her before the banquet. Are you coming?" Atticus questioned his friend, hoping he wouldn't have to attend this dreaded banquet without her.

"I will be there, I assure you, but let's go." Sybilla amused herself, smiling, excited to meet the Ivory Fawn.

Chapter Twenty-Seven

Hazel

Arabella and Hazel strolled through the castle grounds, laughing as they came to a willow tree, sitting down beneath it. Spreading her skirt around herself, Hazel reached into the wicker basket Arabella had brought with them. The sandwiches were cut into perfect triangles, with the crust carefully removed. Each one was made with pepper jack cheese and sliced ham—Hazel's favorite. She reached in, grabbing some pickles that were also packed in their basket.

The sun shone warmly, casting dappled light through the willow's long, sweeping branches, and a gentle breeze rustled the leaves, bringing a refreshing coolness to the air. The pleasant weather made their picnic all the more enjoyable, as they relished the perfect balance of sunshine and shade. The idyllic setting enhanced the flavors of their meal, making each bite of the sandwich and pickles even more delightful.

"Hungry?" Arabella spoke up holding a sandwich out to Hazel.

"I am starving, thank you Arabella." Taking a bite of her pickle, Hazel smiled, enjoying the sting of the dill and vinegar as it slid down her throat.

"All right, pop question. Hazel, what is the proper way to curtsy?"

Hazel stopped chewing as she thought back to what Arabella taught her this last hour: "Right, you put your right leg back and bend your left knee. If you do it the other way, it means you are ill-mannered."

Beaming with pride in her question, Arabella grins "Correct. The proper way to hold a teacup?"

Retrieving a teacup and saucer from the basket, she poured tea into the cup.

Swallowing, Hazel, once again, tried to recollect everything Arabella taught her before taking the cup, trying to remember how to hold it. It was important for her to know this before tonight. Her index finger and thumb joined through the handle as her middle finger supported the handle beneath the handle, and her pinky finger stuck out as she drank from her tea.

"Tsk tsk tsk."

Seeing Arabella's disapproving glance at Hazel's extended finger, she swallowed, tucking in her pink, remembering it was improper to extend it. "Good. See? You're getting it. These lessons may seem unnecessary, but you want to leave a good impression on the king when you meet the court." Removing a book from the basket, Arabella rose to her feet before offering a hand to Hazel.

Taking the hand, she stood up, looking at the book, chuckling "What is that for?"

Arabella stood on her tippy toes, balancing a book on Hazel's head. "You need to learn to walk like a lady." Resting her hand on Hazel's stomach, she smiled. "Stomach in." Moving her hand to Hazel's shoulders, she smiled. "Shoulders back, lift your chin, slowly turned your head from side to side," Arabella instructed with a smile. "Remember to be charming, yet detached and amused and always step lightly."

There was so much to be a court, yet Hazel was relieved that Arabella was guiding her through the court lady etiquette, so she didn't make a fool of herself more than she already had. Arabella's patient instruction helped her feel more confident and prepared.

The banquet was being held in Hazel's honor tonight. She was so excited to dress up again as a princess, but she also needed to make a better impression on the court in hopes they would forget her first day.

Slowly, the sun began to set, signifying that it was drawing closer to the banquet's start. Hazel and Arabella giggled amongst themselves like two teenage girls getting ready for their first ball.

Excitedly, the pair hurriedly made their way back to Hazel's suite. Arabella made sure Hazel smelt of roses and ivy for tonight. Wanting Hazel to captivate the entire court, Arabella sorted through the closet trying to find the perfect dress.

Hazel heart raced with a mixture of excitement and anxiety as she thought about her first official appearance at court. She worried about remembering all the etiquette rules and making a favorable impression on the nobles. The fear of tripping over her dress or saying the wrong thing loomed in her mind, but she trusted Arabella's guidance to help her shine.

Hazel was soon beckoned from her bath, and she wrapped herself in a red silk robe with Arabella's help. She then walked through the bathroom archway to sit at the vanity mirror. Arabella displayed all kinds of jewelry for Hazel to pick from. Against Hazel's shoulders, Arabella reached out and picked up a strand of her blonde hair, her fingers brushing against the delicate accessory nestled within it. It was a barrette shaped like an autumn leaf, its edges kissed with shades of crimson and gold, as if caught in the peak of fall. Tiny flecks of amber gemstones adorned its surface, catching the light with every movement. The elegant piece held Hazel's hair in place, a small yet striking contrast against her fair locks.

Hazel's long, curly hair was pulled up into a ponytail that hung down on her back. Arabella painted Hazel's lips red and blended a mocha color onto her eyelids to bring out her blue eyes.

Hazel gasped, surprised at her appearance once. She didn't even recognize herself in the mirror. With her makeup, Hazel looked young, yet mature.

Standing up and beaming in excitement, Hazel pulled Arabella in to hug. "Ara, you truly can work miracles. I don't even recognize myself." Turning to look back at her reflection, she stared. She was in disbelief at how she looked.

"Wait till you see your dress," Arabella replied before walking over and removing the crimson silk sheet from the mannequin. Both of Hazel's hands rose to her lips, careful not to smudge them, as her heart leaped in her chest. She thought the last dress Arabella had picked was gorgeous. This one was far more breathtaking.

It was a ruby red mermaid trumpet-style gown with a layer of ivory lace that swirled all along parts of the dress that showed off her waist and chest. Strolling over, Hazel ran her hand along it. This was the finest silk she ever felt, even nicer than her bath robe.

Seeing the flaring skirt of that train was so long that it, too, had the same swirling design down the length of it. Hazel's attention went to the back of the dress, and her breathing hitched when she saw there was no back, but instead an ivory dragon attached from one side of her dress to the other.

Hazel's eyes welled up with tears of joy as she felt a rush of emotions overwhelm her. She could hardly believe that the dress in front of her was meant for her, and the thought of wearing something so exquisite made her heart race. Her hands trembled slightly as she reached out to touch the delicate lace, a wave of gratitude and admiration for Arabella washing over her.

"I am relieved I found this dress when I did , but I had the tailor add a special detail to the back of it. The ivory dragon is my own little touch to drive a certain dragon at court a bit mad for how he has treated you, but the coloring was picked by me to help complement your skin tone, and the style is to help show off a few special features you have," Arabella admitted with a grin.

Unable to wipe her smile Hazel ran over to Arabella, wrapping her arms around her. "It is perfect."

Arabella beamed with pride as she stared at Hazel. "I figured if this banquet is in your honor, as Lady Hazel of Alexandria, then I wanted you to give them something amazing to talk about."

Pulling back, Hazel smiled wide before looking at the dress with a grin. "This will not only stop a certain lady of the court from gossiping, but it will definitely catch the eyes of everyone else," Hazel replied cheerfully. Her initial nerves about attending the banquet dissipated as she imagined herself in the stunning dress. The anticipation of making a grand entrance and silencing her critics filled her with newfound confidence. She felt a sense of empowerment, knowing that she would be the center of attention and admiration. With her necklace resting just above her cleavage.

Arabella gestured to the dress with a widened smile. "Well then, shall we get you ready before your uncle comes and escorts you?"

Hazel only nodded her head carefully so as not to mess up her hair that Arabella spent so much time on.

Not long after, Hazel was cinched up in her new dress as she smoothed out the fabric to fit perfectly around her curves.

Soon, there was a knock on her front door. After Arabella glided out of the room to retrieve their guest, Hazel put the dress on with the help of Arabella, smoothing out the fabric before looking in the mirror. She took in the drastic change from a simple village girl to a court lady with fine taste. Walking into the room led by Arabella, Archibald wore a black tunic with a crimson ribbon to tie it closed with a pair of crimson pants.

His eyes came up to look at his niece, widening at her appearance. His mouth opened slightly, and for a moment, he seemed at a loss for words. "Hazel, you look absolutely breathtaking," he finally managed to say, his voice filled with pride and admiration. Archibald faintly smiled, shaking his head before taking his niece's cheek into his rough calloused hand, and leaning on his black cane with the other. "You look just like your mother," Archibald commented with a silver lining in his eye.

Hazel mouth quirked into a subtle smile taking his hand and kissing it before she looked at him. "She would have loved this, wouldn't she?"

Archibald Let out a quiet chuckle.

"Oh yes. She would fuss over how you looked like a worried hen, before she told you how beautiful you are." Hazel laughed faintly at his words. A bittersweet smile crossed her face as she recalled her own motherless childhood. The memory of such tender care and affection brought a pang of sorrow, reminding her of the nurturing presence she longed for.

Archibald cupped Hazel's head, stroking her head, smiling down at his niece. "I'm sorry I haven't caught up with you after the garden. The king welcomed me back into the guard. Light duty, of course." He reassured her, tapping his leg..

Hazel's eyes drift down to Archibald's leg, the one that had been injured in battle years ago. She remembered the countless nights she sat by his side, helping him through the pain and recovery. "Is it still hurting you?" she asked softly, her voice tinged with the familiar worry she has carried for so long.

"I will need some of that elixir you make me soon."

Hazel chuckled, nodding before crossing her arms and looking at her uncle.

Their bond had always been strong, forged through shared hardships and countless moments of support. Archibald had been more than just an uncle to Hazel. he had been a father figure, protector, and confidant. Despite the years and the battles, their connection remained unbreakable, a testament to the love and resilience they both carried within them. "I can make some, but I don't want you exerting yourself. I'm surprised the king agreed with your leg."

Archibald laughed, shaking his head before kissing his niece's head. "I am doing just simple patrols. Kingsly said I can take guard shifts with him if I like till I am more confident with my leg."

Surprised that Kingsly offered that, she swallowed a bit, thinking about what transpired in his bedroom.

"He is a good man. I like that one," Archibald commented.

Hazel's cheeks flush slightly, and she quickly averted her gaze, trying to hide the rush of emotions that Archibald's comment stirred within her. She managed a small, appreciative smile, but her mind raced back to the intimate moments shared with Kingsly before she found out he was betrothed. "Yes, he is," She murmured in response., her voice barely above a whisper. Hazel's eyes widened before she gave a soft laugh, patting her uncle's chest. "That's only because he isn't Atticus."

"Exactly, he would be a good-" He started, but Hazel put her hand on his shoulder

"Uncle," she cut in, giving him a glance. Thankfully, Archibald got the hint she didn't want to talk about Kingsly any further.

"Shall we get you to your banquet?" Archibald asked as he fixed a strand that had fallen on her face.

Hazel nodded before she looks at Arabella, reaching over, giving her hand a squeeze before linking her arms with Archibald as he leads her to the banquet hall.

As they entered the banquet hall, Hazel was greeted by the warm glow of candlelight illuminating the grand room. The scent of roasted meats and freshly baked bread filled the air, mingling with the faint aroma of exotic spices. Laughter and the soft murmur of conversations created a lively and welcoming ambiance, making the hall feel both majestic and intimate.

The two tall pillars at the entryway were elegantly draped with cascading ivy and vibrant wisteria flowers, creating a natural archway of greenery and blossoms. In the center of the ballroom, a magnificent chandelier hung from the ceiling, its crystal facets sparkling above the deep cream-colored marble floor. The royal family crest, featuring a majestic lion with wings, was prominently displayed, encircled by delicate ivy and wisteria, symbolizing both strength and grace.

Hazel glided into the ballroom as her uncle led her further in. The soft strains of a string quartet floated through the air, their harmonious melodies weaving a tapestry of elegance and refinement. Each note resonated with the gentle plucking of violins, the rich tones of a cello, and the delicate harmony of a viola, creating a symphony that perfectly complemented the opulent surroundings. The music added an extra layer of enchantment to the evening, making Hazel feel as though she had stepped into a dream.

"I present Lady Hazel Hilliston of Alexandria, escorted by her uncle, Archibald Randall of Alexandria," the herald announced.

Hazel looked at her uncle, who only patted her hand in reassurance, recognizing how she was a little on edge before he guided her into the ballroom. She took a deep breath, her heart pounding in her chest as they stepped into the grand room filled with elegantly dressed guests. She felt a mix of awe and apprehension, the weight of so many eyes on her causing her to grip her uncle's arm a bit tighter. Despite her nerves, she managed a graceful smile, determined to make a good impression.

The ballroom was a stunning display of opulence, with crystal chandeliers casting a warm, golden light over the room. The walls were adorned with intricate tapestries and gilded mirrors, while the floor was a polished marble that gleamed underfoot. Lavish floral arrangements and elegant candelabras added to the grandeur, creating an atmosphere of timeless elegance.

There were three long tables ten feet long. At the table directly facing the door sat the royal family. Reed was dressed in fine ivory and gold attire. The king wore solid black attire and sat in the middle of the table to Queen Sage's right, and Kingsly sat on her left.

As Hazel's eyes turned to Kingsly, she felt her face flush. She saw his mouth slowly parting as their eyes met, but he said nothing.

He wore a gold and navy-blue tunic with golden lapels. Sitting beside him was the viper herself, Lady Duvessa, who glowered at Hazel as she approached the table.

At last, Hazel's eyes met Atticus, and her heart lurched. He stared at her with such hunger in his eyes. He had a hand across his lips, leaning on his elbow, sitting beside his father on the opposite side of his mother. Hazel wasn't sure if Atticus was growling or smirking, but the look in his eyes made her cheeks warm even more than before.

Atticus was dressed in a striking ensemble of black and red, his dark tunic embroidered with crimson threads that glimmered in the candlelight. His jet-black hair was neatly combed back, accentuating his chiseled features and intense gaze. The contrast between the deep red accents and the dark fabric gave him an air of both danger and allure, making it impossible for Hazel to look away.

Finally approaching the table, Archibald bowed best he could with his cane while Hazel curtsied to the royal family. Just as she and Arabella had practiced.

"It is an honor to be here, Your Highnesses. thank you for allowing me to join your court, King Kai," Hazel said softly, keeping her head lowered.

She was waiting to move until the king spoke, but instead, the sound of chair legs scraping against the hard floor filled her ears. Hazel didn't dare rise, till she felt a calloused hand under her chin raising her head. It was King Kai.

Her blue eyes locked with the woman's gray ones, and something in the depths of those cold, lifeless orbs made Hazel's skin crawl. It was an unsettling feeling, like an itch just beyond reach—she couldn't pinpoint why, but her instincts screamed that something was off. The woman's gaze wasn't just watchful; it was calculating, as if she were sizing Hazel up, weighing her like a pawn in some invisible game. There was a quiet malice behind those eyes, masked by a practiced smile that never quite reached them. Hazel couldn't quite put her finger on it, but the sensation coiled around her, tightening with every passing second. It was the feeling of being watched, studied, hunted—and no matter how hard Hazel tried to shake it off, the feeling lingered like a shadow, cold and persistent. The longer she stared into those eyes, the more her mind raced, searching for an explanation, but it was as if the woman's very presence was a puzzle that didn't quite fit, and it made Hazel's gut twist with a gnawing unease.

King Kai was renowned throughout the kingdom for his ruthless and unforgiving nature. His decrees were often harsh, and those who dared to defy him faced severe consequences. Many whispered tales of his cold-blooded decisions and actions, and the fear he instilled in both nobles and commoners alike, made his unexpectedly gentle gesture towards Hazel all the more unsettling.

"Oh, no. Lady Hazel, it's an honor to have you here at my court. Come sit beside Wylana's heir. I am sure you met my son, Prince Atticus," Kai purred out with pride as he offered Hazel his hand to lead her away from Archibald.

Atticus's fist-where she could see the tip of a dragon's tail wrapped around his wrist-was clenched so tight his knuckles were white. Hazel's mind raced as she took King Kai's hand, her heart pounding in her chest like a war drum. She couldn't shake the feeling of being a pawn in a game far beyond her understanding, every instinct screaming at her to be cautious. As she approached her seat beside Atticus, she tried to steady her breath, determined not to show the fear that threatened to consume her as he stood up pulling out.

"I hope you two enjoy tonight's festivities in each other's company." Kai's voice was laced with warning, as if, for some reason, if Hazel refused, she would be punished Hazel's thoughts swirled like a tempest as she took her seat, every muscle in her body tensing with unease. Despite her best efforts to appear composed, her mind was a battleground of fear and determination, each vying for control as she prepared to face whatever came next.

Atticus took Hazel's hand, kissing it softly. His lips on her skin sent hot shivers up her spine, drawing a smile from her lips.

"It's an honor, Lady Hazel. I hope you will allow me the honor of a dance tonight." Atticus' honey eyes met the swirls of ice blue with swirls of emerald.

Seeing his infamous feline smirk, Hazel swallows a bit. ""Of course, Prince Atticus," Hazel said, her voice tight with forced sweetness, though every word felt like it was being pulled from her against her will. She struggled to keep her tone civil, though her frustration simmered beneath the surface. It's not every day a lady gets to meet a handsome prince, she thought, the sarcasm almost slipping past her lips. But she swallowed it down, biting back the snark.

She forced a smile, keeping her eyes on the prince, doing her best not to let her annoyance show. "How could I possibly refuse such an... honorable invitation?" Her words were as polite as she could manage, though the edge in her voice was almost imperceptible.

Despite the irritation gnawing at her, she agreed to the dance, the polite gesture feeling like a compromise she was willing to make—at least for King Kai's sake. The prince's rudeness still lingered in her thoughts, but there was something in his eyes now, a subtle change that made her hesitate. She had glimpsed something... different in him, a flicker of gentleness that contradicted the arrogant shell he wore so well. Hazel found herself begrudgingly curious, even if it irked her to admit it.

With clapping of the king's hands, the musicians played louder, and the staff brought out various platters of food for the attendees. The aroma of roasted pig, veggies, and potatoes filled the ballroom as servants brought pitchers of wine.

The table was laden with an array of dishes, from succulent roasted chicken and buttery mashed potatoes to vibrant, colorful salads and freshly baked bread. There were also platters of cheese, a variety of dips, and an assortment of desserts, including a rich chocolate cake and a bowl of fresh fruit.

Once the food was set down and Hazel's goblet was filled with the finest wine she had ever smelt, Hazel waited until King Kai began to eat, not wanting to upset the order of things in court. Her stomach churned with a mixture of excitement and nervousness, and her hands trembled slightly as she held her goblet. She couldn't help but marvel at the opulence surrounding her, feeling both out of place and deeply honored. As King Kai took his first bite, Hazel felt a wave of relief wash over her, and she eagerly yet cautiously enjoyed the feast. King Kai clung a fork to his goblet to get the room's attention as he rose up. Raising his goblet he looked at Kingsly.

"To my son Kingsly, may your marriage to Lady Duvessa be all you hope and dream for," Kai proclaimed to his court, who cheered for the happy couple. Duvessa stroked Kingsly's arm before smiling widely, drinking in all the praise and affection from the applauding guests. The court erupted into a symphony of clinking glasses, hearty cheers, and warm applause, filling the grand hall with a palpable sense of joy and celebration. Guests exchanged congratulatory smiles and nods, some even rising from their seats to offer toasts of their own. The atmosphere buzzed with excitement as conversations turned to the forthcoming wedding and the promising future of the young couple.

Hazel bit back the growl that threatened to escape her throat, her irritation flaring at the thought of Kinglsy letting Duvessa kiss him like that. The image of it twisted her stomach, and she could feel the sharp sting of betrayal gnawing at her. In her eyes, Duvessa was nothing more than a snake—slithering and manipulative, always lurking in the shadows with a smile that could turn venomous in an instant. She couldn't understand why Kingsly couldn't see it, but she picked up her goblet, raising it as the others did.

The king then turned to Atticus and Hazel with a grin on his face. This not only made Hazel straighten up, but also Atticus. "And to Lady Hazel of Alexandria, who has traveled very far to join us. Welcome to my home." Once again, there were cheers and applause, but then the king cleared his throat, and the room fell silent, with all eyes turning expectantly towards King Kai. "I also have a very exciting announcement."

The air was thick with anticipation, and the flickering candlelight seemed to dance in rhythm with the collective heartbeat of the court. Hazel felt the weight of the moment pressing down on her, the curiosity and intrigue of the gathered nobles almost tangible.

Atticus leaned toward his father and ground out something Hazel couldn't hear. However, whatever he said warranted Atticus a glare from his father. Hazel's heart pounded in her chest as she witnessed the tense exchange, a knot of anxiety tightening in her stomach. She couldn't help but wonder what Atticus had said, fearing it might complicate her already precarious position at court. Despite her rising unease, she maintained a composed exterior, her eyes fixed on King Kai, waiting for an announcement that could change everything.

"Hazel and Atticus, rise for me," the king continued, now looking directly at Hazel with an intense stare.

Despite Atticus's displeasure, he rose to his feet, offering Hazel his hand. His look was apologetic, which made Hazel's nerves shake as she slowly took his hand and stood.

"My sons went to Alexandria to rid the land of the Netherian people, but instead my son and heir has brought home the Ivory Fawn."

A roar of cheering and applause roared through the ballroom, but Hazel's eyes widened in shock. The crowd's reaction was a mix of astonishment and jubilation, their cheers echoing off the grand hall's walls. Cheers rang out, quickly giving way to a murmur of whispers, as noblemen and women exchanged speculative glances. The air buzzed with a mixture of admiration and curiosity, each hushed conversation swirling with intrigue.

Hazel felt the weight of their expectations, realizing that her newfound title as the Ivory Fawn would bring not only honor but also scrutiny and challenges she could scarcely imagine.

This ball was only to have welcomed her as a newly appointed court lady to Wylana, not announce her as the Ivory Fawn. Hazel could feel Atticus's anger rising in his grip as it was so tight she thought it would break her hand.

"Now we wine and dine in honor of the Ivory Fawn," King Kai bellowed out before sitting down to devour his food and wine.

The atmosphere shifted, charged with a mix of excitement and curiosity, as the crowd buzzed with speculation. Hazel could feel the weight of the attention on her, each whisper from the nobles buzzing in her ears—some filled with admiration, others with suspicion. But underneath it all, a sense of unease settled in, both within her and Atticus. The moment King Kai's proclamation rang out, revealing her as the Ivory Fawn, Hazel knew there was no more hiding. The truth was out, and every eye in the room would be watching her now, waiting for a slip. Her heart raced, the realization sinking in that she would need to stay vigilant from this point on. Beside her, Atticus's grip tightened, his own internal turmoil evident in the tension of his hand, as the crowd's whispers grew louder, each murmur unraveling more questions than answers.

Music began, as did the conversations around them as people feasted. No longer feeling hungry thanks to the growing storm of emotion in her chest, Hazel turned to look at Atticus, putting her hand on his hand as her throat bobbed, trying to swallow the ever-growing lump. "I would very much like that dance." His grip loosed before her hand was brought to his lips, kissing it as if he was thanking her silently.

Chapter Twenty-Eight

Hazel

Atticus lead Hazel to the dance floor with such grace. The music was a gentle waltz, enveloping the dancers, that joined them on the dance floor, in its romantic melody. The floor was a sea of swirling gowns and sharp male attire, creating a mesmerizing display of movement and color.

"Is it too late to tell you I don't really know how to dance? I only know dances from Alexandria," Hazel admitted, but only got a smirk from Atticus.

He chuckled softly, his eyes twinkling with mischief. "Don't worry," he whispered, pulling her closer. "Just follow my lead, princess, and we'll make our own steps."

Resting his hand on her hip while he raised the other he was still holding up. "There you go, just like that, Princess. we will give them something else to discuss." Atticus purred.

Hazel gasped faintly as he pulled her in close, arching her back as she looked up at him. Slowly, she took a deep breath to envelop herself in the music. The only time Hazel had ever really danced back in Alexandria was around the festival fires.

She remembered the vibrant festivals, where laughter echoed through the streets and the air was thick with the scent of spices and blooming flowers. The villagers would gather around the bonfires, their faces illuminated by the warm glow as they moved to the rhythmic beats of drums and the melodious tunes of flutes. Hazel could almost feel the heat of the flames and the joy of those carefree nights when she danced with abandon under the starlit sky.

Her throat bobbed softly as Atticus gazed down at her, as if the pools of honey in his eyes were now taking her in more fully in that dress as they scan down her body then back to meet her eyes. Just then, Hazel's eyes flicked down to the intricate design of her gown, and the realization hit her like a sudden wave. She and Atticus were dressed in the same color palette—deep, regal shades of crimson red and gold, the hues strikingly similar, almost identical. Her gaze shifted to him, taking in how the colors complemented his features, the way the fabric draped over his form with an ease that made him seem even more princely. She couldn't help but feel a twinge of admiration for how perfectly Arabella had executed the look. The woman had an eye for detail, that was undeniable.

But then, the flicker of irritation crept in, souring the moment. Hazel's jaw tightened, and the warmth she'd felt toward the craftsmanship of her gown turned cold. *Of course,* she thought bitterly, *Arabella would do something like this.* She couldn't deny the elegance of the design, but the fact that it matched Atticus's so perfectly—especially considering how much he grated on her nerves—left a bad taste in her mouth. It wasn't just the clothes, it was the implication, the idea that she and Atticus were somehow linked through this shared attire, as though they were meant to be seen together. Hazel wasn't sure why it bothered her so much, but she couldn't shake the sense of unfairness. After all, Atticus was still very much not her favorite person, and seeing him in the same colors only served to remind her of that fact.

Hazel felt a rush of warmth and excitement as she danced with him, he fell so easily into step with him as he leads her. the familiarity of past dances blending with the thrill of the present moment. Though the setting was different, with its opulent decor and formal attire, her connection with Atticus was undeniable. As their movements became more synchronized, Hazel's initial nerves melted away, replaced by a blossoming confidence and a sense of belonging. She wondered if it was a simple coincidence or if Arabella had secretly planned it for her and this dragon prince to match.

Soon, they glided around the dance floor as if it was just them. Her icy blue eyes never came off his as her heart raced in her chest. Feeling Atticus's hand at the small of her back, holding her so close in a waltz, a heat crept over her cheeks and ears as she followed him as best she could.

"One, two, three, one, two, three," Atticus quietly repeated to her, helping prevent Hazel from stepping on his feet as they floated through the ballroom.

Hazel was now once again seeing the same man she saw in her bedchambers after the queen had visited her. Was this the real Prince Atticus ? Or was this just another part of his game of the Wylannian Immortal Dragon? Hazel's mind whirled with the memories of their encounters, and she couldn't help but feel uncertain. Was this genuine affection she sensed from Atticus, or was he merely playing another role in his intricate game? As much as she wanted to surrender to the magic of the moment, a part of her remained guarded, wary of the dragon prince's true intentions.

Whoever she was dancing with now was beginning to like this side of him. It wasn't so rough and mean to her, which was, for once, refreshing.

Soon, the music became livelier, with drums and a gorgeous singer. A song she was familiar with from back home began to play—one she had danced countless times to over and over when they played it in Alexandria. It was a song made to woo men into a dance back home. Hazel's heart swelled with nostalgia as the familiar melody filled the ballroom. Each note brought back cherished memories of carefree days and laughter with her friends and Darius in Alexandria. Her feet moved effortlessly, guided by the music, and for a brief moment, all her worries about Atticus and his intentions melted away, replaced by sheer joy and the comfort of home.

This time, Hazel let the music completely consume her. Her steps became more confident and fluid, matching the rhythm perfectly. She twirled gracefully, her skirts flowing around her legs like a cascading waterfall. Every movement was imbued with a newfound grace and freedom, as if the music had unlocked a part of her soul she had long forgotten. Letting out a joyous laugh at the sweet memory, she leaned her head back, laughing softly for once now, enjoying herself as she felt the music filling her bones and senses. Everything around her no longer mattered, as it melted away from her.

Soon, Hazel stepped back, feeling the music take hold of her, and began moving her hips with a fluid grace, lifting her skirt slightly as she swayed to the rhythm. She let herself get lost in the movement, the music urging her to forget about the crowd and the tension that had been building. As she danced, her eyes flicked briefly to Atticus, and she couldn't help but notice the surprised look on his face. His brows furrowed for a second, as if trying to process the unexpected turn in the evening.

Then, to her surprise, the corner of his mouth lifted into a grin, and he took a step toward her, mirroring her movements with an ease that left her momentarily stunned. His footwork was flawless, and the way he matched her rhythm was almost effortless. Hazel blinked in surprise, watching as Atticus, the same prince who had seemed so arrogant and stiff just moments ago, seamlessly joined her in the dance. She hadn't expected him to know the steps, let alone execute them so gracefully. For a moment, their eyes locked, and Hazel could see the amusement dancing in his gaze, as if he were enjoying the fact that she hadn't pegged him for this. Despite herself, she felt a small smile tug at her lips, impressed by his skill—though she would never admit it aloud.

Her entire body fell in rhythm as she danced before finally looking to meet Atticus's eyes, which were not only filled with that hunger she saw before. Hazel's heart skipped a beat as she noticed a new intensity in them. Was it admiration or something darker? Her mind raced with questions, but she pushed them aside, determined to savor this moment of unbridled joy.

Hazel swore there was a faint purring coming from Atticus before he reached over, took her hand, and spun her into his chest. Her back was now pressed against him, and his hand was on her shoulder, pinning her arm across her chest. Atticus's other hand was holding her arm across her waist, as his hips matched the rhythm of hers.

In this intimate embrace, Hazel felt a connection with Atticus that transcended their previous encounters. The shared rhythm of their movements spoke volumes, hinting at deeper and unspoken emotions between them. This dance was not just a fleeting moment of joy, but a pivotal point that blurred the lines between their past conflicts and the potential for a future together. As Hazel inhaled the intoxicating scent of bergamot and cedar emanating from Atticus, a wave of warmth and comfort washed over her. A serene sense of belonging enveloped her, making his arms feel like a sanctuary .

This wasn't how a lady and prince should dance outside the privacy of the chambers, but it wasn't just Hazel who didn't care. The guest who were watching them dance murmured, their whispers a mixture of intrigue and disapproval. Such a public display of affection could not go unnoticed in a society governed by strict decorum and propriety. Hazel and Atticus's actions risked scandal and potential repercussions from the court.

Hazel was so lost in the music that the melody wrapped her in a warm embrace, unaware that Atticus was drinking every bit of her as she danced. One of his hands slid down her body, feeling every bit of that lace layer from her ribs down to her waist, stopping to rest on her hips as they swayed so effortlessly.

Feeling his hand now on her hips , freeing the hand on her shoulder. Her hand reached down to brush his hand as her hips swayed. Than , Atticus releases her hand across her waist to rest it on her other hip. Hazel trailed her hand up her body, coming behind her head to cup on the back of his neck.

Pulling him closer to her as they danced, not realizing her dancing was slowly becoming his undoing. Hazel's mind raced with a whirlwind of emotions, torn between the propriety she had been taught and her undeniable attraction for Atticus. She wondered if this moment was a fleeting illusion or the beginning of something profound, something that could alter the course of both their lives.

Hazel leaned her head back against the strong chest of the man, feeling his heart beat match the drums of the music. Feeling his hot breath against her neck, shivers shot down her body, relaxing into him more.

Hazel didn't want this side of Atticus to go away and vowed to do whatever she could to keep this side of him with her. Here, dancing with her, like nothing else in the room mattered.

"That's it, princess, let the music consume you." Atticus's chest vibrates from how low his voice dropped..

It made Hazel's body warm like a fire coming alive in her. Inhaling nothing but cedar and bergamot, she whispered a faint moan from her lips, and as a faint growl escaped from Atticus, it sent another wave of shivers through her body. It was as if her moan had stirred something primal in him, a raw desire that matched her own. The sound made her pulse quicken, intensifying the fiery connection between them.

Suddenly, Atticus spun Hazel out of his arms, causing her dress to fan out in an array of red and ivory. The light from the chandelier illuminated every detail of her dress. Before the fabric could fall back down to its original place, Atticus spun Hazel back into his arms. This time, their faces were so close that they shared breaths. Hazel's breath caught in her throat as she met Atticus's intense gaze, feeling both exhilaration and trepidation. The hunger in his eyes mirrored the longing she felt, but also reminded her of the vulnerability she feared. Despite the whirlwind of emotions, she couldn't deny the magnetic pull between them, making it almost impossible to look away.

"What can I say? I have a good dance partner." Hazel grinned for once, actually enjoying herself as she stared into his eyes, unable to wipe away the wide, joyous smile on her face.

When the song came to an end. Hazel looked to in her surroundings, seeing the entire ballroom's eyes on them, including Kingsly, whose expression was nothing but anger.

Hazel's heart sank as she met his furious gaze, her joyous smile faltering. The weight of his disapproval was palpable, casting a shadow over her moment of happiness.

She tried catching her breath as she realized the scene they had just caused.]

Scanning the ballroom, Hazel turned her head to see Atticus bowing before her. As he straightened, he took her hand and kissed it gently. A rush of warmth spread through her as his lips brushed against her skin, a stark contrast to the cold, judgmental stares from the onlookers. She managed a soft, appreciative smile and a curtsy, her fingers trembling slightly in his grasp.

Despite the tension in the room, his act of chivalry bolstered her courage, reminding her that she wasn't alone in facing the night. Atticus's unwavering support and his public display of affection gave Hazel a surge of confidence she hadn't felt in a long time. It was as if his strength and assurance were transferred to her, fortifying her resolve to face the judgmental eyes around them.

After the dance, Atticus led her back to their table, the murmurs of the crowd still lingering in the air as they moved through the room. Hazel could feel the weight of all those eyes on them, their whispers now sharper, more curious. She could feel the tension creeping back into her muscles, a tightness she hadn't fully noticed until now.

When they reached the table, Atticus pulled out her chair with a courteous smile, but Hazel, needing a moment to herself, gave a small shake of her head.

"I think I need some fresh air," she murmured, her voice soft but firm.

Atticus seemed to hesitate, a flicker of concern crossing his features, but Hazel was already stepping away. She didn't want to explain, didn't want to get caught up in more conversation right now. She just needed space.

As the minutes passed, she felt a sense of clarity slowly emerging from the chaos within. It was slightly chilly, but nothing she wasn't used to in Alexandria. Admiring the moonlight hitting the ocean, Hazel couldn't help but watch the waves ripple in the moonlight. Feeling the air hit her overheating body, it was a nice welcoming feel against her skin to help cool her off.

She pondered her growing feelings for Atticus, torn between the excitement of this new connection and the fear of repeating past heartbreaks. The push and pull of her emotions were exhausting, leaving her unsure whether to open her heart or retreat behind her walls. Hazel knew she had to find a balance between vulnerability and self-preservation.

The trees swayed in the breeze as the soft romantic music played in the ballroom, which was a light humming from where she stood. Filling her lungs with the cool winter air, she slowed her heart and mind from the spectacle that Hazel and Atticus had just caused. Playing with the diamond necklace Arabella had her wear tonight instead of her mother's, Hazel couldn't help but think of her mother and father. Their love story had always been her guiding star, a beacon of hope that true love existed and could endure. Yet, it also served as a reminder of the high stakes involved in matters of the heart.

As she gazed at the sparkling necklace, she wondered if she could have such unwavering devotion, or if her fears would always hold her back. Hazel pondered if her parents were proud of or disappointed in her for what she was doing, and what they would think of Prince Atticus and her together.

What was she thinking? She had been warned by Kingsly of how cruel Atticus was, and had heard stories of the awful things he had committed on the battlefield. Ignoring Kingsly's advice could lead Hazel down a path of heartbreak and regret, shattering the fragile hope she held for a future with Atticus. She had to weigh the risks carefully, understanding that a wrong choice could cost her more than just her heart. Sighing softly, Hazel shook the idea of Atticus out of her mind, turning to go back to the ball.

Her eyes laid upon a beautiful woman with long black hair pulled up in a bun, wearing the most gorgeous jade green dress Hazel had ever seen. It shimmered under the soft lights of the ballroom, capturing her attention like a beacon. It wasn't just the beauty of the dress that struck her. It was the way the woman carried herself with such grace and confidence.

It was like the woman glided on the water as she walked over to Hazel with a faint smile. "You caused quite a scene in there, Lady Hazel. I saw you come out here, and I wanted to introduce myself formally." This woman's voice was not as soft as Duvessa's, but she held herself more confident in her words than Lady Duvessa's. "I am Sybilla Asher, a scribe from the castle Andromeda, where the Aestival temple resigns."

Then it clicked. This was the woman Hazel was supposed to learn everything about her mother's people from. Her heart quickened at the realization, and her curiosity piqued by the unexpected encounter. She felt a mix of excitement and nervousness, knowing that Sybilla could hold the key to understanding her heritage.

Sybilla was not as Hazel expected. She figured the one who was going to teach her would be an older woman. "You know about my mother's family," Hazel breathed out.

"What do you mean by your mother's family?" Sybilla tilted her head in question.

Hazel studied this woman closely, not sure she could trust her, before taking a deep breath. "I can tell you everything once we are in a quiet place, maybe the temple?" Her hesitation was palpable, revealing her lineage was a delicate matter, fraught with potential danger. Yet, the desire to understand her roots outweighed her fear, compelling her to cautiously extend an olive branch to Sybilla.

Chuckling softly, Sybilla nodded in agreement before joining Hazel on the balcony overlooking the sea. The two women stood there quietly, admiring the calm and quiet scenery together.

"Hazel, there is something I must tell you." Sybilla finally broke the silence.

She turned her head to look at the lady in jade, but seeing her expression made all alarms go off in her head Her mind buzzed with a thousand possibilities, each more unsettling than the last. Taking a deep breath, she steeled herself, ready to hear whatever revelation Sybilla had to share.

Sybilla looked conflicted, as if trying to find the right words. She painted worry across her brow. It caused Hazel to straighten back, as if readying herself for all this bliss to vanish with a few simple words. It wasn't until the ladies heard a male clear his throat at the archway doors that drew their attention from each other.

It was Kingsly.

Hazel's heart skipped a beat, her palms growing clammy at the sight of him. She forced a smile, trying to mask the unease that churned in her stomach. Their last encounter had left an awkward tension between them, and she wasn't sure how to navigate this unexpected, private meeting.

Sybilla's eyes went from concerned to sharp as a blade as the prince made his way to Hazel and Sybilla. Kingsly's eyes were locked on Hazel, taking her in as she stood in the moonlight.

"Prince Kingsly, wouldn't your fiance be looking for you?" Sybilla chimed, crossing her arms across her chest with a glare that Hazel would never want to be on the receiving end of.

The atmosphere in the room felt thick with unspoken words and simmering emotions. The tension was palpable, as if the very air between them crackled with electricity. Hazel's forced smile faltered slightly, and the silence that followed Sybilla's pointed question hung heavily around them, amplifying the weight of the moment.

"She is currently cleaning herself up in a powder room. She claims she wants to look perfect for our dance together." Kingsly narrowed his gaze to Sybilla, cocking his head slightly. "Besides, I came to speak with Lady Hazel privately, if she would allow me." Finally, his gaze came to Hazel, and her heart raced in her chest.

Hazel felt a surge of panic mixed with curiosity, and she glanced nervously at Sybilla, seeking some form of silent support or guidance. Despite the turmoil inside her, she nodded slowly, her voice barely a whisper, "Of course, Your Highness." Hazel has been hoping to avoid him since their encounter in his chambers. "It's alright, tell Atticus to save me another dance." Hazel reached over to Sybilla to rest her hand on the lady scribe's shoulder.

"Of course, Lady Hazel. Shout if you need anything." Sybilla bowed her head and gave Kingsly one final glare before she made her way inside to find Atticus.

Watching Sybilla leave, Hazel turned her back to Kingsly, looking out to the sea, wishing she was down there instead of on this balcony with him. Her mind was a whirlwind of emotions, as she still felt betrayed by the news of Kingsly's engagement to Duvessa, a sting that was only made sharper by the prince's attention.

Feeling a warm cloak being draped across her back, she looked to see it was Kingsly as he now stood beside her. Shrugging it off, Hazel steps away from him, taking a deep breath; the last thing Hazel needs to add to her plate is Kingsly being romantic, or even overly friendly with her. It would not turn out well for either of them if Lady Duvessa or Atticus were to come out to the balcony. Hazel turned to face Kingsly, her eyes burning with a mix of defiance and vulnerability. "Your Highness, I appreciate your concern, but I think it's best if we maintain our distance," she said firmly, stepping further away to create a clear boundary. Determined to regain her composure, she excused herself, moving swiftly towards the ballroom to find Sybilla and Atticus.

"Hazel, I-" Kingsly began to speak, but Hazel quickly turned to look at him, stopping in her approach towards the ballroom.

"How long were you going to wait to tell me you were engaged? You let me kiss you and almost took me—"

"Hazel, please—" Kingsly cut in, but she once more put her hand up to silence him, feeling naïve about what she had done.

She was overwhelmed by a storm of conflicting emotions, ranging from hurt to frustration to betrayal, and tears threatened to spill over. Hazel's voice trembled as she struggled to maintain her composure.

"Kingsly, you are supposed to marry Lady Duvessa, yet you let me make a fool of myself by kissing you and almost..." She trailed off, remembering how Kingsly hovered over her, just like Darius had so many times. Shaking her head, Hazel took a deep breath and let out a shaky exhale.

"Hazel, I am going to call it off. I don't care about Lady Duvessa, I -" Kingsly began reaching for Hazel, but she stepped out of his reach. "—I only agreed to the engagement out of family obligation," he explained, his voice filled with desperation. "My heart has always been with you, Hazel. I can't go through with a marriage to someone I don't love, especially when I know what we could have together."

"You know nothing about me, Kingsly. You just met me! You can't tell me you care about me more than the lady you are betrothed to," Hazel ground out. Hazel's mind was a whirlwind of thoughts, each one clashing with the next. Her heart yearned for the possibility of true love, yet her rational side screamed at her to protect herself from further pain. Hazel wished Sybilla didn't leave her alone with him. "I have been through enough in these last three weeks. The last thing I need is to have any more enemies that wish me dead than I already have because I'm this so-called Ivory Fawn who is supposed to save all of Wylana. Especially not here at court, where I want to find peace after being raised in a village where we had very few peaceful days," Hazel confessed as her voice wobbled.

Growing up in that village had been a constant struggle for survival, with every day bringing new challenges and dangers. The hardships she faced there had shaped her into the resilient yet guarded person she was now. Despite its beauty, the village held too many painful memories, and Hazel longed for a place where she could finally let her guard down and find solace.

Kingsly's face softened into not only surprise at her confession, but melted into what appeared to be anger. His eyes narrowed, and his jaw clenched, a storm of emotions brewing within him. "And you think being with my brother won't cause you to collect more enemies? I saw how you two were dancing; he was showing you off as his shiny new toy. You're both practically wearing the same outfits!" Kingsly roared in anger.

Hazel flinched at Kingsly's harsh words, her cheeks flushing with a mix of embarrassment and anger. She took a step back, crossing her arms defensively over her chest. "It's not like that," she retorted, her voice steady, despite the turmoil inside her. "You have no right to judge me or assume my intentions." Her breathing picked up again as she stepped back from Kingly, reaching towards her chest as if she could find her mother's necklace.

"He is not good for you, Hazel. I warned you already how cruel and harsh he could be. Atticus is nothing but a soulless monster who doesn't care about who he hurts in the process of getting what he wants. If you think for once he cares about you, why don't you ask how the trail of women he has seduced into his bed makes them think he cares about them just to leave them brokenhearted?" Kingsly roared once more before he gripped her arm, where the bruise that Darius had left was still healing.

Hazel winced in pain as Kingsly's grip tightened on her arm, the throbbing bruise reminding her of past wounds, both physical and emotional. Struggling to pull away, her voice quivering as she cried out, "Let go of me, Kingsly!" She yanked her arm away from him before the sound of a slap echoed across the winter night air.

Kingsly held his face, growling even more in anger before the general prince finally snapped. His eyes blazed with fury as he took a menacing step closer to Hazel, his hand still pressed against his reddened cheek. "You dare strike me?" he hissed, his voice low and dangerous. In a swift motion, he grabbed her other arm, his grip like iron, and pulled her face close to his, their breaths mingling in the cold night air.

Hazel pulled her face away from him, trying to push him off her. Her heart pounded in her chest, the icy grip of fear wrapping around her as Kingsly's rage engulfed them both. Her mind raced, seeking any possible escape from his overpowering presence. Tears welled up in her eyes, blurring her vision as she whispered desperately, "Please, Kingsly, let me go."

His lips trailed down to her neck, hovering right over the healing bite mark. Hazel's body stiffened in terror, every muscle tensing as she felt Kingsly's breath on her neck. She shuddered, a wave of revulsion washing over her, and with all the strength she could muster, she tried to twist away from his grasp.

Her voice, barely more than a choked sob, pleaded, "Stop, Kingsly, please..." Hazel gasped as the memory of Darius crashed into her. The pain of him ripping into her neck, the feel of blood trickling down it. She closed her eyes, trying to shake away the memories, failing as his lips trailed down her neck to her shoulder, ravaging her.

Each touch from Kingsly brought back the agony and helplessness she felt with Darius, fueling her determination to escape. Motivated by the haunting recollections, Hazel's struggle intensified, and she fought back with renewed vigor, driven by the need to never relive that torment again.

Yet again, she couldn't push him off her, just as Hazel couldn't push Darius off her. The fact that he was stronger and taller than her made her feel weak and useless.

Then he stopped. Hazel's breathing was heavy as tears flooded her face. Her mind raced, drawing disturbing parallels between Kingsly and Darius. The way Kingsly's grip tightened mercilessly, his breath hot and invasive against her skin, mirrored the haunting memories of Darius' cruelty. Both men reveled in her helplessness, feeding off her fear and pain, and Hazel couldn't shake the terrifying realization that she was trapped in a nightmarish cycle.

A flash of silver in the moonlight caught her attention. It was a sword; there was a sword to Kingsly's neck. Hazel's focus followed the blade up to the hilt, where her eyes fell upon the White Dragoness. Relief washed over her, momentarily eclipsing her terror, and she allowed herself to believe that rescue was at hand.

Seeing the silver sword at Kingsly's neck gave her the courage to hold on just a little longer, knowing she might be free from his grasp. Ardnaxela was dressed in a bold black dress that made her look like a goddess of death. Her long, silvery hair flowed like liquid moonlight down her back, contrasting sharply with the darkness of her outfit. Her eyes, a piercing shade of embers, glinted with a fierce determination. The intricate patterns embroidered in silver thread on her dress shimmered with every movement she made, giving her an ethereal, almost otherworldly presence. Her shoulders were decorated with dragon-scale armor lapels connected by a black choker of a dragon charm hanging from it where two sheer capes of fabric laid loosely down her side, ending at the end of her dress.

"I suggest to you release the girl, General Kingly, ," she growled at the prince, and after a moment, he released her.

Hazel stepped out of his reach, hastily moving toward Ardnaxela, whose free arm guided the fawn behind her, protectively hiding her. Hazel's heart pounded in her chest, a mix of fear and relief washing over her. Her hands trembled slightly as she clung to Ardnaxela's dress. Kingsly slowly turned to face Ardnaxela,. His eyes narrowed as he met her unwavering gaze, a silent battle of wills unfolding between them. Ardnaxela's posture remained rigid and unyielding, while Kingsly's jaw clenched in barely suppressed anger. The air between them crackled with palpable tension, each daring the other to make the next move.

Holding his hands up, Kingsly looked at the tip of the sword, now aimed at his chest, then to the dragon's golden eyes. "I see you are far too comfortable in your position at Ardnaxela to have the audacity to point that needle at your commander," Kingsly warned the Dragoness, who only scoffed, tilting her head back.

A low, rumbling laugh escaped her throat, echoing through the early winter air. "Comfortable, you say?" she taunted, her golden eyes gleaming with a dangerous light. "I would be more concerned about your own comfort, General. Prince Atticus put me in charge of Lady Hazel's safety. His orders trump your rank. Be lucky I point my sword at you, and not your brother . You remember the last time you were on the receiving end of one of his attacks, don't you?"

Kingsly's eyes darkened, his lips curling into a snarl. "You dare speak of that incident?" he hissed, taking a step forward, only to be met with the unwavering point of Ardnaxela's blade pressing against his chest.

"One more step, and you'll find yourself regretting it," she warned, her voice a cold whisper that sent shivers down Hazel's spine. Kingsly's expression softened, and even though his hands fell, Ardnaxela didn't relax. "I'd get back to Lady Duvessa if I were you. Wouldn't want your father finding out about this and how you're jeopardizing your engagement with her," Ardnaxela crowed with satisfaction, knowing she won.

Kingsly's face paled, and his eyes flickered with a mixture of fear and fury. His hands clenched into fists at his sides, but he didn't dare move them. With a final, scathing look at Ardnaxela, he turned on his heel and stormed into the ballroom, his retreat marked by the echo of his boots against the stone floor.

Hazel felt as if she finally could breathe, but it came out in a sob as she remembered how Kingsly touched her just as Darius had. Ardnaxela turned toward her, pulling her into her chest with one arm . Hazel's body trembled as she clung to Ardnaxela, her sobs wracking her frame with the force of a storm. Her mind was a whirlwind of memories and emotions, each one more painful than the last.

A servant came out to see what was going on as Hazel and Ardnaxela made their way towards the doors. Hazel's heart raced with an overwhelming fear that gripped her it so tight she thought it would explode from such tight pressure. Each memory of Darius's touch was like a brand, searing her soul and leaving her feeling powerless and violated. Yet, she knew she couldn't let her fear control her. she had responsibilities and people who depended on her strength.

"Find Prince Atticus and Lady Sybilla, tell them I took the Ivory Fawn back to her chambers because she isn't feeling well," Ardnaxela demanded before she led Hazel away from prying eyes before leading her to her chambers.

Chapter Twenty-Nine

Atticus

Atticus took a glass of wine from a platter as a server walked by. As he sipped the Cabernet sauvignon, his mind wandered back to the softness of Hazel's hand in his and the way her laughter had filled the air around them. The memory of their dance together lingered as a reminder of the unspoken connection that grew stronger with every shared glance.

He couldn't help but wonder if she felt the same magnetic pull, or if it was just a fleeting moment in the midst of the evening's festivities. He took a large sip of his wine before plucking a piece of fudge from the dessert table and popping it into his mouth. The rich, velvety chocolate melted on his tongue, its sweetness mingling perfectly with a hint of sea salt that added an unexpected depth. The creamy texture made him close his eyes in pleasure, momentarily distracting him from his thoughts of Hazel.

Turning to overlook the ballroom , his eyes scanned the guest as they mingled among one another. Occasionally his eyes spotted a few guest whose eyes lingered on him with disapproval.

Atticus knew very well how inappropriate his dance with Hazel was, but he honestly didn't care. The connection he felt with her was unlike anything he had experienced before. The intensity of their shared moments overshadowed any societal expectations or consequences. For Atticus, the feeling of being truly alive in her presence was worth any potential fallout.

He was enjoying himself for once, attending one of these obnoxious events. Atticus never cared much for being shown off like a prized pony. He often found these gatherings to be superficial, filled with empty chatter and forced smiles. The extravagance and pomp were a stark contrast to his preference for authenticity and meaningful connections. Yet, midst the glittering façade, Hazel had been a rare gem, making the evening unexpectedly memorable.

His mind kept wandering back to the smell of vanilla and sandalwood that still lingered in his nose. Hazel smelt so good he wanted to devour her in more ways than one. The way her body felt beneath his hands, he wondered what her bare skin would feel like beneath his hands. His heart raced with a mixture of desire and trepidation, the pounding in his chest almost drowning out the ambient noise of the party. He felt a primal urge to be closer to her, to explore the depths of their connection beyond the constraints of polite society. Every thought of Hazel ignited a fire within him, a yearning that was both exhilarating and terrifying in its intensity. He wondered how soft her skin was, how her lips tasted, and how a few other things tested on his lips.

What was he thinking? He couldn't let himself get attached to her. Not when she could possibly die and never come back. The consequences of his attachment to Hazel loomed large in his mind. Atticus knew that allowing himself to fall deeper into this infatuation could lead to heartbreak, especially if circumstances tore them apart. The fear of losing her gnawed at Atticus like a relentless specter, whispering doubts into the quiet corners of his mind. It wasn't just the thought of her absence that unsettled him—it was the certainty of the hollow, gaping wound it would leave in his soul. He had suffered loss before, had felt the slow, suffocating ache of grief coil around his rib cage and squeeze until he could barely breathe. But *her*—losing *her*—was something else entirely. It wasn't just pain he feared; it was the unraveling of something intrinsic to who he was, as if she had become so deeply woven into his existence that without her, he wouldn't know where he ended and the emptiness began.

The fleeting moments of joy, those stolen seconds of laughter and warmth, were intoxicating, yet tainted by the knowledge that they could never last. He questioned whether it was foolish to indulge in them, to allow himself the luxury of happiness when he knew the inevitable end would be agony. And yet, despite his best efforts to guard his heart, to keep himself detached, he found that he could not stop *choosing* her. Again and again, he reached for her, drawn to her like a moth to a flame, knowing full well he might be burned but unable to resist the light she brought into his world.

What terrified him most wasn't just the idea of losing her—it was the knowledge that he would never recover if he did.

Sighing, Atticus raked his hand through his hair before feeling his pants straining. Clearing his throat, he straightened up as if his mind wasn't wondering about things he would do to Hazel in the privacy of a bedchamber. his mind was a battlefield of conflicting emotions.

The best thing for them both was for him to maintain his distance. If he didn't guide Hazel like the prophecy said, then maybe she wouldn't die when she became the Ivory Fawn, which made logical sense to him.

Hearing someone approaching him, he turned his head, taking in Sybilla with her everyday jade green attire. Atticus bowed her head to her. "Glad to see you can make it, my friend, enjoying the party?" he said softly, grinning at her, knowing she wasn't much for fancy balls, either.

A faint chuckle escaped her lips as she crossed her hands in front of her with a devious grin.

"I see you enjoyed your dance with Lady Hazel, although I came to warn you, I just left her out on the balcony with your brother. She said for you to save her another dance." Sybilla relayed her message with a hint of concern on her expression.

"What?" he growled. Atticus somehow knew the request wasn't the actually message she wanted relayed. His eyes narrowed as a surge of jealousy and protectiveness coursed through him. His relationship with his brother had always been complicated, marred by rivalry and unspoken grudges. The thought of Kingsly being alone with Hazel only deepened his suspicion, making him question his brother's intentions and whether this was another ploy to undermine him. Remembering the conversation he had with Hazel in her bed chambers, Atticus felt something was wrong. She was trying to send a message for him to help her. Atticus knew he couldn't waste any time and excused himself from Sybilla with a quick nod before making his way toward the balcony. His mind raced with various scenarios of what could be happening.

Determined to confront his brother and ensure Hazel's safety, he steeled himself for the inevitable confrontation. Atticus grumbled as he set down his glass on a passing tray of champagne.

The Immortal Dragon moved to storm his way out there, but Sybilla stepped in his path, putting her hand on his chest. Atticus's heart pounded furiously as he looked down at her, torn between the urge to protect Hazel and the need to maintain his composure.

His mind was a whirlwind of conflicting emotions—anger, fear, and a gnawing sense of urgency. The possibilities of what could have happened between Hazel and Kingsly weighed heavily on him. Atticus knew he had to tread carefully, for one rash move could lead to disastrous consequences.

"If you cause a scene, it could make things worse for her here at court. Don't go charging out there, powder lit and steel drawn, like some overzealous prince in a tragic ballad."Sybila warned.

Atticus clenched his fists, trying to rein in the tempest of emotions swirling within him. He knew Sybilla was right. Charging in without a plan and without all the information would escalate things and put Hazel in an unfavorable situation. Taking a deep breath, he forced himself to calm, his mind working rapidly to devise a strategy that would protect Hazel. Looking at Sybilla's hand on his chest, Atticus's eyes return to her face before he sighed.

As his lips parted to say something, a servant came running up to the pair with a panicked look in his eyes, bowing to them both. Atticus's felt a cold dread settling in the pit of his stomach. He leaned in slightly, his eyes locking onto the servant's, silently urging him to speak.

The servant's trembling voice barely reached his ears, but the urgency in his tone was unmistakable. "Prince Atticus, I'm glad to see you with Lady Sybilla. Ardnaxela wanted me to tell you she has taken the Ivory Fawn to her room because she isn't feeling well."

Atticus tried to hold the snarl curling on his lips , to no prevail, from the servant before he waved his hand to dismiss them. Atticus's mind raced as he processed the servant's words, a mix of relief and frustration washing over him. The fact that Hazel was with Ardnaxela meant she was safe for now, but the underlying tension of the situation remained. There was a reason she feel the need to escort Hazel to her room.

Atticus clenched his jaw, determined to get to the bottom of what had caused Hazel's distress.

"I am going to kill him if he hurt her." His voice dripped in venom, as he slowly looked at Sybilla.

"Go after her. I am right behind you," she said before she scanned the ballroom.

Atticus stormed out of the ballroom into the hallway, it was dimly lit by flickering torches mounted on stone walls, casting eerie shadows that danced with every step he took. The cold, hard floor beneath him echoed his hurried footsteps, adding to the sense of urgency that gripped his heart. If Kingsly had harmed his fawn in any way... Atticus had already warned his brother once—stay away, or he'd get far more than a busted lip.

Atticus's heart pounded in his chest, and each beat a drum of worry and anger. Why was Ardnaxela there with her? Hazel was fine earlier, said she just needed to get some air. What changed? Did Kingsly say or do something?

His mind was a whirlwind of thoughts, the fear of Hazel's safety mingling with the burning frustration towards Kingsly. The cold air of the hallway did little to cool his temper, and every shadow seemed to mock him with shadow spectators flicking against the light cast on the wall by the torches as he quickened his pace, desperation pushing him forward. The last thing he ever wanted to happen to Hazel was for that viper to make Hazel's life harder than it already was. Hearing a panicked cry for help come from Hazel's room, Atticus sprinted for the door. It was Hazel who was crying out. Someone was hurting his fawn, and he was going to drive a sword through them. He didn't care if he was running too fast for Sybilla to catch up. He needed to get to Hazel now.

Chapter Thirty

Hazel

Hazel stumbled into her receiving room, removing herself from Ardnaxela's grip after the dragons had caught her by her arm to stabilize her. She stumbled to a long rectangular table against the right wall. Hazel's heart pounded in her chest, and she could feel the adrenaline coursing through her veins. Fear and confusion clouded her thoughts as she tried to make sense of what had just happened. She leaned heavily on the table, struggling to steady her trembling hands.. It was like all the air was being ripped from her lungs. Hazel couldn't breathe as she felt the phantom touches of Darius and Kingsly touching her in places she wished he never had. As Hazel shook her head, she swatted her arm, wishing it would make her skin stop prickling from the memory of his touch.

Waves of dizziness washed over her, and black spots danced at the edges of her vision. Hazel's thoughts spiraled out of control, each one more terrifying than the last, trapping her in a relentless cycle of panic and despair. Her chest tightened as if bound by unseen chains, every breath shallow and ragged. A cold sweat clung to her skin, her hands trembling as an unbearable weight pressed down on her shoulders. The walls of her mind closed in, suffocating her with visions of failure—of the faces she couldn't save, the blood she couldn't stop spilling, the screams that still echoed in her ears.

Her heart pounded, a frantic drumbeat in her ribs, drowning out reason. Despair coiled around her like a viper, its venom seeping into her veins, whispering cruel truths—*You weren't strong enough. You never will be.* She clenched her jaw, biting back the sob that threatened to escape, but the ache in her throat only grew, raw and unyielding. Her body shook under the weight of exhaustion, yet her mind refused to still, dragging her deeper into the abyss of guilt and hopelessness.

No matter how hard she tried to claw her way out, panic's icy grip held firm, sinking its talons into her soul. The world blurred at the edges, her surroundings distant, unreal—only the suffocating turmoil inside her felt real. It was a storm she couldn't outrun, a shadow she couldn't escape.

Hazel clenched her head with one hand as the other clenched her stomach. She couldn't stop seeing Kingsly and Darius's face as so many memories of him and her together clashed in her mind.

"Hey! ~Hazel, you're okay. You're safe. Tell me what to do to help," the Dragoness soothed, trying to bring her out of her panic state.

She scanned over Ardnaxela's face rapidly before shaking her head as Ardnaxela reached out for her, but Hazel smacked Ardnaxela's hand away.

Hazel took a step back, her mind too consumed by fear to process the Dragoness words. Her breaths came in shallow, rapid bursts as she tried to battle her mind that made it feel like she was drowning. However, just the idea of being touch made her heart pound faster. The only thought running through Hazel's mind was to find safety—to escape the tormenting memories that clawed at her from the depths of her mind. "Get away from me!" she cried out, stumbling back from the Dragoness.

She knew, logically, that it was Ardnaxela standing before her. She could hear the concern in her voice, see the way she reached out—not in malice, but in comfort. And yet, no matter how hard Hazel tried to ground herself in reality, her mind refused to listen.

It wasn't Ardnaxela's outstretched hand she saw, but Lilura's blood-stained grin. The past bled into the present, twisting her vision into a waking nightmare. Flickering images of crimson-soaked steel, of the cruel curve of Lilura's smile as she stood over the fallen, filled Hazel's mind. The scent of blood and the bark of the Raven Palm trees clung to her senses, suffocating her, drowning her in memories she couldn't escape.

Her breaths came in ragged gasps, her pulse a frantic rhythm against her ribs. Every time she blinked, the images only grew sharper—Lilura's glowing eyes piercing through the darkness, Hazel's own screams of the her throat being torn into echoing in Hazel's ears, the unbearable feeling of helplessness sinking its claws into her chest.

She squeezed her eyes shut, shaking her head as if she could dispel the vision, but it was useless. The past had her in its grip, and no matter how much she reminded herself that Lilura was gone, that Ardnaxela was not her enemy, her body still recoiled in terror, trapped between what was real and what her mind refused to forget.

Remembering the way she had devoured Darius's lips painted with Hazel's blood before they began mocking how she was scared, Hazel's knees buckled, and she collapsed to the floor, her body wracked with uncontrollable shivers. Her hands clawed at her own skin, desperate to rid herself of the invisible taint.

Cold sweat dripped down her forehead, and her heart pounded so violently that she feared it might burst from her chest. Clawing at her dress, Hazel gasped for air, the fabric suddenly feeling too tight, too constricting, as though it were suffocating her. The desperate need to be free of it consumed her, panic surging through her veins like wildfire. Her trembling fingers fumbled at the seams, yanking at the fabric, trying to tear it away from her skin. But Arabella had cinched it too perfectly—the laces held firm, refusing to budge no matter how hard she pulled.

Her breaths came in short, frantic bursts, her chest heaving as if the dress itself were crushing her ribs, squeezing the air from her lungs. The more she struggled, the more trapped she felt. She dug her nails into the delicate material, tugging with all her strength, but it wouldn't come loose. All she managed to do was tear jagged holes into the fabric, her fingers slipping against the ruined threads.

Tears burned at the corners of her eyes as frustration and fear twisted inside her. She needed it off. *Now.* The sensation of being caged, of being unable to move, only fed the rising panic. Her hands shook as she clawed at the bodice again, her vision blurring. It didn't matter that it was just a dress—her mind screamed at her that she was trapped, suffocating, drowning.

Hazel's mind was a battlefield, torn between the desire to flee and the paralyzing terror that held her in place. No matter what she did , it was like she was trapped in her own body, powerless against the surge of emotions that threatened to drown her. The walls around her seems to be closing in on her, drawing her into a sense of being trapped.

The sound of hurried footsteps barely registered through the roar in Hazel's ears. Her vision swam, her frantic struggle with the dress consuming every ounce of her awareness. The laces still wouldn't give. The fabric still clung to her like a second skin, suffocating, unbearable.

Then, a presence—solid, unyielding.

The doors burst open with a force that rattled the walls, and suddenly, Atticus was there. A storm of movement, of urgency, his broad frame silhouetted against the light beyond the threshold. Hazel barely managed to lift her gaze, but when she did, she was met with the fierce intensity of his eyes.

They burned into her, sharp and searching, taking in every detail—her trembling hands clawing at the shredded fabric, her heaving chest, the wild panic in her gaze. His own expression tightened, a flicker of something raw flashing across his face.

"Hazel—" His voice, usually so steady, was laced with something almost like fear. Not fear *for* himself, but for *her*.

She couldn't speak. Couldn't breathe. But the moment her frantic eyes met his, the chaos in her mind hesitated. The walls weren't closing in as fast. The crushing weight on her ribs, though still there, loosened just a fraction.

She was still drowning, still caught in the storm of panic—but Atticus was an anchor, a tether to something real. His presence didn't erase the fear, didn't undo the horrors clawing at the edges of her mind, but it *slowed* them. It reminded her that she wasn't alone. That she wasn't trapped, even if her body still believed she was.

Her lips parted, a shaky breath escaping as her fingers trembled against the ruined fabric of her dress. She was still struggling, still fighting against something unseen—but she wasn't fighting *alone* anymore.

Backing away, she placed herself in a corner beside the fireplace. Hazel's mind was a tempest of conflicting emotions, torn between the primal urge to protect herself and the desperate need for solace. Each step backward in the corner was a retreat deeper into her own torment, the corner becoming both a sanctuary and a prison. Her vision blurred with tears as she fought to regain control over her spiraling thoughts.

Hazel's eyes shot to Sybilla the moment she stepped up beside Atticus, her sudden presence sending a jolt through Hazel's already frayed nerves. Panic tightened its grip again, her body tensing as if bracing for another threat. Sybilla's widened eyes mirrored the concern in Atticus's, but in Hazel's fractured state, all she could register was movement—another figure, another presence pressing in when she already felt trapped. Her breath hitched, her hands still trembling against the torn fabric of her dress as her mind warred between fear and the faint, fragile thread of reassurance Atticus had given her.

"He is going to kill me, he is going -!" Hazel cried, trying to press her back into the wall further. Looking to the door beside her leading into her bedroom, Hazel lunged for the opening, trying to close it as quickly as possible.

A black boot jammed itself in the doorway as Atticus's firm yet gentle voice called out, "Hazel, wait! No one is going to harm you. We are here to help." His presence exuded a calm strength, an anchor midst her storm of fear.

Hazel's heart pounded as she stared at the boot, her breath catching in her throat. Panic surged through her veins, and she frantically pushed against the door, trying to force it shut. Her hands trembled, and tears streamed down her face as she screamed, "Please, just go away!" Swallowing hard, Hazel backed away from the door, trembling, as Atticus slowly came into the room. Wincing, her back pressing into the side of her wardrobe. Hazel's eye shifted from the wardrobe to the exit, then to Atticus.

His expression was a mix of concern and determination, his brow furrowed, and eyes soft yet focused. He moved slowly, hands raised slightly in a gesture of peace, trying to convey his intentions without words. "Hazel, listen to me," he said gently. "We're not your enemy."

Reaching for her mother's necklace, feeling its absence, Hazel wished she had it on. The absence of her mother's necklace, a talisman of comfort and strength, left her feeling even more vulnerable and exposed. Every fiber of her being screamed for her to flee, yet she was frozen in place, her fear rendering her immobile. Seeing Atticus now approaching closer without any words, his hands outstretched to her, she held her hand out to Atticus, shaking her head silently, pleading for him to stop. "Please, please, please," she whimpered as tears drenched her face, her mascara now running.

"Princess... It's me ... you're safe," Atticus coaxed her, trying to take a slow, gentle approach.

Two guards ran in, swords drawn, and Hazel tensed. leading her to quickly back further into the corner of the fireplace.

Her fear rattled her bones, and the young woman's shifted to Ardnaxela. The sight of the guards with their swords drawn intensified her panic, and she felt trapped, like a cornered animal. Hazel's breathing hitched, seeing the quick movement of Ardnaxela's hand signaling the guards to stop.

Ardnaxela's expression was one of fierce authority, her eyes sharp and commanding. There was no hesitation in her movements, and her jaw was set with determination, making it clear that she was in control of the situation. Her gaze softened slightly as it shifted to Hazel, conveying a mix of concern and assurance. "Get the lady's handmaiden and tell her it's urgent," Ardnaxela said softly.

"Princess, come back to me. You're safe. I won't let anyone harm you," Atticus's voice was soft and tender as he placed his hand on her hip.

Hazel lunged at Atticus, pinching his jaw. He stumbled a bit as Hazel attempted to dart past him, but he grabbed her wrist. "Hazel, please," he pleaded, his eyes filled with concern and confusion. "I'm trying to help you."

Ardnaxela quickly moved in to help Atticus in restraining Hazel.

Hazel's eyes were wild with fear and desperation at Atticus's grip, her breaths coming in sharp gasps. "Let go of me!" she shouted, her voice trembling.

Catching from the corner of her eyes the fast movement as strong shoulder moved quickly behind her. Her eyes locked on to meet the honey brown of his. Atticus gently turned her to fully face him, cupping her face as blood trickled down his lip. "Hazel." his voice wobbled for a moment. Hazel wanted to trust him, but memories of his cruel behavior and the phantom pain caused by Darius clouded her judgment. Could she really believe that a man would protect her without any hidden motives? As if his words had power over her, Hazel slowly ceased her fighting, relaxed in his grip, stared up into his eyes, and finally heard his voice.

Letting herself fall apart in his touch, Atticus pulled her into his arms, holding her tight into his chest. Relief washed over her as she felt the warmth and security of Atticus's embrace, but the shadows of her past still lingered, making her heart ache with uncertainty.. Hazel held onto him for dear life, afraid if she didn't, she would crumble into a million shards of broken glass.

Atticus didn't let her go as Hazel released all her pent-up fears and frustrations. . It was like he knew this was what she needed. Resting her head against Atticus's chest, she felt a shift within her. The walls she had built around her heart cracked, and for the first time in a long while, she allowed herself to believe that maybe, just maybe, she wasn't alone.

In three weeks, Hazel had her life ripped away from her, nearly died twice, and there was already people here at court that didn't like her. Her entire world felt like it was crumbling out from under her feet.

"You're safe. I swear. I won't let anyone hurt you, Hazel," Atticus swore softly.

He stroked her golden hair, laying a kiss on her temple, rubbing soothing motions up and down her back. In that moment, the bond between Hazel and Atticus deepened.

She could feel the sincerity in his actions and words, which healed the wounds etched into her soul. This newfound connection offered Hazel a glimmer of hope, suggesting that perhaps trust and love were still possible in her fractured world. Hazel may have been reading it wrong, but she didn't care about his reasoning. In this moment, all she cared about was how safe she felt in his arms. Holding him closer to his words, Hazel inhaled the aroma of bergamot and cedar, using it to ground her. Hazel wished she could bottle up his scent and just carry it with her.

The Immortal Dragon was known for being cruel and heartless, but after last night, their dance, and now this, Hazel didn't know what to think. Her mind was a storm of doubt and hope, questioning whether this side of Atticus was genuine, another layer of his complex nature. Despite her confusion, she couldn't deny the comfort and safety she felt in his presence, leaving her heart caught between skepticism and burgeoning trust.

Still caught in the remnants of her panic, Hazel clung to the steady rhythm of Atticus's heartbeat, grounding herself in the warmth of his embrace. Slowly, the storm in her chest began to settle, leaving exhaustion in its wake. Just as her mind started to clear, a familiar scent drifted through the air—lavender and chamomile, gentle and soothing, pulling her further from the edge.

"What brought this on, princess?" Atticus asked softly before slowly releasing Hazel to take her chin in his hand, scanning her over. His gaze sweeping over her with quiet intensity—until his thumb brushed gently against her cheek. Hazel parted her lips to tell him she was fine, that Ardnaxela stopped him before Kingsly could do anything. Yet no words came out. It was as if her voice box was taken out.

Hazel's capability to speak fought against her in fear if she even spoke up, things would get worse. *If she spoke up, would Kingsly try to manhandle her again?*

She couldn't even tell this prince how she was feeling so he could help her not feel this way anymore. "It's okay if you're not ready to talk; you don't have to," Atticus said, stroking a strand of hair from her face to look into those icy blue eyes.

"Why don't we get you in the bath? If you like, I can sleep in the chair tonight, so you are not alone," Atticus offered, gently brushing her cheek with his thumb.

Hazel's throat bobbed as she nodded her head. She didn't want to be left alone. Hazel was scared to sleep, for fear Kingsly and Darius would haunt her dreams.

Finally, Hazel saw Arabella. She came out of the bathing room still in her Pantone blouse and beige skirt as if she had never changed out of it.

Hazel's heart swelled with gratitude for Arabella, whose intuitive kindness provided her with exactly what she needed at that moment. As the lavender and chamomile scents filled her senses, Hazel felt calm wash over her.

Offering her hand to Hazel to assist her out of the dress and into the bath, she hesitantly took it, stepping away from Atticus' arms. The room was filled with a quiet tension of what Hazel had just endured at the hands of Kingsly, the only sounds being the soft rustle of fabric and the distant murmur of water. The air was thick with unspoken words and lingering emotions.. "Why don't I fetch a servant to make tea while you help Hazel into the bath? Will you be okay with Arabella?" Atticus asked low and steady, laced with warmth. It looked, from how white his knuckles were, that he was struggling to keep his calm.

All Hazel did was nod her head as her arms wrapped around her body like a security blanket.

Hazel's mind swirled with a mix of gratitude and apprehension. She appreciated Atticus's concern but couldn't shake the feeling of vulnerability that had taken hold of her. As she nodded, she silently hoped that Arabella's presence would provide her desperately needed comfort.

"Lavender and chamomile would be the most appropriate option for her now." Arabella smiled faintly.

Hazel glanced briefly at Arabella before glancing back at Atticus, who nodded his head, appreciating the suggestion, before his eyes met Hazel's. He bowed his head to Hazel and then to Arabella before turning and walking out of the room.

Chapter Thirty-One

Atticus

Closing the door gently behind him. Atticus knew Hazel was in good hands with Arabella. That's why he chose Arabella to be her handmaiden. Atticus trusted her with his own life, just as he relied on Sybilla and Ardnaxela. If it wasn't for Arabella in the battlefield of Strull. He would have died from infection. He considered them to be his personal inner court, where he could be himself.

Having an inner court was crucial for Atticus, as it gave him a sanctuary of trust and loyalty in a world rife with betrayal. These individuals were not just protectors, but confidants who understood his true nature and ambitions. Their unwavering support and discretion allowed him to navigate the complexities of his position with confidence and peace of mind.

The look of pure fear and panic on Hazel's face played endlessly in his mind. Atticus understood her panic attacks all too well because he had experienced them himself. He knew the overwhelming sensation of dread and the suffocating grip of anxiety that could strike at any moment.

This shared struggle deepened his bond with Hazel and fueled his resolve to ensure she always felt safe and supported. It was one of the reasons why Atticus didn't get upset when Hazel punched his face. His jaw still ached from the impact, a dull throb that served as a constant reminder of Hazel's fear and desperation. Each time he moved his mouth to speak or eat, a sharp pain shot through his teeth, but he bore it without complaint.

The physical discomfort was a small price to pay for Hazel's moment of release. How her eyes glowed with ivory with flecks of gold, how her body faintly glowed. He knew Hazel must have yet again lost control. Her magic seemed to respond to her emotions. Atticus often marveled at Hazel's magical abilities, seeing them as both a blessing and a curse. He admired the raw power she possessed, but he also worried about the toll it took on her emotional well-being. Her magic, unpredictable and tied so closely to her feelings, made it imperative for her to master self-control, a challenge that weighed heavily on both of them. Rubbing her jaw, he was surprised Hazel's punch felt as if it was a grown man twice his size who hit him in the face. Rubbing his jaw, he sighed, wiggling it. It wasn't broken, but it would be bruised in the morning.

Atticus was all too familiar with flashbacks, especially ones that were still raw. He had a fair share of his own from his encounters on the battlefield, memories that haunt his dreams. The battlefield was a relentless and unforgiving place, where the air was thick with the sound of swords clashing and the cries of the wounded echoed in his ears. Atticus had seen comrades fall beside him, their faces frozen in expressions of pain and terror. The chaos of combat, with its deafening explosions and the constant threat of death, had left indelible scars on his psyche, scars that mirrored the ones Hazel carried from her own battles with her magic. One memory stood out among the rest: the night his closest friend, Lucerius, was struck down. The two of them had been fighting side by side, their backs against a crumbling wall when an enemy arrow found its mark in Lucerius's chest when he threw himself in front of Atticus to protect his crown prince from death. Atticus had watched helplessly as the light faded from Lucerius's eyes, his last words a whispered plea for Atticus to take care of his family, a promise that still haunts him to this day. The prince prayed to the goddess Morana that his death was peaceful as he held him till his last breath so Lucerius didn't feel alone in his last moments.

Still holding the door knob tight in his hand, Atticus's knuckles whitened. Kingly would pay greatly for whatever he did to trigger this panic state. Atticus felt a crushing weight of guilt and responsibility pressing down on him. He believed that if he had been just a bit faster or more alert, he could have saved Lucerius's life. Every decision he made since that day was influenced by the promise he made, a constant reminder of the friend he couldn't protect. From the corner of his eyes, Atticus saw a shift of black and green fabric. Of course, they would stay around to see if Hazel was okay. Sighing, Atticus released the doorknob, raking his hand through his hair. Atticus stood in the dimly lit hallway, its stone walls adorned with flickering torches casting dancing shadows. The corridor was eerily quiet, save for the distant murmur of voices and the occasional clinking of armor from the guards patrolling the perimeter. The heavy wooden beams overhead creaked softly, adding to the somber atmosphere of the ancient fortress.

"What happened on that balcony?" he grins, keeping his voice low, and looks at Ardnaxela, her arms crossed over her chest. Atticus's anger simmered just below the surface, his eyes narrowing as he awaited Ardnaxela's response. "Tell me everything you saw, every word exchanged," he demanded, his voice a low growl. The thought of Kingsly causing harm to Hazel made his blood boil, and he needed to understand every detail to ensure justice was served.

"I was going to the balcony to get some air from the stench of desperate ladies of court. As I came out, I saw Kingsly yelling at her for how you two danced. He went on about how he warned her once about you. Painting you as if you were a monster. I must say I was impressed by her fire. Kingsly overstepped in, grabbing her arm, and before I could act, Hazel slapped the daylight out of him." As Ardnaxela recounted the events, Atticus's mind raced with a mix of fury and admiration. He admired Hazel's bravery in standing up to Kingsly, but the thought of her being manhandled filled him with rage. Each word from Ardnaxela's mouth only solidified his resolve to confront Kingsly and protect those he cared about. "I was glad she did, but then I saw him kissing her neck even when she told him to stop. Well, I wasn't going to let that fly, and I put a sword to his neck." Ardnaxela emphasized the last part with a grin on her lips. The torches flickered more intensely, casting sharp, erratic shadows that mirrored the turmoil within Atticus. The tension in the air was palpable, thick enough to cut with a knife. Ardnaxela's voice, steady and unwavering, echoed softly off the stone walls, adding to the gravity of her account as Atticus's grip on the hilt of his sword tightened involuntarily.

Kingsly would beg for his life when he was done with the general prince. He would kill any man that laid their hands on his Ivory Fawn, on his Hazel. Squeezing his eyes shut, all he could see was his brother's hands all over Hazel. Atticus felt a storm of emotions churning within him—rage, helplessness, and a fierce protectiveness that bordered on possessiveness. His heart pounded in his chest like a war drum, each beat fueling his determination to make Kingsly pay for his transgressions. The image of Hazel's frightened eyes haunted him, deepening the resolve in his soul to ensure no harm would ever come to her again.

Sybilla steps closer to Atticus, resting her hand on his shoulder. His honey eyes looked to his friend's soft emerald eyes. "I'm going to kill him," he growled out slowly. "I know, and I don't blame you. Although you know if you do, your father will punish you or worse, Hazel." Atticus's jaw clenched as Sybilla's words sank in, the weight of her warning pressing heavily on his conscience. He knew she was right; acting on his rage could have dire consequences not just for him, but for Hazel as well. Torn between his desire for vengeance and the need to protect Hazel from further harm, he struggles to find a path to bring justice without endangering those he loves: " He thinks your brother has no fault. King Kai will say Hazel is just trying to interfere with Kingsly's engagement to Duvessa." Sybilla spoke calmly to Atticus, bringing him to reason. Atticus's mind raced, torn between the urge to exact immediate revenge and realizing that his actions could escalate the situation, putting Hazel in greater peril. The thought of his father siding with Kingsly and dismissing Hazel's plight as mere jealousy filled him with a sense of betrayal and frustration. Deep down, he yearned to protect Hazel at all costs, but the fear of losing her to his own recklessness gnawed at his resolve, leaving him caught in a web of conflicting emotions. That's why Atticus enjoyed having her around; Sybilla was his voice of reasoning. He had one hell of a temper, but she always knew what to say to calm him down. "What am I supposed to do? Let him get away with assaulting her?! I told him once if he doesn't leave her alone, I will-"

"You will do what? Cause more issues for the poor girl? She has already been through enough. Come on, you are smarter than this. Stop thinking with what lies between your legs and start thinking with your head." Sybilla intervenes in Atticus' words with a raised eyebrow. Atticus's fists tightened at his sides, his knuckles turning white as he took a deep breath. He knew Sybilla was right, but the thought of doing nothing infuriated him. Slowly, he unclenched his fists and nodded, his eyes softening slightly as he met Sybilla's gaze.

Atticus looked at Sybilla before looking at Ardnaxela, taking a deep breath, grinding his teeth, knowing Sybilla was right. He didn't like the response, but he wanted to know his best friend's opinion.

When Atticus turned to look at Ardnaxela, she crosses her arms and raised an eyebrow, pressing a thin line between her lips. Her eyes narrow slightly, expressing her irritation. In Ardnaxela's tone, she bit his skin with death-like coldness. "I think you're being an overprotective, hormonal, territorial prince. I believe you're putting more drama on that poor girl. Knock it off." Taking a deep breath, he rubbed his face and licked his bloody lip before nodding his head.

"Then what do you suggest I do?" Atticus groaned out, rubbing the back of her neck. Atticus felt conflicted because, despite his protective instincts, he understands that his actions may be causing more harm than good. He wanted to ensure the girl's safety but is also wary of overstepping boundaries and creating unnecessary tension. This internal struggle leaves him seeking guidance on striking the right balance. "You let me train her tomorrow." Atticus opened his mouth to protest, but Ardnaxela raised her hand to silence him. "From what I saw on that balcony, now in that room. Hazel has displayed a fighting spirit that makes her a strong leader. She needs proper training." Ardnaxela admitted, "Seeing her eyes like that, how she glowed during her panic. I want to start her immediately on learning to control it. I will search the archives for anything about controlling her magic tonight," Sybilla chimed in. Sybilla's voice quivered with urgency, her eyes wide with determination. "I can provide Hazel with practical exercises to help her harness her abilities. We can tailor training to Hazel's weaknesses and challenges."

Atticus took a deep breath, raking his hand through his hair again. Hearing both their suggestions, he considered them for a moment before he looked at his two friends, nodding his head in agreement. As Atticus listened to Ardnaxela and Sybilla's confident plans, he felt a weight lifted from his shoulders. The thought of Hazel receiving structured training gave him a sense of relief, knowing that capable hands would guide her power. Though his protective instincts remained, he believed their collective efforts could help Hazel flourish.

"As for my brother, I think letting him wonder when I will strike for what he did tonight would be sweet revenge. You two get some sleep. Thank you both again for helping her." Atticus rested his hand on Sybilla's hand, which is still resting on his shoulder. Soon, Sybilla removed her hand. Atticus' feelings towards his brother were a complex mixture of anger and disappointment. While he couldn't deny his deep-seated love for his sibling, the betrayal he felt was hard to ignore. The thought of revenge was tempting, yet he knew it would only deepen their rift, making reconciliation even more difficult.

"I'm planning to get Hazel some tea and sandwiches for her. I will also let her know about her training. Good night to you two." Bowing his head to them both, Atticus strolled off to the kitchen. As Atticus made his way to the kitchen, his mind churned with conflicting emotions. The desire to protect Hazel was overwhelming, yet he feared that in doing so, he might stifle her growth or make her overly dependent. He wrestled with the balance between shielding her from harm and allowing her the freedom to discover her strength. Flickering sconces dimly lit the kitchen, casting long shadows across the stone walls. The air was filled with the earthy scent of herbs hanging from the rafters and the faint crackle of the fire in the hearth. As Atticus moved about, the clinking of metal pots and the soft hiss of boiling water provided a soothing rhythm to his thoughts. Atticus carefully selected a blend of calming herbs from the hanging bundles, crushing them gently between his fingers before placing them into a teapot. He then sliced fresh bread and layered it with cheese and cured meats, creating simple yet comforting sandwiches. As the tea steeped, he arranged everything neatly on a tray, his movements a meditative process that helped clear his mind.

Atticus couldn't quite grasp why he felt compelled to prepare Hazel's meal personally when a maid could easily handle the task. It puzzled him that he cared so deeply for her well-being, a feeling that transcended mere duty. As he sliced the bread and arranged the tray, he questioned whether his actions were driven by genuine affection or an unconscious need to atone for past failures. Was it because she was supposed to be the prophesied hero destined to save their land, or did he genuinely care for her as an individual? The weight of expectation and prophecy loomed heavily over his thoughts. Yet, there was an undeniable warmth in his heart whenever he considered her smile or the determination in her eyes. As he poured the tea, Atticus realized that perhaps it was a blend of both, a complex intertwining of duty and affection, that bound him to her fate.

Chapter Thirty-Two

Hazel

Hazel's head leaning back on the rim of the bathtub , soaking in the warmth of the lavender and chamomile bath, helped settle her nerves. Her body felt heavily drained from her panic attack. She closed her eyes, allowing the gentle aroma to transport her to a serene meadow. Hazel focused on her breathing, each inhale drawing in peace and each exhale releasing the tension that had gripped her so tightly. For the first time in hours, she felt a glimmer of tranquility.

Arabella was letting her soak for as long as she wanted. After her night, Hazel was grateful for the peace and quiet.

The only sounds were the occasional drip of water and the soft rustling of Arabella's movements, ensuring Hazel had everything she needed for her recovery.

She told Hazel if she needed anything, just to shout. It was a relief to know someone she trusted was just outside her bedroom door. Hazel felt a deep sense of gratitude for Arabella's unwavering support and gentle presence.

Over the last 3 days, their bond had evolved beyond that of merely a lady and her handmaiden. they had become confidantes and friends. In moments like these, Hazel was reminded of just how much she relied on Arabella's kindness and understanding to navigate her most vulnerable times.

Hazel's lids grew heavy as the soft aroma of lavender curled around her, wrapping her in a warmth she didn't think she could sink into. Her mother had loved lavender—from what she was told, even if it was a little overpowering to Hazel—but here, steeped in the gentle mix of lavender oil and steaming water, it lost its sharpness, melting into something almost comforting. Before she could think to resist it, sleep pulled her under.

Sways of orchid and lilac leaves swayed in and out of her vision. The lavender wisteria tree was surrounded by a glistening pound that rippled with gold. The tranquility of the garden surroundings was unparalleled. Each delicate petal and leaf moved in harmony with the gentle evening breeze. The soft rustle of the orchids and lilacs provided a soothing symphony, while the golden ripples in the pond mirrored the last light of the setting sun. Hazel's bare feet made their way across the cool stone path, lining its way across the pond to the familiar tree. As she approached it, a profound sense of calm washed over her. The weight of the evening's turmoil lifting with each step, replaced by a serene clarity. Standing beneath the wisteria's fragrant canopy, she felt a deep connection to the natural beauty around her, grounding her spirit and soothing her weary heart. Identical to her mother's necklace, but also the one she dreamed of before.

Running her hand up the bark of the tree, it was so smooth. Her eyes scanned up towards the tree canopy, watching the lowering rays of light peer down from the skylight and through the leaves. Closing her eyes, she inhaled the aroma of tuberose, jasmine, and freesia spices. The white gown that hung loosely around her swayed in the breeze before she heard a familiar voice.

"Welcome home, Ivory Fawn."

Turning around, Hazel saw her great-great-grandmother, Queen Asteria, standing there.

Hazel's breath hitched in her throat, her eyes widening in both surprise and confusion. "Great-great-grandmother?" she whispered, hesitating. Her mind raced with questions—why had Queen Asteria chosen this moment to appear, and what message did she bear this time? "Why am I here? What is this place?" Hazel asked, staying beneath the tree and watching the queen.

"Castle Andromeda This is your home,. It was home to so many Aestival people before the war, but currently, you're standing inside the Mother Grove Tree's temple," replied the queen.

Hazel's gaze shifted from the queen to the great tree. The air here was warm—surprisingly so, given that the skylight had been broken at the start of winter. Even as the first winter rain pattered softly against the shattered glass above, the pond and the cobblestone surrounding the tree remained untouched, as if the water never reached them. She frowned slightly, curiosity stirring in her chest. Was there some kind of magic shielding this place from the elements?

"Castle Andromeda once stood as the heart of our kingdom," Queen Asteria began, her voice tinged with nostalgia. "It was a place of wisdom and celebration, where the Aestival people once thrived in harmony with nature. But when war came, the castle bore the scars of battle, its walls crumbling as our people were scattered, leaving behind only fragments of a once-glorious past

Queen Asteria's expression grew grave, her eyes reflecting a deep-seated worry. "Dark forces have begun to stir once more, seeking to claim the power that lies within this sacred grove," she continued. "You must be vigilant, Hazel, for they will stop at nothing to seize what rightfully belongs to our people." The queen's warming was like a phantom grip, pulling Hazel's gaze to turn towards Asteria with alarm. "He is coming for you, and he plans to not only eradicate you before you become the Ivory Fawn, but to eradicate your Crimson Dragon and your loved ones."

"Who is coming?" Hazel's heart pounded in her chest, a cold sweat breaking out on her forehead as her hands trembled. The weight of the queen's warning pressed heavily on her, making it difficult to breathe. "Who is coming?" she repeated, her voice barely a whisper, filled with a mix of fear and determination. "Why me? Is it because I'm the Ivory Fawn? If so, can't you just choose another?"

Queen Asteria's eyes softened with a blend of sorrow and resolve as she stepped closer to Hazel. "No, my dear," she said gently, reassuringly touching Hazel's shoulder. "You were chosen for a reason that only time will reveal, but know this: your strength and courage are unmatched, and you are the key to restoring our world." Queen Asteria pushed a strand of Hazel's hair to sit behind her ear. "Because you are my great-great-granddaughter. When you ascend as the Ivory Fawn, you will be queen. With the help of your Crimson Dragon, you will rule valiantly and lead your people into a new and brighter era." The queen rested her hand on Hazel's chest with a proud smile.

Pushing her hand away, stepped back, she shook her head. Hazel didn't want any of this. She didn't know the first thing about being a queen, let alone how to lead people thought were extinct. Hazel's mind raced with doubts, feeling overwhelmed by the immense responsibility suddenly thrust upon her. How could she, an ordinary girl, possibly live up to the expectations of being a queen and a warrior? The fear of failure gnawed at her, making her question whether she had the strength or wisdom to guide her people through such perilous times.

"And what if I fail? I can't even control my gift. The last time I did, it nearly killed me," Hazel breathed out as she recoiled into herself.

The queen let out a quiet sigh, shaking her head. Hazel couldn't quite place the expression on her face—it wasn't disappointment, but something else, something unreadable. Their eyes met, and the queen's voice was steady, yet gentle.

"You underestimate yourself, child. Trust those around you—they will help you see the warrior you refuse to recognize within yourself."

The sound of thunder clapped loudly above them, drawing Hazel's attention of the clouds now blocking out the rising moonlight. Hazel's eyes refocused to the tree behind her before she looked at the queen, but when she looked, the queen was gone.

Hazel sat up with a start, realizing the water was colder on her skin upon moving. Her mind swirled with a mix of fear and determination as she processed the queen's words and the storm startling her from sleep. The idea of relying on others for strength was foreign to her, yet it getting easier for her to trust Ardnaxela, Sybilla , and Arabella. It planted a small seed of hope midst her doubts. She wondered if perhaps, just perhaps, she could find the warrior within herself that the queen so firmly believed was already there.

In her bathroom, it was dark because the storm's winds opened the archway window.

The howling wind rattled the glass panes while the distant rumble of thunder echoed through the night. Rain pelted the balcony floor, creating a rhythmic, almost hypnotic sound. The occasional flash of lightning illuminated the room in brief, eerie burst of thunder.

Getting out of her bath, Hazel shivered from the cold removing her wet bathing gown. She quickly dried off before wrapping the warm robe around her. Her bare feet pattered across the cold wood floor, and Hazel felt a slight sense of relief as the door shut out the storm's fury, but her heart still raced from the unexpected wake up call from the storm outside. She took a deep breath, trying to steady herself, and listened to the muffled sounds of the tempest outside.

Despite the warmth and comfort of her robe, the eerie atmosphere left her feeling unsettled and on edge. The only light in her room was from the fireplace. The soft, flickering glow of the flame that was nearly embers, provided a small comforting contrast to the chaotic storm outside. Hazel found solace in the gentle warmth, which seeped into her bones, easing the tension that had gripped her. Adding in some fire wood beside the fireplace to bring it back to life. The familiar crackling of the embers was a soothing reminder of safety and home, gradually calming her nerves.

Grabbing a box of matches, she carefully struck one and began relighting the candles scattered around her bedroom. The storm's winds had snuffed them out earlier, leaving the room in unsettling darkness. One by one, the flames flickered to life, casting a soft, golden glow that pushed back the lingering shadows. The candlelight wavered and danced across the walls, mingling with the steady flicker of the fireplace, creating an almost magical ambiance. The illusion of shifting darkness, born from her lingering unease, began to fade as warmth and tranquility settled over her. Her fingers trembled from the cold, making it difficult to hold the matches steady, but she pressed on, eager to chase away the night's lingering chill.

Walking over to the bed, ,Hazel admired the delicate silk nightgown Arabella had set out, which shimmered softly in the candlelight. The fabric felt incredibly smooth against her skin, almost like a second layer of warmth. Its pale lavender hue and intricate lace detailing added a touch of elegance, making her feel both comfortable and refined. She dropped her bathing robe onto the floor before sliding into the nightgown.

Hazel gazed at the mirror hanging above her headboard to see a man's silhouette behind her sitting in the chair beside the bookshelf and balcony doors. Hazel's heart skipped a beat, and a gasp escaped her lips as she spun around, her eyes wide with fear. She stumbled back, clutching at her chest, but the silhouette had vanished, leaving her questioning whether it had been real or just a trick of the lighting. Trembling, she scanned the room, her mind racing with both dread and disbelief.

Hazel reached for her mother's necklace, but remembered she hadn't been wearing it that night due to the ball. Her heart pounded in her ears as she scanned the room again, looking for the tall person she could have sworn was sitting in the chair Were her eyes playing tricks on her? She steps closer to investigate as her head tilted slightly, as if it would let her see better in the dark. A flash of lightning lit her entire bed chambers up, and she saw no one was in the chair. The pounding in her ears from her heart slowly became less of a deafening roar to nothing.

Brushing out her wet hair in the vanity mirror, she wondered if her eyes had been playing jokes on her earlier. Was there someone in her room? Or was it just adrenaline lingering from her abrupt awakening or the dream?

Making her way towards the vanity mirror , she retrieved her mother's necklace returned to where it belonged: around her neck. It was like it hummed in satisfaction to be back there. Then, there was a knock on her door. Covering her mouth to hold back the scream , Hazel quickly spun her body to face the door of her bedroom. Waiting a moment Hazel took a deep breath to calm her once more racing heart. "Come in."

Atticus opened the door walking in holding a silver tray of tea, a platter of something that smelled like roast beef. She could smell lavender and chamomile tea mixed with honey.

"I brought you some food and tea." he set the tray at the table by the balcony.

Hazel watched him closely, waiting to see which side of him she was going to get. She was hoping she would get the gentle prince side and not the Immortal Dragon side. Hazel's feelings towards Atticus were a tangled web of fear and fascination. On the one hand, she admired his kindness and the sense of security he provided, but on the other, she was deeply unsettled by his darker, more unpredictable nature.

Hazel couldn't help but wonder which version of him would emerge tonight.

His dark brown eyes softened into warm pools of honey as they met hers.. Hazel could see the concern on his face as his gaze swept over her. She wasn't sure if he was checking for any signs of harm or simply taking in her nightwear.

Every moment with Atticus felt like walking a tightrope, balanced precariously between affection and unease for what she just experienced before he showed up. Whatever it was, the expression made her want to melt.

"How are you feeling?" Atticus Spoke in a hushed tone, as if not wanting to pressure her.

Hazel opened her mouth to tell him about her vision with Queen Asteria, but the words faltered on her tongue. Her gaze flickered to the chair in the corner of the room—the same chair where, just moments ago, she had seen a figure sitting. Or at least... she thought she had.

Her brow furrowed as she tried to recall the details, but they blurred like a dream slipping through her fingers. Was it real? Or just a trick of the light, shadows cast by the flickering candle? For a moment, she swore she had locked eyes with the figure—whoever it was—but the next, the chair had been empty.

She swallowed hard, suddenly unsure if she should say anything at all.

Her facial expression must have given her away her hesitation, for he strolled over to her, kneeling before Hazel as she sat at her vanity mirror, careful not to touch her. "What is it, Hazel?" His tone was so warm and smooth, like a hug wrapping its arms around her.

Hazel hesitated, her mind racing to find the right words. She didn't want to reveal too much, fearing it might provoke the side of Atticus she dreaded. Yet, the warmth in his voice tempted her to confide in him, to seek the comfort she desperately needed.

She took a deep breath and realized she had stopped brushing her hair as the brush lingered in her wet hair. Setting it down, her throat bobbed. Hazel looked into the vanity mirror as if wondering if she would see that silhouette again, but nothing. "I saw Queen Asteria." Hazel released a breath.

Glancing at Atticus's reflection in the mirror, she could see Atticus's posture shift as his eyes widened.

"When? How?"

Turning to look at him, Hazel saw it was now pale. His throat bobbed, but he remained calm. Seeing Queen Asteria again unsettled her. Did it mean she was connected to the realm of spirits? That she had some larger role to play in a fate she didn't yet understand? Or was there something more—some warning buried in the vision that she had yet to grasp?

Atticus's reaction lingered in her mind. He hadn't brushed it off. If anything, his unease had only confirmed what she feared—this wasn't just another dream. It meant something. And whatever it was, she wasn't sure she was ready for it.

"It was like a dream, but yet it wasn't. I was at this wisteria tree with purple leaves. I could see the moon just as it was before the storm came. She was warning me." She played with her mother's necklace and chewed on her lip, trying to keep her mind on the dream and not the figure she swore was in her bedroom. "She told me that I am not safe here... that someone is coming for me. Didn't say who, but he plans to kill not only me but you as well." Her eyes finally met his, and all she saw was anger.

His jaw clenched tightly, and his eyes burned with a fierce intensity. His hands formed fists at his sides, trembling with barely contained rage. Leaning to the side, away from him in her seat, her throat nervously bobbed, seeing his expression. It was much like the one in the carriage a few nights ago. She wasn't looking at the prince she was starting to take a liking to but the Immortal Dragon.

"Was there anything else?" he ground out, as if trying to hold his temper back. All Hazel did was shake her head. She felt that if she told him about the shadow man she saw in the mirror, Atticus would lose it.

He sighed, raking his hand through his hair before standing up. Hazel's mind raced with apprehension, each heartbeat echoing her escalating fear.

His expression returned to that calm prince. offering her a hand to stand up, which she took without hesitation as Atticus led her to the table where the tray he brought in was sitting.

"Think you could eat something? I know after a panic attack, it can make you not want anything, but I also know you burn up a lot of energy." Despite his hands being calloused, this time, it somehow seemed soft and gentle.

Candlelight flickered, casting wavering shadows on the walls, the silence heavy with unspoken words.

Hazel's eyes kept darting to the corners of the room as if expecting the shadow man to materialize at any moment, while Atticus's presence, though calm, made her chest tighten not knowing how to process the new side of him, a gentle and caring side she was unfamiliar with.

Sitting down at the table, she nodded her head, pushing a semi-dry stand from her face. Looking at the tray, she took a cup and saucer from it. "I can try. Thank you." Her voice was soft and light as a feather as he poured tea for her. The aroma of the tea wafted up, calming and soothing, with notes of chamomile and a hint of honey. The fragrance enveloped her in a comforting embrace, momentarily easing the tension in her shoulders.

"There is some honey and sugar in the smaller dished. I didn't know how you liked it. Although I know the honey will soothe your throat from feeling raw," he chimed in, handing her the small saucer before sitting down himself.

Hazel watched the tea steam up the sides of her cup before her eyes went to his. How did he know her throat felt raw? "You act as if you are speaking from experience." She regretted the words the moment they came out not meaning for them to come as sharp a they did.

His eyes shot to hers, but she relaxed, seeing a soft, almost sympathetic look in them. "Being on the front lines fighting for my father often comes with a lack of peaceful night's rest," Atticus admitted to her. Hazel's eyes fell back to her cup for a moment as she heard his confession, and a flicker of understanding passing between them when her gaze returned. She felt a twinge of guilt at his words. Hazel never considered the horrors he had to see on the battlefield because of his father, or what it would have done to him mentally. Her heart ached with a mix of empathy and sorrow, realizing they were both haunted by their pasts in different ways. She sipped her tea after putting some honey and two sugar cubes in it. Was that why he acted so cruelly and harshly? Was it because of his father?

"How long has it been since you slept without the nightmares?" Hazel asked shyly, hoping she wasn't overstepping

Leaning forward in his chair, Atticus's fingers interlocking with each other. A shadow of pain crossed his face, and his brows furrowed slightly, as if recalling a distant, unpleasant memory. His eyes, usually so guarded, showed momentarily a wall coming down, revealing a vulnerability that he allowed Hazel to see.

"The night before I found you, I dreamed of Queen Asteria. She told me you were alive and in danger, and then told me where I could find you." He didn't even look at her, but kept his focus on the floor. So, Queen Asteria not only came to her but also him. His words solidifying that he was not lying about their destinies being intertwined.

Hazel's heart pounded in her chest, each beat echoing the unspoken bond that was forming growing further between them. The crackling of the fire in the hearth was the only sound since the storm avenging the night sky had passed. A gentle reminder of the warmth that contrasted the cold reality of their shared burdens. Hazel couldn't shake his words. His last peaceful dream had been about her.

It didn't make sense. Atticus had been nothing but arrogant and insufferable since the moment they met—always challenging her, pushing her buttons, making sure she knew exactly what he thought of her. And yet... in the quiet of his mind, when the weight of the world wasn't pressing down on him, she was what brought him peace?

The thought unsettled her more than it should have. It wasn't anger, not exactly—more like a strange, disorienting shift, as if the ground beneath her had tilted just enough to throw her off balance. She didn't know what to do with this softer version of him, didn't know how to reconcile it with the man who so often met her with sharp words and cold stares.

She told herself it didn't matter. That it didn't change anything. But a part of her, small and stubborn, wasn't so sure.

"And now? Are you still having them?" The young woman wanted to get to know this side of Atticus more. Hazel wasn't scared if he touched her, unlike how she was with Kingsly, where his touch sent her into a panicked state.

Atticus said nothing, only nodded his head.

Hazel thought she heard her heart breaking for a moment before she poured him a glass of tea, sliding it over to him. His eyes went from the floor up to to hers. Hazel found herself melting into his gaze, the warmth in his eyes disarming in a way she hadn't expected. There was no arrogance there, no sharp edges or teasing smirk—just quiet intensity, steady and unwavering. It held her in place, drawing her in before she even realized it, like a force she wasn't sure she wanted to resist.

For a moment, the world around them faded, the air thick with something unspoken. It unsettled her, the way he looked at her—not with challenge or indifference, but with something deeper, something she couldn't quite name. And yet, she didn't pull away.

Hazel's mind raced with a whirlwind of emotions, a mix of empathy, curiosity, and a deepening affection for Atticus. She felt a pang of sorrow for his torment, yet a glimmer of hope sparked within her, knowing that their connection might offer him some solace.

As their eyes were locked with one another, she sensed an unspoken understanding pass between them, a silent promise to stand by each other through the darkness. It was like there wasn't a wall she was so used to in the last several day of being here, in that pool of honey. Pools of honey she wanted to dive into.

He broke his gaze and took the teacup. "You need to eat something," he said softly, gesturing to the platter he had brought her.She could see his walls come up, the shift almost imperceptible—but she felt it. The warmth in his eyes dulled, guarded now, like a door quietly closing between them. His posture stiffened just slightly, his expression smoothing into something unreadable, carefully composed.

It was a defense mechanism, one she recognized all too well. A silent retreat behind carefully built barriers, keeping her—or anyone—from seeing too much. From getting too close. And just like that, the moment between them was gone, slipping through her fingers before she had the chance to hold onto it.

"You will need to build up your energy for tomorrow. Ardnaxela and Sybilla are going to start your training in the morning." Straightening up in his seat, he sipped his tea before setting it down, looking at the chair beside her bookshelf.

Hazel noticed the shift in Atticus's demeanor, a stark contrast to the vulnerability he had just shown. It was as if he had retreated behind a carefully constructed facade.

She couldn't help but wonder what had caused him to withdraw so suddenly, but she knew better than to press him.

"I can sit in the chair tonight and watch over you." Hazel breathing hitched hearing his offer and the tone he always spoke with, Firm and steady. The Immortal Dragon was now sitting in the chair where that gentle prince had been. Hazel felt a mix of disappointment and understanding at Atticus's transformation. She longed for the gentle prince who had briefly appeared to return instead of having to deal , but respected the Immortal Dragon's need for distance and protection. Determined to support him, she resolved to be patient, hoping he might let down his guard again one day.

"But I thought Ardnaxela wanted to-" Hazel began to say, but Atticus interrupted with a growl on his lips.

"After tonight, we all agreed—it's best for you to start learning how to defend yourself and control your magic now rather than later." His tone was like ice biting her skin.

Hazel felt a cold shiver run down her spine at the sharpness of his tone.

Hazel sighed, shaking her head before setting her cup and saucer down and looking at him with narrow eyes. "Why? Because I'm not the Ivory Fawn you envisioned? Because to you—and this court—I'm just some helpless damsel in distress? Too weak to fight back against your brother on that balcony, too powerless to stand against Darius, who is still out there?" She didn't realize what she had blurted out till it was already said.

Hazel's cheeks flushed with a mix of anger and embarrassment as she realized the intensity of her words. She had exposed her deepest insecurities, and now she feared his reaction more than ever. A part of her regretted the outburst, but another part felt liberated, having finally voiced her frustrations and fears.

Atticus's eyes went from that welcoming pool of honey to almost black. "You are so far from the truth, princess." A low, feral growl came from his lips that made Hazel stiffen. He stood up, stalked over to Hazel, put his hands on her chair and arms, and hovered over her. "You are *far* from a damsel in distress, so get that thought out of your head. My brother will be punished for touching something of mine, as will Darius. Hate me all you want, princess, but you will see what I see soon enough." The aroma of bergamot, cedar, and amber filled her senses as her head arched back to look up at him as they were so close they shared breaths. Hazel could feel her eye twitching at the word Princess, a term she despised for its often condescending undertone.

The proximity made her feel trapped and strangely exhilarated at the same time, her body betraying her with a shiver that had nothing to do with fear. She hated the power he held over her, Hazel was acutely aware of the intoxicating pull he had on her.

"And what is that, *dragon*?" Hazel couldn't help herself. She felt compelled to challenge him because she refused to be seen as weak or submissive. Deep down, she needed to assert her strength and independence, despite his overwhelming presence. Her defiance was a way to reclaim some semblance of control in an otherwise suffocating situation.

"A warrior goddess," he breathed as his eyes trailed to her lips, before he licked his own. His gaze held a mix of desire and admiration, a potent combination that left Hazel feeling both empowered and vulnerable.

It was as if he saw through her bravado to the fierce spirit within, acknowledging her strength in a way no one else had. This unexpected recognition sent a confusing swirl of emotions through her, making it difficult to discern whether she wanted to push him away or pull him closer.

Her heart raced in her chest, feeling like he was sucking all the air out of her lungs. Hazel wanted to crash her lips on his, but she held herself back.

She couldn't be falling for this prince, not now. She couldn't let herself love again, not after her last relationship nearly cost Hazel her life. If she let her guard down again, she risked her emotional well-being and her personal safety. Falling for the prince risked manipulation or betrayal in their treacherous political world. The stakes were too high—another heartbreak could shatter the strength she had rebuilt.

He was the Crimson Dragon to this prophecy she was fulfilling. Maybe what was between them now wouldn't go up in flames.

Hazel wanted his hands on her just as they were on that dance floor. The memory of their dance was seared into her mind, a perfect blend of elegance and raw emotion. They had moved in perfect harmony, his strong hands guiding her effortlessly across the floor while their bodies communicated in a silent, intimate language.

The music had been a soft, haunting melody that echoed the unspoken connection between them, each step bringing them closer to an inevitable, unspoken truth.

Watching him straighten up and move towards the fireplace, leaning an arm against it, he didn't even look at her. The silence was heavy, broken only by the occasional crackle of the fire, as if the room was holding its breath, waiting for the next move. Hazel's heartbeat slowed the intensity of their close proximity dissipating, leaving behind a poignant emptiness that filled the space between them.

"Sleep. I'll watch you tonight."

Hazel took a big gulp of her tea before going to the bed, pulling back the sheets and climbing in. But the moment she settled, her mind was awash with worry. Atticus's words, though well-meaning, only seemed to make things worse.

"Atticus..." Hazel began, her voice soft but filled with anxiety. "You can't stay here. Not after everything. The court—"

"I'm not leaving, Hazel." He cut her off, his voice firm but gentle as he moved closer. "I won't leave you. You need rest."

Hazel sat up in the bed, wringing her hands together as she struggled to find the words. "It's not about that," she said quickly. "It's about what the court will think. They've already seen me running from Kingsly's room earlier. And now they'll see you, Atticus. You—*a prince*—coming out of my room, after being here just three days? They'll *talk*. And they'll twist it into something worse, something I can't control. They know your reputation."

Atticus's jaw tightened, but he stood his ground. "I don't care about their whispers. I'm here to protect you, Hazel. Nothing else matters."

But Hazel's worry only deepened. She pulled the blanket closer around her, her voice shaky as she spoke. "You don't understand. They'll think... they'll say that you've been in my room all night. A prince, known for his... his reputation with women, coming out of my room after *three days*? They'll say I'm—" She broke off, swallowing hard, her fear taking over. "They'll say I'm another conquest. A game to you."

Atticus took a deep breath, his expression softening as he stepped closer. "I know what you're afraid of. I saw the panic in your eyes earlier. I saw how hard you're fighting to keep it all together. But I'm not going anywhere. And I'm certainly not going to leave you when you need rest the most."

Hazel shook her head, eyes wide with worry. "But you don't see it, Atticus. The court *will* twist it. It doesn't matter that I'm not like the others. They won't care. All they'll see is a prince leaving my room, and I'll be branded as just another one of your... your fleeting interests." Her voice cracked, frustration and helplessness lining her words.

Atticus's expression hardened, but his voice was unwavering. "Then let them talk. Let them try to make something of it. I'll stand beside you, no matter what they say."

Hazel looked up at him, her chest tightening with both gratitude and fear. "I just can't afford to make things worse. I can't handle the weight of it all right now."

Atticus met her gaze, his eyes unflinching. "Then you don't have to. Let me carry it for you. Let me stay."

Hazel took a big gulp of her tea processing what he was saying before giving in. Raking her hand through her hair she stands up going to the bed, pulling back the sheets and climbing in. The crackling of the fireplace filled the room with a comforting warmth, while the distant hoot of an owl echoed through the night.

Atticus settled into the chair by the window, the creak of the wooden floorboards beneath him adding to the ensemble of the fire crackling inside the room.

The bedding wrapped her in a warm embrace, making it difficult to fight sleep as she watched him from the fireplace. Hazel felt her eyelids grow heavy, lulled by the rhythmic crackle and the sense of security Atticus's presence provided. Wishing he were beside her, sharing the warmth of the bed and the intimacy of the moment. She longed for the reassurance of his touch, the steady beat of his heart next to hers. As her eyes finally closed, she whispered a silent hope that one day, he might be more than just a guardian by the window.

Chapter Thirty-Three

Atticus

Hazel's serene state of slumber as the moonlight was cast on her skin, made her seem more radiance than usual as if she were indeed the long-lost queen they were waiting for.

His fingers rested on his lips as he watched Hazel's chest rise and fall slowly as she slept. He couldn't help but feel a profound sense of awe and reverence, as if he were standing before a force far greater than himself—something ancient, untouchable, and undeniably powerful. It was the kind of presence that commanded respect without a single word spoken, the weight of unspoken history and untold stories pressing down on him like an invisible force. His chest tightened, his breath catching for just a moment as he tried to process the gravity of what he was witnessing. There was admiration, yes, but also a humbling sense of insignificance, as if, in that moment, he was merely a fleeting spark in the presence of a roaring fire. His heart pounded with a mixture of awe and unease, torn between the desire to step closer and the instinct to bow his head, as though he were in the presence of something sacred.

The night held its breath, mirroring his anticipation and the weight of the possibilities that lay ahead. The dim glow of candlelight flickered against the stone walls, casting shifting shadows that seemed to dance and stretch, as if whispering secrets only the darkness could understand. The air was thick with the scent of aged parchment and the lingering traces of smoldering incense, clinging to the fabric of the heavy velvet drapes that barely stirred in the faintest draft. Outside, beyond the window, the night loomed vast and watchful, the moon's pale glow seeping through the glass in fractured slivers, illuminating dust motes that hung suspended in the air. The silence was deep, not empty but expectant, as if even the very walls of her chamber were holding their breath, listening, waiting for what would come next.

Atticus's eyes focused up to the necklace she wore of the Mother Grove Tree. If someone was truly going to come after her, then he would cut them down before they could take a step towards her. Atticus decided he would always stay close to Hazel, blending into the shadows to avoid detection. He would also enlist the help of trusted allies within the court to keep a watchful eye on her. Additionally, he devised a series of escape routes and safe havens throughout the palace in case they needed to make a swift getaway. She was his to protect, and Atticus was going to do everything in his power to do so.

Rubbing his fingers together, imagining them back on that soft, warm skin was almost maddening. His feelings towards Hazel were a complex tapestry of admiration, devotion, and an unspoken love that he dared not fully acknowledge. Each glance at her stirred a mixture of tenderness and fierce protectiveness within him. Atticus knew that his loyalty to Hazel went beyond duty. It was a deep-seated connection that bound his heart to hers in an unbreakable bond. Atticus felt an almost magnetic pull towards her, an overwhelming need to be beside her. Yet he restrained himself, wanting to avoid any kind of scandal as well as not wanting to disturb her peaceful slumber. Every fiber of his being yearned to be close, but he remained in the shadows, content to watch over her from a distance.

He hated that no matter how hard he tried to create distance between them, he kept finding himself being close to her. Atticus didn't understand why. She was naïve, reckless, and had no regard for common sense—infuriating, really. And yet, he still found himself wanting to protect her, to pull her close, to trace his fingers over her skin like she was something fragile and untouchable. It made no sense, but neither did she. What was so aggravating to him was how she always had something smart to say,. frequently challenging Atticus's patience

Normally, he would have dropped a girl like her without a second thought, but with Hazel, it was different.

He never wanted to settle down. He would rather drink his fill of spiced wine, bed the court ladies when he wasn't with his mistress, and survive his way through this court under his father's reign until he became king. However, Hazel's presence had begun to shift his perspective on his future. The thought of ruling alone no longer seemed as appealing as it once did. Atticus found himself imagining a different kind of kingdom, one where Hazel stood beside him. Her influence reshaped his dreams, making him question whether his former ambitions were truly what he desired.

It was maddening. Atticus had only just met Hazel, yet something about her kept pulling him in, like an unseen force he couldn't shake. Was it the prophecy binding their fates? Or was it something far more infuriating—something he couldn't name, a feeling he had never experienced before? Atticus found himself watching her every move, drawn to her in a way that unsettled him. It was as if she lived in his mind, needling at his thoughts even when she wasn't around. And gods, that irritated him more than anything.

The sounds of her shifting positions in her sleep brought him out of his thoughts, but to his surprise, he saw fear on her face. Against his better judgment, he went over to her bed, gently brushing his knuckles across her cheek, pushing a hair from her face as he did. "Shh, you're safe."

To his surprise, the look on her face melted away into pure bliss. A wave of tenderness washed over him, and he marveled at how peaceful she looked, her vulnerability tugging at something deep within him. He found himself lingering here,. feeling the desire to get into bed with her and wrap his arms around her in a comforting embrace. Yet he held himself back, battling the urge with every fiber of his being. The rational part of his mind reminded him of the dangers and implications of such a move, while his heart yearned to bridge the distance between them. Torn between his deepening emotions and his cautious instincts, Atticus stood frozen, the weight of his dilemma pressing heavily on his soul. Yet he held himself back not wanting to scare her or wake her.

Instead, Atticus walked back to his chair, where he had been sitting before. Taking his seat, he scanned the room before his eyes shifted to the balcony watching for any movement, making sure nothing posed a threat to him or her. From where he sat, he could see the bruises from Darius fading away.

Atticus's protective instincts were deeply ingrained, shaped by a past filled with loss and responsibility. Growing up, he had always been the one to shield his younger siblings from the harsh realities of their world, a role that had honed his sense of vigilance and care. This innate drive to protect those he cared about was now directed at Hazel, a testament to his profound connection with her. He was glad her other wounds were healing fast, and they were very minimal. Each time he looked at it, a surge of anger and guilt coursed through him, fueling his determination to defend her from further harm.

Atticus didn't realize he had fallen asleep until her fearful cry woke him up. He bolted upright, his heart pounding in his chest as he scanned the room for the source of the cry.. Getting up, Atticus quickly advanced toward her bed as she began to toss and turn in her sleep. He gently placed a hand on her shoulder, murmuring soothing words in an attempt to calm her down. His concern grew as her cries continued, and he couldn't help but feel helpless. Atticus watched in tense silence as Hazel tossed and turned, her breaths coming in short, panicked gasps. Her fingers curled into the sheets as if grasping for something—someone—just out of reach. A soft, broken whimper escaped her lips, raw with fear, and his jaw tightened. Whatever nightmare held her in its grip, it was relentless.

Her body jerked suddenly, as if she were trying to flee from something unseen, her muscles tensing like a cornered animal. The furrow in her brow deepened, her expression contorted in a silent battle against whatever haunted her dreams. It wasn't just fear. It was desperation. A kind of terror that dug its claws in deep, refusing to let go.

He shouldn't care. Shouldn't feel the strange urge to shake her awake, to chase away whatever ghosts tormented her. And yet, he stayed, watching, fists clenched at his sides, irritation and something far more complicated twisting in his chest.

Atticus climbed into her bed, laid in front of her, pulled her to his chest, and stroked her hair as he rested his chin on top of her head.

Atticus couldn't shake the feeling of dread that something terrible was haunting her dreams, he was no stranger to post traumatic stress. He wished he could enter her mind and fight whatever monsters tormented her.

"Shhh, Shhh, it's okay. I am here. I got you." He made soothing strokes up and down her back, trying to subdue the nightmares plaguing her sleep. Hazel clung onto the black tunic he wore. Atticus wrapped his arms more tightly around Hazel, feeling the rapid beat of her heart against his own. He whispered gentle reassurances in her ear, hoping his presence would offer her some semblance of comfort. The warmth of his embrace gradually eased her tension, and her trembling subsiding as she nestled closer to him. A faint smile formed on his lips as he pulled the blanket over her to keep her warm from the winter air outside that the fireplace couldn't chase away.

Glad she didn't wake up, he now found it hard to keep his eyes open. The room was shrouded in a soft, shadowy glow cast by the waning moonlight seeping through the curtains. Outside, the wind howled, a distant lullaby to the otherwise stillness that enveloped them.

At this moment, he felt relaxed and at peace with where they lay. Sounds of the leaves skittering outside on the two story balcony, the bare tree branches hitting a corner of the balcony railing beside the archway doors. The calm windy night provided a stark contrast to the turmoil that had just unfolded. The serene ambiance washed over Atticus, calming his restless thoughts. As he listened to Hazel's soft, rhythmic breaths, he felt a profound sense of calm and purpose, as if the stillness of the night was a silent promise of better days to come.

As the morning sunlight crept into the bedroom, Atticus tightened his hold on Hazel pulling her closer to his chest. Raising his hand to shield his eyes, the golden light filtered through the curtains, casting a warm glow across the room and illuminating chasing away the remnants of the night's shadows. The gentle rays of sunlight crept through the window, casting a soft golden glow over Hazel's face. Atticus caught himself staring, his breath hitching as the light traced over her features—over the faint crease in her brow that remained even in sleep, over the freckles dusted across her cheekbones like constellations, over the way her lashes fluttered slightly as if she were caught between dreams and waking.

It irritated him. How the sight of her, bathed in morning light, made something tighten in his chest. How the warmth of it softened the sharp edges of her usual defiance, leaving her looking almost... peaceful. Almost vulnerable. It was a fleeting moment—one that would vanish the second she opened her eyes and snapped at him—but for now, he let himself look. Just for a moment. Just until the feeling passed.

The room, bathed in the soft hues of dawn, felt like a sanctuary filled with the promise of a new beginning. Hazel held him close in her sleep; her fingers curled around his tunic.

Turning his head to look down at Hazel, Atticus brushed a strand from her face, kissing her temple before carefully sliding out from under her. The previous night's events forged an unspoken bond between them, built on vulnerability and trust. Atticus felt a newfound depth in their connection, as if their shared raw honesty had woven their souls closer together. As he gazed at Hazel's serene face, he knew that whatever challenges lay ahead, they would face them together, fortified by the strength of their shared confessions.

The last thing Atticus wanted was for Hazel to wake up in his arms—yet, at the same time, he couldn't bring himself to let go. Holding her close, feeling the steady rise and fall of her breath against him, was a quiet comfort he hadn't expected. For once, there was no biting sarcasm, no sharp glares, just warmth. Just her.

But if she woke up like this? It would be a disaster. She'd shove him away, probably with a sharp remark or a well-aimed slap , and the fragile, unspoken truce between them would shatter. She'd accuse him of something ridiculous, and he'd be forced to act like he didn't care—that he wasn't affected by the way she fit so perfectly against him.

He should move. He knew he should. But his arms refused to listen.

Stretching his arms up high, he turned side to side, popping his back. As he moved and stretched, realization washed over him, He'd had a relatively undisturbed night of rest. No nightmares plagued his dreams. Only peaceful sleep. Looking back down at Hazel as she stirred but didn't wake up, Atticus couldn't help but marvel at Hazel's expression, noting how the early morning light accentuated her delicate features.

Getting out of her bed, Atticus walked over to the tray of food and tea left over from last night and carried it to the receiving room, careful not to wake Hazel as he closed the bedroom door. He wasn't surprised to see Arabella read silently in a chair.

Hearing the creak of the door, Arabella glanced up from her book, her eyes widening in surprise. She set the book down with a soft thud on the table, her gaze flicking first to Hazel's bedroom door and then to Atticus, who stood there looking far too at ease. For a brief moment, she hesitated, her brow furrowing as the unexpected scene registered.

Inhaling deeply, she stood, her movements slow and measured, suspicion creeping into her expression as she made her way over to Atticus. Her eyes flickered to the tray in his hands, then back to him, a quiet curiosity playing on her features. "Good morning, Prince Atticus," she said, her voice soft, laced with concern. "Is she still asleep?"

But there was something more beneath her calm exterior—a spark of surprise. She had no idea what had transpired the night before, no clue that Atticus hadn't originally slept in Hazel's bed, but rather the chair beside it. That had been the plan until Hazel had woken from a nightmare, thrashing and terrified, and in his haste to calm her, he had stayed, now entwined in this tangled mess of unexpected feelings.

Arabella's gaze lingered a moment longer on him, a flicker of something unreadable crossing her face as she processed the oddity of the situation.She had always been a steadfast pillar of support for Atticus, serving as a confidante and advisor through his most trying times. Their bond was rooted in years of shared history and mutual respect, while with Hazel, it was the blossoming of a deep and nurturing friendship. Taking the tray, she strode over to the door, setting the food down on the round table, and ringing the service bell. The gentle chime blended seamlessly with the tranquil ambiance of the room, adding a soft, melodic note to the morning's quiet.

Atticus felt a sense of serenity settle over him as if the room offered reassurance and solace. Arabella's calm presence only enhanced this feeling, her composed demeanor starkly contrasting the chaos that had become all too familiar.

"Yes, she is. I let her sleep a little longer, but we both know Ardnaxela is already awake and probably headed this way." Atticus rubbed the back of his neck, his voice gravely from just waking up. Moving towards the couch in front of the fireplace , he sits on the couch inhaling deeply. With its gentle, crackling fire, the fireplace added an extra layer of warmth and comfort to the room.

There was a knocked on the door, after a momentary pause Arabella moved to open it, smiling at the young servant girl who collected the tray. "Please fetch a tray of tattie scones, bacon, fried eggs, and some orange juice for your prince and Lady Hazel."

The servant nodded her head. "And you, miss Arabella?"

Arabella smiled, shaking her head. "I will be fine. I already had breakfast. Oh, and some coffee for the prince."

After the servant left, Arabella joined Atticus by the fireplace, sitting in her chair and looking at him. "I thought Ardnaxela was waiting for Hazel to heal. Does this change in plans have anything to do with last night?" she asked with a look of concern.

Atticus sighed deeply, his eyes reflecting a mixture of worry and resolve. "Yes, Arabella," he replied, his voice tinged with frustration. "Ardnaxela said we shouldn't wait any longer. You saw the state she was in last night. I couldn't bear seeing her there. From what Ardnaxela and Hazel both told me, my brother got handsy with Hazel, and after she slapped him, he didn't take kindly to that. Ardnaxela, Sybilla, and I all agreed it's better for her to learn sooner than later." Atticus didn't have to explain his reasoning, except Arabella was one of the few he trusted in court. She was one of the few who would play along to his cruel, harsh, Immortal Dragon persona he played without being offended by it.

"What was he thinking? He is engaged to Lady Duvessa. He must have been mad," Arabella released a breath of disbelief.

A faint smirk tugged at the corner of Atticus's lips as he heard Arabella's reaction. "Mad, indeed," he said, his eyes twinkling with amusement. "It seems my brother's sense of propriety is as fleeting as ever." Rubbing his face, Atticus faintly chuckled, "He wants to break the engagement off with Duvessa."

Dis-believable laughter broke from her lips. "And what marrying Hazel? He lost his ever-loving mind to think your father would approve." There was a knock on the door, and Arabella rose, walking to the door. Seeing the food being brought up fresh, the young lady's maid reached into a small pouch and handed the servant a few silver coins of appreciation, taking that tray. "Thank you, Cressida."

Bringing the tray over to a small round table in front of the couch where Atticus sat, she set it down. "I don't think your father even knows of his plans. If he did, King Kai would have punished Kingsly just for considering breaking an alliance with the Forrester family." Arabella muttered

"That's exactly what I'm trying to say. I don't think he will tell my father, which is entirely another problem. My brother tends to be rash and reckless. I pray to the goddess Aena to watch over Hazel," he added, leaning over to grab a tattie scone. Biting into the buttery scone made of mashed potatoes, he brought a satisfied smirk to his lip. "Enough of my brother. Can I enjoy this delicious breakfast with my friend?"

A faint chuckle escaped her lips as Arabella sat in her chair. Atticus took a few more bites of his tattle scone. "As for training, Hazel has very few clothing items suitable for training in the winter. I can see if the tailor can make some for her," She said aloud to herself.

Arabella directed her attention to Atticus and asked, "How did she sleep? I upped the chamomile and lavender in her bath, hoping it would help her. Seeing her like that last night was heartbreaking."

Atticus stuffed a piece of bacon into his mouth. For a moment, he was silent, and then his expression softened, and a hint of sadness clouded his eyes. "She slept fitfully, but she managed to get some rest," he replied, his voice tinged with concern. "Seeing her in such distress is a heavy burden on my heart, and I wish there was more I could do to ease her suffering." Reflecting back on the night he spent with Hazel, "She appeared to be quite shaken. I was hoping you could make her some of that tea you gave me when I first came back from the battle of Strull?" His voice was laced with concern.

Arabella nodded softly. "Of course, I can add the mixture to her baths as well. It will be better absorbed that way."

For a moment, she was quiet before Atticus focused his gaze at the bedroom door that was not being opened with Hazel standing in the doorway.. Exhaustion still clear on her face.

"But I don't have anything to train in," Hazel replied in her groggy state. Arabella rested her hand on Atticus's shoulder, offering a smile. "I can lend you some clothing. It may be slightly loose, but that's alright. You can wear a winter cloak to keep you warm until your body warms up in training."

"I want to wear my mother's cloak," Hazel insisted. "It may still have ill patched tears on it from when Darius attacked me."

Atticus and Arabella looked at each other before looking at Hazel. "I can see if the maids can fix those tears. For today, would you be alright with wearing something else?" Hazel was quiet as Arabella silently stared at him. After a moment, Hazel nodded, "Yes."

Atticus took a deep breath. "Well then, I should let you enjoy breakfast. There are some things I need to attend to." Looking at Hazel, he bowed his head before rising to his feet with a faint smile. Turning to Arabella, he bowed his head again, stood up, and left his beloved friend to tend to Wylana's future.

Chapter Thirty-Four

Hazel

Arabella pulled Hazel's hair back into a high pony, but not before weaving a triquetra braid into it first. Hazel was dressed in a dark gray Henley long-sleeve shirt with a belt across her waist to hold it close to her body.. The top was paired with black trousers, and she wore comfortable black boots instead of her normal flats. Her mother's necklace was hidden under her the fabric. Hazel took a deep breath to calm herself down.

Soon, there was a knock on the door , followed by Ardnaxela walking in. The White Dragoness was dressed in a long-sleeved dusty blue V-neck training attire. Her hair was woven in intricate braids, leading to a high-rise ponytail. Her collar was open, showing off a bit of cleavage along with a faint scar peeking out from the left side of her breast. A sword hung around her waist. On the hilt, she saw a dragon's head at the base of the hilt.

Hazel couldn't help but notice how Ardnaxela's muscular frame filled out the sleeves with each movement revealing her strength and power. The sight of the scar only added to her intimidating presence, making Hazel feel even more apprehensive. It was clear that Ardnaxela was a seasoned warrior, and her imposing demeanor left no doubt about her capabilities.

"Come on, let's go, small fawn. We got work to do before I hand you over to Sybilla." Ardnaxela held herself with great confidence as she leaned against the doorway. "Come on, we don't have all day!" Ardnaxela ordered.

Hazel felt a knot tighten in her stomach, her heart pounding faster with each passing second. She nodded quickly, not trusting her voice, and hurried to follow Ardnaxela. Despite her fear, she couldn't help but admire the Dragoness commanding appearance and how she embodied grace and ferocity.

Hazel assumed they were going to the barracks, but to her surprise, they weren't. She turned her head from Ardnaxela to the barracks and then back to the woman training her. "Aren't we heading to the barracks to train?" She asked, her voice a bit confused. Hazel's mind raced as they walked, trying to piece together where they might be headed instead.

Each step seemed to amplify her anxiety, but she steeled herself, determined to prove her worth and learn from the formidable Dragoness beside her.

Ardnaxela only shook her head, not even looking at her as Hazel tried to keep pace with her. "Oh no, we are going outside. Atticus briefed me you barley know how to use your magic. So, if you lose control of your magic, I want it to happen away from people. Do you have any experience with weapons?" Ardnaxela finally looked at Hazel, waiting for her reply.

Her cheeks flushed slightly as she shook her head. "No, I've never handled any weapons before," she admitted, her voice barely above a whisper.

Ardnaxela's expression remained unreadable, but Hazel thought she saw a flicker of understanding in the Dragoness eyes. Hazel had occasionally helped her uncle hunt when it was too cold outside. So *technically*, she had some experience, but only for hunting, not fighting.

"I can shoot a bow, but as far as a sword, I never held one," Hazel replied softly.

With the look on her face, it appeared Ardnaxela was coming up with strategies in her head before, turning her head slightly to Hazel. "Good, that means you have some shoulders, back, arms, forearms, core, and hip muscles. This is good. I can work with that," the Dragoness said as she made her way to the back courtyard.

Hazel shielded her eyes from the bright sun with one hand, as her other hand began to rub her arm to generate heat against the cold. Her black velvet cloak flapped behind her in the breeze. "Isn't it a bit cold to be training outside?" Hazel asked with caution.

Stopping, the White Dragoness looked over her shoulder with a raised eyebrow as she clenched her jaw. "Do you think your enemies care if it's too cold? First lesson, little fawn: You should never underestimate your enemies. No matter the weather, they will still find ways to kill you." Her tone was so unamused and dead that Hazel felt foolish for asking the question. "Now come on, once we start warming up your muscles, the cold won't bother you," Ardnaxela continued her stride to the back courtyard where the two walked toward the forest behind the castle.

After about a mile, they stopped walking. The training ground was a secluded clearing in the dense forest, surrounded by towering trees with thick canopies that filtered the sunlight into a soft, dappled glow. The air was filled with the earthy scent of moss and damp leaves and the occasional rustle of wildlife moving through the underbrush. The sounds of their exertion were accompanied by the distant calls of birds and the gentle whisper of a nearby stream. The pine trees stood tall above them, and the smell of salt in the air told Hazel they were not from the sea. Except the smile brought to her lips by their surroundings vanished as Ardnaxela began barking out orders.

"Show me your stance."

Pausing for a moment, Hazel took up a position as if she were about to fight. She'd never been in a proper battle until the Raven Palm ambush, but instinct and memories guided her. Her feet were shoulder-width apart, knees slightly bent to maintain balance. She placed her left foot forward and her right foot back, weight evenly distributed. Her hands rose—left in front, right near her waist, as if ready to draw an invisible bowstring.

Ardnaxela sucked her teeth, letting out a sharp sigh as she walked over. Her hand rested on the hilt of her sword as she slowly circled Hazel, eyes narrowed in silent scrutiny.

"Where in the Veiled Hells did you learn to stand like that?" Ardnaxela finally asked, eyebrow raised.

Hazel's voice was quiet but steady. "I used to hunt for my uncle when it got too cold for his body to handle the trek. This stance helped me keep steady when lining up a shot."

Ardnaxela's eyes flicked to her, then back to the stance. "Ah. That explains it." She stopped in front of Hazel and gave a faint smirk. "It's not bad—for shooting a still target. But in combat? You'll be laid flat on your back before you can notch an arrow."

Before Hazel could respond, her feet were swiped out from under her. Slamming to her side, she yelped before looking up at Ardnaxela. "What was that for?" Hazel exclaimed

"Like I said, you will be laid out on your back in seconds." There was an actual smirk on this woman's face as she offered her hand. Hazel's eyes narrowed, and she reluctantly took the woman's hand, pulling herself up. Her pride was bruised, but she couldn't help but feel respect for the woman's confidence.

Hazel hissed in pain as Ardnaxela yanked her arm up and pinned it against her back. "Try to get out of this hold. I want to see what you already know."

Hazel winced, her teeth gritting as a sharp pain shot through her arm and shoulder. She twisted her body instinctively to alleviate the pressure, but Ardnaxela's grip was unyielding. Sweat beaded on Hazel's forehead as she struggled to find a way to escape the hold. She swung her free arm back, almost hitting Ardnaxela in the ribs, but the Dragoness caught her other arm.

"That is a smart move, but not good enough to break free. Try to throw me over your shoulder. Do it over your wounded one." Again, the Dragoness barked.

"Are you crazy? I can reopen my stitching if I do," Hazel objected, still trying to get out of the Dragoness grasp. Hazel's mind raced, weighing the risk of reopening her stitches against the necessity of proving herself. She had a feeling that Ardnaxela wasn't one to offer idle challenges. There was a lesson hidden in the pain. With a deep breath, she trusted the process and braced herself for the maneuver.

"In a real fight, you do what you must to survive. If that means sacrificing your shoulder over your life, then you take it. "In a real fight," Ardnaxela said, tone sharp, "you do what you must to survive." She circled Hazel, eyes scanning for hesitation. "If that means sacrificing your shoulder over your life, then you take it." Hazel gave a slight nod, jaw tight. Ardnaxela stopped behind her. "Grab onto my belt." Hazel hesitated. "Now," Ardnaxela barked. "Pull on it while throwing your heel to the back of your head—"

"What?"

"To throw me off balance," she clarified. "Shift your weight to one side *as* you pull me over your shoulder. Don't overthink it. Move."

Hazel did as she was instructed, and it worked. The White Dragoness grunted as her side met the hard ground. A hot flash of pain shot into Hazel's shoulder, and she reached up to grasp it. Pulling it away, she looked at her hand, glad to see there was no blood. A surge of triumph mixed with relief washed over Hazel. Despite the pain, she felt a newfound sense of confidence and capability.

Hazel looked down at Ardnaxela, her breathing heavy, but proud of her accomplishment. "Good, not only did you throw me over your shoulder, you also made sure there wasn't too much weight on your wounded shoulder to damage it." Standing up, Ardnaxela stood up and dusted herself off. "Now, again."

The two sparred for hours. Hazel sat up against a tree, holding her shoulder as her chest burned. Sweat dripped down her face, mingling with the dirt and grime that clung to her skin. Her breaths came in shallow, ragged gasps as she struggled to regain her composure.

"You did better than I thought. You're stronger too."

Hazel couldn't help but feel a flicker of pride, knowing she had exceeded the Dragoness expectations. Determined to prove herself even more, Hazel resolved to push her limits further in the next round of training.

"However, you tend to keep your left side open. You're small, so don't go to big, wide attacks. They leave you open. Go for smaller ones that are closer to your body."

Was that supposed to be a compliment? Huffing, Hazel shook her head but nodded in appreciation. "Thanks, I guess?" she said, trying to catch her breath between words. Hazel's limbs trembled from exhaustion, her muscles screaming in protest with every movement.

Soon, Hazel turned her head to look at Ardnaxela. "About last night, thank you. I hope you don't get in trouble for coming to my defense," Hazel muttered.

After tightening her ponytail, Ardnaxela looked up at Hazel before nodding. "Prince Atticus told me to watch over you till you can handle yourself here at court."

Hazel's eyes glanced up slightly towards Ardnaxela at the mention of Prince Atticus as a wave of gratitude washed over her. She felt renewed determination, realizing the depth of trust and responsibility placed on her.

Ardnaxela continued, "Besides, Kingsly was lucky I didn't pierce my thought through him right there."

Hazel remembered what the Dragoness told Kingsly. How he should be glad she was on the sword's hilt and not his brother. Could Prince Atticus truly be that formidable in combat? Hazel's curiosity was piqued. She wanted to learn more about the prince's prowess. The notion that someone as fierce as Ardnaxela deferred to Atticus only deepened her respect—and her determination to prove herself worthy of their protection.

"Ardnaxela, what happened last time Atticus had a sword pointed at Kingsly? Why did Kingsly look startled when you said that?" Hazel asked with caution.

As she waited for Ardnaxela's response, her mind raced with possibilities. She wondered what kind of warrior Prince Atticus must be to instill such fear in someone like Kingsly. The thought of witnessing his prowess firsthand sent a shiver of anticipation through her, mingling with her exhaustion and fueling her resolve to become stronger. Ardnaxela chuckled, shaking her head with a smile; what the hell? Why was she smiling like that?

"When I was first appointed as Kingsly's second, it was after the battle at Fortuna against the Netherian warriors wreaking havoc on it. These warriors were and are known for their unparalleled ferocity and dark magic, making them formidable opponents that few can withstand. Prince Atticus led the charge against them at Fortuna. This victory solidified his reputation and sent a clear message to his enemies that he was a force to be reckoned with." Ardnaxela reached for her water skin to drink before continued, "No one at court knew I was training to become a warrior, despite being a lady waiting for his mother."

Tilting the water skin in her hand, she let the cold water soothe the back of Ardnaxela's neck.

"He saw something in me when a man tried to get handsy, and I nearly put him in the ground for it. I don't tolerate that kind of disrespect."

Hazel's gaze hardened, the memory sharpening her voice.

"But it wasn't just that. It was when the tide turned against us—when we thought we'd lose. The dead piled up faster than we could blink, and morale? Gone."

She inhaled slowly, then continued.

"I spotted a break in their right flank. Just a few yards of uneven ground and a patrol that got too comfortable. They thought no one would be crazy enough to crawl through a blood-soaked trench half-collapsed from cannon fire."

Her lip curled slightly, almost amused.

"I was. I covered myself in dirt, ash, and the blood of our own fallen so I'd blend in. Slid through that trench like a ghost, silent and small. I waited until their sentries passed, then slipped into their back line during the shift change."

Her voice dropped, almost reverent.

"Once inside, I didn't need force—I used their own weapons. Cut their comms. Sabotaged their munitions. Set fire to their supply carts. They didn't know what hit them."

She leaned back, a faint smirk playing at her lips.

"By the time our front line realized what happened, their defenses were already crumbling—and he was watching. He saw what I did. That's when he decided I was worth something."

"But it wasn't until Kingsly found out a *woman* was the one who claimed victory for Wylana that he called for my head on grounds of treason. Said I disobeyed command. Would've made it stick, too—if Atticus hadn't stepped in."

She shook her head, a bitter laugh under her breath.

"They crossed swords over it. Kingsly fights with brute strength, but Atticus? He's all precision. Calculated, fast. He left a deep slash across Kingsly's chest—just enough to make him yield and never forget who the heir really is."

She met their eyes, something flickering in her expression.

"Kingsly's been careful to stay in his brother's favor ever since... or at least, he *was*—until you came along."

Listening to Ardnaxela's story, it was surprising to hear that the White Dragoness was once a lady waiting for Queen Sage and that Atticus took up for her when Kingsly wanted her head.

"Now come on, let's get you back. You're supposed to train with Sybilla on your wielding ability." Ardnaxela stood offering her hand to Hazel, who didn't take it this time. It earned a smirk from the Dragoness, who also chuckled softly. Hazel didn't take Ardnaxela's hand because she wanted to prove her independence and strength. She had been working hard on her training and felt confident enough to stand independently. She remembered what had happened the last time and took the Dragoness hand.

Standing up alone, Hazel started heading back to the castle, but stopped, realizing her necklace was getting warm on her skin. She looked around them to see if she could spot anything moving in the trees.

Hazel's reaction to the warming necklace was one of cautious alarm. She knew that the necklace had magical properties, often as a warning signal for impending danger or significant events. Her heightened awareness and instinct told her to stay alert, and she took a quick, scanning glance around their surroundings, ready to respond to any potential threat.

There was someone out there with Netherian magic watching them. All alarms were going off in her head. "Hazel, is something wrong?" Ardnaxela's voice snapped Hazel's attention back before she shook her head.

"I thought I heard something, maybe a rabbit." Hazel replies before they both headed to the castle. Her decision stemmed from a mixture of fear and protection. She didn't want to worry the Dragoness unnecessarily.

The trek back to the castle seemed shorter this time while they made small talk about little things .

Walking into the hallways, her necklace did not ease its warmth, making Hazel's eyes scan every inch of the hallway. Suddenly, Lady Duvessa stepped into view, separating

Hazel and her female guard. Which from glancing over Duvessa's shoulder. Hazel can make out Ardnaxela's eyes sharpening on the woman.

Hazel's heart pounded as she faced Lady Duvessa, whose cold, calculating eyes pierced through her. The air between them crackled with unspoken tension, a mixture of mistrust laced with dislike at her entitled behavior towards Arabella. Lady Duvessa's presence was beginning to unnerved Hazel, as if the noblewoman could sense the hidden powers of the necklace and the danger it signaled.

"Lady Hazel, there you are; I have been looking all over for you." The woman caught Hazel by surprise, Hazel forced a polite smile though she remained wary. "Is that so, Lady Duvessa?" she replied, her voice steady but guarded. Internally, Hazel needed to tread carefully, knowing that any interaction with Duvessa can possibly cause issues later on.

"I was wondering if you wanted to have some tea with me later today. What do you think?"

Viper was all Hazel thought, the moment she has left that training field, her necklace hasn't stopped feeling warm, but now with Duvessa standing infant of her it was much warmer.

Hazel's mind raced, torn between the necessity to remain composed and her necklace's urgent warning. Hazel didn't know this woman, and now she was exposed as the Ivory fawn. She needed to be more cautious with who she spent time with alone..

"Thank you for the generous invitation. I will think about it, but for now, I must be on my way. Sybilla is expecting me." Hazel said, wanting to keep their conversation as short as possible without rejecting Lady Duvessa's invitation in a rude way.

As Hazel walked away, she could hear the scoff of disbelief of being rejected. Something Hazel assumed Duvessa was not used to.

Hazel couldn't help but replay the interaction in her mind, dissecting every word and gesture. The warning from her necklace felt like a storm cloud hanging over her, its significance impossible to ignore. She knew she needed to speak with Sybilla, not only because of their arranged meeting, but also to seek her counsel and unravel the meaning behind her necklace and what else it can do.

Hazel stepped around Lady Duvessa, closing the distance between her and Ardnaxela, who reached for Hazel's arm. The Dragoness eyes were locked on Lady Duvessa. Ardnaxela's grip on Hazel's arm was firm, a silent signal to just keep walking and disregard the Lady. Hazel could feel the Dragoness muscles tense, ready to spring into action at the slightest provocation.

Lady Duvessa's smile never wavered, but the subtle narrowing of her eyes betrayed her awareness of the silent exchange of looks that made a chill creep up Hazel's spine. Almost like she was a viper sizing up her next meal. Nodding her head, Duvessa rested her hands in front of her, looking at Ardnaxela before her attention turned back to Hazel. "Don't keep me waiting too long, Lady Hazel. I would love to get to know you better."

Everything about Kingsly's fiancée grated on Hazel. She'd never heard of Duvessa's family name, and the woman's sudden shift from venomous to serene only deepened Hazel's distrust. Beneath the polished facade and honeyed words, Hazel sensed a coiled viper—charm hiding anything but benign intent.

Hazel and Ardnaxela walked toward Hazel's room so she could change into clean clothes before heading to the temple. As they walked away from Lady Duvessa, Hazel realized her necklace was cooling.

Was she one of them? She couldn't be, not when there was no sign of her fingers darkening or when she heard rumors about people going missing here. Why did her mother's necklace warm even more when she appeared? Anxiety gnawed at Hazel's insides, each unanswered question amplifying her unease. The cooling of her necklace only added to her confusion, leaving her torn between fear and suspicion. She felt a growing urgency to uncover why it warmed around Lady Duvessa before it was too late. Her mind racing with possibilities that chilled her to the bone.

Once they were inside her bedroom, Hazel turned to look at Ardnaxela. "What do you know about Lady Duvessa?" she blurted

Ardnaxela stopped at the doorway before turning to look at Hazel, tilting her head confused before crossing her arms, "Not more then what the royal family knows I'm afraid," she admitted, her voice tinged with curiosity.

"I know she's engaged to Kingsly. Honestly, it came out of nowhere. None of us even knew she was a noblewoman until King Kai announced the engagement—right after Prince Heath turned it down. He was supposed to marry her, but Prince Heath turned down the arrangement, saying it wasn't his place and that Atticus should be the one to marry her. King Kai did not like that and well , the king's third-born has been away on a diplomatic mission to locate where the druids went after the blood war. This alliance was meant to benefit both Wylana and the Forrester family. Beyond that, I haven't bothered trying to understand it. Why?" Ardnaxela fully turned to look at Hazel, taking a step closer.

Her eyes widened in surprise, her mouth opening slightly as she processed the new information. "Wait, is Prince Heath another brother? I didn't realize Atticus had more siblings other than Kingsly and Reed," she said, her voice tinged with confusion.

Ardnaxela sighed, a look of realization crossing her face. "Right, your still new to all this. Yes, Atticus is the oldest, then came Kingsly, followed by Heath, and finally Reed," she explained patiently. "It's important to understand the dynamics at play here."

Hazel looked confused for a moment before asking, "So, what are these family dynamics and how do they affect the current alliance? Does each brother have a specific role or influence in decision-making?"

Ardnaxela nodded at Hazel's curiosity. "Yes, each brother plays a unique part in the family's political and social strategies," she explained. "Has Arabella not explained this to you already?"

Shaking her head, Hazel tucks a strand of hair down her face.

"But why the sudden interest in the Forrester family's affairs?" Ardnaxela asked, her gaze narrowing. "You don't seem to be the type to engage in gossip—so what is it about Lady Duvessa that has you asking questions?"

Taking a deep breath, she pulled out her mother's necklace, showing it to Ardnaxela, whose eyes widened at it. "The last three times I have been in danger because of the Netherian people. And all three times this necklace warmed. I don't know why, but it did."

Ardnaxela's eyes widened in shock and curiosity as she took a closer look at the necklace. She reached out delicately, her fingers hovering just above the intricate design. "This... this is no ordinary piece of jewelry, Hazel. Where did you get this?"

Hazel looked at Ardnaxela, ignoring the Dragoness question and continuing the explanation of its working. "It warmed when I ran for my life from Darius and his gang, and it intensified when we were ambushed by the mercenaries. Just now, it warmed again when we were in the forest. It grew even hotter as *she* got closer. I am not accusing her, but it's quite the coincidence," Hazel explained.

Ardnaxela's face turned from soft to stone "Who else knows about this necklace and what it does?"

The alarm in her voice made Hazel tense before she responded, "Just me and my uncle. As far as I know," Hazel replied truthfully.

Ardnaxela sighed in relief, nodding her head and heading towards the door with an almost predatory look. "Change quickly. We need to let Atticus and Sybilla know right away," the Dragoness ordered firm leaving no room for argument in her tone closing the door.

Hazel's heart pounded as she felt a surge of adrenaline. She had never seen Ardnaxela so alarmed, and the urgency in her voice made it clear that there was something the three of them knew about what her necklace is or what it might do. With trembling hands, she hurried to change, her mind racing with questions and a growing sense of unease.

Chapter Thirty-Five

Hazel

The ride to the temple on horseback wasn't as long as Hazel thought it would be. The silent ride made Hazel feel bit unnerved at the urgency Hazel's horse was an exquisite, gentle palomino gelding who stayed close to her. He was the right size for her small stature. She had never had a horse before, but she fell in love with this gelding the moment they brought him out. The stable boy said his name was Phoenix, and it was the most appropriate name for him.

She tried to catch glimpses over her shoulder at Atticus and Ardnaxela's expressions as they rode behind her, hoping for some reassurance. Instead, she found herself lost in her own doubts and the weight of the journey ahead.

Once they got to the castle of Andromeda, Ardnaxela dismounted her chestnut mare. Its black mane was braided into a woven design with metal beads in it. Her muzzle was black but had a white star and stripe design on its face. The mare was smaller than Kissem. Hazel remembered Ardnaxela calling her horse Emmy back at the stable.

As they approached the temple, Hazel's anxiety grew, each step of the journey amplifying her inner turmoil. The Castle's silhouette against the horizon seemed ominous and alluring like a siren song on the wind, a stark reminder of the challenges ahead. Hazel felt awe as she tied her horses to the post outside the castle Andromeda, marveling at its intricate architecture. Hazel still sensed a humming from the castle as the trio climbed the stairs to the doors. It was like it was called to her.

Each footstep echoed against the stone walls, amplifying her apprehension and curiosity. She couldn't help but feel as though the very essence of the castle was watching her, waiting to reveal its secrets. Her necklace hummed as if reacted to being inside of the castle. Hazel's heart thundered in her chest as she crossed the threshold, the air inside heavy with the weight of ancient power and a hush of forgotten mysteries

Hazel excitedly brushed her hand over the large archway door leading into the large entry way of the castle. Pausing momentary to admire the design hidden under the dirt that came from the elements from outside. She took in the large entryway.

"Hazel?" Atticus called out from the stairwell. Coming to , Hazel looks up to see her and Ardnaxela -Who was staring at her- was falling behind.

Quickly gathered herself, offering a reassuring smile to Ardnaxela before hurrying to catch up with him. The sense of urgency in his voice fueled her determination to uncover the secrets that awaited them.

"This place... it's alive," Hazel whispered, rooted in the center of the lobby as she turned in a slow circle, taking it all in. The feeling thrummed deeper than sound—it was a call that echoed through her very soul.

She wondered if the castle held answers to questions she hadn't even thought to ask. The connection between her necklace and the castle's energy left her both intrigued and slightly unsettled, but she knew she had to find out what it all meant.

She didn't realize Atticus had returned until he was at her side, touching her arm gently. Hazel flinched at the sensation as it pulled her back to reality. She turned to meet his concerned gaze, relieved for his steady presence midst the overwhelming sensations.

"What do you feel?" Curiosity filled his voice.

Hazel looked at him momentarily before looking around her and stepping away. There was a welcoming wave of calm washing over her as she admired the marbling patterns of lilac and gold. Winged warriors depicted in various stained-glass windows. It was like she realized she was at home despite never being here.

"This place feels... Alive... It's like it welcomes us in here... Like it is slowly waking up. It doesn't feel like we are alone here. It feels like the Aestivals are still here. Waiting...Watching," Hazel mumbled out as her hand trailed up a marble pillar supporting the balcony overlooking the lobby. Perhaps it was because the castle's energy resonated with something deep within her, something long forgotten.

Hazel had always felt a strange sense of longing growing up in her village, a feeling that she belonged somewhere else. Now, standing in this ancient place, she couldn't help but feel that she had finally found where she was meant to be.

"That's because it's a welcoming home in its Ivory Fawn." Atticus's fingers took her chin in them, turning her head to look at him. He held her gaze longer than he has before. Hazel's breath caught in her throat as she stared into Atticus's gaze, feeling a warmth spread through her chest. His eyes held answers to questions she didn't know she had, and for a moment, the overwhelming sensations of the castle faded into the background. She felt a newfound sense of peace and purpose, as if being here with Atticus made everything clearer, with him being her Crimson Dragon.

"We need to speak with Sybilla about your necklace." Atticus released her chin before stepping back, motioning with his head to follow him up the stairs.

"What necklace?" Sybilla's voice came from above.

Looking up, she saw the woman on a balcony connected to She stood at the top of one of the two stairways leading from the ground floor to the second level, a white cloak draped over her shoulders and parting just enough to reveal the rich green velvet of her gown. The ancient balcony where Sybilla stood was adorned with intricate carvings of mythical beasts and delicate vines, its weathered stone still holding a regal grandeur. The ornate railings, appearing as if woven from ivory marble, gleamed softly in the golden light streaming through stained-glass windows. A mosaic of color spilled across the floor below, casting the entire scene in timeless beauty.

Hazel clenched her necklace softly, waiting to feel any slightest bit of warmth coming from the necklace. Yet it was cold from their ride. "This may sound far fetched but," pausing momentarily before continuing "I fear there is a Netherian wielder is inside the court," Hazel called up to Sybilla as she walked down the stairs to Hazel, concern in her eyes. Hazel herself didn't know how or why her necklace did what it does, but we needed to trust these people. Which means not holding back her suspicions.

From the corner of her eyes, Hazel saw Atticus turned quickly to look at her, his expression shifting from curiosity to alarm, his eyes widening. He moved closer to Hazel, a protective urgency in his posture. "A Netherian wielder? At the castle?" he echoed, his voice low and tense.

"She thinks it might be Lady Duvessa." Ardnaxela chimed in, crossing her arms over her chest and leaning on the wall beside the stairs.

Atticus's jaw tightened at the mention of Lady Duvessa, his eyes narrowing as a flash of anger crossed his face. He glanced toward Sybilla before turning back to Hazel with a mixture of disbelief and concern. "Lady Duvessa has always been an enigma, but a Netherian wielder?" he murmured, his voice laden with the gravity of the situation.

Sybilla's gaze shifted from the warrior to Hazel, confusion on her face. "Hazel, that's a rather big accusation. Do you have any proof?"

Hazel took a deep breath, understanding the weight of her words. "If I'm wrong, it could cause a rift within the court, leading to mistrust and chaos," she acknowledged, her voice steady but laced with worry. "But if I'm right, and we do nothing, the danger she poses is far greater." Taking a deep breath, she removed her mother's necklace, holding it up to Sybilla to see from the balcony, whose eyes widen at it. "The last two times, Netherian wielders such as Darius, along with the ambush in the woods, attacked me. It somehow magically acted as a beacon and grew hot when they were near. I don't know why or how it warms, but it does."

Sybilla's eyes widened further, and she leaned over the balcony for a closer look, her expression a mix of awe and apprehension. "That can't be," she whispered, her voice trembling slightly.

"Then earlier, when I was training with Ardnaxela, I felt it warm again but didn't see anyone. When I got to the court, Lady Duvessa cut me off from Ardnaxela to invite me for tea. That's when I felt it warming up. I think she is the wielder," Hazel replied.

"Did you know about this?" Sybilla asked Atticus "Then earlier, when I was training with Ardnaxela, I felt it warm again but didn't see anyone. When I got to the court, Lady Duvessa cut me off from Ardnaxela to invite me for tea. That's when I felt it warming up. I think she is the wielder," Hazel said, unease curling low in her stomach.

Sybilla turned sharply toward Atticus. "Did you know about this?" she asked, her tone clipped, almost alarmed.

Hazel glanced between them, catching the flicker of something unspoken pass between their eyes. Atticus's expression faltered. For a heartbeat, he looked utterly undone—like someone had ripped a page from history and laid it bare in front of him. He didn't answer right away. His gaze dropped to the pendant at her neck, and his breath caught so subtly Hazel almost missed it.

He shook his head, but it felt delayed—like he was still processing something only he and Sybilla understood.

"No," he finally said, voice tight with disbelief. "I didn't know."

Hazel's brows drew together, a question poised on the edge of her lips—but Sybilla was already turning, her pale cloak catching the light as she moved. Hazel climbed the stairs to meet her, each step light but laced with urgency. The air felt heavier here, like secrets had sunk into the very stone over centuries.

On the balcony, Sybilla stood motionless in the mosaic of stained-glass light. Without a word, Sybilla extended her hand—not with force, but with reverence. As if reclaiming a piece of a story long buried.

Atticus was in tow with Hazel as she climbed the stairs.

"Where did you get this, Hazel?" Atticus' voice had a tone of urgency as his eyes were locked in on her.

Shaking her head, Hazel looked between the pair, trying to recall if Archibald ever told her where he got it from came from. "It was my mother's. That's all I know about it other than it warms itself somehow when there are Netherian wielders nearby."

For a moment, they were both quiet. Sybilla's eyes widened as she processed Hazel's revelation. Her fingers trembled slightly as they hovered near the tree pendant with lilac and orchid shaded leaves. "This changes everything," she whispered, her voice filled with awe and concern. "If your mother possessed such a powerful artifact..." Sybilla looked at Hazel, motioning with her hand to follow them as Atticus and Sybilla made their way up the stairs. Hazel's heart raced as she followed them, her mind swirling with questions.

Hazel didn't know where they were heading. All she knew was that they both looked alarmed seeing her necklace.

Walking into an enormous library, Hazel's eyes widened in amazement. It was a vast, cavernous space with towering book shelves accompanied with slider ladders that almost to the ceiling. It stretched on endlessly, appearing to hold ancient text and scrolls. Ornate candlelit chandeliers cast a soft, golden glow illuminated the large space. Rich mahogany tables were scattered throughout, each accompanied by ancient tattered velvet chairs, inviting scholars to delve into the library's countless secrets. The dome-sized roof had paintings of aerial warriors and clouds with hues of rising morning sun. There were paintings all around of various parts of landscaping, architecture, wars, and portraits of people she didn't recognize.

Walking into the center of the room, one of the book stacks had a portrait hanging on the end. The four of them stopped in front of it to see a winged woman sitting on a throne with a tall, winged male standing beside her with a hand on her shoulder. This woman held nothing but elegance and grace in her posture in the throne for the painting.

Sybilla pointed to the woman and said, "This is Queen Asteria, the last ruler of the Aestival realm before it fell into chaos."

Hazel's heart skipped as she realized the connection. Asteria was dressed as if she were a warrior goddess with a white dress accompanied by a corset that went from her neck down, stopping at her waist to protect her throat, chest, and torso.

While taking a good look at the painting, Hazel's eyes went to Asteria's neck, where she saw a familiar-looking necklace.

It was her mother's necklace—it was originally Queen Asteria's necklace.

"How did your mother come across the necklace Hazel?" Sybilla asked from behind the stunned fawn who stared at the painting, not turning her attention away from it.

"My great-great-grandmother was Queen Asteria. Which would make me the last direct bloodline to her," Hazel confessed before looking at the trio to see their reactions, not surprised to see their jaws drop to the floor. "I didn't know anything about it till recently. I thought my mother died of a broken heart because of my father's passing. Although my uncle recently told me she actually died protecting me. I used my gifts as a child despite being told to hide them. It drew the attention of the Netherian wielders, and she and my uncle fought to keep me safe while my father was away hunting." Inhaling the musk of the ancient library around her, she tried to steady her heart as she told her trusted companions about her past. Hazel's voice wavered as she continued.

Her eyes glistened with unshed tears, her words pressing heavily on her chest. "When my father came back, my mother died under a wisteria tree we had in our backyard. My father was devastated when he saw her. He kneeled beside her, sobbing." Rubbing her clammy hands on her riding pants, she took another deep breath as if it stopped the trembling at her confession of everything she knew.

"My father blamed me for killing my mother. He tried to dispose of me in his fit, but my uncle stopped him. That's all I know about my mother's side. I know that when I used my gift before coming here to save a farmer's boy, I saw Queen Asteria in a vision. She didn't say anything, but she touched my chest with this glowing light. I saw her again last night, warning me that a man was coming for me with plans not only to kill me, but also Atticus. Asteria told me how you three are the only ones I can trust. So, that is why I am telling you everything I know."

Atticus walked up to her, wiping her tears away before putting a hand on her cheek and stroking it with his thumb. "I won't let that happen, princess." He stood there in amazement and disbelief at what she was hearing.

Hazel felt an overwhelming mix of relief and vulnerability after sharing her story. The weight of her past lightened, even if just a little, now that her friends knew the truth. She hoped that she could finally find the strength and support she desperately needed by opening up.

Atticus's eyes softened as he gazed at Hazel, his thumb gently tracing her cheek contours. His touch was tender, almost reverent, as if he understood the immense courage it took for her to share such a painful part of her past.

Sybilla's eyes stayed on Atticus, whose eyes were caution-laced. "Thank you for your honesty, and I will be just as honest with you," she said. Soon, the scribe's eyes met Hazel's before softening from the icy look she was giving Atticus

"Sybilla." Atticus growled in warning.

The scribe's expression hardened momentarily at Atticus's growl, but she took a deep breath before continuing. "I understand the stakes, Atticus," she said, her voice steady and calm.. "There is no way to sugarcoat this. I am sorry." Sybilla's expression shifted more into remorse or pity for what she was about to say. Her shoulders slumped slightly, and she took a deep breath as if bracing herself.

"Don't, Sybilla." Atticus stepped between Hazel and Sybilla, blocking the view. The room felt charged with unspoken words, a palpable tension hanging in the air. Atticus's eyes darted between the two of them, his jaw clenched as if holding back a torrent of emotions.

"She has a right to know Atticus. It's her life, not yours," Sybilla snapped at him.

Hazel pushed Atticus aside. "What do I have the right to know?" she blurted out, frustrated that they were talking about her like she wasn't even there.

Sybilla's eyes locked onto Hazel's just as Atticus stepped back, his expression hardening. The movement was subtle, but intentional—he was creating distance. Hazel barely had a moment to process it before she heard it: a low, guttural rumble rising from Atticus's chest. Not pain. Not surprise. Fury. Quiet, barely contained.

He turned away sharply, one hand rising to rub at his face as if he could wipe the moment clean. His fingers dragged down his jaw, trembling slightly with restrained emotion. Hazel's stomach turned.

She looked back to Sybilla—and instantly regretted asking the question.

Gone was the woman of poise and quiet power. In her place stood someone carved by grief, her face etched with a sorrow so raw it cut straight through Hazel's chest. It wasn't just sadness—it was a mourning of what had to be said.

Hazel didn't even know the truth yet, and already she felt the room shifting around her. The dread settled like frost beneath her skin, crawling up her spine. Whatever this was, it was heavy enough to leave scars.

"You may not survive this prophecy," Sybilla said, her voice thin with effort. "There may be a small chance you'll die... and not come back."

The words landed like a blow to the ribs.

Hazel's breath hitched. She couldn't speak. Couldn't move. The floor beneath her felt suddenly too far away.

Sybilla closed her eyes for a moment, as if steadying herself. "I'm sorry, Hazel. But you had a right to know."

Hazel's heart plummeted before she looked at Atticus, who was leaning on a bookshelf with his back turned to the trio. Ardnaxela stepped forward, her voice trembling but determined. "We can't let this happen. There must be another way to fulfill the prophecy," she said, her eyes pleading with Atticus and Sybilla.

Hazel felt a storm of emotions swirl within her—fear, anger, and a profound sense of betrayal. "And you knew about this?" Hazel's voice was sharp as a knife as she turned to face Atticus, who had tried to silence Sybilla from revealing the truth. "Why didn't you tell me?" she demanded, her voice trembling with a mix of rage and hurt.

Atticus visibly flinched at her words, keeping his back to them unable to meet her gaze. "How could you keep something so important from me? How could you let me walk blindly about this?"

"We will give you both a moment to talk." Ardnaxela said from behind Hazel and Sybilla.

As she and Sybilla quietly exited the room, the atmosphere grew even more tense, the silence almost deafening. The air felt heavy with unspoken words and unresolved emotions, making it difficult for Hazel to breathe. She could feel the weight of Atticus's presence, even with his back still turned, and the chasm of betrayal between them widened with each passing second. Watching Atticus just stand leaning against a stack of shelves without saying anything only made her frustration grow.

"Atticus, look at me! Why would you not tell me?!" Hazel exclaimed, watching him stand there leaning against the bookshelf as if she wasn't yelling at him. She had trusted Atticus implicitly, believing that after last night he would be honest with her. The realization that he had kept such a monumental secret shattered that trust, leaving her feeling isolated and betrayed.

When he turned, Hazel saw the Immortal Dragon peering at her as he stalked over to her. Hazel's breath caught in her throat, and she instinctively took a step back. The familiar warmth in Atticus's eyes had been replaced by a chilling intensity that made her skin crawl. For the first time, she truly saw the formidable power he possessed, and it both terrified and mesmerized her.

"You really want to know, Princess?" His voice was loud and heaving as he stalked toward Hazel.

Swallowing deeply, seeing such hunger in his eyes. Her mind raced with conflicting emotions. Part of her wanted to flee from the dangerous aura emanating from Atticus, while another part felt inexplicably drawn to his raw, unrestrained power. Her heart pounded in her chest as she grappled with the situation's intensity, feeling both vulnerable and inexplicably intrigued.

"Because, Hazel, I care about you. I don't know why I do , but I do. You are intoxicating. The prophecy says you will be guided by the Crimson Dragon. If I don't guide you, then you won't become the Ivory Fawn, meaning you might not die because of it. Call me selfish, but I am with you because I cannot bear the thought of losing you. I would kill anyone that hurts you...Including my brother."

Hazel's breathing hitched, and she didn't know what to think. Her emotions were a tangled web of confusion, fear, and a reluctant sense of understanding. She felt the weight of Atticus's words pressing down on her, realizing the depth of his conflicted loyalty and the lengths he was willing to go to protect her.

"You are selfish and condescending, thinking you know what is better for me because you don't want to lose me, congratulations. You did exactly that." Hazel knew she hit her mark when a flicker of pain crossed his features as he absorbed Hazel's words. Silence enveloped them, broken only by the sound of their heavy breathing, each grappling with the gravity of their fractured bond.

"Hazel, wait." His voice wobbled as he reached for her hand, but she pulled it away, stepping back from him.

The significance of their shattered connection lay in the delicate balance between destiny and choice.

"I was beginning to believe I cared for you... maybe more than I should have. And for a fleeting moment, I let myself hope you might feel the same. But now I see it for what it was—just another illusion. Just a foolish little fawn, stumbling into the fire, falling for the Immortal Dragon. I should've known better. Happy ever afters were never written for people like me. And it seems fate has made sure I never forget that."

Hazel averted her eyes, her throat bobbing hard enough she could hear the swallowing down of her heart.

Did Asteria lie to her? Asteria told her she would rule as queen. Was Asteria telling her that so Hazel would fulfill the prophecy? Hazel's mind ran wild, worried about how much of her life she had left. She questioned every word Asteria had ever spoken, wondering if the promises of a throne were merely a manipulation to ensure she played her part in the prophecy. Doubt gnawed at her, making her question whether she was just a pawn in a grander scheme. Was her love for Atticus real, or had it been planted to bind her to a destiny she never chose?

"Hazel, I-" Atticus took a step towards her again, likely in an attempt to comfort her, but was abruptly interrupted by Ardnaxela, who barged in hand on the hilt of her sword with a look of concern on her face.

Ardnaxela's sudden entrance signified the urgency of the what ever situation has risen.

Her hand on the hilt of her sword indicated that immediate action or defense might be necessary, breaking the emotional tension between the two. It was a stark reminder that their personal struggles were entangled with larger, more perilous stakes.

"It's the queen, she has been attacked. We need the Ivory Fawn now." Hazel's face dropped in horror, hearing they needed the Ivory Fawn, not just some normal healer. The one being was known for possessing rare and powerful healing abilities that no ordinary healer could match. Legends spoke of its ability to cure even the most fatal wounds and diseases. Without its intervention, the queen's life hung by a thread.

Hazel broke into a sprint, racing through the hallway. Instead of taking the stairs properly, she leapt onto the stairwell railing, sliding swiftly toward the lower level. The wind rushed past her as she rode the curve, urgency driving every move. Behind her, Atticus was close—right on her heels as they both rushed toward the waiting horses.

Every second counted, untying her horse, Hazel felt like she had wings from how easily she mounting her horse. Phoenix jumped from the abrupt mounting. Hazel's mind raced with fears of failure and the looming possibility of losing the queen. As Phoenix reared up, Hazel whispered a silent prayer, hoping they would reach the queen in time. Hazel pulled the reins into the direction of the Wylana, nudging his sides with her heels to spur him into a gallop.

Ardnaxela took the lead as they rode to the castle. Hazel's mind was racing. Why would someone attack the queen in her own castle? It makes no sense. Who would do this?

The early winter landscape stretched out before them, a stark contrast to the urgency of their mission. The ground was hardened by the cold, and their horses' hooves kicked up small clouds of frosty mist as they galloped through the forest.

The cold wind bit her cheeks as her hair whipped around her. Hazel held tight to the reins with one hand while the other held the saddle horn to keep her balance. Riding as fast as she could. Hazel's heart pounded in her chest, a mix of fear and determination fueling her every breath. The cold air stung her eyes, but she blinked away the tears due to the wind drying her eye out.

Anxiety gnawed at her insides, but she clung to a fragile hope that they could save the queen in time. Hazel needed to get to the castle as fast as Phoenix can run. Seeing the castle come into view, Hazel's heart hammered in her ears as she rode into the courtyard where a few armed guards waited to escort her in.

Ardnaxela was the first to dismount, then Atticus before Hazel leapt off her horse, stumbling from the impact. Regaining her footing, she ran quickly up the stairs after Atticus and Ardnaxela. Each step felt like a race against time, and her mind focused on the urgent need to get to Queen Sage to see what state she was in. Hazel's breath came in short, sharp gasps, but she pushed through, adrenaline fueling her every move.

The guards quickly led them to the where they were keeping Queen Sage. As Hazel entered the royal chambers, her hands trembled slightly, but she clenched them into fists to steady herself.

The weight of responsibility pressed heavily on her shoulders, but she knew she couldn't afford to falter now. The royal bedroom were opulent, adorned with plush velvet drapes and intricately woven tapestries. A grand chandelier hung from the ceiling, casting a warm, golden light across the room. The bed was a four-poster masterpiece, draped in silk, and embroidered with the royal crest. At the sound of Hazel's footsteps, Kingsly's head snapped up. Instinct moved faster than recognition—his hand shot to the hilt of his sword, eyes flashing with sharp-edged alarm. But the moment he saw her, truly saw her, the tension bled from his frame. His fingers loosened their grip, though they didn't fall entirely away from the weapon.

There was something else in his eyes now—something that flickered just beneath the surface. Shame. Quiet, unspoken, but unmistakable. It clung to him like smoke, hard to define but impossible to ignore. He looked away first.

Lady Duvessa, however, did not. Hazel's necklace warmed again meeting her gaze, one that found Hazel the moment she stepped into the room, and it did not waver. Her face was devoid of warmth, every line sculpted into perfect stillness, like a statue carved of frost. Hazel couldn't tell if it was suspicion or strategy behind that expression, only that she was being weighed—measured in silence.

Hazel saw the queen lying sick in her bed, her face was pale and gaunt, her eyes sunken with dark circles beneath them. Her breathing was shallow and labored, sapping what little strength she had. Beads of sweat dotted her forehead, and her once vibrant hair lay limp against the pillows.

King Kai paced like a caged predator at the foot of the bed, each step measured yet restless, a storm wrapped in silk and gold. His sharp features were drawn tighter than Hazel had ever seen them, a flicker of something almost human carved into the lines around his mouth and brow—worry. Real, tangible worry. But even that emotion twisted uneasily on him, like a mask he wasn't used to wearing.

He kept glancing toward his wife, as if expecting her to vanish between heartbeats. Yet the longer she remained unmoving, the more volatile he seemed to become.

His hands flexed at his sides, then curled into fists. Not from helplessness—Kai did not suffer such weaknesses—but from rage barely held in check. The kind that built under one's skin, hot and festering. The kind that turned into blood.

Someone had dared to harm his wife. Not outside the kingdom. Not in some far-flung battlefield. Here. Inside his castle. His walls. His domain.

Hazel felt the air tighten around him like a vice, the weight of his fury barely restrained. And yet even amid that seething rage, even as he prowled like a beast circling a fallen mate, there was no tenderness in his eyes. Just fury. Ownership. Possession.

Hazel didn't see Reed until he ran over to her and wrapped his arms around her waist. "Please save my mama," he cried, holding onto her waist.

Hazel's heart ached at Reed's desperate plea, and she felt a lump form in her throat. She gently placed a hand on his head, her eyes filled with both determination and sorrow. "I'll do everything I can," she whispered, her voice firm despite the tears threatening to spill.

Atticus came running in until he stumbled back upon seeing his mother's state. Atticus's eyes widened in horror as he took in the sight of his ailing mother. Hazel looked at Atticus, catching her breath while stroking Reed's head. His face turned ashen, and he froze momentarily. Atticus turned and approached Reed, kneeling down, and gently pulling him off Hazel. "She will, but give her some space." He picked up his brother, holding him tight as Reed wrapped his arms around Atticus's neck.

Hazel watched the brothers with a mixture of admiration and sadness, noting the fierce protectiveness Atticus displayed for Reed. Atticus murmured reassurances into Reed's ear, his strong embrace providing the comfort and security that both of them desperately needed at that moment.

Lady Duvessa's eyes narrowed slightly into a piercing glare as she observed Hazel intently. Her lips curled into a subtle, knowing smile as if she was anticipating Hazel's next move.

Walking over to the Hazel, King Kai grabbed her arm tightly. Hazel winced at the sudden pressure, a sharp pain shooting up her arm. She looked up at King Kai, her eyes wide with a mixture of surprise and unyielding. Despite the intensity of the moment, she refused to show weakness, meeting his gaze with unwavering determination.

King Kai leaned in closer, his voice a low, menacing whisper. "If you fail to save her, there will be consequences you cannot begin to imagine," he hissed, his grip tightening ominously. Their eyes locked in a silent battle of wills, the air thick with tension. Hazel's heart pounded in her chest, but she refused to let fear take hold, her resolve hardening with each passing second.

Out of the corner of her eye, she saw Atticus shift—saw the subtle tightening of his jaw as he took a step forward after setting Prince Reed down. His hand twitching near the hilt of his blade. Ready to intervene. To protect her.

Hazel didn't even look at him. "It's fine, dragon." Her voice was slow and controlled, the words razor-sharp and cold enough to cut. Not now. Not from him.

Atticus halted mid-step, his brow furrowing—but he said nothing. The unspoken wound between them lingered, a chasm neither of them was ready to cross.

Hazel yanked her arms away from the king, tearing her gaze from him as she turned her head toward Kingsly. He refused to meet her eyes, his shoulders hunched as if the weight of shame had finally found him. "I need everyone to give me some space

There was silence before they stepped back, except for Atticus who stepped forward to join her side. The smell of bergamot, cedar, and amber wafting through her senses. "Use me if you need a teether again.." His voice was low as it brushed her ears.

Hazel's heart skipped a beat at Atticus' unexpected offer, and a whirlwind of emotions crashed over her. Beneath the layers of hurt, she sensed a flicker of hope, a possibility that perhaps he could be a source of strength in this dire moment.

Looking down, Sage's pained expression broke Hazel's heart. She began her examination, trying to find the wound's source. Hazel's mind raced as she grappled with Atticus's offer. Part of her wanted to reject his help outright, to push him away as she had been hurt by him. Yet, another part of her yearned for his support, craving the familiar comfort and strength they once shared. As she hovered over Sage, her hands trembling slightly, Hazel realized that accepting Atticus might be her best option to not over do it again. Last time she did this , she went to far and almost didn't come back.

To Hazel's horror, Hazel found a rash—white blisters speckling over a blackish purple rash rising up Sage's hand. Taking the queen's hand, she turned the queen's palm up and saw a very tiny prick on her finger. Hazel's breath hitched as she recognized the severity of the rash, her eyes widening in alarm. She quickly glanced at Atticus, the urgency of the situation erasing any lingering doubt about accepting his help. "We need to act fast," she whispered, her voice trembling with a mixture of fear and determination.

Atticus' eyes sharpened with focus as he stepped closer, his earlier hesitation vanishing. "Tell me what you need," he said firmly, his voice steady and unwavering.

Hazel focused her magic on the queen's wound, taking Atticus's hand in her. Plunging into the darkness of her mind, Hazel searched for the mother's grove tree and her great-great-grandmother, but found nothing. She needed to find that tether again. As Hazel channeled down into the source of magic, a tingling warmth spread from her fingertips into the queen's wound as she rest her hand on it. She reached for the magic.

And it recoiled—wild, stubborn, fractured.

It pulsed beneath her skin like lightning in a bottle, burning to be used, but never how she needed it. Never when it mattered. Her heart thudded painfully against her ribs, the memory of Darius slamming her into the tree still vivid in her mind. The way she'd screamed for her magic then, begged for it to come, to protect her, to *do something*.

It hadn't.

She'd been powerless—humiliated and broken, magic simmering just beneath the surface like a cruel joke she couldn't quite grasp.

But this time, someone else's life was on the line.

Hazel squeezed her eyes shut, fingers curling as she reached inward, pushing past the chaos in her chest, the fear that she wasn't enough. That she'd never be enough. Her magic stirred, hesitant and flickering like a flame starved of air. She clung to it, breathing through the pain, through the heat crawling up her spine, whispering to it not like a weapon—but like a wounded thing needing to be *more*.

"Come on," she murmured under her breath. "Please."

A soft glow sparked beneath her palms.

And Hazel held on, teeth clenched, willing herself not to lose it again. Not this time. She felt an intense, almost electrifying energy coursing through her veins, mingling with a deep-rooted connection to the earth. Her senses heightened, and she could hear the ancient whispers of her ancestors guiding her through the intricate dance of healing. The darkness obeyed Hazel, to her astonishment. The same ribbon appeared from when she saved Kingsly. The tether that tied her to the moral world... to her Crimson Dragon. She took the ribbon and pulled it.

When Hazel emerged from the darkness, she felt warmth behind her. Atticus stood close, allowing her to lean back on his chest for support. His steady presence provided a surprising sense of calm, even as the situation pressed down on them.

"You did it," he murmured, his voice a blend of admiration and gratitude. He gently squeezed her shoulder, offering both reassurance and silent comfort.

Hazel panted heavily before looking at the queen, who lay in her bed peacefully in her slumber.

Her silver hair cascaded over the silk pillows, and her skin, pale and smooth, seemed to have the returning glow as if her skin was bathed in the moonlight. She wore a serene expression on her face, appearing to be dreaming of a world far removed from the troubles of her kingdom. Looking at the hand, Hazel held to see there were no signs of sap poisoning.

Atticus kissed Hazel's temple. Feeling the kiss , Hazel took a deep breath too exhausted to move away.

It was then she noticed her own hand was trembling, and she pulled it toward her chest, trying to settle her nerves.

Hazel's mind raced with mix of relief seeing the queen was safe for now. However , there was a lingering concern feeling of worry about what dangers might come next, knowing that their journey was far from over.

When Hazel's eyes came up, she saw that Lady Duvessa was missing, as was Kingsly. Hazel's worry grew as she scanned the room. Lady Duvessa and Kingsly's sudden disappearance at such a critical moment didn't make any sense to her , especially not with how Kingsly reacted when she barged in.

She turned her attention to the king, who didn't look relieved for his wife, but had an amused smirk on his face. "So, you truly are the Ivory Fawn," he purred.

The smile on the king's face must have caused Atticus some unease, she could feel his body tensing behind her, wrapping an arm around her waist protectively.

"She will recover. I can search the infirmary and kitchen to see what herbs and spices you have. Make a special tea for the Queen to help her recover smoothly." Gesturing to the Queen Sage sleeping, she continues on. "She just needs some rest. I may have revered the effects of her wound, but the tea will help her body recover her energy and strength-"

"I would suggest increasing the guards around the queen for her own protection." Atticus spoke up cutting off Hazel.

Atticus tightened his grip on around Hazel the king walked over to the pair, taking her hand and kissing it. "There shall be a grand ball in a month's time to celebrate what you just did here. Give my wife time to recover properly. You saved her and for that I am grateful," the king's voice was gentle to her surprise, she could hear the sincerity in his tone.

Hazel felt a surge of conflicting emotions at the king's declaration and gentle nature he now had shown. Although, She have polite smile, masking the turmoil within, and nodded in response.

Atticus cleared his throat. "If you will excuse us, Father, the fawn has something to do."

Hazel felt a mixture of relief and apprehension as she stepped out of Atticus's protective embrace. A part of her still felt hurt by him withholding some crucial information about the prophecy from her. The king nodded his head, waving his hand to the door before sitting beside his wife.

Reed came running after Hazel and Atticus, giggling. "Can I come?!" The young prince's face was full of excitement and wonder at what he had just witnessed. "Maybe next time, Reed, but our Ivory Fawn has work to do," Atticus replied.

Reed's face fell slightly, his earlier excitement giving way to disappointment. "But I want to help, too," he pleaded, looking up at Hazel with hopeful eyes.

Hazel crouched down to his level, offering a reassuring smile. "Next time, Reed, I promise. For now, you must stay and keep an eye on the king and queen for us," she said gently. Seeing the saddened expression on his face, Hazel took his chin in her finger with a wide smile. "I can spend all day with you tomorrow, okay? We can go for a ride and have so much fun. What do you say?" Hazel asked in the hope of cheering him up.

Reed wrapped his arms around Hazel's neck, holding her tight before moved behind Hazel over to Atticus hugging his leg. "Can I? Can I? can I?" Reed begged Atticus.

Hazel couldn't help but smile faintly, chuckling at the two brothers.

"Of course you can, that is, if I can come with you?" Atticus's eyes met her with a soft, pleading expression. Hazel's heart ached at Atticus's expression, but the sting of his betrayal still lingered. She forced a smile for Reed's sake, not wanting to dampen his spirits. "Of course, you are the Crimson Dragon, remember," she replied, her voice steady but her eyes betraying the turmoil within. It hurt to say it, but she didn't want Reed to know that his eldest brother and she were currently on thin ice.

"Yay!" Reed exclaimed before he ran off to his bedroom excitedly. Hazel looked at the King, bowing her head in farewell before she left with Atticus behind her.

Chapter Thirty-Six

Hazel

Hazel's heart raced as she left the king and queen's chambers. He kept crucial information from her about the prophecy, and for what? It stung, she felt a mix of hurt and confusion. *Did he think she wouldn't do it if she knew the consequences? Or was there something even more sinister that he was hiding from her?*

How could he do that to her? She finally started to trust him and care for him. Hazel knew confronting Atticus further than she did back in the library wouldn't be easy, but she couldn't let his deceit go unchallenged. She needed to find the right moment, gather her thoughts, and demand answers.

The hallway was a blur as she hurried past Ardnaxela who guarding the door leading into the royal chambers. "Hazel?" Ardnaxela called out to Hazel , but she didn't stop moving towards her bedroom.

She was hurt and angry at herself for allowing him to get so close. He was the Immortal Dragon, someone known for being cruel and harsh. Yet, despite everything, a part of her still yearned for the soft, tender moments they had shared. The laughter and warmth had seemed so genuine.

"Hazel, please." Atticus' voice rang out behind her. She froze momentarily, her breath hitching as his voice echoed down the corridor. She clenched her fists, every muscle in her body tensing with the urge to run. Without turning around, she quickened her pace, determined to put as much distance between them as possible. Hazel didn't want him to see her fighting to keep her tears away.

Walking into her room entryway, Hazel felt a storm of emotions swirling within her—anger, sadness, and a deep sense of betrayal. The weight of the situation crashed down on her. Tears finally escaped her eyes, each one a testament to the hurt and confusion that had now consumed her heart. She was going to close the door, but Atticus intervened, following her inside. "Hazel, please let me explain." He grabbed her hand, pulling her to a stop. After he spun her around, she saw his eyes were filled with a mix of desperation and regret. His usually steely demeanor was softened by the gravity of the moment. His grip on her hand was firm but gentle, as if he was afraid she might slip away forever if he held her too tightly. "Hazel," he began again, his voice trembling slightly, "I never meant to hurt you."

She yanked away from him, slapping him hard across the face as tears streamed down her cheeks. "Get out." she growled, watching him hold his face.

He stood there silently as her breathing was heavy. The room grew colder, the air thick with tension and unspoken words. The shadows cast by the dim light flickered ominously, reflecting the turmoil in Hazel's heart.

Despite her fury, a small, fragile part of her heart ached for him to stay, to somehow make everything right again. As she stood there, torn between her anger and lingering affection, the battle within her raged on, leaving her feeling more lost than ever. Hazel wanted him to stay and fight for her.

"I deserved that. But Hazel, I had my reasoning for not telling you," he said, staying where he was, his eyes on the floor.

"I don't want to hear it. Get out!" Hazel's fists clenched at her sides, her knuckles turning white as she fought to maintain control. Her shoulders were tense, and she took a step back, creating more distance between them. Her eyes, still filled with tears, bore Atticus with a mix of defiance and pain. Her shoulders sagged under the weight of exhaustion, yet her spine refused to bend, held straight by sheer will alone. Every breath she drew felt heavy, laced with the ache of magic nearly burnt out, but her chin remained lifted, defiant in the face of her own weariness. Her hands trembled slightly—betraying the toll the battle had taken—but remained clenched at her sides, a silent vow not to falter again. In her stillness was the echo of a storm just passed, fragile in the aftermath, yet undeniably resilient.

. "I want to be left alone!" Hazel growled out again raising her tone a bit higher before she watched him bow his head and leave.

As the door closed behind him, she collapsed onto the floor, her body wracked with sobs. The room felt emptier than ever, and the silence now seemed to mock her pain. She wrapped her arms around herself, trying to hold together the pieces of her shattered heart, wondering if she would ever feel whole again.

Hazel rested her head on the door frame barricading the door shut with her body. Hazel walked through her bedroom door, hastily moving through the archway into her bathroom, and held her stomach as if she was going to be sick. She caught a glimpse of herself in the bathroom mirror and almost didn't recognize the person staring back. Her eyes were swollen and red from crying, her cheeks streaked with the remnants of her tears. She looked like a shadow of her former self; the pain etched deeply into her features.

There was a chance she was going to die fulfilling this prophecy, and the thought made her stomach curdle. Hazel turned on the faucet with trembling hands, splashing cold water onto her face in a desperate attempt to steady herself. She gripped the edges of the sink, taking deep breaths to keep the nausea at bay. For a moment, she closed her eyes, trying to gather the strength to move forward despite the overwhelming heartache.

Part of her wanted to believe Asteria was telling her the truth. The truth is, one day, she will be queen. Yet, part of her was terrified it was a ploy to use her as a pawn to bring back the Aestivals. Feeling her stomach beginning to roll , she raced towards the toilet.

Hazel held onto seat of it as she emptied the contents of her stomach into the toilet. Her body shook with each heave, and cold sweat dripped down her forehead. She felt both physically drained and emotionally overwhelmed, tears mixing with the perspiration on her hairline. Despair washed over her as she clung to the porcelain, praying for the nausea to end. After she finished, she sat on the cool marble floor leaning her head against the wall.

She wanted to be angry with Atticus. A part of Hazel knew he did it out of his own self way to protect her. Despite his good intentions, his actions hurt her deeply. She couldn't ignore the pain she felt, even though she understood his motives.

Hazel wanted to find happiness so much. She thought she had that with Darius, but not only had he been lying to her in the years they had known each other, but he had also tried killing her. Hazel and Darius had shared what seemed like an unbreakable bond. They had built a life together, filled with shared dreams and intimate moments that made Hazel believe they were meant to be. However, the discovery of his deceit and his attempt on her life shattered her trust and left her questioning everything she thought she knew about love and loyalty.

Now she was starting to fall for Atticus.

Pulling her knees to her chest, Hazel laid her head on her them, wondering if she could ever find her happily ever after. With this prophecy, it didn't seem like she would. Closing her eyes for a moment, she inhaled deeply. Trying to ignore the smell of her bile on her breath. Hazel's heart ached with the weight of her conflicting emotions. She desperately wanted to trust Atticus, to believe that his actions stemmed from a place of love and protection. Yet, the fear of facing another betrayal gnawed at her, making it hard to fully open herself to the possibility of happiness.

Hearing the doors open in the receiving room, she pulled herself up from the marble bathroom floor walking towards the door expecting to see Arabella.

Reaching for the door, she gasped, seeing the door open to her bedroom, stumbling back when she was who it was. Atticus. Hazel let out a sigh seeing him there looking at her with that soft expression she was warm up to. She tenses slightly as he quickly approached her, wrapping his arms around him, his lips crashing into hers.

Hazel's initial shock melted into a mixture of longing and hesitation as she felt the warmth of his embrace. Her heart raced, torn between the desire to surrender to the moment and the lingering fear of another betrayal. Slowly, she found herself responding to his kiss, allowing herself to feel a flicker of hope midst the chaos. Her breathing hitched as he entangled his hand in Hazel's golden hair, pulling her closer until there was no space left between them—just heat, tension, and the thundering of her heart against his chest. His lips crashed against hers, hungry and unrelenting, and the world around them blurred into nothing but the taste of him and the feeling of his hands anchoring her like she was something precious he couldn't afford to lose. Her fingers gripped the fabric of his shirt, clinging to him like he was the only steady thing left in a life full of chaos. Every kiss was a spark, igniting a fire she'd tried so hard to smother, and as his mouth moved against hers—demanding, desperate—her mind spiraled in a thousand directions. This was dangerous. Reckless. Forbidden. But gods, it felt like coming home.

Midst the passion, she clung to the hope that maybe, just maybe, this kiss could be the first step toward healing her fractured heart.

His lips were on her as if he desperately needed her. Hazel felt his hands running down her body as she gripped onto him even tighter, not wanting him to stop

Her body ignited with a fiery passion, every touch sending electric shivers down her spine. Her pulse quickened, and she felt a sudden, insatiable hunger for him, each kiss stoking the flames of her desire. As his hands roamed her body, feeling his hand trailing down her curves of her body. Hazel could no longer deny the magnetic pull between them, her longing overpowering any remnants of doubt.

Melting into his embrace, one of his hands gripped her hip, holding her where she was in the middle of the room. The hand in her hair trailed down to her cheek, intensifying the connection they shared, breaking down the walls she had so carefully constructed. Every caress, every whisper of his touch, communicated an unspoken promise of love and protection.

Arching her head back to allow him to devour her lips even more. Hazel needed more of the taste of cedar and bergamot, and wrapped her arms around his neck, locking him in closer to her. Atticus leaned down, hooking his arms under her knees to lift her. The scent of lavender mingled with the aroma of cedar and bergamot, creating an intoxicating atmosphere.

Hazel wrapped her legs around him effortlessly. Her heart raced with a mixture of exhilaration and vulnerability, the intensity of her emotions overwhelming her. She felt a profound sense of connection, as if every kiss and touch was setting a blaze in her lower half. In that moment, she allowed herself to believe in the possibility of love and healing, letting go of her fears and doubts.

Moving to the wall beside her vanity mirror, Hazel's back is pressed to it as Atticus pinned her there with his body. His lips trailed from hers to her soft heart-shaped jawline, down her neck where it was once ripped open. Hazel shivered at the sensation, her breath catching in her throat as Atticus's kisses traced the delicate path down her neck. She closed her eyes, surrendering entirely to the pleasure and the promise of something deeper between them.

Pressing his full height into her, like he needed to become one with her. "You taste like honeydew," he growled in her ears.

Before she knew what was happening, Atticus lower her from the wall, impatiently removing her pants with a fluid motion. Hazel's skin tingled as the cool air brushed against her newly exposed flesh, contrasting sharply with the warmth radiating from Atticus's body.

Her pulse quickened, every nerve ending alive with anticipation and desire. The sensation of his hands, firm yet gentle, exploring her curves, sent waves of pleasure that made her knees weak and her breath hitch. Picking her up again, he lead them to her vanity desk. Laying Hazel on her back, he knocked over various perfumes and loose powders on the vanity desk.

Hazel felt breeze brush her now exposed center, dripping in need of him. Exhaling sharply, his hot breath brushed her intimate center. Hazel's pulse quickened, every nerve ending alive with anticipation and desire. The sensation of his hands, firm yet gentle, exploring her curves, sent waves of pleasure that made her back arch and her breath hitch. Cold surface of the vanity desk contrasted starkly with the heat of Atticus's body, adding to the sensory overload that consumed her. Hazel's senses were overwhelmed. Between the mingling scents of their bodies, the faint perfume lingering in the air, and the electrifying touch that promised unspoken depths of passion, Hazel's leaned her head back on the flat surface under her head. Hazel's world narrowed to the pulsing rhythm of his tongue, each stroke sending ripples of ecstasy through her core. She cried out in pleasure, feeling his tongue plunge into her without warning.

The intoxicating mix of sensations—the slick warmth of his mouth, and cold air against her fevered skin—created a symphony of pleasure that built to a crescendo within her. Every moan and gasp was a testament to the exquisite arousal that coursed through her, leaving her utterly breathless and yearning for more.

Hazel arched her back, moaning, gripping his hair to hold him there. Grasping her wrist, Atticus pulled it off his head, pinning it above her head, releasing a growl that vibrated her center. The atmosphere was charged with an electric intensity, each moment crackling with unspoken desire and raw emotion. Every touch, every breath, and every whispered word added layers to the palpable tension, creating a world where nothing existed but the two of them and their insatiable need for each other.

Hazel couldn't stop the whimper leaving her lips. "Gods, you are my undoing."

Atticus lifted her off the table, carrying her toward the bed, and tossed her onto it with a bounce. He then climbed onto the bed and leaned over her, his eyes locking onto hers with an intensity that sent shivers down her spine. Reaching out, he gently brushed a strand of hair away from her face. Hovering over Hazel, he returned his affection.

She didn't want this to stop. She loved how his body felt on hers, how his hands felt on her skin. Hazel felt a whirlwind of emotions surging through her—excitement, desire, and a deep sense of connection. Her heart raced with anticipation, and every touch ignited a fire within her. Hazel had never felt more alive or more in tune with someone. The way he moved his tongue was her undoing.

"Hazel," he breathed.

Her skin tingled under his touch, each caress sending electric sparks through her veins. Hazel's breath hitched as waves of pleasure washed over her, her mind swirling with a heady mix of passion and longing. She felt as though every nerve in her body was on fire, and she surrendered completely to the overwhelming ecstasy coursing through her.

A loud crashing sound woke her abruptly, looking around the bathroom. Her chest heaved as she registered where she was. A dream, it was just a dream. Seeing a branch hitting the window of her bathroom.

Hazel's heart was still pounding as she tried to shake off the remnants of the dream. She felt a confusing mix of disappointment and relief, her mind grappling with the intensity of what she had just experienced. As reality settled in, she couldn't help but feel a lingering sense of longing that left her both exhilarated and unsettled.

Taking a deep breath, Hazel recollected her dream, which only confirmed that she was indeed wanting to be just more than what she already was to Atticus. He couldn't know. She didn't want him to know, especially since Atticus broke her trust. It hurt that he kept something that big from her. Yet, Hazel somewhat understood why he kept the information to himself. It was because he did actually care for her.

In all honesty, if she were in his place, Hazel would do whatever she could to find a way around the prophecy. This is so he doesn't die if she was in his shoes. There there would be another way to fulfill this prophecy without losing him.

Running her hand through her hair, a soft sigh escaped her lips. Getting up from the floor, she rinsed the lingering bile taste from her mouth before looking at herself in the mirror and taking a deep breath.

Tucking hair behind her ear, Hazel wished she knew what to do. Hazel felt a deep sense of fear and uncertainty about her death that was inevitable, but was it sooner than she thought? The thought of leaving Atticus alone filled her with a profound sadness. Despite her courage, the looming prophecy made her feel vulnerable and trapped in a fate she desperately wanted to escape.

Hazel wrestled with the weight of her destiny, torn between her desire for Atticus and the ominous shadow of the prophecy. Each choice carried its own peril, and the fear of making the wrong decision gnawed at her constantly. In the quiet moments, she questioned whether she had the strength to defy fate or if she was simply prolonging the inevitable.

At least at court, Hazel would learn how to fight as well as use her magic. If she truly needed to die to fulfill the prophecy, then Hazel wouldn't run from it; She would embrace it because then her home and loved ones would be able to be freed from the Netherian tyranny. She would be reunited with her mother and father. That honestly didn't sound all that bad.

Chapter Thirty-Seven

Atticus

Atticus stormed into his room, slamming the door shut, and paced in his receiving room angrily. Someone had dared attack his own mother in their castle, where was his father? Where was the guards? Did anyone see how it happened? Who ever it was, he is going to suffer. Thank gods to Nophy, Hazel was able to bring his mother to at least a stable state from how she looked regaining her color to her face.

Soon him mind wondered to Hazel and how she reacted in the library. Why would Sybilla do that? Why would she tell her? He wanted to keep it a secret until they found a way to save Hazel from dying. His mind races, a whirlwind of frustration and desperation. Him foolishly keeping that secret had now fracture what ever trust they had built, jeopardizing their mission to help Hazel become the Ivory Fawn. Atticus knew that every move must be calculated, or they risk losing everything.

Seeing that look of pain and betrayal in those glowing ice-blue eyes was like a dagger plunging into his heart. He never intended to hurt her; all he wanted to do was protect her, even love her.

Atticus was outraged by Hazel's statement that he lost her by hiding this knowledge from her. His anger clashed with his guilt, creating an unbearable storm within him. Part of him wanted to lash out and blame Sybilla for the chaos, but another part knew he couldn't ignore his role in this mess. The weight of his decisions pressed heavily on his shoulders, leaving him wondering if he could ever make things right again.

He couldn't blame anyone else but himself for withholding that knowledge from Hazel. How could he be so stricken with her that it blinded him to what was actually right for her? Atticus took a deep breath, realizing the only way to mend their fractured relationship was through honesty and open communication.

He resolved to speak with Hazel, to explain his reasoning and truly listen to her feelings and concerns. By confronting the issue head-on and working together, he hoped they could find a path forward—maybe even rebuild the trust they once shared.

Raking a hand through his black hair, he groaned in frustration at the mess he had caused. The prophecy could cost her life. And still, despite everything, she lingered in his thoughts like a fire he couldn't put out. He didn't understand the hold she had over him, the quiet strength that made him want to be better—greater than his father had ever been.

He had been content with who he was: the cold, calculating prince who bedded women as he pleased and swore never to take a wife. But Hazel made him want more. Made him *need* more. Not because she doesn't fall for his charm, but because she is the only woman who will tell him when he is arrogant. When he is an asshole.

Hazel challenged him. She made him want to chase her, knowing she might slap or punch him for his attempts. It was thrilling, and he loved it. She had a warrior spirit, unlike most women he had met. Her fierce independence and unyielding spirit ignited something within him, pushing him to strive for more than just power and pleasure. Hazel's courage and resilience made Atticus question his own values and the legacy he wanted to leave behind. Her unwavering strength became a mirror, reflecting his flaws and inspiring him to become a better leader and a better man.

Women had always swooned at his feet, wishing for his favor. However, with her, he would happily get down on his knees and beg for her if she asked him to.

He would die for her, kill for her.

The bliss Atticus experienced while with her could not be overstated. When they danced the other night, his heart soared with joy, seeing her finally let go and enjoy herself. Atticus' internal struggles were a constant battle between his inherited arrogance and newfound humility.

Hazel's laughter was like a melody to him. The way she felt so relaxed at that moment made his heart melt with desire. He could be so carefree like her, but he couldn't, unless he wanted his titles taken from him. Although, if that made her happy, he would seriously contemplate it.

He realized he was falling in love with her, not because of who she was prophesied to be, but because of who she really was. He was falling in with Hazel because she was Hazel.

Although Atticus knew he had to respect her wishes. If she no longer wanted to see him or be around him, fine. But if anyone ever hurt her, they would burn.

There was a knock on the door before his courtier walked in. "Lady Sybilla, your Highness."

Stepping aside, Sybilla entered the room, her hand gracefully hovering over her sternum, playing with her ring. Her emerald eyes were fixed on Atticus, waiting for the courtier to leave.

Atticus stared at her, his anger rising. Waving his hand, the courtier left them alone. Retrieving his goblet from the table next to the fireplace, he poured the dry red wine into it. "She had a right to know, Atticus. It is neither of our places to withhold that information from her."

Scoffing faintly, he sipped the contents, not looking at his friend in fear he would lash out. "No, it isn't, but I wanted us to find another way for her." Turning his head, he looked at Sybilla, who now stood by the couch in front of the fireplace, her hand resting on the back of it. "I have been looking through everything surrounding the prophecy. Nothing in the library of Andromeda has turned up that can help us other than what we already know." Approaching Sybilla, he handed her a goblet of wine. The mood in the room was tense, a palpable sense of concern hanging in the air.

Sybilla's eyes reflected her worry as she accepted the goblet, her fingers brushing against his. The crackling of the fireplace did little to dispel the heavy silence that filled the space. Taking it, she sips the wine.

"Wasn't Asteria a prophet? Maybe she had a journal." Atticus inquisitively spoke. Asteria's journal might contain crucial information about the Netherian and their plans. It could also reveal hidden identities and provide clues about their next moves. Accessing the journal could be the key to understanding and countering the threat they pose.

Sybilla inhaled slowly, her eyes lowering for a moment. "Yes, it was said she was the one who saw the prophecy. I can search her old chambers for one. I am not sure if she would have written it down, but it's worth a try," she replied.

Atticus nodded his head, walking back to the table to retrieve his own goblet of wine, thinking back to that look on Hazel's face. Sighing, he took a deep breath before looking over his shoulder at Sybilla. "Did you find the scrolls needed to help control her magic?"

Sybilla takes another drink, her hand remaining on the back of the couch as she approached him. "It was a blessing that they wrote down the basics. Although that's only it. Let's just pray it will be enough for her to be able to defend herself."

Atticus sighed softly, raking his hand through his hair. "It has to be enough. She said someone was coming for her. I am worried it may be Darius."

Sybilla stepped closer to Atticus, lowering her tone, "As in her ex-fiance? You said he was one of them, correct?" Nodding silently, Sybilla inhaled deeply before sitting on the couch arm. "If Hazel's accusation about Duvessa is correct, she could be in more danger than we know. What if Duvessa is working with him?"

"If she is, her head will be with his. I will not let anyone harm her." Atticus gripped his goblet tightly. It didn't take long for a soft hand to begin resting between his shoulders. Turning his head, her looked down to see Sybilla sitting on the couch arm, "I know, but we must approach this very cautiously."

Sybilla's expression was a mix of determination and worry. Her brows furrowed, and her lips pressed into a thin line. "We can't afford any mistakes," she whispered, her voice steady despite the turmoil inside her. "We are talking about Hazel's life. This stays between us. I can keep a close eye on Duvessa. I'll also ask my ladies maids to keep their ears out about anything from her ladies maids." Sybilla paused for a moment before continuing. "Let me handle Lady Duvessa. You focus on Hazel. You cannot guide her if you are distracted," she advised him.

His childhood friend had always seemed wise beyond her years, something he admired so much about her. "Be careful, Syb. If she is, in fact, a Netherian woman, we need caution. Who knows who else could be one of them? If you investigate this further, keep your head low. The last thing I would want is to lose someone I see as a sister."

Sybilla's hand touched Atticus's arm with a faint smile. "I will, I promise. I am planning to go see if I can find Asteria's journal."

Chapter Thirty-Eight

Hazel

The rest of the evening was quiet and peaceful. When the morning light crept into Hazel's bedroom, she was already sitting up in her bed, running her hand through the disheveled mess of her hair. Outside her window, a thin layer of frost coated the castle grounds, shimmering in the gentle dawn light. The bare branches of the ancient oak trees stood stark against the pale sky, and a crisp, cool breeze carried the faint scent of pine. Snowflakes drifted down lazily, adding to the serene winter landscape.

Hazel knew she couldn't always relying on other people to save her or protect her, there may be a time where she wont have a bodyguard around. Getting up, Hazel walked over to her vanity mirror. After braiding her hair, rising from the chair, she walked over to her wardrobe opening it. The wardrobe was full of various dresses but thanks to Arabella now had a few Henley shirts and trousers to train in.

Hazel felt a mixture of determination and resolve as she prepared for the day ahead, a routine she had fallen into the last few days of training. She knew that embracing her own strength and independence was essential, and today was the beginning of that journey. Changing into a red Henley tunic and pairing them with black trousers. Hazel didn't wait for Arabella. She needed to distract herself. As she retrieved her mother's cloak, she wraps the cloak around her, she clasped it closed. Hazel left the castle towards the back courtyard.

Jogging around the yard, Hazel's mind had taken on so many things. When it came time to fulfill the prophecy, would she even come back? Was that women she saw in the pool of water under the mother grove tree actually her? If she did survive , what would that mean for her? Would an Aestival take the throne and she just be an champion? No matter what would happen , she will do what she must to fulfill the prophecy in order to at least give Wylana a fighting chance.

She held a new determination in her. Hazel continued her pace along the woodland path she had traveled with Ardnaxela before reaching the training spot, catching her breath in the opening. Hazel wanted to get there earlier then normal , before breakfast. Once she was done training she would have Arabella get her something from the kitchen like bacon and eggs to help muscles recover. Stretching her limbs and concentrating, she looked over at the surprised White Dragoness , who was stretching her limbs while she leaned on the trunk of a tree. It appeared she had just finished her warm up with the light sweat on her hair line.

"Your up early, you sure your up for training? You did save the Queen last night. I think that earned you a day off from training." Ardnaxela said.

"I will be fine , and I can check on the queen after this , make sure the tea is helping. As for right now I am ready to learn how to fight." Hazel replied

Ardnaxela sighed before approaching. "Hazel, about yesterday in the library," the Dragoness started.

"I don't want to talk about it." Hazel lunged to catch Ardnaxela off guard, but the Dragoness side stepped the attack.

"Hazel, Atticus was trying to do what was best for you." Hearing Ardnaxela trying to defend him, Hazel growled, going to swipe her leg out from under Ardnaxela, but missed her target. The Dragoness grabbed her leg and twisted to where Hazel's face now met the ground.

"I don't care what he is trying to do, he shouldn't have hid that from me." Hazel ground out, getting up off the ground before dealing a combination of punches she was shown in their last session.

"No, he shouldn't have, but wouldn't you have done the same thing? Or would you have run to him and tell him how he would die?" Ardnaxela argued blocking the blows with ease.

"I would have been honest with him, simple as that," Hazel replied, going for a kicking combo.

Ardnaxela's eyes narrowed as she deflected Hazel's powerful kicks, their sharp motions slicing through the cold air. Each movement was fueled by Hazel's unyielding anger and desperation to prove herself. With every block and counterattack, the intensity of their sparring escalated, the sound of their collisions echoing like thunder in the stillness of the forest.

"Lying to yourself won't help the matter, Hazel." Once again Ardnaxela dodged her blows like they were child's play.

"I am not lying to myself. I would have been honest with him!" Hazel yelled before aiming for a punch to Ardnaxela's jaw only for her arm to be caught swiftly being pinned behind her back.

Ardnaxela forced Hazel's face to meet the pine tree bark. "Yes, you are because you would have done exactly what he tried to do; you would have tried to find a way to save him."

Ardnaxela scoffed, holding her there.

A sudden flash of Darius in her memory of him as Ardnaxela pinned her to the tree flooded Hazel. Tensing, she shook her head, trying to break free from the Dragoness grip, "Ardnaxela, let go!" Hazel cried out, closing her eyes in an attempt to shake the memory.

Only Ardnaxela held her grip, growling into her ear, "Make me, Hazel, Fight me off!"

Hazel's mind was a tumultuous storm, her heart pounding with a mix of rage and fear. Memories of Darius stirred a deep devastating betrayal within her, and the physical struggle with Ardnaxela only intensified her inner turmoil. Desperation clawed at her, fueling her determination to break free and fight back with all her strength.

Finally, Hazel's eyes flashed in anger and she pushed the memory to the back of her mind. She tossed her head back, almost bursting Ardnaxela's nose open from the sound that followed, forcing the Dragoness to step aside. Swinging her elbow backward, she almost caught Ardnaxela in the head, but the Dragoness caught it with ease, moving away.

Hazel swung her leg out of anger, catching the warrior woman in her ribs. The Dragoness grunted, stepping back. Staring at Ardnaxela, her gaze softened as she realized she was no longer pinned to the tree. Hazel landed a blow on the woman that she had been unable to land before.

"See? There you go. You're learning," Ardnaxela praised before motioning with her hand to continue. "Come on, let's keep going."

Hazel was felt a twinge of pride to hear this before shaking the expression off her face to continue to fight. Her movements, once more launching herself into sparring, became more fluid and purposeful, fueled by the ardent desire to earn Ardnaxela's approval. She launched herself back into the fight with renewed vigor, ready to tackle whatever came next.

After hours of training, both Ardnaxela and Hazel sat on the ground panting, catching their breaths. Hazel stared at the sky, watching the birds and trees before looking at the Dragoness. "Did you know as well? About the outcome of what may happen?"

Ardnaxela turned her head to look at before looking up at the tree, shrugging. "I didn't, but if Atticus would have told me to keep it hidden till we found a way to save you, I would have. I serve him, and if there was a way to save you from death, I would have helped," The Dragoness held a blank expression as she looked at the sky.

"Yeah, but he didn't have the right to keep it from me," Hazel said, her voice trembling slightly with hurt. She sighed, shaking her head in disbelief. "If I were in his place, I would have told him everything. I wouldn't want to hurt someone like that."

Ardnaxela chuckled softly, her gaze drifting towards the sky. "Hazel, sometimes we think we would act differently, but it's not always that simple. Atticus had his reasons, even if his actions weren't perfect. Maybe he was trying to protect you, in his own way." Ardnaxela argued before turning to her side, watching Hazel.

Thinking for a moment, Hazel sighed, running her hand through her hair not caring if she messed up her hair. "I just... I just wish there wasn't even a prophecy...Then, yet again, I wouldn't have met him. Although you're right...I can't really blame him because I would do the same thing. I would try everything in my power to save those I care about. Although, it hurt that he kept it from me...I could have helped him search, I can still help." Hazel admitted to herself out loud. Ardnaxela sat up, running her hand through her ponytail and shaking her head before getting to her feet and offering a hand

"You can still help. Become the Ivory Fawn and help him save his kingdom. Who knows? Maybe you will survive. There is no guarantee you will die over this silly prophecy," Ardnaxela said, sounding a bit bored by their conversation.

Hazel took her hand, standing up before adjusting her braid. She looked down, contemplating Ardnaxela's words. "The prophecy has controlled so much of my life, dictating my every move and decision in the last month," she murmured. "But it's time I take control and shape my own destiny, regardless of what it foretells."

Ardnaxela smirked, patting her back. "Come on, we don't want to be late. Sybilla will have my hide," Ardnaxela joked before ushering her back to the castle in order to prepare for their ride for the temple.

Arriving at Andromeda, Hazel was still amazed by its design. Dismounting Phoenix, she patted his neck before heading inside. Once Hazel opened the door, Ardnaxela waited for her to walk inside. She then left to go to Wylana's castle to deal with her own responsibilities.

Admiring the architecture, the weight of the door helped it close slowly behind Hazel, and she heard it close with an echoing thug. Hazel watched the door for a moment before looking at the castle.

Making her way up the stairs, Hazel felt drawn somewhere. Following the pull, she walked down the corridor to a long hallway and found a large archway door, unable to read the clear writing that appeared on it. Opening it, she saw the Mother Grove Tree.

Her breathing slowed at the sight of the tree standing before her. Hazel remembered the countless times she had seen it in dreams and vision, its branches reaching out like welcoming arms, its leaves whispering secrets of the past and future. Each vision filled her with peace and purpose, guiding her steps even when the path seemed uncertain. Now, standing before it, she felt a powerful connection, as if the tree held the key to unlocking her true destiny. Walking over to it she steps on the stones as its leaves swayed toward her.

Her eyes filled with amazement as she stepped up to the bark of the gorgeous lavender leaves of the wisteria. The trunk was even enchanting with a hue of lilac and gold shimmer on the. Gently resting her hand on it, a burst of golden light erupted from the tree. A pulse of magic pushed her braid to fall back behind her as she turned to see the room looked more vibrant than it did before. The once dim room now glowed with vibrant colors, the walls adorned with intricate patterns that seemed to dance in the golden light coming from the ancient tree behind her. The air was filled with a sweet, floral scent, and the soft whisper of leaves created a soothing melody.

As Hazel looked around, she noticed that the stones beneath her feet were now emanating a gentle warmth, and the entire space pulsated with energy and life. Hearing joyful cheerful voices, Hazel walked out of the room to see the castle was no longer covered in dust, vines, and age-old wear. There was instead, vibrant arrays of gold, ivory, and lilac pillars. The grand chandeliers sparkled with renewed brilliance, casting intricate light patterns across the polished marble floors. Tapestries that once hung tattered and faded now displayed vivid scenes of ancient lore, their colors rich and inviting. Hazel could hear the distant laughter of children playing, and the harmonious music of a string quartet, making the castle feel like a place brimming with joy and life once more.

Wisteria flowers added a touch of ethereal beauty, as they cascaded down the pillars, their lavender blooms swaying gently in an breeze. Hazel walked down the hallway, following the sound of music and laughter

When she turned the corner, she saw the goddess in the pond's reflection from her vision before she came to Wylana. Hazel's breath caught in her throat as she beheld the woman, her eyes widening in awe. She radiated an aura of divine grace and power, her ethereal beauty almost surreal against the backdrop of the enchanted castle. Hazel felt a deep sense of reverence and curiosity welling within her; the young woman's breathing hitched as she stared in shock. "It's you, the one in the pond reflection" Hazel breathed as she approached her.

She turned to Hazel, offering a smile before gliding over to her with her ivory wings loosely behind her. Hazel's heart pounded in her chest, a mixture of awe and trepidation flooding her senses. She felt like she was in the presence of something profoundly sacred, a being of immense wisdom and power. Tears welled in her eyes as she struggled to find words, overwhelmed by the sheer magnitude of the moment.

Cupping Hazel's face, the ethereal beauty smiled wide before kissing the top of her head. She guided her to look at one of the many mirrors lining the hallway. Although, Hazel only saw the goddess in the mirror, not her own reflection.

"I-I don't understand," Hazel stammered out before staring at the woman in confusion. Her mind raced with questions, her thoughts a whirlwind of disbelief and wonder. Why could she not see herself standing in the mirror ? What did this vision mean?

Despite the confusion, a sense of destiny and purpose took root within her, as if she was being called to understand a deeper truth. The goddess said nothing, only turning Hazel's head to look at the mirror and motioning to their reflection.

The scars on Hazel's neck and shoulders matched the goddess's appearance in the mirror.

She gasped as her chest was filled with not just wonder but amazement there reflection she was staring at in the mirror wasn't a goddess. it was her own.

Hazel as the Ivory Fawn was what she was seeing.

Hazel's head turned quickly to look at the goddess, who she now realized was herself. Her eyes were lined with silver as the goddess gave her a faint smile.

"Does this mean I won't die when I become the Ivory Fawn?" Hazel asked as her voice broke at the words.

The Ivory Fawn laughed, but there was no sound. They way her chest raised and fell with her shoulders, along with the smile on her lips, was enough for Hazel to know.

The future vision of herself, accompanied by the vibrant colors surrounding her, gently kissed her head before disappearing.

Hazel now stood in a dusty and worn-down hallway she had walked into only moments before.

Looking around, confused, she clutched her mother's necklace, which now was no longer humming, but instead, glowing. Hazel's hand went to her head to see if she could feel the crown , turning her head to look over her shoulder wondering if the wings were there.

"Hazel?" Sybilla called from a distance.

The sound brought her fully back into the present, and Hazel took a deep breath before turning around hastily and heading in the direction of the sound . She smiled widened at what she had just witnessed.

Once Hazel found Sybilla walking down the hallway Hazel traveled down, she told her scribe mentor what she had seen, and the woman's eyes widened in shock. Her heart pounded in her chest, knowing the gravity of her discovery. She watched Sybilla's reaction closely, hoping for validation but fearing the implications.

"So, there's a chance you won't die? Are you sure it was indeed the Ivory Fawn you saw?" Sybilla's question poured out with excitement

"Yes. When I saw her in my visions before, I thought she was just some goddess to the Aestivals. I didn't realize it was actually *me* as the Ivory Fawn. Queen Asteria told me I was supposed to rule valiantly as a queen. What if this was confirmation that I survive?" Hazel rejoiced, holding Sybilla's hands.

"I am so happy for you, but we can't celebrate now. You first need to learn to use your magic and fight before you can become the Ivory Fawn. We also have to consider that she warned you about someone planning to stop the prophecy from coming true. We need to be vigilant," Sybilla reasoned Hazel.

Nodding, she knew Sybilla was right. Smiling widely, Hazel held herself up with more confidence and a smile. "Then let's start teaching me how to use my magic so I can save all of Wylana," she said with a cheery voice.

Chapter Thirty-Nine

Hazel

After a very long day of training, not only in combat but also from training with her magic, Hazel was absolutely exhausted. After she made her way down the hallways and opened the door to her receiving room, she removed her cloak and draped it over the back of the couch.

Hazel took a deep breath, stretched her arms up high, walking through the doors of her bedroom. Stretching her limbs up high feeling the weight of her exhaustion weighing her down. She groaned before stopping, realizing she wasn't in her room. Her eyes widened in confusion, scanning the unfamiliar surroundings. Panic set in as she glanced around for any sign of familiarity. Hazel's heart raced as she tried to piece together how she had ended up in this strange place.

As Hazel took in the sight of the bedroom, her heart lurched in her chest as she saw Atticus lying there, shirtless, and under the sheets. A shirtless woman was on top of him, breathing heavily and kissing him as his hand speared into her raven-black hair. She stopped moving her hips , glancing over at the sudden intrusion.

Hazel's mind went blank for a moment as she processed the scene before her. A mix of betrayal, anger, and heartbreak surged through her, making it difficult to breathe. She felt a lump form in her throat as she struggled to find the words to express the whirlwind of emotions consuming her. It was very evident what was transpiring between them. Hazel stammered, unable to get any words out in general .

Kingsly was right.

Atticus didn't care at all about her. All he wanted was to whore around, which was why he was being so kind to her. The room was filled with a tense, suffocating silence, broken only by the sound of Hazel's ragged breathing. The air felt thick with unspoken words and raw emotions, making it hard for her to stand upright. The dim lighting cast eerie shadows on the walls, amplifying the sense of betrayal that hung heavily in the air.

Hazel slowly stepped backward as Atticus looked her way. There is a flare of fire and hunger in his eyes as he sat up, watching Hazel. He scanned her over, but was that hunger and fire for her because he wanted her, or was it because he was furious she walked in on his playtime?

Atticus's eyes narrowed as he locked onto Hazel, his expression now becoming a turbulent mix of surprise and irritation. He clenched his jaw upon seeing her saying nothing. The woman sitting on top of him shifted uncomfortably, sensing the sudden shift in his demeanor, but Atticus's focus remained unwavering on Hazel, as if daring her to make the next move.

"I'm sorry," Hazel breathed before quickly grabbing her cloak and running out of his room. The hallway was dimly lit, with flickering torches casting long, wavering shadows that chased her as she ran. Her footsteps echoed loudly in the silent corridor, each one a painful reminder of the scene she had just witnessed. The cold stone walls seemed to close around her, amplifying her isolation and despair.

Hazel ran momentarily before finding her chambers, barreling straight for her bedroom and closing the door behind her. Holding her stomach as her mind was racing. She couldn't shake the image of that woman riding Atticus. Hazel stumbled into the bathroom, her hands trembling as she gripped the edge of the sink. Staring into the mirror, her reflection was a stark reminder of her anguish as tears streaming down her cheeks. A guttural sob escaped her lips as she sank to the floor. *Why is she feeling this? Why did seeing him with another woman make her heart hurt? They're not together, they are just foretold to be the ones to bring back the Aestivals. It didn't mean they end up together.*

The way his hands were on that woman was the way she wanted his hands on her. Taking off her sweaty Henley tunic, her breathing was fast and unsteady as she clutched her chest, trying to shake the memory. Hazel's heart pounded erratically, each beat echoing the chaos in her mind. Her thoughts were a whirlwind of confusion, anger, and a deep, aching sadness that gnawed at her soul. The realization that Atticus's touch was meant for another tore at her, leaving her feeling hollow and utterly broken.

"Hazel, came out." She heard Atticus coming into her bedroom without even knocking.

Hazel's entire body tensed, her breath hitching as she heard footsteps approaching. Panic surged through her, and she frantically wiped away her tears, trying to compose herself even as her heart screamed in agony. *Man did she wish she locked that door.*

The prospect of confronting him now, with her emotions so raw and vulnerable, was almost unbearable. Hazel turned to face him, but stood frozen in awe as she saw him. Her eyes locked onto Atticus's, searching for solace in the depths of his gaze. Every muscle in her body was tense, ready to either fight or flee, as the tension between them crackled like a live wire.

Atticus's eyes took her in as she stood there with just her bralette and pants on. Atticus's eyes widened as he took in Hazel's disheveled state, her bralette and pants clinging to her form. A flicker of desire mixed with guilt flashed across his face, and his breath caught in his throat. He took a tentative step forward, the intensity of his gaze betraying the turmoil within him.

Hazel's breathing picked up as it became more unstable, taking him in, seeing his fist clenched at his sides. Taking notice that his pants starting to strain more. Her chest lurched, wanting to wrap herself around him and see what it felt like to have his hands on her, and not just in her dreams, but she was frozen to her spot. Her heart yearned for his touch, but her pride and the sting of seeing him with another held her back. She struggled to reconcile the love she still felt for him with the pain he had caused, leaving her stranded in a limbo of indecision and heartache.

As he stalked over to her. Hazel lips parted to get words out, but she couldn't say anything as he now towered over her. The smell of bergamot and cedar filled her nostrils. He trailed his fingers down her neck to her collarbone as she closed her eyes, shuttering at the feel of his hand on her skin. It felt just like she dreamed it would feel.

A shiver ran down her spine, electrifying every nerve and sending waves of conflicting emotions crashing over her. She felt a dangerous mix of longing and resentment, her body betraying her mind's desperate attempt to remain distant.

Hazel wanted him even more as he touched her. There was such hunger in his eyes as Atticus stared at her with the intensity of a dragon looking at a small fawn ripe for the taking.

Unable to stop herself, Hazel's hand cupped his neck, pulling down, and kissed him deeply. It was like she needed him to breathe in this moment. His air was hers.

The sudden kiss lit an explosion of pent-up emotions and unspoken words. It was fierce and desperate, a clash of lips that spoke of both anger and longing. In that moment, the world around them faded away, leaving only the raw intensity of their connection, as if their very souls were colliding in a tempest of unresolved passion.

Atticus gripped her hip, pulling her towards him as he nipped her bottom lip, groaning. His hand went into her golden hair, pulling her head back, allowing him the ability to bite her neck. Normally, she would have panicked and run, but not with Atticus. She didn't want him to stop. His lips trailed down her body as he pinned her hip to the sink with his. Pressing himself more into her, Atticus devoured her neck with his soft lips.

Every touch sent shivers down her spine, igniting a fire within her that she had never felt before, not even with Darius, The urgency in his movements matched the pounding of her heart, each kiss and bite leaving her breathless. She clung to him, lost in the whirlwind of passion that consumed them both.

He suddenly stepped back from her and forced himself to let go. A longing filled her as she immediately hated the absence of his hands and lips on her body.

"You don't want to do this," he replied, his chest rumbling with the sound.

Her eyes widened in confusion and hurt. She reached out, her hand trembling slightly, desperate to close the distance that had suddenly formed between them. "But I do," she whispered, her voice barely audible, laden with the intensity of her feelings. Rubbing his face, he appearing to be attempting to gain control again. Control she didn't want him to regain.

His resolve shattered at her soft whisper, and with a growl, he pulled her back into his arms. His lips crashed against hers with renewed fervor, hands roaming her body as if he couldn't get enough.

The control he so desperately tried to maintain was lost in the heat of their desire. Grabbing her hair, he pulled her away from the sink, pushed her back to the wall, and kissed her with more desire and need for her.

Hazel gasped, feeling his hot breath on her neck as his lips hovered over her racing pulse.

"Don't come to my room again, Princess, or I will regret it," he growled before releasing her, stepping back from Hazel with such hunger and desire in his eyes as he created distance between them.

Hazel's chest heaved as she struggled to catch her breath, her mind a storm of conflicting emotions. The fire in Atticus's eyes mirrored her own, but his words cut through her like a knife. "Why do you keep pushing me away?" she demanded, her voice trembling with frustration.

He turned his back to her, fists clenched, clearly fighting his own internal battle. "Because if I don't, I'll lose control, and you deserve better than that," he replied, his voice barely above a whisper.

"What?" Hazel watched him turn hastily out of the bathroom without saying anything else to her.

Why now? Why make her feel as if her head was soaring in the cloud with his touch, only to walk away?

"Atticus wait!" She cried out after him.

Racing out after him, she flinched as his hand suddenly coiled around her throat and pinned her to the wall. Her eyes widened in shock, her heart pounding wildly against her rib cage. The fear and confusion in her gaze were unmistakable, but beneath it all, a flicker of determination remained.

Hazel's breath hitched as she met his intense stare, refusing to let the fear consume her.

"I said don't come to my room again," he growled.

The tension in the room was palpable, and an uneasy silence settled between them. The air was heavy with unspoken words, and she could sense the intensity of his anger pressing down on her. She hesitated, torn between leaving and attempting to bridge the sudden chasm that had formed between them. Nodding her head, she saw the Immortal Dragons glaring back at her with no hint of the man who had just made her come undone in the bathroom. She felt a mix of fear and sadness, her heart aching with the loss of the warmth they had shared just moments ago. Confusion clouded her mind as she struggled to reconcile the man she loved with the cold, unfeeling presence before her. Tears welled up in her eyes, but she blinked them back.

When Atticus releases her, Hazel could have sworn she saw hurt in his eyes. Stepping back for a moment, Atticus stared at her before turning his eyes away and leaving quickly.

Why would he make her feel so much bliss, only to leave her wanting him more? Hazel's internal conflict stemmed from her deep desire for Atticus. Torn between her desire to reach out to him and the fear of further rejection, Hazel felt trapped in a whirlwind of emotions. Was this some kind of game?

Chapter Forty

Atticus

Slamming the mahogany wooden door behind him, Atticus leaned all his weight against it, his forehead resting on its cool frame. His hands barricading it, not wanting Hazel to follow him back into his room. He was so careless not to lock it beforehand. His heart pounded in his chest, a mix of frustration and regret coursing through him. He could feel the adrenaline surging, his breaths coming in ragged gasps as he tried to regain control. The thought of Hazel witnessing his vulnerability was unbearable, leaving him feeling exposed and desperate for solitude.

Atticus wouldn't be able to stop himself next time, not with the taste of vanilla still lingering on his lips. There couldn't be a next time. He'd told her that. Now, he had to convince himself of that. Why did that one faint whispering plea escaping her lips cause him to lose all control of holding himself back? It was maddening to pull himself away from her.

Atticus struggled to reconcile his intense desire for Hazel with the need to protect her from his darker impulses. The dichotomy of wanting to hold her close while fearing the consequences of his actions tore at his conscience left him in a state of inner turmoil. He understood the urgency of mastering his emotions before they overwhelmed him completely.

After witnessing the fear in her eyes when he had her by the throat, he realized there was a high probability that he could be turning into his father. The way her heart raced under his pulse. Atticus had a good feeling that she wouldn't be coming after him. She needed to stay away from him. For her sake.

He wasn't right for her. He wasn't what she needed. Maybe his brother would be the better option for her. Perhaps he should just go to his father and brother to convince them that Lady Duvessa should marry him instead. Let Hazel marry Kingsly.

Revulsion filled him at the thought. What was he thinking? Atticus knew Kingsly wasn't good for her, either. In fact, he was worse for her. Kingsly's actions sent her into a hysterical episode not once, but twice.

Letting out a long sigh, he rubbed his face, trailing his hand down his skin, feeling the stubble starting to poke through. His hand made its way down a strong, marbled jawline to his neck, rubbing its tense muscle.

Turning to look at the empty receiving room, , he saw two elegant armchairs sitting on top of a large Decorative maroon rug in front of a large fireplace, adorned with a mirror above it, caught his attention. As he gazed into the well-lit room, he was met with a horrifying sight—his own reflection staring back at him. Disgusted, he averted his gaze, unable to bear the sight of himself. His actions only exacerbated the situation, causing pain and suffering for both him and his beloved.

Finally stepping away from the front door, he moseyed his way across the room to two large mahogany wooden doors, opening the one on the right as he moved into his bedroom.

Looking up, he wasn't surprised seeing his mistress hadn't left, nor dressed herself after his abrupt exit when Hazel walked in on the two of them having intercourse. Atticus lowered his head before sauntering over to a large black canopy bed with maroon silk sheets as his mistress crawls across it, going to her knees.

Her raven hair hung loosely in a tangled mess over her right olive-colored shoulder to rise up on her knee, trailing a finger down his jaw to his neck.

"Why are you still here, Jasinda?" Atticus' voice raspy as he didn't look at the raven-haired woman.

Jasinda was known throughout the kingdom as Atticus' public mistress, a role that had sparked endless whispers and gossip. Their relationship was complex, marked by both passion and political maneuvering, with Jasinda often acting as a confidante and advisor.

Atticus, despite the public scrutiny, couldn't deny the comfort and strategic advantage her presence provided.

Taking her hand away from his skin, Atticus felt contrite for what he had done to Hazel. Jasinda's touch only made it worse. Releasing her hand, he sat down on the bed beside her.

"I was going to ask you the same thing." Pushing hair from Atticus's face, her eyes were empathetic as she stared into his. "You need to be with her, not me."

They'd had this arrangement since Jasinda first joined the court years ago. He wanted a mistress to try to avoid marrying any court ladies, and she needed protection from a previous lover. So, Atticus made the arrangement with Jasinda that if she became his mistress, he would protect her.

They came to the agreement that their relationship was strictly confined to the bedchamber, nothing more and nothing less. A simple way to relieve one another from their adult desires when needed.

Jasinda took his chin into her soft hand and turned his face to look at her with a look of concern in her eyes..

Atticus's jaw tightened as he struggled to find the right words. His eyes flickered with a mix of frustration and sorrow, revealing the conflict within him. He finally sighed, his shoulders slumping in resignation. "I cannot. If I allow myself to get any closer to her, more than I already am, I will only end up destroying her. I won't let that happen. I *can't* let that happen. It would be better for her if I stayed away."

Soon, an exasperated expression painted his face as he rose from the bed, putting himself out of reach from Jasinda's touch, and paced up and down the mahogany wood floors. All Atticus could think of was how Hazel's skin felt under his hand, how warm it was beneath the calluses of his fingers, the taste of vanilla on her soft lips—they were softer than he imagined—and how her hair smelled of rosewater and ivy.

"Atticus, you can't predict the future or shoulder all the blame for what might happen," Jasinda spoke gently. "Sometimes, the best thing you can do for someone is to be there for them, no matter how scared you are. Did you ever ask what *she* wanted, Atticus? Doesn't she have a choice in any of this?"

Atticus froze mid-stride, his pacing coming to an halt as Jasinda's question pierced his thoughts. His brow furrowed, and he turned slowly to face her, a look of dawning realization mingled with uncertainty in his eyes. "I... I haven't," he admitted quietly, the weight of his oversight settling heavily on his shoulders.

"I saw how devastated that young woman looked when she came in. She truly cares for you, and you are sitting here acting all sanctimonious, thinking you know what is better for her because you're wallowing in your own self-sorrow, which isn't the Atticus I know."

He felt a tumultuous storm brewing inside him, a wave of guilt and fear clashing with the undeniable truth in Jasinda's words. He had always prided himself on being closed off, but now he questioned whether his actions were more about shielding himself from pain than safeguarding her happiness. The realization cut deep, leaving him feeling exposed and uncertain about the path he had chosen in distancing himself from Hazel given they duties to the prophecy..

"The Atticus I know is never afraid to make the first move and loves taking hazardous risks and paths. Yet here you are, hiding from your yearning for that girl who obviously wants you," Jasinda remarked, watching him closely.

Atticus said nothing because she observed everything correctly. He wanted Hazel, but was scared of the outcome of the prophecy would cost her, and what let himself fall for her would do to him. He was startled by these unfounded, unprecedented feelings for someone that he knew nothing about other than she was supposed to be this legendary hero, one who was prophesied to eradicated the dark cloud hanging over his kingdom. Yet she was so naïve.

Instead, he sighed, not looking at his mistress.

Making his way around his bed to further the distance between them, he leaned against the large mahogany archway leading into his bathing chambers. Looking at the large oval-shaped black marble bathing tub, his eyes trailed to the mirror that hung just above his bathroom counter to see his reflection once more.

He had never felt so guilty in his life over actions with a woman before. It made him avert his head away from the reflection and down to the floor. Hearing the sound of his mattress creaking from the shift of weight and the sound of fabric scraping the floor signaled to Atticus that Jasinda was finally changing back into her clothes.

Atticus was underwhelmed to find Hazel in the Raven Palm forest. Initially confused and disbelieving, he expected a grand, confident figure but saw a young woman out of place among the trees. He questioned the tales he'd heard, expecting a valiant hero wielding Aestival magic, but found a village girl struggling against her assailant. However, when he met her alone and felt her powerful slap, saw her eyes, and heard her speak, he realized she was a warrior in mind, not strength.. "It doesn't matter now, Jas. I think I took it too far this time. I acted just like my father with her." Atticus lowered his voice to an almost brittle tone.

A smooth hand glided up his bare skin from the small of his back to his shoulder right where the dragon inked into his skin rested. He felt a hand pulling to turn Atticus's head to look at the young woman who barely came up to his nose.

When Jasinda's eyes met his bleak expression, her gaze held that same empathetic expression. Jasinda raised her hand to his cheek. She now wore a simple silk peach gown that hung loosely to her waist, with a green embroidery bodice showing off her finest assets. "The only way you will ever know is to go to her." Her voice was angelic yet soft as her eyes stared into his

His eyes misted over as he pulled Jasinda's hand away from his face, looking down at her hands. Feeling his face twitch, trying to fight off the tears that were threatening to fall, he sighed. "You don't understand. If I let myself fall for her and be with her. She will could possibly die to save us all."

Jasinda blinked in shock, pulling her hands away from his, as she stepped back. "Wait, are you saying..." Not finishing her sentence,

Atticus knew what she was asking, only nodded. He forgot Jasinda wasn't at the banquet when his father announced she was the Ivory Fawn to everyone at court.

"Yes. Lady Hazel is the Ivory Fawn."

Atticus took a deep breath, leaning his head back like it would stop the tears threatening to leave his eye. Feeling a stream of wetness down his cheek, he knew he had lost the battle on keeping his tears at bay. Atticus was overwhelmed with a mix of sorrow and relief. The weight of the revelation bore down on him, and the tears were a release of the pent-up emotions he had been carrying. His heart ached, but there was also a sense of catharsis in finally acknowledging the truth to Jasinda.

"I thought it was just a silly court rumor she was the Ivory Fawn." There was hope in her eyes for a split moment before it faded to a frown. "Wait, you said she will die to save us all? How is Hazel going to be the Ivory Fawn if she is dead? That makes no sense." Jasinda retorted, not wanting to believe it was true

"I was told by Queen Asteria herself."

Jasinda's eyes widened in shock, and she took another step back, as if the information physically struck her. Her hands trembled, and she clutched at her chest, trying to steady her breath. "In order for her to save all of Wylana, she must sacrifice herself." Atticus' voice became more unstable as he gripped onto Jasinda's hips to anchor himself.

"Then doesn't that give her the right for her to choose what she wants to do with the time she has left? Atticus, don't let yourself be the one who denies her that." Pulling his face down to hers, Jasinda stared deep into his heart, her eyes pushing another strand of hair from his face.

"I hurt her. I kept the secret that I knew she could die while fulfilling the prophecy. Then, she saw me with you. Not to mention, I lost control of myself after I saw her standing in her bathroom, completely naked except for her pants and bralette. I almost took her right there and then. I foolishly allowed myself to taste her lips, even though I knew I needed to protect her. I thought if I scared her, she would stay away." Atticus's voice broke as he stepped closer to Jasinda, resting his chin on her head, not wanting to see that look she was giving him anymore.

Jasinda stepped out of his arms and crossed her arms over her chest, raising an eyebrow at him. "Atticus, stop hiding behind a wall. You're only hurting yourself and her by denying what could be something great. And why? Out of fear of what ifs? If she does die in order to save Wylana, then at least she dies with some happiness in her life. If you keep denying her, then what if the last memory of you she has was of you being cruel and harsh?"

Atticus's face contorted with a mix of anguish and guilt, his vision burned with hot tears. He opened his mouth to speak, but no words came out, his throat constricted by the weight of his emotions. Finally, he nodded slowly, acknowledging the painful truth in Jasinda's words, and a single tear escaped down his cheek.

"You don't want that for her, do you?"

Atticus sighed, swallowing hard, before he stepped away, turning his back to Jasinda, not wanting to further their conversation. The idea was already painful enough, and he needed more time to think. "I don't need your services anymore tonight; you are dismissed."

He knew he would regret dismissing Jasinda when she was only trying to help him, but Atticus just wanted to be left with his thoughts so he could figure out what he truly wanted.

The sound of her light footsteps were barely audible as she made her way back to the bedroom, grabbing her lace-up boots. The sound of her rubber soles hitting the wood floor was quickly followed by the sound of his door closing.

Atticus was now alone

But was he going to allow himself to stay alone forever, or would he finally let himself find love and happiness with Hazel? His heart still pounded with the fear of losing Hazel if he allowed himself to get close to her. The idea of opening up and then watching her slip away, either through danger or his own inadequacies, terrified him. He worried that his love might not be enough to protect her, and that the pain of losing her would be more than he could bear.

The rays of the morning sun crept slowly in through the split in the maroon curtains, bathing Atticus's fair skin as he lay tangled up in his maroon silk sheets. Slowly, his eyes fluttered open, tailoring to the brilliant rays of the sun illuminating his bedroom.

Looking about his room, he glanced to the fireplace . Turning his head to the right, he looked to the empty bedside, his fingers trailing over the maroon silk pillowcase, feeling how cold it was. For once, he felt lonely lying in his bed.

His tall armoire mahogany dresser had his formal uniform hanging up on it. He was supposed to meet with his father, but he dreaded having to sit through a meeting with his brother and father.

Sitting up, he rubbed his eyes, removing any lingering fatigue in his eyes. Hearing a knock at his bed chambers, he turned his head slightly to look at his door.

"Enter," Atticus called out, not even getting out of bed. The dragon's mouth, which was inked on his skin, flecked as he stretched his limber to see Arabella coming in.

He straightened up and was surprised to see her here and not with Hazel. Her auburn hair curled loosely around her face as she entered the room, closing the door behind her, fully turning to look at him.

As she stepped closer to Atticus, her peach-like face showed unease. Immediately alarms went off in his head "Is everything alright?"

Nodding her head, she walked up to the mahogany bedpost, resting her hand on it before looking at him and taking a deep breath. "I am worried about Hazel. She was already dressed this morning when I came in, and didn't want her breakfast."

Atticus's eyes widened with concern, his grip tightening on the maroon silk sheets. He sat up straight, his expression shifting from curiosity to alarm. His jaw clenched slightly as he absorbed Arabella's words, the worry evident in his gaze.

"She made a comment about just wanting to train and be left alone for the day. It's out of character for her. I was hoping you had some idea what might have brought this on."

Atticus's mind raced back to the heated argument they had the previous evening. He recalled the hurt in Hazel's eyes and the sharpness of his own words, regretting how his temper had flared. Perhaps this sudden change in her demeanor was a reaction to their confrontation, and now he felt compelled to make amends. Lowering his head, he rubs the back of his neck, frowning. "It could be partially my fault. We kissed last night, but the visit ended in a fight."

Light footsteps approached before he felt the young woman sit beside him. "What happened during your fight?" Arabella's soft voice asked.

Titling his head back, he sighed before closing his eyes. "She walked in on me and Jasinda sharing an intimate moment. I didn't realize the door was unlocked until she arrived. I went to try to talk to her, but my control slipped."

Hesitant to tell Arabella about what he learned about Hazel's proclaimed death, he looked at Arabella, who reached a hand over to touch his leg gently. "I pushed her away because there is a chance this prophecy will take her life, and I don't know if she can come back from it."

Arabella's eyes widened slightly, and a mixture of concern and understanding was washing over her features. Her grip on his leg tightened, offering silent reassurance as she nodded slowly, processing the weight of his words.

Her soft features faded into what looked like heartbreak. "And you're falling for her, aren't you?" Atticus only nodded his head in response. Arabella reached over to fix a strand of his hair with a mournful look, sighing softly. "Don't you think the poor girl deserves at least a chance of happiness, even if it's only a sliver?"

Atticus felt an overwhelming sense of guilt because he believed that if he allowed himself to get closer to Hazel, he might inadvertently seal her fate.

Atticus turned his face away, rubbing his stubble a bit before he shakes his head, running his hand through his hair. "She does, but not with me."

A hard slap to the back of his head made him groan, and he reached up and rubbed the sore spot, looking at Arabella's expression, which had now gone from mournful to pure annoyance.

"Atticus, since I have known you in these last five years at court, you have *never* allowed yourself to get close to any court lady, but Hazel is far more than some court lady, and you know it. What if she is your happiness waiting for you to accept her? Are you truly too scared to let her in because you don't want to get hurt? That isn't very princely, is it? That sounds more like the Immortal Dragon you pretend to be."

His face falls, knowing she was right. Arabella was always good at knowing just what to say when he needed a boost of confidence. "But if I do then she may die and never come back, I can't lead her to her death."

Scoffing and shaking her head, Arabella crossed her arms over her chest, raising an eyebrow at him with a faint smirk. "So, what, you are going to hide from your feelings for her? And what if hiding your feelings and pushing her away leads her right into a death where she never becomes the Ivory Fawn? Hmm? What then?"

Once again, Arabella always knew what he needed to hear. Swallowing, he looked up into his friend's kind eyes, sighing before nodding and putting his hand on her shoulder. "Thank you, Ara. Unfortunately, I have to meet with my father soon and can't talk to Hazel right away, but please see if you can get her to eat."

Chapter Forty-One

Hazel

The winter air from where she just left the training field left a lingering chill in her bones. Rubbing her arms together to get herself warm. All she could think of was warming herself up at the fireplace.

As Hazel walks down the hallway, her boots sounded on the marble floors. Heading towards her bedroom, she could practically smell the chamomile bath with just a dash of lavender calling her name.

Not only could she smell it , but the feeling of her stomach growling from the appetite that Hazel has worked up training. When she gets to her room, she will Arabella order her a nice heaping plate of maybe some steak. Oh not to mention some of those succulent brussel sprouts steamed with butter, accompanied by some mash potatoes with the skins on them still.

It only made her stomach gurgled even more at just thinking about it.

Her pace quickens down the hall , the idea along putting a spring into her step at having time to finally relax.

Hazel has been dog tired from having Ardnaxela again and again put her face first in the snow. The young woman was growing somewhat comfortable now with her new routine. Part of her somewhat forgetting her troubles.

As she left down the hallway, Hazel feet kept going but when her eyes fell onto Kingsly. Hazel's upper half came to a dead stop as she stumbled a bit, her lower half of her body's way to realign with the top.

Hazel's hand moves slowly to her mother's necklace not feeling any hint of its warmth. Part of her wish it had, that way she could use it to gather herself.

He was speaking with some guards, he hadn't spotted her just yet. Turning quickly on her heels, Hazel turned to go back down the hall from once she came in an attempt to avoid him.

"Hazel."

Closing her eyes, she swallowed the massive lump in her throat. However, her heart felt like it had already left her body through her feet, from how fast it dropped.

Move damn it, Fucking move, don't just stand here.

Hazel cursed to herself. Alas her feet did not move, no they stayed planted right there. She could hear the heel of his boots approaching.

Desperately, she clawed at the invisible force in her mind that held her there. She had trusted this man, let him see even the rawest part of herself that Atticus hasn't even seen.

Yet, she made a fool of herself by kissing him without getting to know him. Hazel curses at herself. Stupid naive girl, you wouldn't even know what love would feel like. Not even if it hit you so hard in your face, you were seeing stars.

The sound of Kingsly's heeled boots became silent behind her. Hazel stared down the empty hallway in front of her. Hoping or wishing someone would come and save her.

What is she even thinking? Ardnaxela hasn't been training her just so she can go back to being an damsel.

Trying to build her wall up, she straightened her spine not realizing her hand was braced against the wall slightly hitched. Removing her hand, she felt the sweat on her palm but dried it on her pants.

"I know you don't want to see me," he said quietly, taking a hesitant step forward. "But I need to say this."

Hazel's jaw tightened. "There's nothing to say."

Turning to look at Kingsly she steeled her nerves, inhaling deeply imaging with every breath. She fueled the fire in her chest to stand her ground.

The first step into overcome your demons, is face them directly and show they no longer have power over you.

"There is." His voice was softer than she expected, remorse laced in every syllable. "I was drunk. I was jealous. And I was an idiot. I never should have—"

"You shouldn't have," she cut in sharply, taking a step forward as her heart pounded against her ribs. Her hand shaking but she clenched her fist in attempt to stop it. "You don't get to make excuses, Kingsly. You don't get to act like that and then just apologize like it never happened."

He exhaled, rubbing a hand over his face before looking at her again. "I know. I know I hurt you. And I hate myself for it. I don't expect you to forgive me, but... I want to make things right. Somehow."

She stared at him, at the raw regret in his expression, the weight of his guilt pressing against the air between them.

Hazel wanted to believe him. She wanted to believe that he wasn't like Darius, that he wasn't another shadow waiting to consume her. But the fear still coiled deep in her gut, a reminder that trust wasn't something she could hand out freely anymore.

"I don't know if you can," she admitted, her voice barely above a whisper.

"Hazel, look I know I messed up-"

She let out a bitter harsh laughter cutting him off. "Messed up? Kinglsy you made me believe you were someone I could lean on. I let you see a side of me that I wouldn't dare show Atticus at my mother's grave." Hazel sneered standing tall before poking Kingsly in the chest hard. "Then in your called drunken mess as you called it , which by the way is not an excuse, tried to force yourself on me after I slapped you for being an arrogant fucking prick!"

"Hazel please-" Kingsly began to plead, but Hazel's sharp words cut him off.

"I am not finished." She barked clenching her fist glaring at Kingsly.

"You think saying you hate yourself for it makes a damn difference?" she snapped, stepping closer, her voice shaking with fury. "You think your guilt matters to me? Kingsly, you didn't just 'mess up.' You betrayed me. You destroyed any trust I had in you." She jabbed a finger into his chest again, her eyes burning with unshed tears. "I confided in you. I let myself believe you were different, that you weren't just another person waiting to use me, to twist my trust into something ugly. But that's exactly what you did."

Kingsly opened his mouth, but she cut him off with a sharp glare.

"No. You don't get to talk. You don't get to explain. You don't get to fucking defend yourself," she hissed, her voice a blade that cut straight through him. "Do you even understand what you did to me? You made me feel powerless, Kingsly. You made me afraid in a way I never wanted to be. And you don't just get to stand here and act like your guilt is enough to fix that."

She took a shaky breath, her fists trembling at her sides. "You don't get to ask for my forgiveness. You don't get to beg for another chance. Because I am done. Done making excuses for people who hurt me, done pretending that their remorse makes it okay." She stared him down, her voice sharp, final. "You are not someone I trust. You are not someone I even fucking know anymore. And I sure as hell am not giving you the chance to hurt me again."

She let the words hang between them, let them sink in, let him feel the weight of everything he had done.

She turned sharply, done with this conversation, but Kingsly reached out, his fingers grazing her wrist

Hazel reacted instantly.

Her hand flew across his face in a vicious slap, the sound echoing like a thunderclap in the tense air. Kingsly staggered back, his head snapping to the side, a bright red mark blooming across his cheek.

Before he could say anything, a new voice cut through the air.

"That's enough."

Ardnaxela's voice was calm, but it carried an unyielding command. Hazel turned, still shaking with rage, her chest heaving. The warrior's golden eyes flicked between them, unreadable, before settling on Hazel. "This isn't the way."

Hazel's hands clenched into fists, her nails biting into her palms. "Then tell me what is, because I can't—" She sucked in a sharp breath, swallowing down the lump of emotion clawing at her throat. "I can't keep carrying this."

Ardnaxela studied her for a moment before nodding. "Then let it out." She turned to Kingsly, her expression hard. "Get to the mat."

Hazel blinked, her pulse thrumming. Kingsly looks at Ardnaxela his breathing heavily looking between Hazel than to Ardnaxela. "I don't see how this is-" Kinglsy started "Mat now!" Ardnaxela growls "Kingsly you fucked up , you possibly can't expect Hazel to just forgive you." "Excuse me , last time-" Kingsly started once more , but neither women would let him speak. "Last time I checked , you were told to stay away from Hazel. Yet here you are." She sneered stepping between Hazel and Kingsly looking up at him. "So, get on that fucking mat. Hazel said herself she cant keep carrying this...So, you will be her punching bag." "Ardnaxela , I-" Hazel began reaching for her, her finger brushing the Dragoness wrist before it was yanked away.

"No , Atticus entrusted me to help you train. If you keep holding onto this , you will not get better. Therefor will not improve if you keep tiptoeing around to avoid the prick."

"Hey!" Kinglsy exclaims.

Ardnaxela only shot him a glace that made him tense. For a beat he didn't move , then Kingsly began stepping past Ardnaxela and heading toward the training mat without a word.

Saying nothing , Hazel followed. Her movements stiff, her fury still coiled tight inside her.

"Don't hold back," Ardnaxela said after catching Hazel's wrist. "Kingsly won't."

Hazel scoffed bitterly. "Like hell he will."

Hazel walked up to the mat , the one she had previously saw in Ardnaxela's office inside of the male barracks of the castle. Instead of wearing a ballgown , this time she was dressed for a fight and she was planning to make sure Kingsly walked out of here with more than a hand print on his face.

"Alright , rules are the first one to tap out looses" Ardnaxela commanded handing Hazel a bamboo pole. "I will not step in unless I feel it's necessary. The whole purpose of this is to squash what is going on between you both."

Hazel for a brief moment took her eyes off of Kingsly who took off his tunic shirt. Her eyes moved to Ardnaxela taking to pole from her.

Kingsly was allot bigger than her, if he did not hold back neither would she. He may have a size advantage on her , but she has her wits.

"I don't care if you draw blood , or knock each other out. We don't leave this room until Hazel can work though what she needs." Ardnaxela hands the bamboo pole to Kinglsy before releasing it before he even has a chance to take it. Her silent way of showing where she stood in this sparing match.

"I don't see how-" Kingsly started

Ardnaxela lets out a sharp, derisive laugh, shaking her head. "You still don't get it, do you?" Her eyes narrow, gleaming with cold amusement as she steps forward. "This isn't about you, Kingsly. This isn't about your pride, your excuses, or whatever self-pitying bullshit is running through your head right now."

She gestures at Hazel without looking away from him. "She needs this. She needs to break you down, piece by piece, until she isn't afraid anymore. Until she knows—deep in her bones—that she can fucking destroy what once destroyed her. And you? You're going to stand there and take it."

Ardnaxela leans in, her voice dropping to a deadly whisper. "You don't get to hold back. You don't get to run. You fight her, or you become just another weakness dragging her down. And I don't tolerate weakness."

She steps back, her expression cold, final. "So pick your poison, Kingsly. Either she beats the fear out of herself, or I beat the stupidity out of you."

Kingsly narrows his eyes before gripping the stick , but the sound of a crack could be hear in the air. Hazel had already lunged just a mer second sooner and she would have caught Kingsly in his shoulder if he hasn't been fast to parry her attack.

"I trusted you , You took an arrow for me in that ambush on the road-" Pushing hims back she snarls striking low to go for his legs but he rolled out of the way. "-I let you sit with me at my mother's grave!"

Kingsly stands on his feet squaring them staring Hazel down as her chest heaved. However, he didn't move a step.

Cowardice bastard.

Hazel threw the bamboo stick to the side without even looking. From how Ardnaxela *side stepped* in her preferential view. Looks like it nearly hit her. However, the Dragoness said nothing.

"You took advantage of me when I was vulnerable." She sneers before watching him hold his bamboo stick still. Hazel circled him on the mat, like a predator studying her prey.

"Hazel , that was not-"

"Shut up , I'm not done!" She sneers lunging, he went for a strike but Hazel catches it with her hand before lowering her shoulders to his stomach. Ramming her body into him , he stumbled back.

"I'm sorry! Fuck, okay!" Kingsly growled, clutching his stomach, his breath ragged.

"I don't care! Your apologies don't mean shit to me!" Hazel spat, her voice cracking as she lunged with reckless fury.

Kingsly barely managed to side-step, shifting behind her with swift reflexes. Before she could react, he pressed the bamboo stick across her chest, restraining her. "Let me fucking explain, damn it!"

Hazel's blood boiled at the restraint—at his audacity to think he could stop her, control her, silence her. Her mind flashed red-hot, a whirlwind of rage and panic spiraling in her gut. She slammed her heel onto his foot, feeling his weight falter. Without hesitation, she threw all her strength into her right shoulder, flipping him over and sending him crashing onto his back with a forceful *thud.*

The impact rattled through her bones, but she didn't stop. She *couldn't* stop. Before Kingsly could recover, Hazel straddled him, her knees digging into his ribs. Her breath came in ragged gasps, her grip shaking as she pressed the bamboo stick hard against his sternum. Her entire body burned with fury, but beneath it, something else writhed—a sick, suffocating fear clawing up her throat.

"Not only did you fucking deceived me—" her voice wavered, but she pressed the stick harder, willing herself to focus, to stay in control, "*you made me believe you were someone I could trust!*"

The word *trust* shattered inside her like glass.

Her fingers tightened around the bamboo stick. Heat flared beneath her skin, radiating from her palms as her vision blurred with rage and something far worse—*memory.*

Darius.

The Raven Palm tree bark scraping her skin

His teeth ripping into her neck

That sickening nickname that used to be endearing but now made her revolt

A sharp pain, a helpless struggle—

She gasped, the present snapping back into focus, but the panic still gripped her chest like a vice. The stick in her hands was burning—no, *she* was burning. The heat surged, spreading up her arms, her power feeding off the chaos storming inside her.

"You made me relive the one fucking moment I never wanted to!" Hazel roared, her voice raw with fury and pain.

She *hated* how her voice broke. How the tremble in her hands betrayed her.

She wanted to hurt him. To make him feel the weight of what he'd done. But beneath the rage, she hated something else even more—how much this moment made her feel small again. Like she was trapped, pinned beneath someone stronger, powerless to stop what was coming.

Kingsly struggled beneath her, his face twisted in shock, but Hazel couldn't see him—only ghosts of the past clawing their way into the present.

The heat surged hotter, searing the bamboo in her grip. The fear in her chest warred against the fury in her gut. Was this what she had become? Was she still that helpless girl, drowning in panic, or was she something more?

She wanted to let go. But she couldn't.

Because if she did—if she stopped now—she wasn't sure what would be left of her.

"You have *no fucking idea* what that feels like!" she spat, pressing the stick harder against Kingsly's chest. Her whole body trembled now, not just from anger but from the sheer weight of the past crashing over her. "To have your power ripped away. To *know* you're strong, that you could fight, that you *should* fight—" her voice cracked, and she hated it, hated how much of herself she was laying bare, "—but you *can't*."

She clenched her teeth so hard her jaw ached. "To feel your body *betray* you. To be too weak, too scared to fucking *move*."

Her breathing hitched. The phantom feeling of Darius's hands pinning her down made her muscles lock up, a sickening chill running down her spine despite the heat radiating from her skin. "Do you know what it's like to scream and know no one will come? To fight so hard and still lose? To *know* you're going to die and that no one will ever find your body?" Her voice wavered, but her grip never did.

Kingsly didn't speak. He barely breathed beneath her.

Hazel's chest heaved, her vision swimming. Her power swelled, the heat in her palms intensifying, the bamboo now smoldering against his shirt. "You don't know that kind of helplessness," she hissed, her knuckles turning white. "*You* don't know what it's like to be used, to be tossed aside like you're nothing. To feel like you're going to *die*—not just in body, but in soul, in everything that fucking *matters*."

Her breaths came in ragged gasps now, her pulse hammering in her skull. Her hands burned, shaking.

And for the first time, she realized—

She wasn't sure if she wanted to hurt Kingsly.

Or if she wanted him to understand just how much he'd *broken* her.

"Hazel!"

A voice cut through the haze, but it felt distant, warped, like she was underwater. The burning in her hands spread up her arms, her vision tunneling as the raw energy inside her pulsed, uncontrolled, *hungry*. She could feel it radiating off her skin, feeding off her rage, her hurt, her fear.

She didn't realize she was still pressing down—harder, harder—until Kingsly choked beneath her, his body jerking as he struggled to breathe. His fingers clawed weakly at her wrists, but she didn't feel them.

She was back there again.

The dark room. The suffocating weight. The way her own body had turned against her, refused to move, refused to fight—

"Hazel, stop!" Ardnaxela's voice shattered through the storm in her head, and then—hands, strong hands, were yanking her back. The sudden force sent her stumbling off Kingsly, her grip ripped from the bamboo stick as she gasped for breath. The moment she was free, the magic inside her flickered, and the burning heat in her palms abruptly snuffed out.

Hazel's vision spun as she staggered backward, her chest rising and falling in sharp, panicked breaths. Kingsly was coughing violently on the ground, his hands clutching at his chest where she'd nearly crushed his windpipe. She blinked down at her hands, still shaking, the heat in her fingertips slowly fading but leaving a lingering burn.

She hadn't even realized she was *killing* him.

"You're right." Kingsly's voice rasped, weak but still somehow steady.

Hazel's heart clenched, her anger twisting into something darker, heavier. She felt his eyes on her, but she couldn't meet his. Her hands trembled too violently, the shame and panic flooding her veins too fast for her to fight it.

She wanted to scream. She wanted to shout at him—at the world—for making her feel this helpless again. But more than that, she wanted to run. To bury herself somewhere far from everything she had done.

But she couldn't move.

She just stood there, paralyzed by her own fear and her own power. She couldn't trust herself. Not anymore. Not after this.

Kingsly slowly rose to his feet, and for the briefest moment, Hazel thought he might walk away, leave her to stew in the mess she had made of herself. But instead, he stepped toward her, his footsteps slow, deliberate, like he was afraid she might break beneath his gaze.

When he reached her, he stopped just a breath away. Hazel stiffened, her pulse hammering in her throat, but he didn't reach for her. Instead, he held out his hand—soft, steady.

Her eyes flickered to his hand, the weight of it anchoring her to the moment. She didn't pull away, but she didn't take it either.

"Hazel," he said, voice gentle, with something vulnerable in it. He reached out slowly, his palm hovering just above hers before it finally settled there, warm and firm. His touch was grounding, but it didn't make the shaking stop. Not entirely.

"The demons don't want you letting it out," Kingsly murmured, his thumb brushing over the back of her hand, coaxing the tremors to settle. His voice lowered, just a bit, like he was sharing something personal, something important. "That's why the claws dig deeper the more you fight. But the more you fight..." He paused, and for a heartbeat, Hazel could feel the sincerity in his words before he finished softly, "...the less hold it has."

Her chest tightened, her breath catching in her throat. It was like he understood. Like he could see through the storm in her mind, the way her demons gnawed at her from the inside, wanting to consume her. She felt the weight of his words settle on her shoulders, and for the first time in what felt like forever, Hazel didn't feel quite so alone.

She blinked back tears, her body shaking less now, though her heart was still pounding. The fear inside her was still there, still clawing at her, but it felt different now. Softer.

She let out a shaky breath, the tremors in her hands finally slowing, and she slowly lifted her eyes to meet his. What she saw in his gaze wasn't just understanding—it was compassion. Maybe even a little bit of *hope*.

And for the first time in a long while, Hazel wasn't sure if she was still drowning. Maybe there was a way out.

Maybe she didn't have to fight alone.

The silence hung between them, and she didn't pull her hand away. Instead, she allowed his warmth to anchor her, the small, tentative connection between them doing more to steady her than anything else ever had.

For a moment, just a moment, Hazel felt like she could breathe again.

"I believe that is enough for now." Ardnaxela spoke up approaching the two rubbing Hazel's back looking at Kingsly. "Next time you do something fucking stupid , I'll let her kill you."

Chapter Forty-Two

Hazel

The next few weeks since she last saw Atticus in her room, he has been cold and distant. Yet she didn't allow him to disrupt the routine she had fallen into with Ardnaxela and Sybilla. However, This morning Hazel let her mind wander during her training with Ardnaxela and Sybilla. Her thoughts were running wild from the disorder that had been her life since she came to court almost a week ago. She longed for normal life again.

She missed her cottage home in Alexandria, her mother's tree, and the lavender in the garden. She recalled the mornings spent with her uncle, sipping tea on the porch as the sun rose over the hills. The scent of freshly baked bread would waft through the air, mingling with the fragrance of blooming lavender. Those peaceful moments felt like a lifetime ago. God, was this how it felt to be homesick? It was such an awful feeling.

At least she was learning to better her stances with Ardnaxela and could finally summon a ball of light without spiraling into darkness, but now Atticus had her mind in a ditsy state, switching between the prince she was falling for and that Immortal Dragon she was scared of.

Reaching her hand to her throat, she remembered how his hand felt on her neck as he stared into her eyes. It was oddly not terrifying like how Darius had done it. Hazel had never seen him like that, and now she knew why people feared him. One look made her want to crumble and beg for her life which the ideal how just how dangerous he can be had oddly made her feel drawn to him more. However, what she couldn't understand was why he looked pained, like *he* was the one being forced to that wall by the throat.

It had been weeks since she had a moment alone with just him, and whenever she saw him, he was that Immortal Dragon. Now he was starting to take the responsibility of overlooking her training sessions with Ardnaxela. Correcting her at the smallest missteps during training with Ardnaxela. Making her take new stances, having Ardnaxela teaching her more advance moves. He even went to the length of personally challenging Hazel during training sessions, throwing her around like she was some rag doll he could take his anger out on when he wanted.

She rowed her hand through her high-raised ponytail. Hazel debated on cutting it off to prevent it from being a hazard during a fight, but she loved her long hair so much. It was more than just a part of her appearance. Each strand held memories of her past, from the times her uncle lovingly braided it to the way it flowed in the gentle breeze of her hometown. Cutting it off felt like severing the last ties to her true self, a sacrifice she wasn't ready to make.

What was this new game was Atticus playing with her? Was it some sick game? Or maybe he didn't know which role he should play with her? Kingsly was right about him wearing two masks, one of the immortal, cruel, harsh dragon prince and the other a gentler and caring prince. She just wished she knew which one was the real side of him.

In these last few weeks, Kingsly had become somewhat of a friend to her once more. Their shared experiences and mutual frustration with Atticus had brought them closer. Kingsly's insights and candid conversations offered Hazel a perspective she desperately needed.

Despite the chaos around them, Hazel found a small measure of solace in rekindling this friendship. She wasn't really bothered by him touching her arm or back or being around her. Ardnaxela even let Hazel and Kingsly duke it out on the mat. Hazel found herself pushing herself to limits, but the match ended in a draw, and each of them equally matched. They both lay on the mats after sparing, panting heavily, exchanging tired but genuine smiles before he helps her up, and they go again. Kingsly had slowly become that gentle general prince again she met at her mother's grave. Hazel's trust in Kingsly was evolving slowly but surely, built on the foundation of their shared struggles and honest exchanges. She found herself confiding in him more, leaning on his strength as she navigated the complexities of her new life. With each passing day, Hazel saw Kingsly not just as an ally, but as a friend she could rely on.

Laughing with Sybilla on her way back to her chambers to change before dinner, a court nurse hurried past Hazel, carrying a bowl of water that smells rancid, with a bloody rag in it. Hazel's laughter faltered as she caught sight of the nurse's urgency, realizing that something serious must have happened. The rancid smell and the bloodied rag hinted at an injury or perhaps a sudden illness that required immediate attention. It was a stark reminder of the ever-present dangers and tensions within the court after the attack on Queen Sage, pulling Hazel abruptly back to the reality of their precarious situation.

The nurse turned to look at Hazel to apologize but stopped. "Oh, Lady Hazel, thank the gods. We need you quickly. It is your uncle."

It felt like the words were a kick to her chest as she stepped back. Hazel's immediate reaction was a whirlwind of emotions, Panic surged through her veins like ice, and her chest tightened painfully. Her mind raced with worst-case scenarios, making her feel dizzy and unsteady. She took a deep breath, unsure if she misheard the nurse. "Take me to him now!" she demanded. The nurse led Hazel down a mahogany hallway lined with wisteria and ivy, the sweet scent contrasting with their urgent steps. Her heart pounded, each step echoing and heightening the tension. Anxiety grew, fearing something terrible awaited. Despite the beauty, a sense of doom made it hard to breathe. She clenched her fists, trying to steady her emotions.

The nurse led her through a large archway door with the words infirmary on a wooden plank hanging above it. Inside, the room was filled with rows of wooden cots, each draped with stained linens. The dim light from flickering candles cast long shadows across the walls, revealing shelves lined with glass jars containing various herbs and potions.

Hazel's nostrils were filled with a putrid, decaying smell. It took everything for Hazel not to vomit. Each wooden cot was occupied by a patient. Their faces were pale and gaunt. Some were while others lay almost lifeless just on the edge of life, barely breathing. A few groans escaped their lips, while others stared blankly at the ceiling, their eyes reflecting pain and resignation.

The sound of shattering glass was the only way Hazel could describe her heartbreak. She saw her uncle with no shirt on, lying in the infirmary bed, a deep, blackening gash on his sternum. The flesh around looked to be eating itself away.

How long had he been like this? His skin was ashen, almost translucent, with veins that stood out like dark, twisted roots. The wound on his chest oozed a thick, black fluid, and the smell of rot emanated from it, mingling with the other scents in the room. His eyes, once full of life and mischief, were now sunken and hollow, barely recognizing Hazel as she approached.

Stepping closer, she blinked the tears away in her eyes, hoping they would wash away the sight of her uncle like this and that he was perfectly fine. Swallowing the small bits of vile, she covered her mouth, stepping closer in horror. It only worsened as Hazel closed the distance. Archibald's eyes were not opened as he lay in that metal infirmary framed badly, his chest rising and falling slowly.

Taking his hand into her, it felt like she had just placed her hand into a pile of snow that started to fall this afternoon. Her tears fell from her eyes and onto his hand as she took in the severity of her uncle's condition. As a village nurse, Hazel was accustomed to tending to a few patients at a time, but the sheer number of people in the infirmary was overwhelming. The oppressive atmosphere pressed down on her, making it hard to breathe. The low, murmured prayers of the attending healers blended with the labored breaths and occasional coughs of the patients, forming a somber symphony that echoed through the room. Shadows danced eerily on the walls, playing tricks on Hazel's mind and intensifying the already daunting sense of dread.

Hazel knew in her heart that when he told her he was going to be a guard, she should have told the king he was unfit. Archibald had always been frail, often falling ill with even the slightest change in weather. His reflexes were slow, and his stamina was lacking, making him unsuitable for the demanding role of a royal guard. However, she knew her uncle would push himself to prove he was fit for duty.

Now, as she watched him suffer, the weight of that decision crushed her. She couldn't shake the feeling that she had failed him. Each tortured breath he took was a painful reminder of her inability to protect the one person who had always been there for her.

Did this happen to him while he was on duty? If he was on duty, was Kingsly with him? Hazel and Archibald's bond was unbreakable, forged through years of shared stories, laughter, and hardships. Archibald had been more than just an uncle to Hazel. He had been her confidant, her protector, and her guiding light. As she held his cold hand, memories of their happier times flooded her mind, intensifying the ache in her heart.

"Are you able to help him?" A warm and calm familiar voice came from behind her. Hazel didn't even know there was someone else other than the nurses and healers in the room. Turning around, she saw Kingsly sitting in a chair, his hair disheveled, his right arm bandaged, and his left hand bandaged. Oh gods, he was there. If he was there, then maybe he could tell her exactly what happened. Kingsly's injuries spoke of a fierce battle, one where he had risked life and limb to protect those he cared about. The deep gashes on his arm suggested a close encounter with a blade, while the bruises on his face hinted at relentless, brutal hand-to-hand combat of fate. Her eyes went to Kingsly's wounds, seeing they looked minor with him having the use of his arm and hand.

The bandages on his arm were stained with dried blood, hinting at the severity of his injuries. His face was etched with lines of pain and exhaustion, and his eyes carried a haunted look that spoke volumes about the ordeal they had faced.

Hazel's heart clenched as she realized that Kingsly, too, had not emerged unscathed from whatever tragedy had befallen them.

The general prince stood up, using his unbandaged hand to push up off the chair, and walked over to Hazel with a deep grimace as he joined her side, resting a hand on her arm.

Her chest constricts as she looked at Kingsly's wounds, and then her eyes go to the ice-blue eyes that bore into her soul.

"Your uncle and I were on patrol," Kingsly started.

Hazel inhaled deeply, shaking her head. She now regretted wanting to know what had happened.

She didn't need to ask who did this—she already knew. The yellow scorch patches mottling his skin were unmistakable, a telltale sign of Netherian corrosive magic. The acidic burns were damning enough. But then her gaze dropped to the deeper wound—a jagged laceration that hadn't just been caused by raw magic. The stench hit her next, thick and metallic with a bitter, sweet rot. Her breath caught. The skin around the gash was discolored, blistered in a way she recognized all too well. Raven Palm sap. The only ones who used it were the Netherian wielders. Whoever struck him hadn't just relied on magic—they wanted this to linger, to kill slowly.

"We were ambushed by Netherian swordsmen," he continued, his voice strained. "Despite our best efforts, we were outnumbered and forced to retreat."

Hazel's heart pounded as she imagined the chaotic clash of blades and the desperate struggle for survival.

"I insisted he stay behind since his leg was bothering him today."

Starting to choke up, her emotions ripped into her. She warned him about that damn leg. It was a haunting reminder of the last great war against the Netherians, a conflict that had raged before Hazel was even born. The injury had never fully healed, leaving him with a persistent limp and a constant source of pain. Every step he took was a testament to the sacrifices made and the horrors endured during that brutal campaign.

"While patrolling the western side of the wall I wasn't paying attention to my backside. There was a Netherian group of men that ambushed us," Kingsly continued, "Your uncle saw the attack and shoved me out of the way, taking the blow to his sternum from a sword."

Hazel inhaled deeply trying to calm her raging heart as she looked at her uncle. Tears filled her eyes as she saw her uncle's battered body. Her heart ached with sorrow and fury, her hands trembling as she struggled to stay composed. Helplessness weighed heavily on her shoulders, making it hard to breathe.

"I-I tried stopping the bleeding, but it didn't work. Can you save him like you saved me?"

Archibald weakly reaches for her. Taking his hand, she turned her back to Kingsly to fully look at her uncle. Hazel's mind raced back to her childhood, where her uncle had been a constant source of strength and wisdom. He had taught her how to tend to the garden, how to read the stars, how to shoot a bow, and had always been there to offer a steady hand when the world seemed too overwhelming. Now, seeing him so vulnerable, she felt an overwhelming surge of love and desperation, willing to do anything to save the man who had always been her hero.

Hazel shook her head, cupping her uncle's face. "Hey, hey, keep your eyes open, okay? I can't help you if you close your eyes." Her voice cracked, but she tried to stay strong as her uncle looked up at her.

"I-I just need a bit of rest my dainty fawn," he said, weakly.

Trying to hold back her emotions, she shook her head. Tears welled up in her eyes, and her lips trembled as she forced a brave smile. Her brows furrowed in concern, revealing the depth of her worry.

"Once I heal you, you can. Then you and I are going to have a talk about you and this guard job," Hazel scorned softly. She would not, like hell, accept him dying here and now, not when they came this far together.

Hazel pushed the hair from his cold and clammy, stroking his stubble. His body felt so hot from the fever that it was almost too uncomfortable to touch.

Hazel had never seen Raven Palm sap poisoning this severe before. His skin had taken on a sickly, grayish hue, almost waxen under the low light, as if life itself were slowly being leached from his body. A thin sheen of sweat clung to his brow and neck, but his skin was cold to the touch—clammy, like something left too long in the dark. His breathing came in shallow, uneven draws, each one a brittle thread barely anchoring him to consciousness.

The wound at his side pulsed an angry, inflamed red, the flesh around it blistering and raw. Veins branched outward in deep purples and sickly blacks, crawling like ink beneath the surface of his skin.

The stench was unmistakable now—metallic, sharp, and laced with the bitter, almost sweet rot of Raven Palm sap. She had smelled it once before in a controlled environment, safely bottled behind alchemical glass. But here, it was real and alive, saturating the wound like poison steeped in hate.

This hadn't been meant to subdue. It was meant to ruin—slowly, viciously.

Hazel's heart pounded in her ears. This wasn't just a tactical strike. This was personal.

His breathing was shallow and labored, with occasional bouts of coughing that sounded wet and painful.

"Just keep your eyes open for me, okay? I know you're tired, but if you go to sleep, I can't help you," Hazel softly reminded her uncle.

Reaching her hand down to look at the gash, it was so deep, if the sap didn't kill him it would be the blood loss or corrosive magic that ravaged his body. This had to be some horrible nightmare. It had to be. She couldn't lose the one person she saw as a father.

Hazel kissed his scarred knuckles as tears streamed from her eyes. Hazel realized that her magic was the sole barrier preventing Archibald's imminent death. The poison was advancing swiftly, and every second was crucial.

She could feel the energy within her, ready to be unleashed, but she had to focus.

Turning her attention to his wound, she swallowed all her emotions down to focus on task at hand.

Hazel, having been diligently training for this moment, possessed the ability to heal the victims of the Netherian people.

She took deep, calming breaths, like Sybilla had taught her to help her keep her control and focus instead of burning out. As Hazel's hand hovered over her uncle's chest, a faint, golden light began to emanate from her palm. After a few moments, her heart race beginning to see the dark veins of the poison continued to spread from the gash, inching further up Archibald's sternum. His skin twitched and convulsed as the poison resisted her magic, and Hazel could see the battle between her healing light and the encroaching darkness.

Focusing harder on pushing her magic into his wound, it glowed brighter. However, nothing happened. He wasn't getting better, and his skin wasn't healing. Hazel needed him to get better.

This wasn't the end of their story. This wasn't where he would leave her. He was supposed to watch her build a life for herself, watch her have a family of her own, and walk her down the aisle whenever she got married. Archibald wasn't just her uncle, he was her father.

Hazel could see his pain, seeing her magic not working to help him get better. Her light only sputtered as she continued her attempt to heal him. It was gutting her not being able to take away his pain.

"Please." Hazel's voice broke as she whispered a prayer that the goddess Nophy would lend her power to heal him. However, all she heard was a deafening silence.

Tears streamed down her face, mixing with the sweat of her efforts as desperation clawed at her heart. Each pulse of her failing magic felt like a stab to her soul, the helplessness nearly suffocating her. A part of her even knew she wasn't going to be able to, not when he should have healed by now, but he hadn't.

She was too late.

Hazel's heart shattered as Archibald raise his hand taking his niece's chin and turning it to look at him one last time. She pulled her chin away, her eyes burning as she shook her head. "I need to focus, just a little more." Hazel's voice cracked as she held her focus to his wound.

She remembered a time when she was just a child, scraping her knee while playing in the garden. Archibald had scooped her up, his laugh booming as he reassured her that a little kiss and a bandage would make everything better. That memory now felt like a cruel echo of the past, a stark contrast to the harsh reality she faced.

Praying harder to the goddess of healing to help her heal him, Hazel refused to say goodbye. He would live. He had to live.

The goddess of healing had always been a beacon of hope and strength for her, guiding her through many of her toughest battles. From a young age, Hazel had dedicated herself to mastering the healing arts, believing that Nophy's blessings would allow her to save those she loved. Yet now, in this moment of dire need, the absence of the goddess's aid felt like a betrayal, deepening her despair and fueling her desperate determination to keep fighting for Archibald's life.

The young woman refused to pull her focus from his wound as hot tears flooded her eyes, blurring her vision.

"My little fawn, please." His voice was so raspy and hoarse that Hazel closed her eyes upon hearing his voice. She knew in her heart this situation would steal him from her.

Hesitantly, Hazel pulled her hand away from his wound to grasp her mother's necklace around her neck, silently praying to Morana that the goddess of death would listen to her in her plea for this poison not to take her father away from her. Hazel had so many plans for them, and the idea that they would never come true was earth-shattering. Hazel's heart pounded with a frantic rhythm as the weight of helplessness pressed down on her.

Despite her extensive knowledge and unwavering faith, for the first time, she felt utterly powerless against the insidious poison ravaging her uncle's body. The cruel reality that her healing abilities might not be enough to save him gnawed at her soul, filling her with a crippling sense of despair and frustration.

"Let me see your face one last time," Hazel's sob ripped out of her throat as she turned to look at her uncle's fading brown eyes, seeing his life slowly slipping away from him. Holding his hand, Hazel felt a tumultuous mix of emotions surge through her. The cold clammy touch reassured her, yet it was tinged with the cold dread of impending loss. Grief, love, and desperate longing intertwined within her, making every heartbeat feel like an echo of their shared past and a reminder of the fragile present.

"You look so much like your mother."

"No, you can't leave me. Please hold on just a little longer."

Archibald only faintly smiled at her, stroking his niece's soft face as a tear fell from his eyes, taking in every last detail of his niece. "I wish I could have seen you grow up, walked you down the aisle of your wedding day, watched you build your own little family."

She could not look at him as hearing his words just ripped her heart out more slowly and painfully.

"You would have been an amazing mother, Hazel. Follow your heart, for it will lead you correctly," Archibald continued, his voice strained.

Tears streamed down Hazel's face as she struggled to hold back sobs threatening to escape. Her chest tightened with a mix of sorrow and longing, making it hard to breathe. She wanted to speak, but the words caught in her throat, leaving her overwhelmed by a wave of grief and love.

Hazel couldn't control the sobbing coming from her as she held her uncle's hand close to her heart.

"Please don't talk like this. You will be okay. Nophy will heal you. I prayed to her. I willed it to happen. You will live. This isn't the end," Hazel choked out.

Archibald gave her a weak smile, his eyes filled with sadness and acceptance. "My dear Hazel, sometimes even the strongest prayers can't change fate," he whispered, his voice barely audible. He gently squeezed her hand, offering what little comfort he could in his final moments. "Please promise me something, Hazel, my sweet precious Hazel." Archibald's raspy voice broke for a moment as he tilted her head to look at him as her tears flooded from her eyes. "Your heart is too big for this world. You are so good and kind. Promise me you will follow your destiny and save our home."

Hazel bit her lip before starting to shake her head. How could she fulfill a prophecy if she couldn't save the one person she loves the most?

Archibald continued stroking her cheek, wiping away the tears. "I know it will be scary, that you may feel alone, but you are never alone. Those who love you truly will never leave your side."

Hazel leaned her head into his touch , before silently nodding to him in acceptance.

"When I am gone, will you burn my body so I may join your mother in the stars? I don't want people to mourn me, but to celebrate my life and the memories I made with them."

Hazel crumbled, hearing his words. Her heart ached at the thought of losing him.

Despite the unbearable pain, she steeled herself, realizing this was the first step in fulfilling her promise to him. Not letting him see how much she was breaking His last wishes for her. Standing and then leaning over the bed, she wrapped her arms around his neck to prevent him from leaving her. Hazel needed to hold him to this plane of life.

"Dad, I-I can't." Hazel choked out, holding him tight, ignoring the putrid smell flooding her nostrils. She was overwhelmed with grief and fear, unable to process the reality of the situation. The thought of losing her uncle, who had become her father, was unbearable, and the stench only made the moment more painfully real. Her trembling hands clung to him, desperate to hold on to their little time.

"My little fawn, please. I don't have much time." Archibald wrapped one arm around her, holding his niece close to him. Hazel felt his tears slide down his cheek falling onto her cheek, which only gutted her more.

"I promise, there will be a grandest feast in honor of you, I swear it." Hazel steeled herself to look at her uncle one more time so the last thing he saw was a smile on his niece's face as she stroked his cheek. She kissed his head before pushing hair from his face as more tears fell from her eyes. "Tell mom how much I love her and miss her, I swear I will make you both proud of me. I will fulfill my destiny and become the Ivory Fawn."

Archibald smiled weakly, taking his niece's hand and kissing it softly as his tears fell before reaching up to his niece's face to stroke away her tears. "She already knows, Hazel, and you already have made us both very proud. Never stop chasing what makes you happy. It was an honor being your uncle and your father. I love you, Hazel."

She leaned forward and kisses his head. When his last breath hit her cheek and she felt the life leave Archibald's body, Hazel's heart shattered into a million pieces. A guttural sob escaped her lips, and she clung to him even tighter, unwilling to let go.

Hazel collapsed to the ground beside his bed, wailing as she held her uncle's hand tight, pressing her head on his cold knuckles. He was gone. The only thing she had to remind her of home was gone. The one father figure she had was ripped from her because of the people who took joy in hurting others for their sick pleasure.

Her mind raced with memories of their shared moments, each one now a painful reminder of what she had lost. Anger and sorrow intertwined within her, fueling a burning desire for justice against those who had caused this pain.

Hazel wailed as if her sobs would wake her from this nightmare. This wasn't real. This couldn't be real. Hazel didn't lose Archibald. When woke, she would find him and give him the biggest hug she could..

A pair of arms wrapped around her shoulders, holding her close to their warm chest. Hazel shook her head. "No, no, I won't leave him!" she cried out, trying to push the boulder frame away from her, but it held firm. Snapping her attention to the face linked to the sing; arm that now held her.

Kingsly's face was so soft yet anguished, his eyes filled with tears, mirroring the agony Hazel felt. His voice, choked with emotion, barely managed to whisper, "Hazel, I'm so sorry, but you need to let him go."

Trembling, Hazel stared at him with such devastation of her lost. She finally released her uncle's hand, crumbling further as she did, screaming in sorrow. Kingsly pulled her tight to his chest, so tight she heard and felt his racing heartbeat. Kingsly gently rocked her back and forth, whispering soothing words of comfort into her ear. "I'm here, Hazel. You're not alone," he murmured, his voice steady despite the tears streaming down his face. He held her as she sobbed, offering her the only solace he could in that moment of unbearable grief.

Hazel let out all the pain and sorrow. Her vision was blurry, she could tell from how the room looked that her magic was responding to her emotions.

Hazel barely heard the door leading into the infirmary opening as she yowled with sorrow and pain. Soon, she felt the familiar touch of a hand brushing the hair on her face before wiping tears from her face. Looking to her right to see through her blurred vision, she saw a soft peach-like face of a woman with brown hair pulled back.

"Come on, my sweet girl." Smooth honey, soft familiarity washed over, realizing Arabella was now at her side.

Seeing her trusted friend, Hazel broke down once more, breaking from Kingsly's arms before wrapping her arms around Arabella as she raced towards her , holding Arabella close to her chest.

Soon, Hazel felt a strong, calloused hand helping her stand. Leaning on Arabella, Hazel held a hand over her mouth, trying to silence her sobs before looking at her uncle's body lying in the bed as the healers covered his face with a white cloth. Waves of grief washed over her, mingling with a profound sense of loss and helplessness. Her knees buckled slightly, and the tears flowed even more freely, each one a testament to the love and sorrow she felt. However, Arabella and Kingsly kept her upright as the pair guided her out of the infirmary.

The young fawn didn't even remember how they got back to her bedroom, all Hazel could see was Archibald's body lying there and how she couldn't save him. Hazel's mind was a whirlwind of guilt and helplessness, each thought sharper than the last. She kept replaying the moments leading up to her uncle's death, wondering if there was something she could have done differently. Every breath felt heavy with regret as if she had failed him in his final moments.

Leaning on her ivory wood bedpost, Hazel held her stomach, feeling absolutely sick. She was also scared that if she let it go, she would crumble all over again.

Arabella helped her out of her training attire to slip Hazel into a comfortable nightgown before leading her into the bed.

The ladies maid tucked her in before sitting on the bed, rubbing Hazel's arm in soothing motions. "I will not be going anywhere. You tell me what you need." Arabella's honey voice was soothing, as was her touch.

Hazel took Arabella's hand and pulled her into the bed, wrapping the young woman's arm around her trembling body. "Please just hold me and stay the night. I don't want to be left alone." Her voice was so brittle and hoarse from crying as her eyes were so heavy she couldn't keep them open before she let sleep take her in the hope she would wake up from this horrific nightmare.

Chapter Forty-Three

Hazel

The rays of the morning sun woke Hazel from her slumber, and her eyes fluttered open as she lay in her bed. Recollecting what happened last night, she felt a calamitous feeling inside her chest. She remembered her uncle would no longer hug her, kiss her head, or even call him her little fawn.

Forcing her eyes shut, Hazel desperately wanted to wake up from this nightmare. She didn't want to believe this was now her reality—one where her uncle was no longer in her life.

A guttural sob broke from her strained vocal cords as she remembered last breath on her cheek. He was gone.

Pulling the silk gold sheets to her chest, Hazel tried covering her mouth to muffle the sobbing. Forcing her eyes closed, she hoped when she opened them, her father would be there soothing her from this nightmare, but Hazel knew in her heart that wasn't going to happen.

A soft, warm finger brushed across her face before the hands pulled her weeping form into their lap. Stroking her hair softly, the gentle hand rubbed up and down her arm. Hazel didn't need to open her eyes as she knew Arabella was taking care of her, once again.

The feel of her ladies maid's chin resting on her head as she rubbed her arms made Hazel sob even harder.

"I want my uncle!" Hazel yowled out, holding onto Arabella before opening her eyes , her room was blurred by her tears.

Hazel thought she heard Arabella's heartbreak against her eardrum from her words, her grip tightened around Hazel's shoulders, holding her closer.

"I know, Hazel, I know." Arabella's voice wasn't the normal soft honey-smooth tone, but now brittle and hoarse as if she had sobbed herself.

"This isn't right! It's not fair!" Hazel argued not with Arabella, but as if she was arguing with the goddess of death. How dare the goddess take her uncle? How dare they abandon her when she needed them the most to save her uncle? Damn the Aestival gods as well for not helping her save her uncle.

If she could go head-to-head with whichever god took him from her, she would fight so damn hard to her very last breath just to see him one more time.

"I am so sorry, Hazel." She felt a kiss on her head while Arabella's hands continued to rub the young fawn's arms, trying to soothe her.

Her throat felt so raw it hurt to speak. Holding her throat as she sobs in her friend's arm, unable to stop the tears.

Soon, there was a knock from the entryway beyond the bedroom doors. Arabella kissed the young fawn's head, helping her lay back in the bed. "I will be right back."

Hazel watched her friend walk out of her bedroom into her receiving room. She heard soft voices, but they weren't loud enough for her to identify the visitor. Moments later, Arabella walked back inside the bedroom with a frown. "It's Atticus. Do you want to see him?"

Hazel didn't have the mental strength to talk to him. She shook her head and turned in her bed, putting her back to Arabella. She was in no mood to talk to anyone. Not when she just lost her uncle. She especially did not want comfort from him, not now. After their moment a few weeks ago,

Hearing more indistinct conversation before the doors closed, Hazel kept her eyes shut tight trying to fall asleep, not wanting to be in this reality where Archibald wasn't alive. She wanted to see him, to hold him, to hug him, even if it was in her dreams.

Once more, Arabella's footsteps approached before she sat on the bed. "What did he say?" Hazel asked curiously.

A faint sigh came from the soft lips of her lady's maid as her thumb rubbed soothing patterns on her arm. "He wanted to check up on you, and also to ask about what to do with your uncle's remains and possessions."

Of course, he did. He was still a inconsiderate of her feelings. She had just lost her uncle, and he asked her these things. Taking a deep, shaky breath, she sat up, clutching her mother's necklace, and remembered what her uncle said. He didn't want people mourning him, but celebrating his life.

Hazel wasn't ready to face the world without her uncle. However, her uncle wouldn't want her to lay in bed wallowing in what could have been. She knew Archibald would want her to keep trying and pushing forward, despite it being challenging. On his deathbed, she swore she would become the Ivory Fawn, and she reminded herself of that promise.

"Is he still out there?" Wiping her tears away, she took a deep, shuddering breath.

Arabella nodded to Hazel's question.

"Let me get dressed first, and then I will talk to him." Hazel's voice wobbled as she tried to stay in one piece and be strong.

"Death leaves a heartache no one can heal, and love leaves a memory no one can steal. Remember that, Hazel." Arabella's smooth, honeyed voice wrapped her in a warm sensation before the handmaiden leaned over, kissing her forehead.

Hazel rose from her bed, sauntering over to her vanity mirror before taking a deep breath and gazing at the woman staring back at herself. A woman who had her entire earth shattered beneath her feet, losing the last living member of her family.

However, instead of plummeting into that darkness and letting it consume her, she would rise to her feet and be who she was destined to be. Touching her mother's necklace, Hazel took a deep breath, removing it from around her neck before running her finger along the lilac claw mushrooms.

Remembering what Archibald told her about her heritage and destiny, Hazel gazed into the mirror, seeing the eyes of a simple village girl pleading with her to return to bed and avoid meeting the prince, urging her to flee back home. She blinked away her tears and looked at the mirror again, now seeing the eyes of the woman and fearless warrior she was becoming.

Archibald saw that warrior inside her, and Atticus, too. It was time Hazel became that warrior they saw.

She set her mother's necklace on the desk of her vanity mirror and braided her hair in a waterfall braid she had learned over the years. Rising to her feet, she strode over to her gold wardrobe, picked out a simple ivory knitted blouse, slid it over her head, and pulled her golden hair out from under the fabric. Reaching for a brown skirt, the maturing fawn stepped into it, pulling it up to her waist before lacing the back tight.

Hearing a peck at the balcony archway window doors, Hazel turned and spied a cardinal pecking at the glass. Seeing the crimson bird, she slowly made her way toward it Her hand trailed off her bedpost as she approached. she stared at this bird pecking at the glass door. Running her hand along the ivory oak wood bed frame, she took a deep, shuddering breath as she walked towards the doors.

Opening the glass doors, the cardinal flew away, but circled back around and landed on the white-marbled balcony's railing. Hesitantly, her hand rested on the door frame, wondering if she should continue to approach as the cold winter air bit at her skin.

There was something familiar about this bird as she approached it.

As she made it to the railing looking down to the courtyard where Hazel saw them building the pyre for her uncle's cremation ceremony. Hazel noticed the faint crackling of the courtyard torches mingling with the soft whispers of the winter wind. The scent of pine and burning wood filled the air, grounding her in the bittersweet moment.

Feeling her heart shatter all over again, she couldn't pull her eyes away from the reality that was slamming its presence into her heart.

The small red feathered creature rubbed its small redhead on Hazel's finger, chirping a happy song. Looking down, she smiled warmly, looking at the preparations being made in the courtyard below her. Her friend spread its wings, ruffling its feathers before hopping up Hazel's arm to nuzzle its head against her falling tears.

Chuckling faintly and nuzzling her own cheek gently into the creature's head, the small bird took flight and headed west. It then finally hit her that it was her uncle saying his final farewell to her. Hazel watched it fly away for a moment. "Goodbye, Father." she breathed

Inhaling deeply she turned back toward her bedroom. Seeing Atticus standing there in the archway, his hair combed back with his normal prideful strong stature,

As Atticus stepped forward, his boots echoed softly against the marble floor, breaking the delicate silence.

Hazel sighed, seeing him straightening her shoulders back as she strode to the dragon, not wanting to give him the satisfaction of her crying village girl he saved back in Alexandria. Not with how he been acting these last few weeks "You wanted to see me, Prince Atticus?" Hazel's voice held firm as her shoulder brushed his arm as she strides over to the chair sitting beside her bookshelf, sitting down and looking at him as if his very presence didn't shake her, but her eyes never left him in fear he would have his hand around her throat once more.

The air between them crackled with unspoken tension, one revolving around unresolved emotions. Hazel's heart pounded in her chest, but she refused to let it show, maintaining her composed facade.

"Hazel." Atticus' voice trembled as he said her name.

Her steeled expression to protect her heart holding a stern tone, not letting herself fall for him.

"You wanted to talk about my uncle's remains and possessions. I see you already decided what would happen to his remains. As for his possessions, I want them packed and brought to my receiving room so that when I am ready, I can sort through them."

Atticus took a few steps towards Hazel, whose body tensed as he did. The Immortal Dragon must have seen it, for he stopped. "Please, Hazel." His voice actually broke as he said her name. It was almost pleading.

Hazel felt a tumult of emotions crashing within her. His vulnerable voice tugged at her heartstrings, threatening to break down her defenses. She longed to comfort him and bridge the gap between them, but memories of betrayal and pain held her back. Her mind wavered between old affections and the need to protect herself.

Hazel couldn't prepare for how he sounded saying her name. Her breath shuddered as she looked away from him, walking to her bathroom.

The morning rays light the ivory and gold marble bathroom, and her eye glanced up to the sink Atticus once had her pinned to.

"If you only wanted to discuss my uncle's belongings, then you have my answer. I have nothing else to say. I shall see you the weekend following next at the ball." Hazel couldn't look at him. She couldn't bear to see the expression on his face.

After she caught him sleeping with another woman, and left her alone in the bedroom. She wanted him to finish what he started because she wanted his hands on her so badly, like she'd seen Atticus's hands all over that woman. At the same time, Hazel couldn't let herself fall for him, for anyone, not when the last person she let into her heart nearly killed her.

"Hazel, please talk to me." It sounded brittle. His voice was a dagger to her heart. How dare he ask that she talk to him about what she was going through when all he had been was this cruel, harsh prince who held her by her throat and threatened her , then never let up on her in training,? No, she wouldn't let him in.

"Why should I?" Hazel couldn't stop the words from tumbling out of her mouth as she turned to look at him.

His face contorted with pain and desperation, his eyes pleading as if searching for a glimmer of the connection they once shared.

"Since I've been here in court, one moment, you are this gentle, compassionate prince who I can see myself loving. But then you become this cruel, vile, harsh prince who doesn't care who he hurts while satisfying his own agenda and needs. I don't know who is worse, you or Darius."

The prince's face fell, his shoulders slumping as though the weight of her words crushed him. He opened his mouth to respond, but no sound came out.

"At least with Darius, he had the guts to reveal his true colors to me before he tried killing me. You? You would rather play with me like this is some cat-and-mouse game." Hazel's sounded with a thunderous voice was as if it was lightning striking Atticus, causing him to step back from the blow of her words.

"I don't have to talk to you because you are the so-called Crimson Dragon. No matter what you say or do, you cannot fix the damage you have caused. I will become the Ivory Fawn, not for you or for your kingdom, but because I swore to my uncle while he lay dying in that bed that I would. Whatever we had, Atticus, went up in flames because you set fire to it."

Desperately trying to keep the tears from pouring out, and refraining from punching him, Hazel clenched her fists tight, her nails cutting into her palm. "You don't get to come in here and act like you care. You had plenty of chances in these last weeks to apologize for how you been acting, what you caused, but you let your pride stop you." Hazel turned her back to Atticus, not wanting him to see her cry, her heart raced in her chest as the blood trickled between her fingers from how hard they pressed into her palm. "It's best you go, Prince Atticus. I am sure there are some royal duties you need to tend to or some women who need your attention."

There was no sound of shifting weight on the wood or of his clothes rustling from any moving limbs. Standing there, Hazel didn't even look at the mirror in her bathroom to see if he was still behind her.

"If that is what you wish, princess." His tone was so cold. It bit the back of her exposed neck.

Hazel had just lost her uncle. The last thing she needed was for this prince to come along and cause further heartbreak than there already was.

There was a creak in the wood flooring as Atticus silently left Hazel's bedroom. Turning her head slightly, she watched the prince's backside leave her. She wondered if she was being too harsh, but she couldn't let herself fall for his charm again.

Atticus held open the mahogany door before glancing over his shoulder, looking indirectly at her. "I give my condolences, Hazel. Your uncle, from the small time I knew him, was a great man."

Hazel bit her lip, holding back the breakdown threatening to come back to the surface.

He stared at her, as if she would respond to him, but she said nothing. If Hazel did, her words would give away how badly she wanted him to hold her and comfort her.

The sun was slowly reaching the ocean's medium red-violet waters as Hazel stood at the funeral wood pyre created for her uncle. Walking towards the pyre that was decorated with red roses from the queen's garden as a tribute to his sacrifice for the queen's son, Hazel carried a bundle of lavender and wisteria flowers in her arms. Dressed in a simple black dress with a black lace veil and black winter cloak, Hazel's eyes were flooded with tears to the point she barely could make out her uncle's face. For the funeral, she requested they didn't cover his face so she could see him one last time before the cremation.

The setting sun cast an ethereal glow over the scene, its warm hues blending with the cool tones of the unlit pyre. Shadows danced across the floral decorations, creating a somber yet beautiful contrast. The air was thick with the scent of flowers and the salty breeze from the ocean, adding to the poignant atmosphere of the moment. Hazel adjusted the fur blanket to cover him a bit more, as if the cold would bother him in this state. Leaning down, she kissed Archibald's cold head,

The lavender and wisteria she chose held deep meaning. Lavender symbolized peace and serenity, reflecting her hope that her uncle would find rest in the afterlife. Wisteria, with its cascading blooms, represented her enduring love and remembrance, ensuring that his sacrifice would never be forgotten. These flowers, combined with the red roses from the queen's garden, created a tapestry of emotions honoring both his noble deeds and the personal bond they shared.

Hazel took in every detail of him to remember him in this peaceful state and remind herself he was no longer hurting.

Laying the bundles of lavender and wisteria on his chest where the brown fur sat, tears slipped out, making the cold bite her skin more. "I love you so much, and I will miss you more than you know."

His pyre, adorned with his sword and flowers, was set on a cliff overlooking the ocean. Ancient trees surrounded the clearing, their branches swaying in the breeze. Hazel felt warmth seeing the offerings, including flowers, food, and a fur blanket from the castle staff who loved him.

Taking a deep breath, Hazel stroked Archibald's hair once more before feeling Kingsly's calloused hand rest on her arm. "I'm so sorry, Hazel. This was a loss that this castle will never forget."

Feeling brittle beneath his touch, sorrow threatened to consume her, but Hazel held it back as Kingsly kissed her head and pulled her away from the pyre to join the royal family.

The queen's hand reached for Hazel as if to keep her stable. The queen had treated her with the utmost respect, but she started treating Hazel more like a daughter after she saved her life, offering guidance and support in times of need. This gesture of comfort was a testament to their deep bond, forged during her short time here at the court. When the queen pulled Hazel into a hug and rubbed her back, it was her undoing. More tears came out, and she held the queen tight as if she were her own mother.

"Easy dear, it's almost over," the queen soothed before releasing the young fawn, wiping away the tears before handing her the ceremonial bow and arrow to light the pyre.

As Hazel took the bow and arrow, a surge of conflicting emotions welled up inside her. She felt the weight of grief pressing down on her shoulders, mingled with a sense of honor for being entrusted with such a sacred task. Her hands trembled slightly, but she steeled herself, drawing strength from the queen's comforting presence. Staring into the fire inside of the fire pit. Hazel was hesitant to light the arrow.

Feeling a calloused hand come to her shoulder, Hazel looked over to her shoulder, seeing Kingsly standing behind her once again. He said nothing to her as he looked into her eyes, stroking a tear from it before nodding his head, almost as if he was trying to reassure her everything would be just fine. Kingsly's gesture was filled with unspoken empathy and support, conveying his deep understanding of her pain. His silent reassurance provided Hazel with a sense of comfort and solidarity, reminding her that she was not alone in her struggles.

Turning her head to the torch, she raised the arrow to the sacred flame, lighting it before notching it into her bow. Taking a few steps forward, Hazel filled her lungs with cold, crisp air before raising her bow up. A black feather brushed her cheek as she pulled back the arrow. Not ready to let him go, she released it with an exhale knowing he wouldn't want her to hold on to that grief for too long.

Hazel felt a mix of anticipation and dread as she watched the arrow soar through the night sky. Her heart pounded in her chest, each beat echoing the significance of this moment. As the arrow blazed a trail of light, she hoped it would bring the peace her uncle deserved in the afterlife. Watching the arrow hit true, Archibald's pyre went up in flames.

Hazel stood silently, and observed the embers rise into the night sky. Leaning her head back, the flames warmed her skin. She lost count of the minutes she stood there watching the flames consume her uncle. They grew so bright and high that Hazel couldn't see his body anymore.

Soon, the attendees headed indoors to warm up and eat the feast prepared to celebrate Archibald's life.

While Hazel continued to watch the flames roar and consume her uncle, she remained frozen in place with the bow lowered. A part of her waited for him to walk through the flames unharmed. She felt a mix of grief and hope, her heart pounding in her chest. Tears welled up in her eyes. The uncertainty of the moment left her paralyzed, unable to move or look away.

A soft hum came from Hazel, which transitioned into her singing a soothing melody. Leaning her head back, her voice became louder as tears continued to roll from her eyes. As she sang to the stars, the melody became heartbreaking.

This song was one her uncle sang, a lullaby meant to comfort Hazel during nights of fear and uncertainty. In this moment of profound loss, it was the only thing that could ground her. It connected her to a time when she felt safe and loved. The melody carried the weight of her grief, acting as a farewell and a desperate plea for solace. There were no common spoken words, but how Hazel sang in another language. All her sorrow and pain were being sung to release her heart from its pain.

The lullaby was a well known song throughout Tresian. It tells the story of a beloved hunter who fell in love with the goddess of the hunt. Her brother, misunderstanding the situation, accused the hunter of wrongdoing and demanded he betray the goddess. When the hunter refused, the brother sent a beast to kill him. The hunter convinced the goddess that a man had defiled her priestess, leading her to mistakenly kill him. In sorrow, she placed his body among the stars to be remembered forever.

Tears fell from her eyes as the snow fell, as if the goddess of winter was crying with her. Lowering her head at the end of her lullaby, Hazel couldn't hold the bow anymore. Her fingers released it before her palms met with her eyes the moment her knees met the cold, soft snow.

Hazel couldn't hold it back anymore, couldn't be strong anymore, and a heart-wrenching scream ripped from her throat. Her magic burst out around her, clearing the snow in a fairy-like circle, leaving nothing but green grass and flowers. Her magic, a rare and powerful gift, had always been tied to her emotions. This moment of profound sorrow and release manifested as a burst of life midst the barren winter, symbolizing her deep connection to nature and the raw, untamed power within her. This display not only showed the depth of her pain but also her resilience and the hope that still lingered in her heart.

She let it all out, the pain of losing the only father she had growing up. Hazel knew death was inevitable for everyone, but she never lost someone she cared for as much. She was too young to remember her parents. Her mother died before she could have any memories of her. Hazel never made any friends in her village, and the ones she did befriend were taken as Blood Brides. Hazel didn't even bothered to get attached to anyone other than Darius because every month someone was being plucked up like a pig for a monthly meal. Hazel's isolation had forged her into a solitary figure, fiercely independent and wary of forming attachments. Her self-reliance was a shield against the pain of loss, but it also left her yearning for connection, making her bond with Darius all the more significant.

Two calloused hands wrapped around Hazel's shoulder, pulling her a thunderous beating heart, and she held onto whoever came to comfort her. All Hazel could see was black fabric of a cloak wrap around her, which was common for a funeral. However, when Hazel saw the strands of white in the wind, she knew it was the White Dragoness who was holding her. Her presence signified a bond that transcended ordinary companionship, offering Hazel a sense of protection and understanding that few could provide. In this moment of profound sorrow, Ardnaxela's embrace reassured Hazel that she was not alone and that even in her darkest times, she had a powerful ally by her side.

Burying her face into the Dragoness' arms, Hazel's sobbing screams grew louder as the Dragoness embraced her tighter. The Dragoness hand held her head close to her chest, letting the fawn get everything out.

Hazel felt another hand gently touch the small of her back before she realized her back was now warm from someone wrapping her arms around her and Ardnaxela.

Seeing a sliver of jade green, Hazel crumbled further as Sybilla kneeled beside them, joining the embrace. Ardnaxela and Sybilla enveloped Hazel in a cocoon of warmth and solidarity, starkly contrasting to the isolation she had known for so long. Each touch and comforting gesture from her companions melted away the jagged edges of her grief, allowing her to feel a sense of belonging she had almost forgotten existed.

In this shared moment of vulnerability, Hazel discovered that even the fiercest independence could not replace the healing power of genuine connection and support. More limbs joined in, followed by the aroma of peaches of Arabella who held Hazel's hand tightly, wiping her eyes from the tears streaming down her face.

For once, she didn't feel alone in her sorrow. Hazel remembered while she may have lost Archibald, the last remaining blood family she had, she still had family—a family that was now forming a circle around to shield her.

It was now clear that Hazel would not be alone on this journey. She didn't know where it would lead. Hazel had Sybilla, Ardnaxela, Arabella, Kingsly, and even Atticus. This was now her new family, and she would do what she must to protect them, no matter what.

Chapter Forty-Four

Hazel

Swirls of lilac and orchid leaves danced in the wind, and
the aroma of wisteria flowers and oak wood filled Hazel's senses as storm clouds
gathered outside the temple archway windows. It was spring outside. But how? Hazel
stood perplexed, her eyes wide with wonder and confusion. Just moments ago, the sky
was heavy with winter's chill. Now, she felt an inexplicable warmth and the unmistakable
scent of blooming flowers.

Hazel's eyes turned to the tree, and the vines of wisteria flowers brushed her cheek, the
petals soft against her skin. She looked to her right, seeing a bright golden light coming
from her peripheral. As she focused her gaze to it, she saw Queen Asteria standing in all
her golden glory.

The queen's platinum hair laid loosely in curls, and her golden halo-spiked crown
matched her dress and wings. The look of unease on the queen's face and how she was
hastily walking toward her made Hazel refrain from speaking.

Taking the young fawn's hand, the queen stroked her soft, golden hair before taking
Hazel's chin with her other hand.

"It is almost time, my young one. He is on his way. You must only trust your dragon
and those close to you. You are nearly ready to become the Ivory Fawn." The urgency in
the queen's voice made Hazel's spine straighten.

"Who is coming? You keep warning me about a man coming for me, but you don't tell me who or what he looks like." Hazel's heart pounded in her chest, a mix of confusion and fear swirling within her. Her mind raced with questions and doubts, but the queen's grave expression only deepened her anxiety. A cold shiver ran down her spine, despite the warmth of the queen's touch, as the weight of the unknown pressed heavily on her. "How can I be prepared to defend myself and my family if I don't know any details?"

Scanning her surroundings, as if something in the room would tell Hazel who was coming, the queen pulled the young fawn's attention to her. "He wishes to eradicate you before you become the Ivory Fawn so he may plunge Wylana into darkness."

"How am I supposed to become the Ivory Fawn if I couldn't even save my uncle?"

The queen's face softened with a mix of compassion and resolve. "Hazel, your strength lies not in your past failures but in your willingness to rise above them," she whispered, her voice steady but gentle. "You have more power within you than you realize, and your uncle's spirit guides you still."

Hazel's mind churned with doubt and fear, battling the seeds of hope the queen's words had planted. She felt the weight of her uncle's memory pressing on her heart, a constant reminder of her perceived failures.

"Isn't that what the Ivory Fawn is supposed to do?" Hazel whispered, her voice barely holding together. "Heal. Protect. Save the ones who can't save themselves." Her hands hovered over the chest, shaking—not from fear, but from the weight of everything she wasn't sure she could be.

"I can cure the sap poisoning," she went on, quieter now, like the truth might shatter her if she said it too loud. "But I can't undo what their magic has done. I haven't figured out how to stop it without burning myself out."

She swallowed hard, her throat tight. "I couldn't save him," she said. "My uncle—he died right in front of me. And I tried. I tried so damn hard, but it wasn't enough. So tell me—how are we supposed to be certain I'm this great savior everyone keeps whispering about? What if you're wrong? What if I'm not the Ivory Fawn? What if I'm just... the girl who got there too late?"

Hazel's voice ripped from her throat as she looked at the queen, how could she become this righteous destined hero when she can't do the one thing she was destined to do.

"Hazel, your uncle's passing was not your fault. You alleviated his suffering, ensuring a peaceful end. You also saved those men from the carriage ambush. You are my great-great granddaughter. Your ancestors' magic resides within you. Hazel, you possess the ability

to wield my magic; you simply need to learn how to harness it. You are the Ivory Fawn."
The queen held a heartbroken expression.

Hazel ripped her hands away from the queen, stepping back and shaking her head.
"Peaceful? There was nothing peaceful about his death. How can I be this Ivory Fawn
like you want me to be? If I can't even save my loved ones, what makes you think I will
be able to help all of Wylana!" A mist clouded Hazel's eyes as she stared at the queen's
blank expression. "You tell me to trust the dragon, but all the dragon has done is conceal
secrets from me, hurt me, and confuse me. Were you ever going to tell me that I would
die from this prophecy? Am I just a pawn to bring the Aestivals back to life?" A growl
escaped Hazel's lips as she took a step toward the queen wanting to see her reaction.

The queen's eyes softened with a mix of sorrow and understanding, her regal composure momentarily faltering. "Hazel, I would never use you as a pawn. The burden of
prophecy is heavy, and I have faced its harsh truths and made my own sacrifices. But you
are not alone." The queen sighed softly, looking down, not meeting Hazel's eyes. "In order
for you to become the Ivory Fawn, there must be a sacrifice." That was all the queen said.

Hazel's eyes widened. It was as if the blow had struck her heart, and the queen had
revealed what worried Atticus so much. She could possibly die to become the Ivory Fawn.
"So, am I just learning to become the Ivory Fawn so I can die? You know what? Forget the
dragon and forget your cryptic messages. I will become the Ivory Fawn like I swore to my
father, but I will not die. I will become the Ivory Fawn on my own without your help or
Atticus's help.."

The queen observed Hazel, gently pushing her shoulder back as Asteria's posture
improved with the slight tilt of her chin. "Hazel, you must be cautious. There is a war
coming, and you need his help preparing for it and winning it."

Hazel clenched her fists, her jaw tightening as she struggled to keep her voice steady.
"Why must I always rely on someone else?" she muttered, her eyes flashing with defiance.
Shaking her head, Hazel scoffed, glaring at the queen. "I am aware there is a war approach-
ing, but I will trust the one dragon who hasn't wronged me. *She* is who I will follow. The
Dragoness. Not the Crimson Dragon. When I become the Ivory Fawn, I will rid Wylana
of this Netherian plague and rid myself of your insufferable, vague warnings."

Hazel walked down the stone path to the Mother Grove Tree, running her hand up the
oak, before taking a deep breath, and closing her eyes. Once they opened, she was lying in
her soft silken bed sheets. Sitting up with a gasp, she saw how dark the room was. The only

light that illuminated it was the moonlight coming in through the glass archway doors leading into her bedroom from her balcony.

The morning after waking up , all she could think of was the vision she had with Ast eria.The snow was still soft from this morning's fall. Dressed in warmer fighting attire, Hazel jogged through the white-covered courtyard to where she was planning to meet with Ardnaxela for their daily morning training.

She was urged to let herself grieve, but the young fawn didn't want to sit around and mope about the loss of her uncle. She wanted to honor the promise she made to him and put her anger and rage towards the Netherian people,.

Panting heavily, her breath clouded with every huff, Hazel let her mind wander during her warm-up. She remembered what her Queen Asteria said to her about a war coming and trusted the prince. Trust the prince that had kept information from her , threatened her , and had her by the throat. It was hard to trust him like she used to.

Hazel slowly approached Ardnaxela and her routine training spot, panting heavily. Hazel's heart tightened as she saw Atticus, her emotions conflicting between betrayal of her trust and duty. Her eyes narrowed slightly, masking the pain she still felt from his past actions. Despite her inner turmoil, she kept her voice steady, not wanting to reveal just how much his presence affected her. "What's this?" she asked, confused about why the prince was even here.

"He is training you today in a new fighting style to keep you on your feet," Ardnaxela responded by strolling over to a pine tree and leaning back on it.

Hazel's mind raced with uncertainty and a touch of resentment. However, she knew that mastering a new fighting style could be crucial for her upcoming battles, and she decided to push her personal feelings aside, focusing on the opportunity to grow stronger.

"Plus, whatever tension you two have going on right now, you can get it out during training. It is a healthy way to release some of that anger and frustration."

Shaking her head, Hazel faintly laughed in disbelief at what was being said, tightening her ponytail hair as she looked at Atticus, who was wearing a sleeveless black tunic and trousers. She could see the dragon tattoo wrapped around his arm. She remembered seeing the full length of that dragon tattoo the night he came to her bedroom, how well built he was. But Hazel shook her head clearing her thoughts.

"So we are going to beat the crap out of each other, and for what? For your entertainment or because it will actually help us?" Hazel's attention was fully on the White Dragoness crossing her arms over her training attire.

Atticus smirked, a glint of amusement flickering in his eyes as he raised an eyebrow. "A bit of both, I suppose," he replied, his tone laced with confidence.

Hazel couldn't help but feel a surge of irritation at his nonchalant attitude, yet she knew she had to maintain her composure.

"What, you can't handle me, princess? Scared I would embarrass you?" Atticus purred with amusement.

Ardnaxela pushed off the tree with a smirk, walking to stand between the two. "Both. You will learn how to handle a larger opponent along with new skills while also working out whatever is going between you two. You are the Ivory Fawn and he is the Crimson Dragon. You both are vital in bringing peace to Wylana, but neither of you can do that if you are being insufferable children."

Hazel looked at Atticus, tilting her head back, seeing him give her that feline smile. she narrowed her eyes, removed her mother's cloak. and to draped it over a tree branch. If she wanted Hazel to get all her anger out on him, then she would. Maybe a few good kicks to his jaw would knock him down a few notches.

Ardnaxela turned her back to Hazel, walking over to Atticus and patting his shoulder. "Don't hold back," the Dragoness said to him before she looked at Hazel with a grin. "Show him what you can do, little fawn." She winked at Hazel before walking back to a tree and leaning on it.

Hazel's heart pounded in her chest, a mix of excitement and nervousness swirling within her. She clenched her fists, determined to prove herself. Taking a deep breath, she stepped forward, ready to show Atticus the extent of her abilities.

He approached her with a grin, rolling his shoulder, making the tail of the dragon look as if it was adjusting itself on his arm. Hazel's icy blue met honey before she scanned over his body. Even though he was an arrogant ass, she had to admit he looked so damn good in his fighting attire.

"Shall we make this interesting, princess?"

Hazel's attention shot to his mischievous eyes as he removed his shirt, tossing it aside. Her cheeks flushed a deep crimson as she tried to maintain her composure. She couldn't help but steal a quick glance at his chiseled physique, her breath catching momentarily. Determined not to let him see her flustered, she smirked and replied, "Only if you're ready to lose, Atticus."

Hazel took in his figure more. In the bathroom, how did she not see his muscles before? Maybe because she had another emotion other than anger and frustration on her mind.

I can't let him distract me. Focus, Hazel, focus. This isn't just about impressing Atticus or Ardnaxela but proving my strength and capability. Her thoughts raced. I've trained hard for this moment. I won't let a pretty face throw me off.

"Like what you see, princess?" he chuckled as he and Hazel circle each other. Atticus's grin widened, his confidence radiating with every step. "I hope you can keep up," he teased, his voice dripping with playful arrogance. His movements were fluid, each one a testament to his battle-hardened experience and unwavering self-assurance. Atticus had the upper hand in strength and size, but she was quicker and more agile with her size.

Hazel watched for the slightest muscle twitch to give away where he would strike, just like Ardnaxela taught her.

Suddenly, his left forearm tensed. Hazel quickly ducked his left hook, noting that his fighting side was his left. Seeing her opening, she went to kick at his exposed ribs, but he must have predicted because he smacked her foot away.

"Impressive," he praised, before lunging a step towards Hazel.

This caused her to keep her fist up while stepping back to keep the gap between them.

Atticus prowled around her like she was some prey for him to devour. Seeing his lunge, she quickly shifted her feet. Hazel kept her hands up, she blocked his left hook, but wasn't fast enough to block the right hook.

Making sure she kept her defensive stance, she glared at him. He hit harder with his right. A sharp pain spreads across her face as her lip bled from Atticus's strike. She tasted the metallic tang of blood, fueling her determination.

She needed to be careful of his right side. Hazel wondered if he only used his left as a distraction before he struck with his right. She decided to feint towards his left side, hoping to draw out his right-handed punch. As soon as he committed to the attack, she planned to dodge and counter with a quick jab to his exposed side. This strategy might give her the upper hand she needed.

"Hazel, stop being on the defense!" Ardnaxela called out. The Dragoness had moved around them without her realizing it. She must have been examining Hazel during the training.

She recalled the countless hours spent sparring with Ardnaxela, each session pushing her to her limits. The Dragoness had drilled into her the importance of agility and strategic thinking, always emphasizing that raw strength wasn't everything. Hazel knew she had to employ every lesson learned to outmaneuver Atticus and turn the tide in her favor.

"I'm not. I am just getting a feel," she argued back, but she was lying to herself. Hazel was worried that if she went on the offense against Atticus before knowing his weak points, she wouldn't be able to hold her own.

"You won't always get that luxury in a real fight. Your opponent can overwhelm you and knock you on your ass before you blink," the White Dragoness said sternly, watching Hazel.

Seeing Ardnaxela's movement in her peripheral vision, Hazel turned her head to snap at her. Realizing her error, she quickly returning her attention to Atticus as he let loose a combo of punches and kicks.

It was a struggle to block the unexpected array of attacks. After taking a few hits to the jaw and ribs, Hazel growled before slamming her foot into Atticus's chest, pushing him back and glaring at him. "Are you kidding me?!" Hazel ground out, holding her jaw and moving it around to make sure it wasn't broken, creating some distance between them.

Atticus grinned, adjusting his stance before raising his hand to the beacon Hazel to let loose. "Oh, is the damsel getting mad? I'm quivering."

The smug look on his face only made Hazel want to pummel him into the ground. He was enjoying this; he was enjoying beating her.

The air crackled with intensity as her eyes locked onto Atticus, her anger bubbling just beneath the surface. Every taunt he threw at her only fueled her determination to prove him wrong. With her muscles coiled like springs, Hazel knew this was her moment to unleash everything she had trained for.

Wiping her busted lip, she tightened her hair. Atticus's gaze shifted from feline to serpentine as he bettered his stance.

Hazel lunged for him. He swung with his left, which she dodged with ease but caught his right hand.

Quickly shifting her weight, she put her foot behind his, and yanked him over her shoulder. A loud grunt escaped his lips as his back came into contact with the snow. "I'm not a damsel!" Hazel snarled out to Atticus, who laughed, taking a handful of snow and throwing it into Hazel's face. She blinked rapidly, the cold shock momentarily blinding her.

Wiping the snow off her face, Hazel felt her breath leave her body as her back met the snow, biting at her exposed skin. All the air leaving her lung as Atticus managed to get her hand pinned beneath her. Throwing her free hand, Atticus caught it, slamming it to the ground.

Hazel didn't know how he had the upper hand so quickly, but he was positioned over her, so she couldn't even move her legs.

"Fight me off!"

Icy blue snapped to those honey eyes that now darkened into a deep brown. Her heart pounded furiously in her chest as frustration and determination swirled within her. Her cheeks burned with a mix of humiliation and anger, but she refused to let defeat take hold. Adrenaline surged through her veins, fueling her resolve to break free from Atticus's grip and prove her strength. Hazel tried to free her hand, but his grip held. Grunting in aggravation, she wasn't able to get free.

She tried lunged her head forward to catch his face, but he leaned back before grinning, his eyes rolling down her body before they met once more. The young fawn's face darkened as she narrowed her eyes at him. "You proved your point! Let go!" Hazel snapped at him.

"Atticus," Ardnaxela warned, stepping closer to the pair;. Her expression was stern, her brows furrowed, and lips pressed into a thin line, conveying her readiness to intervene. Her eyes flickered between Atticus and Hazel, a clear warning in her gaze that demanded immediate compliance.

"I haven't even gotten close to proving my point," Atticus argues back to Hazel, ignoring Ardnaxela's warning.

The tension between the trio was palpable, each moment stretching tighter like a drawn bowstring.

Feeling how he had positioned himself above her. Hazel's lip curled up into almost a snarl as she remembered Darius used to do the same thing. Like hell, she would submit to this arrogant prince today. Hazel's left knee came up, catching Atticus in his manhood. In that moment, her knee striking out was not just an act of physical resistance, but a declaration of her unyielding spirit.

Hearing him groan and curl up from her attack, Hazel acted quickly before he could recover. Getting her leg out from under him as he leaned back, wrapped her leg around his shoulder, and shifted her weight to dislodge him off her, scrambling back getting to her feet once he was off. Her anger was boiling as she launched another attack, aiming to tackle him before he could recover.

Although Hazel didn't anticipate his rapid recovery, getting to his feet so soon.

He planted his them into the ground to keep him standing up before driving his elbow into her back, forcing her to her knees.

Hazel's mind raced with a mix of fury and frustration as she felt the sharp pain radiate through her back. Her thoughts were a whirlwind of determination, as she refused to let this setback break her spirit. She gritted her teeth, vowing to find another way to stand her ground and reclaim her power.

Atticus's hand tightly grasped her throat, drawing Hazel's face close to his getting Hazel to her feet. Their heavy breaths mingled in a shared exchange. Turning them around, Atticus pinned her against the pine tree. Her eyes widened seeing the Immortal Dragon staring at her. Hazel tried her hardest to shove him off, but his grip held firm, and all that anger melted away into panic.

Feeling the familiarity of bark biting her skin, she thought back to how the Raven Palm bites her skin with Darius first betrayed her

"That's enough, Atticus," Ardnaxela shouted out, the sound of snow crushing as the Dragoness approached hastily.

"Stand down!" Atticus' voice thundered in command to the White Dragoness, who stopped behind the dragon prince.

Hazel's breathing picked up as she clawed at his wrist, trying to get him to release her throat. She wouldn't let herself go through this again. If she had to fight dirty, she would. Closing her eyes, she reached into her pool of power. Her plan was to summon a burst of energy to strike the prince, temporarily giving her a chance to escape his grasp.

Feeling the familiar warmth of her power building up, Hazel focused on directing it toward her hands. Ready to unleash the blinding flash that would secure her freedom.

Her eyes shot open, and when they met with Atticus's, she no longer saw the ferocity that belonged to the Immortal Dragon, but a look of remorse from the prince behind the mask. Slamming her foot into his knee, it buckled before his jaw met her glowing fist, sending him flying backward into Ardnaxela, who barely caught him. The expression on their faces made Hazel stop her prowl towards them as they held not only shock, but wonder if she had actually controlled her magic.

"There she is," Atticus hummed in amusement.

Hazel blinked a few moments, realizing there was a burn mark on Atticus's jaw where her fist had just met. Looking at her hand, it was slowly dimming from bright gold to dull amber.

"We are done here." Ardnaxela snapped out, standing between Hazel and Atticus.

Hazel just stared as her hand dimmed back to normal before looking at Atticus, her eyes widening. She didn't mean to hurt him. Yes, she was angry with him, but she didn't want to hurt him.

Atticus rose, reaching to touch his jaw, but winced in pain. Staring at him in disbelief at her actions, Ardnaxela's touch sent a shiver down Hazel's spine, causing her to swing as a reflex.

However, the female warrior caught her hand gently, releasing it. "You need to control your emotions during training, especially when you don't have a hold of your magic. Head back inside and cool off before you go see Sybilla."

Hazel only looked at Ardnaxela before looking at Atticus, who turned his back to her while he rubbed his jaw and rolled his shoulder. Swallowing, she hastily grabbed her cloak, wrapping it around herself to make it appear she was calm before being out of eyesight of the two dragons.

Once Hazel was safely inside, she pressed her back to the wooden archway, holding her pounding chest. She really didn't want to hurt Atticus. She glanced over her shoulder through the double doors that were opened to the courtyard to see if she could catch a glance of Atticus and Ardnaxela. Hazel didn't see either one of them, to her relief.

Sauntering down the hall and into her bedroom, she laid her mother's cloak over the ivory and gold antique chair inside of her receiving room, warming herself in front of the roaring fireplace.

Looking to her hands, Hazel took a deep breath, remembering what both Ardnaxela and Sybilla had warned her about: letting her emotions take control of her powers. Hazel needed to keep the gates of her powers closed off from her emotions.

A soft knock startled Hazel, drawing her attention away from her faintly glowing hands. She had let out a trickle of power to warm them—just enough to keep the cold from setting in—but the glow was already fading, swallowed by exhaustion. Her eyes drifted toward the door.

She rose slowly, stepping around the couch. A breath hitched in her chest as she approached, silently praying it wasn't Atticus. She wasn't ready to see him—not after today. But when she opened the door, it wasn't Atticus.

"Kingsly," she said, surprised.

"I—" Hazel glanced down at her loose training tunic and worn leggings, brushing a stray curl from her face. "I wasn't expecting company. I was just warming up before heading back out to meet with Sybilla."

She stepped aside, gesturing him in with a tired flick of her hand. Kingsly entered with that usual composed stride, posture perfect, eyes alert. His gaze swept across the room, noting the faint embers still on her fingers before settling on her with quiet curiosity.

"I didn't mean to intrude," he said softly, his voice calm and reassuring, a warmth she'd come to recognize over the last few weeks.

"You're not," she replied, closing the door behind him.

Since that moment on the sparring mat—when her magic had surged through her and caught him off guard, when he'd taken her hand afterward instead of pulling away—they had started piecing together the remains of their fractured friendship. He had already apologized for the balcony incident then, his sincerity as sharp as the bruises they both wore from the fight. They hadn't needed many words. Just effort. Respect. And he had given her both.

Kingsly lingered at the edge of the room, hands clasped behind his back. "I just wanted to check on you. Sybilla mentioned training didn't go... well today."

Hazel let out a shaky breath, arms crossing over her chest. "That's an understatement."

She walked past him and sank into the chair by the fire, curling her legs underneath her. "Atticus is pushing me harder than necessary. Not in a way that helps. It's like he's trying to prove something—and it's not even about me." Her voice lowered. "I can feel the resentment when he looks at me."

Kingsly didn't speak at first, just moved closer and took a seat across from her, his expression unreadable. "He doesn't know how to handle people who challenge him," he said at last. "Especially not someone like you. You don't bend. You don't break. And it scares him."

Hazel gave a bitter laugh. "Well, I feel like I'm breaking." Her fingers curled slightly, heat rising in her palms before flickering out again. "I'm not upset because I can't keep up. I'm upset because I let him get under my skin. I let myself believe... that he saw me. Really saw me. And maybe—maybe there was something real there."

She glanced away, ashamed of the crack in her voice.

"I found him with another woman," she said quietly. "And after that, I still—gods, I kissed him when he came to my room. Like some foolish girl clinging to a dream. Hoping he'd be different."

Kingsly's jaw tightened, but he said nothing. Instead, he rose and crossed the space between them slowly. He didn't touch her until she looked up at him. When she did, his hand gently tilted her chin up.

"You're not foolish," he said softly. "You just have a heart that still believes in people, even when they don't deserve it."

Hazel's breath caught in her throat. She remembered how he had stood between her and Atticus when things got too heated back in her childhood home. How he had held her when she broke at her mother's grave. How, over the past few weeks, he had been kind without expecting anything in return.

"I wish things were different between us," he continued, voice low. "But I've made vows to Duvessa. I won't break them. That doesn't mean I can't still care about you."

His hand brushed a strand of hair from her face, and for a moment, Hazel let herself lean into his touch. A single tear slipped down her cheek, and she gave a small nod.

"I know," she whispered. "Thank you... for seeing me. For not giving up on us."

Kingsly opened his arms, and Hazel didn't hesitate. She stepped into him, resting her head against his chest as he wrapped his arms around her. There were no sparks, no confusing promises—just warmth, and the comfort of a friend who had come back when she needed him most.

Chapter Forty-Five

Atticus

The snow fell once more as Atticus and Ardnaxela stood in that training yard. He rubbed his jaw, wincing anytime his fingers touched the scorch mark on his skin. He had wanted her to fight back, wanted Hazel to learn how to get him off. What Atticus hadn't anticipated was for her Aestival side to kick in.

Seeing her eyes opening after what he thought was her submitting and giving up, he didn't expect to see the Ivory Fawn staring back at him. He knew the moment her eyes opened, he overstepped. Hazel moved too quickly for him to recover from her knocking him off balance. That strength he heard about in stories about the Aestivals was nothing he imagined.

When that charged punch met his face, Atticus knew he pushed it to far. He was ready to restrain her and calm her down, but what he didn't predict was to see two glowing wings made of golden light forming behind her as she radiated that bright or seeing her eyes turn ivory and gold. She didn't look like the village girl he met over a month ago, but looked ethereal, as if her Ivory Fawn was showing itself for the first time.

Atticus was amazed by what he saw, but when Ardnaxela moved away, causing him to fall back against the snow, he saw Ivory Fawn revert to the frightened village girl she truly was. At least now she was capable of removing an overpowering opponent from pinning her.

He was proud of her progress. Hazel was becoming stronger in stature and strength than when she first arrived. He knew a war was coming, and someone was going to be coming straight for Hazel. Atticus needed her to become stronger and tougher to beat in case he couldn't be there to help her.

The Crimson Dragon didn't know who would be coming for his Ivory Fawn, although he would be damned if he allowed anyone to take her away from him. Atticus was finally coming to terms with the fact that she may die from the prophecy, and there was nothing he could do to stop it. What he could do was to do everything in his power to make sure she was prepared for that time to come, even if that meant he had to be the villain prince in her story.

"What the hell was that, Atticus!? This was supposed to help her , not set her back!" the Dragoness shouted out, punching him hard in the shoulder and glaring at him.

Grunting, he held his shoulder, looking down at the warrior who came up to just below his nose, glaring at her. "I wanted her to stop acting as if she was some damsel and fight back!" he snarled at the Ardnaxela. Atticus didn't care if she was pissed off at him, Hazel not only got him off once but twice. Just like he hoped she would, that is why he pushed her so much.

"By getting her so angry, she lost control of her magic on your face!" she argued back, crossing her arms. "How is that supposed to help her?"

Atticus scoffed, rolling his sore shoulder from being tossed like a rag doll over Hazel's shoulder and than Ardnaxela's strike. "Because now she knows how to get out from under an opponent who has the upper hand."

Ardnaxela huffed out a cloud of hot breath, shaking her head and crossing her arms over her chest. "You pushed her so much she lost control and she scorched your jaw. How are you going to explain that to your father? Hmm?"

Pausing for a moment, he took a deep breath, realizing her point. Raking the snow from his hair, Atticus felt his body cooling off. "I will handle my father. Please make sure she sees Sybilla."

Putting his hands in his pants, Atticus looked at Ardnaxela and then at the castle, glancing up toward Hazel's room.

His eyes widened as he saw Kingsly through the second story window. He had his arms around Hazel in what looked like an embrace. A growl came from his throat, but he forced it simmer down, tearing his eyes from the sight.

Sounds of a gasp slipped from Ardnaxela's lips as she joined his side. "You gotta be kidding me."

Her words were full of irritation, but Atticus's eyes were fixated on the window, watching Kingsly stroke Hazel's cheek. It made his blood boil. "He can't just stay away from her, can he?"

Ardnaxela looked at Atticus putting her hand on his shoulder. "Don't read into it, Atticus. She just lost her uncle. The last thing she needs is for you to make things worse than they already are for her," the Dragoness warned, tightening her grip on his shoulder. "He can simply be giving her his condolences. If you keep acting like a territorial male, you will just push her further away."

He took a deep, calming breath, nodding his head before shoving her hand from his shoulder and stalking into the castle.

Chapter Forty-Six

Hazel

As she held Kingsly, a sense of calm washed over her, mingling with the lingering sadness she kept buried deep inside. The weight of her promise to Archibald was a constant presence, but in this moment, she allowed herself a fleeting respite. Hazel's resolve remained unshaken, but the quiet comfort of Kingsly's embrace gave her the strength to carry on.

This prophecy wasn't going to take her life. She would survive, live for herself. and choose her own future. Nuzzling her face into Kingsly's arms, Hazel held him closer. She needed this embrace more than she knew.

A gentle stroke to her head opened the floodgates to her tears. Not wanting him to see her cry, Hazel turned her face to press it further into his arm.

When Hazel's hands gripped his sleeves to his gray tunic, his arms around her tightened even more. Trying to keep her crying silent, she couldn't keep her body from trembling from her silent sobs.

Kingsly said nothing but tightened the embrace. Remembering Archibald's laughter, warm hugs, and playful taunts, Hazel wished that, more than anything in the world, Kingsly was the uncle she was hugging. She would give anything in the world to hold him one last time.

His hand went between Hazel's shoulder, holding her closer, resting his head on her head, his free hand on the small of her back. "I got you. Let it out." It was as if his words amplified her silent cries as they tore from her lips.

A heart-wrenching sob escaped as Hazel clung onto him; she didn't care how much her throat hurt from sobbing as loud as she did. Hazel needed to get the pain out She needed to be stronger from here on out, but at this moment, she needed to let herself grief one last time before she put up a wall and did her best to move on.

Digging her finger into Kingsly's back. Hazel kept him in a tight embrace in that receiving room, scared that if she would let go at this moment, she would melt into the floor.

"He isn't in pain anymore." Kingsly spoke gently into her hair, holding Hazel as she poured her heart out. "Archibald was the bravest warrior I ever saw in the small time I knew him."

Feeling a kiss on her soft, dirty blonde hair, she took a deep inhale to calm herself. Hazel stood there in Kingsly's arms for a long moment, getting out everything she could.

Her throat was raw, but she slowly built up that brick wall to stop the tears and the heart-wrenching sobs coming from her throat.

Straightening up, Kingsly wiped her red, puffy eyes, kissing her head before he cupped her hot face. "Would you like to spread his ashes back home?" He asked, pushing hair from her face.

Hazel nodded taking a deep, shaky breath. "Yes, tonight, if possible. I have to meet with Sybilla soon, but we can leave tonight." Hazel's voice was hoarse as she looked at Kingsly's soft, gentle eyes, taking another calming breath. "I need a change of scenery away from this castle and Atticus. I swore to my uncle I would become the Ivory Fawn. I can't run off and skip on training with Sybilla." Kingsly nodded before taking Hazel's lilac cloak and handing it to her. "Of course. I'll have Arabella pack you a bag. It's a two-day trip from here. We can take horses instead of a carriage, so we aren't so obvious."

Hazel nodded to his suggestion, taking her mother's cloak and wrapping it around herself. She decided to change out of her training attire, dressing as if they hadn't just planned to leave Wylana. "Good idea. I will see you tonight after dinner."

Hazel carefully closed the tall wooden door behind her, leaving behind the echoing corridors of Castle Wylana. She stepped out into the cool morning air, her breath visible in the crisp atmosphere. With determination in her stride, she crossed the cobblestone courtyard and made her way to the stables where a sleek palomino horse awaited along with Ardnaxela. She mounted the horse gracefully, patting its neck reassuringly as she turned its head towards the path that led through the dense forest separating the two grand estates.

The journey to Castle Andromeda was both familiar and soothing, with the rhythmic clopping of hooves on the well-trodden path and the gentle rustle of leaves in the breeze. Ardnaxela leading the way as normal , them both riding in silence due to her exhaustion , and Ardnaxela scanning the area as they rode. The towering trees stood like sentinels, their branches weaving together a canopy that dappled the ground with shifting patterns of light and shadow.

As the day wore on, the sunlight filtered through the trees, shifting into a warmer hue, and Hazel could see the spires of Castle Andromeda appearing in the distance.

Upon reaching the castle, she dismounted and tied the reins of her horse to the horse post before making her way through the grand entrance and into the heart of Castle Andromeda, where the expansive greenhouse awaited her discovery.

Hazel now standing in the enormous greenhouse in the courtyard of Castle Andromeda. It could have been a secondary castle with how large it was, which made sense. If the Aestivals had wings, they would have needed room to move around and fly up high to reach the fruit of the apple and pecan trees that were now bare any fruit.

"I figured we could practice your magic outside today. You're getting better at creating balls of light, which you learned can be used to blast an opponent away, and how to anchor yourself, so you don't lose control or burn out too quickly. Today I want to work on your shields. That will be vital in battle, especially if you want to protect allies," Sybilla said softly before she looked back to the scroll . Glancing it over, Sybilla then returned her gaze at Hazel, giving her a faint smile. "Atticus told me you did it once before, during the attack on the carriage right before you first arrived. From what the scroll mentions, when you want to create a shield, you envision where you want it and how large you want it to be, Then, you must graze that small pool of magic we've been working on, only allowing a trickle of power to enter into your mind. How about you try creating a small shield between us." Setting the scroll down, Sybilla gave Hazel an encouraging smile. "Clear your mind, and remember to anchor yourself."

Taking a deep breath, Hazel nodded, adjusting her posture and stance before she slowly held out her hands. She reached into her mind, seeing that golden stream of power, allowing a little of it to trickle into her mind like a calm waterfall.

Keeping her breathing steady, she raised her hands a little more, picturing she was building a small wall of golden light. Nothing happened. There was no shield of light, just her glowing hands.

Thinking back to the emotions pelting her during the attack, she took a deep breath and tried to replicate them, pushing those emotions into her hands. She tried visualizing stacking imaginary bricks in her mind to create the shield. Again, nothing happened. Soon, her hands dimmed as they fell to her side. "I can't. It was different the first time. I lost control last time. I don't know how I did it," Hazel breathed out apologetically to Sybilla, who glided over, putting her hand on her shoulder. "Don't rush it, Hazel. Don't try to force it. Let the magic flow through you. Instead of bricks or a wall, imagine it like the water in a field of lavender. If there's too much, the plant drowns, but if you don't use enough water for them, they can't grow. Try to find that medium ground where there's not too much or too little of water." Sybilla's voice held so much encouragement before she moved aside to stand behind Hazel. "Try again."

Hazel nodded her head, taking a deep breath before she closed her eyes, allowing the essence of the Aestival magic that lingered to rise up in her. She exhaled, opening her eyes. Her hands glowed once more. She needed only a small amount of that power, which she let trickle in. Cupping her hand under that stream of her power, she re-imagined that brick wall building once more.

Seeing the glow from behind her, Hazel turned to see a wall of light building between her and Sybilla. It wasn't exactly where she wanted the shield, but at least created one.

Sybilla grinned and tapped the shield, which held. "Good. Now let's work on the placement of your shield. If you had an enemy behind you, it would work, but if there was an enemy coming from in front of you, then it wouldn't have been of any use. Let's try that again." Hazel nodded her head softly, a look of new determination on her face.

Sitting in the greenhouse, relaxing her muscles, Hazel played with a small ball of light between her fingers. Sybilla joined her side, offering her some water. "Here, it's important you stay hydrated after that. You did good today," she praised the young fawn pushing hair from Hazel's face.

Sybilla was becoming like an older sister to her. Hazel loved their training sessions this last month. When they weren't training, they were in the library reading about the history and lore of her people. Although, neither one of them could find anything specific about the prophecy of the Ivory Fawn. Just vague retellings of how the Ivory Fawn would rise from the ashes of their home. What did that even mean? The castle Andromeda and the temple were untouched. Would this coming war change that? Or was it referring to her home Wylana? Will this war try to burn Wylana down?

A soft hand took Hazel's hand, drew the young fawn from her thoughts, and looked at Sybilla, whose expression softened into concern.

"Kingsly mentioned you had a garden at your cottage and laid lavender on your mother's grave. If you like, this greenhouse could use some life. You are more than welcome to use this as a way to bring some normality back into your life and give you a change of scenery from the Wylana castle. You can grow as much lavender as you want."

Hearing the offer, Hazel's heart warmed before looking at the bare greenhouse, already picturing it bursting with flowers and vegetables. Her eyes went back to Sybilla, and she pulled her young scribe friend into an embrace. "Thank you, Syb." Pulling away from the embrace, Hazel took the scribe's hand, holding it gently for a moment before watching the dusk sky dance with shades of pink, blue, and violet. "We should probably head back to the castle. Wouldn't want to miss dinner." Hazel said softly to her friend.

Hazel planned to keep her trip with Kingsly to Alexandria hidden for the moment, she didn't need Atticus to stop them. She would get her bag for their trip from Arabella, except she hoped that Arabella wouldn't tell Atticus. She knew Atticus would try to stop her if he got wind of her leaving.

Hazel needed spread her uncles ashes , so he could be with her mother. Plus she could use a scenery change from the ivy and wisteria flowers that decorated the mahogany walls.

She wanted to go lie down in her old bedroom and wake up from this long-lasting nightmare to her uncle bringing in wood for the fire and the smell of cinnamon, oranges, and vanilla when he would hug her. Hazel needed to have her old life back one last time.

Sybilla smiled, standing up and offering a hand to Hazel. "I heard the cook made roasted lamb with potatoes and asparagus, which is by far my favorite. Plus, you need to wash up. you aren't the most pleasant-smelling one at the moment," she teased while helping Hazel to her feet.

"Like you smell any better, you smell of dust and dirt, my friend," Hazel teased right back, giving a playful smile.

The pair made their way through the courtyard to where the horses were tied up. Stroking Phoenix's soft palomino neck, she smiled at her companion, who only nickered at her. "I know, you're ready to go home and eat, too," Hazel said softly, kissing the leathery nose of her horse before mounting her steed. Waiting for a moment for Sybilla to climb onto her chestnut mare, they made their ride back to Castle Wylana.

Chapter Forty-Seven

Hazel

Hazel didn't pay much attention to the conversation at the dining table. Kai spoke with Atticus mainly about politics. Her focus was glued to the roasted lamb, scallop potatoes, and asparagus on her plate. Using her fork, she moved the food around occasionally, eating a bite or two, but Hazel really wasn't hungry. Her mind was back home at her mother's tree, which she would see in a few days.

A nudge to her shoulder from Ardnaxela, who sat to the left of Hazel, drew her from her plate to look up to the Dragoness who had been watching her. Those golden eyes went from Hazel to her plate as if saying, *eat your food, don't play with it*. Swallowing, Hazel cut into her roasted lamb, taking a bite.

"Lady Hazel, have you picked a dress for the upcoming ball? Hopefully its grander than the one you wore last ball" Duvessa's mocking tone made her want to just put her in place.

She looked at Duvessa, who leaned back in her chair, sitting tall with her head tilted back. "I haven't given it much thought. I have had my hands and mind a bit preoccupied," Hazel replied, keeping a watchful eye on her. There was something off with this woman, and she didn't know what it was.

"Well, you should tell that handmaiden of yours to put you in something darker so you don't look as flushed as you do now in that beige dress. It brings out the puffiness of your face," Duvessa spouted out like some siren trying to lure her in her prey.

Hazel wasn't buying into it. "I was going to suggest the same for you. Maybe a more saturated color would improve that bleak face of yours. You might consider pulling your hair up in to a stylish design, or would you rather not show off what your bedroom activities have done to your neck?"

Duvessa's hair was draped over her shoulders and around her neck, instead of being elegantly pinned up like a princess. The woman did her best to keep her hair in place, but Hazel saw the mark on her neck when they first entered the dining room from the faint gust of wind caused by Kingsly's swift movement past her.

"That's enough," growled the dragon prince sitting across from her.

Hazel's eyes met the cold brown brick wall in Atticus's eyes, yet it didn't phase her. She held a blank expression on her face, keeping her walls up to prevent herself some showing even the slightest hint of anger towards Duvessa, who hid her neck more. Fuck him. With how he had been treating her in this last week or so, even after Archibald's funeral, Hazel wished she punched him harder than she did during training. He deserved it. Looking at the King, she bowed her head to King Kai and Queen Sage. "My apologies to your majesty. I am not quite myself. I think I shall retire for the night."

Ruffling Reed's hair with a smile, Hazel stood up, striding out the door, acting as if she was perfectly fine.

After about an hour, Hazel was down in the courtyard with Kingsly, securing the straps around Phoenix's girth . As they traveled through the snow, she wore a brown cloak with fur lining her neck, she left her mother's cloak not wanting to be easily recognizable. Fur blankets were strapped to the back housing of her ivory saddle. Looking off to the west where Alexandria lay, Hazel took a deep breath before her hand moved to her saddlebag. She rested her hand softly on it, feeling the urn safely stowed away.

Taking a deep, shaky breath, Hazel lowered her head, trying to hold back tears. "I wish we would have been able to return home one last time, visit moms tree together. Tell Mother I love her."

Kingsly approached on his white dappled stallion from behind Hazel. She stood there for a moment, trying to build the strength to get into her saddle. Looking up at Kingsly, she nodded her head before putting her foot into the stirrup and hoisting herself up.

Adjusting the reins, Hazel looked toward the castle, only to see what windows were lit. Her room and a few others were dark, but her eyes lingered on Atticus's room. Relieved he hasn't tried to spot her just yet.

Sighing, she glanced at Kingsly before nudging her horse into a canter. The sooner they got on the road, the sooner they could get to Alexandria.

Hazel knew in her heart it was wrong not to tell Atticus she was leaving, but she knew he would stop her. Try to tell Hazel it was too dangerous, but she needed some normality back in her life. A few months here at court and all of it had left her confused and heartbroken.

Hazel needed to get away, needed to see her old home. Spread her uncles ashes. Speak with her mother at her grave. Bring her more lavender to her grave, since the bundle there now was long withered.

Riding in silence beside Kingsly for a bit, Hazel swayed as her horse walked. A blank expression was on her face as she rode. Hazel didn't even hear Kingsly talking. All she did was tilt her chin up and nod her head when she heard Kinglsy asked if Hazel wanted silence as they rode.

It was a few hours into the night before Kingsly pulled his stallion to a halt, looking at Hazel with a worried expression. "We should rest here." His voice was soft and gentle as his blue eyes met Hazel's.

Looking down at her companion, seeing how Phoenix's breath made him appear as an angry dragon huffing out plumes of smoke with the cold night air, Hazel nodded her head, leaning over and rubbing her gelding's neck.

"Do we camp here or should we find a cave?" she asked curiously, looking around and pulling her cloak close to her to shield her body from the cold.

"I believe there is a cave up ahead about an hour away. We will make camp there." His voice held so much confidence in his words.

Hazel took a deep breath, nodded her head, and looked behind them, making sure no one was tailing them. Noticing the snow clouds rolling in.

"Let's go, before it starts snowing," Hazel replied, nudging her horse to a gentle walk.

Riding the last stretch of the night, they finally arrived at the cave Kingsly mentioned. The snow-covered a good portion of the ground, possibly about four inches now the clouds moving on. Hazel was grateful to be done riding for the night as she could barely feel her legs from the cold.

Hazel and Kingsly made their way into the cave, its large mouth was perfect for leading the horses in on horseback. Dismounting her horse, Hazel stroked his neck, taking a deep breath and rubbing her gloves together to generate heat. Leather gloves were a smart choice.

Kingsly walked over, taking a deep breath. "I am going to grab up some firewood. I packed some starter materials in my saddle bag if you want to get them out. It shouldn't me take long."

The young fawn nodded her head. It was dark in the cave, but not too dark that she couldn't see anything thanks to the moonlight hitting the snow .

Staying by Phoenix, the heat radiating off of her gentle gelding helped her stay warm.

Kingsly returned shortly with an armful of timber for the fire and went to work on starting it. When the fire came to life, Hazel was relieved the cave had lit up. There were fewer shadows for anyone to even attempt to hide in.

Taking a bag of oats out of her saddlebag for Phoenix, he nickered, greedily stuffing his nose into the bag.

They had been riding nearly a full day of riding, before they finally decided to sleep for the night. With the ground they covered, they should arrive in Alexandria tomorrow night.

"I can roast up some of the pheasants I took from the kitchen , if you're hungry," Kingsly offered, untacking his own horse and stroking the dapple-gray stallion's neck.

Hazel heard men use their riding gear to get some sleep, so she would do the same. "I can go for some food," was her only reply. Hazel walked over to kneel by the riding gear she set down to retrieve the fur blankets from the back housing and sprawled it over her bedroll. Using her hands to smooth out the fur of the blanket, Hazel took a deep breath, looking at the saddlebag that contained her uncle's ashes. It was such a bitter taste on her tongue staring at those ashes.

It was such a guttural feeling that made her feel so hollow on the inside. Holding her arms close to her body, she tried to keep in her tears. Her eyes stung as she lowered her eyes from the saddlebag that held her uncle's ashes. The tears she tried to desperately keep away blinked away from her eye. That solid brick wall Hazel built to keep her grief buried down deep cracked, and her grief trickled out of those cracks. As if that dam she desperately wanted to keep the flood of her grief at bay, no longer could withstand it.

The tears fell rapidly causing her vision to blurred, forcing her eyes shut, it would not stop the burning along with stop the overwhelming flood of the grief and sorrow she desperately tried to bury.

Feeling a calloused hand rest on her shoulder, it was like what little hold that dam finally gave as caved into the overwhelming devastating she was trying to suppress.

"I'm here." Kingsly soothed as his hand stroked calming circles up and down her spine.

Hazel crumbled into the general prince's arms, continuing her sobs. She had been holding back something she had been wanting to express. The sheer volume of her screams made her feel lightheaded, and her throat was now even more raw and irritated.

Hazel felt a fur blanket being wrapped around her, closing off the world to her to allow her privacy to get everything out.

Her cries became more faint as she grew more and more lightheaded before her vision blurred around her. When she stopped, Hazel had nothing left in her. She slowly melted into hollow shell of herself. Letting out all she had in her.

Slumping into Kingsly's arms, Hazel didn't care as he moved an arm to rest behind her neck while the other cradled itself under her knees. She was lifted from the ground and lowered down to her bedroll. She didn't have the energy to say thank you.

The warmth of the fire kisses her cheek as if kissing her goodnight with the warmth of the fur blanket. There was a soft kiss at her temple by Kingsly. Through her exhausted, narrowed vision, she watched him brush hair from her face before he rose to his feet. Kingsly made his way to the fire where the small pheasant was cooking from some of the provisions he brought with them.

Even through her bedroll, the cave floor felt so cold, but it was a welcoming mixture of the cold floor and the warmth of the fire. The weight of the fur blanket beckoned her to sleep. Slowly, Hazel's eyes became too heavy for her to keep open, and she fell into a deep slumber

Chapter Forty-Eight

Atticus

Moonlight penetrated Atticus's bed chambers. Watching from the corner of the large archway glass door leading to the balcony, he ground his teeth as his eyes were locked on Hazel and Kingsly's cloaked figures riding away on their horses.

It wasn't difficult for Atticus to guess it was her under that cloak seeing the tips of her golden hair sneaking out from it. This was for the best, to keep himself distant from her.

During the funeral procession, he wanted to reach out to her and comfort her, but he knew she was angry with him and didn't want to make her more upset. Atticus would wait as long as it took for her to come back to him on her own terms. He would not force himself on her because of who she was supposed to become. For the nearly three months he knew her, she had power over her life. So, he let her have that small of control over who she keeps company during her moments of apprehension, because Hazel deserves to finally have some say in her life.

Even if that meant letting her be happy with someone else.

Atticus grew irritable seeing her with Kingsly because of his engagement to Lady Duvessa and how he has treated her in the past. He didn't want Hazel getting her hopes up to be with Kingsly. He could only pray to Amias, that his brother would honor his engagement to Lady Duvessa and not lead the poor girl on.

Tearing his eyes away from her, he went to his bathing room, and stared at the face of the dragon resting on his pectoral, admiring its scaled body coiling down his right arm. Its mouth was still open in a snarl on his chest. Running his hand over the ink-scaly head as if his touch would soothe the snarl coming from the dragon. However, that threatening appearance of the dragon will never leave, just as the title of the Immortal Dragon he earned on the battlefield would never go away.

Sighing, he tore his eyes from the dragon, and drew himself a hot bath. Steam filled the room and fogged up the mirrors with condensation. Undoing his pants, he let them drop to the ground before he stepped into the tub. The hot water nipped his skin, forcing a hiss out of his lips, but slid further into the soothing warmth.

He wanted to burn the image of Hazel and Kingsly together from his mind. He relaxed into the bathtub, resting the crook on his neck on the rim of a black marbled claw-tooth tub. Inhaling the bergamot and cedar scent of the oils he dripped into the tub, it was the only thing that soothed his mind and body from its aches.

Atticus's eyes closed, and he basked in the moonlight, enjoying the rays on his face when he heard his front door leading into his receiving room open. His eyes opened to footsteps from the hallway into his receiving room. Expecting a knock on his bedroom door, he heard the knob turn instead. Slowly, his eyes shifted to the archway that led from the bathroom into his bed chambers. He didn't care if he was naked or not. Whoever allowed themselves in without permission would feel his teeth at their throats.

Standing in the archway, the moonlight brushed the pale features of the viper woman engaged to his brother. Atticus never cared for the lady, and didn't trust her from the moment she came to this court. She had a reputation for manipulating those around her to get what she wanted, leaving a trail of broken alliances and shattered trust. Atticus had witnessed her deceitful nature firsthand when she had orchestrated a scheme that nearly toppled his closest ally. Her sudden engagement to his brother only deepened his suspicion, making him wary of the true intentions behind her every move.

Her black raven hair was draped over her right shoulder, allowing the moonlight to illuminate the serpentine smile on her lips as those dark midnight black eyes scanned his naked body in the water.

Atticus sighed, looking at the skylight and closing his eyes. He felt his face twitch, trying to hold back the snarl. "What do you want, viper?" he snapped in irritation that his moment of peace is ruined.

The shifting shadows in his peripheral vision were the only indication she was no longer leaning on the door frame. She approached him slowly. "I wanted to see if you were still awake. Seeing Kingsly was occupied by your Ivory Fawn, I came to occupy my time with the infamous Crimson Dragon." Duvessa's tone was now only low and sultry, giving away her intentions of interrupting his bath. But was there a twinge of jealousy he heard?

"And why would I sully my moment of peace with my brother's sloppy seconds?" His attention slid to those pools of black as she stood beside his claw tooth bath, her silk nightgown leaving nothing to the imagination.

Atticus's mind drifted to the night of the winter solstice ball where Duvessa had cornered him in the garden maze. Cloaked in shadows, she had whispered promises of power and pleasure, her breath warm against his ear. He remembered the way her fingers had traced along his jawline, her eyes gleaming with predatory intent as she tried to lure him into her web of deceit. Atticus could see the mark his brother had placed on the lady's neck from their bedroom activities. From that moment it solidify his reasoning on why he couldn't trust her, especially after noticing the missing details in her story of who she truly way.

"Because you and I both know we are the better match. Why settle for a weak little fawn when you can have a lioness?" Duvessa's hand slowly stroked the dragon's head on his chest, trailing it down, only to be snatched up by Atticus in a snarl.

"Please. You're not a lioness, just a snake in the grass."

Shoving her hand away, he stood up, dripping water onto the floor, reaching for a towel to wrap himself up with. Walking into his bedroom, not caring about the amount of water he tracked across the wooden mahogany floor.

"So sour. Why is that? Is it because your brother is off playing with your fawn? I never took you for a jealous type. Although seeing you around that little fawn of yours, I took you more of a possessive prince." Her words made his blood boil.

Reaching into the large mahogany wardrobe he slipped on some pants so he could walk away from this conversation and from the venomous woman in his chambers. "Whatever game you're playing here, Duvessa, I advise you to walk away before you get hurt." His voice was low and threatening as he turned to look at the woman who now was behind him instead of standing in the archway of his bathroom, leaning on the bedpost before moving to lower herself down on the maroon silk sheets of his bed with a grin.

"No game. Just two grown powers having a civil conversation, or would you rather have your lips on something else?, I would happily arrange that. Since your brother probably his lips occupied with that little fawn of yours," Duvessa purred before rising off the bed to close the distance between Atticus and her trailing a finger down the right side of his neck to where that dragon rested before planting a soft kiss to his neck. "From what he told me, they are going to Alexandria together and will stay at her old cabin. We both know what will happen when they get there."

A gasp slipped from her lips as Atticus's curled his fingers around her throat in a bruising grip, bringing her face to his as a deep growl emanated from his lip, staring down into those black eyes. "What did you say?"

Duvessa's hand came up to Atticus's wrist, staring into the dark, dangerous expression on the Immortal Dragon. A faint chuckle came from the viper woman as her lips curled upwards. "Why am I not surprised they didn't tell you?" she purred, running her hand up his arm, not phased by the grip around her throat.

Slamming her back into the bedpost, Atticus closed the distance between them, leaving no gap. His voice was dangerously low as he tightened his grip.

"We both know your brother can't keep his hands to himself. I heard what happened on the balcony. Maybe he will actually succeed in bedding her this time."

Her body tensed as she inhaled sharply as the grip on her throat tightening. Atticus glared at Duvessa with a blazing fire in his eyes. Like hell, he would let Kingsly sleep with Hazel, especially not when she was in a mourning state. Not to mention he is engaged to this viperous woman. Shoved her away by her throat, his eyes never left the woman's onyx eyes. "Get out," Atticus commanded with a tone that would make any man cower for his life.

Watching the woman grinning at him before striding out of the room, Atticus waited till he heard the door open and close before roaring in anger and slamming his fist into the wardrobe behind him. The wood bit his hand in retaliation for the hole he left in the wardrobe door. Withdrawing his hand, now splintered with wood and blood, Atticus grabbed his long-sleeved Henley shirt, his rut sack, and cloak to pack for a two-day trip in the snow.

He was going after her. Alexandria was the most dangerous place for Hazel to go without the proper protection. She almost died saving Kingsly the last time they traveled that road. He wouldn't let that happen again.

Once Atticus saw his brother, he was going to drive him into the nearest tree and give him a much-needed beating for putting Hazel at such great risk.

Atticus was going to go to Alexandria and bring Hazel back home, where she was safe and far from that dreadful place.

Chapter Forty-Nine

Hazel

The snow crunched beneath the hooves of the mellow-tempered palomino gelding, who shook his platinum blonde mane, huffing a plume of hot air that swirled in the crisp, cold afternoon air.

Hazel and Kingsly knew Alexandria was a simple few-hour ride downhill at their current pace.

When she woke up this morning, the young woman wasn't expecting Kingsly to give her his only fur blanket to make sure she stayed warm. When she asked why, he simply said she looked cold. Hazel was also surprised that he stayed up so late to make pheasant jerky from the leftover meat from last night's dinner.

"Are you nervous about returning home?" Kingsly asked, trying to spark a conversation, since Hazel hadn't spoken much during this trip.

All she could think of was her blissful moments with her uncle in that family cottage and the small festivals they used to have. Alexandria wasn't always chaotic; it was sometimes joyful. "If I am being honest, I don't know... I have so many good memories, but with everything that has happened in these last three months... I don't know what was real and what was people pretending to be my friends because they also were secretly Netherian. If Darius knew who I was, who else knew?" Hazel's voice didn't hold the normal softness, but was now a little bitter

Leaning her head back, she could feel tears filling her eyes. Taking a deep breath. Hazel huffed in disbelief, shaking her head and gripping her reins tighter. "It feels like my whole life was decided for me before my conception. I wish sometimes I wasn't this Ivory Fawn, and I wish this world weren't so corrupted. Maybe then I could have some power over my life and choose what I want to do instead of it being decided for me. I never signed up for any of this. I had my home ripped away from me. The first man I ever truly loved and wanted to spend my entire life with turned out to only want to lower my guard so that he could exploit it..." Hazel's voice became more brittle as she turned her face away from Kingsly , she said, "I feel utterly out of place in this world. My entire life was spent as a healer in a small village, and now I'm thrust into the harsh reality of being a prophesied heroine for people I didn't even know existed. How can I possibly become this Ivory Fawn, destined to vanquish the Netherian dark cloud that plagues this land, when I can't even find my way out of my own inner darkness?" Pulling her horse to a stop, she wiped her cheek from her tears before she looked at Kingsly "As the feathers are covered in red, the Ivory Fawn will rise from the ashes guided by her Crimson Dragon. That is how the prophecy goes. How am I supposed to become the Ivory Fawn if your brother, who is supposed to be this Crimson Dragon, does nothing but give me emotional whiplash and confuse me? I'm grateful for him training me , but I wish the whiplash didn't come with it."

There it was. Hearing her own words was a smack in the face. Hazel lowered her eyes, frowned, and took a deep breath. If she were to be the Ivory Fawn, then she must find the courage to stop looking for someone to take her away from all of this , and stand her own ground to confront Atticus for his actions.

Kingsly opened his mouth to say something, but she raised her hand to him and shook her head. "Let's get to Alexandria." Looking behind her, she could see dark clouds forming to the south of them. Sighing, she nudged Phoenix forward. "We need to beat the storm, or else we will be stuck in it with no shelter."

The wind whipped Hazel's braid into her face they rode into the barren streets of Alexandria. Dismounting Phoenix once they arrived at her cottage, Hazel tried to keep her hair out of her face. Turning to look at the storm that was quickly approaching, she watched the lightning light up the dark clouds, and the thunder rumbled across the sky , as the threatened snow cloud promising to bury both Hazel and Kingsly.

Feeling Kingsly take Phoenix's reins from her, Hazel's attention snapped to him.

"Get inside!" he called out over the howling wind and snow falling.

Hazel reached into her saddle bag, removed her uncle's urn, and placed it under her cloak, keeping it safe from blowing away.

Hurrying inside, holding her uncle's urn close to her. Hazel turned her attention to the dark, cold cottage. Hazel's chest grew heavy as she looked around the cottage, holding the urn closer to her chest keeping her cloak wrapped around her. She trembled from the cold, but stood frozen in place in the entryway as reality of how empty it felt hit her in the face.

Her hot breath swirled around the crisp, cold air in the cottage as Kingsly closed the door behind them both , Making his way to the fireplace to start building a fire to warm themselves up. Thankfully, there was still timber from when her uncle last chopped some wood for the winter months.

A rough callus hand brushed her cheek, causing her to jump, stepping back out of her frozen state as her eyes met Kingsly's soft, ice-blue eyes. "Come sit by the fire. I can find us something to eat other than the jerky."

Hazel nodded silently, walking toward the fireplace, refusing to let go of that urn as she sitting down in a rocking chair in front of the fire. Kingsly draped a cold yet soft knitted blanket over her shoulders. Hazel took a look around the cottage, realizing that it had been ransacked while she was away in Wylana thanks to the light coming from the fire. Hazel bit her lip, taking in what was left of her home.

Standing up slowly, Hazel stared at a wall of portraits of her mother, father, uncle, and her as she grew up. Setting the urn down on the table beneath the array of pictures of her family on the wall, she removed the portrait of her mother and father holding Hazel as a baby.

She wondered what they would think of the woman she became now. Would they be proud? Or would they be disappointed?

Walking to the west side of her home, she peered out a bay window to see where her mother's tree was thrashing in the storm. They couldn't spread her uncle's ashes in this storm.

"Are those your parents?" Kingsly asked from behind Hazel. She turned her head toward the portrait in her hand before looking up at his inquiring expression as he glances down at her. She nodded her head and hands it to him before sniffling from her running cold nose. "Resemblance of your mother and you is like your looking in a mirror," he said in attempt to comfort her before resting his hand on the small of her back. "I found some food in the kitchen. It's not much, but it's better than pheasant jerky."

Hazel looked to her mother's tree, whipping in the wind. Then focused her gaze to the cottage, nodding her head.

Walking back to the fireplace, she sat on the couch in front of it, trying to warm up.

Hazel could hear Kingsly in the kitchen preparing whatever he had managed to find. Slowly, she melted into the warm embrace of the heavy-knitted blanket around her and drifted into a blissful slumber.

The sudden sound of the front door slamming against the wall abruptly woke Hazel from her slumber. Shooting up to her feet, she saw a black-cloaked figure barging into her cottage. Remembering what Sybilla taught her, she summoned a ball of light to her hand as she stood her ground and stared at the figure. Hazel didn't know where Kingsly was, but she sure as hell wasn't going to run to get him like some frightened girl needing protection.

The cloaked intruder straightened their postures before slowly prowling closer. Hazel steeled herself to stop the trembling, watching the intruder step around the couch. Her hand beginning to glow as she took a step back to keep the distance between them, Hazel couldn't see any of their features the cloak. Narrowing her eyes, she tried her best to see any hint of body language that would give her the slightest hint of this cloaked figure's intentions of barging in. It hit her, what if this was Darius. Instantly a wall of light shielded her.

"Look who is no longer a damsel," the figure spoke, in a like tone purr, before reaching up with a black leather glove to remove the hood showing the wet damn onyx hair. Those honey-brown eyes stared into her icy blue eyes.

The light in her hand dimmed when she saw how pale Atticus looked. Did he ride through this storm?

"Oh my gods, Atticus?" Hazel quickly hurried toward the couch to grab the blanket she had been sleeping with. Going to look at him, she said, "Strip, or you will catch a cold." However, she heard a thud behind her, and Atticus had already stripped off his soaked cloak.Thank goodness for the Henley black shirt now clinging to his skin, or she would see how sculptured that body was once more.

Handing him the blanket, Hazel went to pick up his cloak, but Atticus gripped her bicep, stopping her. Atticus was freezing to the touch, yet the fire in his eyes must have warded off his notice. "Where is Kingsly?"

Was that a growl she heard from his lips?

Looking around the room, she couldn't see any sign of where the general blue-eyed prince was. "I don't know. I fell asleep while he was making us some food," Hazel replied before her eyes went back to him, pulling her arm away from Atticus. "Wait? Who told you we were here?" There was no way he could have known unless Arabella told him.

"Does that really matter? You shouldn't be here, especially now that people know who you are!"

Hazel shook her head, turning her back to Atticus to walk towards the fireplace. "Like people didn't already know. You wasted your time and breath coming here, dragon," Hazel snapped back to him before adding more wood to the. Footsteps approached from behind her, causing her to whirl around, stand up with the fire poker in one hand, and glare up at the crown prince staring down at her.

"Be angry with me all you want, princess. Hate me for all I care, but know this: I am trying to help you protect and guide you as best I can. This little stunt you and my brother just pulled, walked right into the lion's den. When the storm clears, do whatever you came here to do, and then we are leaving." His voice was low and deep.

Hazel wasn't going to let him get in his way this time. Shoving him back, her hands illuminated with a dim, gold light. "Protect and guide me? Other than that night when I had a panic attack , All you have done in the time I have known you have taken away my choice in deciding what I can do with my life. You keeping your little secret about the prophecy was not your choice to make for me. Let's not forget the *one time* I needed you, the *one time* I needed you by my side, not only as my Crimson Dragon, but as someone I considered a friend. You did not even acknowledge me at my uncle's funeral, and have yet to give your condolences for his passing. You don't get to act all high and mighty with me because your upset about the consequences of your jealousy," Hazel snarled, adjusting her stance in preparation for if he would get physical with her. Just like he did in her bedroom a few weeks ago almost a month.

"Jealous of who? My brother, of all people? Oh, my sweet little fawn, you couldn't be more wrong," he replied.

Tilting her head back, Hazel didn't let him see the nerves threatening to make her stomach turn.

"Is that so, Brother? Because from the looks of it, you are a wreck of rage and jealousy that she is here with me and not you," Kingsly's dangerously low voice called from behind Hazel from the top of the stairs.

"Why the hell would you bring her here?" Atticus roared in as he made his way down the stairs to stand behind Hazel.

The air grew taut as the two princely brothers glared at one another. The general prince wore no shirt, which caught Hazel's attention for a moment, seeing that bare chest one more made her think of the kiss they shared in his bedroom. Shaking off the image from her mind, she than shifted her focus to Atticus glaring at him. She stepped closer to the crimson dragon, grinding her teeth. "Because I asked him to. I wanted to spread my uncle's ashes. If you have a problem with that, you can take it up with me! Kingsly is only here for moral support because I can't trust you." Hazel's words were meant to go for Atticus's throat and from his softened expression she knew it hit its mark. Yet, it made her feel a certain way on the inside she couldn't explain.

"Is that how you feel? Or is that what Kingsly has put in your head?" Atticus's voice no longer held anger but something else. From the look in his eyes and the tone of his voice, it felt like it hurt. "Kingsly, can you give us the room?" Hazel asked without taking her eyes off Atticus, crossing her arms over her thunderous heart. Feeling a hand on her shoulder squeezing it, she took a deep breath.

"I can go get some more firewood since the storm is dying off," Kingsly replied softly, his hand lingering for a moment before he released her shoulder.

Both Atticus and Hazel stood there staring at each other waiting for Kingsly to come back down the stairs, bundled up for the winter air outside and leaving them alone.

The air became thicker as the room felt more enclosed around them as the two stood there alone. Hazel's glare never wavered from Atticus's soft expression that rested on hers. "You better make your plea good for me to not throw your ass back out in the snow." Hazel's words were clipped, trying to keep her nerves steady.

Chapter Fifty

Hazel

There was a long silence between them as Hazel watched the Crimson Dragon. She didn't know what to think about watching him standing there. She took a deep breath and motioned upstairs. "Let's get you out of those wet clothes." Turning to walk upstairs, she felt a rough callus hand grasp hers, halting her departure. The coldness of the hand nipped at her skin. Hazel looked over her shoulder, seeing Atticus's soft, gentle honey eyes, and it was like he had stolen her breath.

"I can handle some wet clothes, but what I *can't* handle is the way you're looking at me." His voice was hoarse, like trying to hide the true emotions behind his voice.

Hazel didn't pull her hand away as she stared at him. She wasn't moving away, even though her mind screamed for her to shout, yell, and possibly slap him. Hazel's heart cried something different, screaming a feeling she had never felt before. "Atticus, I don't know if the version I am looking at is the real you or a mask." Hazel's kept voice stern. "One moment, you are this wonderful, gentle prince with whom I could see growing a future. However, then you turn into that cruel, harsh, cold prince your court knows well. You have been acting as if because of this prophecy, I don't get to say what I can do with my life, including a life with you." Finally pulling her hand away from him, she continued glanced over her shoulder steadying her pounding heart as the fire crackling filled the silence between them.

"This prophecy may take my life, and you kept a secret about it. Do I not get the option, if this prophecy takes my life, to choose what I want to do with my remaining time? Or has that *also* been chosen for me?" Hazel's voice turned rough and bitter She turned her back to the stairs and stepped backward to create some distance between them. Hazel feared she would give in before him if he stayed any closer to her. "I thought you genuinely cared for me, that I could find happiness after my world was flipped upside down. You and Darius cast me aside like a temporary plaything. I don't think I can forgive either one of you." Hazel fought the break in her voice, crawling up her throat. "I am nothing like that bastard. He didn't deserve you,"

Atticus growled, stepping closer to her, who only retreats a step back.

Hazel, remembering hearing that growl, remembered how just as she thought she finally broke through to him, he had her by her throat to the wall. "Yet, you hurt me far worse than he ever did." Hazel's voice finally broke as she spoke up. She witnessed her words cutting deeply into his heart, evident in the look on his face. "You thought keeping that secret from me would protect me. And maybe part of me understands that now. I was willing to forgive you for not telling me about the sacrifice, because I was starting to see why you held it back. But what hurts... what really hurts... is that you didn't trust me enough to face it with you. I would've helped you. I would've fought to figure it out with you, no matter what it cost."

She paused, her chest rising with a shaky breath.

"I tried not to let you in. Gods, I tried. After everything Darius did—after he tore through every part of me and left me questioning my own worth—I didn't want to feel anything for anyone again. But then you—" Her voice cracked slightly. "You saw me when I was at my lowest. You sat with me through a panic attack and didn't flinch. That night, when you finally let me in... I thought maybe—just maybe—I could let you in too."

Her hands trembled slightly at her sides.

"And I did. I let myself feel something real. I let myself hope. That was the terrifying part. Because I wasn't just scared of what you were hiding—I was scared of what I was starting to feel for you."

Her breath caught as she took a slow step back, her next words sharp and brittle.

"At least with Darius, he had the gall to drive that dagger into my heart face to face. You were a coward and stabbed me in the back, right as I was beginning to fall for you."

Her eyes shimmered, but she didn't tear them away from him. She wanted—no, *needed*—to see how he reacted to that truth. To see whether he would flinch at the weight of her pain or stand there like it meant nothing.

"But finding you with her... after all that? After finally believing there might be something real between us? That hurt worse than anything Darius ever did. Because I never gave him all of me. I was always holding something back. But you—" she shook her head slowly, tears sliding down her cheeks, "you had the part of me I'd buried. The part I didn't think I'd ever give to anyone again."

Her voice softened but lost none of its edge.

"I want to be with you, Atticus. That hasn't changed. But your actions—they terrify me. Because I don't know if I can survive giving my heart away again just to have it shattered like that. And I need to know... if you ever really meant any of it. Or if I was just another game you could afford to lose."

Tears streamed from her eyes as Hazel finally opened the gates to her heart. He didn't speak.

Hazel watched as the weight of her words landed, striking harder than any blow she could've delivered in training. Atticus's posture shifted—subtle at first, but then unmistakable. His proud, straight-backed stance faltered, his shoulders sagging like the wind had been knocked from his lungs. The tension in his jaw slackened, and for a moment, he just stood there—still, silent, unraveling.

His hands, which had always held power with such confidence, now hung limply at his sides. One twitched slightly, as if debating whether to reach for her—but never did. His fingers curled into a fist, then relaxed again, a restless movement that betrayed how uncertain he suddenly was.

Hazel felt her heart clench, even as her chest burned with betrayal. She hated that part of her still longed for him to close the distance. Still waited for him to *do something*.

But he didn't.

He just looked at her, and gods, he looked *wrecked*. Not the version of him she'd seen in court or on the battlefield. This was the man beneath the armor, stripped bare. Regret shadowed every inch of his face. Not the performative kind, not the usual smooth-talking prince with a clever excuse waiting on his tongue. This was real. And it hurt to see.

His gaze dropped, unable to meet hers. That, more than anything, made her stomach twist. Because for the first time... he looked ashamed.

And still—*still*—he said nothing.

Hazel's hands trembled at her sides, and her heart screamed at the silence between them, too loud to bear. If he had just said something—anything—maybe she could've believed there was still something left to salvage.

But instead, he stood there like a man who realized too late what he'd lost

"You were right. You were selfish when it came to me, but for all the wrong reasons. You are a jealous, scared, cowardly prince who hides behind the Immortal Dragon reputation you built on the battlefield because you would rather be alone. Where it's safe from being harmed from taking risks such as love and affection." Hazel's voice cracked looking at him. "You were so scared you would lose me, yet you were the very one pushed me away."

Through her blurred vision, Hazel shoved him away, feeling anger erupt.

Deep down, she felt a pang of regret mixed with her fury, questioning whether pushing him away was the right choice. Despite her dismissing words, a part of her longed wanted him to stay while the other was scared of the idea of what could be. Why wasn't he arguing with her or fighting back like he did in that carriage? He just stood there not looking at her.

"I am all that you said and more. I am jealous. I am jealous because you came here with Kingsly and not me. Hearing Duvessa tell me that you both went to Wylana together..." Stepping closer to Hazel, closing the distance, he stared down into her icy blue, and it made her whole body lock up, not knowing what to say or do. "Yes, I am scared. I am scared that I am falling for you, Hazel. "Yes, I am scared." His voice cracked with the weight of everything he'd buried. "I am scared that I'm falling for you, Hazel. And not in some fleeting, passing way—not like every meaningless flirtation I've had before. This is different. *You're* different."

He dragged a hand through his hair, pacing a single step before turning back to her, his eyes pleading.

"I've spent my whole life pretending love didn't matter, like it was just another weapon to use or a mask to wear. But you... you make all of that impossible. You make me question everything I thought I knew. And it terrifies me."

He exhaled sharply, voice lowering. "Because every time I start to feel something real, I hear his voice—my father's. I see what he became, what loving someone the wrong way did to him. To my mother. To me. And I think... what if I end up just like him? What if I ruin you too?"

He looked at her like she was already slipping through his fingers.

"That's why I pushed you away. Why I let pride and fear keep me from being honest with you. Because the thought of letting someone in—*really* letting them in—is terrifying. Especially when it's *you*. Because you're not just anyone."

He stepped forward, just enough for his voice to soften, to crack at the edges.

"If this prophecy takes you away from me, I will burn all of Wylana down for taking the greatest light from my life. And yes... you're right. I *am* selfish. Because I want you. I want you to be with me, even if I don't deserve you."

His hand hovered near hers but didn't touch.

"The idea of another man's hand on you makes my chest twist in ways I can't even explain. I've met so many women in my life—bedded them, flirted, played the part. But not a single one has ever made my heart stop just from a trace of vanilla and sandalwood on the breeze."

A broken chuckle escaped him, full of guilt and longing.

"You make me feel everything I've spent years trying to bury. And I ran because I was scared. Scared of you. Scared of *me*. Scared that if I let myself love you... I'd lose you. Or worse—I'd break you."

He shook his head, almost like he couldn't believe he was saying the words out loud. ""In spite of everything... I'm here now. And the walls? They're gone. I've stripped myself bare so you can see every part of me—every flaw, every truth I've been too much of a coward to say before. And I won't set foot back in Wylana until I say all of this. Until you know."

His voice lowered, but it carried a fierce intensity.

"If, after everything, you still hate me... then I'll take that. I'll carry it. I deserve it."

He stepped closer, no longer hiding from her eyes.

"But what I *won't* accept—what I *refuse* to let you believe—is that you're not good enough. Not for me. Not for anyone. You are powerful, brilliant, maddening in the best ways, and more heart than most people even know what to do with."

He took a breath, voice thick now with unspoken emotion.

"You are not some broken thing to be pitied, Hazel. You're the one who walked through fire and kept going. And if you don't see that yet... then I'll stay right here until you do."

Atticus reached for Hazel's hand, but a loud slap sound filled the air, and his face whipped to the side as he stumbled back.

"I never said I wasn't good enough for someone—don't you *dare* put words in my mouth!" Hazel's snarl cracked through the room like a whip, her voice trembling with fury. Her hand still throbbed from the slap, and Atticus stood there, frozen, one palm to his cheek, his chest rising and falling in staggered breaths—equal parts pain and disbelief.

Her breath came in ragged pulls, and though her eyes gleamed with tears, there was no weakness in them. Only the fire of a girl too used to being broken and too stubborn to stay that way.

"You don't get to decide how I feel. And you sure as hell don't get to tell me what I deserve." Her voice cracked but didn't fall. She backed away, the space between them charged like a drawn bowstring, steps faltering only when she felt the solid edge of the bookshelf behind her.

Atticus's jaw clenched. He stepped forward—not in anger, but desperation.

"Then *why*, Hazel?" His voice was a low thunder now, raw and scraping like it had been carved from bone. "Why do you push yourself so hard that you burn? Why does your face twist with guilt every time you stumble? I *see* you—you think no one does, but I do. The self-doubt when your magic doesn't obey, the way you scan the room like you're waiting to be replaced by someone stronger, prettier, more... perfect."

He took another step, and she swore the air between them vibrated.

"Tell me the truth. Are you afraid you won't be good enough to be the Ivory Fawn? That you'll let everyone down the way you think you did with your uncle?"

Hazel flinched like he'd struck something buried so deep, it still bled.

Atticus's voice cracked now, too—barely a whisper. "You think your worth is tangled up in fate and prophecy, but it's *not*. You are where you are because of *you*. Not because some stars aligned or ancient gods whispered your name. You clawed your way here. You bled for it. You *broke* for it. And damn it, Hazel—you are *more* than that prophecy. You are the only one who doesn't see it."

His words landed like a punch to her ribs.

She inhaled sharply, backing into the shelves as if they could steady her. Her mouth opened—but nothing came out. Nothing could. Because deep down, every word he said had hit a nerve she thought she'd buried long ago.

And now, there they stood—two people on opposite ends of the same hurt, stripped bare under the weight of truths they weren't ready to say but couldn't stop from spilling.

As Atticus leaned forward, he rested his right hand on the bookshelf behind her, towering over her as his left hand nearly brushed her cheek, but he hesitated. Hazel saw how close his hand lingered, her mind was clouded . Hazel's breath hitched as she felt his hand warmth inches from her skin. Her eyes searched for his, silently begging for the connection her heart yearned for. All she could focus on was how hard she was breathing, the way his hand felt so soft against her skin the night he was in the bathroom. Hazel looked down and away from his eyes. "I am not worth anything to anyone without fulfilling that damn prophecy."

A rough, calloused hand cupped her chin, tilting it to look at him. "If that was true, would I be here risking my title, reign, and life for you? I didn't fall for the Ivory Fawn. I fell for you." His voice was low and deep as his lips hovered closer to hers.

Hazel pressed her hand into his chest, stopping him. "What about that woman in your bed?" Hazel's voice broke at the memory, but Atticus pulled back to look her in the eyes with no hint of a wall up. "Jasinda is nothing more than a release. She was to be a broodmare for her ex-fiancee. I agreed to take her as a mistress so she wouldn't have to marry him because then she would be ruined. When I am king, she will wed whomever she chooses with my blessing. She meant nothing to me unlike you mean something to me and actually scolded me that night in the bathroom."

Hazel was shocked to hear his bluntness about the woman. Seeing the dragon inked onto his skin, Hazel swallowed and undid the buttons on his soaking-wet Henley shirt. Tailing her hand along its scaly head, she said, "In my bathroom, why did you say I would regret it? Not that *you* would regret it. What did you mean by that?" Hazel looked up into his eyes that stared deep into her own, making her feel bare beneath him.

"Because if you came to my room, or we had shared a bed, I wouldn't be able to resist you like I had before. Even now, I am fighting the urge to prove how much I would worship you. If you want control in your life, here it is. You choose whether you want me by your side or if you wish to cast me aside into the snow, as you swore earlier."

Hazel felt the air shudder from her lungs like the ground had been yanked from beneath her. For so long, she'd kept her heart wrapped in iron and silence, too scared to hand the pieces to someone who might shatter it all over again. She had survived betrayal, bloodshed, and the unbearable silence left behind by those who never stayed. But this—**this** was different.

Atticus wasn't begging. He wasn't demanding. He stood before her, unguarded and raw, letting her decide. And despite every reason she'd built not to trust him... she *did*.

She saw him—not the crown, not the cold exterior, not the war-torn prince—but the man who looked at her like she was worth burning the world for. The man who had slipped past her defenses and somehow made her feel like she was *more*—not because of a prophecy, but because of *who* she was.

And gods, she was tired of holding back.

With trembling fingers, she reached for him, tracing the line of his jaw before sliding to the nape of his neck, right beneath the edge of his hair. His breath stilled under her touch.

She didn't speak.

She didn't need to.

Because in this moment, she was choosing him—despite the fear, despite the risk, despite every wound she'd tried to hide.

Hazel pulled him down into a kiss that wasn't gentle or uncertain—it was everything she'd been afraid to feel. It was fire and desperation and the ache of finally *letting someone in*. Her magic sparked beneath her skin, not wild or dangerous this time, but warm—like it finally understood what it meant to feel safe.

His arms closed around her, grounding her, anchoring her in a way nothing else ever had.

And just like that, the walls crumbled.

This wasn't surrender.

This was *freedom*.

Chapter Fifty-One

Atticus

Gods, she was his undoing. How many times had he imagined having her like this? Every touch ignited a blaze of desire that threatened to consume him entirely. His heart pounded fiercely, each beat echoing the depth of his longing. At that moment, nothing else existed but the intoxicating sensation of her presence, overwhelming his senses with an almost unbearable intensity. Although he controlled that tether, he was at her mercy. This moment marked a turning point in their relationship, where unspoken emotions finally found expression through touch and connection. It was a silent admission of their mutual desire, breaking down the barriers that had kept them apart for so long. Their bond, once simmering beneath the surface, now blazed brightly, promising a future neither had dared to hope for until now. Atticus silently vowed to her that he would give her the control she never had.

Feeling her pull her lips from his, her breast rose and fell in the brown corset that pushed those gorgeous mounds so high up that he wanted to capture them on his lips. Her eyes met his, wide and shimmering with surprise and longing. A blush spread across her cheeks, betraying both her vulnerability and desire. A soft smile played on her lips as she caught her breath. This smile revealed the joy and relief of finally succumbing to the passion they'd both suppressed for so long.

The room was bathed in the soft, flickering glow of candlelight, casting dancing shadows on the walls and enveloping them in an intimate cocoon. The subtle crackling of the fire in the hearth added a layer of warmth and a rhythmic backdrop to their shared moment. The scent of old books mixed with the heady aroma of her perfume created an ambiance that was both nostalgic and electric, heightening the intensity of their newfound connection. Remember how fiery she was when he first had the chance to speak with her in this room. Resting his forehead on hers, he yielded to her, letting her see the most raw parts of him.

They slowly moved towards the plush sofa by the fireplace not breaking their kiss, their fingers intertwined, unwilling to break the physical and emotional bond they had just forged. Settling down, they let their bodies mold into each other, savoring the profound intimacy that words could never fully capture.

Atticus couldn't help but marvel at how the firelight played across Hazel's features, casting a golden hue that accentuated her every curve and contour. The flickering flames highlighted the delicate lines of her face, making her appear ethereal and almost otherworldly. Her eyes sparkled like the frost on the window seal, reflecting the warmth and intensity of their shared moment. Atticus's heart swelled with a blend of awe and gratitude, feeling as if he were witnessing the very essence of beauty and strength emodied in Hazel. He marveled at how her vulnerability made her even more radiant, deepening his admiration and love for her. At that moment, he realized that he wanted to spend the rest of his life cherishing and protecting the woman who had become his entire world. Atticus gently cupped Hazel's face with his hands, his touch tender and reverent. Leaning in, he pressed his lips softly against hers. A kiss that was both a promise and a confession of his unwavering love. As they kissed, he poured all his emotion, commitment, and devotion into that single, heartfelt gesture, sealing their bond with an unspoken vow.

Hazel said nothing as she pulled her lips away, resting her head on his to catch her breath. Her soft hand took his rough, calloused hand in a warm, as she stands beckoning him to follow her up the stairs. Atticus could feel the heat rising more as it awakened down into his groin. Hazel led him into her old room, where he first met her. The fireplace was the only light in the room. It still looked like it had when they left it two months ago. The familiar scent of vanilla and lavender wafted through the air, instantly transporting Atticus back to their first encounter. The worn, leather-bound books lined the shelves.Standing by the fireplace where she released his hand, Atticus watched hr start undoing the buttons to his wet Henley shirt, helping her remove it over his head.

Watching her remove his shirt and discard it to the side, Atticus eyes locked onto those icy blue eyes taking in every detail of his body. Feeling her finger trace that dragon inked into his skin, Atticus sucked in a breath.

"You don't want this." Hazel broke the silence. Her icy blue eyes looked into his soft, honey eyes. That's what he had told her in her bathroom where he last lost control. Was she mocking him? A low chuckle escaped his lips as Atticus took her chin into his forefinger and thumb and tilted it back. Her breath hitched, and a slight shiver ran down her spine. Her eyes fluttered closed for a moment, as if she was savoring the sensation, before she opened them again, showing her desire and determination. Hazel's lips parted slightly, and she leaned into his touch, her expression softening.

"You were my undoing in that bathroom, but," he breathed haughtily, brushing his lips gently over hers before trailing them up her ear. He whispered, "Is this what you had in mind that night, or would you rather have me on my knees before you, worshiping you like the goddess you are?"

Hazel's hands rested on his chest as a soft moan escaped her lips, and it was the most beautiful sound he had ever heard. Their eyes met as she stroked his cheek, kissed him deeply, and ran her hand through his onyx-damp hair. "Would you get on your knees for me?" It was not a question, but almost a demand.

As Atticus obediently kneeled before her, he never took his eyes off hers.. The only woman he would give all his power and strength to was a queen he would be proud to rule beside his sovereign. "For you, Hazel, I would also give you my heart and mind, body, and soul." Atticus watched her fall silent, lips parting, eyes wide with something raw and unspoken. The tear that slipped down her cheek hit him harder than any blade ever had.

She wasn't pulling away. She wasn't running.

"If you're gonna kneel, you better be ready to worship—because I don't take devotion lightly."

A surge of emotions coursed through him, and he a profound sense of surrender and devotion, a willingness to be vulnerable and open in a way he had never experienced before surged through him. At that moment, he realized that surrendering himself to her wasn't just an act of submission, but an affirmation of their deep, unbreakable bond.

His eyes scanned the body sculpted perfectly in that burnt orange dress and brown corset. He felt a mix of awe and intimidation as she stood so close. He couldn't help but be mesmerized by her commanding aura. Gods, she was a picture of perfection.

Hazel leaned down putting her finger under his chin, kissing him deeply, as she took his hand and puts it on her hips. Standing up slowly, Atticus backed them towards the bed. Once the backs of her knees meet the bed frame, she sat down on the bed.

However, instead of crawling on top of her like every instinct begged him to—of letting his hands worship every inch of her body—he chose restraint. That time would come later.

For now, he sank to his knees before her with deliberate grace.

"Atticus," she breathed, her voice laced with pleading.

He only answered with a slow, feline smile.

"You wanted me on my knees. I plan to worship every part of you, starting with this."

Atticus felt her skin prickle beneath his lips as he pushed the fabric of her skirt up to reveal her core already soaked in undergarments. Lowering his lips to her inner thigh. He felt the heat radiating from her skin, the slight tremble of her muscles under his touch. The softness of her skin against his lips was a stark contrast to the firm grip of his hands on her hips. Her breath hitched, becoming a soft, sensual sigh, as his kisses trailed higher, leaving a path of warmth and yearning in their wake. He took his tongue and licked the soft fabric, watching her head fall back as her breathing became heavier. Looking up, her cheeks were already flushed, and her breath was coming out in soft, needy gasps. Hazel's fingers tangled in his hair, gently pulling him closer, as her hips instinctively arched toward his touch. A deep moan escaped her lips, echoing through the quiet room, as the intensity of his worship sent shivers coursing through her entire body.

As Atticus continued his tender ministrations, he couldn't stop the awe that bloomed in his chest at every sigh, every arch of her back, every soft gasp that escaped her lips. The way her body responded—so instinctive, so trusting—ignited something fierce and reverent inside him. It was more than desire; it was worship. Each shiver he drew from her felt like a silent praise, and gods, he wanted to earn every last one.

At that moment, he felt an overwhelming sense of reverence and devotion. Trailing a hand up her leg, he felt the pebbling forming almost instantly where his hand met her skin. Hazel raised her hips to assist Atticus in removing her wet undergarments. The smell of her arousal caused a hungry groan to escape his lips. "Does the sight of me on my knees really make you this wet?" he teased softly. After blowing onto her core, Atticus let his tongue separate her soft wet lips, not giving her the chance to speak.

She tasted so sweet, almost like honeydew. The flavor brought back childhood memories of summer picnics and carefree days in the sun. It was a comforting and nostalgic sweetness that lingered. Gods, he could feel his cock twitching in his pants for how she tasted and those little gasp. Not yet, he will let himself have her in a moment. He wanted her to come undone before him, before sinking into her. Hazel deserved to be worshiped for the goddess she was.

His mouth claimed that sweet, swollen bud with a hunger he barely restrained, tongue flicking and teasing as if he were memorizing every reaction. The soft, desperate sounds spilling from her lips spurred him on, each moan a symphony he never wanted to end. He explored her with slow, deliberate strokes—each movement designed to unravel her, to make her tremble beneath him. She tasted like sin and surrender, and he was determined to indulge until she was utterly undone. Damn, she was so tight. Her body trembled with each flick of his tongue, her fingers clutching the back of his hair in a desperate attempt to ground herself as he worshiped her. Every gasp and moan that escaped her lips only spurred him on, her hips arching and pressing against his mouth in a rhythm that spoke of her rising pleasure. Her skin flushed with heat, a sheen of perspiration forming as she came closer to the edge.

His mind wandered to how tight her slick, sweet core would feel around him. Atticus shoved those ideas down and focused on pleasing his future queen. Sucking and exploring her sensitive bean with his mouth, he groaned in excitement, feeling her back arched upward as her hips moved slightly away from him. Atticus's hand came up, pinning her waist down, growling as their eyes locked. "You're interrupting my feast."

Their eyes locked with an intensity that sent shivers down his spine. Hazel looked so breathtaking like this. Her face was so beautiful with that red across it and her neck. Hazel's gaze was a mixture of desire and vulnerability, her pupils dilated with lust. The connection in that moment felt almost primal, a silent communication of their deepest cravings and unspoken promises. Continuing his worship of her sweet core, a cry escaped her lips as Atticus felt Hazel find a blissful release.

He couldn't hold back the satisfied groan that escaped his lips as he savored every drop on his tongue and lips. "Atticus, I-I-" Hazel was so breathless she couldn't even finish her sentence, tell him what her needs. She didn't need to, her eyes told him everything.

"Have you laid with a man before?" Atticus asked. He knew Hazel had been in a relationship with another man before, but didn't know if they had been intimate as they were at this moment.

Hazel was hesitant, but shook her head. That would be good. Then he wouldn't need to be gentle.. Atticus rose to his feet, pulling her to stand in front of him. Leaning down, he pulled her hair aside, kissing her shoulder up to her neck, stopping just below her ear. "May I take this off?" he whispered as he pulled on the corset. Hazel nodded her head. Atticus' heart raced with a mixture of anticipation and reverence as he untied the laces. Each knot undone was a step closer to unveiling a precious treasure, and he wanted to savor every moment. He marveled at her trust in him, feeling a profound sense of responsibility to make this experience as gentle and unforgettable as possible.

As Atticus turned Hazel to face him, she was holding her unlaced corset to her chest, his eyes found her soft ice-blue eyes, noticing a green swirl around the irises. Was that always there? Forcing the corset to come off her wide hims and fall, he watched as Hazel slowly removed her burnt orange dress, also letting it hit to the ground. His thoughts raced as he took in the sight before him, marveling at her natural beauty and the vulnerability she displayed. He felt a deep sense of privilege, knowing that she was entrusting him with such an intimate moment. Every curve, every inch of her skin seemed to beckon him closer, and he was determined to honor her trust by making sure their connection was as profound and tender as it was passionate.

Watching Hazel fall to her knees before him, Atticus let out a faint growl, gripping her chin, pulling her back up to stand, and shaking his head. He gently caressed her cheek, his voice soft but firm. "Hazel," he whispered, "I want you to always stand tall beside me. You deserve to be cherished and respected, not kneel before anyone. Especially not to me"

Atticus squatted down picking Hazel up by the back of her knees, hoisting her up. Hazel's legs wrapped around his waist as he lowered her gently down onto the bed. Her golden hair sprawled out under her head on the pillow, creating a perfect halo around her, making her appear even more like a goddess.

"Slap me if you want me to stop, princess," he teased before lowering his lips down, capturing those soft vanilla lips with his. Her breath hitched, her arms draped around his shoulder . Her hands gripped his shoulder, pulling him closer, and the world around them faded away, leaving only the electrifying connection between their lips. "I'm at your mercy. You tell me what I can or cannot do. So, princess, what do you desire?" His voice was low and deep in invitation. This was him letting her have that control.

"I want all of you," Hazel said. Her voice was like silk.

Hearing her words, he was relieved that Hazel was allowing him this. This moment marked a profound turning point in their relationship, solidifying a bond that transcended mere physical attraction.

Standing up, Atticus removed his trousers. He knew where her eyes were staring and smirked before joining her on the bed. Positioning himself between her legs and hovering over her body, he gently guided the tip to her entrance, but he didn't push all the way in, not yet. Looking at Hazel, he checked on more time to see if there were any objections or second thoughts.

Hazel wiggled eagerly, biting her lip. "It's alright," she breathed.

Slowly, Atticus pushed himself into her tight entrance, and a shared gasp of pleasure slipped from their lips. His breath hitched as her body welcomed him, warm and trembling beneath him. Leaning down, he captured her mouth in a deep, lingering kiss, pouring every ounce of his need and reverence into it. As she adjusted to his size, he let his hand roam across the curve of her waist, then up—fingertips brushing over the soft swell of her bare chest, savoring the way her breath caught beneath his touch.

Atticus began his thrust, slow and deep, and her core swallowed every inch of him in a needful manner. The room was filled with the intoxicating scent of desire and their intermingling fragrances. Heat radiated from her body, and each thrust sent waves of pleasure through him. The sound of their breaths, heavy and synchronized, mingled with the rhythmic slap of skin against skin, created a symphony of passion that enveloped them both completely.

Hazel's head arched back, exposing her neck to him. Leaning down, he scraped his teeth along her throat, trailing his lips and nibbling on her soft skin. His thrusts were soft and slow. He wanted their first time to be gentle and passionate. Not like he had ever done before with any other women because Hazel was nothing like the other court ladies he's been with.

Hazel was his air, his world, and his salvation.

For Atticus, this wasn't just pleasure — it was surrender. A rare instance of vulnerability, where the walls he'd built with iron and pride crumbled at the sound of her soft gasps and whispered moans. Each breathy plea she gave him was a melody he never knew he'd crave, and the way she whispered his name — like a prayer, like a promise — threatened to undo him entirely.

Every inch of her was a revelation, and he wanted her to feel that — to feel how sacred this was to him. His lips trailed down her neck to the slope of her collarbone, leaving a path of soft, reverent kisses that made her shiver. Her fingers tangled in his hair, tightening just enough to ground him in the moment, and the quiet, broken sound that escaped her lips made his chest ache.

She was letting him in — not just into her body, but into the guarded, aching parts of her soul. That trust was a gift he didn't take lightly. His name fell from her lips again, breathless and sweet, and he answered it with another deep, steady thrust, unable to hold back the groan that tore from his throat as her legs wrapped tightly around his waist, pulling him deeper, locking him into place like she never wanted to let go.

In that moment, Atticus wasn't just making love to her—he was giving her everything he had.

Feeling her meeting his thrust with the arch of her hips, Atticus groaned into her skin, trying to keep control and not falter into a punishing thrust. Secretly wanting to hear her scream his name,

"Why are you holding back?" Hazel's voice was exasperated as her eyes locked onto his.

"Do you want me to punish you? To make you scream my name like the pretty pillow princess you are," Atticus taunted, stroking her cheek.

"You said to yourself you wanted to worship me, yet I don't feel I am being worshiped," Hazel taunted right back to him, biting her bottom lip.

It was as if that tether snapped at her words. His eyes darkened with a mix of frustration and desire, and he took a step closer to her. "Is that so?" he murmured, his voice low and challenging. "Perhaps I need to show you just how *devoted* I can be."

Atticus grinned before he started to thrust again. This time, a far more punishing pace, driving harder as he lifted her hips to plunge himself deeper. "Careful what you wish for, princess."

Hearing those beautiful sounds erupt from her as she grabbed the headboard, crying out in pleasure. Hearing her moan his name like that, soft and breathless, sent a jolt straight through Atticus — a primal, reverent kind of hunger laced with awe. The way her body clenched around him, how she whimpered when he hit that perfect spot, it wasn't just arousing — it was addictive. It was *everything*. It made him feel powerful and helpless all at once, like he would do anything to hear that sound again.

In that moment, he wasn't just chasing pleasure — he was worshiping her with every thrust, every breath, every heartbeat. And that sound? That moan of his name falling from her lips? That was the sound he wanted to chase for the rest of his life.

Gods, Hazel was going to be the death of him.

He couldn't get enough of her, enough of those beautiful sounds she made, how her breast bounced from his punishing plunges. "Hazel, I'm-" Atticus breathed out her name, feeling his release building in his core.

"Don't hold back," Hazel cut him off, her voice a breathless command as her fingers twisted into the sheets.

A wicked smile tugged at Atticus's lips. "As you wish," he purred, his voice rough with desire.

He drove into her harder, deeper—each thrust sending ripples of pleasure crashing through them. Hazel cried out his name, her back arching as her body trembled beneath his.

"*Gods, Hazel*—" he groaned against her mouth, losing control as her walls clenched around him.

Their moans tangled together, breathless and raw, as they spiraled over the edge—falling apart and coming together all at once in a rapture that stole the air from their lungs and left them trembling in each other's arms.

Collapsing on the bed beside Hazel, Atticus's chest rose and fell rapidly. He tried to catch his breath as he admired how those pools of blue captured the firelight.

Pushing the damp strands of hair from her face, Atticus brushed his lips against her forehead before his thumb traced the soft curve of her cheek. His hand lingered as he took her in—the flushed warmth of her skin still glowing from their shared heat, the way her lashes fluttered like a sigh over dazed, golden eyes. He admired the delicate slope of her nose, the subtle fullness of her lips still kiss-swollen and parted from breathless moans, the faint freckle near her jawline he'd never noticed until now.

To him, she looked like ruin and salvation all at once—gorgeous in her vulnerability, and devastating in the way she made him feel so utterly *hers*.

"You know there is no going back after this, Atticus warned as he rested his head on hers, pulling her close into his arms. Needing her to be closer to him to breathe.

"I wouldn't ever want to go back," Hazel replied before nuzzling her head under his chin, snuggling in closer.

"I wish I could take everything back on how I treated you," he started, but Hazel's finger stopped his words as she looked up at his honey-brown eyes.

"I know, but what we can do from here is move on and learn from previous actions. No more secrets, no more walls. Just us," Hazel said before brushing her lips against his, stroking his cheek. "No matter the outcome, we need to live in this current moment, not in the what if moments. Okay." Atticus only smiled, kissing her head. "As you wish, princess."

Pulling her close to his chest, Atticus rested his chin on top of her head, reaching to grab the blanket at the edge of the foot board, and covering them with it. Feeling her skin against his, it felt so right. He never wanted this moment to end, never wanted to leave this room.

He felt his eyelids grow heavy as he held Hazel close. Rubbing soothing strokes up and down her spine, he coaxed her into a deep slumber. Her breathing and slight snore let him know she had fallen asleep in his arms. Scanning the room for any threats, it was a struggle to keep his eyes open. Looking down at Hazel, he stroked her cheek, admiring her sleeping state.

Hazel looked utterly breathtaking, so at peace. Finally, for once in his life, he felt genuine joy and happiness to have her in his arms. Kissing her head, he held her closer to him. As if his arms would shield her from anything that wished them harm.

He would lay his life on the line if she asked him to. Soon, his eyes became so heavy it was no use trying to keep them open. Atticus didn't care if Kingsly came back or not. All he knew was that Hazel finally accepted him as hers, just as he accepted her as his.

When they returned to Wylana, he would speak with his father about allowing Kingsly to take the throne instead of him so he could marry and rule by her side. He truly hoped he was wrong about this prophecy and that she would survive and be the queen all of Wylana needed. A queen like his mother, kind and gentle. He would give it all up if that meant being by her side. Soon, sleep befell him, and Atticus slipped into a blissful sleep.

Chapter Fifty-Two

Atticus

It was hard to breathe. Only darkness surrounded him as Atticus choked on the thick air.

A familiar female voice echoed in his ear.

"The cottage is on fire. Get up Dragon!" the voice once again bellowed out. It soon hit him it was Asteria when she used his title

Opening his eyes, his eyes burned as he looked around, seeing smoke filling the air. He grabbed the still-wet shirt from the ground and urgently moved to Hazel, who was starting to cough, coming to consciousness from the difficulty of breathing. He quickly wrapped a hand around her wrist, pulling on it, urging her to stand. "We need to get out now, Hazel!" he shouted over the crackling flames Grabbing her dress from where Hazel discarded it, Atticus handed it to Hazel to get dressed. His heart pounding with fear and adrenaline. Atticus hands her his shirt in hand "Cover your mouth with this. Stay close to me."

His ears were filled with the crackling roar of the fire devouring wood, the sharp pops of beams splintering under the strain. The once-familiar creak of the floorboards was now replaced by a chaotic symphony of groans and snaps as the cottage fought to hold itself together. Smoke curled in thick, choking tendrils, burning his throat with every breath, wrapping around his lungs like chains of ash.

The heat was unbearable—clinging to his skin, pressing in from every side, a suffocating blanket that made his heartbeat thunder in his ears. He could feel the walls trembling, the floor beneath him trembling like a creature about to collapse. And still, through it all, the only thing he could think about was Hazel—and getting them both out before this place became a tomb.

Every breath felt like swallowing fire, and the weight of responsibility for Hazel's safety pressed heavily on his shoulders. Determination surged through him, knowing that her life depended on his every move.

"Atticus, what's going on?" Hazel's voice was hoarse from coughing and groggy.

Sliding on his pants, he fastens it, looking at her as she gets dressed. Atticus took that black Henley shirt, raising it back to her face.

"The cottage is on fire. We need to go!"

Hazel's eyes widen with terror as the gravity of the situation sank in. Her hands trembled as she fumbled to secure her dress, the panic evident. Tears well up, both from the stinging smoke and the overwhelming fear, but she nodded resolutely, trusting Atticus to lead them to safety. "Keep your mouth covered," Atticus emphasized his last words, not wanting her to inhale any more smoke. Covering his own mouth with his free hand, he looked for something to cover his own mouth. Atticus knew the closet was empty because he watched Hazel on the day they left to pack everything.

Hearing fabric tear behind him, he turned to see Hazel handed him a piece of his shirt to cover his mouth. Without arguing, he took it and covered his mouth. Grabbing her hand, he led her toward the door leading.

Atticus hissed at how hot it was before he opened the door, shielding Hazel from the sudden blast of hot air. Atticus inhaled sharply at the hot air, licking his bare skin. "Let's go. Hold on to my trousers," he demanded before heading out into the hallway, looking both ways to see the source of the fire.

The smoke clouded his vision as Atticus blinked the hot tears from his eyes. "Hazel, where is the nearest exit?" he called out over the roaring flames, turning to look at her, but she wasn't behind him anymore. "Hazel!"

"I need to get my uncle's ashes!" She called out, running for the stairs.

Atticus' heart dropped, watching her run towards the flames before chasing after "Hazel, wait!" Racing after her, ignoring the burning in his eyes, he grasped her hand just at the top of the stairwell. The heat was unbearable, and the smoke made it nearly impossible to see or breathe. The wooden beams above them groaned ominously, threatening to collapse at any moment. Every step they took was fraught with danger as the floorboards creaked and splintered under the intense heat. The wood beneath their feet caved from their weight.

A scream ripped from Hazel's throat as they plummeted to the base level of the cottage. Atticus quickly pulled her into his chest, turning them as they fell, so it was his back that took the brunt of the impact. Sharp pain radiated through Atticus's spine, and he felt a burning sensation in his lower back. His breath came in shallow gasps as he tried to mask the agony, unwilling to alarm Hazel further. A pained grunt escaped his throat feeling the impact of Hazel's weight falling onto him. Atticus felt his breath escape his body before looking at Hazel, pushing the hair from her face. "Are you hurt?"

As she shook her head, Atticus realized the shirt she used to cover her mouth was now burning up in the flames. The acrid smell of smoke filled the air, stinging their eyes and throats. The crackling of the burning wood and the roaring flames created a deafening cacophony around them. The heat was unbearable, intensifying the urgency as they struggled to find a way out with the front door being blocked. Handing Hazel the sliver of his shirt, he held it to her mouth, "Go, get out of here. I will get your uncle's ashes." Getting up, he winced in pain, holding his ribs.

Hazel's eyes widened in fear and defiance. "No, I'm not leaving you!" she cried, her voice cracking with emotion.

Groaning and getting to his feet, Atticus saw an open opportunity for an open window. The window, partially obscured by the encroaching flames, offered a glimmer of hope. Shattered glass edges reflected the flickering firelight, creating a kaleidoscope of chaos around them. Smoke billowed through the opening, but the cool night air beyond it promised a chance of escape.

Yanking Hazel to her feet, he shoved her toward the open window. "Go! I am right behind you!" Atticus called out before looking around the room to find Archibald's urn.

Atticus stumbled through the smoke-filled room, his vision blurred by tears and the acrid haze. His mind raced as he tried to recall where the urn was last placed. Desperately, he pushed aside burning debris and broken furniture, his heart pounding in his chest. Finally, through the thickening smoke, he spotted the familiar shape of the urn on a shelf, partially hidden by a fallen beam.

Atticus continued to cover his mouth with the crook of his arm to keep the smoke back. Maneuvering around the burning cottage, he made his way over to the urn. Picking it up, he wanted to cry out in pain from how hot it was in his hand and how the sudden movement hurt his ribs. Despite the searing pain and the overwhelming heat, Atticus's resolve never wavered. Every step was a battle, but his determination to honor Hazel's request kept him moving forward. Clenching his jaw, he cradled the scorching urn against his chest, preparing to make his way back to the window and the promise of safety outside.

Turned to make his way toward where he saw that opportunity. Hazel was right there, reaching in to take the urn from him. "Hazel! I told you to-"

"I am not leaving you here! We leave here together!" she snapped back at him.

The flames roared louder, consuming the wooden beams and threatened to collapse the structure at any moment. The heat was unbearable, and the smoke somehow thickened, making it harder to breathe with each passing second. Time was running out, and their only chance of survival was to make it through the window before the entire cottage turned into an inferno. The sound of creaking wood brought their attention to the roof, where a beam was falling.

"Atticus!" Hazel cried before a sharp pain erupted along his body, shoving him back into the floorboard behind him. Atticus's pain momentarily blinded him with its ferocity. He struggled to stay conscious, his vision dimming as he focused on Hazel's panicked face. Through the agony, he gritted his teeth and tried to push himself up, refusing to give in to the darkness.

Shaking the distorted vision away, he turned to see the urn now laid on the ground beside him, unopened, thankfully. To his horror, when he whipped his head around to see Hazel buried under the beam. As the flames tried to engulf her.

"No!" His terror ripped from his chest as he rushed to push the beam off her. His hands trembled with desperation and fear as he struggled to lift the heavy beam. Sweat dripped down his forehead, mixing with tears of panic. Each second felt like an eternity as he fought against the crushing weight, his heart pounding in his ears. Hazel was pinned underneath the beam that would have taken him out if she hadn't shoved him out of the way.

"Hazel!" Atticus prayed she was okay, prayed She was conscious, pale, with blood trickling from a forehead gash. Her breathing was shallow, and her eyes fluttered weakly. Her legs were pinned under the beam, and Atticus feared the worst as he pushed. Hazel tried to get up but groaned in pain; her left leg was broken and twisted. The forehead gash was deep, seeping blood into her hair. Bruises and scrapes on her arms indicated she bore the brunt of the impact.

His ribs screamed in protest as he stood up and pushed all his weight into that beam, trying to push it off of Hazel. Atticus would be damned if he let them die like this.

Atticus's mind raced with thoughts of their shared past, the moments of joy and laughter that now seemed so distant. He couldn't lose Hazel, not after everything they'd been through together. The pain in his ribs was excruciating, but the thought of life without her was a far greater agony. Atticus turned, using his shoulder and full body weight to push the beam once more, but it didn't budge. Atticus couldn't breathe with how much his lungs burned, but he refused to leave Hazel like this.

Holding his side, he looked around before kneeling down and pushing hair from her face. Her skin was clammy and cold to the touch, a stark contrast to the heat around them. Her breaths came in short, labored gasps. The light in her eyes was fading, and Atticus knew they were running out of time.

"Just hold on. I will get you out." Sheer determination was in his voice as he looked for something to help him free her.

"Please," Hazel pleaded before reaching for his hand.. "Get out. I will be okay. Wylana-"

"All of Wylana can burn in hell for all I care!" he roared in anger, his voice strained as his strength gave on him. A heavy weight was now pressing on his body. He refused to submit, not when Hazel was trapped like this.

Groaning, holding his ribs, he looked around the burning cottage. Seeing there was no way out now, he couldn't even find a way to get her out did get her out. Outside the cottage, the world was a stark contrast to the inferno within. The icy wind howled through the trees, carrying with it the bitter chill of winter, but none of it mattered compared to the fiery chaos inside.

Hazel's gagged coughing brought Atticus's attention to her. He took her hand in his, trying to think of something to save them both. "Hazel, I-" He struggled to finish his thought as tears flowed from his eyes, not only burning from the smoke but also from the horrifying realization that this could be their final moment together.

"No, Atticus, please! Hey, stay awake!" Hazel choked.

It was hard to keep his eyes open as he felt the weight of his body dragging him down to the ground, forcing him to submit to its weight. The sound of the burning cottage was fading, as was his misty vision, as he lay on his unwounded side. "I'm sorry," he breathed out hoarsely.

Hazel's eyes welled up with tears, mixing with the soot on her cheeks as she squeezed his hand with the little strength she had left. "No, Atticus, don't be sorry," she whispered, her voice fragile but filled with unwavering love. "We've encountered perilous situations in the past, and we're prepared to face them once again."

Atticus had failed her. He tried to get her out, but he should have been the one to shove Hazel out of the way—not the other way around. He failed Queen Asteria. He was supposed to guide her to become the Ivory Fawn, but instead, he led her right to her death before she could fulfill the prophecy.

If this was the sacrifice Hazel needed to make to become the Ivory Fawn, she would already have wings and be glowing, but there was nothing. She hadn't become the Ivory Fawn, which meant he helped the Netherian plague on his home win. Nothing would stop them from taking the precious kingdom he loved over because the one person who could stop him was now going to die.

He felt himself slip into darkness, unable to stop falling deeper and deeper into the abyss. Soon, a golden light erupted from the darkness.

Looking toward it, he could see Queen Asteria walking over to him. His heart swelled with a mix of hope and awe as the radiant figure approached. The darkness receded with each step she took, filling him with a profound sense of relief, wonder, and salvation in her presence.

The queen's golden hair stroked the hair from his face with a gentle smile. "You did well, Crimson Dragon, but there is much more to do. She is on the right path. Stay by her side, and she will be safe. He is coming for her, and he will not be alone. Protect her with all your might until the Obsidian Tiger awakens and aids you both."

Atticus' eyes widened hearing there was supposed to be another person to aid them, but in what sense? Opening his mouth to question further, no words came out, and she vanished from view, leaving him to continue his plunge into the dark abyss.

Chapter Fifty-Three

Hazel

The smoke was so dense and suffocating it hurt to breathe. The weight of the beam hurt as the hot wood bit at her skin. "Atticus! Atticus please!" she pleaded to her unconscious prince. They needed to get out of there, but how, with her trapped under the beam? Trying to raise off the floor and push the beam off her, her muscles strained as it was getting more and more difficult to breathe.

Hazel's icy blue shot to Atticus, she reaches for his hand and grabbing it tight in hers before she looked at the dire situation they were in. Her home was engulfed in flames, and if they didn't get out, they would be as well. Looking at Atticus, her heart broke seeing him like this. If she wouldn't have gone after her uncle's ashes, they wouldn't be in this situation. Blinking the tears from her eyes, a cough erupted from her throat, pushing a strand from his face. "We will not die here," she swore to him in his unconscious state.

"for I am the Ivory Fawn, and I will not die!" she cried out to the flames, as if challenging them. Feeling her strength coming to her, Hazel rose off the floor, the beam now weightless on her back. She threw the beam to the side, the beam ripping her dress. She turned to put it over Atticus's mouth, but she caught a glance of herself in the reflection of the mirror beside the entryway, and her eyes widened. Two wings made of golden light were behind her. Not wanting to dwell on it, Hazel quickly turned to Atticus, kneeling down before him.. Hazel then reached toward his neck, feeling for a pulse. It was there, but it was faint.

She grabbed his arm and wrapped it around her neck before hoisting him up. He didn't feel heavy at all. Looking towards her uncle's urn, she took a deep breath. She couldn't carry Atticus and her uncle's urn.

Turning her head, she saw a silhouette in the flames. Staring for a moment, her heart dropped into her stomach as her eyes met her uncle's.

The look in Archibald's eyes was one of aching understanding—an acceptance laced with heartbreak. There was no anger, no blame, only a quiet resignation that spoke volumes. His eyes shimmered with unshed tears, proud and pained all at once, like he was silently telling her *"Go. I know you must."* It was the kind of look that would haunt her, not because he didn't fight her decision—but because he didn't have to. He already knew she was choosing the greater good over the love they could've had.

Dragging Atticus towards the entry, she created a small ball of light, blasting the door open. Adjusting his weight in her arms, she carried him outside to the winter air and the chaos of the villagers trying to put out the fire.

Regulus, the farmer whose son she saved, ran over to her, his eyes widening. "Hazel! Thank the gods!"

Looking at her cottage home engulfed in flames, she couldn't let this fire possibly spread to the village. Turning her head towards the Regulus, she gently handed Atticus to the farmer. "I need you to take him. I have to stop the fire," Hazel said softly. It felt like getting that beam off her had cleared both her head and her lungs. Her wings must've disappeared too, because no one was staring or gawking at her anymore. Hurrying over to some men throwing snow onto the fire, Hazel's hand rested upon the butcher's shoulder. "Get everyone back. The flames are too high. I can handle the rest."

Hazel's determination and confidence in her voice must have been enough to convince the butcher to listen, because he immediately started moving the crowd.

Hazel's thoughts spun as fast as her heartbeat. *Was Darius really the butcher's son? Or just another lie sewn into the fabric of her past?* She didn't know—but she'd find out. When the fire was out. When people were safe. Right now, there was no time for truth or confrontation—only action. The blaze came first. Everything else could burn later.

Reaching into that magic pool, Hazel raised her hands as golden light began to fill the cottage. Taking deep and calm breaths, she focuses on the image inside her mind of her home wrapped in a shield. If it can kept things out, what if she reversed it to keep things in?

"Start throwing snow onto the fire now!" Hazel called out to the bystander, who stood in amazement, but it was the butcher who spoke up.

"You heard her!" he yelled.

The villagers tossed buckets and buckets of snow onto the fire. To her amazement and relief, it worked. The snow passed right through the shield, but the flames never came out, no matter how hard they beat against it.

Slowly, Hazel shrank the size of it, as if snuffing out the flames. With the teamwork effort made by her and the village, the flames soon died out.

Letting the shield fall, Hazel felt overwhelming pride in herself. She had not only protected the rest of the village from catching fire but also controlled her magic, and burn herself out.

"Hazel!" a familiar voice cried out in worry, leading her to turn around to see Kingsly running over. He wrapped his arms around her in a tight embrace. "Oh, thank gods you're okay!"

Returning the embrace, Hazel then remembered Atticus and the state he was in. Pushing Kingsly away, she looked to where she left him with Regulus. "Atticus!" Hazel cried out in worry.

Rushing over to the wagon that had been brought to help carry supplies to put out the fire, Hazel climbed into it, pulling Atticus into her lap and holding him close. Lowering her head, she listened for a heartbeat. A sigh of relief left her chest as she heard the strong, steady rhythm.

Resting her hand over his heart, Hazel took a calming breath to control her emotions and focused on the pool of her magic. She couldn't lose him, not after what they had just done together before that fire. Because for the first time in a long time, Hazel had let herself feel something real—raw, terrifying, and beautiful. She had dropped every wall, every shield, and given herself to Atticus in a way she never had with anyone. It wasn't just about passion—it was the trust, the vulnerability, the whisper of hope that maybe, just maybe, she could have something more than pain and loss. And now, that hope was in danger of being ripped away by the fire. She couldn't lose him—not after giving him all of her. Not after realizing how much she *wanted* to love him.

Slowly, her hand glowed, and that light spread up her arm and throughout her body to where she radiated brightly.

Murmurs from the villagers could be heard, but she blocked them out. Hazel needed to focus on the task at hand. She had already used a lot of her power to get them out of the cabin and extinguish the fire. This was the last thing she needed to do before she could let herself rest. She needed Atticus to be okay.

"Hazel," Kingsly said softly, reaching for her while Atticus lay still in her arms. Pulling away from him, Hazel gathered more of her power to heal him. Atticus would not die in her arms.

"Hazel." Kingsly's voice sounded louder this time, in almost a plea.

Her eyes snapped to his in a sharp glare. "Kingsly shut up!" She snapped before her eyes went back to Atticus. When she saw his eyes flutter open, a joyous sob left her chest. "Oh, thank gods you're okay," she cried, stroking the hair from his face as her glow faded out.

Atticus reached up, wiping the tears from her cheek before he pulled her head down, holding it into the crook of his neck. Hazel didn't care how badly he smelt from the smoke. She was just glad he was alive and well.

"How did you?" he asked hoarsely, holding her close to him.

She ignored everyone else, as if it was just the two of them, relieved to be alive.

"I-I don't know. All I remembered was seeing you laying there nearly dead, and I knew I couldn't let you - let us die in that fire." Hazel pulled away, brushing hair from his face with a small smile. Atticus's eyes filled with a mixture of awe and gratitude as he listened to Hazel's explanation. His voice trembled slightly as he responded, "You saved me, Hazel. I owe you my life." The weight of her sacrifice sank in, and he pulled her even closer, a silent promise of never letting her go.

"Whatever you did, it saved our asses. Thank you, Hazel," he said before softly cupped her chin to brush his lips to hers.

Atticus looked at the crumbling cottage, its walls standing but the roof mostly consumed by flames. Hazel followed his gaze, her heart breaking at the sight of her family home. She slowly climbed out of the wagon, leaving Atticus behind, and approached the ruined house. Kingsly came up behind Hazel and placed a hand on her shoulder, Hazel glanced at the strong, blonde man beside her without turning away from her home.

However, no words came out as she walked towards the ruined home.

Walking across the charred remains of what was once her front door, Hazel stepped into the ruins of her home. The overwhelming scent of burnt wood mingled with scorched herbs and spices from the kitchen, filling her lungs with bitter smoke and memories. Her heart ached as she took in the devastation—where there had once been warmth and laughter, only ashes remained.

Each step felt heavier than the last, her breath caught somewhere between her chest and throat. Her gait faltered, knees threatening to buckle under the weight of grief. She blinked back tears, forcing herself forward, searching for anything worth salvaging—anything that would prove this place had once been a home.

Then her eyes landed on what used to be the leather armchair by the fireplace, now reduced to blackened fragments. A sob caught in her throat. Archibald used to sit there—telling her stories, laughing with her, sometimes falling asleep after long days. The chair was gone, but the memories clung to the air like smoke.

Hazel's knees slammed into the wood floor, biting her knees. Ashes flew up into the air like snow falling around her. A guttural sob escaped her throat, as her eyes never strayed from the burned remains of her uncle's chair.

She can't bear staring at it anymore. Hazel lowered her gaze, closing them, wishing this nightmare would end. Wishing she never lost her home or her uncle.

Why was this happening to her? Was it because she was the Ivory Fawn?

Taking a deep, shaky breath, Hazel looked around her cottage—well, what was left of it—when she remembered she had left her uncle's ashes in here when she was saving Atticus. It was like her body moved on its own as she dug through the rubble, her sobs became louder the longer she searched.

"Hazel, what are you-" Kingsly began, but stopped as Hazel turned quickly cutting him off "I am not leaving my uncle in this rubble!" She lashed at him in her fit of grief. Realizing who she was lashing out at , she was lashing out at Kingsly. Hazel wiped her tears away, smearing more of the ash and soot that now covers her fingers onto her cheek.

Pushing away brittle beams, Hazel ignored the biting pain of the hot embers on burnt wood. She needed to find her uncle. She had lost her home, and she wasn't going to lose her uncle for a second time.

A sound came from the left of her a beam moved. Some naive, foolish side of Hazel hoped her uncle would magically rise up from under it, hug her tight, and tell her everything was okay.

As her head moved toward the sound, she watched as Kingsly shoved it aside to aid her in her search for her uncle's ashes. Her heart swelled in admiration. he was willing to assist her sort through the rubble.

It was like her heart stopped in her chest as she watched the villagers trickling in. They lent a hand to remove the rubble and debris from her home. Regulus came into the cottage along with his son, helping pick up the debris and carry it out. Regulus came over to her, cupping Hazel's soot-covered face as tears poured out of her eyes as if a gusher of water was released.

"You and your uncle have done so much for us and this village. Let us repay that," he said softly as his own broke. Watching all the villagers lending a hand from the children she saved, from Ratherian alongside their parents to the farmer boy and his father who begged Hazel to save them. Her heart swelled even more seeing Tanja, the local healer and her mentor, help clear the debris from her home.

Walking over to Tanja, she took the elder woman's hand. Her long, wavy hair was peppered with brown and gray. Her round glasses hung around her neck, and she smelled of myrrh and bergamot.

The woman said nothing except to pull her into a long and comforting hug, rubbing soothing strokes up and down her back.

"I am so sorry, honey." Her voice wrapped Hazel in a soft and welcoming hug. "He was a great man," Tanja continued before she pulled away, stroking the tears from her face. "Here, my darling," she hummed before removing an Apache tear necklace from around her necklace putting it around its new owner's neck, cupping her cheek. "It won't stop the pain you're feeling, or bring your uncle back, but it will help you navigate your grief." Kissing her head softly, she pulled her in for another hug.

Holding the young woman's hand, Tanja turned Hazel to look around at not only the villagers helping clear the rubble of her home but Kingsly and Atticus helping as well.

"Mama Tanja?" She turned to look at Tanja. She felt lost—utterly confused and conflicted, her emotions a tangled storm. Taking a deep breath, she fought to hold back the tears threatening to spill, desperate to find clarity in the chaos.

She wanted to stay in Alexandria, where she spent her whole life growing up, but she knew there was something calling her back in in Wylana.

It was like Tanja saw the doubt, pain, and fear all in her eyes. Taking her hands, Tanja kissed them softly before stroking her head. "You belong with those princes. There is nothing but pain and grief for you here in Alexandria. Go with them, be happy, Hazel. That's what Archibald would want for you. I am relieved you are with people who love you and want to help you grow."

Her tears fell more from her eyes, washing away the soot and ash on her cheek. Tanja pulled her back into her embrace. Hazel wished the elder healer woman could come with her. "Thank you, Mama Tanja for all you taught me." Hazel breathed as she held Tanja, who only pulled away and smiled.

"I will miss you tremendously, my little spice. I am excited to see all the amazing things you will do in Wylana."

Chapter Fifty-Four

Hazel

Morning rays greeted the somber village of Alexandria as they rose over the mountain tops. Covered in soot, Hazel helped the villagers clear the last bit of her fire-bitten cottage.

The flames had devoured so much of her once joyous cottage, where she first learned to walk with her father, her uncle teaching her how to hunt and sew. As the light of the morning sun came through the holes in the roof, Hazel's ash and soot-covered face embraced its warmth, and a tear fell down her cheek.

The fire had consumed her clothes, leaving her shivering in the winter air. Regulus offered her his cloak for warmth, as she arrived in Alexandria wearing only a burnt orange dress. The fire had destroyed the brown cloak she had originally worn.

Standing in what used to be the kitchen, Hazel looked to what was left of her apothecary her mother built. The was nothing more than some empty jars on the counter, broken jars from falling off the shelves, and whatever plants she had were now ash.

It felt like Hazel's heart was being clawed out of her chest, examining the damage caused by the fire. Slowly her head turned to look towards the dining room. So many memories were now in ashes.

Truly Hazel had nothing left now of her home. It was so difficult to swallow that thought. Her heart pounded in her ear.

Atticus had join her side, his calloused hand on her shoulder was cold to the touch. Giving her a quiet comforting moment. Slowly looking up, Hazel felt as if she was swaying from shock at the extensive damage to her home.

One of Archibald's cloaks survived the fire with just a few minor holes and burns, which now wrapped around Atticus's bare chest since he sacrificed his only shirt to keep Hazel from breathing in the smoke. Lowering her hand to the cloak, Hazel's hand to stroking the fabric. Feeling herself choking up at the memory of her uncle and her in the woods while he wore this, she bit her lip, looking down as she tried to hide the pain.

The overwhelming scent of bergamot and cedar mingled with hints of cinnamon, oranges, and vanilla as Hazel's face pressed against Atticus's cold chest. She wrapped her arms around him tightly.. Hazel imagined the arms that held her tight into a comforting embrace weren't of the prince she fell for, but her uncle.

"It's gone," Hazel said with a breathless cry as she held him.

Atticus wrapped that cloak around her holding her close to him. "Not entirely," he replied before releasing her, tilting her chin up to look at him. Pain, sorrow, and remorse painted his eyes as he stroked her cheek. "It will forever be in your heart."

Wiping her tears away, Hazel took a deep breath, leaning in slowly, brushing her lips to his before resting her head on his chin. "What about my mother's tree?" She was terrified to ask, but in the midst of the chaos of the fire, and nearly losing Atticus, the thought never crossed her mind until now.

His silence was the only answer she needed, she felt her heart clench threatening to break further then it has already loosing her childhood home.. Her mother's tree was gone. There was now truly nothing left for her in Alexandria. Thankfully, they were able to find her uncle's ashes still in one piece and not scatted in the ashes left by the fire, along with the safe return of their horses. However, that was all that remained.

Closing her eyes, she tilted her head back, inhaling deeply before looking at the remains of her home. "Let's go home, please." Hazel's voice held no emotions, just a flat dead tone. "We will, but we first need to get proper travel clothing, a bath, and some food. We can leave tonight." Brushing a strand from her face, Atticus pulled her chin to look at him. A look of concern lined his face. "You know this village better than me. Is there a village or an inn where we can stay for a few hours?"

Hazel only nodded "It's right next to the butcher. It's called the Scarlet Tavern," was all Hazel could voice before she lowered her head to appear down to see she was covered in soot. Hazel didn't even manage to get shoes during the chaos.

Kingsly walked over, looking down at her with a somber look. "I am so sorry, Hazel." Reaching over to stroke her shoulder, Kingsly hesitated at the growl that slipped from Atticus's throat.

Closing her eyes, she didn't care Atticus was being possessive. she just wanted to go back to sleep and wake from this nightmare.

"Hazel said there is a tavern called the Scarlet Tavern beside the butcher. We can eat some proper food and rest there before heading home. Think you can get us some provisions for the road, brother?" Atticus's voice was firm leaving no room for argument.

"Yes, of course," Kingsly replied softly, looking at Hazel, rubbing her arm reassuringly, before leaving.

Clinging onto the borrowed cloak provided to her by Regulus, she walked closely to Atticus and Kingsly. After last night's ordeal, Atticus was at her hip. Hazel didn't care how close he was to her. All she wanted was to get to this tavern where she could soak her sore bones and fall into a much-needed slumber after her night.

Making their way into town, it was as if nothing happened last night. The market was lively, with shop keepers yelling out various things being offered in their shops and booths. Hazel paid no mind to them as she led the way to the Scarlet Tavern. Walking up to a brown archway door, Hazel pushes it inward, stepping onto the entryway balcony. Looking over the railing down to the stone-floor tavern with a larger horseshoe-shaped bar, a wall towered with barrels of various meads and ale. There was a small stage beside the bar where Hazel had heard bards perform different ballads, and different dances performed on that same stage. Hazel remembered the night her uncle brought her here to celebrate her coming of age. How she used to laugh alongside the few friends she had before they were either killed by the Netherian people or taken as Blood Brides. An elderly man was wiping down the bar counter as a few patrons sat at the various tables. Each had a breakfast laid out in front of them.

Atticus and Kingsly walked down the stairs that connected the entryway balcony to the tavern floor. Following them, she held her cloak tight around her, looking around the tavern. "Can we get two rooms for a night? Also, we will have three bowls of whatever you're serving for breakfast, please," Atticus asked the elderly male, who had shaggy gray hair and a long, shaggy gray beard.

The bar keep let out a rough grunt before taking in the trio. From how he looked at her, it was clear the barkeep already knew their predicament. "Thirty silver pieces for the two rooms and breakfast," his gravel-like voice croaked out.

Atticus fished out payment from his pants, which he thankfully recovered in the forest. He handed the coins to the barkeep. Examining it, the barkeep reached down and retrieved two room keys. He handed one key to Atticus and the other to Hazel.

"Thank you," Hazel said softly to the elderly man. She turned to take an empty table directly in front of the bar. A long tablecloth runner ran across it, and four small oval stools surrounded it. The wood table had carvings of tally marks, and a game of tic-tac-toe was also on it.

Sitting down, Hazel scanned the area, keeping herself vigilant, but also hoping that her uncle would walk through those doors by some miracle. However, no one appeared, except for the elderly barkeeper who handed them their food. The aroma of fresh eggs, bacon, and hash browns brought a warm smile to her lips. Feeling him rest his hand on her shoulder, she looked at him, seeing the apologetic frown on his face.

"I'm sorry, missy, for your loss. Archibald was a great man."

Taking his hand, Hazel gave it a squeeze before she released it, watching the bar keep head back to the bar to continue on with his day. The two princes didn't wait to dive into their breakfast, devouring every bite. Kingsly sat in front of her with the same leather armor he wore into town. It will be nice to get cleaned up from the chaos they were faced with last night. Atticus slide closer beside her before nudging her food closer to her, leaning in, and whispering, "You need to eat, princess. You look like you haven't in a few days."

Hazel only looked over at him before forcing a fork full of eggs and hash browns before chewing up a few pieces of bacon. She wasn't very hungry, but it tasted really good. Shoving a bit more into her mouth, she pushed the food away, looking down. "I am going to wash up before I get some rest," Hazel said softly, not to either prince in particular.

They both looked at her before Kingsly spoke up. "I can get you a warmer cloak and attirc for you in the market. What is your favorite color?"

Hazel didn't look to meet Kingsly's eyes, who stared at her attentively. "Lavender is my favorite color. It reminds me of my mother. As for shirt and pants size, a medium is just fine." Atticus's hand went to the small of her back, rubbing soothing strokes up and down.

"When you're in the market, Can you fetch me a warm cloak and shirt? Preferably black. I will leave you in charge of getting provisions," the crown prince chimed in, looking at his brother. "I will stay here with Hazel till you return," Atticus continued as he looked to Kingsly who only nodded in agreement to the plan. He led Hazel to the room they were staying in together.

Opening the rusty wooden door, Hazel glances up at an oak wood bedroom, two windows where the morning sun now lit the tavern room. A small chest sat under the window, beside a room divider, but she could tell from the silhouette of the rays coming from the window that on the opposite side was a large oval bathtub. Atticus came in behind her, closing the door behind them while taking in the room. A nightstand sat beside a bed with red comforters neatly made with a long ivory pillow beneath two golden pillows. Although that was the only bed in the room, it shouldn't have bothered her after what they did last night, but for some reason, seeing they were sharing another bed tonight made her nervous.

Hazel's eyes went to Atticus's as He looked at her, tucking a strand behind her ear. "Do you want to get some rest before I run you a bath?" he asked gently, seeing the exhaustion in her face.

Hazel only leaned into his touch, taking his hand into her. "I want to clean up before I get some sleep. Would you help me?" she replied softly, looking up at him. There was a look in his eyes that was so soft and desirable, like the gentle glow of a candle flickering in the evening breeze. It was a gaze that seemed to envelop everything it touched with warmth and affection, as if his very eyes were speaking a language of their own. Hazel wondered what was going through his mind, but she didn't care. She was just glad he was alive and, more importantly, with her.

Atticus walked towards the room divider, starting to warm up the bath for them both. Thankfully, it was big enough for two. Looking out the window beside the bath on the other side of the divider, Hazel looked down into the busy streets of Alexandria before looking up to watch the swaying Raven Palm trees in the distance, remembering how far she had come since she had last been here.

She was no longer that scared little fawn, but a warrior in the making. She finally knew how to defend herself. After last night, Hazel realized she was mastering her magic and no longer needed her mother's necklace to prevent burnout. There was a new feeling in her chest. Not know if it was pride in herself or sorrow that the one person she wanted to tell all the progress she had made was dead.

Rough, calloused hands met the small of her back. The steam filling the room helped give it more warmth. Hazel looked over her shoulder at Atticus, who now stood towering beside her with no shirt on.

Her eyes met the dragon's eyes, inked forever into his chest. Reaching for his tattoo, she turned to face him. She stroked the dragon's head, closing her eyes softly, biting her lip, her breath becoming shaky.

"It's okay to cry. It means you're healing, Hazel."

It was like his words melted that wall made of steel she had built around her heart, making her feel so numb. Was now flooding her with the overwhelming sorrow and pain she tried to keep locked out.

Atticus wrapped his arms around her and pulled her into his chest, holding her tightly to him until she was ready to move. Weeping into his arms, Hazel held onto him, trembling as an agonizing sob pooled out of her. He did nothing but stand there holding her, stroking a calming stroke up and down her back. "He would be so proud of you, Hazel. You have come so far."

Her weeping became a bellowing of sorrow as Hazel held onto him tighter.

Atticus said nothing further as she sobbed to the point she had no more tears coming from her eyes and her throat was too sore to continue making any sounds.

The crown prince removed her cloak and dress, lifted her into the bath, and lowered her into the hot water.

She slowly melted into the water. Letting her sorrow and pain fading away in that same bath water as she relaxed. Closing her eyes softly, Atticus took a sponge and dipped it into the water. "Let's get this soot off you."

Hazel didn't protest as he raised her arm out of the water and scrubbed her with that sponge. Hazel's mind went blank as the crown prince washing her down. *Her* crown prince. Atticus was hers and she was his. Finally. At last, they could find happiness with one another.

Atticus stopped his hand right above her collarbone. "Who did that to you?" His voice sounded low and menacing, causing Hazel's eyes to open.

She looked to see the small scar that was a few five inches on her right breast. "My father... He tried to get rid of me when I was a child." Her voice was so dead and emotionless that Hazel wasn't surprised to see Atticus's face was a tableau of conflicting emotions as she told him bluntly why the scar existed. His eyes widened, then narrowed, absorbing every word like a slow-motion punch, the muscles in his jaw tightening involuntarily.

"Why would he do that?" Atticus growled out.

"My father blamed me for the death of my mother. I accidentally caught the attention of a Netherian man by using my magic. If I had listened, my mother wouldn't have died.

My father slashed my chest open with a knife. My uncle intervened to protect me and killed my father. I was merely a toddler. I didn't know he did it until my uncle told me when I was older."

Atticus leaned down, running a hand over that small scar with a somber look. The touch made Hazel shiver. His face was a storm of emotions, a mix of confusion and something deeper that tugged at her heart. She reached out, her fingers brushing against his cheek, feeling the warmth and the subtle tension beneath her touch. "Don't look at me like that," Hazel said, which caused Atticus to look at her.

"Like what?" he replied.

Hazel frowned before leaning in and kissing him deeply, stroking his cheek. Resting her head on his forehead, she said, "Like I am some little girl who needs someone to protect her from her past. I have come to terms with what happened to me in the past. Although, I wouldn't change it, because if I did, I wouldn't be here with you right now."

Atticus was taken back by her words but chuckled, kissing her forehead and stroking her cheek with a smile. The icy blue met with those pools of honey. "The moment I saw you, I knew you were a warrior. I was just waiting for you to finally admit how brave, strong, and resilient you were. Why do you think I was so hard on you? It drove me mad seeing you doubt yourself so much when I saw so much more."

Hazel smiled before pulling him closer to her, nuzzling her cheek into his. Placing his hand into the water towards her exposed core, a feral smirk grew on his lips as he pulled back, looking at Hazel. "Gods, you're going to be my undoing and my beginning."

Chapter Fifty-Five

Hazel

The warm duvet cover wrapped Hazel around in the most nurturing embrace, cradling her into slumber. She was wearing a clean cream long-sleeve linen nightgown brought by Kingsly, who had returned from his market shopping to get her something to sleep in. Kingsly got her a lovely golden fleece cloak, a simple brown skirt, and a beige puffy long-sleeve blouse. Hazel was impressed with his eye for shopping for a woman, but when she learned he had help from Tanja, it explained why it was right for Hazel.

Atticus helped her braid her hair. When she questioned him how he even knew how to braid, he explained Atticus would help Kingsly braid his hair. Now her prince was looking into getting them a wagon to carry their provisions for the trip home, Kingsly gathered for the three of them back home.

Hearing voices in the other room beside hers, Hazel's eyes fluttered open. So much for getting some sleep. Lying in her bed, she rolled to her back, stared up at the ceiling, and took a deep breath. The room wasn't all that pleasant, with its faint musky smell and floral aroma. Looking to her right she could see on the nightstand there was a fresh bundle of lavender in a vase. Rolling to her side, she reached for the note, smiling.

Lavender is supposed to symbolize grace and serenity, but it also means devotion. Let this bundle be my symbol of my devotion to you, my fawn princess.

-A

Atticus must have left these for her when she slept, hence why she slept so calmly. Leaning over, she stroked the petals with a faint smile, worried if she applied too much pressure to her stroke, the lavender bud would fall. Hearing the voices in the other room rising, she paused for a moment, realizing the room the voices she was hearing from was actually Kingsly. Getting out of the bed, the cold wooden floor creaked under her feet, Hazel grabbed her cloak walking over to the door, opening it. Listening for a moment in the hallway, she left it open, afraid if she closed it, it would alert the commotion to a halt.

Silently walking over to Kingsly's room, she reached to knock on it.

"This is not what I had in mind when Duvessa said I would be King!" Kingsly's voice ground out. There was pure rage behind his voice, which caused Hazel's body to freeze.

"What did you expect, Prince? That your brother would be exiled and would you get to live happily with the girl?"

Where had she heard that voice before? It sounded so familiar. "Come now, you can't be king, *and* also get the girl, especially with who she is."

Hazel's breath snagged in her throat. Hearing this.

Who was this person? Why did he sound so familiar?

"What I didn't expect was for you to not only nearly kill my brother, but nearly kill her as well. Hazel is not to be harmed, am I clear?" he growled out to the stranger.

"I cannot make any promises she won't be harmed with her being so close to your brother. There is a possibility she can be collateral damage if you don't keep her away from him." The voice was familiar, yet cold.

Her heart was racing inside her chest. Was this really happening? Was she really hearing that Kingsly had some sort of connection with her cottage burning down?

"Then our deal is off. I will not allow her to be so-called collateral damage for my desire to rule. I will find another way," Kingsly replied sharply.

There was only a dark, deep chuckle behind that door in response.

She knew that chuckle. Her heart plummeted into her chest as she covered her mouth, trying to keep the bile that crept up her throat down. Sounds of footsteps came towards the door, and Hazel's heart dropped more. She went to move, but it was like her feet were rooted to that tavern floor. The door opened, revealing an amber-shaded room illuminated by setting rays and two wall-mounted candles above the bed. Hazel froze in disbelief at what she heard, then saw a cloaked figure standing there. She couldn't see the wearer, but a black hand emerged to adjust the hood.

"Hazel?" Fear and panic lined Kingsly's voice as he looked at her, whose eyes were fixed on the other figure.

The aroma of salt and iron filled her senses, causing her body to seize up. There is only one person she know that smells like that.

The cloaked figure walked towards the door with a faint chuckle. "I shall take my leave."

The voice, the chuckle, that scent. Every alarm in her body screamed at her as the cloaked figure walked past her and down the hall.

"Hazel, let me explain." Reaching for her hand with a pleading expression, but she ripped it away from Kingsly, stepping back. Pure horror filled her face as it paled. Shaking her head, she headed towards her bedroom. "Hazel, wait!" Kingsly called out as he gave chase as she rushed out of the room down the hallway.

She tried to close the door on the general prince, but he was too fast.

He pushed it open, closing the door behind them. "Hazel, it's not what it sounded like," Kingsly began pleading his case once more, but all Hazel could hear was a roaring in her ear.

Bracing herself on the sink, her chest rose and fell as she forced air into her lungs. There was no way this was actually happening. Hazel forced out her flooding memory from three months ago.

"You're working with Darius?" Her words came out sharp and clipped as fear turned to hurt, now knowing the truth.

She didn't know it was Darius, not till she smelt the iron and salt. It was something she will never forget..It was as if hearing the name Darius made Kingsly freeze. His expression went from confusion before gradually transforming into horrifying realization .

Scoffing softly, Hazel shook her head. "He didn't even tell you who he was, did he?" Hazel swallowed the bile. Turning her body to fully look at him, her eyes narrowed. "What deal did you make with him in order to become king, huh? You would honestly kill your own brother to take the throne?"

Kingsly stepped forward, narrowing his eyes to Hazel. "Watch your treasonous mouth."

"Or what, Kingsly? You will kill me, too?" Hazel replied, showing no fear as she stared at him down despite her trembling hands.

Kingsly sighed softly, shaking his hand and running his hand over his braided gold hair. "Derek, well, Darius said if I helped him and Lady Duvessa in framing Atticus, they would convince my father to allow me to become king instead of my brother. You were not supposed to be..."

Hazel's eyes widened in shock, her mouth was slightly agape as she struggled to process the betrayal. Her brow furrowed deeply, and she took a step back, trying to distance herself from the harsh reality of Kingsly's confession.

"Lady Duvessa? You're telling me you and Lady Duvessa have been working together? She is one of *them*, for fucking sake, Kingsly! How blind can you be?" Hazel's voice erupted in anger as her hands began to glow from her growing rage.

Shock lined Kingsly's face as Hazel could see his mind racing. "But she is—"

Hazel cut in with a disheveled laugh broke from her. "She isn't Netherian? That necklace I wore when you first met me, I learned from experience that it warms when someone who uses their magic is near. It has warmed on several occasions with her near."

Kingsly lunged for her arm. "Hazel-" but a cone of golden light wrapped around him, holding him in place. He struggled against it, and looked at Hazel with a mixture of anger and panic.

"Hazel." His mouth wrapped around with that same golden light as a tear fell down Hazel's cheek.

There was a slam of a door so hard the door hinges rattled. "Hazel, what is this?" It was a cold, lethal, calm voice that came from Atticus.

Hazel's eyes went to his now deep onyx eyes. Eyes that were now locked onto the restrained Kingsly. She swallowed, looking back at Kingsly, whose face whirled from his brother before snapping his attention back to Hazel, shaking his head, as if silently pleading her not to say anything. She refused to cover for him. "He is working with Darius, the fire was his fault, and I'm pretty sure the only reason he brought me here was so he could speak with Darius. Kingsly was planning to frame you to be seen as unworthy of your crown so he could take it." Hazel's voice clipped as tears fell. Her eyes burned into Kingsly's panic-filled ones as she confessed everything she heard. "Darius, Lady Duvessa, and Kingsly were all in on this plan." Her voice broke for a moment as she looked down, unable to see the rage she felt pooling off of Atticus and the panic in Kingsly's eyes.

She thought being betrayed by Darius hurt. This hurt far more.

How did she not see this? Hazel knew Kingsly was jealous of his brother, but this—to go to this length and use her in the process? She turned her body away from the princes, bracing herself against the sink again, inhaling sharply from the blow of the betrayal.

"You bastard!" Atticus roared.

Watching Atticus slam his full strength into Kingsly's jaw, causing his face to whip to the side.

Letting her focus slip for a moment, the shield fell around Kingsly, who quickly rose to his feet, standing up and rubbing his jaw with one hand.

"Atticus, wait!" Kingsly pleaded. Hazel saw the fear in his eyes as he backed away from his brother.

"Your jealously nearly got her fucking killed!" Atticus bellowed, swinging on his brother, who ducked beneath the swing.

Kingsly's foot met Atticus's chest, shoving him back. "I didn't mean to! It wasn't supposed to happen this way!" he replied, getting ready for his brother's next attack.

Hearing the singing of steel ring out, Atticus gripped his sword tightly. "I'm going to rip you to fucking shreds!"

Hazel's eyes widened as she saw how heated their fight was getting. At first, she wanted to let Atticus and Kingsly fight this out, and even thought she was beyond angry, she didn't want either one of them to get seriously hurt.

Running to stand between the two, Hazel gripped Atticus's wrist holding the sword, before reaching a hand up to stroke his cheek. He shoved Hazel aside hard enough that she tripped on her own feet.

Atticus lunged for his brother, who, with his combat skills, managed to dodge the attack in time. Taking advantage of his brother's momentary recovery, Atticus launched a counterattack.

He swung his sword down, but his brother had recovered swiftly and caught the wrist holding the sword. To Atticus' surprise, it wasn't Kingsly who held his wrist, but Hazel, who had grabbed his hand. The force of Hazel's fist connecting to his jaw caused him to lose grip on the sword, and he stumbled backward, landing on his back.

"Enough, Atticus!" Hazel held such command and strength as she stood her ground, staring down the enraged Immortal Dragon. Hazel gripped the sword tightly in her hand not knowing who she was more upset with, Kingsly for betraying her, or Atticus who was now trying to kill his brother

"I trusted you. I let you comfort me at my mother's tree. You were so sweet and caring. When you messed up on that balcony *and again* in your bedroom, I gave you another chance. You were there for me when my uncle died and at his funeral. How could you do this?" She did not look at the general prince, who was directly behind her, as there was a shift in her.

Turning to look at Kingsly, who stared up at her in disbelief she disarmed Atticus so quickly.

"Get up," she ground out. Not wanting to be on the receiving end of her wrath, Kingsly rose to his feet, his focus shifted between Hazel and then to the sword, whose eyes now stayed on the sword. His eyes widened.

"Hazel." Atticus's voice seemed calmer now as his hand touched the smalls of her back but she didn't pull away or look at him

"Don't touch me." Hazel's rage and pain bubbled over as her hand continued to glow brighter.

"Hazel, the sword," Atticus replied, his eyes just as wide as Kingsly's.

Gazing down at the sword in her hand, it blazed with an electrifying glow, and suddenly, a mysterious inscription appeared, igniting her spirit with anticipation and power! It vibrated in her hand like Hazel felt when she was at the Andromeda castle.

Chapter Fifty-Six

Hazel

As Hazel glanced down at the long hilt, it looked ordinary, but as she looked closer, the leather wrap seemed bulkier than a normal sword's would be.

Her eyes spied a part of the leather was not unraveling from the humming of the handle which was vibrating. Slowly peeling if off, Hazel revealed the original wrap, which was a breathtaking lilac color, with ivory and gold swirls engraved into it. Slowly unraveling that black leather more, the air grew taunt, with no words being exchanged between the trio as their eyes were solely focused on the sword.

Hazel held up the vibrating steel to examine it further. The cross guard was an array of gold vines to set a barrier between the fuller and the cross guard. sword. Running her hand over the inscription, a sharp gasp fell from Hazel's lips, feeling the surge of power the sword erupted into her touch.

"Is that..." Kingsly breathed in disbelief, but Hazel's attention never came off that blade.

Its fuller was gold along the edge, but the middle was ivory steel. On the edge, it had a glowing inscription on the

Her eyes shot up as the room around her faded away. She now saw Queen Asteria, lying in the arms of a male with long silver blonde hair, his wings in an array of caramel, earthy tones like a tawny owl, holding her under the tree.

Asteria's eyes went to Hazel as she muttered under her breath,

"You are almost ready. He is nearly upon you. Use the sword to help bring back our people beside the Obsidian Tiger." Her voice was filled with so much pain and sorrow.

As if slamming back into her body, Hazel inhaled sharply.

When her eyes went to a slowly dimming sword, the inscription no longer glowing. Her hand trailed over the blade before Hazel's eyes slowly rose to look at the two princes, who now stared at her in disbelief. She took a deep breath to steady herself as the humming of the steel dimmed to a quiet buzz. Who was the Obsidian Tiger? Was she not supposed to be ruling beside Atticus?

"Where did you get this?" Hazel asked Atticus as she watched Kingsly. The general's face was awestruck by what she held inside her hand.

"It was inside the water pool beside the mother's grove tree," he replied softly. "I took it because I knew it belonged to the queen, and I wanted to keep it safe."

Not allowing her eyes to come off her ancestral blade, Kingsly processed the information along with what she learned.

"How long?" Hazel's voice was cold and flat.

"Since you arrived at court two months ago." His voice was hesitant.

Hazel glanced in Atticus' direction, who stood behind her. "You didn't think of giving me the sword sooner? Were you planning to keep it for yourself?"

Did Atticus know this sword was the key to returning her people? Was this just another secret he kept from her?

"It's not like that, Hazel." He stepped toward her, reaching for her.

Hazel backed a step away from Atticus before looking at Kingsly. "We leave now for Wylana. There is something I need to do. The sooner we are there, the better." Her voice was powerful and demanding as she looked at the sword belt around Atticus. "I will take that."

Without protest or question, he handed it over

Her focused back to Kingsly, who still stood there in awe. He didn't even moved an inch as Hazel put the sword in the sheath.

"Dragon, tie him up and prepare for the ride home. Wagon or not, we are leaving," Hazel ordered, Atticus did exactly as she commanded.

Her prince approached to help her in the saddle, but Hazel climbed into it without any complications.

"Hazel, listen, I was planning to give you the-"

"And I thought we agreed on no more secrets. You should have told me at the cabin at least before I let you take me to bed," she replied quickly, cutting him off.

Looking at Kingsly, whose hands were now restrained with rope and tied to his saddle horn, he kept his eyes toward the ground.

"I swear to you, Hazel, no more secrets, but, what are you planning? Let me help." Resting his hand on her knee, Atticus watched her closely.

Hazel's eye turned to his hand, swallowing for a moment. If what the queen told her was true, it only confirmed that she would survive this prophecy, but Atticus wouldn't be at her side. Who was the Obsidian Tiger? She was praying to the gods. it wasn't of all people, Darius. no, she knew he wanted her dead.

Her gaze was drawn to the sword on her hip, feeling how it buzzed in response to her presence. "We can talk about it when we get home. However, right now, we need to leave if we want to get home on time for the ball. It's a week away. Once home, I need you, Sybilla, and Ardnaxela to teach me the history of the sword and how to fight with it."

Atticus exhaled silently, nodding his head without arguing or protesting, "As you wish, princess." He winked at her causing her cheeks to warm up along with her core.

However, she shoved it down before taking the lead. Atticus rode behind both Kingsly and Hazel to watch his brother and her backs.

Hazel didn't remember much of their ride home, remembering bits and pieces of their ride as well as the light conversations. The sun rose in a warming orange glow, painting the winter sky with hues of lilacs, orchids, pinks, and burnt orange. It rose above the ocean peak, lighting up the Wylana castle in all its glory as ivy vines crept up its white pillars.

During the two-day ride, Hazel and Atticus did not touch one another, not with Kingsly tied up the whole trip. It was a challenge for Hazel to see him as a prisoner after they were just now working on their friendship , but he didn't even try to plead his case to either one of them or demand they let him go. Hazel could sense the deep emotional turmoil his foolish deal with Darius had left him in. She observed the silence, the averted eye contact, and the distancing himself from Hazel.

Hazel almost felt sorry for him seeing that guilt eating away at him, but then she reminded herself that Kingsly helped Darius burn down her home, and would have succeeded in killing both Atticus and herself if her magic hadn't saved them.

Looking to her saddle bag, Hazel found Atticus had packed her uncle's urn after they retrieved it from the rubble of their cottage home. Without her mother's tree, she couldn't bear the thought of scattering his ashes there.

Ardnaxela rode up to the approaching guards on horseback, mounted on a beautiful white mare. She must have spotted their return to the area so quickly.

"What in the hell is going on?" she asked, looking at Kingsly. Ardnaxela's eyebrows rose as she turned her head to Atticus. Her jaw twitched as she stared in an accusatory look, opening her mouth, but it was Hazel who spoke first.

"I had him tied up. He was aiding Darius and nearly cost Atticus and me our lives in a fire he caused ." Her voice strained at the last part, but she held herself high.

Ardnaxela's eyes widened before she looked at Atticus, who nodded his head in confirmation.

Kingsly remained silent as Hazel observed the icy, piercing gaze directed at him by the White Dragoness. "I can take it from here. You got some rest, and you." Her glare went to Hazel, who swallowed, seeing that look now on her. "Don't think you get to skip almost a week of training without any consequences."

Hazel's throat dried up at what the Dragoness had planned for her, but she took a deep breath and held her head up. "I welcome it, Dragoness." Offering her disappointed friend a smile, the Dragoness lip quirked into a wicked grin.

"Although, there is something urgent I need to speak with Sybilla about. Is she at the Andromeda castle or temple?"

Atticus turned in his saddle to give Hazel a look similar to the curious one Ardnaxela once gave her, but Ardnaxela relaxes in her saddle. "She said she was going to do some research, so I am assuming the castle library." Nudging Phoenix to join Atticus and Kissem's side, Hazel focused her attention to Ardnaxela and Atticus, lowering her voice. "Meet Sybilla and me at the castle library. I've discovered something, but I need to investigate further. Based on my hunch, I believe the answer lies there."

"Are you sure you don't want to wait for us to come with you?" Atticus asked cautiously..

Hazel shook her head with a faint grin. "I will be okay. I can take some guards with me of your choosing to ease your mind."

Ardnaxela glanced over her shoulder at the women who rode up with her. "Raven, Ivy, escort Lady Hazel to the Andromeda castle. Any sight of danger, you get her and Lady Sybilla to safety."

Raven, a guard with medium-length hair pulled up into a ponytail with purple ombre coloring, was decorated in black dragon-scaled armor. Hazel was impressed to see how well this woman held herself but there was nothing feminine with her dressing in that armor.

"This is Raven. They are one of the guards I have, who have defended me in many fights." Ardnaxela gestured to the guard on her right before gesturing to the woman on her left. "And this is Ivy."

Hazel could have sworn fire licked up the woman's red hair and into the high raised ponytail to show off the sharp figure's piercing green eyes. The way she held herself in the saddle with a hand on the pommel of her broadsword. Hazel swallowed hard, feeling slightly intimidated by the black armor that matched Raven's, except for the white cape over her right shoulder. "These are my most trusted friends and some of the finest guards in the Wylana arsenal. They will keep you safe."

Taking a deep, steadying breath steadying herself. Hazel thought that Ardnaxela was intimidating. However these two came a close second to being just as frightening. Hazel knew she needed to find Sybilla and ask her what she knew of the prophecy. What if there was more to the prophecy than they knew? Hazel knew Sybilla would be the one to know.

Looking at Atticus, Hazel leaned in and kissed his cheek. "We can talk later, I promise," she spoke in a soft, low tone, stroking his cheek, not caring that people were now watching.

Atticus only took her hand and kissed it softly. "Just be careful."

Turning her gaze to the two female warriors, she pulled her reins to steer her horse in the direction of the Andromeda castle, nudging Phoenix's soft side with her leather riding boots to a canter towards Sybilla and the truth that may lay in the immense-sized library.

Chapter Fifty-Seven

Hazel

Arriving at the Andromeda castle, Hazel's heavy breath swirled in front of her in the crisp winter air as she pulled Phoenix's reigns to a halt. Adjusting her reins in her beige buckskin gloves, she stared up at the castle.

Feeling Raven joining her right side, Hazel looked to her right slightly, taking in the woman adorned in black armor. With everything she has endured, she has a hard time trusting strangers now. It helped they came with Ardnaxela's blessing, but she still struggled.

"Are you alright, Lady Hazel?" Ivy asked from her opposite side in a flat tone.

Hazel nodded her head before looking to the castle and nudging Phoenix to continue on.

Dismounting her horse once they came to a halt, she handed Ivy the reins, rubbed the gelding's neck, and looked up to the scarlet-haired guard. "I shouldn't be long," Hazel assured but before heading up the grand stairs leading to the castle doors.

Raven spoke up. "Then I will accompany you while Ivy stays here with the horses." Glancing at the guard she nods her head before heading inside.

Walking into the library, Hazel's hand rested on the pommel of her sword Atticus had concealed from her. She looked around the large white stacks of shelves that held up a secondary floor of more shelves. Hazel's focus fell upon the portrait of Queen Asteria. Slowly walking over to the portrait, she examined it closer.

Those icy blue eyes fell upon the necklace her mother had passed down to Hazel on the portrait. Her hand came up to her chest, where the necklace no longer sat. As Hazel learned to control her magic and fight properly, she didn't feel as if she needed to wear it anymore.

Hazel's gaze came to the bottom right corner of the portrait where she saw the queen's hand relaxed on a sword, the same sword now resided on Hazel's hip. Running her hand over the crackling paint of the portrait as Hazel's hand mirror the placement on the pommel, mimicking how her ancestor was sitting in the portrait.

Unable to peel her eyes away from the painting. Slowly, her hand slid off the pommel of the sword down to its handle, where she felt it warm beneath her hand. Looking down at the blade, it emanated a glow that faded in and out from the sheath as if it were a slow heartbeat.

Looking at the portrait again, Hazel took a deep breath before hearing soft footsteps approaching from behind. Turning upon instinct, she withdrew it, despite having very little skill with it, to see Sybilla's wide doe gaze upon it.

Lowering her blade slowly, Hazel's hand traveled down to the sword, examining it before she walked up to Sybilla. "Syb, what do you know about this and the prophecy?"

"I know that was one of your ancestors. It was named the Light-Bringer. From what I've read, it only emanates a blinding purifying light when in the hands of a true ruler."

Hazel's attention went to the sword that had only given off a soft glow since she'd had it in her possession.

Will it give off that blinding like when she became the Ivory Fawn? Or was it just responding to the magic inside of her?

Approaching the sword, Sybilla examined the writing on it, angling her head to read the inscription, as if trying to decipher it. She then ran her hand along the blade, right over the inscription.

"When I held it, I saw Queen Asteria... It looked like she was dying," Hazel spoke cautiously to her friend, not sure how the scribe would respond. It wasn't surprising to her, seeing the shock on her raven-haired friend's face.

"She said I was almost ready, that he was almost upon us, and that I must use this somehow to bring back my people alongside the Obsidian Tiger," Hazel continued, looking at the portrait before looking to Sybilla. "The only thing is, I don't know how I'm supposed to use it to bring them back or who this Obsidian Tiger is. That's why I need your help. Do you know if the sword can do anything else other than produce blinding light?"

Sybilla stood there with an expression that made Hazel nervous. For a moment the scribe stands there before morning to search the inner archives of knowledge with the Aestival lore in her mind as she ran her hands over spins of books. Sybilla paused for a moment, a look of confusion on her face as she spoke up. "You said he is nearly upon us. *Who* is nearly upon us?"

Hazel didn't know who Asteria was warning her about until now, and it made her stomach sick. "Only one I can think of is Darius. He was my ex-fiancee that Atticus and Kingsly saved me from after he tried killing me. He has a strong connection to the Netherian magic. Darius doesn't want this prophecy to come true."

Sybilla shook her head. "Well, let get you back into training, so when the time comes you are prepared. As for the knowledge of Light-bringer, all I know is it has a blinding light when in the hand of a true ruler. And as for the Obsidian Tiger, I haven't come across anything that mentions an Obsidian Tiger. Did Asteria mention anything about who he be? What he looked like , or when he would come? "

Although seeing something click in Sybilla's mind open up for a moment, no words came out before turning to the rows of shelves, looking for something among them where they stood. "Wait, there may be something."

The scribe, who wore her jade tunic with beige trousers with her hair pulled up into a messy bun, turned with a quicken pace down the enormous stacks of shelves. Turning and walking along one of the large bookshelves of the library, Hazel's eyes widened at the hundreds of thousands of books of various sizes that filled them. They were so high that a sliding ladder was needed to reach the highest shelves.

Sybilla and her companion walked along a long aisle of books until they reached the end. Sybilla slowed down to look up at the shelves and then climbed the ladder, taking about three steps. Reaching her hand over to a title, she pulled out a worn brown leather book. "There you are." Sybilla stroked its leathery spine. Climbing down the ladder, she quickly made her way to a small rectangular table. Sitting down at the table and opening the book, Hazel followed silently, watching the scribe's eye scan the text on the table before "Here!"

Hazel stepped over to her friend, Sybilla, and read the foreign words on the page, looking at Sybilla with confusion. "What am I looking at?"

"Right, you can't read the Aestival script. Sorry. It says that a sword can connect you with your ancestors and previous rulers before you." Hazel's gaze came up to meet Sybilla's bright wanderlust eyes as the scribe continued, "Asteria was the last documented ruler during the Blood War with the Netherian people before they were snuffed out. If you saw Queen Asteria when you took that sword, you might be able to use it to connect with her to answer some questions."

Looking down at the sword, Hazel stared at it before withdrawing it. Light-bringer's appearance was just an ordinary-looking sword. "But how? When I took the sword from Atticus to stop the fight I didn't notice at the time it was glowing, I was scared he was going to kill Kingsly. It was glowing slightly earlier, when I was looking at the portrait of my ancestor, but that's it."

"Wait. What? What do you mean *going to kill Kingsly*? Hazel, what happened while you were gone?" Sheer worry and panic in Sybilla's voice, which only made Hazel's throat tighten up. A lot had happened these past five days.

Opening her mouth to speak, her words didn't come out. Instead, a male's deep voice was heard behind her in an irritated grumble. "Kingsly aided in an assassination attempt on my life. Hazel was caught in the crossfire as collateral damage. If it wasn't for her and her magic, both she and I would have burned alive in her family cottage," Atticus replied to Sybilla before walking over to Hazel, resting a hand on the small of her back and speaking. "Are you alright?"

Nodding, she offered a soft smile "I'm fine." Hazel's mind then slipped to the consequences that Kingsly may be facing, opening her mouth to ask what happened. Atticus spoke softly. "After father lost his cool , I'm shocked he didn't whipped him a bit , but he is getting a fair trial; he has been stripped of all titles till the trial. Till then he will sit in a cell in the dungeon till after the ball when he is summoned."

"Which I think is being too kind for trying to kill his own brother and recklessly endangering others. Treason is treason, no matter who commits it." Ardnaxela's venomous tone made Hazel's skin crawl, swallowing hard being on the receiving end of that anger as the White Dragoness in her armor stood beside Atticus. "Why did you need to come here so urgently? You didn't want to wait for Atticus and I?" The White Dragoness asked. Hazel looked at the sword, showing it to Ardnaxela, whose eyes widen in shock. "Light-Bringer showed me Queen Asteria when she was dying. Asteria told me I was almost ready and that it could be possible that Darius is almost upon us. I have a feeling he is coming here to finish off what he started in the Raven Palm forest and stop me from completing the prophecy."

Atticus' fingers curled into the small of her back as he stood closer to her, The look on his face was pure anger, but he composed himself. "Well then, we cannot waste another moment. We pick up the speed on training, get you able to wield Light-Bringer, and improve your abilities with your magic." Atticus's voice was not one of a request but rather a demand as he looked to Sybilla and Ardnaxela.

They both nodded their heads in agreement.

"I can meet you three in the courtyard back in Wylana. Let me see what spells I can dig up that could be of some use and won't be too difficult to learn," Sybilla replied, closing the book beside her on the table.

"If we don't want to waste time since you got your new sword, lets show you how to use it properly, in the Andromeda courtyard," Ardnaxela suggested, looking among the trio.

Hazel looked down at her clothing,. "seeing I'm not really outfitted to train. Not with me in a skirt and puffy blouse I don't think training in the snow will help me;"

"Syb, do you know if any of the old wardrobes or rooms have clothing in them that could work?" Atticus asked as his fingers unraveled their tight grip as he began a soothing stroke to calm Hazel.

"Not something she can train in. If Darius is likely to arrive at any given time, he won't allow her a moment to change. I think it wise she trains in a skirt and blouse. It's better to learn now than later," Ardnaxela interfered, scowling at Atticus, crossing her arms over her chest.

Taking a step forward, Atticus's mouth opened to say something, but Hazel put her hand on his chest, speaking instead. "Ardnaxela is right. We should practice here. Every minute counts." Hazel could see pride swirling in Atticus's eyes.

"Okay," he said before looking at Sybilla. "See what you can find, and then meet us in the courtyard."

Sybilla nodded her head in response before picking up the book she had on the table. Hazel watched Sybilla pull the book they were reading about Light-Bringer from the towering bookshelves as they walked to them.. Ardnaxela and Atticus followed the scribe in tow.

Hazel bit her lip and grabbed Atticus's wrist, stopping him. She glanced at the White Dragoness, whose eyes followed Hazel's grip where the dragon prince's tail coiled around his wrist.

"Ardnaxela, I need to speak with Atticus. Give us about five minutes and we will join you. I promise," Hazel said not looking at Atticus.

Ardnaxela only scoffed. "Five minutes, nothing more." With those stern words, she vanished into the stacks of books.

Taking a deep breath, Hazel looked up into Atticus's eyes. No more secrets, they promised one another, but he kept that secret of the Light-Bringer. Hazel opened her mouth to start but no words came out.

Rough callus hands met her soft cheek as Atticus lifted her chin. "What did you find out, Princess?" His brows furrowed, his tone laced with concern as the rough palm of his thumb stroked her cheek.

Inhaling the scent of bergamot and cedar that reminded her of a crisp autumn rainy day, Hazel settled her nerves, not sure how Atticus would react to what she learned about the prophecy. "When I saw Queen Asteria, she told me this sword is supposed to help me bring back my people; we haven't figured out how. Sybilla and I found a book that said the it would give off a blinding light when in the hands of a true ruler. With this, I'm supposed to be able to connect myself with Asteria and previous rulers of my people."

"If the sword connects you to her, you can use it to ask how you're supposed to use the sword. Any possible advantages we can get, we need to take." Atticus suggested

"I know, Atticus. We don't really have time to sit and wait for me to learn how to use Light-bringer in that way," Hazel replied before taking his hand that still lingered on her cheek, holding it tight before lowering it to her side. "Till then, we continued as planned. Knowing Darius, he isn't for subtly. He will want to make a show of it. He may even try to show up at the ball, make a grand show of it "

Sighing, Atticus leaned in, kissing her forehead softly before brushing his lips against hers, resting his large calloused hand at the small of her back while the hand she held was now free, resting on her chin to raise it to meet his lips. "Let the Ivory Fawn reign," Atticus purred upon Hazel's lip as a small curl tugged on the corner of his lips.

Chuckling against his lips, she rested a hand on the side of his warm tan cheek. "Alongside her Crimson Dragon."

Walking down the castle steps with Atticus in tow, Hazel rubbed her arms and took a deep breath. Her cloak flowed behind her as she descended. Despite the cold outside, she was now accustomed to training in the snow. Once they began training, her body warmed up. Atticus kept close as she approached Ardnaxela. Hazel stood in the middle, stretching and warming up. Once at the bottom of the stairs, Atticus leaned in, his warm breath brushing her ear, making her pause. "If you need a warm-up, I have a few ideas." His words were cut short by a grunt as Hazel's elbow met his gut.

"Later," Hazel said with a smirk. Not only in pleasure, Hazel found her mark but grinning at the idea of letting him warm her up when they arrived back at Wylana castle after training.

Removing her cloak, Hazel was ready when the Dragoness approached. She took her place in front of Ardnaxela and held the sword in her hand, adjusting her grip. Looking at her feet, Hazel made sure they were shoulder width apart, just as she had learned. Ardnaxela walked over, prowling around Hazel, examining the young woman's posture before Ardnaxela's sword draws and taps Hazel's elbow, angled upwards awkwardly as she brought it up to her shoulder.

"Adjust your stance, Elbows out. With a long sword, you won't be able to use a shield, so you will need to rely on your quick thinking." A schooling tone came from the Dragoness as she came to stand in front of Hazel. "You have an advantage with your magic. So, use it. If you are able to cast a shield or your magic. You use it. When in battle you take every advantage you can get." Ardnaxela continuously scanned over her posture .

Hazel adjusting her position just as Ardnaxela instructed her. Tightening her grip on the sword, she looked at Ardnaxela's sword, admiring the all-steel work of the blade. Returning her eyes to the Dragoness body language as it shifted. With quick thinking, she drew the sword up at an angle to let the steel of her ancestor's absorb the blow, but the cross guard connected with her nose. Hazel swore under her breath, stepping back and holding her nose, but the Dragoness attacked again. Reacting just in time, Light-bringer clashed with Ardnaxela's , but instead of letting it hit her in the face from the blunt force of the collision. Hazel dug her feet into the ground, shifting her weight, and keeping the sword from hitting her face.

"Good. Again," Ardnaxela praised before using the blade to push off Hazel's sword while she adjusted her posture. Although the young woman took offense this time, holding the sword firmly in her hands, swinging to connect Light-bringer to her Ardnaxela's side, but the steel clashed once more. A blunt force met her nose, forcing Hazel's head back. Stumbling backwards, a warm trickle trailed out of her nose.

"You are small. If you go for larger blows, you leave yourself open. You are predictable. Make yourself unpredictable," demanded Ardnaxela as she came towards her, she swinging her ancestral sword.

If Hazel hadn't acted, she would have been slashed vertically across her chest. As Hazel called upon her magic to protect herself, a dome of golden light rapidly expanded and transformed into a shield around her, intercepting the swift steel before it could reach her. Her hand remained steady on her sword as the Dragoness weapon clashed against the luminous barrier.

A grin curled on Ardnaxela's face, seeing the interception of her sword. "Good girl. Again."

Chapter Fifty-Eight

Hazel

The sun slowly dropped from the sky, wrapping the mountains in its dimming light. Hazel's body ached and roared at her from the vigorous training session with Ardnaxela. Atticus approached Hazel with her cloak in hand. Her body was cold to the touch from the outside elements despite the sweat on her brows.

Tying the cloak around Hazel, Atticus rubbed her arms to warm them up, looking down at her. "Let's get back to the castle to warm you up and get a proper meal for you."

Hazel could get used to this caring side of Atticus as he kissed her forehead and wrapped an arm around her.

Sybilla came down the stairwell with a few books in her hands, dressed for their departure. "Did you find anything out?" Atticus asked.

Atticus let go of Hazel, giving Sybilla his full attention now as the scribe approached. Ardnaxela was sitting on a rock just behind the trio, looking at them as she sharpened her blade.

"No. All I found is that the sword belonged to previous rulers of Andromeda. Nothing about what it can do or how it can be used to help bring the Aestivals back. Although, I wonder if there could be something in these books. I can read them during dinner," Sybilla replied.

Atticus nodded his head in agreement before he looked among the members of their small inner court. "Alright then, we should head home. We can pick up training again tomorrow morning."

Strolling out of Atticus' reach to her horse, Hazel put her sword back into its sheath. As Raven and Ivy waited for the group to mount up before leading the way home.

Arriving at the Wylana castle on horseback, Sybilla and Hazel engaged in casual conversation about their attire for the ball. Hazel was so exhausted that during their ride, Atticus allowed her to ride with him on Kissem while Ivy led Phoenix.

Her muscles were already sore from riding the last two days, but now her body ached and groaned in protest after her swordsmanship training with Ardnaxela.

A stable boy came to collect Phoenix, who gladly bobbed his golden head in greeting. Keeping her cloak wrapped around her, Atticus rested his hand on her shoulder before motioning with his head to take the lead inside the castle. As he guided his friends through the grand entrance of the castle, the enticing aroma from the kitchen wafted through the air, instantly captivating their senses. This particular scent was one of her favorites, evoking memories of warmth and comfort, and setting a welcoming tone for their visit.

Feeling a strong pat on her aching shoulder, Hazel winced before her eyes meet the amber of Ardnaxela's eyes. "Go relax and enjoy the rest of your night. You earned it. We can pick up training tomorrow afternoon. You look like you could use some sleeping in." Joked the warrior in front of Hazel, "I can meet with you first thing in the afternoon to fill you in on everything you missed on your...vacation." Ardnaxela's last words came out sharply.

"I can let you both know if I find anything out about the sword and what it has to do with the prophecy," Sybilla chimed in as the four of them came to a stop in the middle of the hallway in front archway windows.

"Then it's settled," Atticus said with pure confidence, possibly what Hazel could have mistaken for hope before he turned to look at Hazel. I can escort you back to your room if you wish." Feeling his eyes now on her, Hazel looked up into his honey-brown eyes, biting her bottom lip, remembering their night in the cabin before nodding her head.

"I would like that, but I want to find Arabella, she must have-"Before Hazel could get the words out, a soft melody, a familiar voice, came from behind her.

"Worried out of her mind that her friend and lady vanished without a word of where she was going?"

She turned to see Arabella standing in the hallway. The once soft, peach-like face is now lined with anger, coming from the body language her friend now held. Her arms were crossed over her chest just below her breast, Hazel swore she could hear Arabella's foot tapping as well.

Turning her head to look at Atticus, Hazel put her hand on his chest, lowering her voice slightly. "I will see you after dinner," she assured him with a smile. Reaching for his hand, she took the rough callus palm in her own, squeezing it.

He nodded his head before leaning down, lowering his voice to a deep, almost animalistic tone. "Good, because I'm planning to have a honey-dew cream pie for dessert tonight." It wasn't like he cared at all that they had an audience as he lowered his lips to Hazel's neck, hovering her breath over her skin, sending chills through her spine before he pulled away. "I need to check in on Reed and my mother before dinner. I will see you then." That primal predator in her ear was now gone. He was back to being the prince his court knew him by, the Immortal Dragon. With his small display of intimacy in the hallway, he made it clear she was his.

Without another word, bowing his head to Sybilla, Atticus turned away, leaving the handmaiden and fawning over their conversation Hazel was now bracing herself for.

"Ara, I can explain everything, but can we do it in my room? I need a bath terribly after my journey."

Arabella's nostrils flared dramatically, twitching with an involuntary response as if capturing an invisible scent trail. Her eyes squinted slightly, a reflexive action to the sharp, unexpected aroma wafting towards her. The sensation seemed to wash over her like a sudden wave, causing her to momentarily halt her thoughts. As the full extent of the odor reached her, Arabella's expression shifted. "Of course."

The walk down the hall from where she and Atticus split ways included a deafening silent treatment from Arabella. Hazel had never seen her this angry in the time she had known her. It was even more unnerving knowing that the anger was directed toward her and not toward anyone else. Although Hazel couldn't blame the young woman, she and Kingsly told no one where they were going and left in the dark of night with no warning.

Hazel never thought of seeing her chambers in the palace with its white and golden interior, her ivory canopy bed with golden drapes and silk linens would be a welcoming sight after a week being away in Alexandra. Inhaling deeply of the ivy and roses oils being prepared for her bath, Hazel stood by the archway window doors that led out to the balcony

"Your bath is ready." There was no softness to the maiden's tone.

Hazel looked over her shoulder to her friend and saw her anger hadn't faded. Walking with her head lowered, as if she had her tail tucked between her legs, she approached her. "Thank you," Hazel replied softly, walking through the open archway into the white marbled bathroom.

The mirror gathered condensation from the steam coming off the bath water. The aroma of ivy and roses grew stronger as she approached. Dropping her robe, Hazel slipped into the bath. It was scolding hot, just like she liked it. A small satisfied groan escaped her lips as Hazel melted into her bath water, leaning her head back on the rim of the claw-tooth bath. She closed her eyes and tried to settle her mind with everything that had transpired in the last week. She nearly dying again, and then learned Kingsly had been working with Darius and Duvessa. The cherry on top was learning that she wasn't prophesied to rule with Atticus.

Hazel wished that, more than anything, her uncle was here to guide her and give her some advice on what to do, but he could no longer be able to be that father figure she needed. This was all too much. Everything felt as if it was caving in on her. Hazel didn't ask for this, nor did she expect her entire life to be uprooted in a matter of a few months. Slowly, she slid further down into the tub, as far as she could go, letting the scalding hot water lick her cheek, neck, and ears. She stared at the sky, through the sky light, the clouds floating by before letting her face go completely underwater, consuming her. Closing her eyes, she listened to her heartbeat, focusing on it.

All that was around her was the sound of the water moving, her heartbeat, and an inaudible mumble coming from above . Letting the world around her melt away as she went deep into herself, as if she went deep enough, she wouldn't be so overwhelmed. Needing air, she slowly came up to breathe where her eyes met a concerned yet irritated Arabella, who was not sitting beside the tub on a small wooden stool. Arabella went to reach for a sea sponge to begin bathing Hazel.

Hazel reached over, taking the soft, warm, lightly calloused hand into her own. "I am so sorry, Ara. I never met to worry you. I wouldn't blame you if you hated-"

"I don't hate you, Hazel. I am just hurt you couldn't trust me with knowledge of where you were going," Arabella said, cutting her off with a somber look on her face before resting her other hand on top of Hazel's and holding it tight. "I was going crazy knowing you were out there without telling anyone else where you and Kingsly went alone." Hazel opened her mouth to ask how she knew, but Arabella continued, "I ran into Atticus when

Kingsly was being dragged down to the dungeon. He filled me in on what happened." She paused hesitantly before continuing. "I am so sorry about your cottage and your mother's tree, Hazel. I knew how much they meant to you."

Hazel's eyes averted away from Arabella, unable to bear the kindness and pity in her lady's maid's soft, peachy expression. "It's all gone, my old life... I have nothing left." It was as if Hazel's heart-wrenching cry was audibly heard in the room before that gentle hand lifted Hazel's chin, forcing her to gaze at Arabella with tears streaming down her face..

"Not true, Hazel. Your uncle and mother will live inside of your heart forever. The memories will stay with you forever. No one can ever take that away from you. Your cottage and mother's tree? Yes, they held sentimental value, but that isn't what made it home. Home is a place in your heart and not simply where you lay your head down. A home is who you have around you and the memories you make. *That* is what makes a home."

Hazel leaned her head into Arabella's comforting touch, her tears flowing freely as if they could wash away her pain and heartache. She felt utterly lost in darkness, with the world around her losing all significance. Every time she tried to rise, life seemed to knock her back down. Arabella gently cradled Hazel's head as her silent cry turned into a sob. Leaning into Arabella, Hazel finally released the grief, sorrow, anger, and betrayal that had been consuming her for weeks. She had tried to bottle up her feelings, hoping they would just disappear, allowing her to continue her days. But there was only so much one person could contain before breaking apart completely.

Arabella stroked the young woman's golden hair as her sobs became louder. Instead of speaking comforting words, she just held Hazel's head to her chest, letting her get everything out.

"Why me? Why, of all people, am I the one who has their life ripped away? What have I done wrong by living a simple life and trying to help people in any way I can? It isn't fair. I never asked for any of this. I want my old life back. I want my uncle back. I want Darius not to be some evil Netherian male trying to kill me to stop this prophecy. I want to be living in my cottage, raising a family," Hazel choked out,

"I know. Change is the scariest part of life. We get comfortable and content in our normal lives, and once we are content, we are blind to unhealthy things in our lives. Without change, you don't grow. Sometimes, those changes in life lead you to something better." Arabella replied before pulling back to stroke away Hazel's tears. "When you first arrived here in court three months ago, you were a frightened village girl who didn't know who she was. However, now I see a brave and courageous woman who inspires others with her light. You learned not only how to defend yourself, but also how to take control of the power inside of you. Hell, you stood up to Atticus *and* Kingsly, of all people. I am so proud of the woman you are turning into."

With those words, Hazel smiled wide, pulling her friend into a hug, holding onto her tight, not caring if she gets Arabella wet. "Thank you, Ara. You always know how to guide me back to the light."

Arabella chuckled before standing up. "Now let's get you smelling like an actual lady and not a cooked sow," Arabella teased as she began to wash Hazel's hair.

Closing her eyes as Arabella massaged her scalp with the bar of soap that was infused with eucalyptus and ivy, Hazel relaxed further into her bath, noticing with her limbs movements the water wasn't as hot as she first got it. "Ara, about earlier-"

"Let's put it in the past and move forward from here. Just promise me not to just stand up and vanish like that anymore," Arabella cut in as she rinses the soap from Hazel's hair.

Without a word, Hazel nodded her head, inhaling deeply the scent of eucalyptus. A thought crossed her mind that Hazel had never inquired about Arabella's knowledge of the Ivory Fawn.. It was clear that if Atticus told Arabella about what happened in the village, he must have told her something when Hazel arrived at court.

"I noticed that while you were away, you and Atticus became quite intimate. From what I saw, it seems like you had a special encounter."

Hazel's face and neck warmed at the idea of Atticus coming back for some honeydew cream pie, as he referred to it. Gods burn her. The idea alone made the fire in her stir in her core. She tried to think of something to say, but only thing that came out as an inaudible muttering, and Arabella laughed at Hazel's flustered state.

"How about I dress you in something that will drive him wild for you at dinner? Just as we did at your feast."

Hazel didn't need to look at her friend to see the mischievous grin on her face before she laughed softly. "I would love that."

Chapter Fifty-Nine

Atticus

Atticus knocked softly on the queen's door, still dressed in the attire he rode in on. When the crown prince opened the door, he was greeted by Reed, who flung his arms around his waist. "Atti! Thank goodness you're back! Where is Lady Hazel?" The young boy looked around, but Atticus could tell there was something off because the young prince didn't even glance at him directly. His gaze wandered aimlessly over the receiving room, lingering momentarily on the ornate tapestries and the flickering chandeliers. Atticus watched him with concern, noting the slight tremor in his hands and the way his shoulders slumped. It was as if the vibrancy and curiosity that usually danced in the prince's eyes had been replaced by a shadow. "Is everything all right?" Atticus asked.

"Reed." His tone came out lower than he wanted, suspicious of his brother's reluctance to glance at him. He didn't see the happy, outgoing ten-year-old at that moment. "What happened?" Reed kept his head down, swallowing audibly before looking up at the crown prince. To Atticus' shock, Reed's eye darkens of his skin and the puffiness of it. Dropping to one knee, Atticus cupped his brother's cheek, examining his slowly healing eye. "Who did this?" Reed didn't have to say anything. The hesitancy to reply told Atticus exactly who was the culprit that hit him while he and Kingsly were away. "Where is Mother?" Atticus's words came out more panicked than he wanted,.

Reed's eyes misted as his lower lip quivered. "I tried to stop Dad, he-"

"What happened? Where is she?" A growl escaped his mouth as Atticus rose to his feet, looking around the receiving room, not seeing his mother. Looking at the archway wooden doors, much like Hazel's chambers, he hastily walked toward them before he barged into his mother's bed chambers. Queen Sage lay on white silk sheets, on her side, with her back toward the door. She wore a low-cut nightgown that showed deep lacerations on her back. Atticus felt bile creeping up his throat threatening to spew all over the white oak floor of her bedroom. Running to his mother's bedside, he rushed to the left side of the canopy bed.

She was sleeping soundlessly on the bed, clutching onto the blanket she had made for Atticus as a child. Kneeling down before her, Atticus gently stroked platinum blonde hair from her face looking her over to see if he could see any other injuries to her body. She startled awake at the touch, her icy blue eyes wide. "I'm so sorry mother." Atticus's voice broke as he wiped away a single tear that clung to her lower lashes.

The gentle queen raised her hand up to stroke her son's cheek as she smiled faintly. "I'm glad to see you back home, How was your trip?" Sage always kept a smile on her face, even when their father was cruel to her.

"He did this, didn't he?" His tone came out low and deep as the anger boiled inside of him. Seeing his father not only gave Reed a black eye, but also gave his mother deep lacerations from a whip fueled his rage.

"Atticus, please don't, I can-"

"Don't say you can handle him. Look at what he did to you! He is a coward for doing this to his own wife and child! And for what?" Atticus ground out in anger before he stood up.

Sage sat up as he rose, grabbing her son's hand. "Atticus, if you go after your father, he will-"

"He can't be allowed to do this anymore!" Atticus roared, pulling his hand away from his mother before he stormed out of her room, feeling only hatred and rage. His father would wait till both Kingsly and Atticus were gone to do this.

It didn't take Atticus long to find his father. He was standing with his advisors in the throne room, discussing politics with the surrounding kingdoms. "King Kai!" Atticus snarled, refusing to call him father. The moment the king turned to speak to the abrupt interruption, Atticus' fist connected with his muscular jaw so hard it sent the king to the ground. Jumping onto his father, he slammed his fist into Kai's face several more times before feeling a crack beneath his fist. Guards ran over, grabbing Atticus, pulling him off their king. He yanked out of their grip, baring his teeth at them.

"Don't you ever lay a hand on my mother or brothers again!"

Kai held his bloody nose , his lip split in the corner , and his cheek cut by the ring Atticus wore before his honey eyes met with his sons. "You dare strike me, boy?"

The advisors in the throne room stood in stunned silence, their eyes wide with shock and disbelief. Murmurs of astonishment rippled through the group as they processed the audacity of the prince's actions. Some exchanged worried glances, unsure of how the king would retaliate against such a brazen act of defiance.

Hearing his father calling him a boy made his inner stomach twist slightly, familiar with how the king referred to his sons as boys when he asserted his dominance, "Tie him to the whipping post," the king ordered. "It seems my son forgot his place." Atticus held up his chin high, showing he wasn't scared of his father. He was used to taking whips as punishment to protect Kingsly, Reed, and even Heath, when they got into trouble.

Two guards grabbed him and dragged him to three large pillars. A guard retrieving a rope keeping the curtains of the throne room open. He restrained Atticus with it to the far left pillar, Atticus was forced to his knees.

"Kai please!" a soft voice called out.

His mother.

Sage didn't even bother to change after Atticus stormed out of her room. He watched over his shoulder at his mother who held Kai's arm that held the whip.

"Be quiet, Sage!" Kai roared shoving her away.

Seeing his father get into place, gripping the whip, Atticus tucked his head under his arms to protect his face as he closed his eyes, tunneling deep into himself.

CRACK

His body naturally tensed up, pulling on the chains, groaning, trying to hold in his pained yelp. Feeling his skin splitting , followed after a few seconds the trickling of blood. As he rested his head on the pole with his back to his father, his arms guarded his face between him and the pole.

CRACK

Another lash. Atticus kept his head down and groped his chains tight, refraining from letting the stinging sensation in his back cause him to cry out. How many times had he endured this for his brothers? He welcomed this lashing because Kai deserved his nose being broken.

CRACK

But this time there was no sting, no feeling of fresh blood soaking his shirt. Vanilla, sandalwood and roses filled his senses. Hazel.

His eyes widened as his head whipped to look over her shoulder, seeing Hazel standing there with her back towards him, in a red silk robe, her curls up in a bun. Oh, sweet Aena. Hazel had lost her mind. What in God's name was she thinking? The whip coiled around her arm as if it were a serpent she had mastered. With a swift, decisive tug, Hazel wrenched it from the king's grasp. The king, taken by surprise, stumbled forward, losing his balance as the whip tumbled noisily to the floor. Atticus, confined to the pillar, strained to catch a glimpse of the scene. Though his view was limited to what he could see over his shoulder, the sight of Hazel's fearless defiance against the king was unmistakable, even in his restricted vantage.

"How dare-" the king started.

"How dare you whip your own son! You are no king. You're a tyrant!" Hazel snapped back, removing the whip from her arm and throwing it to her side.

Atticus could feel such raw power emanating from her from just her rage alone. His heart swelled with a mix of gratitude and fear. He was deeply touched by Hazel's bravery in standing up to his father, but he also worried for her safety. The consequences of her actions could be dire, and he couldn't bear the thought of her facing his father's wrath.

"You think because you are the Ivory Fawn that I won't hesitate to-"

"Do what? Whip me? Do your worst. I have endured so much worse than being whipped by a king who chooses to rule with fear," Hazel replied with pure venom in her words.

Dear Saaos, Hazel was not backing down. Atticus looked up to her, trying to reach for her hand, but the rope make sure they remained on the pillar. "Hazel," the prince warned.

The king stared down her, but said nothing. Instead, he smirked, scoffing slightly before lifting his chin back. "You're lucky you are the Ivory Fawn, or else I would have your head on a stick," Kai ground out before waving to the guards. "Release the Crown Prince."

Atticus couldn't believe his ears when he heard his father allow Hazel to walk away from insulting him. Once the ropes released from his wrists, he stands up, taking his place behind Hazel, and rested his hand on the small of her back. Hazel, from how he could feel her muscles tighten, was scared, but she didn't show it.

"Get yourselves cleaned up. Dinner will be ready in two hours." This was the only response the tyrant king gave before he turned and left Sage, Hazel, and Atticus in the throne room.

Sage ran over to Atticus, cupping his cheek. "My son, why did you do that? You know how he gets it." Her small voice was now raised and lined with concern.

Atticus took his mother's hand and kissed it. "I'm sorry, mother. I lost my temper, but you shouldn't have intervened. I don't want you to end up back on that post."

"I know, my son, but I had to at least try to stop him." Sage then turned her face to Hazel with a look of concern. "Are you able to heal his back?"

Atticus felt Hazel's eyes go to his back before she replied, "I can, but let me heal yours first."

The queen didn't object as she turned her back to Hazel, whose hands began to glow along with her eyes anytime she used her Aestival magic. Sage's back stitched itself together. Hazel then turned her attention to Atticus cupping his cheek. "Come on, let's get you back to your room, and that back healed."

Atticus only nodded his head before wrapping his arm around Hazel's shoulder. To others, it looked as if he leaned on her solely for support from how badly his back now hurt. Sage walked with them silently to his right while Hazel was on his left. Her brazen actions towards his father could have seriously injured her, and although he would have taken whatever punishment his father decided on to spare her from his wrath, Atticus was just glad she was unharmed. Reaching the large archway doors to his chambers, Hazel helped him walk inside and over to the couch. His mother stood in the entryway, watching them.

"You shouldn't have done that, Hazel. I had it-"

"I'm not above slapping your back, Atticus. Don't say you had it handled," Hazel snapped at him before she removed his ripped shirt to look at his back. He only sighed, not wanting to argue.

Knowing exactly what she would see on his back—the scars from previous whippings, if she hadn't already seen them from their night in the cabin—he wouldn't blame her if Hazel didn't see them when they tried to escape with their lives from a burning building.

Feeling her soft hand brush across his back, he tensed, biting his lip, stilling to the touch. "Are these?" Hazel breathed.

Atticus, taking a deep breath, nodded his head. "Yes, all are from him." He looked up at his mother, who has now averted her eyes from her son.

Sage has tried before to stop the beatings, but Kai would turn that rage on her, but then take her beatings behind closed doors.

"Why?"

Once again, Atticus took another deep breath, steadying his heart racing up his throat, feeling a warm, calming sensation over his back, feeling his skin slowly stitched itself together. "My father is cruel and harsh, with no consideration of how his actions will affect others. When any of my brothers and I stepped out of line, he felt the need to put us in place. It was how his father raised him. Said his father's teachings made him a stronger and better king. My fa—" He shook his head. "The king thinks the same will be for his sons. Heath and Kingsly were always the troublemakers. I was the peacekeeper, being the oldest. The one to set the example. Always the one who stepped in when they got into trouble." Atticus swallowed hard before he continued, "There was one night I learned Heath had been sneaking out of the castle to attend the illegal fight pits as a participant. When I got to the fights, my brother was against an opponent I knew he couldn't win against. I watched Heath get knocked around that ring like a sandbag for this man to unleash his rage on. At first, I watched, hoping it would teach him a lesson, but then hearing his grunts and saw the blood coming from his lip and nose. I couldn't stomach it again, so I intervened in the fight. I was recognized by one of the attendees. We got out, thankfully, in one piece after we fought our way out." Pausing for a moment, he calmed his racing heart, feeling Hazel's hand on his shoulder. Reaching up, he gripped her soft hand before his eyes meet his mother's eyes. "When we got to the castle, my father was furious with us. We were treated as if we were simple peasants who disobeyed him. My father forced Heath and I to our knees. My brother shook from either fear or adrenaline from being caught, I still don't know to this day. When my father asked whose idea it was, I told him it was mine. I told him that Heath tried to stop me, but I wouldn't listen. I took full blame because Heath already suffered enough in the fight. My father would have broken him then and there. My brother watched as Kai whipped me to the point I couldn't feel the pain anymore. I remember hearing Heath beg my father to stop, but he didn't." Finally, he turned his head and let Hazel's eyes as silver misted over them, her cheeks wet with tears.

Atticus stroked tears away from her soft cheek. "That's why I would rather bear the pain and suffering instead of seeing those I care for go through it. I became the monster he wanted in this court to protect them. People tend to avoid angering you if you are a man like my... like the king." Seeing her lips part to say something, but no words came out, all he could do was pull her face in and lean his forehead on hers, stroking hair behind Hazel's ear. "I'm not a stranger to the darkness, Hazel. I would rather face the monster that lie in the dark instead of seeing it prey upon those I love."

Hearing footsteps approaching, he looked up to see his mother kneeling to become eye level with her son, taking his cheek in his hand. "My son, without pain, there would be no suffering. Without suffering, we would never learn from our mistakes. To make it right, pain and suffering is the key to all windows. Without it, there is no way of life. You can't bear this pain on your own. Sometimes letting others help bear it is the only way to heal."

Atticus leaned into his mother's hands. Swallowing audibly he couldn't help the tears burning in his eyes, threatening to come out before taking Sage's soft hand that smelt of roses and kissing it.

Hazel rubbed his shoulder and kissed the back of his head. "Let's get you cleaned up and ready for dinner."

"You go ahead and finish getting ready, Lady Hazel. We will meet you at dinner," Sage assured the woman standing in front of Atticus. The one who not only stepped in front of his father's path of wrath to defend him, but who also never escaped his mind.

Hazel nodded her head before leaning down, kissing Atticus's cheek, and whispering in his ear, "I shall see you after dinner, dragon." She straightened up, looking to his mother, "I shall see you at dinner, my queen." Giving a small curtsy, Hazel then left Sage and Atticus together.

Chapter Sixty

Hazel

Standing in front of the mirror, Hazel stared down at the dress, lost in her thoughts. The deep plunge of the crimson-red dress showed how large her cleavage was. It was one of the most revealing dresses Arabella ever put Hazel in. Despite the way the dress's fabric hung loosely from her hips, she couldn't help staring in the mirror, mesmerized by the way the deep, rich color seemed to illuminate her complexion. The soft drape of the dress contrasted with her sharp features, creating an elegant silhouette that exuded a timeless sophistication. As she gently twirled, the fabric caught the light, adding a shimmer to each step and elevating her presence. There was a subtle, understated allure in its simplicity, one that demanded attention not through boldness, but through elegance and grace, making her feel as though she was stepping into a timeless portrait. A small smile crept onto her face, appreciating how the dress transformed her reflection into an image of quiet confidence and beauty.. Two sheer fabric panels hung from the shoulders, draping down each arm. Hazel had to be cautious with how she walked because the high leg slit would reveal more than she liked to the court.

"Hazel?" Arabella's concerned words pulled her out of the trance she was in, and the young fawn turned her head to look at the handmaiden.

She stared at her with a raised eyebrow, holding up two different pairs of earrings. One set was two large gold and pearl stars dangling from the other , the other set was a gold teardrop shape with a crimson gem in the middle.

"I was asking which one you wanted. Are you alright?"

Hazel took a deep breath, smoothing out her dress and looking it over before looking back at Arabella. "The gold stars are perfect."

Arabella handed Hazel the earring for her to put on herself, a pair of dagger made earrings. Hazel's mind wondered what Atticus endured to protect his brothers. She had met Kingsly and Reed, and she wondered why she hadn't met Heath. "Ara, what do you know about Prince Heath? Is he still in court?" Hazel couldn't help herself.

The look on Arabella's face was one of bewilderment. "Prince Heath? What made you want to ask about him?" Arabella continued working as she fixed a few loose strands in Hazel's hair.

"Atticus told me about something that happened with his brother, but he isn't here at court. Why is that?" Arabella stopped what she was doing before looking into Hazel's eyes in the mirror. Resting her hands on both of Hazel's arms as she took a deep breath before she walked to stand directly in front of Hazel.

"He was sent away on a diplomatic mission. Kingsly is the king's general, and as you know, Atticus is the king's heir. Heath was the king's emissary, making relations with the other kingdoms to establish treaties and alliances. However, he caused turmoil in the Taldora kingdom. He was supposed to marry their princess, but he called off their engagement. The Taldora king was furious and threatened war, until Kingsly stepped up and agreed to marry the Duvessa in his stead."

Hazel's eyes widened in shock hearing, and felt the air being sucked out from her lungs. "Wait, you're telling me Lady Duvessa is... Is a daughter of a Duke?" There was no hiding the disbelief in her voice.

"Yes. No one knew what the duke's daughter looked like. The Taldora King asked her not to disclose her title until after the wedding. Although with Kingsly now in the dungeons, who knows what will happen."

Hazel swallowed down the bile in her throat at the thought that the king would force Atticus to marry Duvessa after both Heath and Kingsly have dishonored their king. Is that why the prophecy said he wouldn't rule by her side, but that the Obsidian Tiger would?

Hazel's brows furrowed in confusion as she thought for a moment before looking towards her mother's necklace as it hung from the vanity mirror, the same one that has apparently been passed down the last hundred and fifty years. She thought back on how it warmed when Duvessa was near her and when Darius attacked her.

"Wait. Taldora? Where is Taldora located?"

What if Taldora was ruled by Netherian rulers? Did Kingsly know Duvessa was a Netherian? Was how he knew Darius was because of Duvessa?

Back in the Raven Palm forest, Hazel remembered how Lilura mentioned the queen would be happy with whom he brought home. Her stomach clenched as he stomached rolled. She covered her mouth to hold back the bile until she reached the toilet, where she vomited.. Arabella must have followed Hazel, for seconds after she dropped to her knees in front of the toilet, her friend rubbed and stroked her back.

"Hazel!" Arabella exclaimed in surprise as Hazel emptied her stomach into the toilet.

After a few more heaves, Hazel trembled, tears soaking her cheeks as she felt on fire. She steadied her racing heart with deep breaths. "How sure are you that Duvessa is actually a duke's daughter?" Looking at Arabella, who'd grown concerned and taken aback by Hazel's question, her mouth opened dumbfounded. She can tell Arabella was thinking but she remained silent.

Wiping her mouth with the back of her hand, Hazel stood up, walked over to the sink, and ran the cool water before rinsing out her mouth. "My necklace warms when I am around anyone with Netherian magic. It can get to the point of being so hot I can't bear it on my chest. It happened when Darius tried to kill me, and on our way here from Alexandra when we were ambushed by the Netherian bandits." Turning to look at Arabella, who remained sitting on the floor beside the toilet, staring up wordlessly, Hazel continued, "I had an encounter with Lady Duvessa alone in the halls before Ardnaxela intervened. She invited me along for tea, my necklace warmed in her presence, which meaning she is Netherian, and I doubt that tea part would have been civil."

Hazel faced Arabella, rubbing her face and bracing her hands on the sink as her mind raced with the weight of her recent discovery.

"Wait, where is Lady Duvessa now? If I am right about her, she will try to run," Hazel stated, standing straight and picking up her dress as she hastily left the bathroom to look for her black riding boots. Hazel didn't care that the boots didn't match her dress, but she preferred comfort over coordinating her outfit with her shoes.

"I haven't seen her. Wait, Hazel. What are you doing?" Arabella's concerned voice came from behind.

The fawn didn't need to see Ara's face. She knew from her tone that Arabella was concerned. "I will find Duvessa. If she is still here, she may be planning something. If that viper fled, it may be to flee for reinforcements if my hunch is correct about her." Finding her boots discarded beside her wardrobe, Hazel picked them up, sat on the canopy bed, and put them on.

"Hazel, if she is Netherian, you shouldn't leave alone. Bring Ardnaxela or Atticus with you," Arabella pleaded, joining Hazel's side on the bed, resting her hand on Hazel's lap and squeezing her knee. "Let's say she is Netherian. They want you dead, so the prophecy never comes true. What if she tries killing you?"

Hazel stood up, turning to kneel before her friend, taking both her hands and squeezing them tight. "I will find out if she tries to, I at least know how to fight back. I will take my mother's necklace. The necklace will let me know when she is getting to close. I promise I will be okay and back before dinner."

Arabella took a deep breath before helping Hazel to her feet. "I see there is no changing your mind here." She released Hazel's hand before walking over to retrieve the sword leaning against the wall behind the door. She picked it up and turned to face Hazel with a faint grin. "You can't wear that dress and this at the same time, can you?"

Chapter Sixty-One

Hazel

Hazel knew she couldn't take the normal route to Duvessa's chambers. With a sword on her hip and not dressed for dinner, being seen in the hall would surely raise an alarm. Her cloak covered her black leather arm guards where a matching leather brown corset protected her vital organs. The cold air lashed against her face, whipping her braid from beneath her hood. She clung tightly to the castle's brick wall, inching along a ledge barely wide enough to accommodate her foot. Each careful step she took along the narrow edge heightened the sense of danger, setting her nerves—and perhaps those of any unseen watchers—on edge.

Hazel was determined not to be seen by guards or staff in the hallway. Hazel took a deep breath, her eyes scanning the rough surface of the castle wall, searching for the next secure hold. Her mind was sharp and alert, each movement deliberate and precise. As she inched along the narrow ledge, she was acutely aware of the void below. Her heart pounded in her chest, but she didn't allow fear to overtake her resolve. She focused intensely on the texture of the stone under her fingertips, the cool, unwavering touch of the bricks offering a small sense of stability. Each step required her complete concentration, her muscles tense and ready to adjust at a moment's notice. With each successful sidestep, a wave of determination coursed through her, pushing her onward despite the daunting height. Her thoughts briefly flickered to her mission, a reminder of why she was scaling the wall in the first place, which fueled her persistence. The sound of the wind whistled past her ears, but Hazel's gaze remained fixed forward, her mind locked on the task at hand. She visualized her path, meticulously planning each subsequent move as she continued her careful progress along the wall. Her senses were heightened, aware of every slight shift in her balance as she maneuvered, her instincts guiding her safely to her destination.

When there were large archway windows, Hazel ensured that no one was in the room or could at least see if she stepped onto the balcony before crossing it. Turning around as she neared the castle corner, She swallowed down the lump in her throat seeing she were about three stories high and she wouldn't survive if she fell. However, Hazel wouldn't let that fear of falling make her lose focus. As she nimbly rounded the corner of the castle wall, the necklace beneath her white puffy long-sleeve shirt began to warm.

Climbing over one balcony to a vacant guest room, Hazel calmed her nerves with the cold air, adjusted her hood, and swallowed her anxiety as she approached Duvessa's balcony. Mentally preparing herself, she climbed over the railing of the balcony, finding placement for her foot before securing a grip on the cobblestone wall for her cold fingers. She was regretting not wearing actual gloves for this trek

The blanket of night made this trek easier to hide, but also more nerve-wracking, with little to no light other than what came from the castle windows. Hazel pressed her back to the side of the castle near the large archway window doors that lead out to the balcony, Hazel peered into the bedroom to see if Duvessa in the room. Her necklace became warmer, but she put her hand over it, as if the touch would calm it down.

Seeing no movement, Hazel reached for the door handle, stepping away from the wall to maneuver around the outward-opening balcony door. Leaving the door open behind her, Hazel examined the room. It was almost identical to Atticus's bedroom, with red mahogany flooring and walls. The large mahogany canopy bed was empty and untouched. However, the only difference between their rooms was instead of maroon-colored drapes and decorum, it was decorated with a deep violet and smelled of iron and salt. Her necklace warmed even more beneath her hand as the other hand rested on the pommel.

Stepping further into the room, she stalked towards the vanity mirror, there was a drop of red liquid on the surface. Running her finger through it, it was warm.

Looking around the room, it seemed vacant. But why was her necklace burning so hot now? A slow mocking clap came from the bathroom, causing Hazel hand to draw the sword she barely knew how to use and face the sound.

The aroma of iron and salt became more prominent as she turned, her stomach revolting at the source of the clapping. Standing in the large archway led to the bathing room was Darius. His fingers were now completely black from the Netherian magic as the blackness crawls up his hand like spiderwebs. He must not have taken another Blood Bride after her, which means he was likely very unstable if the look of hunger in his eyes was any confirmation. "Look at you, my Hazel. I thought you looked delicious before, but now..." He bit his lip as he trailed off, not even hiding the moan from his lips as he stalked closer.

Hazel's entire body froze, seeing Darius now in front of her. No one but Arabella knew where she was.

Hazel trusted her friend not to tell anyone where she was. However, she was now hoping Arabella told the guards or even Atticus by now. Her hands trembled as she swallowed , holding onto the sword with both her hands like Ardnaxela had taught her. Although everything she had learned in these past months was fading away from memory as the panic began to settle in.

Darius took another step closer. "Here you are, dressed as if you are some valiant hero who will save everyone, but in reality, you are just that scared, scared village girl who relied on a man to validate her. How pathetic," he purred, his eyes darkening as he got closer with a pure predator look.

"W-Where is Duvessa?" Hazel choked out, trying to act brave, but her attempt failed her.

Darius only laughed deeply before he lunged toward her. Hazel gasped, released the sword, and stepped backward, but wasn't able to move fast enough. As the necklace scorched her neck from how close he was to her, Darius's hand coiled around her throat. Lifting her so her feet now danged from the ground a few feet. "She is the last of you worries, just be glad it is me you're facing and not her." His grip tightened around Hazel's throat as he pulled her closer, inhaling deeply before letting out a low rumble from his chest. "I forgot how delectable you smell when scared."

Clawing at his hands, Hazel tried to release his grip, holding back the whimper threatening to come out. "Why would I be glad about facing you and not her?" Hazel choked out once more, panicking slightly at how it was hard to get the words out.

"Considering you are in this room alone and strapped for a fight? You already know," he replied.

She was right, Duvessa wasn't just a princess, she was the Netherian queen Lilura talked about back in the Raven Palm forest. She clawed at his hands more to loosen the grip. The pounding in her ears was so loud, but she tried calming herself, but with his hand around her throat, that was nearly impossible.

"What was your deal with Kingsly?" Hazel ground.

Darius only chuckled softly bringing her closer to his face, mere inches away as he hovered his lips near her neck, his breath making her crawling from the sensation. "Duvessa and I planned to let him think he was going to have a chance at being king. Just so she could get close to Atticus. That idiotic general prince was just a pawn. Once she got rid of him, it would be easier to make sure the prophecy never came true. We were going to kill you both when you left for Wylana, but that damn general prince couldn't help but protect you. Pesky morals of his."

Hazel's eyes widened as her focus darted to the side where Darius lingered by her ear, whispering into it.

If he was revealing this all now, it meant he wasn't planning for her to leave alive. Hazel needed to fight back, Kicking her feet trying to land any kind of kick but she couldn't.

"Once you were here, we needed a reason for you to return home, get you away from the protection of the castle and far from help of the castle. What better way than to get rid of the one person you had left in your life? Duvessa paid one of the few Netherian guards we have here in the castle to stage an ambush. How clever she was to make that general think he was the target, when it was actually your uncle all along. From what I observed in the four years of getting to know you, Archibald is a man who is of honor."

Hazel's eyes widened as tears misted over her eyes, hearing her uncle's death was because of Duvessa.

"When Duvessa got word from that the foolish general prince Kingsly and you were going to Alexandria alone, well, she had to make sure Atticus went as well. Kill three birds with one stone. Duvessa knew how attached Atticus was to you. How strong his jealousy was over you with Kingsly. How badly he wanted to make sure the prophecy came true. Atticus would have followed you both without a doubt. It was such a riveting feeling setting fire to your pathetic squabble. Although we didn't take into consideration, your magical capabilities you have now."

Before Hazel could open her mouth, Darius threw her body into the vanity mirror. Her face slammed into he mirror cutting her face as it broke. Crushing the chair beneath her as she rolled off the vanity. Sharp pains shot up the left side of her body, making her cry out.

Her eyes whipped up to the sound of Darius's approaching boots before she looked for her sword. It was a mere feet away. Standing up as fast as she could, Hazel lunged for it, but Darius's finger coiled into her hair, whipping her head back. Releasing her mid air sending her soaring into the archway door leading into the bathroom. A grunt escaped her as Hazel's back made contact, almost breaking her back from how much force he used. Without the Blood Brides, the Netherian magic became more uncontrollable the more someone used it.

Holding her ribs, Hazel stood up, looking at Darius, who stalked toward her. Stepping backward, she lured him into the white-marbled bathroom. The trembling fawn swallowed hard. "So what? You plan to kill both Atticus and I off to stop the prophecy? So you can become king?" Hazel baited him. She needed him in a corner so she could use her magic to distort him and make a run for it.

"I don't need to become king when I already am king of Taldora. Once Taldora is done with Wylana, there will be nothing left."

A gasp escaped her lips hearing that Darius was king of Taldora. Hazel was at a loss for words as her body seized up once more realizing that this entire time she was sleeping in bed the last several years with the king of the Netherian. That's why Ratherian backed off in the market, why Lilura listened to Darius, and Why was there a comment about Darius being higher in rank than Ratherian? In an instant, Darius was mere inches away, slamming Hazel's body hard into the marble wall, causing it to crack under her back. She let out a loud scream before his hand was so tight on her throat that she couldn't utter a word. Sharp pain shot through her shoulder, accompanied by a warm sensation spreading down her arm.

Hazel's vision blurred, the world smeared with blood and flame and memory.

Pain exploded through her shoulder, hot and sharp like a blade plunged straight into the bone. Her breath hitched. Her knees trembled beneath her. She couldn't look down—she didn't need to. She knew exactly what was happening.

Darius.

The last time he'd sunk his teeth into her, it had nearly killed her. She'd felt her soul unraveling under his bite, magic fraying like broken thread, life slipping away one heartbeat at a time. She'd barely survived then, saved by sheer luck and someone else's sacrifice.

But not this time.

She wouldn't let him finish the job.

Gritting her teeth against the searing pain, Hazel raised her hand, magic already boiling under her skin, desperate to be unleashed. Her pulse thudded loud in her ears. The world tilted.

"Get off me," she snarled through clenched teeth, voice cracking.

She forced more magic forward, another flare sparking to life—but it fizzled before it left her hand. Her body betrayed her. Her magic slipped out of reach, fraying like static, spitting sparks that licked harmlessly at the floor.

No no no—come on—

She tried again. Her power surged, but it wouldn't listen. It crackled and twitched like a wounded thing, overwhelmed by fear, by trauma, by *him*. Her breath came in short, panicked gasps, her heart slamming against her ribs like it was trying to escape her chest.

Darius didn't move. He didn't need to.

Releasing her neck , her blood coating his lips. He watched her struggle with a cruel, coiled stillness—like a serpent waiting for the last shudder of life before striking again. His hand pressed against her throat, not choking—*containing*. Pinning her there like prey beneath his palm.

When her magic flickered out for the third time, his smile widened. Slow. Cold.

"Still so frightened of me," he said softly, tilting his head, voice thick with mock affection. "All that power... and yet you shake like a cornered lamb."

His fingers traced the blood-soaked edge of her shoulder wound, and she flinched.

Darius chuckled low in his throat. "I remember this fear. You wore it last time too—when I had you against that tree, scared and fragile . You haven't changed, little fawn. Still trembling. Still breakable."

Hazel tried to summon something—anything—but her vision swam. Her magic writhed inside her like it was *afraid* of him too.

He leaned in, close enough that she could see the faint flecks of her own blood in his teeth.

"You've always known how this ends."

His grip tightened slightly—not enough to crush, just enough to remind her she was powerless.

"I'm not here to kill you," he whispered. "Not yet. I want you to *feel* it. The helplessness. The unraveling. I want you to know that when your people scream for their savior... you'll have *nothing* left to give."

Darius released her neck suddenly, followed by a painful yowl. Stumbling forward, gripping her shoulder, calloused hands suddenly caught her by her bicep, holding her up.

Hazel , Looking towards Darius, breathing heavily in a daze from the damage done to her shoulder. Standing there was a man with onyx black hair that was just as black as his puffy obsidian colored long sleeve and pants.

"Don't. Touch. My. Fawn!" Atticus roared in anger as her an word was driven into Darius' side.

Hazel's head turned to look at who was keeping her up by her bicep. A male she had never encountered before had long, brown hair tied back in a low ponytail. His skin was tan, but the most striking feature was the swirling tattoo adorning the left side of his neck. His honey-brown eyes were locked on Darius and Atticus as the square lining of his jaw tightened. He paid no mind to Hazel as he held her up by her bicep.

Darius snarled, drawing Hazel's attention to him as he shoved off Atticus, clutching his side and rushing toward the window. Atticus charged after him, but Darius launched himself out of it, vanishing in the darkness of night. Atticus ran over, looking out the window before growling, slamming his fist into the wall, and turning to look at her.

The man released her, and her feet moved before Hazel knew it as she ran to Atticus. She went to wrap her arms around him, but he stopped her. The look in his eyes was nothing of gentle concern, but downright cold and full of rage.

"What were you thinking, Hazel?" The Immortal Dragon glared at her, gripping her bicep tight, sheathing the ancestral sword with his other hand into her sword belt before looking to her shoulder. "Fuck, Princess."

Before she could say anything, Atticus scooped her up in his arms and looked at the man standing in the bathroom. "Heath, get the medics and send them to my chambers, now!"

Without waiting for his brother to respond, Atticus quickly carried her out of Duvessa's bedroom, where the guards were now standing armed. "Alert my father and mother that the Ivory Fawn was attacked. Find Lady Duvessa and throw her into the dungeons beside Kingsly."

The guards nodded their heads before quickly running out of the room.

Hazel winced as her shoulder rubbed on Atticus's chest, but the aroma of bergamot and cedar help to calm to her. Hazel thought about how, yet again, she had nearly died by Darius's hand. Hazel forced her eyes shut, trying to ignore the pain in her shoulder. How was she going to defeat him if she couldn't even stand up to him? Hazel had no idea what she was going to do. There was no way she was going to be able to fight with her shoulder like this.

"You and I are going to have a serious talk about your impulsive recklessness," Atticus scolded her as he carried her. "I can't keep mending you. Eventually, neither of us will make it."

Chapter Sixty-Two

Hazel

The castle was in an uproar as Hazel was carried to Atticus's chambers. Her body hurt all over, from her arms to her ribs to her back. The decision to chase Duvessa like that with no plan was reckless. Atticus was correct about that, but if she hadn't been reckless, she wouldn't have learned the truth about what Darius and Duvessa were planning next. That was one thing she was grateful for. To know Kingsly wasn't a power-hungry fool who would intentionally killed his own brother.

Hazel felt sorry for the poor mahogany archway door leading into Atticus's receiving room as he angrily kicked it open. Keeping her eyes closed, she let a groan out at the aroma that felt like home. It made her nuzzle her head into his chest. Hearing his thunderous heartbeat against her ear, she counted them. The steady rhythm helped calm her own.

"I got you, princes," he soothed her.

Her face must have betrayed the extent of her pain, despite her desperate attempts to conceal it from him. Alternatively, could he discern her pale complexion due to the blood loss she endured from Darius's repeated ripping of her shoulder?

Another set of fast footsteps approached, followed by a deep, rough voice. "Medics are on their way.".

A cool, calming silk sheet met the exposed skin on her face as she laid her head to the side on a silk pillow. As she kept her eyes shut, something warm and wet brushed against her shoulder, as if someone were wiping the blood from her now exposed shoulder through the fabric. Then, a dry fabric pushed against her wound.

Hazel's eyes shot open as she reached for the wrist holding the rag to her shoulder, feeling a surge of pain from the pressure. It wasn't Atticus sitting beside her, now, but Heath. He maintained a composed demeanor on his face, as if she could discern the intricate workings of his mind, meticulously analyzing and devising methods to assist her. Heath's eyes mirrored his mother Sage's, an icy blue.

His touch was much gentler. Making out the scar from just below his ear to his collarbone that hid beneath a well-kept green tunic. His face was well kept and held not even a shadow of hair on his jaw. Hazel's eyes went towards Atticus, who was now leaning on the foot board of the canopy bed. Still boiling with rage, his grip was tight enough that she saw the whitening of his knuckles. Atticus' eyes locked on her. Hazel could read just what was going on behind those murderous eyes. He wanted to kill Darius for hurting her, rip into her for being reckless. The healers came into the room, but Heath didn't remove his focus from her shoulder as he lifted the rag, relieving the pressure.

"I need beeswax, myrrh, and mint crushed up, along with a needle and thread," he said indirectly to the healers who stood in silence. Their attention went to Atticus as if asking for confirmation.

"Prince Heath gave you a command. Do it!" Atticus growled out as his eyes never leave hers.

The healers straighten up, hurrying off to retrieve the items needed.

"Attic-" Hazel started, but Heath laid his hand on her chest just between the collarbones, being respectful not to touch her breast.

"Please conserve your energy and voice," he interrupted.

Surprised by his manners in contrast to Kingsly and Atticus, Hazel nodded her head in response. She turned her head to look at her shoulder but Heath's forefinger came to her jaw and stopped the motion. "I would advise against looking, Lady Hazel."

Returning with the supplies handed to him, Heath nodded in appreciation before he looked at Atticus. "Can you guard the door, brother?"

The way he spoke was much different from how Kingsly, Atticus, and Reed spoke. It was a pleasant change.

Without hesitation , Atticus went to the door, putting his back to it. Hazel's eyes trailed over Atticus's body, seeing his taut muscles. He was a ticking time bomb waiting to explode.

"This may be unpleasant , but please remain still," Health assured Hazel, waiting a fraction of a second before he set the bloody rag aside.

Taking a deep breath, she braced herself for the uncomfortable sensation she was about to endure. Hazel looked at Atticus, focusing on him.

At first, it was a calm, warm sensation that was short lived before Hazel felt her skin was being stretched and pulled. She tried to hold back the groan of pain, until it became worse.

Leaning her head back into the pillow, she inhaled sharply in pain, biting her lip. The cry came out of her lips, and she began to yell out in pain as tears flooded her eyes, burning them. Closing her eyes, she tried keeping still as the sensation spread down her body.

From the feeling of her ribs mending themselves, they were broken by Darius.

Rough, callused hands brushed her forehead, pushing hair from her face before grasping her hand. "I have you, princess. Shh, it's almost done." Atticus's voice was next to her now, telling Hazel he'd left his post, guarding the door to soothe her during this excruciating moment.

Hazel opened her eyes and looked up at the honey-brown eyes that met hers. Opening her mouth to say something, the pain of another rib mending itself sent her eyes slamming shut and her body arching.

"You're almost there. Please stay still," Heath spoke softly.

"It hurts!" Hazel cried out.

Atticus's hand went from her forehead to her cheek, stroking it. "I know, princess, just focus on me. It will pass."

Going to speak once more in protest against continuing the pain, Atticus's surprisingly soft lips met her. It was like everything around her went blank. She could feel her body mending itself, but no longer felt the pain that came with it.

All she could focus on was his lips, his scent, and the feeling of Atticus's callused hand on her cheek. She leaned into the kiss, opening her mouth for him. To her surprise, he didn't let his tongue slip into her invitation.

"There," Heath said, breaking Atticus and her moment and kiss.

Looking at her shoulder, the wound was gone. Hazel was no longer in pain. She was still tired, but her body was healed of the damages caused by Darius. However, how? The only magic she knew that could do this was her own magic and the druids—except for the druids, who hadn't been seen or heard from since the Blood War.

"Your body is healed, but you will still feel the soreness and tenderness of your wounds," Heath said, standing up, making a mess of the requested materials to make it look as if he had, in fact, used them.Laying some herbs on the table with some water. Making it appear it had knocked over.

"When you told me you found them, brother, I didn't quite believe you, until seeing you picked up a druidic healing trick. Now, I am curious as to where they've been hiding all this time," Atticus said, standing up as he walked towards the bedroom door, removing the chair he had placed there to barricade the door shut.

"I can't divulge their whereabouts, but yes, I found them. As for that trick, it was a simple one. Their young learn that spell early in their training." Heath's attention was directed towards Atticus as he stood up, walking around the bed to the. "I was sent with a message for the Ivory Fawn from their clan leader," Heath called from the bathroom before strolling back in, drying his hands.

Hazel sat up on the bed, propping pillows behind her for some support. Giving her attention to Heath. "For me? Why?"

"The Aestivals and the druids had a close alliance with one another. They fought together in the Blood War against the Netherian invaders," Atticus replied to Heath

"Exactly. Their leaders wish you would continue the alliance." Setting the dry rag on the desk, Heath walked to the bed where he previously sat. "Once you rise as the fawn, they will rise from their shadows and return to the light."

Hazel sat for a moment before she took a deep breath and nodded her head in agreement. "I would be honored to stand beside them."

Heath bowed his head in response before he looked between his brother and Hazel, inhaling deeply. "Then I shall relay a letter to their clan leader."

Heath crossed the room to the left side of the bed, where Atticus now sat on the maroon duvet with Hazel. "I will leave you two alone. I must see our mother." Hazel bowed her head in appreciation before speaking up. "Thank you, Prince Heath, for your help. I hope to see you at the upcoming feast in three days.."

Heath only chuckled, nodding his head, "I wouldn't miss it. Thank you again, Lady Hazel."

With those words, he dismissed himself from the bedchambers, leaving Hazel and Atticus alone.

Chapter Sixty-Three

Hazel

Morning rays kissed Hazel's face as the young fawn stared into the vanity mirror, brushing out her long, honey blonde hair. She braided it in a long french braid to keep it out of her way while training.

After last night's attack, Hazel knew Darius had lost his senses to the Netherian magic coursing through his veins. He wasn't thinking clearly now, acting more brash and reckless.

Thanks to Heath's incredible healing gifts, Hazel felt better than ever before. Which was good, because she couldn't afford to have her shoulder healed after it was ripped open once more. Hazel would have been at a huge disadvantage with a wounded shoulder. Even worse, she would be at a disadvantage if she couldn't get over her fear of him.

Hazel froze like a deer in headlights when she saw him. Everything she worked on during these past months had gone out the window. Hazel felt like that weak, helpless fawn who needed a man to whisk in and rescue her.

If she couldn't get past this fear of him, she may not be so lucky she would be saved for a third time.

Hazel needed to find a way to find the courage in herself and not let him have that power over her anymore, she will not let him best her a third time.

There was a knock at Hazel's bedroom door, and a frantic female voice called through the door, "Haz, it's Syb. Are you decent?"

Hazel, hearing the tone of her friends' voices, hastily walked over to her bedroom, opened it, and saw Sybilla clenching a dusty, purple journal in her hand.

As soon as the door opened, she hurried in and shut it quickly, conveying urgency. "I found something. This changes everything."

"Well, hello to you, too," Hazel replied.

Sybilla's long raven hair swayed as she passed the bed frame. She made a straight path for the table that sat beside the large archway door.

"Read this. I need to make sure I am not translating this incorrectly. You read an Aestival scripture without being taught. With you being the proposed fawn, you will be able to read it clearer than I." Such alarm was in Sybilla's voice, but also excitement and wonder.

She was beaming with curiosity as she opened the book and set it down on the table, pointing to a page.

Hazel slowly approached Sybilla, as her eyes never left the scribe until Hazel looked at the book.

Watching the words morph into a common tongue, she stood in shock before look at Sybilla. "Do I read it out loud?"

Only a shake of her head followed by a glance to the room was answered enough

As Hazel began to read, her heart raced, realizing this was her great-great-grandmother's personal journal with the inscription on the sword was engraved in the leather cover. Her eyes widened as they met with Sybilla's, who only nodded her head. Hazel then looked down to the journal reading.

I know a war is coming, and I fear there is no way of preventing it. With no sign of the Ivory Fawn rising, I am sure my people will fall. My beloved daughter, my only daughter who is wild at heart, didn't question my plea for her to leave with Evander.

I know our champion will get her to Alexandria safely. It's the only place safe from here so far away. I pray to Merikh that she will spare me from death so I may see her once more.

Although these are my last hours in this realm, I will ensure I help guide the Ivory Fawn.

Hazel's knees gave out as she sat down in the chair, reading how her great-great-grandmother had sent her great-grandmother to Alexandria. Was that why her family was raised for generations there? If Sariah was Aestival then how was she able to hide in Alexandria when it was so close to the Netherian borders? Was Taldora always a Netherian kingdom, or was it taken over when Asteria lost the war?

I will make sure my people come back from this. I must protect the Mother Grove Tree and its pool, just as my ancestors before me. Without it, my people's magick will cease to exist, our wings will vanish, and we will be mortal. The Mother Grove Tree's waters may be able to heal or bring back a person once from death, but they cannot restore powers.

If I die, there will be no way to bring me back, since the waters have already done so. I would gladly give my life again if it meant my husband and children survive as I have before. My sons have made me proud of the men they became. Alastor will be an amazing king to our people with his wife. Kaiser couldn't make me any prouder for his ambition and determination when it came to his inventions. And then my beautiful Sariah. I never thought I would be blessed with a daughter with strength in her will and determination makes me admire her more than she knows. With the courage she has fighting alongside her brother, I know she will be an amazing mother to the baby she carries now.

Hazel's vision blurs as she continued to read. These were her great-great grandmother's final written words. She could feel the sorrow in the writing, but also the pride she held for her children. This is where Hazel's story began when her great-grandmother fled from Wylana to Alexandria, where she built a life for herself. What about the champion? Evander? Did he stay with Sariah, or did he come back to fight? Was he the Obsidian Tiger? Or is he one of the brothers?

If you are reading this Ivory Fawn...

The young fawn's heart stopped when reading this journal entry was now directed at her. Was she about to learn about the sword? Was she planning to find out who the Obsidian Tiger was?

I wish I could have lived to see you rise with our people. Please take care of them. Although they may have a few rotten ones, such as the fallen, they are good people. However, don't let the fallen's wings put you off. Evander is one of them. He has shown me that not all fallen Aestivals are untrustworthy.

I have a plan, but I can't tell you exactly what, just in case this journal falls into the wrong hands. The Light-Bringer is the key to returning our people, and the sword will awaken the spell. I hope you hear its call and save our people.

Turning the page, Hazel's eyes widened as she saw it was blank. Nothing else was written. Going back and reading the words again, her heart plummets more as she rose to her feet. How would she know the sword told her something?

"Hazel?"

She slowly turned to look at the scribe, her eyes scanning her face while she tried to process the information.

Sybilla's head was tilted to the side, and her arms were extended, offering to catch Hazel if she fainted. "What did she say about the sword? What does it have to do with the tree?" she inquired with wonder in her eyes

Hazel swallowed to try soothing the dryness in her throat before turning to the sword that hung on the wall. Walking over to it slowly, as if it would bite her if she moved too quickly, Sybilla's words became inaudible mumbling.

Removing the sword from the wall, Hazel stared at it with such intensity, hoping the answer would drop right into her lap. Was there a secret compartment of the sword? "She said the sword was the key to bringing back my people... The tree is much more than a tree... If something happens to that tree... Then there will be no way to bring back my people..." Hazel processed what she had read.

Would it be so horrible not to become the Ivory Fawn? To have a normal life with Atticus, and rule beside him as his queen? Whoever this Obsidian Tiger was, she was going to have to rule beside him. Yet another thing in her life she had no control over.

Her eyes misted as she thought about the promise she made to Archibald—the promise she swore to keep with him on his deathbed. Hazel couldn't break that promise to him. Her heart and conscience wouldn't allow her to. Did he know the full prophecy? Her mind was reeling with so many questions, for the queen and for her late uncle.

"How is the sword going to be the key?" Sybilla's words finally became clear as Hazel looked up at the emerald-eyed lady scribe and took a deep breath.

"I don't know, but she said I will hear its call when it is time." Hazel didn't exactly know what that would be, but she knew in her heart when that time came, she would do what she must to keep her promise to her uncle. When the sword finally awaken for her, she would do what she must.

Hazel would not be afraid to head its call.

Chapter Sixty-Four

Hazel

The cold air was now something Hazel was used to. It wasn't so much of a bother anymore training in the snow. Her mind wasn't on the training field, but was lost in a cloud of wonder and confusion. How was the sword going to help her? Why couldn't Asteria have left an instruction manual for her on how to become this Ivory Fawn they desperately need in order to bring her people back? Or at least left an instruction manual on how to use the sword. *No, that would be easy, wouldn't it?*

Pure raw strength connected to Hazel's ribs, sending her side stepping into a tree. Grunting as her right arm made contact with the tree, it nearly caused her to release her sword, but she stabilized herself with her.

"Get your head out of the clouds, princess," Atticus barked, not giving her a moment to think or recover as he lunged.

Quickly, Hazel dodged under his attack, taking her chance at his exposed ribs, driving her shoulder into them, and shoving him back. "My head is just fine."

There was a huff of disbelief in her dishonesty. "If you were paying attention, you would have been able to block my initial hit," Atticus ground out.

Hazel shook her head, going to an offensive strike. He stepped back, and in one swift move, disarmed Hazel before pulling her so her back was against his chest.

She groaned, trying to break the hold. She slammed her heel into the top of his foot, and if it hadn't been for his quick adjustment, she would have broken from the hold. It only made his grip tighter.

Hazel felt his hot breath against her neck as his lips brushed her ear. "See, you're predictable. You can't be predictable. You must find a way to get the advantage over any opponent," Atticus scorned.

Swallowing, Hazel felt his thunderous heartbeat on the back of her head from how her head was placed against his chest. Testing his strength on his hold, it didn't waver one bit.

Hazel leans her head back feeling his heartbeat, counting the beats, listening to his breathing. There was one way to find upper hand. She was smaller in frame to him, which could be Atticus's disadvantage, but there was one thing Hazel knew would be her chance in this situation: hearing how close his breathing was to her neck.

Quickly turning her head, Atticus's head pulled back as if expecting to be kissed, created enough distance between their lip and body. She needed him to think that long enough so she could turn to reach Atticus's hip. With a swift movement, the blade was kissing his throat as she backed his body into a tree just.

He grunted upon impact, leaning his head back and adding additional pressure to that blade.

"Impressive, princess, using your opponents' own weapons against them. Good."

Giving Atticus a victorious grin, her breath snagged as his fingers entangled in her hair, pulling her head back pulling her closer to him as if he didn't care the blade was still to his throat. For a moment, Hazel's grip loosened, but by the time she recovered from her millisecond error, Atticus had disarmed her and his lips were now crashing into hers. He flipped their positioning where her back was now against the tree and she had a blade to her throat. Grinning at the cold steel touch her throat. "You will need to do so much worse than that."

His eyes darkened, and his eyebrows furrowed. "You must learn to play dirty. Darius won't play fair, and if you try to play fair, he wins, and you die."

Hearing Darius's name, Hazel shuddered before her eyes became like daggers, glaring at him. "I know he doesn't. Why do you think I am trying everything I can to make sure I beat him?" Shoving him away, Hazel rubbed her throat.

A rough calloused hand wrapped around her wrist, stopping her as she walked past him. Hazel turned to look at his hand on her wrist. "What did you learn? Your not making your usual sassy comment I enjoy oh so much, and a servant told me Sybilla brought you some books. No secrets, remember?"

Hazel's mouth dried up thinking about what she read in Asteria's journal about the Obsidian Tiger. If Atticus and she weren't supposed to end up together, what was the point of trying to chase what could happen if she didn't get choose him? Looking back up at him, Hazel took a deep breath. "I thought I found answers in the journal about the sword and the prophecy but-"

"The prophecy? We already know how the prophecy goes, that I, as your Crimson Dragon, will guide you to becoming the Ivory Fawn."

Stilling, Hazel slowly lowered her gaze, licking her bottom lip that felt so dry and cracked. She knew she swore no more secrets, but if she saying it out loud to him, it changed everything and will change what happened between them. "Hazel...What are you not telling me? What did you learn?" His grip tightened on her wrist like it would make her look at him.

"You won't be by my side after I fulfill the prophecy..." Hazel's voice broke for a moment when she finally looked at Atticus, whose expression melted into disbelief.

"What?" was his only reply to the bomb she dropped. "What do you mean?"

"When I took the sword, I saw Asteria... She was dying. It was as if her last words were being spoken to me. Asteria told me that I will rule beside the Obsidian Tiger."

A deafening silence drifted between them, as if time had stopped around them, leaving them wordless. Hazel waited for the explosion, waited for his temper to flare. Honestly, she wanted any reaction other than his emotionless stare into her soul, that his gaze had gone into her soul in search of the evidence that what she said was true.

"I see."

Gods, she hated how those words came out. His tone was so dead, it sounded like had just shattered his world. Hazel reached up to cup his face, but he stopped her hands.

"You honestly think because this prophecy doesn't declare me as your king that I won't be by your side in another way once I serve my purpose? "

"Atticus, wait. No. That -"

"You think I would abandon you because I wouldn't be able to have you to myself? Yes, I can be selfish, but I am not selfish enough to put my own wants over your happiness."

Hazel felt as if her breath was sucked right from her lungs as he dropped her wrist, stepped away from her, and picked up the dagger she had dropped in the midst of their training.

"Atticus! Gods no. I would never think of you like that. It's just-"

"Just *what*, Hazel? You think just because we slept together I can't separate my feelings for you from my duty? If so, you clearly don't know me."

The sheer pain in his tone cut through Hazel's heart. Her mind stumbled for words to say. However, what could she say in order to make this better?

"Atti, please."

His eyes went from her to someone approaching from behind. "You enjoy the rest of your night, Lady Hazel."

Hazel's heart stopped as the wall came up behind his eyes. He was shutting her out, just as he did when they first met. Just like he did when he was that cruel and harsh prince in the carriage

"No, Atticus." Reaching for his wrist, her voice was clear as glass, not hiding the pain in her voice at how her words had harmed him.

He stepped back from Hazel, staring at her as if nothing was between them, and bowed from his waist. "Lady Hazel."

His tone was so cold, she thought his breath was now colder than the winter air around them

"Atticus," Hazel pleaded once more, but the Immortal Dragon straightened to look at the person approaching, ignoring her.

"Good afternoon, Arabella. Make sure she looks her best for tomorrow."

Hazel turned to look at her friend to dismiss her, but she saw the bright smile on her lips as Arabella stroked Hazel's arm, comforting her. "I plan to make every court lord and lady's mouth drop when they see her," she replied with a smile.

Turning to look at Atticus, who now stared at Hazel with an emotionless expression as he took her hand and gently kissed her knuckles, "She already does that. I shall see you tomorrow. Have a wonderful rest of your day."

With no other words, he released her hand and took his leave.

Watching him walking away without even turning back to look sent her heart tumbling into the darkness of despair and heartbreak.

Her hand lingered in the air where Atticus had kissed it. A kiss she wished lingered longer on her hand. It burned without his lips to protect it against the cold. Hazel's eyes never strayed from Atticus's backside as he walked away.

"Hazel? Hazel?" Arabella spoke, squeezing her arm gently to bring her focus back to Arabella.

Looking into her friend's honey eyes, Hazel attempted to speak, but no audible sound came out. Why was she choking up? Tears burned her eyes as she blinked them free from her lower lashes, feeling the cold air nipping her cheek as the salty tear trailed down her cheek.

Why was she this upset? She shouldn't be upset. He has hidden far worse from her. Turning to look for Atticus one more time, he was gone. Her knees buckled, but instead of collapsing to the ground, she sheathed her sword as her legs took off running after her. Her vision was blurred by the tears as she ran as fast as she could after her dragon.

"Hazel!" Arabella's voice cried out as she ran towards the castle. She needed to make things right with Atticus. She had to explain herself. They didn't come this far just for them to fall apart like this.

Shoving through the double archway doors, Hazel's eyes scanned the ivy-decorated halls. All the servants and guards occupying the hall stopped to look at her in the state she was in, but she didn't see Atticus. There was no sign of which way he had went.

Soft, warm hands grip her shoulders tightly from behind. When she turned, Arabella was looking at her.

"Hazel, please." The maid's soft plea made her realize she was causing a scene, and her arms are lowered from the doors she had shoved open. Swallowing hard, Hazel finally takes notice of those staring at her.

"Let's get you cleaned up. I can let Sybilla know you won't be studying with her," Arabella soothed, stroking a strand from her face as she gently nudged Hazel with her hand to head toward her bedroom chambers. Without argument or hesitation, Hazel obeyed.

In silence, she walked into her receiving room, staring at the fireplace, and took in a deep breath before letting out a curse in frustration.

"What happened between you two? Already have a lover's quarrel?" Arabella lightly teased, trying to ease the tension in the room.

After leaning her head back to the ceiling and asking silently for strength, Hazel lowered her head again and turned to look at Arabella.

"I learned all of this, all that Atticus and I have created with one another, is going to be for nothing." Hazel paused on her last words, wondering how to get her point across to her trusted friend. "When I fulfill the prophecy, I will, in fact, live, but I won't have the Crimson Dragon at my side. I'll have someone known as the Obsidian Tiger."

There was a moment of silence as Hazel watched Arabella's reaction, who stood there in disbelief. "I thought because it said I was going to be a ruler with someone else at my side-"

"You thought Atticus would abandon you once you fulfilled it."

Hazel said nothing but nodded her head, looking down, taking a deep breath, and keeping her emotions in check so her magic wouldn't flare up in response.

"Which was stupid. Yes, I know. I don't know why I said it or even think it. I am just so used to-"

"Being abandoned by those you trust?"

Hazel nodded, watching Arabella as the hand maiden gently stroke her cheek, pushing a strand of hair from her face.

"People don't abandon people they love. They abandon the people they are done using. From what I have seen, Atticus loves you with all his heart. I see it in his eyes and in his actions," Arabella continued with a faint smile, tilting Hazel's chin up. "I have never seen him fall so . In all the time I have known him, you are the one who has left the biggest impact on his spirit. Prophecy or not, that man will cling to you as if you are the air he breathes. Give him time. He will come around. Give him his space at the ball tomorrow, then after that. He will be just fine."

Hazel smiled warmly at Arabella before turning around wrapping her arms around her dear friend, kissing her cheek before pulling her into a hug.

"This is why I love you. Please never change," Hazel said into her friend's neck.

"Now, let's get you ready for dinner and then it's straight to bed for you. You have a big day tomorrow."

Hazel smiled before chuckling, looking at her friend. She took a deep breath, stealing her nerves not only to sit through another dinner with the king, but also to get through the awkward tension there was going to be between her and Atticus.

Chapter Sixty-Five

Hazel

The morning of the ball was a busy one, and the sound of cheerful chatter filled the halls. Guards were dressed in special uniforms with freshly polished swords and armor. Court ladies whispered among themselves about which gentleman they wanted to dance with at the ball.

It was about mid-afternoon, and Hazel was in her receiving room with an array of maids attending to her hands and face, making sure she looked perfect for tonight. Arabella was standing by the fire, removing the tea kettle from its whistling placement in the fire before setting it down on the small rectangular table beside the fireplace that held small finger sandwiches and other light snacks.

Sybilla was sitting in one of the large armchairs, reading a book.

"Scylly, are you wearing your normal jade green tonight or are you spicing it up?" Arabella asked curiously.

"Well, I have to represent the Asher household, so yes, jade green it is," she replied with no amusement in her voice, as if dressing up for a ball was not something fun for her.

"House hold? Each household has selected colors?" Hazel asked.

Sybilla looked up at Arabella, "Didn't you cover house colors with her?"

"No, I haven't had the chance to give her the full run down. We were covering etiquette first before we got into history, although history is your thing, my bookworm," Arabella lightly teased walking over to hand Sybilla a hot cup of creamy caramel oolong tea.

"What can I say? Fictional men are so much better than real men," Sybilla playfully taunted back, putting her jade green bookmark into her book, chuckling softly.

"Is that why you are still un-courted?" Arabella laughs in response before narrowly dodging a pillow thrown by the scribe.

Hazel laughed loudly watching her two friends. "Hey, you two, don't break anything in here, please. What about you, Ara? What are you wearing to the ball tonight?"

Arabella stilled for a moment looking at Hazel, slightly alarmed at her question before she smiled faintly. "Handmaids don't attend."

Hazel was shocked at the comment waving away the women who went to apply some kind of serum to her skin before she looked back at Arabella

"Nonsense, you are not *just* a handmaiden, you're one of my closest friends. You are welcome to wear anything in my closet. I don't have anything the shade of green you like, but I have other choices."

A smile curled on her lips softly. "Really? You want me there?"

Standing up from her seat on the couch, she strode over to Arabella in her red silk robe. "Of course I want you there. If it wasn't for you, Sybilla, and Ardnaxela, I would be lost. Without you girls, I wouldn't be here."

Sybilla smiled, standing from her seat and walked over to Hazel. "Hazel, you had the strength inside of you all along. We were only here to support and love you. Although, I am so proud of who you are now. I am honored to be by your side as your friend."

Hazel's eyes misted over as she leaned into Sybilla's touch. "Thank you, Syb."

Arabella and Sybilla wrapped their arms around Hazel, holding her tightly to them in a group hug.

"What is with all the mushy, loving feelings?" said a strong female voice.

Startled, Hazel looked to the front door of the receiving room where Ardnaxela stood with a black dress draped across her arm, her hair for once down.

The hugging trio exchanged glances, laughed softly, and then hurried over to Ardnaxela, pulling her into a tight group hug and laughing softly.

Ardnaxela surprisingly laughed, hugging her friends. "What is this for?"

Hazel smiled as Sybilla picked up her book again and Arabella grabbed a finger sandwich. "I was just telling them how happy I was to have you girls in my life."

Ardnaxela looked at Hazel, raising her eyebrow. "Oh?"

She smiled, holding Ardnaxela's hand. "Thank you for everything, For not giving up on me, even though I am a pain in the ass."

The White Dragoness playfully notched Hazel's chin with her knuckle. "Hey, I don't give up on my friends."

Smiling, Hazel looked at the dress draped over Ardnaxela's arm. "Did you come to get ready with us?"

"Why else would I be here with my dress in hand? ."

There was so much laughter inside Hazel's chambers, between Sybilla and Ardnaxela poking fun at each other, and Arabella helping do Hazel's makeup and hair.

For once in these past few months, Hazel was excited for something. She had temporarily forgotten about all the turmoil in these last few days from her cabin home being destroyed to her nearly dying by Darius's hands once more.

Hazel was surrounded by the women she considered to be her close friends. These last few months had seen them grow close, and she now felt as if they were no longer her friends but her sisters, whom she had never had.

She watched in the mirror of her vanity as Ardnaxela smoothed out her dress attire for the ball. Not only did she look intimidating in it, but she also looked the role of a death-like goddess.

It was a halter top gown made of gorgeous lace that held a deep plunging neckline with a decorated dagger strategically placed between her breast where the hilt of the dagger had shown coming out from neckline, but to the untrained eye, it could have easily been seen as an accessory piece . When Hazel watched her change into it, she was amazed that it had a special quality for in case anything was to go wrong, Ardnaxela would be able to remove the skirt to reveal her black leather pants and her sword. At first glance, she was a divine court lady, but anyone who knew the White Dragoness knew how lethal she was.

Just like hemlock, the beautiful, white, dainty flower seemed harmless at first glance, but in reality, it was extremely deadly.

Sybilla laughed as she walked over to her warrior friend, motioning with her finger to turn around. "Here, let me cinch you up. I don't want that dagger slipping."

Without arguing, Ardnaxela turned around and held onto the back of the couch while Sybilla grabbed the string to the corset and tightened it accordingly.

Hazel laughed, hearing Ardnaxela's grunts as Sybilla yanked on the strings, tightening it. One of her hands was on the bedpost, while the other held the dagger where she wanted it.

"I don't understand how you and Hazel can breathe in these cursed corsets." Ardnaxela cursed out, causing the receiving room to burst out in laughter.

Sybilla laughed, tying up her friend's, and stepped sideways towards the door to admire Ardnaxela's dress. "I still will never get used to how you radiate in that dress. You actually appear like a lady."

Huffing and shaking her head, Ardnaxela crossed her arms and looked at Sybilla. "Yeah, yeah, don't get used to it. It's not practical to wear these. I don't understand how you two love it."

Hazel smiled, turning her head slightly from watching her friends in the mirror, laughing. "When you grow up the way I have, it's nice to feel like a princess now."

Sybilla's eyes widened as she saw her in her stunning green and violet dress, with green lace sleeves trailing down her arms and secured with a loop around her middle finger. The violet corset, adorned with gold swirls, contrasted strikingly with the lace green fabric shaping her breasts. At her waist, a green fabric fan spread out, resembling wisteria petals fallen onto the dress. The under fabric, also violet-purple, extended to cover her feet.

"Sybilla." Hazel breathed out in awe.

"I know it's not my normal green, but I wanted to do something special for today. I had this made for tonight. It's a combination of my devotion to my family house and my devotion to the Aestival lineage. Is that okay?"

Hazel stood up from where Arabella was doing her hair, followed by a disapproval clearing of the throat from the handmaiden. Hazel smiled, walked over to Sybilla, took her hand, and squeezed it. "It's more than okay. It's perfect. Thank you." Hazel grins softly before hugging her scribe friend. "But you will need this," she continued walking over to her vanity, removing her mother's necklace from the mirror. Turning back to Sybilla, she strode over to her friend. "I want you to wear this tonight. Keep it safe for me. As you know, it belonged to my great-great-grandmother."

Sybilla's eyes widened in shock before she looked at the necklace breathlessly. "Are you sure?"

Hazel nodded. "All I ask is that if it starts to warm up, let me or Atticus know right away." She replied as her scribe nodded in response.

There was a knock at the door of the bedroom. Arabella maneuvered around the vanity mirror and the trio standing beside the couch to open it up to see a servant boy holding a large white box

"I have a package for Lady Hazel. It is a gift for tonight." The boy said softly.

Arabella looked at the package, peeking inside before her eyes widened, and then proceeded to take the box. "Thank you," she said, retrieving a small silver coin for the servant boy. "Here you go."

The boy smiled in gratitude before running off. The trio watched Arabella curiously as she made her way to the bed chamber, setting the package down on the bed. "Hazel, you're going to love this."

When Hazel excitedly approached, she opened the box to see a note.

For the Ivory Fawn, long may she reign.

Under the note was a halo-point crown with ivy vines swirling around it. Taking it out, she admired it before noticing a gold dress inside the box.

Pulling it out, Hazel was amazed by it. The dress was a mermaid trumpet halter-style neckline with a deep plunging back. The gold fabric was styled as if it were feather wings shaping it. There was a slit up the right leg and hanging from the back of the neck strap was a sheer fabric that had golden petals falling from the back.

"Try it on!" Arabella squealed out in excitement. Hazel hastily went behind the room divider and, with Arabella's help, changed into the dress, maneuvering it over her hair, which was hanging in loose curls with decorative gold accent hair pins.

"Hurry up, I want to see," Ardnaxela exclaimed in excitement.

When Hazel stepped out from behind the divider, tears filled Sybilla's eyes while Ardnaxela's mouth was open in awe. "Oh Hazel, it's perfect. Who sent it?"

Walking over to the note, there was no name, just that maybe the Ivory Fawn reigned. "I don't know. Maybe Atticus?"

Arabella walked up behind Hazel, stroking her arm. "Well, whoever it's from knows exactly how to compliment your features."

Hazel smiled, turning toward her and putting a hand on her shoulder. "Thank you, Arabella. You helped us get ready, and now it's time to give you a court lady glow-up."

Shaking her head softly, Arabella's face and ears turned pink as a peach. "Oh no, I was just going to wear one of my dresses. It's okay."

"Nonsense, you are one of us, Bella, pick out one of Hazel's dresses. Sybilla will do your hair and I will do your makeup," Ardnaxela replied

Her head turned in surprise to hear Ardnaxela offer to do makeup for Arabella.

"What? Hey, makeup can be a very useful weapon in certain cases," Ardnaxela defended herself, crossing her arms over her chest. "Now come on, we have only an hour before we need to appear at the ball."

Chapter Sixty-Six

Hazel

Hazel, with Sybilla, Ardnaxela, and Arabella by her side, had a wide smile on her lips. She looked around the ballroom, which was decorated with wisteria flowers and ivy dangling from the chandelier, and a violin plays a lovely tune.

Seeing the array of different masks being worn , Hazel did had forgotten in the last few days it was a masquerade. She looked at the trio of friends who stood behind her as a server brought over a tray of masks.

Arabella picked a brown and gold rhinestone mask to match her brown and gold dress she had borrowed from Hazel's closet, Ardnaxela chose an intriguing white and black mask to contrast with her mostly black dress, while Sybilla collected a green and gold mask.

Hazel saw no other masks, and she faintly frowned before looking at the trio. "I should have brought a mask, shouldn't I?"

"No mask is required for you .Its a tradition, every king before Kai believed it took less attention away from the guest of honor."

A strong aroma of bergamot and cedar filled her senses as she turned to see a man in black scale-like attire and a black dragon mask. Hazel knew by his presence that it was Atticus.

Taking in his attire, Hazel's body went still as her breath hitched, seeing how well his attire clung to his muscles looking at his outstretch black gloved hand. "May I be your escort, Lady Hazel?"

Hearing his formality with her, Hazel swallowed hard, seeing he was still hurt from the previous day. Nodding her head, Hazel took his hand and allowed Atticus to lead her to the grand stairway case balcony that overlooked the balcony. Raising his free hand to the orchestra to silence them, Atticus guided them to the railing.

Once the orchestra had silenced, Hazel straightened as Atticus held her hand, then turned to his right to retrieve two glasses of wine, handing one to her. He then raised his glass in the air. "A toast to our Ivory Fawn for saving my mother and your beloved queen. From this day forth Wylana will forever be at the disposal of the Ivory Fawn as a way to show our gratitude towards her actions."

Hazel looked at Atticus, who turned to her and toasted her with a smile: "To the Ivory Fawn. May she forever reign."

A smile she couldn't hold back crept on her face as Hazel held her glass. "Thank you, Prince Atticus. I couldn't have asked for a better ally. To Wylana and its royal family, may Wylana flourish forever its divine glory it is today."

An eruption of cheers Swallowing, Hazel took a drink of her own, not taking her eyes off Atticus. Turning her head she sets it down onto the tray a servant brought her from her right, setting it down.

Atticus raised his hand, which still held Hazel's, and kisses the knuckles before he leads her down the grand stairway. Being guided to the dance floor, Hazel's breathing caught once more as Atticus rested his hand on her lower hip while one held her left hand.

"Attic-"

"Don't say anything, just dance," Atticus cut in before leading her into a waltz.

They glided through the ballroom like butter with every step. Hazel's eyes never came off Atticus as she took a deep inhale of his scent.

"We need to talk," Hazel started, but Atticus caught her by surprise, leading her into an under-the-arm spin.

""You look breathtaking tonight, Hazel. That dress..." His gaze lingered, not with hunger, but admiration, reverence. "It suits you so perfectly, it's almost unfair. I might have to give Arabella a raise for knowing exactly how to steal the air right out of my lungs." Atticus deflected as they glided through the ballroom. Hazel looked at him confused, taking a deep breath.

"Wait, you didn't send the dress?"

A flicker of confusion passed through his eyes before he let out a quiet, hollow laugh. "No, I didn't. Maybe it was your ever-loyal Obsidian Tiger—ready to sweep you away.."

He was most definitely still sore. "Atticus, I didn't know how exactly to tell you. You can't get mad with me when it's not my choice-"

"Right, I can't get mad about you concealing something like this from me that could affect my life. However, it's okay for *you* to get mad when I didn't tell you about the prophecy asking you to sacrifice yourself. Yeah, that totally makes sense," Atticus scorned before spinning Hazel once more, letting the gold fabric skirt of the dress flare out in a show before he pulled her back in.

"Can we please not fight here? We can talk about this tomorrow when it's just us," Hazel pleaded, but Atticus scoffed.

"That sounds like a deflection, Hazel. Besides, I already have plans to speak with my brother and learn where Duvessa has gone."

Hazel's eyes widened in surprise before she stepped closer, speaking slowly. "Kingsly is innocent. He was a pawn for Darius and Duvessa. They used him to-"

"You're so naive, Hazel, thinking my brother wouldn't try for a power grab," Atticus ground out.

Hazel was about to speak, but the orchestra ended their song. Stepping back, she curtsied to Atticus, holding her tongue as she straightened, keeping her hands tightly to herself. The last thing she wanted to do was insult the king by making a scene by slapping Atticus across the face, so she walked towards Arabella and Ardnaxela, who were mingling with each other.

A man stepped in her path, dressed in all black and wearing a raven mask. "My apologies, Lady Hazel, but may I ask for a dance from you?" the gentleman asked politely, extending his gloved hand.

Hazel looked at her friends, who smile at her as Arabella motioned with her hand to go dance. Sighing, Hazel politely grins, nodding her head. "Yes, you may."

Allowing him to lead her back to the dance floor, Hazel caught a glimpse of Atticus, standing beside his mother, glowering at her with a glass of wine in his hand.

Hazel couldn't care less right now about his brooding; she was planning to enjoy her party. The gentleman rested his hand on her hip, just as Atticus had before, as the orchestra started up once more.

"You look so divine tonight, Lady Hazel," the gentleman complimented, bringing her attention back to him.

"Thank you. This dress was a gift from a secret admirer," Hazel replied, offering a kind smile

"I wouldn't say a secret admirer, but more of someone who truly knows you. Someone who would be able to pick such a divine dress to complement not only your skin and shape, but the way your eyes sparkle in the chandelier's light," the stranger said, spinning Hazel, fanning the dress out as if to admire it more.

Hazel considered his words for a moment. His comment was odd, but also struck something in her, setting off all alarms in her head and body. "Would you mind indulging me on who you think could have chosen a dress like this?"

An uneasy feeling crawled up her body as the stranger spun her once more only to spin her into his chest. He leaned in, and the feathers on his raven mask brushed her cheek and ear. "Perhaps you already know who, but you are too afraid to admit he has come back for you."

Iron and salt filled her senses.

No, No this isn't happening

Hazel's entire body tensed as she continued to dance, scanning the room to see if she can spot Atticus or her friends.

"Your scribe friend was surprisingly strong for the dainty persona she carries around the court. Although, it wasn't hard for Duvessa to obtain her."

The contents of her stomach turned to acid, and the bile wanted to creep up her throat.

"You know you smell of sweet vanilla when you're terrified." Pulling her closer to feel his hardness against her, "If you wish for your friend to be spared, you will walk out of this ball with me without alarming a soul. Am I clear?"

Swallowing, Hazel tried to steel her nerves, catching a glimpse of Atticus once more. Now standing at attention with his hand on the hilt of the sword, his eyes stared into her.

Neutralizing her expression to form a smile on her face, she leaned her head slightly to the side before Darius spun her once more and pulled her to his chest, keeping the charade up that everything was okay and that she wasn't dancing with the enemy right now.

"If I go with you, you swear no one gets hurt, including Sybilla?" Hazel replied slowly to Darius.

"I have no interest in them, only you, hence the dress. I want to show off just how divine you will be when I finally drain you of everything," he purred softly.

She nodded her head. "Alright then, Take me to where Duvessa is keeping Sybilla, and I will do whatever you want."

Darius' lips curled up in a wicked grin as the music ended. Hazel curtsied while he bowed, offering her his arm. She didn't want to check where her friends were because they might realize what was truly happening and interfere.

Following Darius out of the ballroom on his arm, she fought back the tears at the realization he was leading her to her death.

Chapter Sixty-Seven

Hazel

Hazel held onto Darius's arm as he led her out of the ballroom. When two guards raised their eyebrows towards the fawn, she spoke up. "My escort and I are going to get some fresh air. I shall be right back." Hazel hoped her words would assure them not to set off any alarms. She feared Darius would somehow get word to Duvessa to kill Sybilla. The guards bowed and remained at their posts as he led them away.

"Very good, my little fawn," Darius purred, leaning into her neck to inhale her scent. "Don't call me that. You lost the right to call me yours when you tried to kill me not once, but now three times," Hazel ground out through her smile to a bystander as she is led to a black carriage outside drawn by four black horses.

"What can I say? Fourth time will be the charm, although I am surprised you aren't crying for your dragon. Why is that, my little fawn?" Darius mocked once more, but Hazel kept her composure as they stepped down the grand staircase leading into the courtyard towards their carriage.

"This fight is between you and me. No one else should get hurt. Once I see Sybilla is unharmed and returned safely, then we shall end this with you and I. Where exactly are we going?" Hazel replied, keeping her eyes on the carriage.

"Where this bloody war started. I thought it would be a suitable place to devour what is left of you at the same place your ancestors failed."

Hazel opened her mouth, hearing someone approaching she turns to speak to the guard , However, she shuts her mouth instantly.

It was Heath, who wasn't dressed in formal attire. He may also be her last line of defense to get a warning to Atticus without endangering Sybilla. "Lady Hazel, you're leaving?"

Clearing her throat, she smiled softly, nodding her head. "Yes, I want to show my newest friend here the temple. I won't be long.. Do me a favor?" The squeeze of Hazel's arm in a warning from Darius made her tense, but she kept her face neutral. "Tell Prince Atticus I adored the dress he chose. I need to pick up my necklace from the temple, as I left it there and want to show it to my guest." Hazel replied, forcing a calm and cheerful tone to her voice.

Heath looked her up and down before nodding and then bowing. Darius pulled her toward the carriage before opening the door for her to step inside.

Hazel looked up, taking in the Wylana castle as if it were the last time. She saw Heath lingering. Offering a nod of her head, she climbed into the carriage. Hazel watched him head back inside, praying to Saaos that Heath delivered her message to Atticus. Looking up to the balcony, her heart still saw Atticus now standing on the balcony of the ballroom.

Swallowing as Darius stepped inside the carriage sitting across from her, Hazel tried to keep her cool.

"You playing a dangerous game, Hazel. If your prince shows up-" Darius started before Hazel cut in.

"He won't. We have been fighting. He will probably take credit for the dress and end up in bed with another woman as he has before."

"You both seemed intimately closer from our last encounter."

"Yes, well, things change when you keep secrets. You should know that from personal experience, since you made me think you cared about me before trying to kill me," Hazel snapped with tightness to her tone.

Darius grinned, taking her hand to kiss it. "Oh don't be so sad, Hazel. I *did* love the pretty sounds you made for me when you submitted like a good little girl." Hazel growled and reached out to slap Darius across the face, but he caught her hand, pulling it close to inhale her scent. "Even though your fear-" He leans in to lick up her neck, sending shivers down her spine. "-you still are feisty."

Hazel's throat dried as she took a deep breath. Holding his gaze, she reminded herself he no longer had power over her. Although, it was so damn hard not to shiver at the idea of him ripping her throat out

"Let's just get to the temple so I can see Sybilla, and then we can finally end this," Hazel huffed out, trying to make herself seem unfazed. But with Darius now restraining her wrist and inhaling her scent ,it made her stomach want to revolt

This was how she was going to die.

Arriving at the temple, Hazel looked up the grand stairwell of the castle, taking a deep breath. She hoped Heath would get her message to Atticus. Hazel was ill-equipped without her sword since she got so caught up in the blissful moment with her friends that she didn't even think to grab it.

"Shall we, my little fawn?" Darius once more taunted Hazel, whose eyes narrowed like sharp daggers.

"If she is hurt in any way, you will regret it," she replied coldly.

Opening the door of the carriage, Darius stepped out, offering her his hand. While waiting for her to take his hand, he removed his raven mask, discarding it into the carriage.

Hazel frustrated with herself not seeing it sooner as the glove wasn't a glove but his own blackened hand from the use of the Netherian magic. Inhaling deeply, she took his hand, stepped out of the carriage, and made her mind and nerves like steel. Once she saw Sybilla was safe, she would attack.

Walking up the stairs in the large entry, Hazel kept her breathing even and calm, thinking of every scenario Ardnaxela taught her and every hidden entryway Sybilla told her about or that she read in one of the many books she studied.

Darius nudged her roughly forward with a sharp growl "Don't even think of trying to escape. It's time you face your death."

Closing her eyes softly she for once prayed to whatever god who might listen to her.

Please, goddess of protection Aena and god of destiny Saaos if you are listening, hell if there is even an ancestor living, I don't care if I make it out of this, but Sybilla needs to make out of this alive. Lend me your strength and will.

Darius took the lead once they approached the Mother Grove temple inside the castle Andromeda's wall and shoved it open with little care as it slammed into the wall behind them. "I brought a guest, my queen."

Duvessa

Hazel stepped into the room. Sybilla was tied to the Mother Grove Tree unconscious, but thankfully unharmed. Hazel's eyes went to the necklace around Sybilla's neck seeing how warm it was making her skin red from how it radiated heat, just like it scorched Hazel in the carriage and when she ran into Darius in Duvessa's bedchambers.

Duvessa stood before Sybilla, where the stone path crossed the pond and led to the tree. Dressed in a black lace gown with a deep plunge neckline and a black point crown, Hazel yearned to smack the smug expression off Sybilla's face.

"You truly are a bleeding heart, aren't you, Hazel? First, defending a pathetic servant, and now handing yourself over for what, a scribe who you barely know?" Duvessa's serpentine grin made her stomach twist in fear of her friends' safety. However, Hazel kept a neutrality to her face, trying to keep herself from trembling. Picking up the skirt of her dress, she went to hurry over to Sybilla, but Darius caught her arm. "Don't even try to play hero when you're still that scared village girl." When she was released, Hazel rushed over to Sybilla, dropping to her knees, beginning to untie her scribe friend. "Syb, Syb, wake up."

Scanning her over, she was glad to see no signs of harm.

Sybilla's eyes fluttered open as she groaned in pain. "Hazel, no... it's a trap."

Hazel stopped right before a faint shuffle of feet made her whirl around, quickly reaching for a sword that wasn't there. A strong black force collided into her jaw, sending her flying into the pool of water beside the tree.

The crown clattered on the stone path as she forced herself up to her hands and knee. The young woman tasted iron and salt in her mouth.

"I will make sure this is a long and painful death for my little pet," Darius said as he approached from behind. Hazel went to stand up and throw her fist in an attempt to fight back. It failed as Darius's hand coil around her throat and slammed her into the pond, submerging her head completely underwater.

Chapter Sixty-Eight

Atticus

Atticus stood on the balcony, watching the carriage drive away with Hazel in it, wondering who the man was and where they were going.

Turning to walk back inside to see what he could figure out from Ardnaxela and the others, he stopped when Heath and Ardnaxela ran up with a look of alarm.

Atticus' stomach dropped. He didn't need to know what they were about to tell him. Somehow, he felt in his bones that Hazel was in trouble. "What happened?" Atticus asked Ardnaxela directly, who looked shaken up was something Atticus never saw unless something horrible happened.

Heath took a deep breath before stepping forward. "I found Arabella and Ardnaxela, but-"

"But we haven't seen Sybilla since she said she needed to use the women's room," Ardnaxela interjected for Heath.

Turning the railing, Atticus leaned on it with his hand, trying to settle his mind so he could think clearly. Not only had the love of his life more than likely sacrificed herself for Sybilla, someone he saw as a sister, but Hazel put herself in danger.

"Hazel told me that she wanted me to thank you for the dress, and that she was taking her guest to the temple to fetch her necklace and would be right back. Does that make any sense to you?" Heath said from behind Atticus.

Wait, the dress. Only one other person would be brazen enough to make a display that grand.

"I can't find Sybilla anywhere. What do we do?" Arabella's panicked voice came out on the balcony, causing Atticus to turn around looking at her.

Glancing at his sword, Atticus inhaled deeply. "Hazel more than likely gave herself over to Darius to save Sybilla." With his words, Atticus very quickly headed towards the ballroom.

Making his way over to his father and mother, who were enjoying the festivities.

Kai glared as his son interrupted his wine. "What is it, boy?" he ground out in irritation.

"The time has come for the Ivory Fawn to rise. I need you to lock down this castle. I'm taking my men to help her." Atticus held firm to his words as he stared at his father, not breaking his glare.

Kai's face, for once, held some surprise. He nodded his head in response. ". Go, do what you must. I will stay here with my men and make sure the guests don't learn what is transpiring."

"I will also need Kingsly."

The king's expression became furious but schooled his tone to keep from their guest over hearing "Why?"

"Hazel trusted him. If she trusted that he is innocent, then so do I. Plus, he is the best strategist we have. We need him for this." Kai's eyes bore into Atticus before he caved, waving his hand. "Fine, but hurry. If the Ivory Fawn dies, then Wylana is lost. Do what you must."

Atticus bowed his head to his father before quickly leaving with Ardnaxela, Heath, and Arabella in tow.

"Where is Hazel's sword?" Atticus asked over his shoulder to Ardnaxela, who stepped up beside him.

"Her bed chambers where we were all getting ready, I didn't see her put it on," she responded.

Inhaling deeply, he tried to ice his nerves. "We retrieve the sword and ride immediately. Hazel will need that in this fight."

While walking down the hall Ardnaxela looked to a guard leaning on the wall flirting with a guest.

"Killian , assemble the dragon guard, meet us outside with them in five minutes." She ordered

"Yes , Captain." Without hesitation he bowed before rushing off to follow orders.

Arabella took the lead, holding her dress up. "I will have the stables ready for your horses immediately. I am no good to you in this fight."

Exchanging looks with the maid, he nodded his head, "Alright, we will be there in five. Ella, are you-" As he turned to Ardnaxela, she ripped away her skirt, showing she was ready for battle. That was one of the things that made Atticus admire her. "Alright, let's go."

Barging into Hazel's room, he searched for the sword but found nothing.

Ardnaxela went to the bed-chambers, after some searching she came out with the sword in hand. "Alright, let's go," she said sternly, but Atticus's eyes were transfixed on the fireplace where an empty chair was. He felt he was going to be sick at the idea of Hazel dying tonight. "Atticus." Ardnaxela nudged his shoulder with hers bringing him back to reality. "We don't have time for you to stare into space," she scorned gently.

Taking a deep breath, he nodded his head, taking the sword from Ardnaxela, and quickly made his way towards the dungeons where Kingsly was being kept.

They were cold and damp, and the odor did not bother Atticus one bit being used to worst smells on the battlefield.

In the small, dim halls of the dungeon, Atticus remembered the cell they kept his brother in. Hastily, he approached it, snapping at the guard to unlock the cell.

Kingsly didn't move hearing the door open. He just sat on the straw bed in the far right of the cell, his hair unkempt.

"Get up," Atticus growled before he removed his sword belt and tossed it to Kingsly. "Hazel has been taken. She trusts you, which was the only reason I am trusting you. We need you to help us get her and Sybilla out alive," he continued

Kingsly caught the sword belt and looked at it, his eyes snapping up to look at Atticus. His eyes widened, "What?"

"Shut up. Get up. We don't have time. Move, or I leave you down here," Atticus snapped back before turning his head back down the hallway and looking at one of the guards. "Castle is on lock down. No one gets in or out."

The guard nodded before Atticus made his way up the stairwell to head into the hallway of the castle, his mind reeling.

Kingsly caught up with his brother, tying the sword belt to his waist and pulling his hair back the best he could with a leather strip offered by Ardnaxela. "Darius took her, didn't he?" He spoke softly as they made their way to the main entrance.

Atticus didn't need his sword, he had his dagger hidden on his personal, and if he needed to, he would be able to slit Kingsly 's neck here for any reckless behaviors. "Yes, and Sybilla. Hazel won't be able to hold herself up against him. She froze like a deer in headlights when she saw him recently." Atticus didn't even look at Kingsly as he continued to say, "I want to trust she can do this on her own, but without the sword, she can't fulfill the prophecy. We need to get it to her and save them both."

We made it to the front doors of the main entrance. Ardnaxela was already on her horse, adjusting the reins, looking at Arabella as the handmaiden patted her friend's leg. Ardnaxela, Atticus, and Kingsly's horses were already saddled and ready to go. Along with several of Ardnaxela's dragon guard already mounted and ready to go.

Walking over to Kissem, Atticus mounted up and adjusted his reins, as he could see Kingsly mounting his gray dappled steed from the corner of his eye.

"Alright, this is it. The time when the Ivory Fawn must rise. We must help Hazel in any way so she can become the Ivory Fawn. We keep any Netherian scum away from her. Kingsly, you take the lead on this since you were working with them." Atticus barked out his orders.

"I don't know much, just that Duvessa is their queen and told me she could make me her king if I helped her," Kingsly replied, lowering his head in shame

"It doesn't matter *why* you were helping them. It matters only that you help us get Hazel and Sybilla back. Now let's ride."

Chapter Sixty-Nine

Hazel

Still under water, Hazel gripped Darius's wrist tight, trying to hold her breath while she tried to break free. If Hazel didn't get he was going to drown her. An idea crossed her mind as if a whisper on the wind, faint but there among the panic. Releasing his wrist, Hazel held her hand up to his chest, channeling her magic. She used it to send Darius flying back from her, which caused him to land in the pond.

Coming up for air, Hazel coughed violently, spewing the water out from her stomach she had swallowed. She struggled to brace herself on her hands and knees, as they felt like jelly from the air she was deprived of. Hazel stood up just as Darius threw a blast off his magic.

This time, her hands came up, creating a shield to deflect the blast. "Sybilla, go!" Hazel demanded to her friend, as she threw a ball of light at Darius, scorching his shoulder. Not allowing him to recover, Hazel charged him.

Tackling him down to the ground, she threw a fist to his face, but he was too quick and caught her hand, yanking it to the side with such force she fell forward landing face first. His teeth connected to her shoulder as he ripped into it. A strained groan escaped her, trying to hold back the scream as her chest pressed against the stone floor surrounding the Mother Grove Tree. Her nails dug into the stone.

Knowing he could kill her while she was pinned like this, she needed to figure out how to escape. Bracing herself, inhaling deeply, Hazel tore her shoulder from the grip of his teeth, ripping her wound open further. She pushed him off, scrambled to her feet, and held her neck, examining her hand.

"You taste so sweet, my little pet. I can't get enough of you," Darius said, standing up as be withdrew his sword from his hip. It dripped with a black sap-like substance.

Raven Palm sap.

"As if I'll let you try that again." Hazel's voice quivered as she tried to appear brave. She stepped back, reaching down into the source of magic within her. Letting it build so when she strikes him again , it would help her get the upper hand. Exploit his weaknesses. Make him think she is too scared to fight back, that she will freeze again.

Darius chuckled, stalking closer, licking his lips softly with a grin, twirling the sword in display. Hazel backed up, her wet hair and dress clinging to her.

"You're trembling like a fawn, my little pet," Darius taunted as he walked closer.

Hazel swallowed and examined his movements, just as Ardnaxela has shown her.

Darius lunged with the sword. Anticipating the attempt Hazel rolled out of the way, there was a slice to her arm. Wincing from the pain, she clasped her arm. Getting to her feet, she looked to see the blade has sliced her arm.

The panic set in as she realized the blade that cut her arm had been covered with the sap. Hazel's chance to win the fight was dwindling with each passing second. She had a limited time to end it and rescue her people before the sap removed her from existence.

Throwing another ball of her magic at Darius, he dodged it. Lunging for her in the process, she blocked his forearm, which held a sword, disarming him. Kicking him away from her, she remained to grip his sword tightly, attempting to disarm him.

Gasping in pain, as Hazel held the sword. She dropped it. Holding it close, feeling her skin blistering from the sap on the hilt. The bastard laced his hilt, too. All the air forced out of her body as Darius tackled her once more.

Grunting in pain as her head smacked the marble floor, everything spun around her. She closed her eyes, trying to get her head to stop spinning. Hazel inhaled sharply, feeling Darius's hands around her throat once more.

"Did you like how that prince's cock felt in you?"

Hazel looked Darius in his eyes, seeing nothing but pure insanity. There was no longer any trace of a sane man. No sign of the butcher boy who used to bring her meat and wood when her uncle was unwell and unable to provide for them. No sign of the man she loved behind those eyes, only a monster.

"W-what?" she managed to sputter out as he held her to the ground by her throat. The panic and memories flooded back. Hazel wanted to escape this hold desperately and run, but all the training she learned from Ardnaxela was now consumed by the panic taking over making it nearly impossible to think.

"That night at the cabin, I heard you both. Oh, the sweet sounds he pulled from you." Darius let out a pleased groan. "I hadn't heard those sounds like that from you before and was half tempted to join you both. I was jealous," Darius continued learning by inhaling her scent. "Mm, your fear is so intoxicating."

Hazel looked at Darius as her breathing became shaky. Hazel's eyes went wide, a torrent of emotions flooding her features as the realization hit her like a freight train. "No..." she whispered, her voice barely audible. "You set the fire?"

Darius chuckled softly with a grin, tightening his hold on her throat. "Who else? Your little prince friend was busy getting drunk at a brothel. I told him to light the fire, and the coward refused. He tried to warn you both, until I rendered him unconscious," Darius confessed as his hand reached down, trailing up her leg, moving the wet fabric up.

"I was jealous he made you make such pretty sounds. I wonder if I can do the same now." Darius raised his hand more, but let out a yowl of pain as a dagger—the only dagger Hazel had on her—was thrust into his side. One she slipped on after she changed into the dress Darius gifted her. If Ardnaxela could conceal a dagger in a dress , why couldn't she?

"Don't fucking touch me," Hazel snarled.

Darius roared in anger, raising her up by her throat. Her feet peddled in the air as he removed the dagger from his side. He plunged it into Hazel's side before abruptly discarding her to the side into the Mother Grove Tree.

A sickening *crack* echoed through the air as Hazel's spine collided with the tree, the force knocking the breath from her lungs. An unholy scream tore from her throat—raw, instinctive, animal—as white-hot pain detonated down her back. Hitting the ground, she lay on her side, removing the dagger from her side, holding it firmly in her grasp, and looking up at Darius as he approached.

"Such a naughty girl. Don't you know it's rude to stab someone?" he mused with a pleased look.

Hazel grunted in pain, getting to her feet and holding the dagger while Darius retrieved his sword. She lunged once more in the hope of catching him off guard. Darius turned in time to catch her by the throat, throwing her across the room again. A cry came out as she slammed into a pillar.

There was no way she could keep this up. He was throwing her around like a damn rag doll. Panting heavily, Hazel supported herself up on the marble pillar bedside her to stand up, holding her side. As she got to her feet , she notice just above her hand was a stained blood hand print not much bigger than her own. This was starting to look similar liked she seen this before. Turning her attention towards the tree, Hazel remembered seeing Asteria dying under the tree, holding a similar wound to Hazel's.

Shifting her focus back to the hand print, Hazel realized it was her great-great grand-mother. Taking a deep breath, she looked at Darius as he stalked towards her.

"You will die the very way your ancestor died, just as my queen killed yours. It's so fitting."

She felt the sap begin to take hold—slow at first, like embers catching on dry grass. Then came the fire.

It surged through her veins like molten metal, setting every nerve alight. Her muscles seized, tendons pulling taut beneath her skin as if something inside her was trying to rip free. She convulsed, jaw clenched so tight her teeth ached, and a strangled cry clawed its way up her throat.

Her legs buckled. Her spine arched. Every inch of her screamed.

Her mouth flooded with saliva, but it wasn't relief—it *burned*, acidic and vile, coating her tongue and throat like poison. Swallowing felt like drinking glass. Breathing was worse. Each inhale scorched her lungs like she'd inhaled smoke straight from a forge.

She couldn't scream. Could barely breathe.

All she could do was *burn*.

I'm sorry Atticus, I'm sorry Asteria, I wasn't good enough

As Darius lunged, she braced herself, closed her eyes, and threw her hand up to shield the attack. The sound of steel clashing made Hazel still, and her breathing stopped.

A small gasp escaped her lips when she immediately opened her eyes to see Kingsly's sword now collided with Darius's. Atticus was at Hazel's side in an instant, grabbing her arm tightly in a snarl. "Thank fuck your alive , don't this ever again!"

Hazel's eyes misted as Atticus handed her Light-Bringer, which now glowed in her presence. She saw the tree beginning to stir, slowly emanating a glowing lilac light.

"No! Traitor!" Darius bellowed in anger towards Kingsly.

he used his sword to push Darius back, standing his ground. His eye never left Darius's. "Get her out of here. I will handle him."

Atticus didn't argue as he grabbed Hazel's arm and pulled her along, but Hazel yanked from his grasp. "No! I'm not-"

"Hazel I said go!" For a moment, Kingsly's eyes went to Hazel, holding that same pleading softness from the night of the carriage during the ambush. The look of that prince who had been so kind to her at her mother's grave, the prince who saved her from being killed by an arrow, the same prince who consoled her when her uncle died.

Hazel's stomach dropped as a sword was thrust through Kingsly's abdomen. A ragged grunt tore from Kingsly's chest as he staggered, blood already spilling from his lips. His eyes stayed locked on Darius—cold, defiant—even as the sword, blackened with poison, drove through his abdomen with a sickening crunch of flesh and metal.

He didn't cry out.

He didn't have time to.

His body convulsed, knees threatening to buckle, but he *held*—held long enough to tear his gaze away from the monster before him and look to Hazel.

Hazel, who was frozen in horror.

Hazel, who he needed to *run*.

His lips parted, forming the first syllable of her name—"*Ha—*"

And then Darius twisted the sword.

The breath caught in Kingsly's throat. His eyes widened. Whatever words he meant to say died there, on the edge of his tongue.

He collapsed like a marionette with its strings cut, the light in his eyes fading before he even hit the ground.

"Kingsly!" Hazel sobbed as she caught Kingsly as he fell, but Darius went to attacked her. Atticus intervened, fighting Darius, while Kingsly collapsed into Hazel's arms, causing her to fall back to the ground.

Holding Kingsly in her lap, tears flowed from her eyes as she hovered her hand over his abdomen. "It's okay. It's okay. I can help you. Just like last time," Hazel spoke softly to him, trying to comfort him.

Her hand began to glow, but then flickered.

"Hey," Kingsly softly said as he took Hazel's hand and squeezed it.

She shook her head before she looked at him. "No. No, I can save you."

The screech of steel on steel tore through the air, sharp and violent. Hazel's head jerked up just in time to see Atticus and Darius crash into each other like warring gods, blades flashing with fury, each strike a blur of vengeance and desperation.

But she couldn't move.

The poison surged deeper into her system, dragging fiery claws through her muscles, locking her limbs in place. Her body screamed for release, for *anything*—but all she could do was lie there, trembling, twitching, *burning*.

Another clash rang out, deafening this time. Sparks lit the edges of her vision.

Beyond the temple doors, she could hear it too—shouts, the thundering of boots on stone, the unmistakable, horrific sound of steel meeting flesh. Her people were fighting. *Dying.*

And she couldn't get up.

Her fingers scrabbled weakly at the floor, nails cracking against stone. Her breath came in short, wet gasps, every inhale searing her lungs. The roar of combat was getting closer, louder, but it all felt so *far away*—like she was listening from the bottom of a well, drowning in heat and noise and helplessness.

Turning her attention back to Kingsly, she looked at him as blood trickled from the corner of his lip. "Please let me save you," Hazel pleaded.

He faintly smiled. "Conserve your magic, my friend."

Hearing him call her friend made the floodgate opened up as she choked on her tears, shaking her head. "Please," Hazel pleaded once more before pulling her hand away from his to hover it over his wound. "I have lost enough people. I can't lose you. Please, *please* just stay with me, Kingsly." She tried to focus on his wound as her tears blurred her vision more.

A rough, callused hand moved her chin to look at him as he faint smile. "I need you to know I never wanted to hurt you or my brother. I wouldn't have agreed to work with them if I knew it would come to this. I was blinded by jealousy. Furious"

Blood bubbled at his lips as he struggled to speak, his voice barely more than a rasp. Hazel could barely keep her eyes open, her body on fire from the poison, her hands shaking as she pressed them against the wound that wouldn't stop bleeding.

"I used to hate him," he breathed, the words broken by pain. "Our father made him cruel... colder than ice. I thought... *he* was meant to be king, and I would be nothing. But then you came."

He coughed, violently, red streaking down his chin. Hazel whimpered, trying to hold him, her fingers slipping in blood and panic, her lungs begging for air through the burn.

"I was jealous... so jealous that *he*—of all people—found someone like you." His eyes flickered, desperate to stay on hers. "Someone *good*. Someone who looked at him and saw more than what our father made him. If a monster like *him* could win a heart like yours..."

His hand trembled as it reached for hers, barely brushing it.

"Then maybe—I thought—I could, too."

Hazel let out a choked sob, trying to shake her head, to deny him this goodbye.

"I was a fool," he whispered, the light dimming in his eyes. "You were never mine to steal. Love him, Hazel. With everything you have. You made him *better*. I saw it. And I'm grateful, even now... *especially* now."

His fingers slipped from hers.

"And thank you... for letting me feel... like I was *enough*—even if just for a moment."

His breath hitched.

And then, nothing.

"No! No! No, Kingsly!" she bellowed out in sorrow as she gripped onto his filthy tunic, cupping his face in her hands.

He was gone. Hazel had yet again lost someone she cared for to the Netherian scum that plagued her life and home.

The sword glowed brighter, catching her attention. Taking deep, shaky breaths, she reached for it. Even as the sap coursed through her and made it harder to move, she stood up.

Hazel's breath hitched, broken and shallow, as the clash of steel echoed like thunder in the temple. She could barely keep her head lifted, her limbs shaking from the poison ravaging her body—but she couldn't tear her eyes from the battle before her.

Atticus and Darius—locked in a storm of fury, blades singing death.

And Darius... *Darius.*

The man who once whispered promises of forever into her hair. Who spoke of quiet mornings and love that could weather any storm. The man who swore she was *everything* to him.

Liar.

Her chest burned—not just from the poison eating her alive, but from the truth that had shattered her heart long before this battle ever began. He had never loved her. He hadn't seen her as a partner or even a person. She had been a *means to an end*. A pawn in his twisted game.

He had made her believe they could have had something real. He had *let* her dream.

And now, he was trying to take *everything* from her.

No more.

Hazel's fingers scraped against the stone beneath her, nails splitting as she forced her arms to move. Her entire body screamed in protest—but her soul, blistering with rage, refused to surrender.

The poison burned—but her fury *blazed hotter*.

Her magic twitched to life, wild and unstable, crackling like a storm trapped beneath her skin. She grit her teeth, forcing air into her lungs, forcing herself to rise—*for everything he stole from her*.

Her life.

Her Uncle.

Her heart.

Just as Atticus's eyes met hers—pleading, searching—he turned. Just for a second. Just enough to glance at his fallen brother.

And Darius struck.

The sound of flesh tearing rang out like a gunshot. Atticus staggered back, blood spilling down his chest in violent rivers.

Hazel's scream ripped through the temple.

Something inside her *snapped*.

She surged forward, the pain forgotten beneath the tidal wave of betrayal, grief, and incandescent rage. Magic exploded from her fingertips, surging in violent, uncontrolled bursts, lighting up the temple in fractured flashes of power.

She didn't care if she burned herself alive.

She would make him *feel* what he did to her.

He had turned her love into a weapon. Now, she would return the favor.

"Bastard!" Hazel roared as she lunged for Darius.

Darius barely blocked her first strike. He had to step back from the sheer force of it.

She slams the pommel of her sword into Darius's jaw, knocking him clear on his ass into the pond. Hazel kneeled beside Atticus, who held his chest from the deep laceration. He tried to breathe the best he could with the sap now poisoning his body. Atticus couldn't even look at her, all he could do was cry out in agonizing pain.

Her rage boiled higher and higher, and she didn't miss how the sword glowed brighter in response. Turning her wrathful attention at Darius as he stood up, holding his jaw as he picked up his sword.

"Look who decided to grow horns?" Darius hissed out.

Hazel stood up, stepping over Atticus, placing herself between Darius and him. Like hell she let this bastard win. If she dies here and now , she is taking Darius with her.

Glaring at Darius, Hazel held the hilt of her sword tight, snarling at him. "You took my uncle from me, destroyed my home, killed my mother's tree, kidnapped my best friend, and killed someone I cared for. Now you have hurt the man I loved. I will no longer run from you. I will not hide behind that fear anymore. I will no longer surrender to you, for I am the great-great-granddaughter of Queen Asteria, the daughter of Ashira Hilliston, and the niece of Archibald Hilliston. I am the Ivory Fawn, and I will protect this kingdom and the people in it from you. You *will* die here and now at my hands."

Darius snarled at Hazel as his hand flew up, sending a blast of dark Netherian energy toward her. She threw her hands up in time to block the strike, but the sheer blow against her shield sent her into the Mother Grove Tree, causing blinding gold light to erupt, filling the room with new life.

Chapter Seventy

Hazel

There was darkness all around Hazel. Her breathing shook from the Raven Palm coursing through her blood. The searing pain felt like molten lava surging through her veins, each heartbeat amplifying the agony. Her muscles spasmed uncontrollably, and her vision blurred with the intensity of the torment. Every breath she took was a struggle, as though knives were slicing through her lungs.

Looking at the sword as it vibrated, it floated from her hand, erupting in a golden light so bright she had to step back and shield her eyes. In the midst of her suffering, Hazel's mind raced with fragmented thoughts. She wondered if this unbearable pain was a sign of her imminent demise or a test of her resilience. As the golden light engulfed her, a flicker of hope ignited within her, whispering that perhaps this was the key to overcoming her torment.

As the light dimmed, Hazel saw they were inside the temple, although everything was brighter. Seeing Atticus lying on the ground, her heart dropped. She kneeled down before him, reaching to touch his cheek—except her hand passed right through, as if she was a ghost. A wave of cold dread washed over her, intensifying the turmoil within her.

Panic surged through Hazel as she desperately tried to grasp him again, tears welling in her eyes. "Atticus," she whispered, her voice trembling with fear and desperation, "please, no..."

Looking up over her shoulder, Darius stood there with a sword, raising it high, but everything moved incredibly slowly around her, as if time had stilled. Hazel's mind struggled to comprehend the surreal slowness of her surroundings, each second stretching into an eternity. Her thoughts became a chaotic blur, oscillating between the urgency to protect Atticus and the paralyzing fear of losing him gripping her heart. The slowed time magnified her helplessness, making every movement feel like a monumental effort against an invisible force.

"Hazel Grace Hilliston," a female voice called from the right side of her.

When Hazel looked, she saw a white flowing skirt in front of her before her eyes trailed up to see ivory wings with gold tips.

Queen Asteria.

Standing up, she watched the floating sword, looking at the queen. Hazel went to speak, but the queen held her hand up to silence her.

"It is your time to rise and take your place, but you must give up something you hold dear in your heart," the queen said.

Hazel looked at Asteria confused, shaking her head as if it would help her understand. "What do you mean?"

She cupped Hazel's chin before turning it.

She looked around, confused to see the Wylana throne room in front of her, it appeared to be early morning from how dark it appear outside the windows . It was empty, but then the doors opened up. A woman with a large, engorged belly walked in with an infant on her hip, while two smaller children ran into the room. Hazel's breath caught in her throat, and her heart pounded with a mixture of recognition and disbelief, emotions swirling chaotically within her. She felt a profound sense of connection to the scene unfolding before her, yet she was unable to piece together why.

"Come on, mama!" the youngest girl said as she ran ahead.

A tall, bearded gentleman dressed like a king came through the doors playing with an older boy with two wooden swords. "You're getting better, Archibald," said the king

Hazel sharply inhaled, hearing the name, and her eyes misted over as she realized what she was being shown. She felt an overwhelming sense of longing and sorrow, wondering if she was witnessing a life that could have been hers or perhaps once was. Each laugh and gentle word from the family resonated deeply within her, stirring memories she couldn't quite grasp, but felt in the very core of her being.

"Careful, Atticus, I don't want our son to have a scratch on his face before his birthday party," the woman scorned, but the king laughed softly and walked over, kissing the woman deeply, careful of the infant on her hip.

Hazel's heart twisted painfully, and she clutched her chest, feeling a pang of envy and sorrow, realizing the depth of the love and connection she had lost or perhaps never had.

Tears streamed down her face as she whispered, "Is this the life I must give up?"

The warrior queen didn't speak.

"I'm sorry, Hazel, just having some fun," the older version of Atticus responded.

As she reached out to touch this version of Atticus, it vanished, and she was back in the temple. Hazel felt hollow and bereft as the vision dissipated, the vivid scene slipping through her fingers like sand. The warmth and love she had just witnessed now felt like a cruel reminder of what she could never have. Desperation and sadness engulfed her, making it hard to breathe as she faced the cold reality of the temple once more.

Hazel whirled to face Asteria, tears streaming down her cheek, realizing if she didn't become the Ivory Fawn, she would be able to live that life happily with Atticus, a life where she could choose her happy ending.

"That is what my life could be with him? If I choose him?"

Hazel stood frozen, her heartbeat a drumbeat of anguish in her ears. Her gaze dropped to Atticus—still crumpled on the ground, blood slick across his chest, his breaths shallow but fighting. And then her eyes lifted, catching the faintest flicker of movement from the corner of her vision.

She turned.

There—by the ancient tree—*herself*.

That version of her leaned against the bark for balance

Her stomach twisted.

Hazel stepped closer, every footfall heavier than the last, her magic humming faintly beneath her skin like the last ember of a dying fire.

Inside her, a storm surged. *Duty or desire. Destiny or love.* Wylana's future pressed against her chest like a blade. But so did *he*—Atticus, with his fire and fury, his unshakable loyalty. A life beside him would be soft and sun-drenched, a balm for every scar. But to take that path would be to leave her people behind. To watch her world fall.

The vision had shown her happiness.

Now reality demanded sacrifice.

Her voice broke when she finally spoke.

"You mean..." she breathed, barely above a whisper, "if I want to save my people... become the Ivory Fawn..."

She turned her head slowly, her eyes finding Asteria, who stood tall beside Atticus, proud and expectant—like she already knew the answer.

"...I'd have to give up *everything*? I'd have to give up *him*?"

The words tasted like ash.

Tears welled in her eyes, her heart fracturing under the weight of it all

Asteria slowly nodded her head before tilting her chin back. "If you wish to fulfill your destiny, there must be a sacrifice. As queen, we must sacrifice our wants and desire to do what's best for our people. When you fulfill it, you will have to not only rule but marry the Obsidian Tiger. It is your destiny and your duty."

Hazel turned to fully look at Asteria, biting her lip and remembering her uncle's promise before she closed her eyes. Archibald had always told her that true strength lies in making the hardest choices, the ones that demand personal sacrifice for the greater good. Both Archibald and her words echoed in her mind, reminding her that leadership was not about personal happiness, but about the welfare of those who depended on her.

She opened her eyes, the weight of his promise giving her the resolve to face the path laid out before her. Was the life of a queen, uncertain about her future, truly worth sacrificing a life filled with happiness and contentment with someone she genuinely loves?

An aroma of cinnamon and oranges with a hint of vanilla filled her senses, causing her eyes to fly open as whirling around to see Archibald standing there beside her mother. Her breath caught in her throat, and her eyes widened with a mix of surprise and relief. The familiar scent and sight of her uncle brought a fleeting moment of comfort in the midst of her turmoil.

Tears blurred her vision as Hazel stumbled forward, her breath catching in her throat like a sob that wouldn't rise. For a moment, she didn't believe it—*couldn't* believe it.

But then her mother turned to her.

And her uncle smiled the way he always had, that warm, grounding presence she'd yearned for in the darkest nights.

Hazel's knees buckled beneath the weight of it, and she collapsed into their arms with a cry torn straight from the hollow part of her soul. Her fingers clutched at them desperately, terrified they might vanish if she let go.

Her mother's scent—lavender and something soft—hit her like a wave, like childhood, like safety. She buried her face in her mother's shoulder and sobbed, her whole body trembling as years of grief poured out of her in raw, choking gasps.

"Mom..." she whimpered, the word cracking on her lips like a broken promise. "Uncle Archibald..."

She felt Archibald's arms wrap around both of them, strong and steady, just like before—when he used to lift her onto his shoulders, or wipe her tears when she scraped her knees, or hold her hand when the world felt too big.

But the world *had* swallowed them. It had taken them both. She had held Archibald hand as he died. Her was buried before she had any memory of her other than what Archibald told her. Their absences had carved holes in her chest that never quite healed.

And yet—here they were. *Warm. Whole. Real.*

Hazel couldn't stop crying. She didn't want to.

Because for one fragile, impossible moment... she had them back.

And it shattered her in the most beautiful way.

"I missed you both so much. How are you here?" Hazel asked

"We knew you needed us so we came," Archibald replied.

"You have been so brave and strong, my little lavender," Ashira said softly.

Little lavender had always been Hazel's favorite flower, symbolizing calmness and grace. Her parents had given her that nickname when she was a child, reminding her that she possessed those same qualities. Hearing it now brought her a sense of comfort and connection to her family.

Looking up at her uncle and mother, Ashira wiped her tears from Hazel's eyes and took a shaky breath. "I am so scared. I don't know what to do." Hazel's voice broke.

Archibald placed a reassuring hand on her shoulder and said, "It's okay to be scared, Hazel. Remember, you don't have to face this alone. We're here to help you every step of the way."

Ashira nodded in agreement, adding, "We may not be physically with you anymore, but we will always be by your side in your heart and spirit."

Hazel felt a wave of warmth and reassurance wash over her. She took a deep breath.S "What if I fail? What if this was all for nothing?"

"The unknown is terrifying, but when you have people who love you and support you beside you, it is not so scary," Archibald said softly to Hazel, stroking her golden hair from her face before kissing her forehead. He turned his head, looking to Atticus, who was rolling to his side in slow motion.

"You have him, your scribe friend, the warrior, and the maid with a lion's heart. With them, you will sore farther than you know." said Ashira as she kissed her daughter's head, before cupping Hazel's chin and turning her daughter's face toward her family.

Hazel felt an overwhelming surge of gratitude and love, her heart swelling with the warmth of their unwavering support. Tears of relief and hope filled her eyes as she realized she wasn't alone in facing the challenges ahead. With renewed determination, she nodded at her family, ready to tackle whatever lay ahead. Hazel focus between her uncle and mother before she looked at Asteria taking a deep breath.

As she looked into Asteria's eyes, building the courage in herself. Stepped out of her uncle and mother's arms, she approached the queen, taking a deep breath. Each step toward the her was one away from her selfish desires, yet she knew deep down it was the right path to take.

"I swore to my uncle on his deathbed that I would fulfill my destiny to become the Ivory Fawn and save my home. If that means sacrificing the happy ending, I want to follow a path of uncertainty and meet it with my head held high," Hazel said with pure confidence as she straightened her posture and rolled her shoulders back.

"Hazel," Queen Asteria said, her voice steady and laced with ancient power. She raised the golden orb in her palm, the light from it casting sacred shadows across the chamber. "Repeat after me. This is not merely an oath—it is the lifeblood of our people. It is the promise that will bind your soul to the legacy of the Ivory Fawn, to the will of the goddess Verity, and to the hope of all who still believe."

Hazel's throat tightened as she turned to look one last time at her family. Her mother—radiant and proud—and Archibald—gentle and unyielding—stood side by side, their eyes shimmering with the love that had carried her through every moment of doubt. They nodded, not with sorrow, but with pride.

This was goodbye.

But it was also the beginning.

Hazel's heart trembled as she faced Queen Asteria once more. The golden light bathed her skin, seeping into her bones, and for the first time, the fear began to fall away.

She took a deep breath.

"I, Hazel Grace Hilliston, chosen by fate and forged in fire, do solemnly swear before the goddess Verity, before the sacred Aestival flame, and before those who came before me, that I shall carry the mantle of the Ivory Fawn with unwavering honor."

She stepped forward, the orb's golden glow reaching for her like it *knew* her. As Hazel repeated the words

"I vow to protect the innocent, even when the world demands their sacrifice.

I vow to uphold justice, even when it is easier to turn away.

I vow to stand as a shield for the helpless, as a blade for the voiceless, and as a light in the darkest of hours."

Hazel felt the magic begin to wrap around her like silk and flame.

"I offer my strength, my will, and my life to the safety and preservation of the Aestival people.

I will not falter. I will not yield. I will not run.

Though the path ahead may demand blood, sorrow, and solitude—I will walk it with my head held high, with love in my heart and courage in my soul."

She looked Asteria in the eye, then raised her chin proudly.

"This is my promise. This is my purpose. This is my power.

So help me, by the unshakable grace of the goddess Verity.

Let my name burn in legend, not for glory, but for hope."

The orb surged toward her—light flooding her chest, her veins, her very spirit.

In that moment, Hazel Grace Hilliston became the Ivory Fawn.

Not because fate demanded it.

But because *she chose it*.

As Hazel spoke the final words of her oath, the golden orb of magic surged into her chest—an explosion of warmth and divinity that swept through her veins like wildfire. The air trembled. The ground beneath her feet hummed. And in that sacred moment, everything began to change.

Her golden feathered dress shimmered, the threads of magic unraveling midair like spun light. In its place, fabric blossomed around her—elegant, regal, *reborn*. The bodice clung to her like a second skin, a soft cream hue with the faintest golden sheen, shaped into a strapless sweetheart neckline that radiated both grace and strength. The skirt flowed down in cascading layers of cream and pale lavender, each one dancing with movement. A sheer layer of tulle settled over it, adorned with delicate, hand-sized purple flowers that sparkled like they'd been kissed by starlight.

Then came the wings.

Two enormous ivory wings unfurled from her back with a sudden, radiant burst—wreathed in soft light and trailing golden shimmer like divine fire. They curled inward for a moment, shielding her like a cocoon, before sweeping open in a breathtaking display. They stretched wide, gleaming in the chamber light, each feather edged in molten gold.

A soft wind, summoned by her power alone, stirred the petals at her feet as a crown materialized upon her head—woven from verbena, cornflower, and deep violet cattleya orchids, symbols of strength, wisdom, and sacrifice. Two majestic golden antlers rose from the crown, curving outward and upward, jeweled chains and crystals draped delicately between their tines, catching and scattering the light like tiny stars.

She looked like the prophecy made flesh.

Not just a girl. Not just a warrior. But the *Ivory Fawn*—protector, chosen, eternal.

And as she opened her eyes—now glowing faintly with the gold of Verity's blessing—every soul in the room knew:

Tresian had its savior.

Hazel took in her new appearance. Her eyes widened in shock she appeared down at her new dress before glancing over her shoulder at her wings. Hazel was taken back by her newest appearance. Before, Hazel returned her attention back to her uncle and mother, who were beaming with joy. Picking up her dress, she ran over to hug them both, saying, "Thank you for everything."

A tear fell from Hazel's eyes as she looked at her uncle and mother one last time before she turned to returns her attention to Queen Asteria with a proud smile. "Tell me how I can bring the Aestivals back."

Asteria smiled softly. "They are already on their way. Ivory Fawn."

Hazel nodded her head before she walked over to her old form, still in slow motion, before looking at Archibald and Ashira one last time. "I love you."

Archibald's eyes glistened with tears as he reached out, his voice trembling with emotion. "We love you too, Hazel," he whispered.

Ashira, unable to contain her feelings, rushed forward and enveloped Hazel in a tight embrace, her laughter mingling with tears of joy. Holding her mother close, she pulled away returning her attention to her older form, still in slow motion.

Reaching out, Hazel's fingers brushed her own shoulder—skin to skin, spirit to spirit.

And then, everything *snapped*.

The weight that had gripped her chest for what felt like an eternity shattered like glass. The searing burn of the poison that once curled through her veins vanished—replaced by something warm, *clean*, and *unshakable*. The ache in her limbs dissolved. The tightness in her throat released with a breath that came out clear and whole, like the first gasp of life after drowning.

The world surged back into focus, but it wasn't the same world.

It was brighter.

The cracked marble beneath her feet gleamed with gold-veined light. The shadows in the room receded as though ashamed to remain near her. Every sound was crisp, layered with clarity—the distant clash of swords, the flutter of wings, the hushed whisper of magic thick in the air. The scent of flowers—fresh and wild—filled her nose, as if the earth itself exhaled in relief.

Her magic, once wild and fraying, now pulsed steady and strong within her chest. It flowed through her like a second heartbeat—elegant, powerful, *hers*. It felt like sunlight poured into a vessel of flesh and bone, and it moved with her as she took a step forward, golden sparks trailing at her heels.

She blinked, and where once the world was blurred by fear and pain, now she saw *everything*. The fine dust dancing in shafts of light. The flicker of magic on the edge of her vision. The faces of the people she loved, etched with hope and awe.

No longer broken.

No longer afraid.

She was whole.

The Ivory Fawn had awakened.

And Hazel—*Hazel Grace Hilliston*—stood stronger than ever before.

Lunging forward, her sword classes with Darius before it could touch Atticus. His eyes widened in terror. Hazel smirked as she flung the bastard back with such brutality he slammed into the pillar with enough force it cracked. Darius's face twisted in a mix of shock and rage as he struggled to regain his footing.His blade wavered.

Hazel saw it—the subtle tremor in Darius's wrist, the way his gaze flicked from her face to the cracked pillar behind him, then back again. The confidence that had once dripped from his every word, every cruel grin, now faltered beneath the weight of *her*.

And she knew.

He was afraid.

"You feel it, don't you?" Hazel said, her voice low but steady, rippling with quiet fury. "That weight pressing down on your chest... that's fear. *Your* fear."

Darius's jaw clenched, but he took an unconscious step back. His eyes flicked around the temple as though seeking an escape, as if the very stones were closing in around him.

"Do you smell it, how enticing you fear smells. Smell like vanilla." Hazel taunted. "This isn't how it was supposed to end," he spat, but the words lacked venom now. "You were *mine*. You were meant to stand beside me!"

"I was never yours," Hazel growled. Her wings flared out, catching the temple light, casting a silhouette far greater than the girl he thought he could break. "You only wanted my power. My crown. My *fear*. But I've reclaimed every piece you ever tried to tear from me."

She advanced, magic crackling at her fingertips—not wild and uncontrolled this time, but *focused. Intentional.*

Darius lifted his sword in a trembling grip, sweat beginning to bead at his temple. "You think you can kill me? I am the rightful king!"

"No," Hazel said, eyes glowing, voice like thunder before a storm. "You're just a man who thought he could control a goddess in the making."

His breath caught.

Hazel tilted her head, gaze piercing. "And now you realize... you're standing alone."

Darius's lips parted, but no sound came. The silence that followed was deafening—until Hazel took one more step and the ground seemed to shudder beneath her feet.

"I am the Ivory Fawn," she said, voice rising like a battle hymn. "And this time, you don't get to write the ending."

Chapter Seventy-One

Hazel

The Ivory Fawn stood between Atticus and Darius with a newfound strength. Glaring Darius down, she gripped her sword tight as her attention went to the tree as emanated a bright lilac light.

Darius, however, took a step back, his face contorted with a mix of fear and anger.

Turning her head to Atticus, Hazel offered him a hand up. As he took it, a look of pure awe appeared on his face. She pulled Atticus to his feet and hovered her hand over his chest, healing his wound with ease.

Hazel dropped to her knees beside Atticus, her movements calm but sure, the storm inside her no longer chaos—but purpose. Her hands, steady and unwavering, moved to his chest as golden light unfurled from her fingertips in radiant streams, flowing effortlessly from a well that no longer flickered or faltered.

"You're not leaving me," she said, voice firm and quiet, like a vow whispered to the stars.

Her magic obeyed without resistance. It surged through her in a steady rhythm, pulsing warm and powerful, responding to her will as if it had been waiting for this moment. The light wrapped around Atticus's wounds, weaving through torn muscle and broken bone with reverent precision, every thread of golden energy laced with love—and power.

Behind her, unseen, Darius stood still as stone. His breath caught in his throat. That *light*—it wasn't wild or panicked like before. It was *controlled*. It was hers.

His disbelief curled into fury. He clenched his fists at his sides, nails biting into skin. His jaw locked. "This changes nothing," he snarled through gritted teeth, though a flicker of fear hollowed the words.

Hazel didn't look at him.

She didn't need to.

The tide had turned, and she knew it.

Atticus stirred beneath her hands, a soft breath escaping his lips as color crept back into his skin. Her magic pulsed once more—gentle, protective—and then quieted, still glowing faintly around her fingertips like embers after a blaze.

Only then did she look up, her eyes glowing with quiet power.

"This changes nothing!" Darius roared, hurling himself at Hazel and Atticus in one final, desperate attempt to win.

But the moment he moved, the air split with a crack of dark magic.

Shadows *lunged* from the temple doors, coiling like vipers around his sword mid-strike and yanking it from his hands with a violent screech of metal. The blade spun through the air before vanishing into the shadows like it had never existed.

Darius's eyes flared wide. He stumbled backward, scrambling, disarmed and breathless. "What—?"

A gust of cold wind swept through the temple. The shadows curled tighter, growing denser, as footsteps echoed against the stone. Slow. Purposeful. Predatory.

From the darkness stepped a man—tall, lean, radiating calm, controlled fury. Wings made of solid obsidian fanned out behind him, spanning nearly the entire width of the chamber. Every step he took bent the room's light around him. His eyes—glowing with silver and smoke—locked on Darius like a storm given form. "While breath yet stirs in these lungs, the Ivory Fawn will not fall. Not to time. Not to war. And never—*never*—to cowards." That voice — gods, that voice — was a baritone dipped in smoke and steel. Rich, smooth, and devastatingly calm, like the kind of lullaby death might hum before it strikes.

Hazel's breath caught in her throat.

She could feel it—the raw power radiating from him like heat off sun-baked stone, but colder. Calmer. Darker. Her knees nearly buckled, not from fear, but from the overwhelming *presence* of him. This wasn't just magic. This was *Aestival*. This was living myth.

Her heart pounded, the reality slamming into her with the weight of prophecy fulfilled.

He moved like someone who had fought wars before the world had names for them, whose bones remembered glory, grief, and godhood. And he was *here*. In front of her. Standing between her and death itself.

A mix of awe, fear, and something dangerously close to hope churned in her chest.

The shadows around him coiled tighter, alive and aware, as though the darkness itself recognized her now. Chose her. Protected her.

Hazel couldn't look away.

And somehow, in the quiet pause that followed, she felt it:

He wasn't just protecting the *Ivory Fawn*.

He was protecting **her**.

Darius's face drained of color, and his bravado crumbled under the weight of the man's ominous presence. His eyes darted around, searching for an escape. Trembling, he took a hesitant step back, realizing that his plan was longer attainable now that she brought back the Aestivals.

Hearing a thud behind her, Hazel whirled, bringing her sword up, ready to cut down whoever dared to sneak attack. Hazel's eyes widened in shock, seeing two large brown wings with tinges of caramel and coffee tones. Her eyes met with the caramel, honey almond-shaped eyes of King Gavriel, who effortlessly caught her hand.

"Is that any way to greet family?" Gavriel teased softly. His voice was low but also commanding.

Hazel turned, her breath catching in her chest as she took in the scene. The obsidian stranger stood with terrifying calm, his wings half-flared, casting wide shadows across the temple floor. His blade—a broadsword black as night—rested just beneath Darius's throat, the edge so close that a single swallow would open his jugular.

Hazel's fingers went slack around her own hilt, her lips parting in stunned silence. The air felt electric, charged with something ancient and raw. Her pulse roared in her ears. She was seeing a real Aestival—a being of legend, of prophecy—standing like a wall between her and the monster who'd haunted her every step.

Darius stood rigid, chest barely rising as he tried not to breathe too deeply. His sword hand trembled at his side, useless, unless he wanted to lose his head.

The stranger didn't move. He didn't need to. The message was clear: Flinch, and you die.

Hazel could see it—the calculation churning behind Darius's eyes. He couldn't overpower the stranger, not in this position. Not with the blade poised so precisely. So he did what cornered beasts always do: he waited for a mistake.

His eyes flicked to the side, searching—for footing, for cover, for any weakness. And then, like a striking snake, he twisted his body—not away, but into the blade. The sword sliced the edge of his cheekbone as he ducked, the cut shallow but enough to draw blood as he rolled out of reach.

Hazel's breath caught.

Darius hit the ground hard, but didn't stop. He scrambled to his feet, blood trailing down his jaw, his sword back in hand. His desperation pulsed in the air like a storm—wild, reckless, cornered.

But the Aestival didn't flinch.

He simply turned his head to follow Darius's movement, the shadows already curling tighter around his arms, ready to strike again.

Hazel's heartbeat thundered.

The fight wasn't over.

But something had shifted.

Darius bled now—not just from the cheek, but from pride, from control, from the fear now rooted deep behind his eyes.

And Hazel? Hazel stood taller, watching not just a savior, but an executioner cloaked in light and shadow, and she knew—

This time, Darius wouldn't escape unscathed.

Hazel watched, transfixed, as the two men clashed in a storm of shadow and steel. The obsidian stranger moved like a phantom, wings sweeping behind him with terrifying grace, catching the light like blades of moonlit glass. Each strike he made was a calculated execution, defending not just himself—but **her**. Every motion was deliberate, every pivot of his heel positioning his body between Hazel and danger.

Darius fought like a man unraveling. His blade tore through the air in wild, furious arcs, desperation driving each movement. His rage spilled into every attack—sloppy, unpredictable, frantic. But no matter how fiercely he lunged, the stranger met him with surgical precision, deflecting the fury with devastating elegance. Hazel could see it now—Darius was **burning himself out**.

The final clash came like thunder.

A deft parry. A pivot. A disarming twist of the wrist.

Darius's sword clattered to the floor with a shriek of metal on stone.

Before he could reach for it, the stranger stepped forward, obsidian blade back at his throat, a mirror of the earlier standoff. This time, Darius knew—he was beaten.

His chest heaved, sweat pouring down his brow, eyes wide with the reality of his fall. The fire in him flickered into dread.

And then the stranger turned his head—just slightly—to Hazel.

Not a word passed his lips, but the meaning was clear.

Now.

Hazel didn't hesitate.

She stepped forward, power simmering in her veins like molten gold. Her own sword glowed in her grip, no longer flickering, no longer afraid. Her steps were steady, boots echoing with purpose. She saw Darius's eyes widen—not with rage, not with defiance.

With fear.

"No more running," Hazel whispered, her voice trembling with conviction. "No more lies. No more pain."

"Why is it, brother, you get to have all the fun?" Hazel heard a sultry female voice, but saw no one. Then, a woman with long black hair and black wings landed beside the stranger. Her eyes were a piercing shade of violet, glowing with an otherworldly intensity, and her lips curled into a mischievous smile. She wore a sleek, dark leather outfit that accentuated her lithe and agile form, exuding an aura of both elegance and danger. With a graceful flick of her wrist, she summoned a dagger, twirling it effortlessly between her fingers as she assessed the situation with a predatory gaze.

"Maybe because you're too slow, Nariana" the stranger laughed out.

Hazel couldn't wrap her mind around the face that not only was there one Aestival, but now three of them in front of her. Feeling the overwhelming emotions of joy, triumph, amazement, and shock. It all hit her that the Aestivals have truly risen as it was foretold. Her knees buckled.

Atticus was at her side, catching her, holding her up. "Easy there, I am here," he said before stroking the hair from her eyes.

Hazel's heart stopped as Darius, with the blade at his throat, vanished in a plume of black smoke. She waved the smoke away, but he was already gone. Her chest tightened, disbelief and rage flooding her. He escaped. Again.

Her fists clenched, nails digging into her palms. Failure. It stung deep, the rush of victory slipping through her fingers. She couldn't let it end like this.

Gavriel's voice thundered across the room. "Find him!"

Hazel stood frozen, her gaze locked on the empty space where Darius had stood. But the fire inside her only burned brighter. She wouldn't stop.

Hazel's chest rose and fell in shallow breaths, the weight of relief washing over her. She was still here. Still alive. The thought lingered, bittersweet—*they were wrong*. The prophecy hadn't been fulfilled through her death.

But then, as the relief faded, a dark shadow crept over her heart. Kingsly. She remembered him, his body crumpling to the ground, the life draining from him as he shielded her from Darius's strike. The memory hit her like a wave, the pain of his loss crashing over her.

He had died for her.

The truth stung. She had lived, but someone else had paid the price.

Hazel's head snapped over to where Kingsly's body lay on the ground. Running over to him, she fell to her knees, stroking his cheek, as tears formed.

Atticus joined Hazel, kneeling beside his brother, resting his hand on Kingsly's shoulder. "He gave his life... For us." His voice was low and broken as a tear fell onto Kingsly's cheek.

Hazel's fingers trembled as they brushed against Kingsly's cold skin, the chill seeping into her bones. She closed her eyes, desperately drawing on the power within her—the power of the Ivory Fawn. She focused, willing her magic to heal, to restore life. Her hands glowed with a soft, golden light as she whispered his name, pushing everything she had into the spell.

But no warmth returned to his body. No breath filled his lungs.

The magic—her magic—pulled at the edges of her consciousness, straining against the weight of what she was trying to do. But the light flickered and died, fading into nothingness.

Her heart shattered as she fell back, the tears flowing freely now, each one carrying a piece of her soul with it. She stared at him, the pain of her failure more suffocating than the loss itself.

"I'm sorry," she whispered, her voice cracking. "I wish I could have saved you."

But no matter how hard she tried, no matter how much power she summoned, it wasn't enough to bring him back.

Hazel looked at Atticus, reaching over and taking his hand. "He loved you, Atticus. He told me with his last words he never wanted to betray you if he knew working with Darius and Duvessa would have caused this. He never would have agreed to their deal."

Atticus's eyes widened with a mix of surprise and pain as he absorbed Hazel's words. His grip tightened on her hand, and a soft sob escaped his lips, the weight of his brother's sacrifice bearing down on him. "I should have seen it," he murmured, his voice cracking. "I should have protected him."

Hazel could see Atticus's heart shattering as he leaned over his brother's body, wailing in sorrow. She rested her hand on his head, stroking it gently. "None of us could have known, Atticus," she said softly, her voice breaking with emotion. "Kingsly's sacrifice wasn't in vain. He saved us, and we have to honor his memory by staying strong and united."

"No."

Hazel turned to look over her shoulder at Ardnaxela and Sybilla standing in the door frame, Hazel's heart dropped into her stomach as she turned toward Ardnaxela and Sybilla, noticing the heartbreak written across their faces. The moment they saw Kingsly's lifeless form, their eyes flickered with a quiet, unbearable grief, one that Hazel knew all too well. Ardnaxela's usually fierce, confident expression crumbled in an instant, her shoulders slumping as if the weight of their shared loss had crushed her in one swift motion. The way she held Duvessa now, her body rigid and tense, was no longer just the victor carrying her foe; it was someone mourning, someone who understood that this battle, this entire war, had taken its toll in ways they couldn't undo.

Sybilla, too, couldn't hide the pain that flashed across her face, her lips trembling ever so slightly as she stepped closer, her eyes darting to Kingsly's body. For a brief, fleeting moment, she seemed lost, her gaze locked onto him, her breathing shallow as though she could hardly bear to look at the man who had fought so hard beside them, now gone forever. Sybilla's posture faltered, as if she was about to crumble under the weight of their collective loss.

Hazel could feel their heartbreak in every small shift of their movements, in the way Ardnaxela's fingers tightened around Duvessa as if holding onto something—anything—that could bring her back from the edge of her own sorrow. It was an unspoken moment of shared grief, an understanding that even in their victories, there was no escaping the pain that lingered in the wake of Kingsly's death.

The room felt colder somehow, the silence heavier. Their brief, victorious expressions faded as quickly as they'd appeared, replaced by the hollow sting of reality. Kingsly was gone. And no matter how much they had fought, no matter how many battles they had won, they couldn't undo that. His absence left a gaping hole, one that even the fleeting defeat of Duvessa could never fill.

Sybilla rushed over, dropping to her knees beside Atticus, wrapping her arms around him, and rubbing his back. She gently rocked him back and forth, her embrace firm and unwavering.

Reaching her hand out to Ardnaxela, the warrior dropped Duvessa's unconscious form on the ground and limped to Sybilla's side just as more Aestival filled the temple. Two Aestivals shrouded in armor took the unconscious Netherian queen away.

Slowly approaching as if it were an illusion, Hazel's eyes never left Ardnaxela as she came closer. Hazel's heart ached with a profound sorrow that echoed within the very walls of the temple. Tears welled in her eyes, blurring her vision as she struggled to reconcile the pain of their loss.

Taking her hands into Hazel's, Ardnaxela dropped to her knees and wept at the fallen prince before them. Hazel's eyes misted over as she wrapped an arm around the weeping warrior, encasing her wings around her mourning family.

Hazel's senses sharpened, a chill creeping over her skin as she felt someone approach. She turned slowly, her heart skipping a beat as she locked eyes with the mysterious Aestival male. His amber gaze held a depth that sent a shiver through her, his presence both captivating and unsettling. With measured steps, he moved closer, his wings folding neatly behind him, each movement graceful yet deliberate.

When he finally knelt before her, the air around him seemed to thrum with power, and Hazel couldn't help but feel the weight of his gaze—a mixture of intensity and something darker, something haunting. Despite his striking beauty, there was an aura around him that made her uneasy, as if he held secrets older than time itself. He was the same shadowed figure who had stepped in during her confrontation with Darius, the one who had turned the tide of the battle, and now here he was, close enough for her to feel the full extent of his otherworldly presence.

Hazel's eyes drifted to the pool of water that surrounded the ancient tree, its surface shimmering softly in the dim light. The memory of Queen Asteria's journal came rushing back—Asteria had written about the pool's miraculous power, how it could bring one person back, but only once. The words echoed in Hazel's mind, filling her with both a flicker of hope and an overwhelming sense of desperation.

She turned back to the Aestival male, her voice barely above a whisper as she asked, "The pool... it can bring someone back, right? Just once?" Her gaze remained fixed on the water, the weight of her question hanging in the air, her heart pounding in her chest as she searched his eyes for any sign of reassurance.

The weeping beside her stopped, and Hazel kept her eyes on the shadow winger warrior, waiting for his reply. He nodded his head only slightly once.

"Then use the pool to bring him back," Hazel said, keeping her trembling steady.

The stranger kneeled there for a moment before he looked at Gavriel, who approached the small, found family, who were mourning the loss of their brother.

"Is he important to you?" Gavriel asked softly to Hazel.

"Yes, he is my brother. He was there for me at my mother's grave and saved my life multiple times. I want to repay him for saving my life," she replied.

Gavriel's eyes softened with understanding as he listened to her heartfelt words. He nodded slowly, "then we shall try," he murmured, determination etched into his expression. Gavriel turned to look at the black-winged male

"Evander, carry him into the pool, please."

Evander? As in Evander, their champion?

Evander bowed his head, rising to his feet before approaching Kingsly lifeless body. "May I touch him?"

Hazel turned to look at the group, who was now staring at her, waiting for their response. The group exchanged hesitant glances, their eyes filled with a mixture of hope and fear. Some nodded in silent agreement, while others bit their lips, unsure of the consequences. Despite their apprehension, they gave their consent. Taking a deep breath, she nodded her head.

Atticus looked up. "You may, just be careful."

"I will treat him as if he is one of us," Evander replied

Once Evander had a clear amount of room to pick up Kingsly, he carried him to the pool at the edge of the mother tree, laying him gently in. Kneeling before the water, Evander removed his sword from his waist as Hazel and the other stood where Kingsly once laid, watching the winged male with anticipation..

"Oh great Mother Tree, cradle of life and ender of sorrow. You who breathe life into the fallen and shelter the brave—Hear me now. This warrior gave everything so others might live. Let his sacrifice not be the end. If your grace still lingers in these waters, let it be enough. Restore him, not for me—But for the world he died to protect," he said, looking up at the tree before he removed a dagger slicing his hand, hovering his slit hand over the water letting a few blood trickled in.

Hazel stood frozen, heart hammering in her chest as she stared into the glowing waters surrounding the great Mother Tree. Her hands trembled at her sides, knuckles white from clenching her fists too tightly. Around her, a heavy silence fell, the kind that seemed to press into the skin—thick with desperation and fragile hope.

She could feel the tension ripple through the room like a second heartbeat. Some of the Aestivals had fallen to their knees, whispering prayers under their breath. Others stood rigid, hands clasped together, eyes locked on the pool. Hazel couldn't tear her gaze away either. This had to work. It *had* to.

Please... she thought, every part of her aching. *Please bring him back.*

Then came the first ripple.

Hazel's breath caught. The shimmering water stirred, soft and slow—too subtle at first to believe it was real. But then the pool lit up in a radiant glow, golden and alive, the light cascading upward to illuminate the twisting limbs of the tree above. A hush swept through the space, and Hazel's knees nearly buckled as her chest tightened with disbelief. It was happening.

The light encased Kingsly's body like a cocoon spun from pure magic. She took a small, involuntary step forward, unable to breathe. Her lips parted in wonder, the breath trembling in her lungs. *Is this the power of the Aestivals?* It was divine—ancient and impossibly beautiful.

For a moment, there was only the light. No sound. No movement. Just a fragile, radiant stillness.

Then—he gasped.

Hazel choked back a cry as Kingsly's chest rose violently and his eyes snapped open. He shot upright, coughing, looking wildly around the space until his gaze landed on the Aestival warrior kneeling beside him.

Hazel's hands flew to her mouth. Her knees hit the earth.

He's back. *He's alive.*

Around her, the others surged forward—Atticus, Sybilla, Ardnaxela—throwing themselves into Kingsly's arms. The sounds of laughter and disbelief mixed with tears, filling the space with the kind of joy Hazel hadn't heard in what felt like forever.

And still, she knelt there, stunned into silence, watching the reunion unfold with tears in her eyes and awe in her heart.

The atmosphere was electric with joy and relief. Laughter and tears of happiness mingled as the group surrounded Kingsly, each taking turned to embrace him and express their gratitude.

Evander rose slowly from where he had knelt, his obsidian wings folding behind him with quiet grace. Without a word, he stepped toward Hazel and extended his cut hand, the fresh wound a quiet testament to the ritual he'd just helped complete.

Hazel's breath hitched at the sight. Tears shimmered in her eyes as she reached for him, her touch feather-light, reverent. She cupped his hand in both of hers, her fingers trembling as she ran her palm gently over the injury. A warm glow pulsed from her skin to his, knitting the cut closed with soft, golden light.

She stared at his hand for a moment longer—large, calloused, steady—and then looked up at him with tears trailing silently down her cheeks. "Thank you," she whispered, her voice barely audible, but rich with sincerity. The weight of what he had done settled on her chest, heavy but filled with awe. Her actions said what her voice couldn't—the trust she placed in him, the respect that bloomed in her heart, the bond forged not through words, but sacrifice.

Evander's golden eyes held hers, steady and unreadable. Then she spoke "You're the champion Queen Asteria spoke of." she took a deep breath. "You're the Obsidian Tiger, aren't you?"

Her mind raced, her heart pounding in her chest as she awaited his response. Doubts and hopes clashed within her. Could it truly be him? Hazel's breath hitched, her eyes searching him for any sign of acknowledgment, her entire being hanging on the precipice of his next words.

The warrior let out a soft chuckle, the sound low and rich like gravel soaked in honey. He gently withdrew his hand from hers, his golden eyes fixed on her with a hint of admiration. "You have done well, Ivory Fawn," he said, voice like dusk and thunder. "But... may I know your true name?"

Hazel raised an eyebrow, tilting her head. "Only if you tell me yours first, mystery man." Her tone was light, teasing—but her eyes searched his face for answers, looking for any crack in the mask he wore. When he remained silent, offering only that same unreadable expression, she sighed, biting back a smirk.

"So that's how we're playing it," she muttered, slipping her hand back into his with a wry grin. "Alright, stranger. I'm Hazel."

But the moment her name passed her lips, the smile faded—just a little. A quiet realization settled over her like a whisper from fate: if this was him—if this man truly was the Obsidian Tiger of prophecy—then the choice had already been made. She had sacrificed her chance at a simple life, at a quiet forever with Atticus, to awaken the ancient powers and restore the Aestivals... and to stand at the side of the man now before her.

Her chest tightened with the weight of that truth. She had traded her happy ending for a crown, for war, for legacy.

And for him.

Her fingers squeezed his once, eyes narrowing just slightly. "You owe me a name, Tiger," she added, softer now. "Especially if you're the reason I just rewrote my entire future."

Evander's smile curved like a secret kept in the dark. He lifted her hand with reverence, his eyes never leaving hers, and pressed a slow, deliberate kiss to her knuckles—warm lips brushing skin with the kind of ease that only came from someone who had done it a thousand times... and meant it every time.

He lingered there a heartbeat longer than necessary before lowering her hand, his thumb lightly grazing over her palm before letting go. "Well, *Hazel*," he said, his voice dipped in velvet and smoke, "the honor is all mine."

His amber gaze glittered with something unspoken, something ancient and teasing, like he was in on a joke she hadn't caught yet. Then, as if he could read the question still burning in her mind, he leaned in just a little closer—his breath brushing her cheek.

"And for what it's worth..." he added in a hushed murmur, "I rather liked hearing you say my name, even if it wasn't *me* who gave it to you."

He winked, then stepped back, a ghost of a grin tugging at his mouth, leaving Hazel caught between a flustered glare and an intrigued smirk of her own. Yes, Gavriel may have said his name, but she wanted him to say it himself.

Kingsly ran to her without hesitation, scooping Hazel into his arms and spinning her around as if he'd never let her go again. She let out a bright, unrestrained laugh, clinging to him tightly, her wings instinctively tucking close in the whirlwind of joy.

"Look at you!" Kingsly beamed, his voice cracking with emotion as he finally set her down. "You're glowing, Hazel!"

Hazel's feet touched the ground, but her heart was still soaring. Her cheeks flushed with warmth as she met his teary-eyed grin, the disbelief and happiness mirrored in her own gaze. She cupped his face for a moment, her fingers brushing over the skin that had once been cold and still.

"I thought I lost you," she whispered, her voice thick with emotion.

Kingsly gave a breathless chuckle, pulling her into another hug—tighter this time, like he meant to anchor them both to this second chance. "You didn't. Thanks to you... and him." He glanced toward Evander with gratitude in his eyes.

Hazel looked over too, her heart tightening with emotion. Evander stood a few steps away, silent but watchful, his wings folded and his gaze unreadable. The weight of everything they'd lost—and somehow regained—settled in her chest.

She turned back to Kingsly, burying her face in his shoulder for just a moment longer. In a world where miracles were few and fleeting, this one was real.

He was alive.

Hazel stepped back, twirling her dress and spreading her wings in display. There was no way she couldn't wipe the smile off her lips. Seeing Kingsly again filled her with an overwhelming sense of relief and joy. The familiarity of his presence and the warmth of his embrace reminded her of the bond they shared, making her feel less alone in the daunting journey ahead. Despite the uncertainties surrounding Evander, having Kingsly by her side gave her a renewed sense of hope and strength.

Atticus walked over, pulling Hazel into him. Cupping her cheek, he kissed Hazel deeply, pouring his heart into it. "Never do that to me again, Hazel Grace. I thought I lost you." Stroking her a strand of hair from her face, he smiled, looking her over before he cupped her face. "You exude such an aura of power and grandeur that it seems as though you possess the ability to shake the very foundations of heaven, and the gods themselves would be compelled to bow before your presence."

Hazel smiled widely as she leaned in, kissing him once more. Atticus returned her affection, Hazel's heart ached with the bittersweet reality of her choices. The warmth of his lips and the intensity of his love clashed with the knowledge of the sacrifice she made. She savored the moment, knowing it might be one of the last glimpses of a life she had to leave behind for the greater good of her people.

Hazel's gaze drifted to Evander, now standing beside Gavriel and Nariana, his amber eyes still fixed on her. Something in his expression stirred a strange ache in her chest—like a memory she didn't yet own.

Turning back to Atticus, she gently brushed her fingers along his cheek, her heart twisting at the warmth of his familiar presence. In the vision, their life together had been perfect—peaceful, whole. But that life belonged to another version of her. One who wasn't the Ivory Fawn. One who hadn't given everything to bring the Aestivals back.

She forced a soft smile through the ache and pressed a light kiss to his cheek. "We should go," she said quietly, stepping back. "Your father needs to know what happened. About the battle... about Kingsly's sacrifice. He deserves to know everything."

The weight of her words lingered in the air, solemn and unspoken, as if part of her still couldn't believe Kingsly had truly died—only to be come back again. She would make sure King Kai knows in hope his sacrifice would pardon Kingsly from his treasonous mistake.

Atticus smiled wide, chuckling before she looked at Ardnaxela and Sybilla, who joined their side.

Hazel hugged her two friends closely. Ardnaxela and Sybilla had been with her through thick and thin, their bond had formed into a sisterly connection, providing each other unwavering support and strength when it is needed most. "Oh, thank the gods. You both are okay."

Her friend's arms wrapped around her, holding her tight as they all let out joyous laughter. "Let's go home."

Chapter Seventy-Two

Hazel

A collective gasp swept through the ballroom as Hazel glided through the open balcony doors, descending like a vision woven from starlight and prophecy. The hush that fell was instant, as if the room itself held its breath. Her ivory wings shimmered under the chandeliers, catching the light and scattering it like fractured moonbeams across the polished marble. Her gown flowed like liquid dusk, ethereal and commanding all at once—undeniably otherworldly.

Behind her, Gavriel, Nariana, and Evander descended with silent grace, their presence alone shaking the foundations of belief. Aestivals—living myths—stepping into the mortal world once more.

Atticus, Ardnaxela, Sybilla, and Kingsly entered moments later, their steps steady and untouched by the aftermath of battle, their wounds completely erased—testaments to Hazel's divine gift. The crowd could barely process the sight.

Whispers rippled through the room like an echo of thunder. *"The Ivory Fawn..."* *"She's real."* *"The Aestivals have returned."* Wide-eyed nobles clutched their goblets tighter, some rising from their seats in stunned reverence, others bowing instinctively, overwhelmed by awe and fear alike. Many had scoffed at the old tales. Few believed in the prophecy. But now, standing before them was the living, breathing truth—wrapped in gold and shadow.

Hazel's gaze swept across the stunned assembly, her expression calm yet resolute. She wasn't just a girl who survived a war. She was the symbol of its rebirth.

And the age of legends had begun again.

Hazel stepped forward, her wings folding gracefully at her sides as she faced King Kai. The entire ballroom watched in silence, breath held. Behind her, the Aestivals—Gavriel, Nariana, and the others—knelt, a powerful show of respect and loyalty. They were here, not only as warriors, but as her people, recognizing her as their queen.

"I stand before you, King Kai," Hazel spoke with unwavering conviction, her voice carrying through the room. "I have fulfilled my duty, as the Ivory Fawn, bringing my people back. But my actions were not without sacrifice."

She met his gaze, unflinching. "Kingsly died protecting me—he gave his life in the battle. But thanks to my people, thanks to the Aestivals, he lives again. He was brought back through magic and faith, a hero."

A stunned murmur rippled through the room, but Hazel pressed on, her tone rising with urgency. "I know the law states that death absolves treason, but I ask you now—no, I *demand*—that you honor that law. Kingsly's death and resurrection should clear his name. I ask that you pardon him."

King Kai's face tightened, the weight of the request settling in. For a moment, his expression remained cold, unreadable. The atmosphere in the room grew heavy, the air thick with anticipation.

Evander, standing just behind Hazel, stepped closer, his presence a silent but powerful reassurance. Hazel could feel the steadying force of his gaze, a reminder that she was not alone in this.

The king finally spoke, his voice low and calculating. "You ask much, Ivory Fawn. You challenge the law with your words."

Hazel didn't flinch. She met his gaze with the same strength that had brought her this far. "I do not challenge the law, Your Majesty. I uphold it. Kingsly's sacrifice speaks for itself. I ask only that you honor his service to this kingdom."

The king's brow furrowed as he processed her words. The tension stretched, thick and palpable, before he exhaled sharply. "So be it. Kingsly's death, and his return, are proof of his loyalty. The court will recognize this pardon... effective immediately."

A collective sigh of relief rippled through the room, and the Aestivals behind Hazel stood tall, their respect and approval evident. Evander's gaze softened as he stepped back slightly, allowing Hazel to absorb the gravity of her victory.

King Kai extended a hand toward her—not out of affection, but as a sign of acknowl-edgment. "You have done this kingdom a great service, Hazel. I will not forget the sacrifices you've made."

Hazel's chest rose and fell as she processed his words, her heart swelling with the weight of what she had just achieved. Kingsly was free. The kingdom had hope. And now, the Aestivals had their queen—one born of battle, magic, and prophecy, who would fight for them, no matter the cost.

The court erupted in applause.

Hazel turned to look at her found family and her recently erected court, and held her head up high. Gavriel's eyes shimmered with pride.

"Long live Queen Hazel, the Ivory Fawn!" Atticus roared out in joy.

The crowd's reaction was immediate and thunderous. Cheers and chants of "Long live Queen Hazel" echoed through the ballroom as guests raised their glasses in celebration. The energy in the room was electric, a shared sense of hope and renewal enveloping everyone present.

Hazel's smile widened as Reed ran over, hugging her. Laughing softly, she kneeled down, smiling, wrapping her wings around him. "Was that Ivory Fawn like of me?" she asked the youngest prince, who laughed, wrapping his arms around Hazel's neck.

"Was it ever!" he cheered out.

Hazel's eyes softened as she lowered her down to be leveled with Prince Reed. "I couldn't have done it without your flaky pastries and kindness, little prince," she whis-pered, her voice filled with affection. Reed beamed up at her, his admiration for Hazel shining brightly.

Queen Sage stepped forward, which led Hazel to stand up, tucking in her wings and bow. She was a vision of elegance and grace, her emerald green gown flowing like a river of silk. Her silvery moonlight hair was intricately braided and adorned with delicate silver leaves that glimmered under the chandelier's light. Hazel spoke up"Thank you for letting me stay in your home."

Sage smiled, bringing Hazel's chin up. "No, thank *you* for being the daughter I always wanted." Hazel teared up before nodding, moving to hug the queen, who in turn opened her arm embracing Hazel.

The room was enveloped in a palpable sense of unity and joy, the air thick with the collective excitement of the guests. Laughter and music filled the space, blending into a harmonious symphony of triumph and togetherness.

Gavriel stepped forward, clearing his throat. "I'm sorry to interrupt, but may I have a word with you, my queen?" Looking at Gavriel, Hazel took a deep breath, nodding before she took Sage's hand and kissed it.

Gavriel then led Hazel up the grand stair way towards the balcony over looked the grand ballroom, and Evander and Nariana stopped just at the bottom of the stairway to ensure their privacy.

Gavriel's gaze softened as he looked at Hazel, his usual confidence tempered by an unspoken understanding of how much she had already carried. "You've done well, my queen, but there are matters we must address," he said, his voice carrying an underlying weight of regret. "Two, in fact." He hesitated, his eyes flicking toward the others in the room as if weighing the situation. "Ardnaxela did great damage to Queen Duvessa. She's in our custody now and will be questioned, but that's not the pressing matter. There's something far larger we must discuss."

Hazel's heart skipped a beat, her mind racing with the possibilities. She could feel the tension in the room shifting, the air thickening with the gravity of what was about to come.

Gavriel's eyes softened further, a rare moment of compassion flickering in his gaze. "I hate to bring this up now, especially after everything you've endured, but it's urgent. You're tired, I can see it, but I need you to hear me. The Aestivals are vulnerable—scattered across Tresian and newly resurrected. Their strength is fragile right now, and we cannot afford to wait. We must act swiftly."

His voice softened, but his words cut through the room with the precision of a blade. "This isn't something we can delay, Hazel. The future of the Aestivals—and all of Tresian—depends on what we do next."

Hazel felt the weight of his words settle on her like a mantle she hadn't yet been ready to bear, but knew, deep down, that she had no choice. This was her path now

Hazel's thoughts swirled with uncertainty as she met Gavriel's gaze, her shoulders heavy with the weight of everything she had yet to fully grasp. Despite the turmoil brewing inside her, she stood tall, determined to embrace her destiny with the same grace and courage that Queen Sage had always carried. With a quiet frown, she inhaled deeply, the sound of her breath steadying her nerves. As she turned slightly to glance over her shoulder at Evander, standing like a silent sentinel behind her, the reality of the prophecy hung in the air like a thick fog.

"About the last part of the prophecy," she began, her voice low, meant for Gavriel's ears alone. "Your champion... the Obsidian Tiger... is he not?" Her words were edged with a hint of hesitation, her mind racing between the duty that beckoned her and the visceral fear she felt at the thought of the marriage it demanded. She wanted to fight it, wanted to reject the very idea of being bound to someone for the sake of prophecy. Yet, the sense of inevitability lingered, pressing down on her like a weight she could not escape. Deep down, she feared she would never truly find happiness in this arranged union, wondering if it was simply a sacrifice she had to make for the greater good.

Gavriel's eyes softened with understanding as he replied, his tone tinged with the memory of a love long gone. "I see my late wife was guiding you and your dragon," he said quietly, acknowledging the weight of the connection between Hazel and Asteria. "You are quite observant. Yes, Evander is our Obsidian Tiger. It was the nickname Asteria gave me when she saw the prophecy. We can hold off on wedding arrangements until you've settled into your role. Let your engagement run for about a year or so until you're ready."

Hazel's heart clenched, the burden of both duty and a future she didn't quite understand pressing in on her from all sides. The sense of urgency in his words, however, made it clear that there was no turning back now.

Hazel appreciated Gavriel's offer, but the thought of delaying the inevitable did little to soothe her unease. She feared that prolonging the engagement would effect her people.

"No, it's alright. I swore I was ready to become the Ivory Fawn. That also meant accepting that I would need to marry. Correct me if I am wrong, but for me to be seen as queen, I would have to marry anyway to take that position. Am I right?" Hazel said, finally turning her attention to Gavriel.

He only chuckled faintly at her observation . His attention went to Evander, whose back remained to them. "Indeed, you are correct," Gavriel responded, his tone softening. "Evander's role as the Obsidian Tiger is not just symbolic. He is also a key protector of the realm. His strength and loyalty are unparalleled, and his union with you will fortify the kingdom's future, ensuring both stability and prosperity."

Hazel stared out into the crowd of people, inhaling deeply before looking at Gavriel. "Then we marry in a year. We will do as you suggested and have a long engagement. This will give our people to recover and piece themselves together. It also allow Evander and I to get to know each other better. Although for now, the remaining day, I just want to be a normal girl one last time. Can you grant me that?"

Hazel stood at the balcony, her eyes drifting over the shimmering ballroom below where her found family gathered, their laughter and conversation filling the air with warmth. The court of Wylana, once strangers, now felt like her own, each face a familiar beacon of love and support. Still, as she watched them, her heart felt heavy with the weight of her future responsibilities. The vibrant chatter and joy around her contrasted sharply with the turmoil swirling within. The freedom she had once known felt like a distant memory, and she knew her life was now forever bound by the path before her.

Her mind swirled with thoughts of the destiny that awaited her. Hazel was no longer just Hazel; she was Queen Hazel, the Ivory Fawn of Wylana, the one chosen to lead the Aestival back from the ashes. From this moment on, nothing would ever be the same.

The soft sound of footsteps broke her from her thoughts, and Evander stepped up beside her, his presence solid and grounding. His gaze swept over the room below before landing on her, his amber eyes filled with quiet understanding. He stood tall beside her, as if silently acknowledging the storm brewing inside her, but offering no words of comfort—only the strength of his quiet support.

His shoulders relaxed before he nodded, the weight of their shared responsibility pressing on them both. "Yes, I can," he said, the assurance in his voice a silent promise.

Hazel turned to him, her fingers brushing his as she reached for his hand, the warmth of his touch grounding her in the moment. She squeezed his hand, the strength in her own growing with every beat of her heart. She knew what was expected of her, what she would have to become. But even with the heavy burden of her title, there was one thing she could promise.

"I swear to you," she said, her voice steady but filled with the fire of determination, "I will be the best queen our people have ever seen."

As the laughter and voices of her family echoed from below, Hazel knew this was only the beginning. She would rise to meet her fate, for them, for the Aestival, and for herself. The future awaited, and she would face it head-on, no matter the cost.

Acknowledgements

To my amazing readers—thank you from the bottom of my heart. Your support, encouragement, and enthusiasm have carried this story farther than I ever dreamed possible. You are the soul of this journey, and I'm endlessly grateful for every message, every review, and every moment you've spent in this world with me.

To my incredible editor, Elisabeth—thank you for your keen insight, steady guidance, and for never letting me settle for "good enough." Your care and dedication have helped shape this book into something I'm truly proud of.

To my phenomenal artist, Allison—your talent has left me speechless time and time again. From the detailed character portraits to the breathtaking map and the stunning cover, your work has brought this world to life in ways I never imagined. Thank you for capturing the spirit of this story so perfectly.

To my grandmother—thank you for being my rock. You've stood by me through every high and low, believed in me when I couldn't believe in myself, and poured so much love into every part of my life. This book carries a piece of your strength and your heart on every page.

To my close friends and family—thank you for holding me up through moments of doubt, for the late-night talks, the pep talks, and for always letting me bounce ideas (and emotions) off you. And a special thanks for letting me use you as blocking references—I promise I only made you fight invisible monsters a *few* times. Your support and patience made all the difference. To my dearest "wifey" best friend, I want to express my deepest gratitude for your unwavering support and the pivotal role you played in my life's journey. Without your intervention, I would never have reached the place I am today. Your prompt attention to the warning signs, your refusal to wait, and your courageous decision to make that life-saving call were instrumental in my success. I am forever indebted to you for your unwavering belief in me and your unshakable faith in my abilities. Your presence in my life has been a blessing, and I am so grateful to have you by my side. Thank you

Creating this story has been one of the greatest adventures of my life, and I couldn't have done it without each of you. Thank you, truly.

With all my love, —Mackenzie Hill

About the author

Born and raised in Phoenix, Arizona, Mackenzie's story is one of resilience, passion, and unyielding creativity. After being removed from an abusive household, she was lovingly raised by her grandmother in Litchfield Park. It was her grandmother's unwavering love and guidance that shaped Mackenzie into the woman she is today, instilling in her a deep sense of compassion, strength, and determination.

In 2017, Mackenzie pursued a degree in theater and creative writing, but life's demands led her to leave college to care for her grandmother full-time, a testament to her dedication to family. During this time, she reconnected with her biological father after a six-year search through Ancestry DNA. Though their time together was tragically brief—he passed away from lung cancer during COVID—his encouragement to follow her dreams became a profound source of inspiration.

Her father's memory and the relationship they were denied became the heart of Mackenzie's Ivory Fawn series. This deeply personal work reflects her longing for the bond they could have shared, the solace of hearing a father's words in dark times, and the painful journey of finding closure for wounds left by his passing. Through her writing, Mackenzie poured her grief, love, and healing into the series, transforming her pain into a story that not only helped her heal but also became a beacon of hope for others.

Mackenzie dreams that her stories will provide the same escape and solace for readers that they gave her. She hopes her books will become a sanctuary for those navigating their own challenges, offering them a safe space to heal, dream, and find strength through her characters and worlds.

www.ingramcontent.com/pod-product-compliance
Lightning Source LLC
Chambersburg PA
CBHW011638010726
47495CB00011B/2812